WORKS BY CHABOUTÉ

Alone
Park Bench
Moby Dick

CHABOUTÉ

Park bench

GALLERY 13

New York   London   Toronto   Sydney   New Delhi

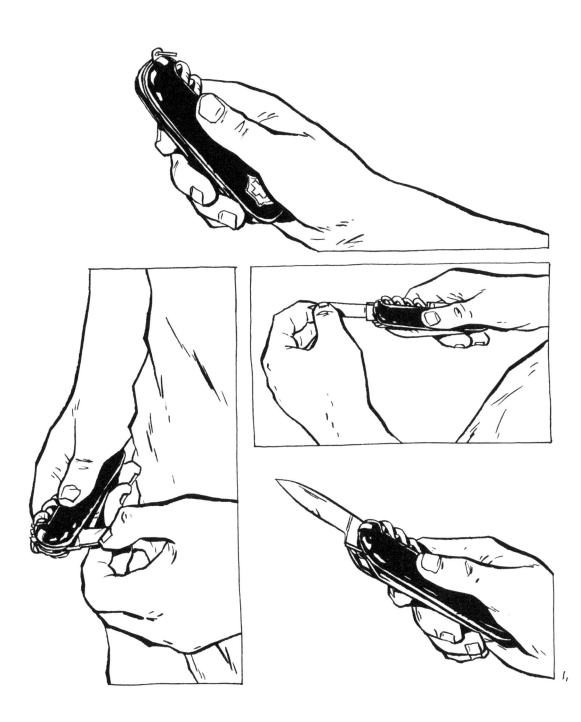

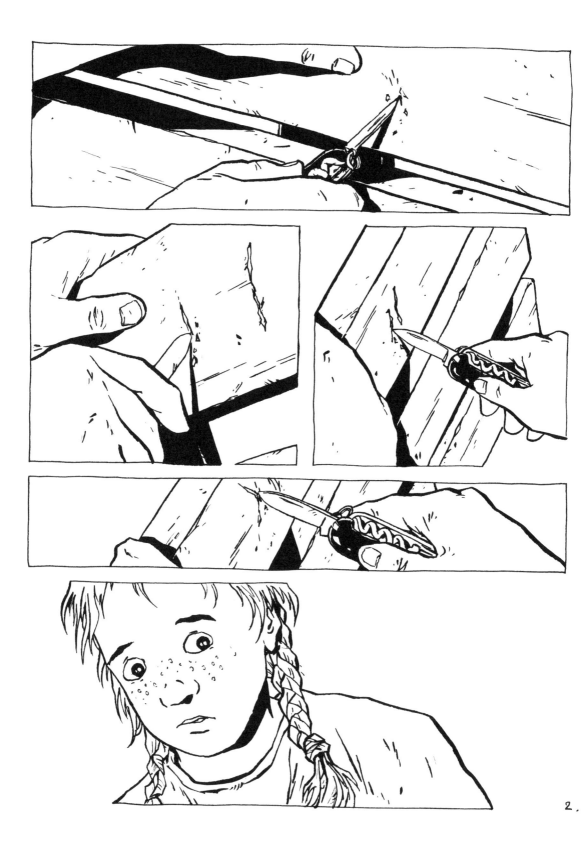

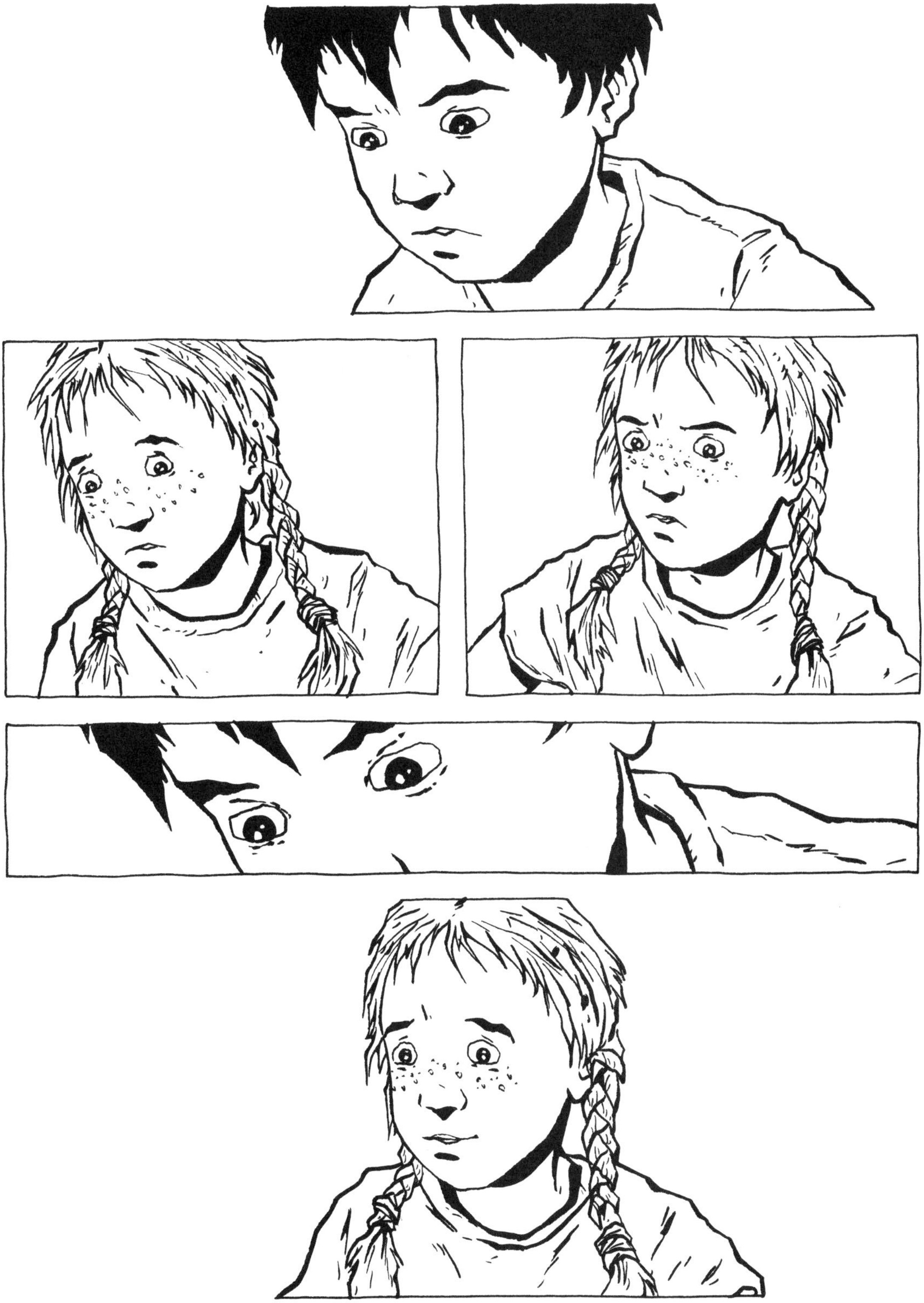

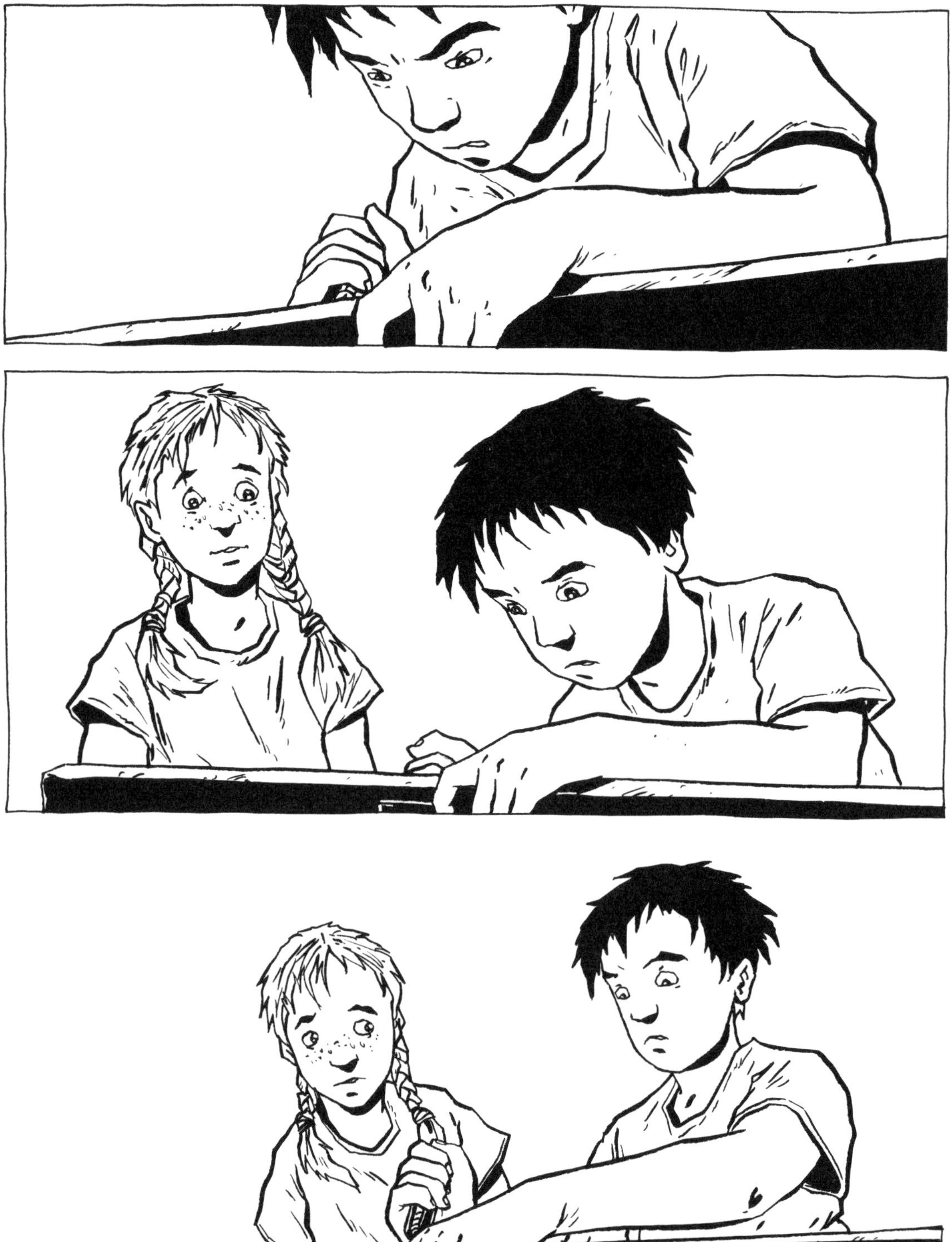

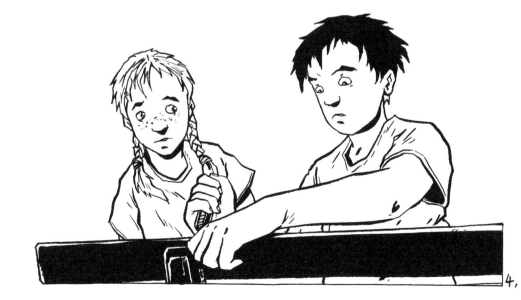

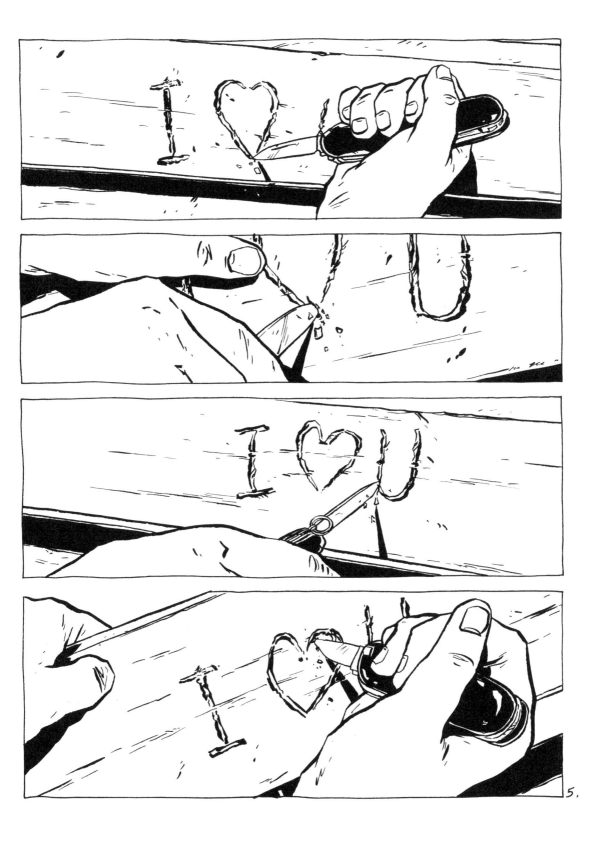

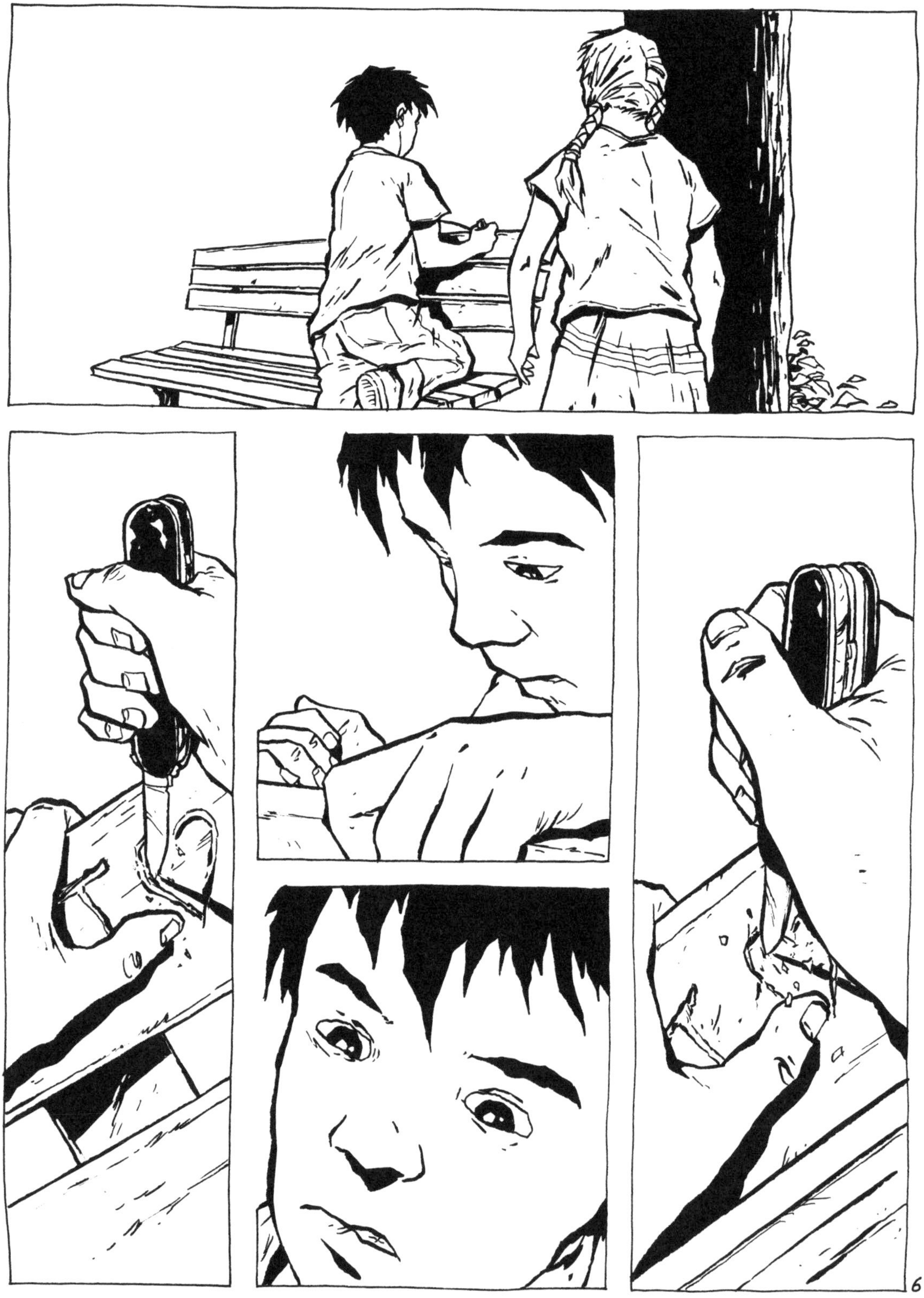

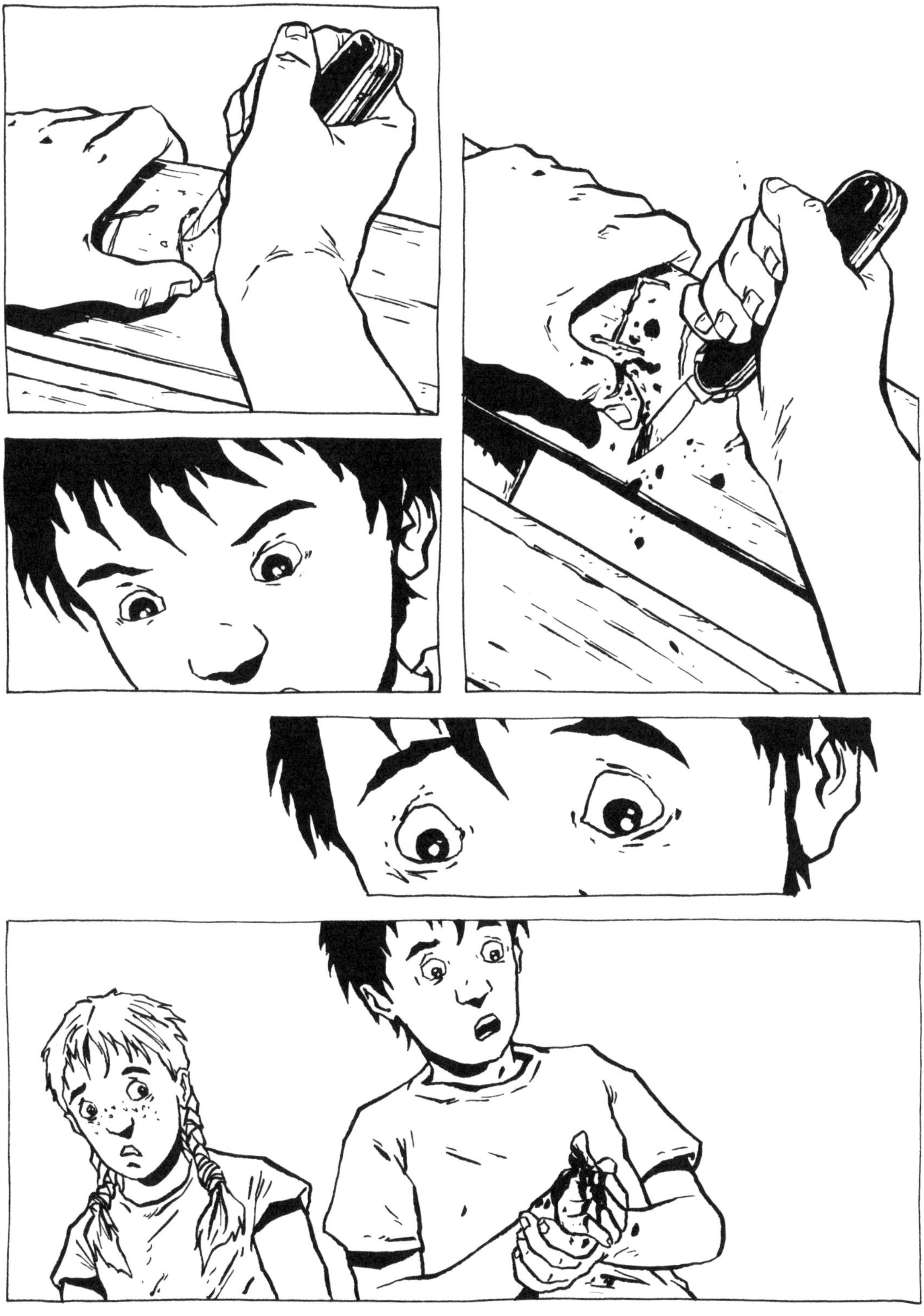

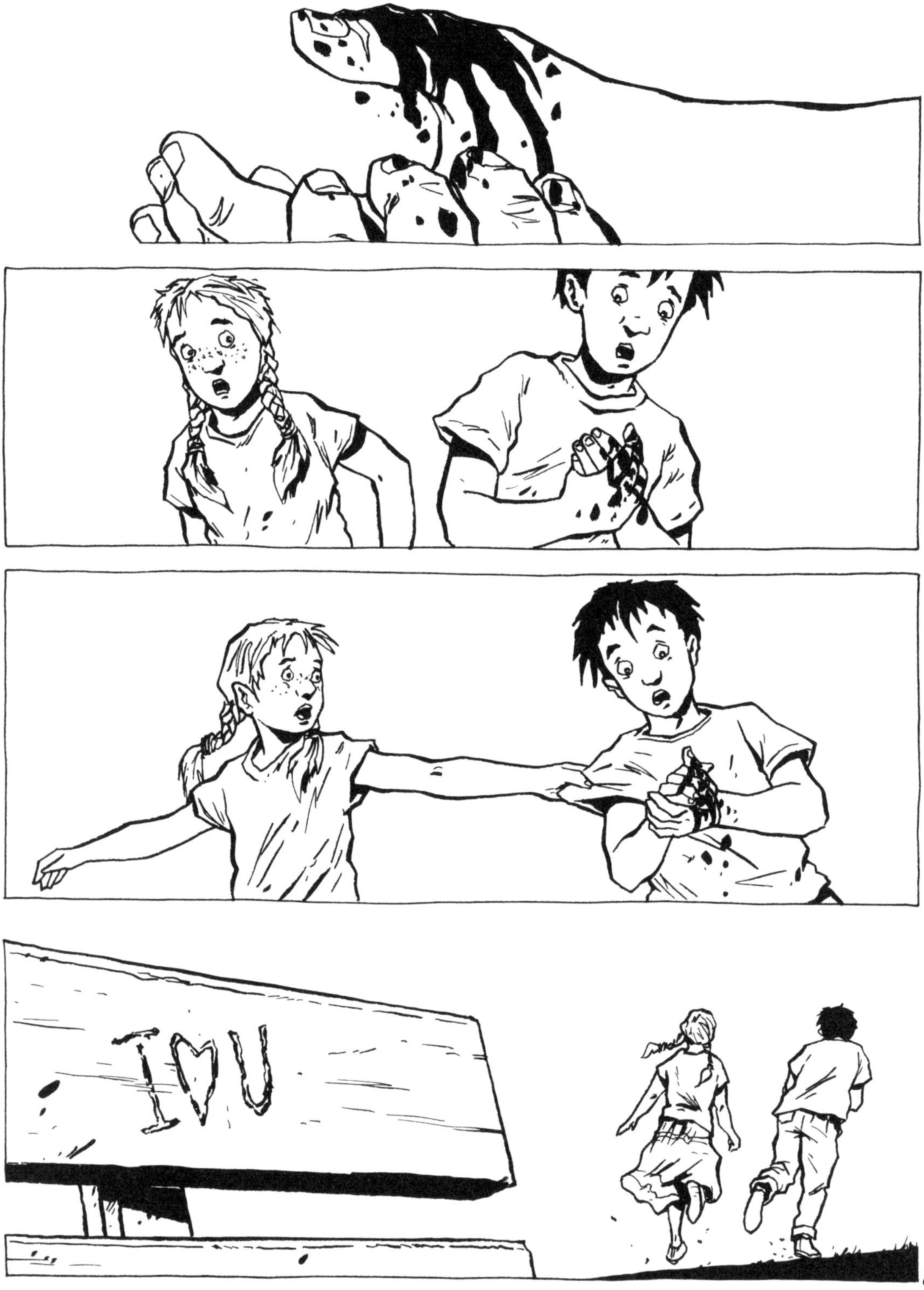
I ♥ U

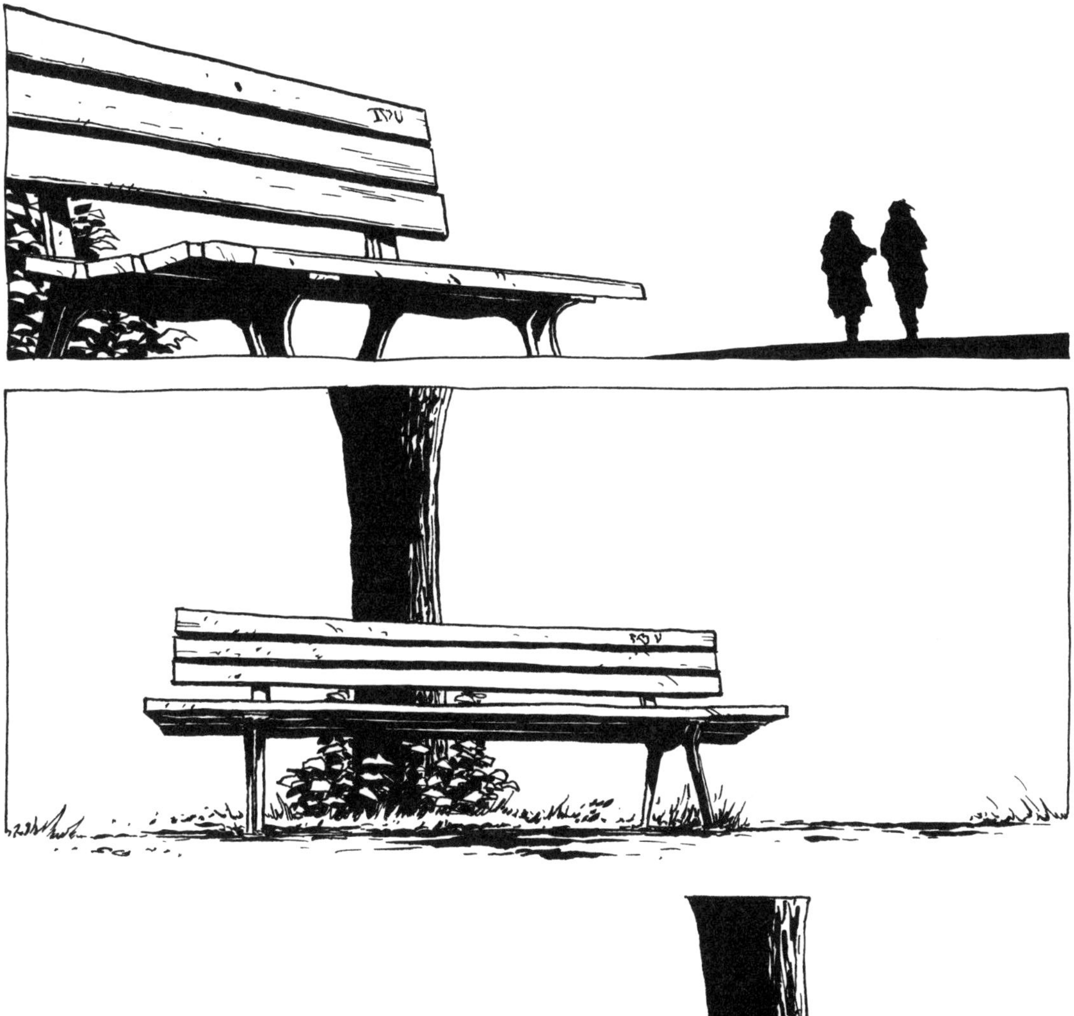

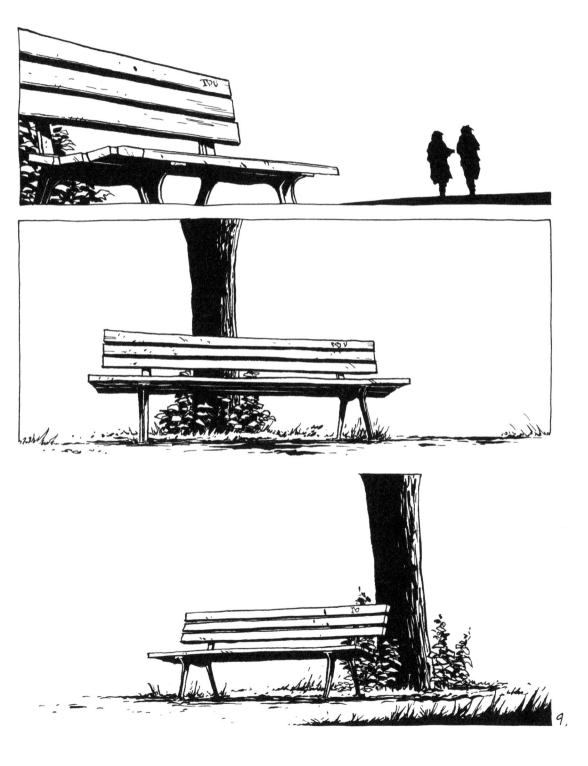

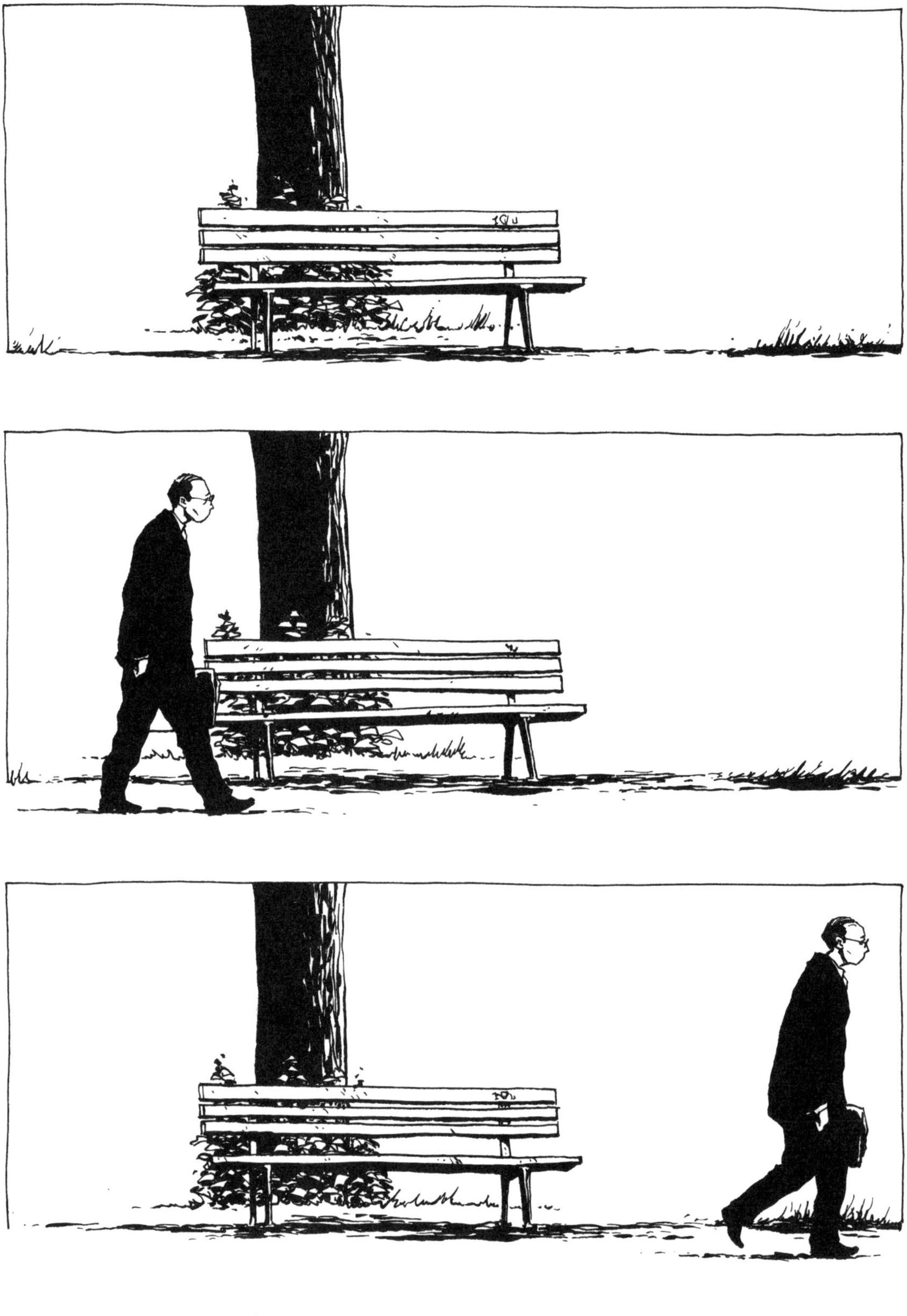

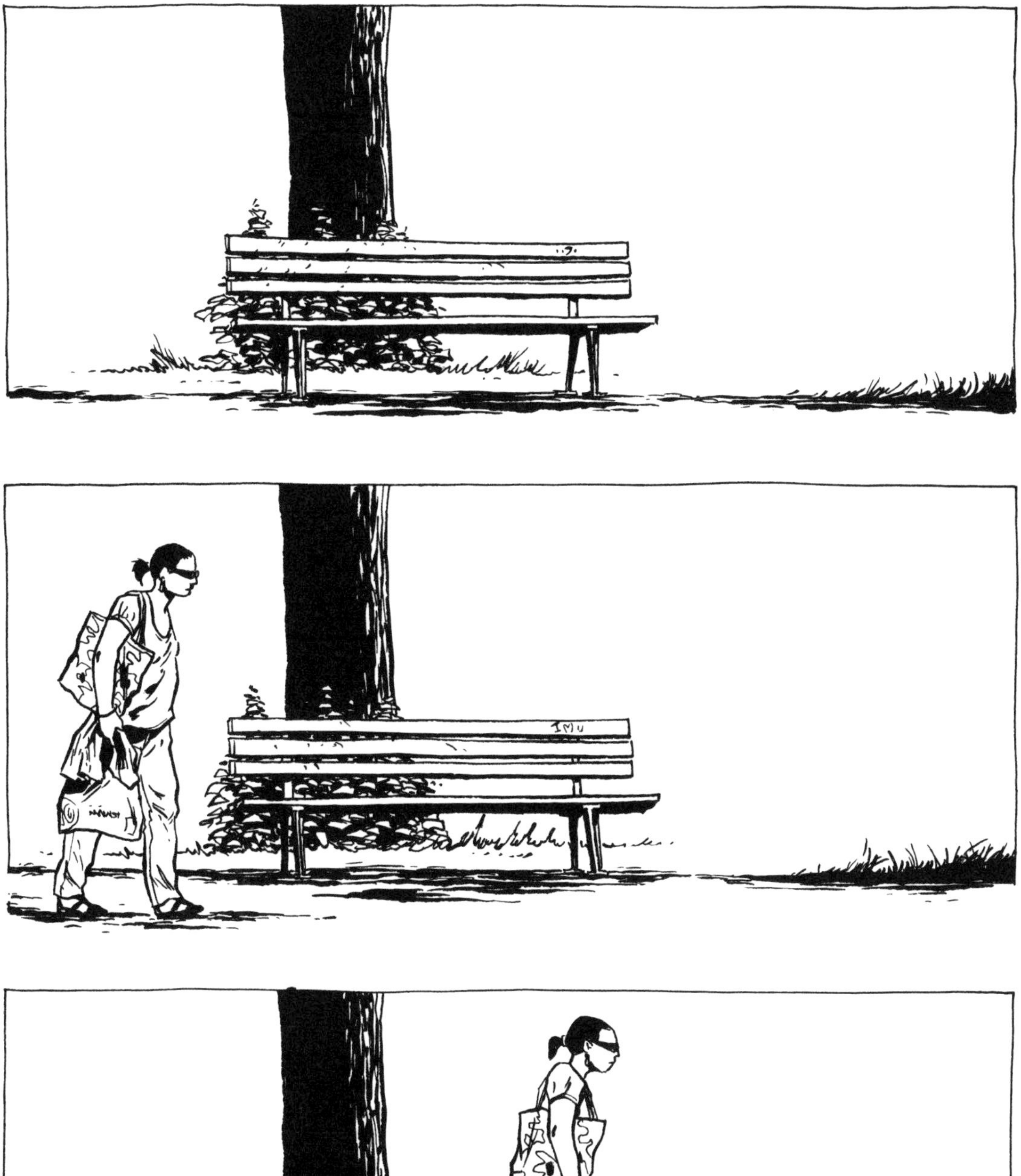

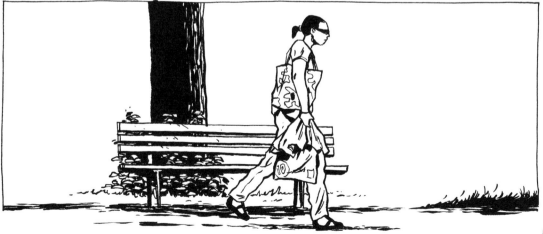

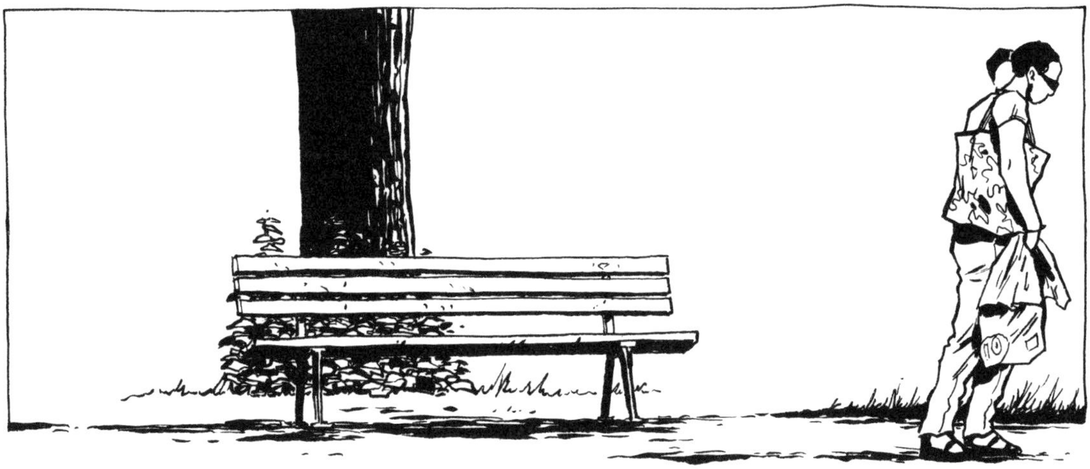

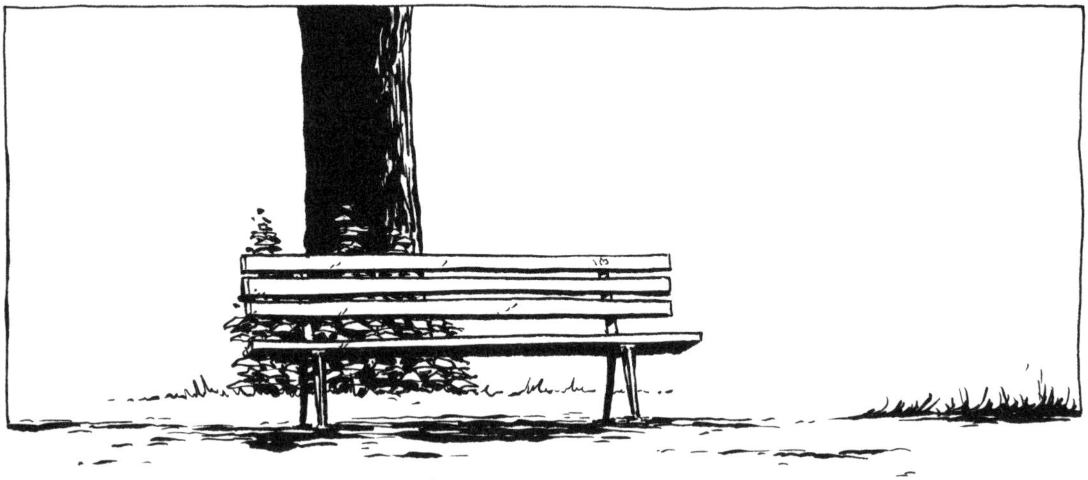

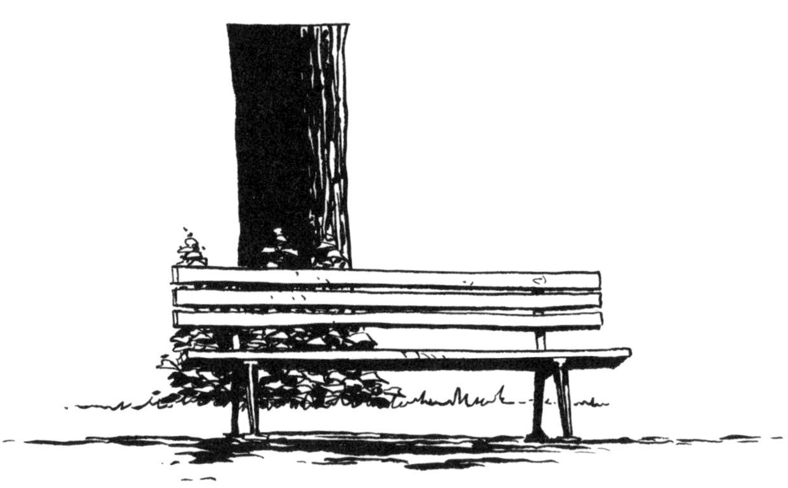

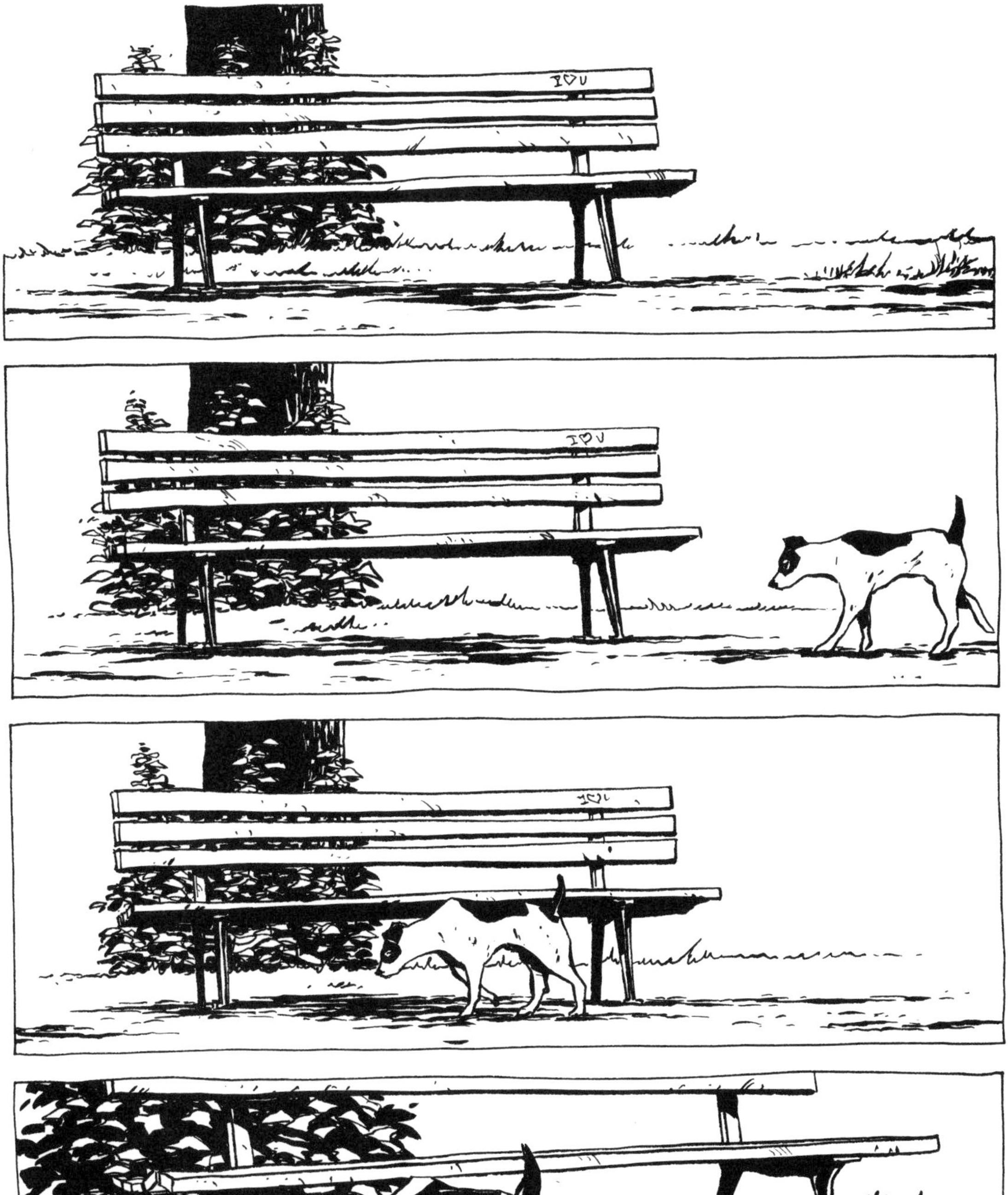
I♥U

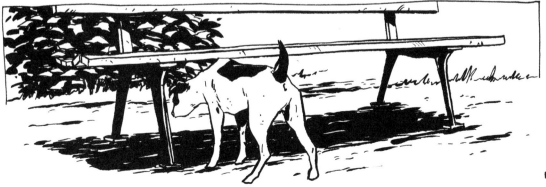

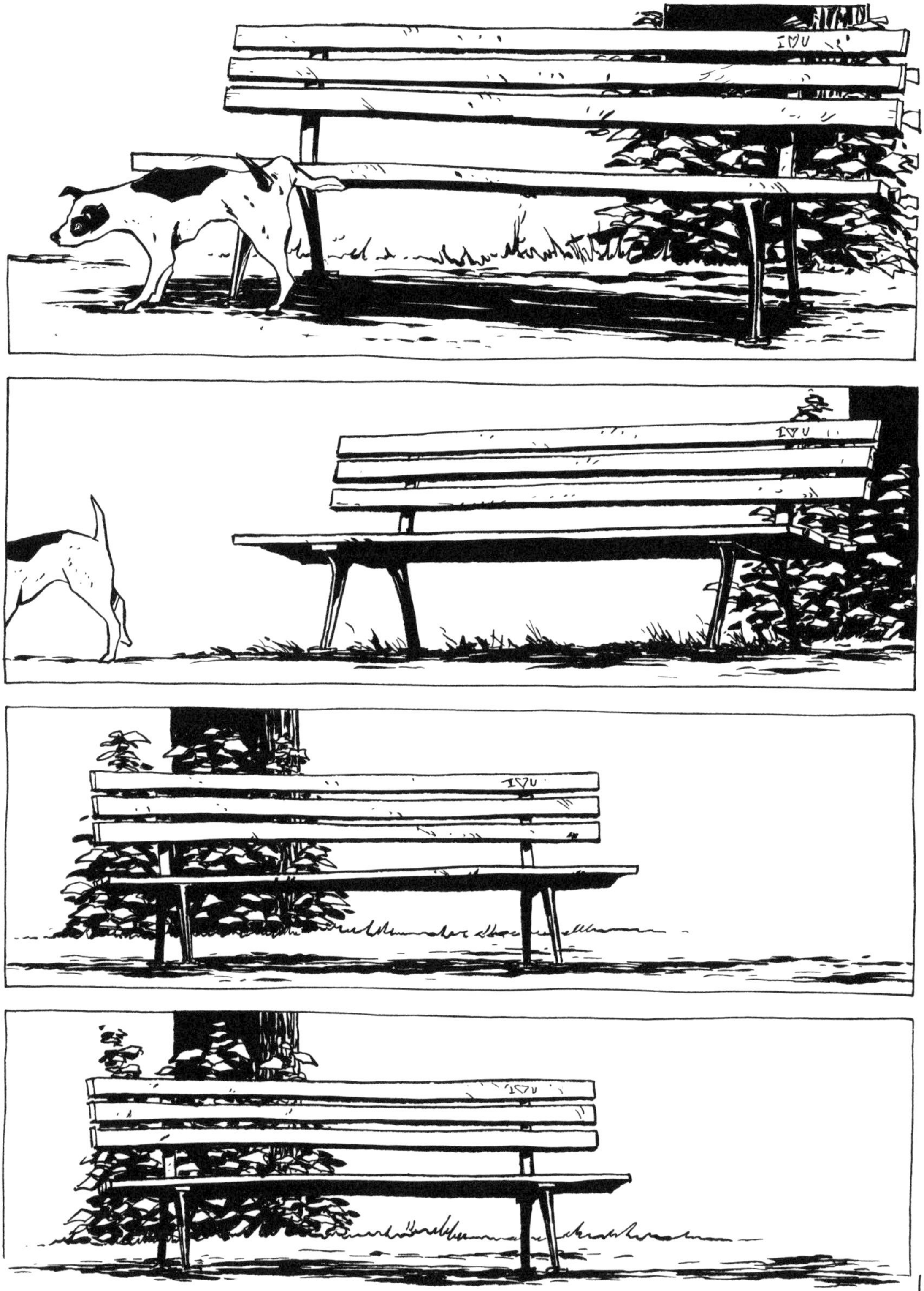
I♥U
I♥U
I♥U
I♥U

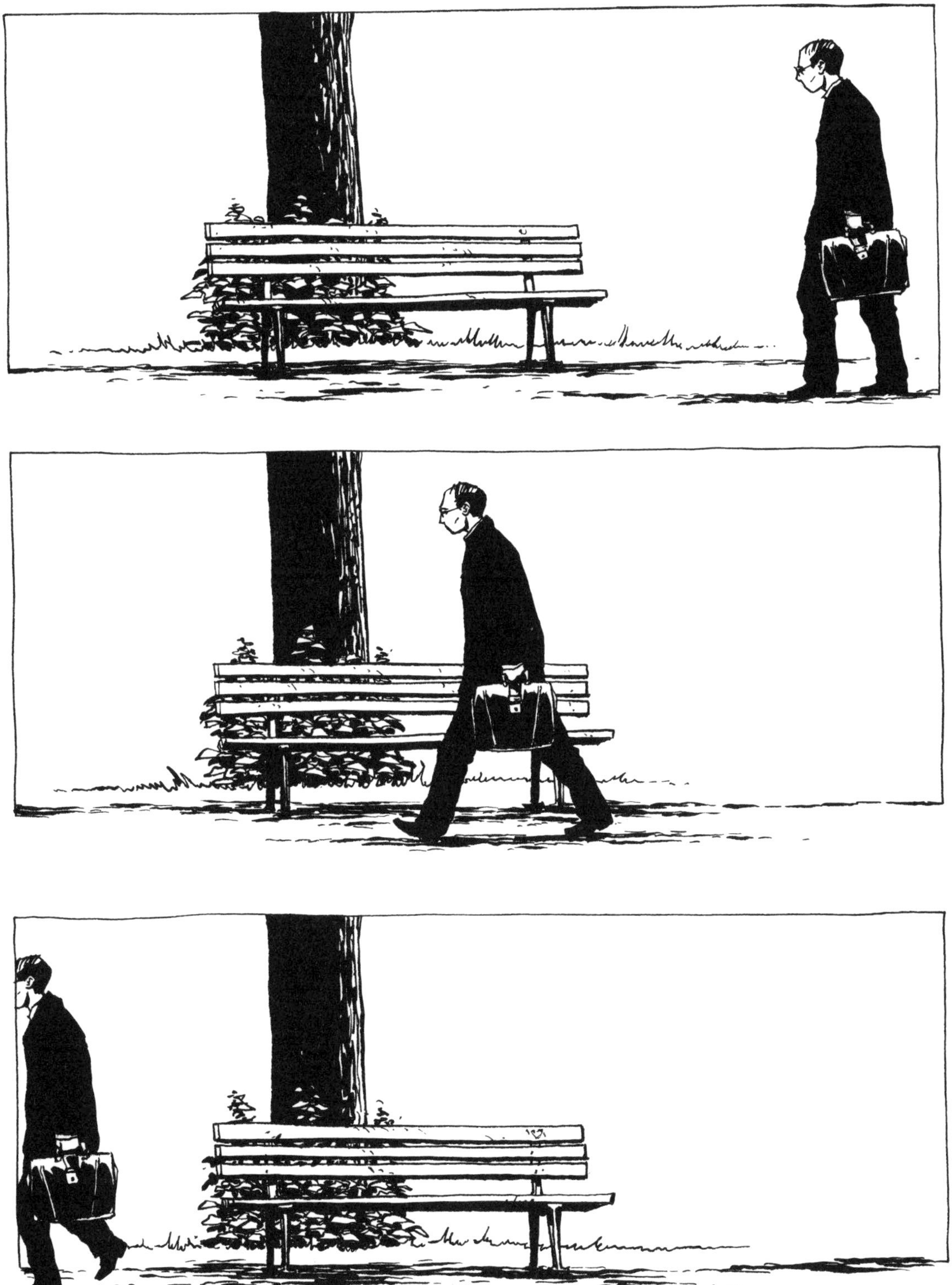

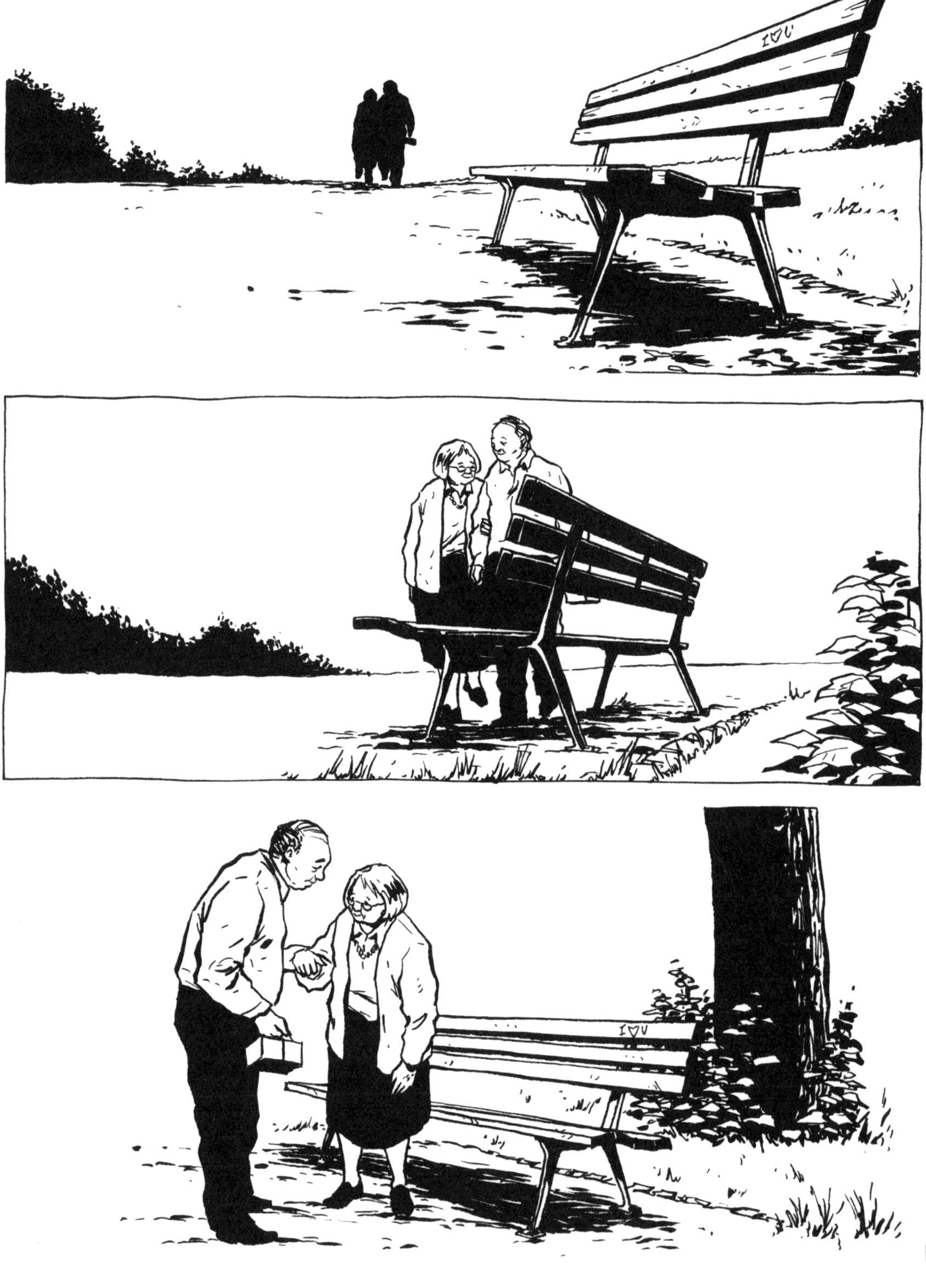
I♥U

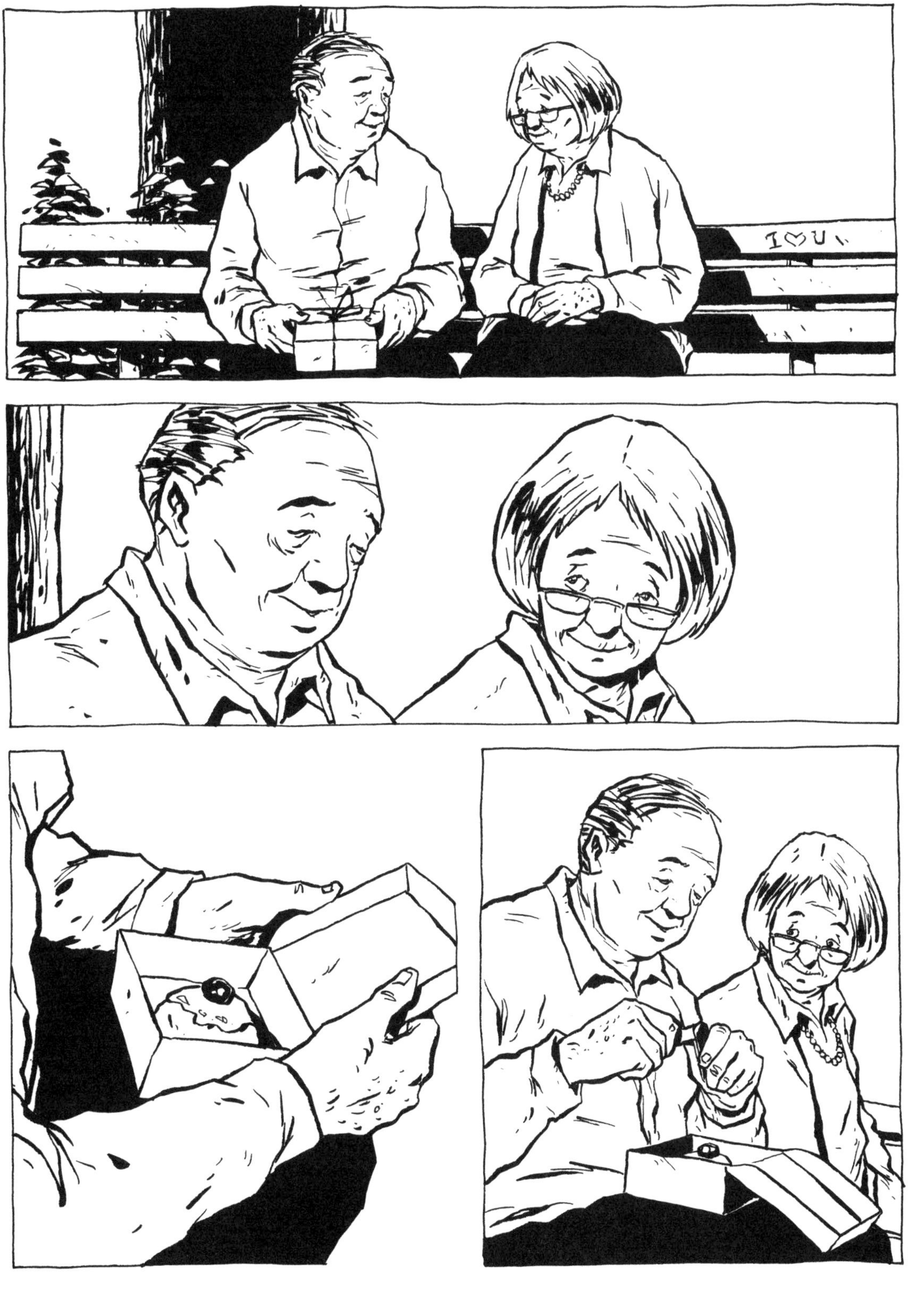
I ♡ U

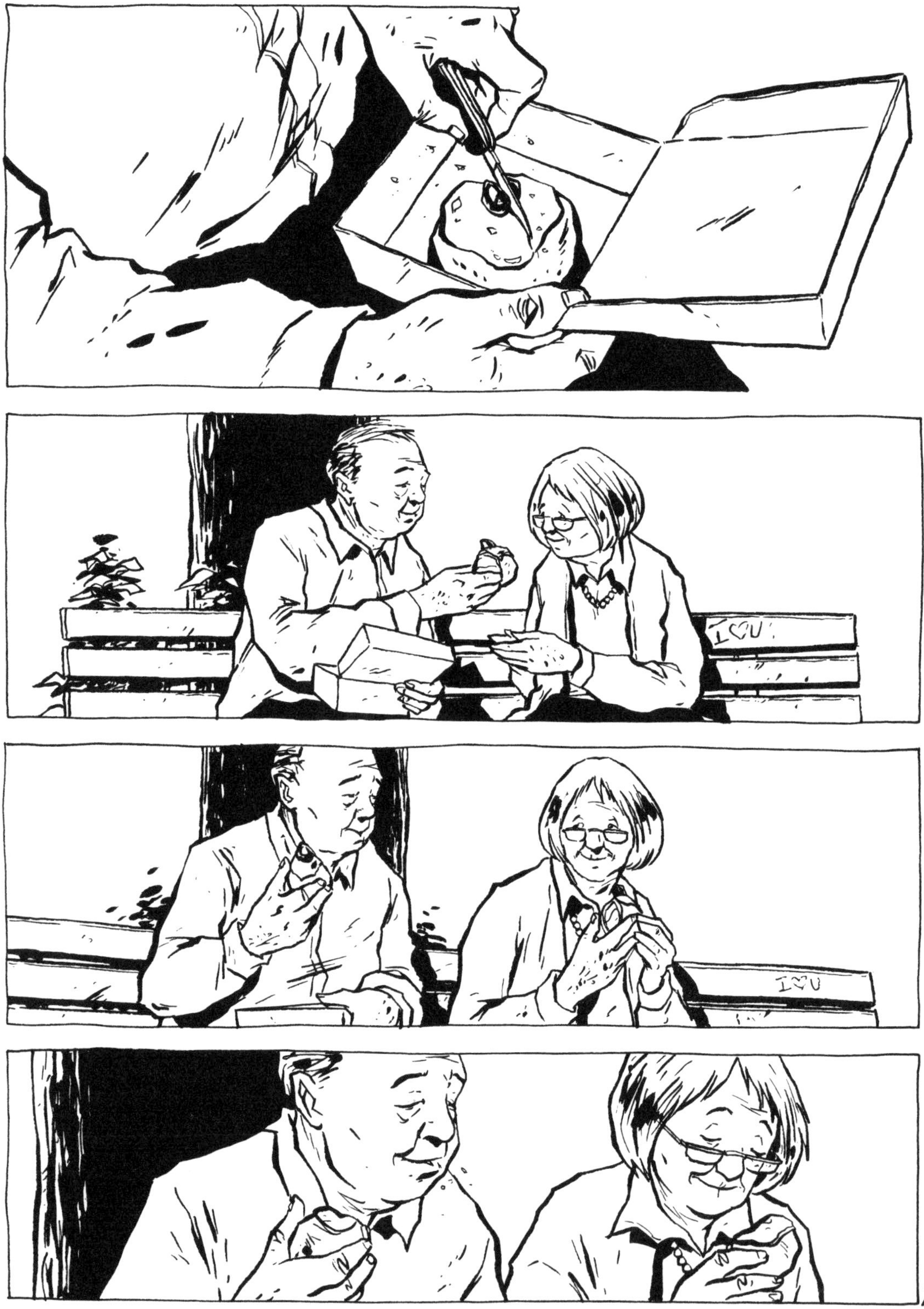
I♡U

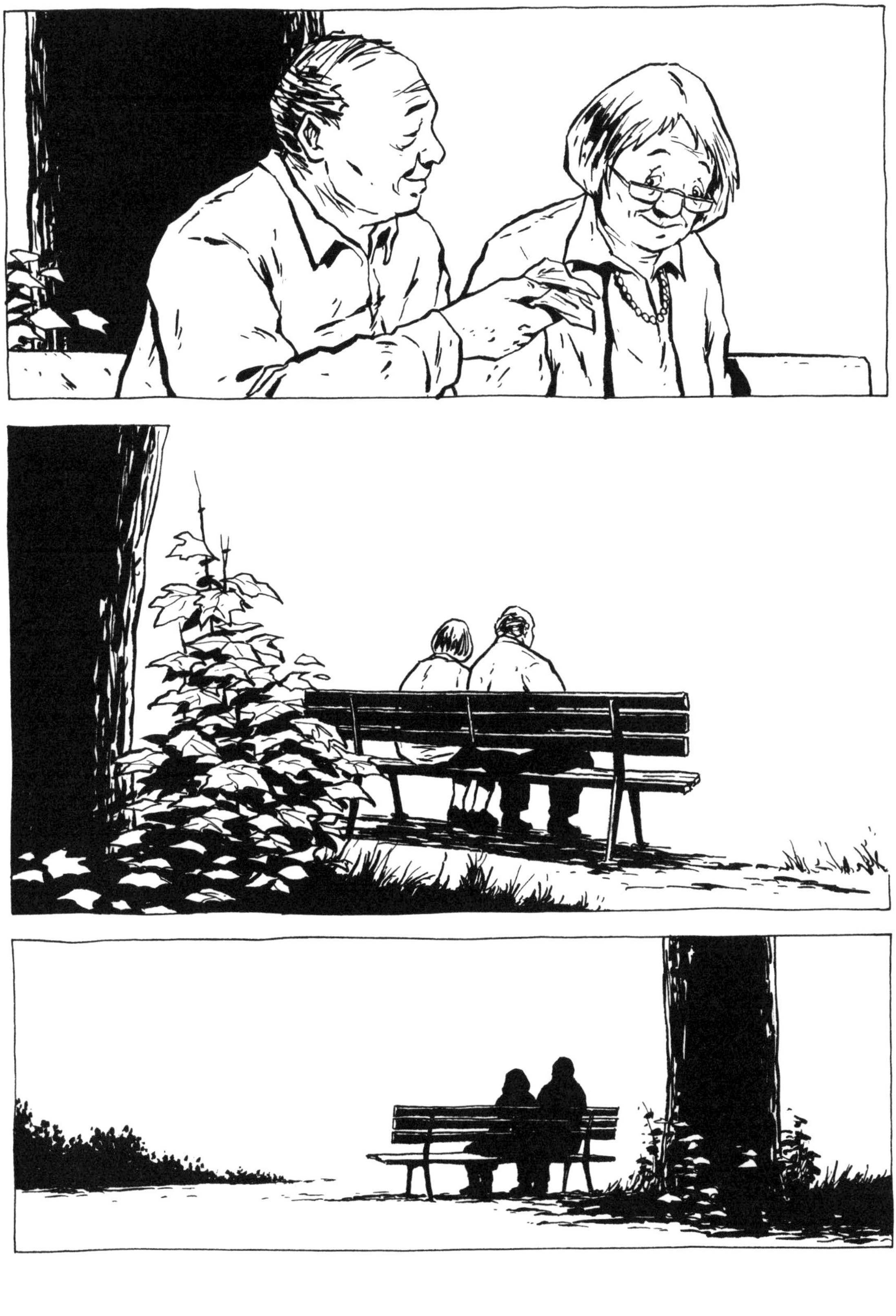

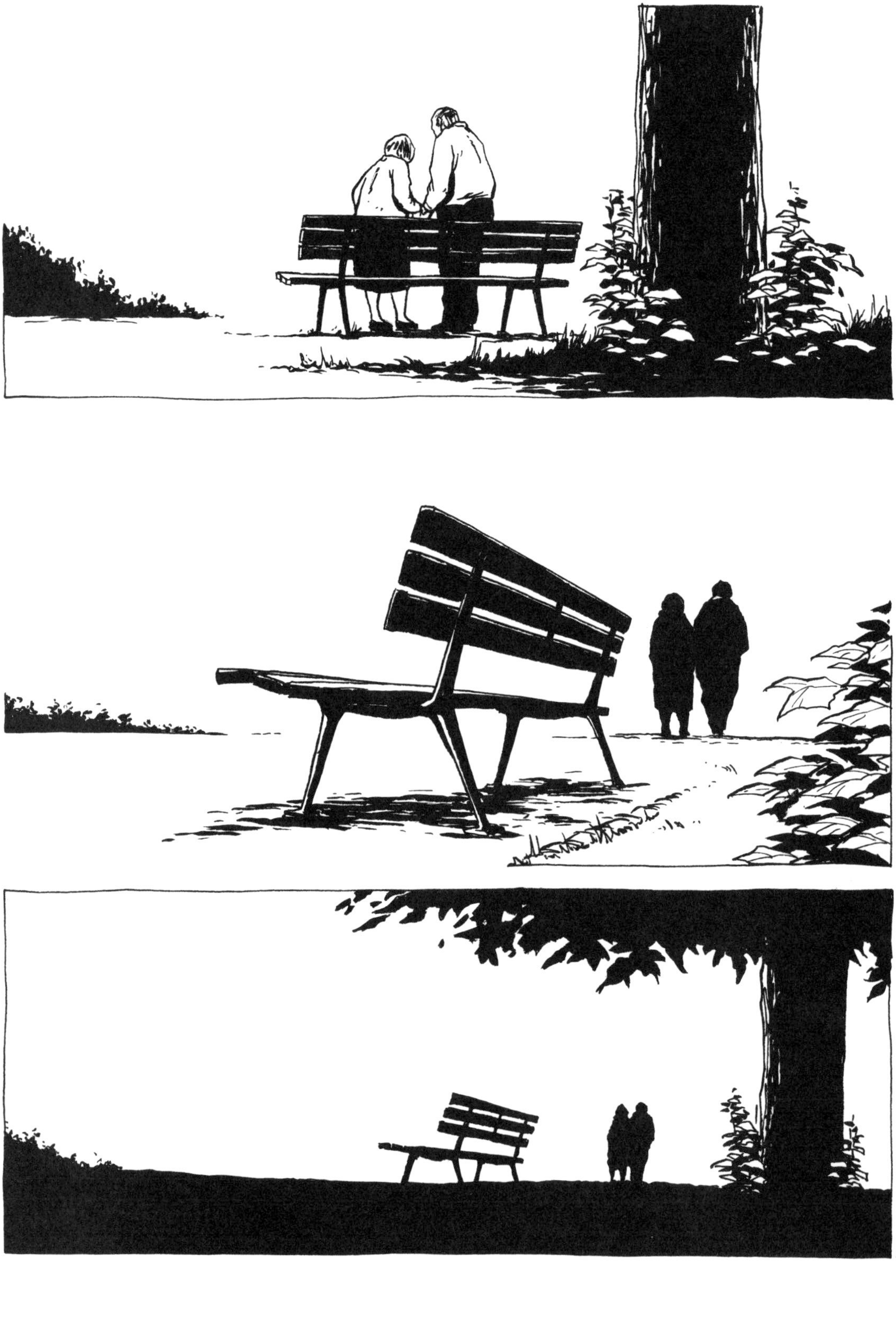

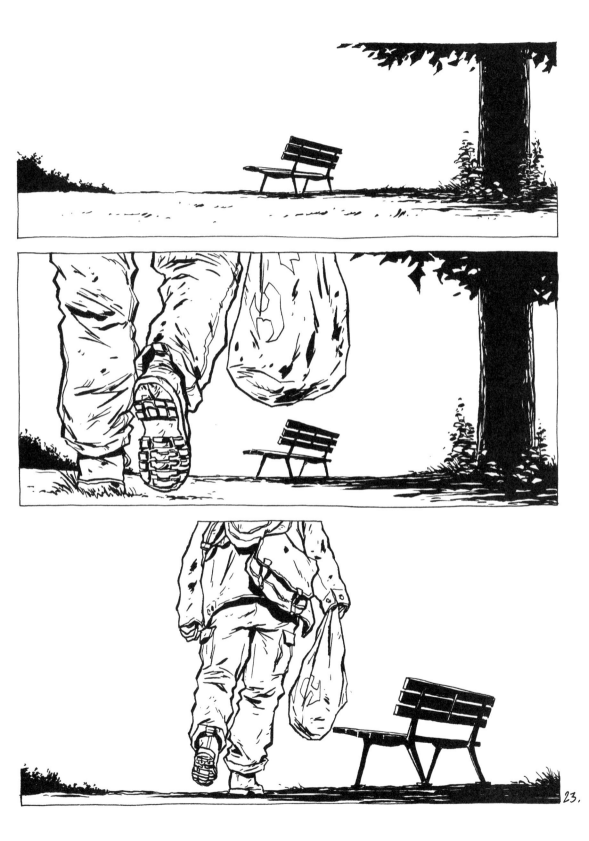

23.

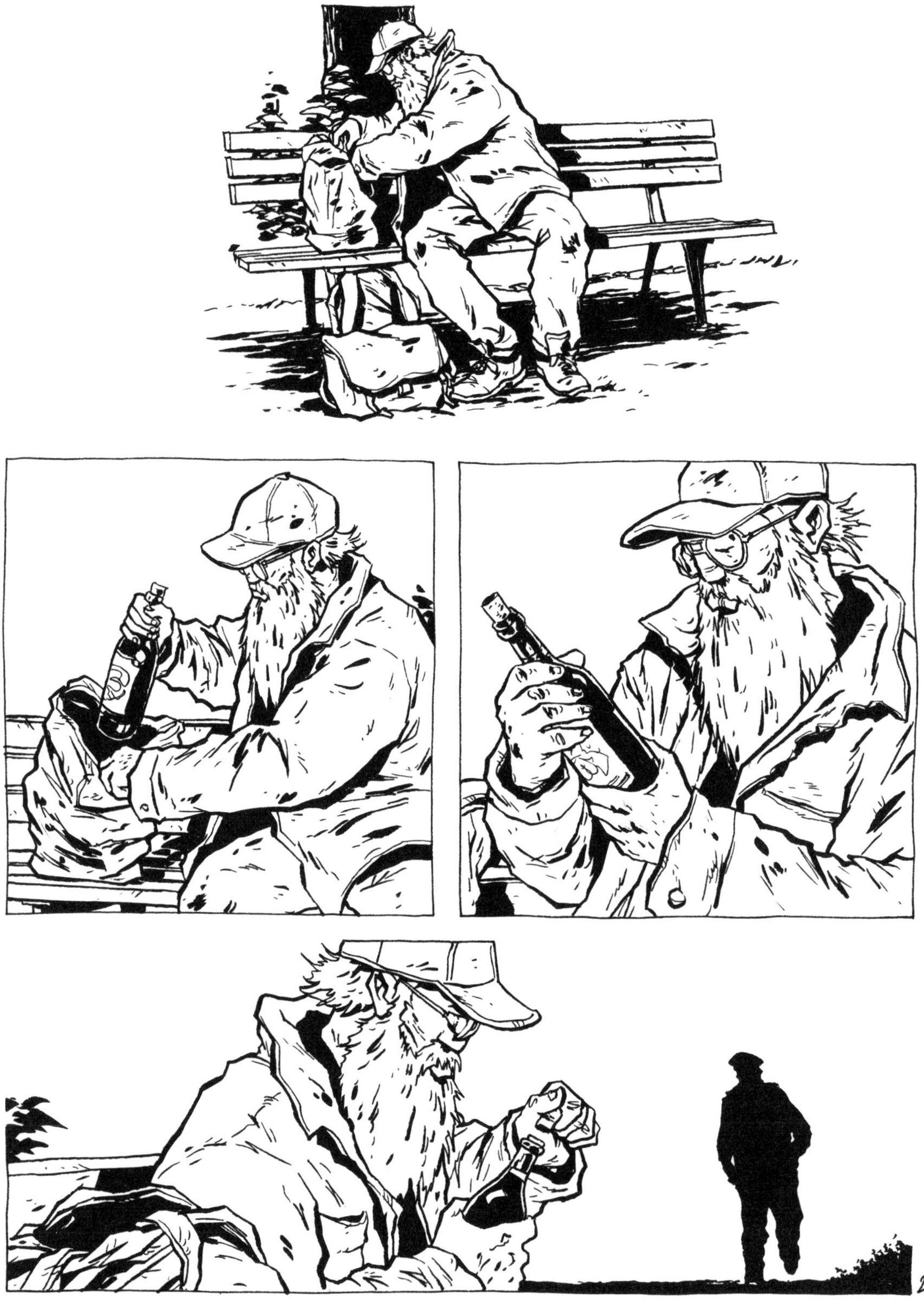

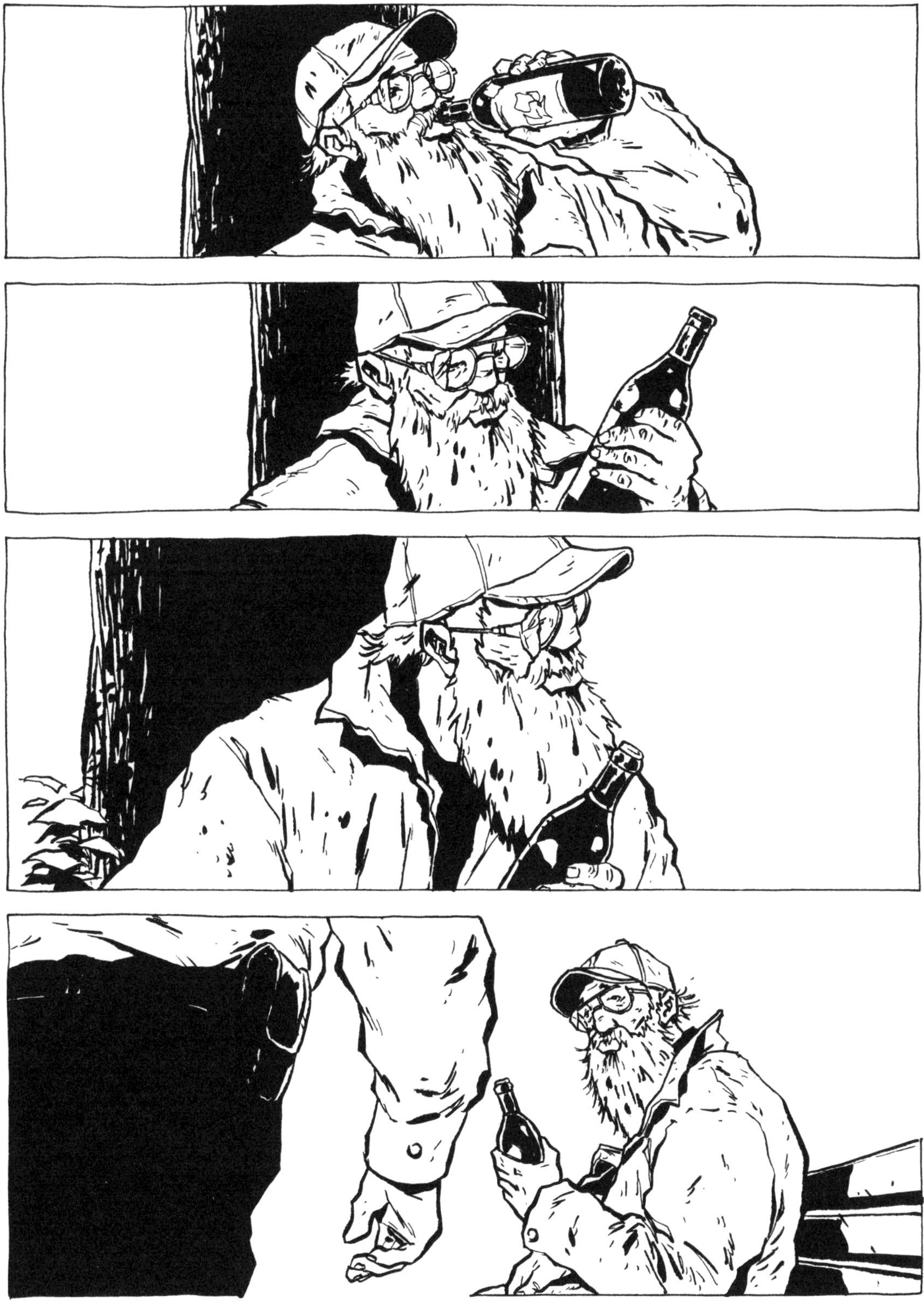

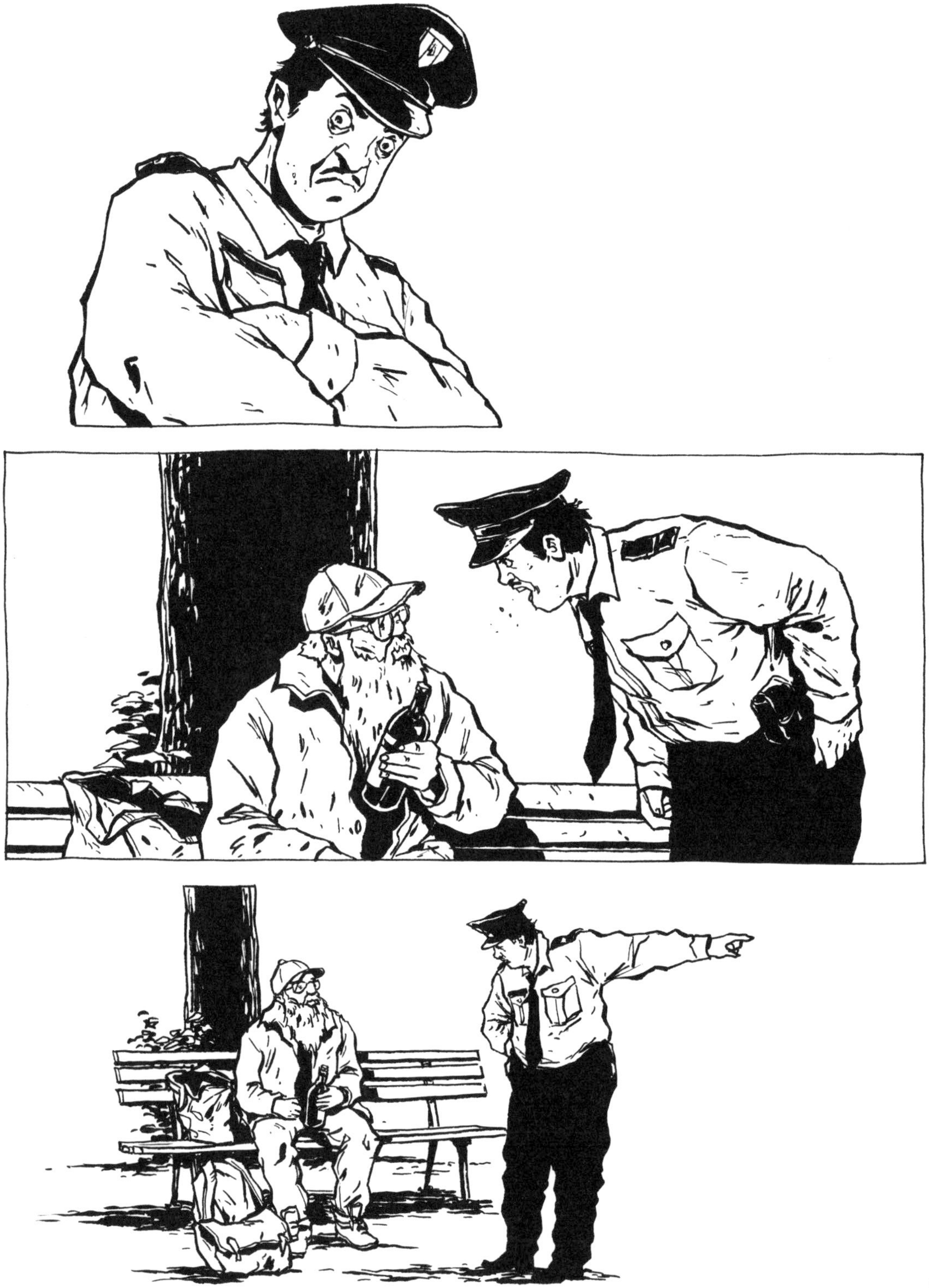

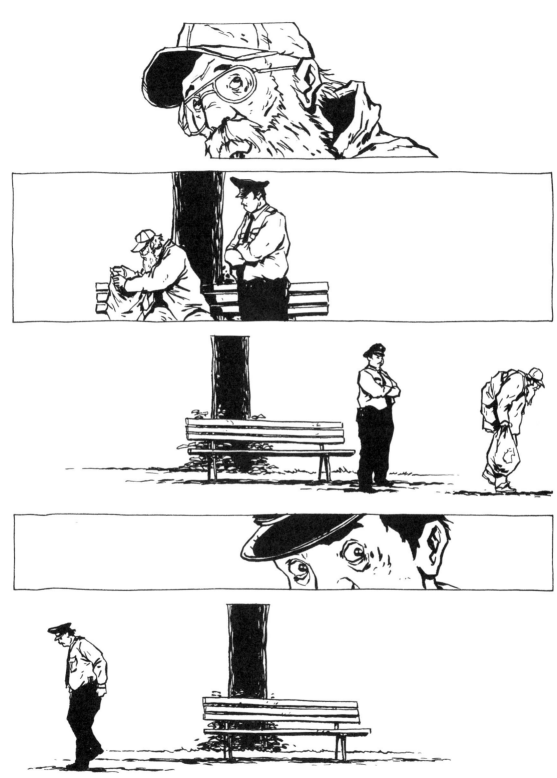

27.

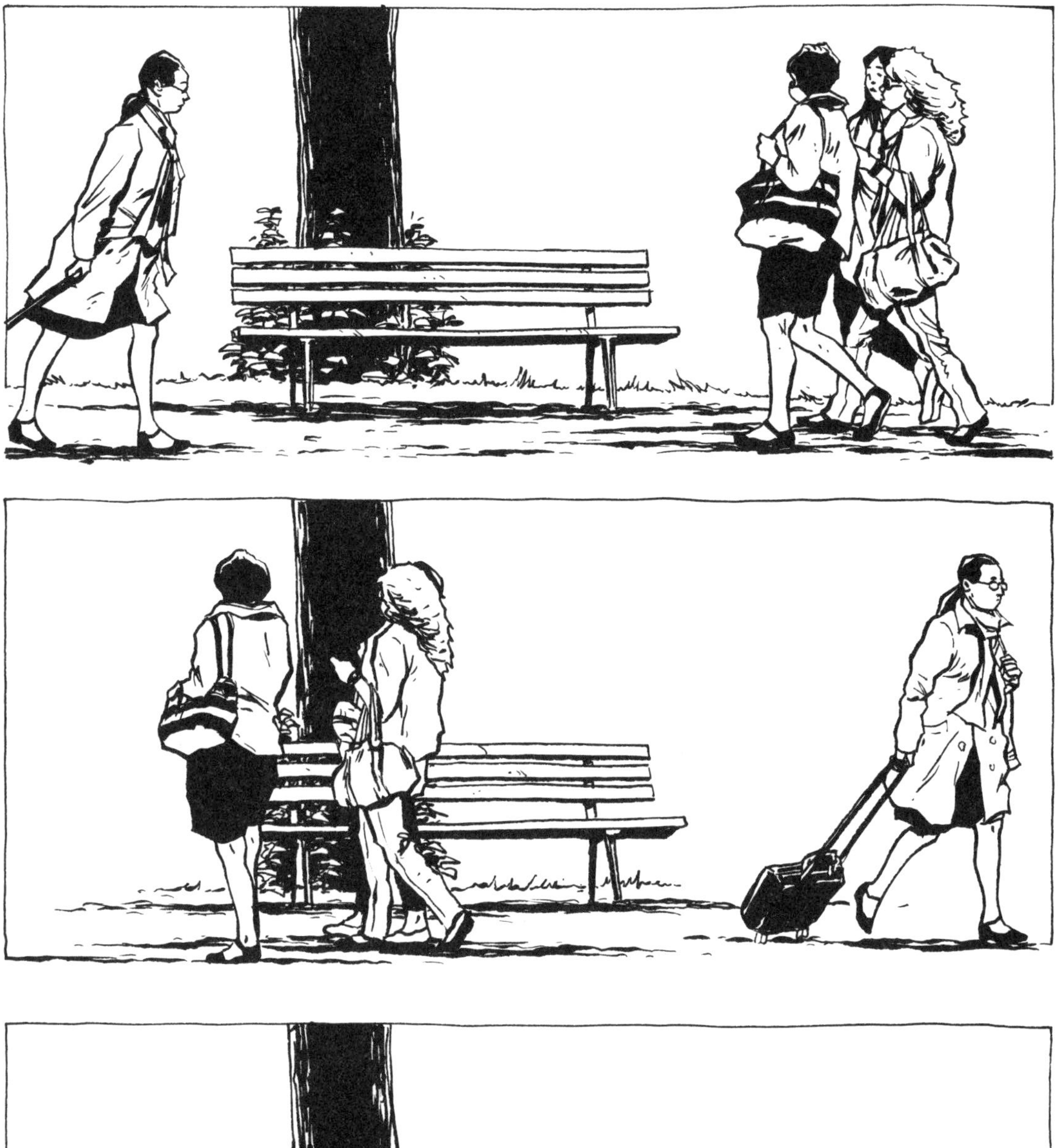

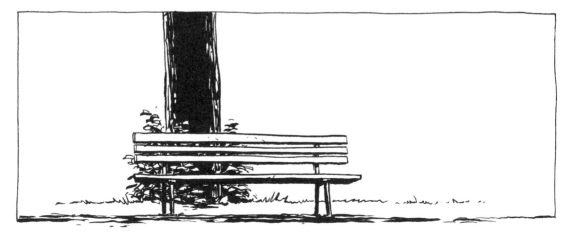

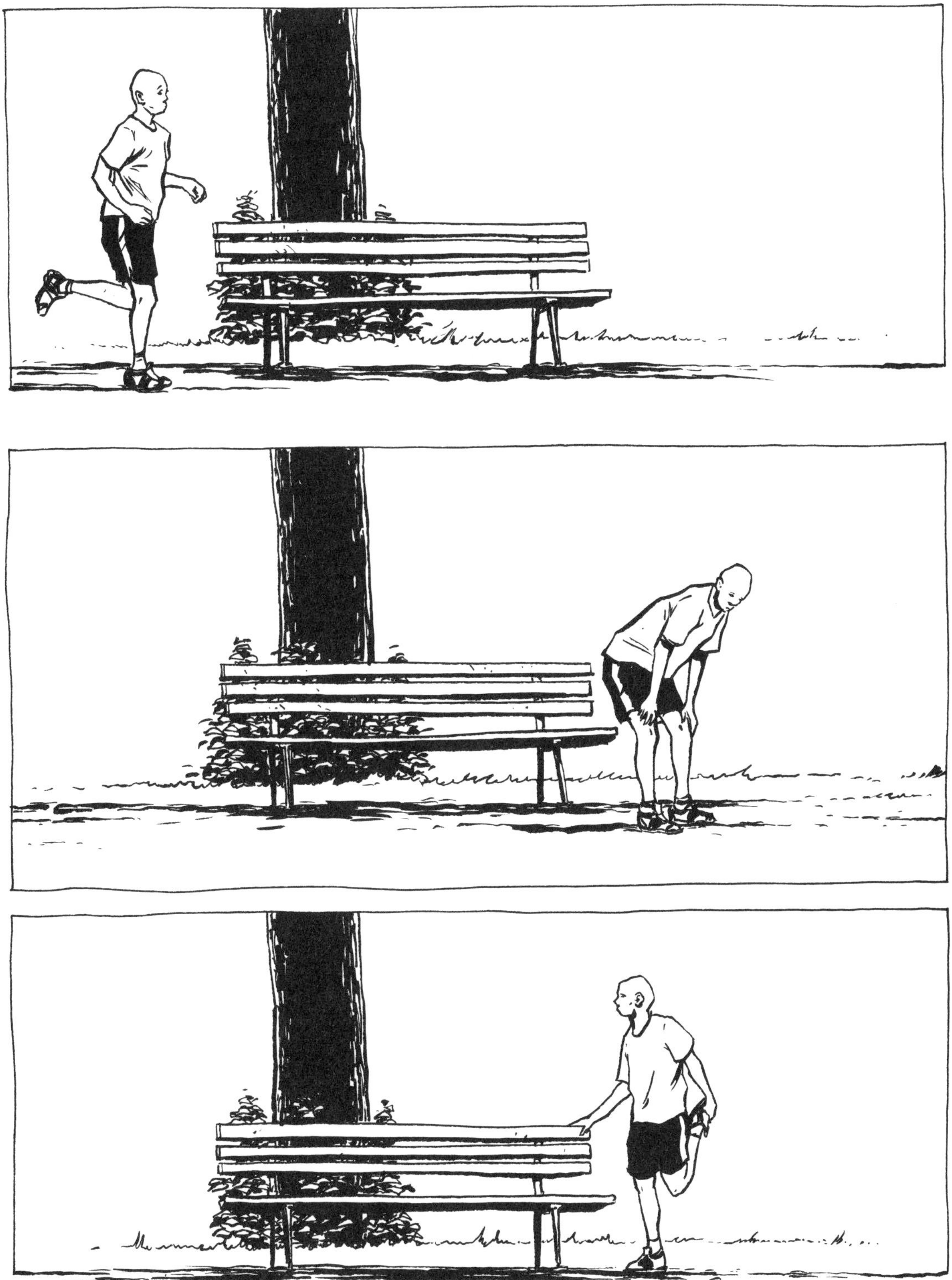

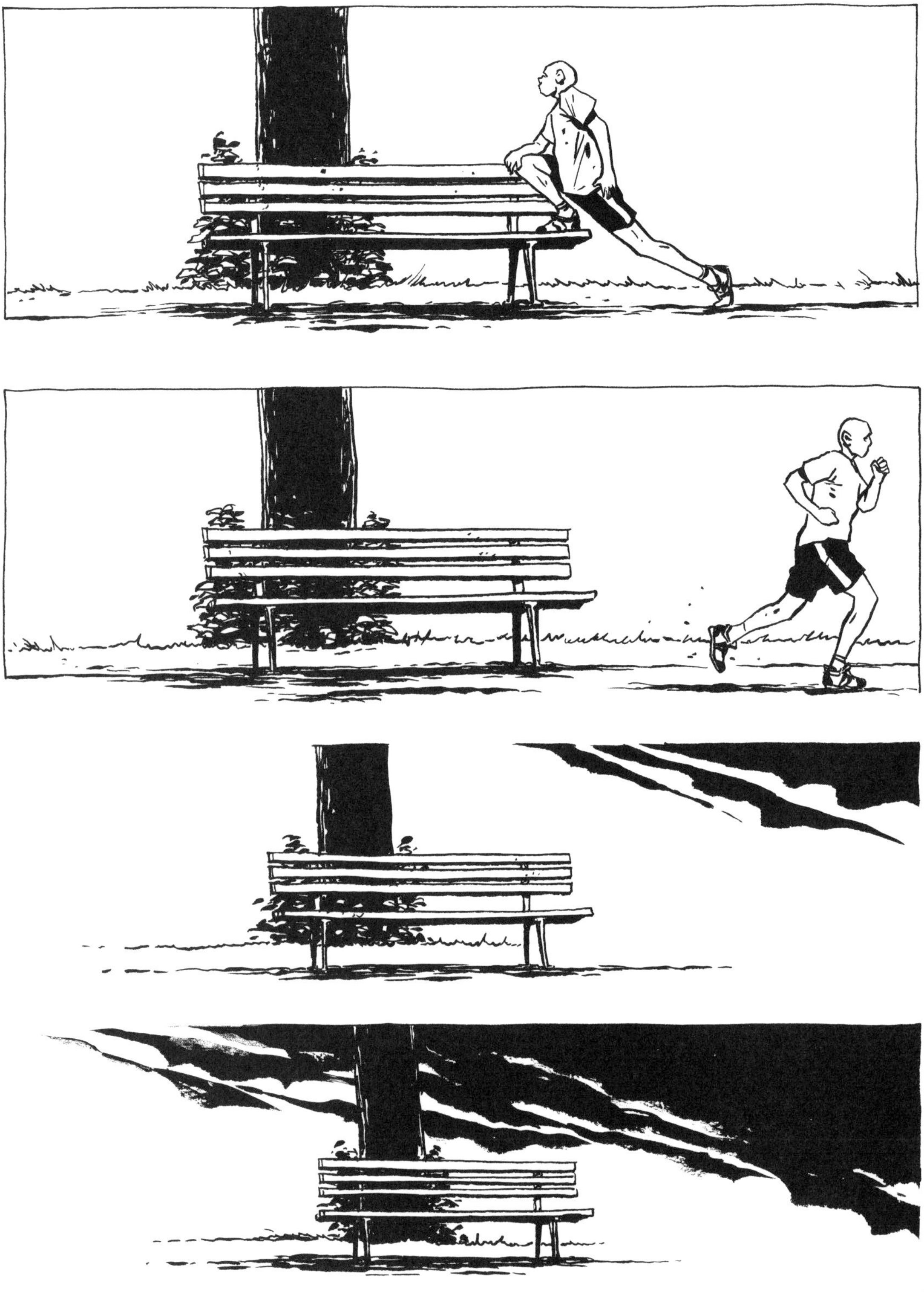

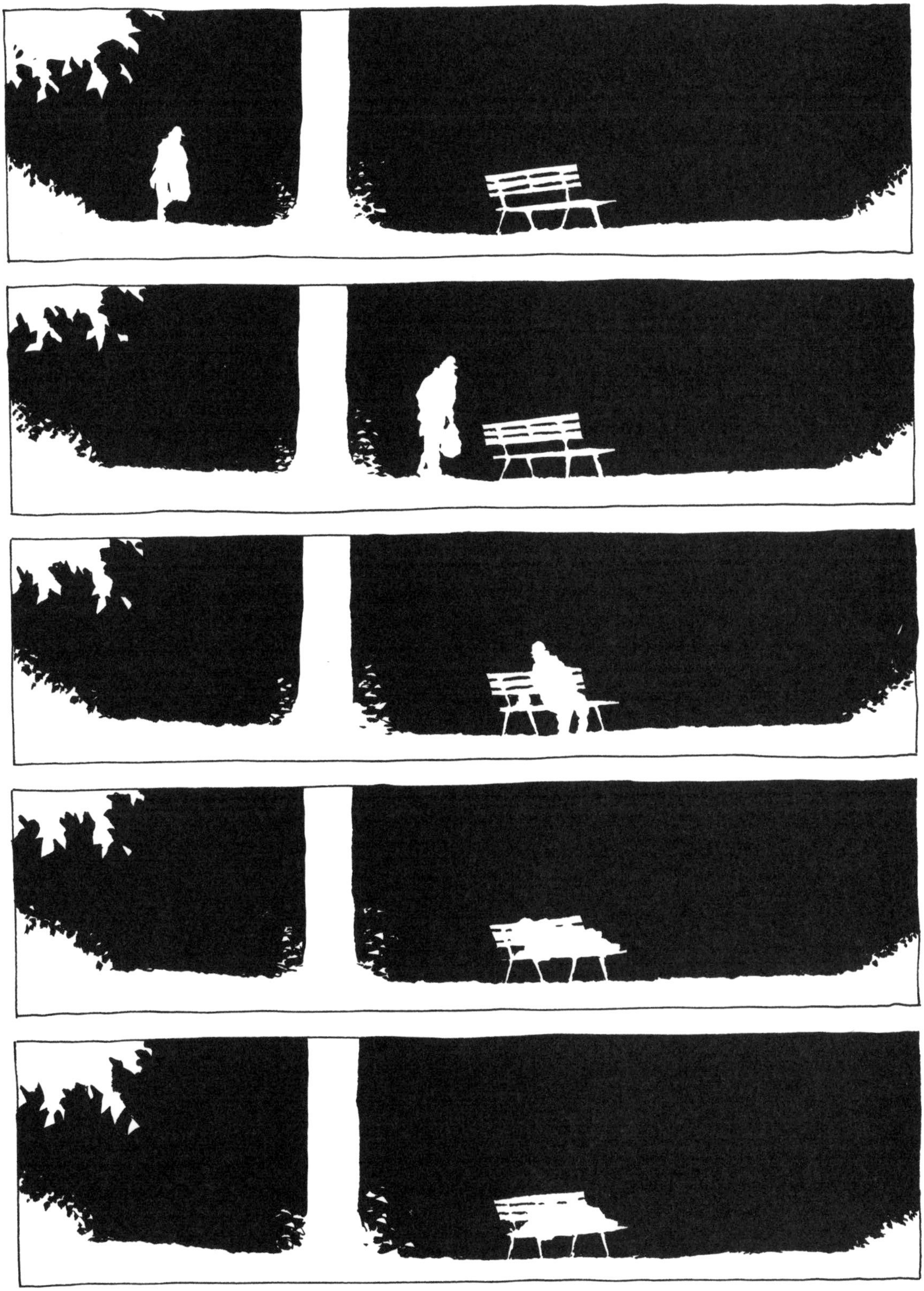

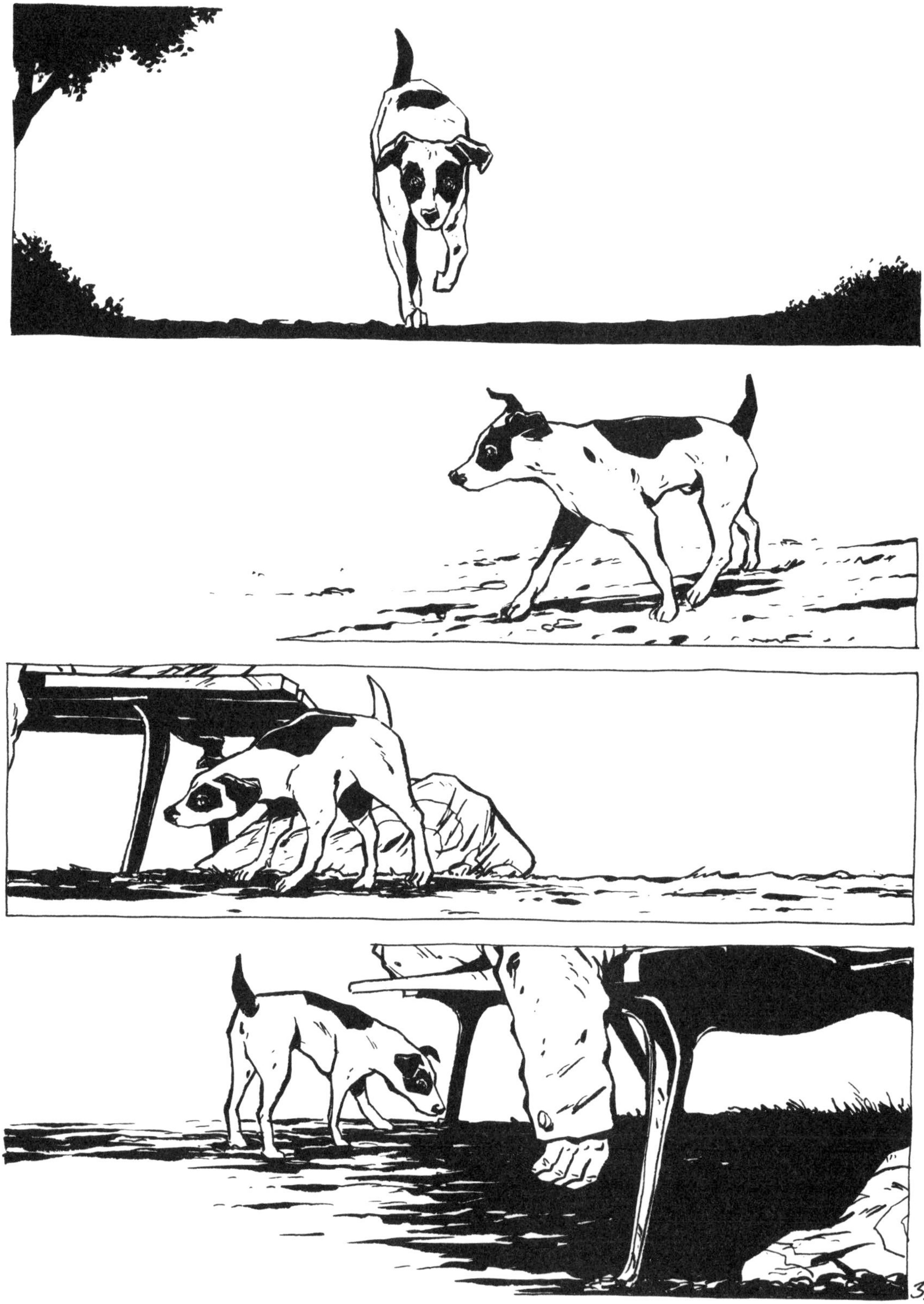

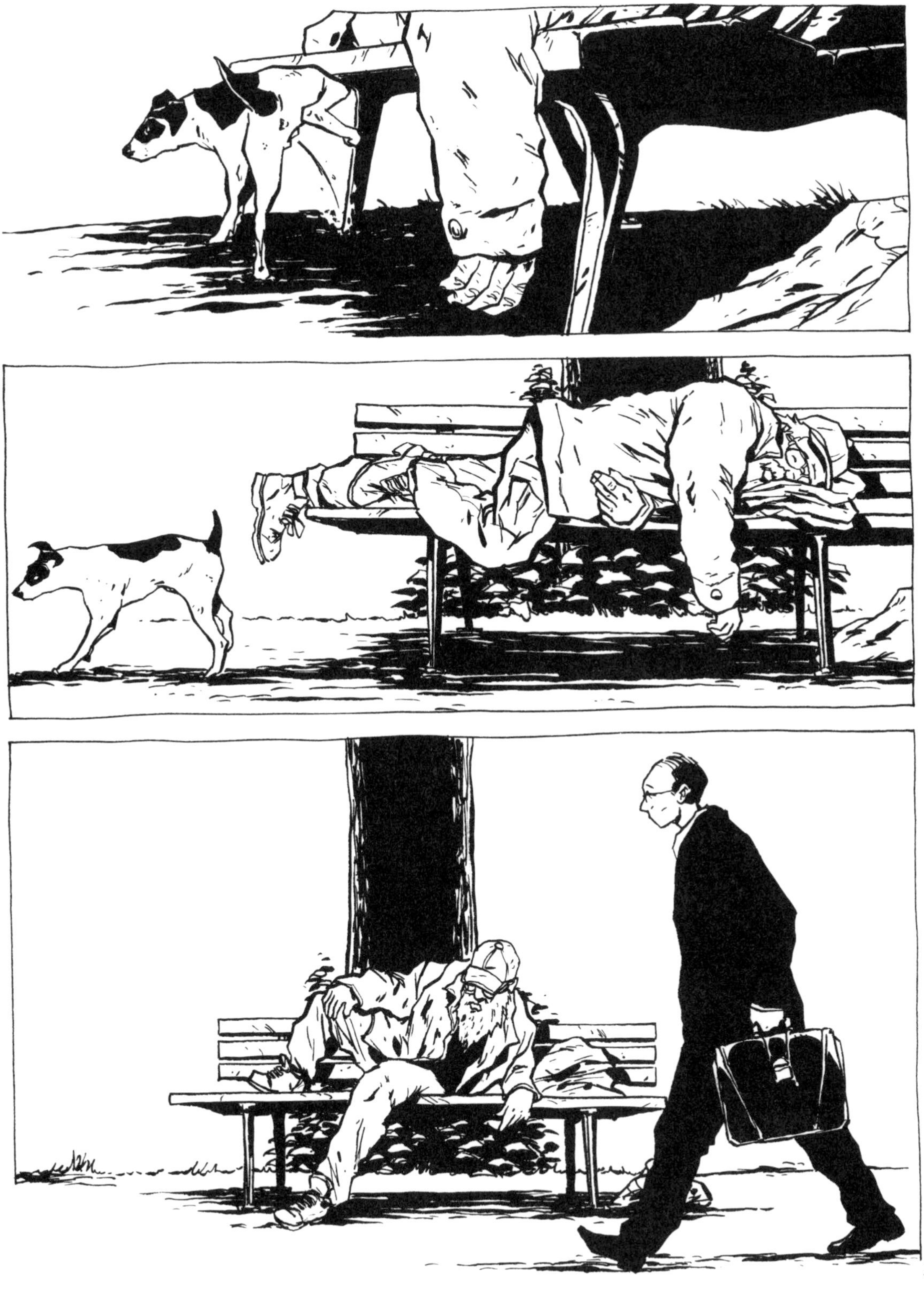

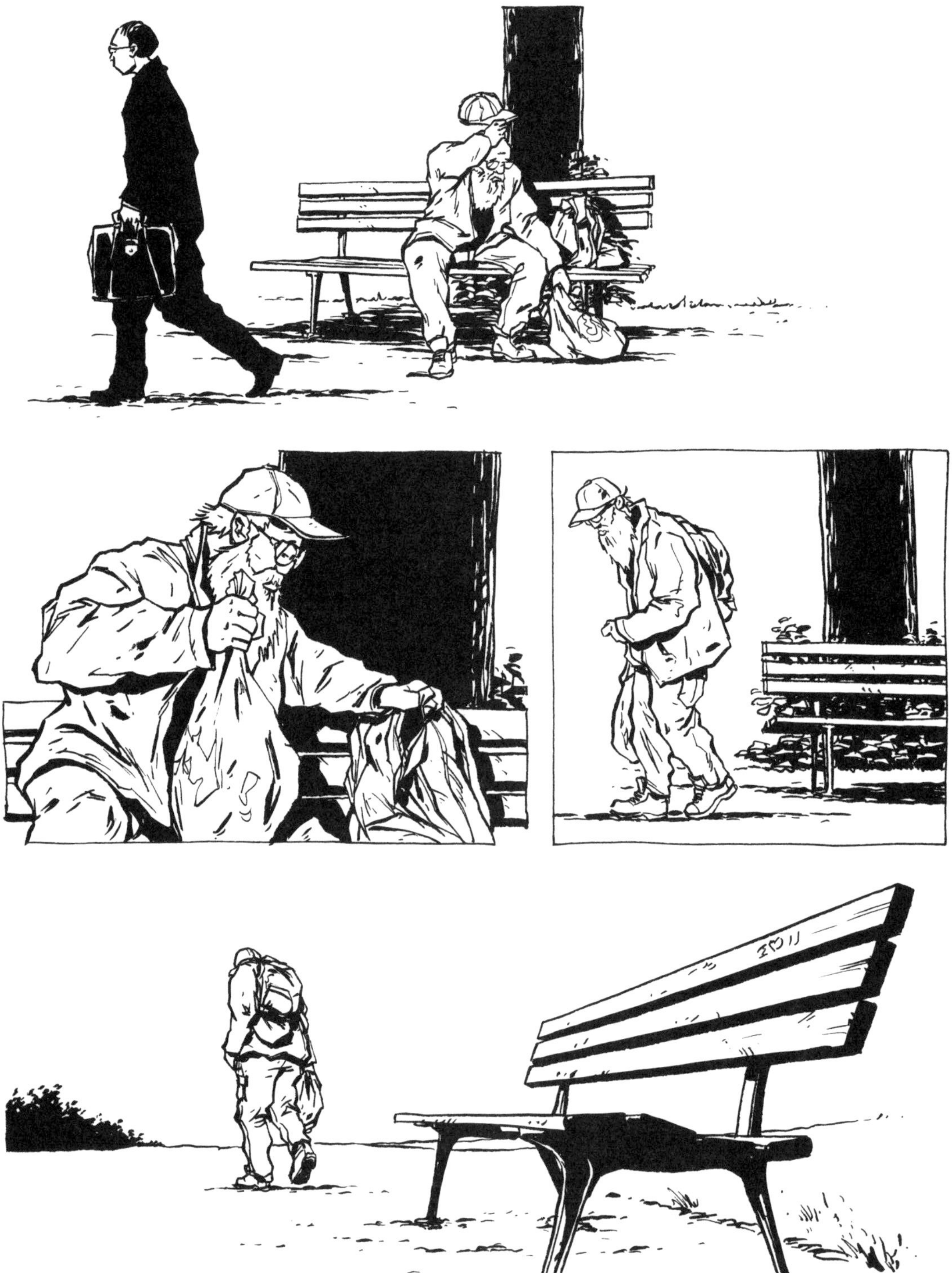

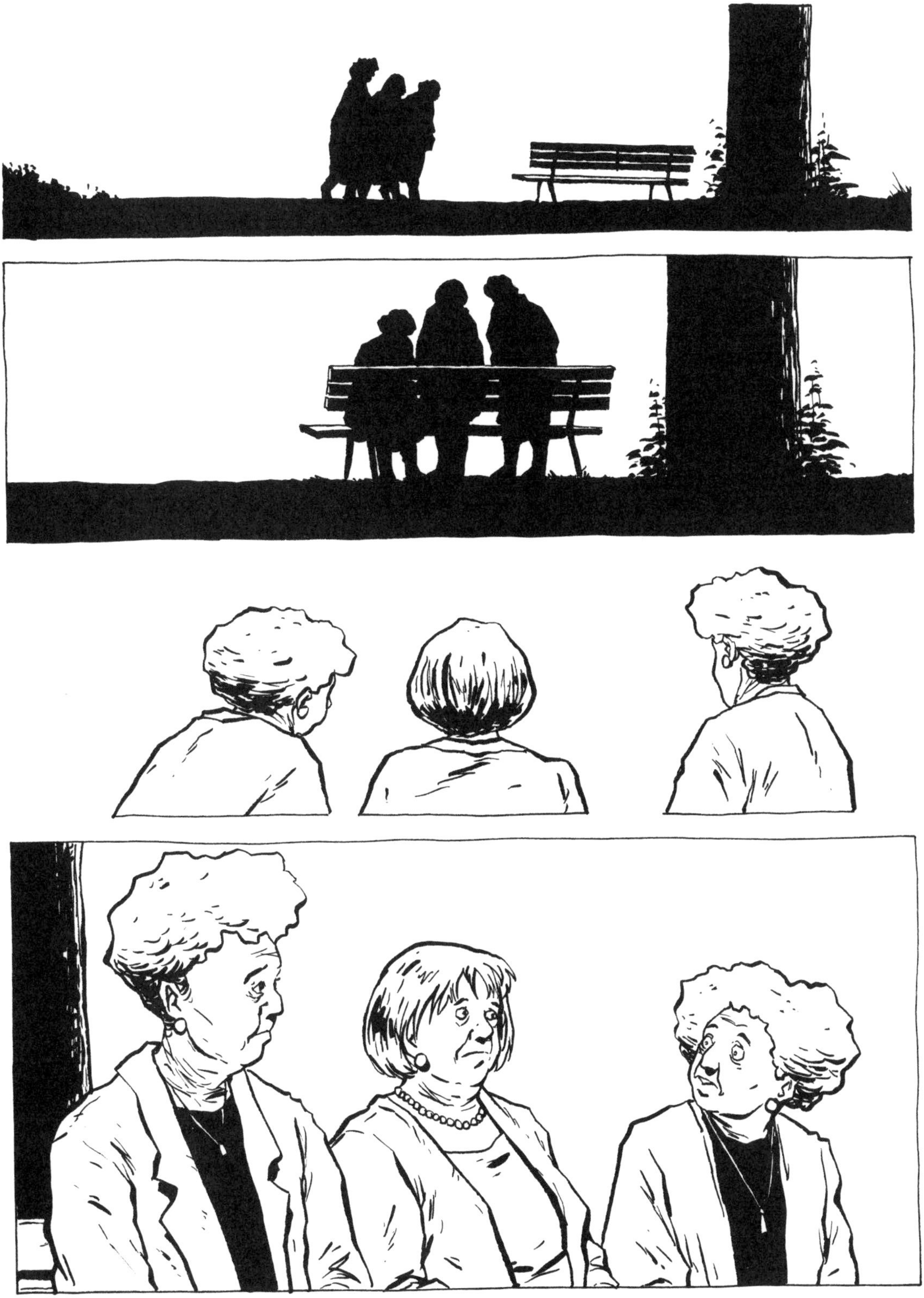

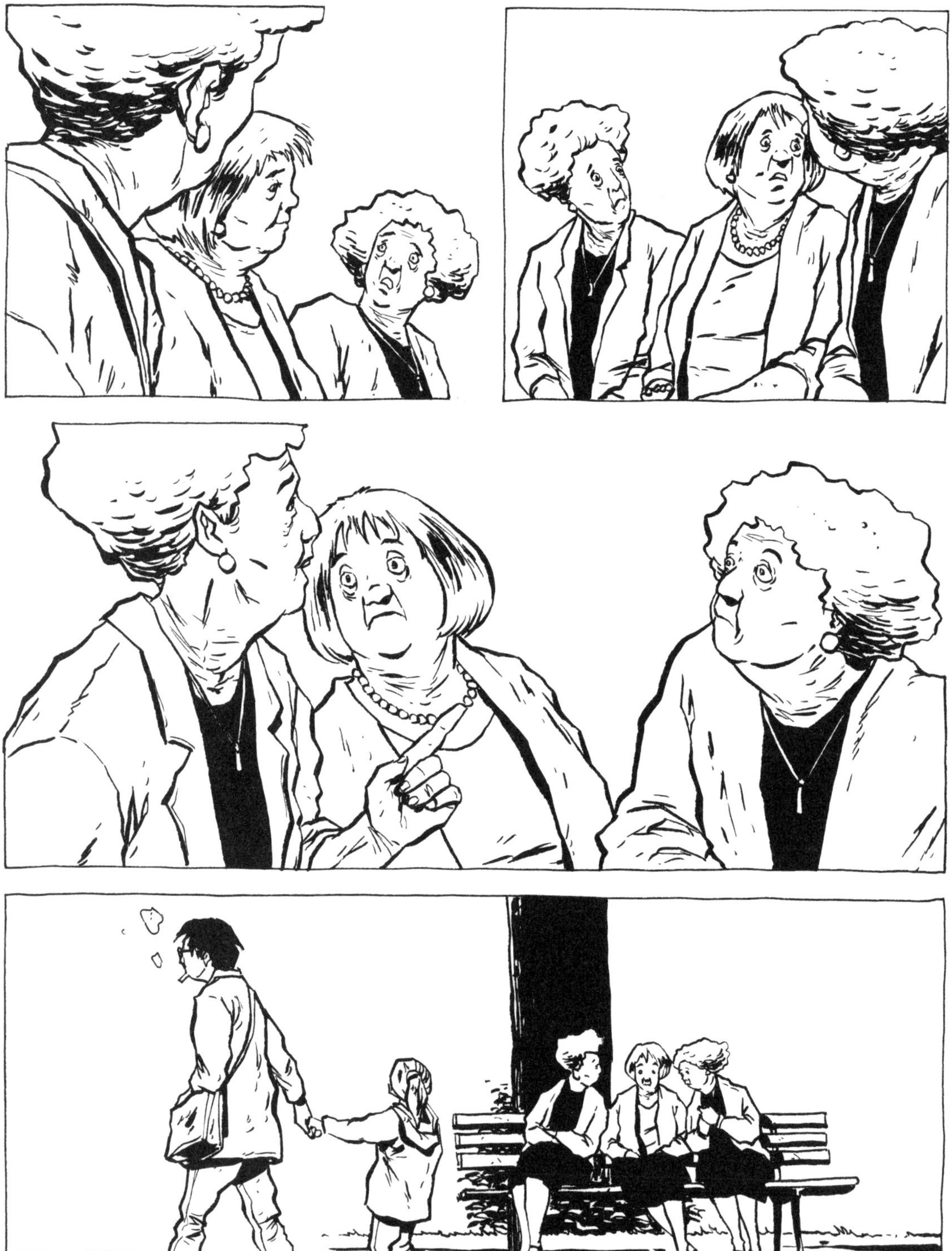

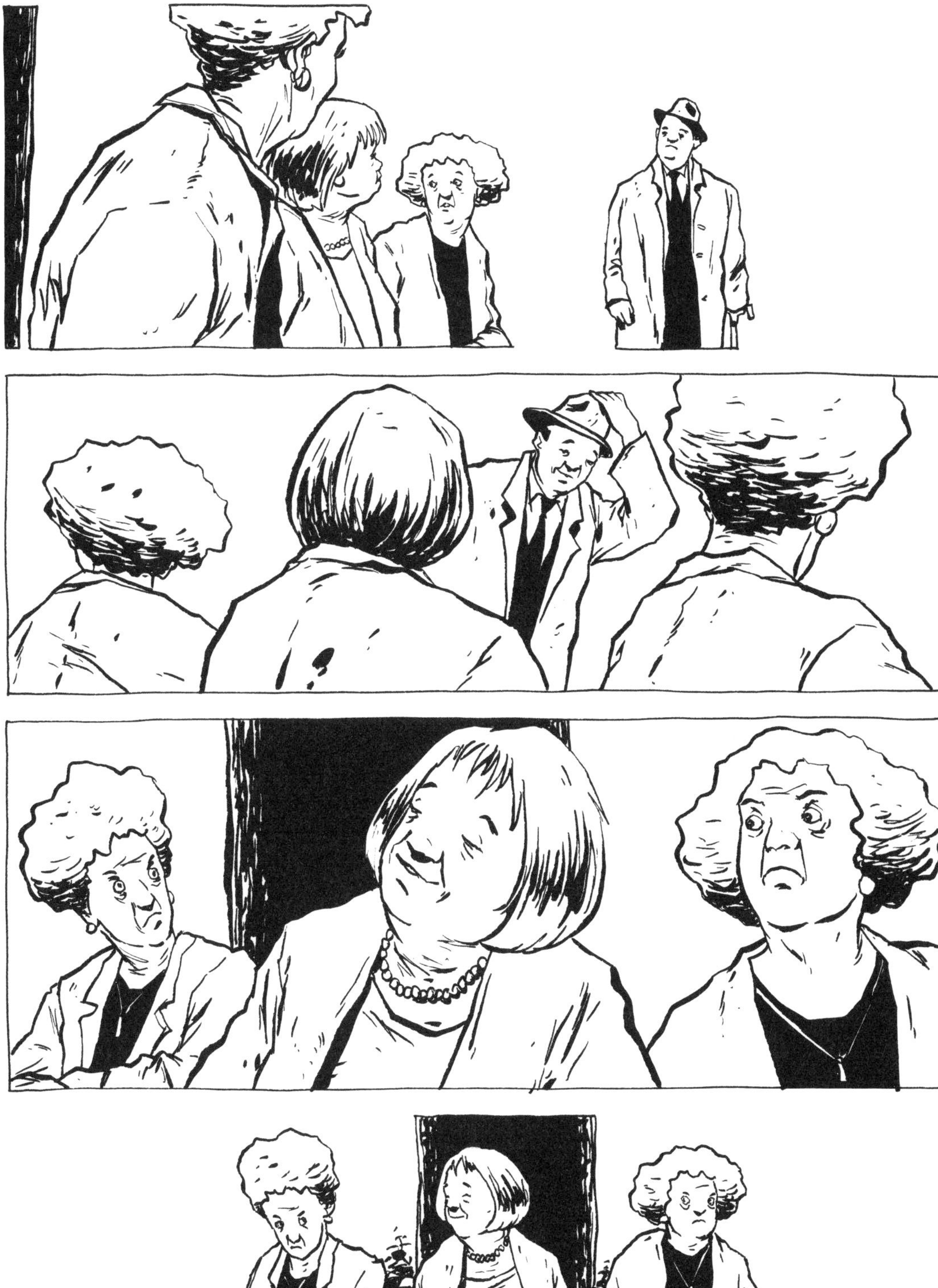

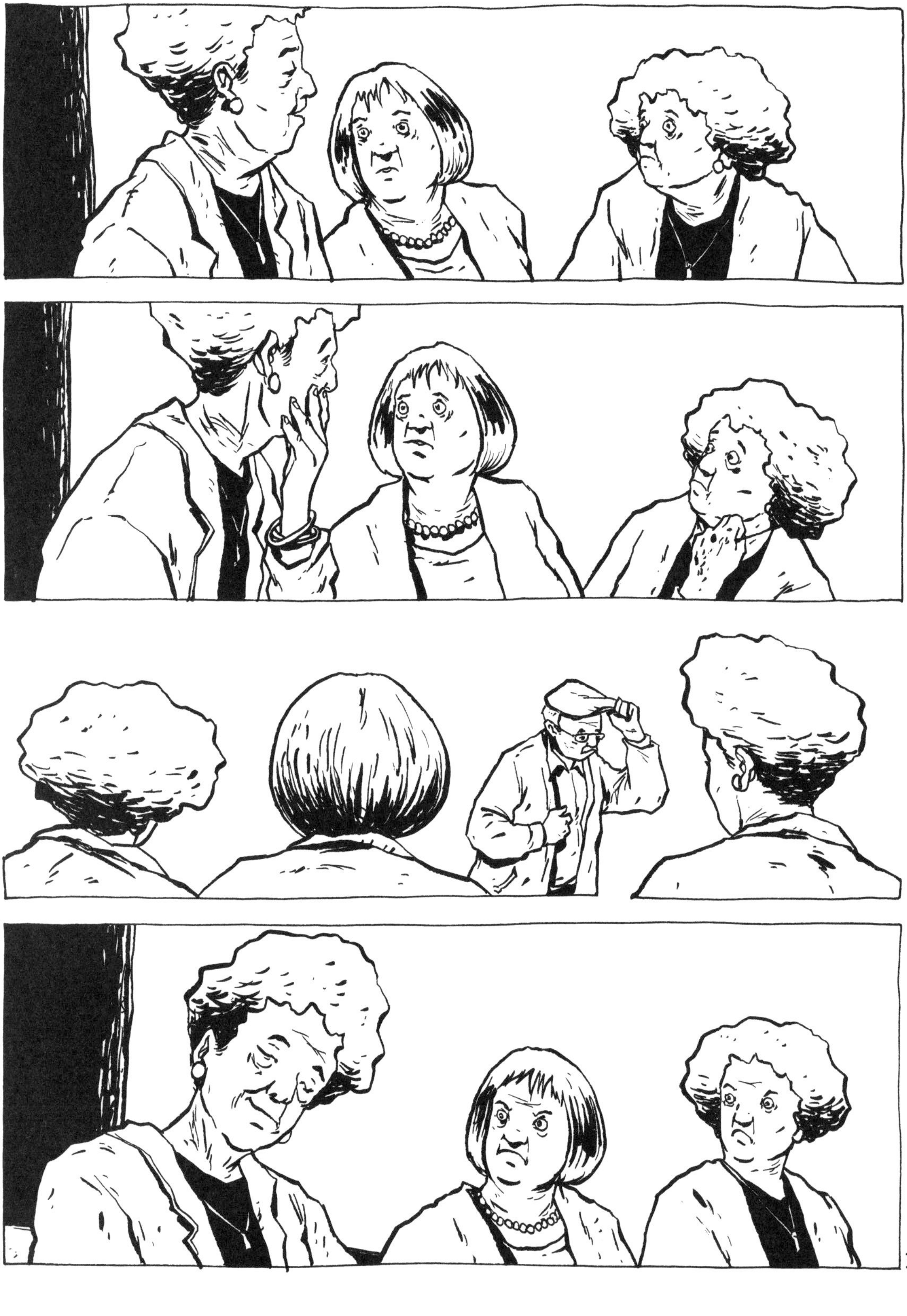

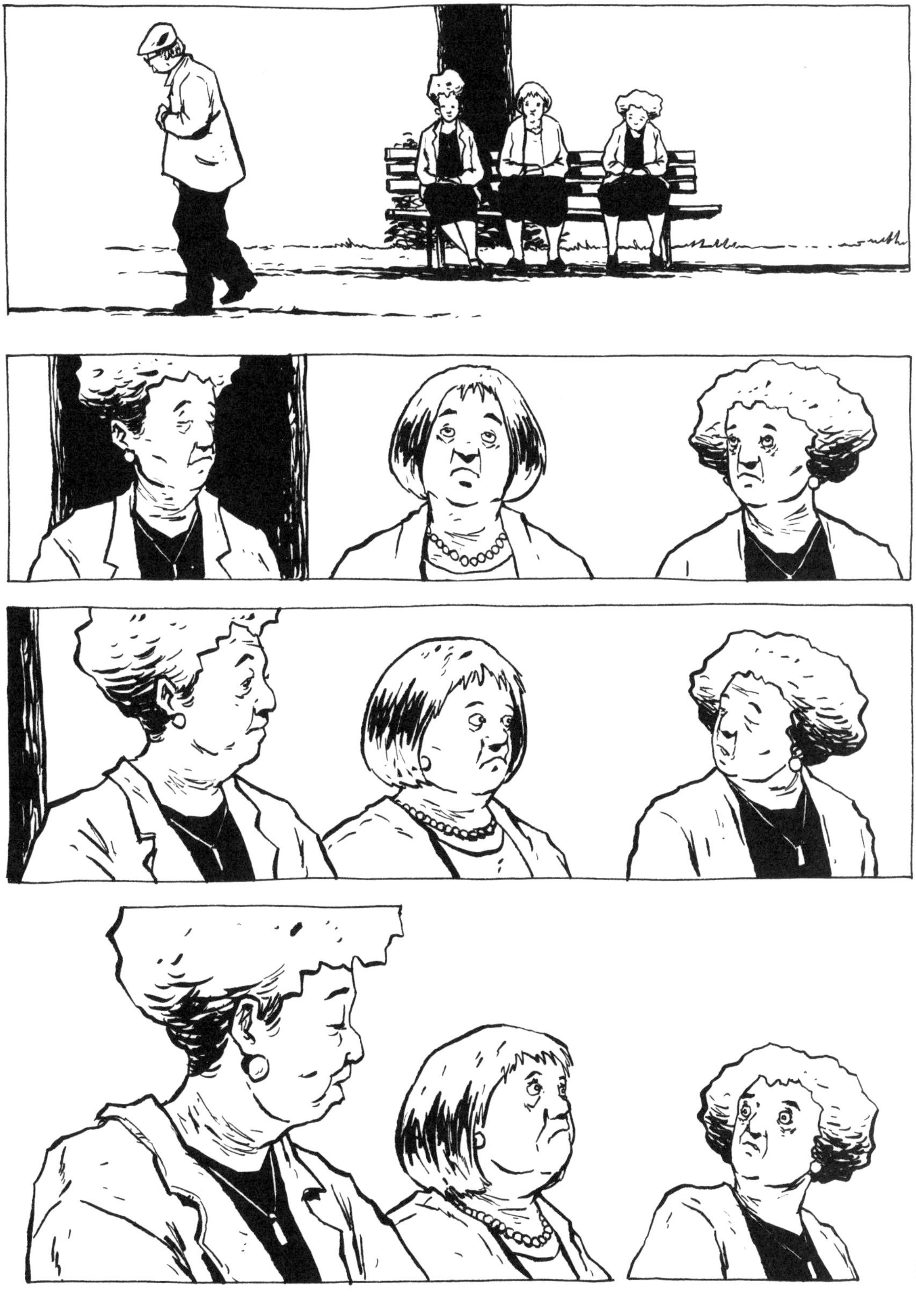

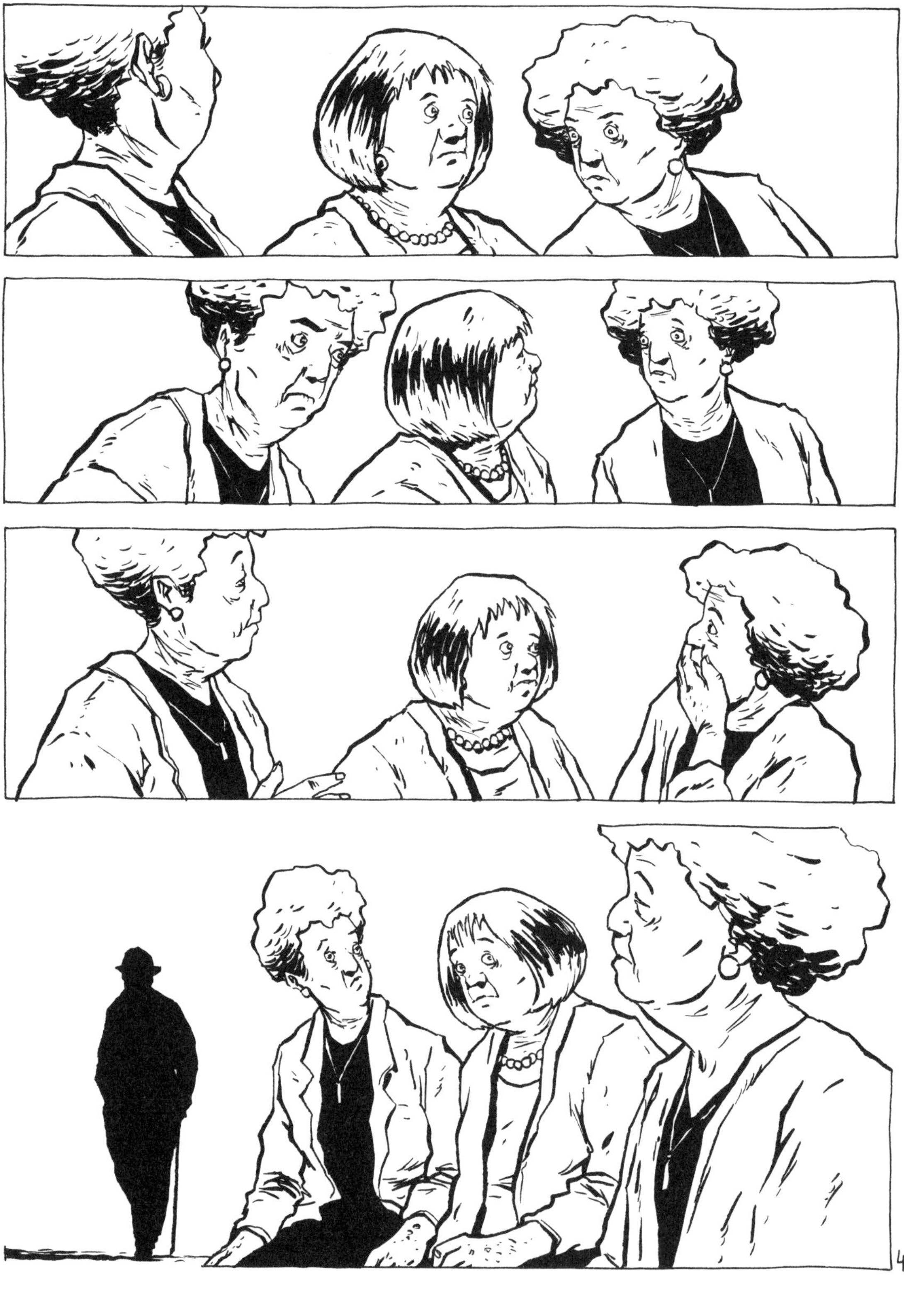

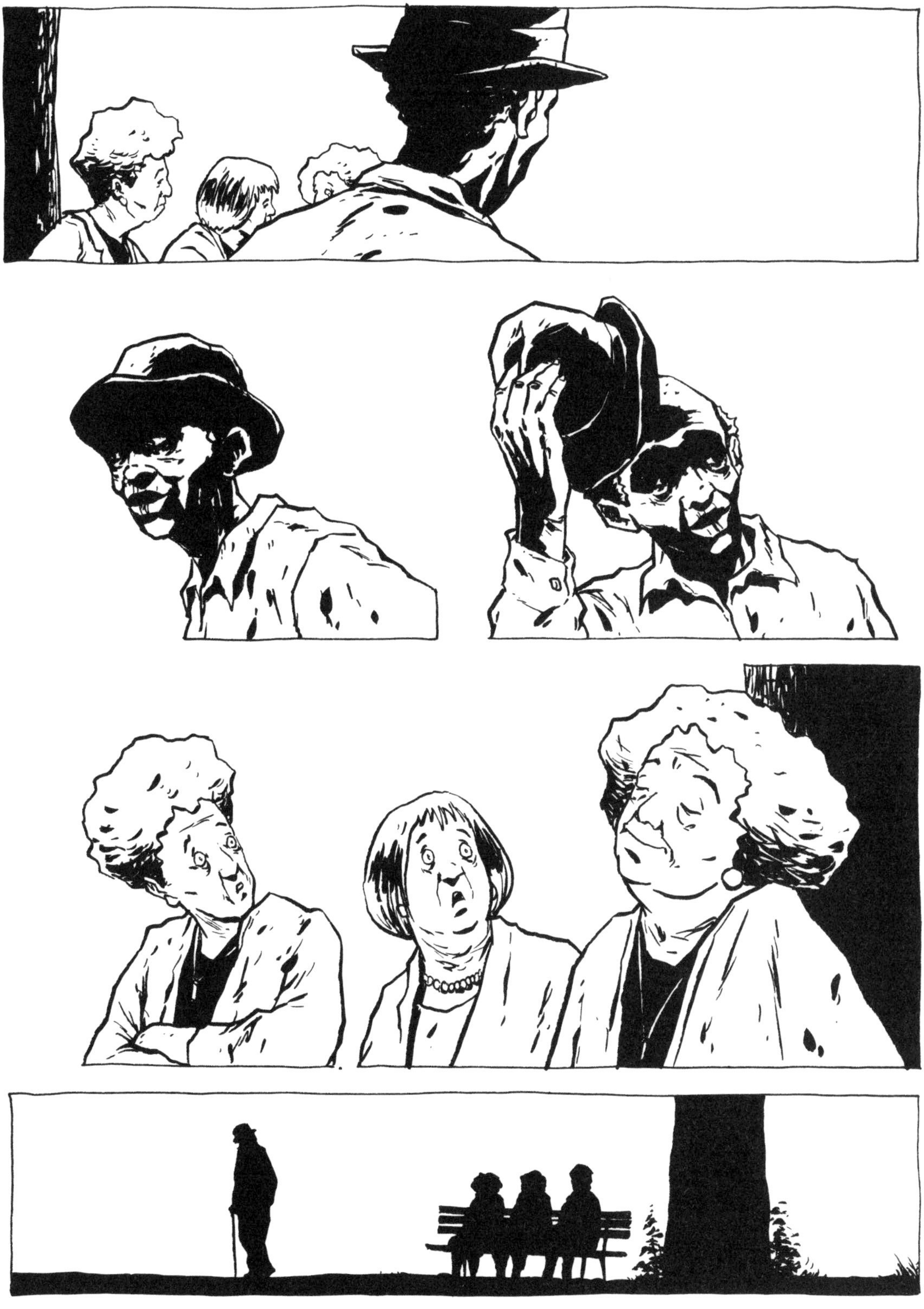

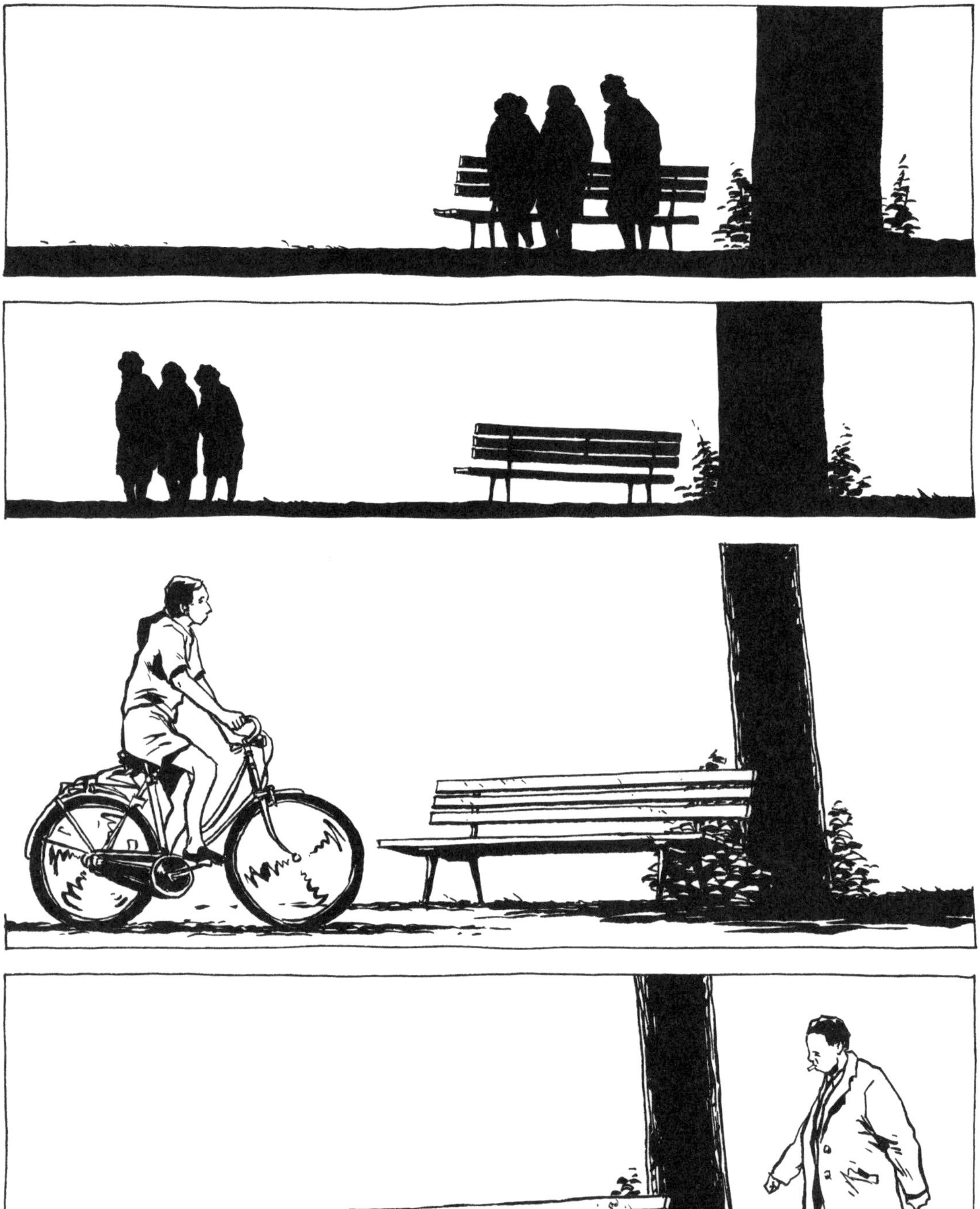

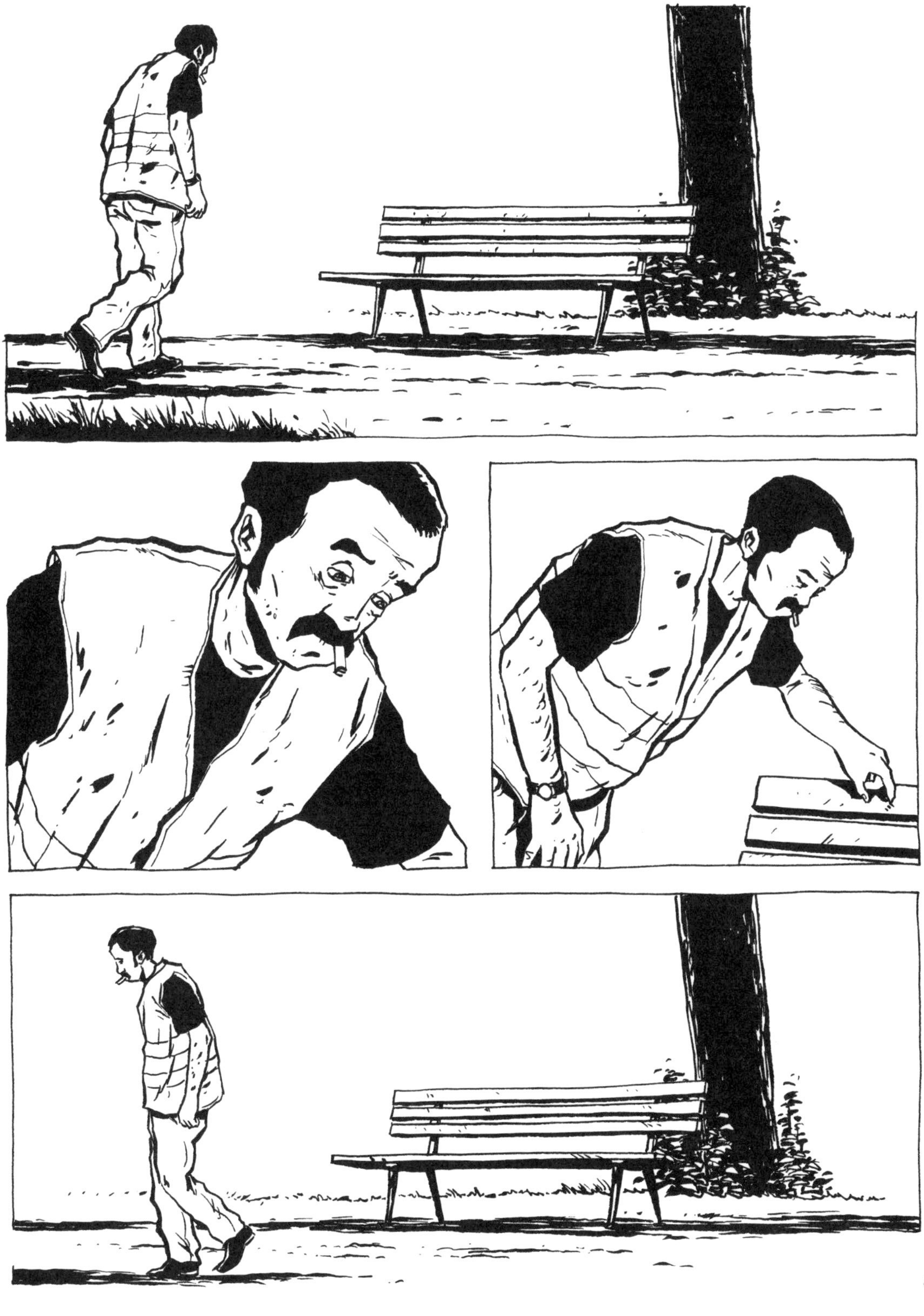

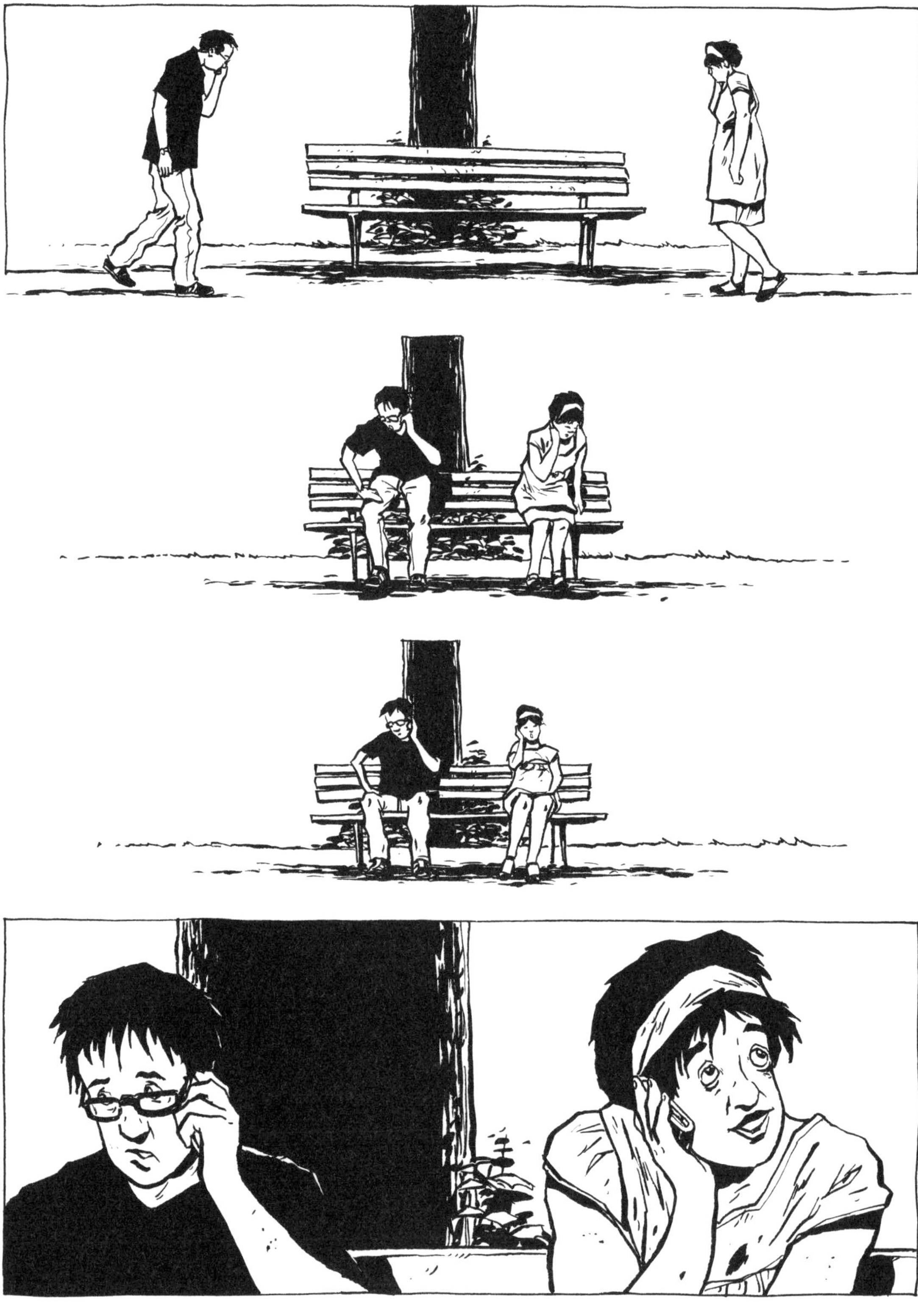

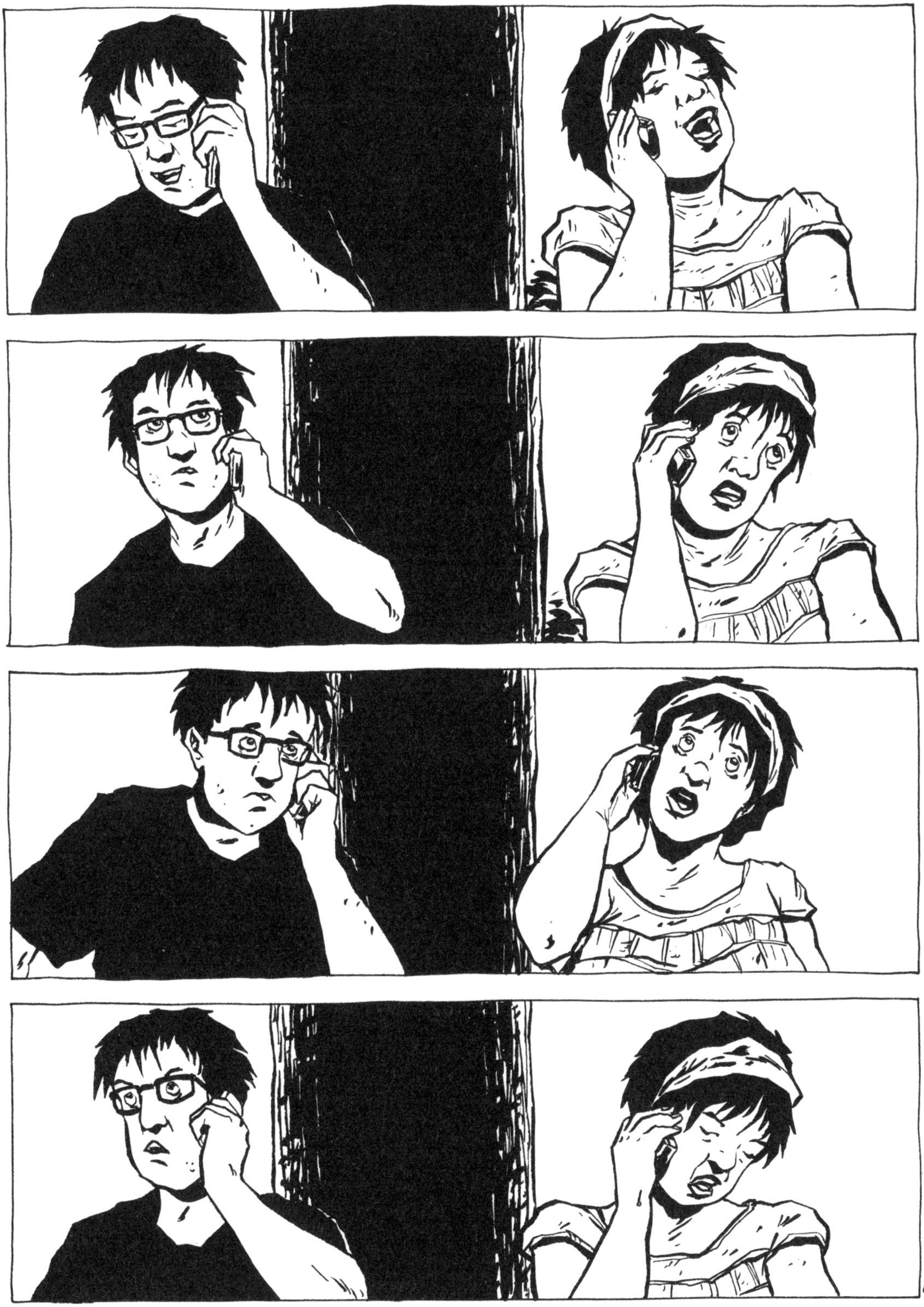

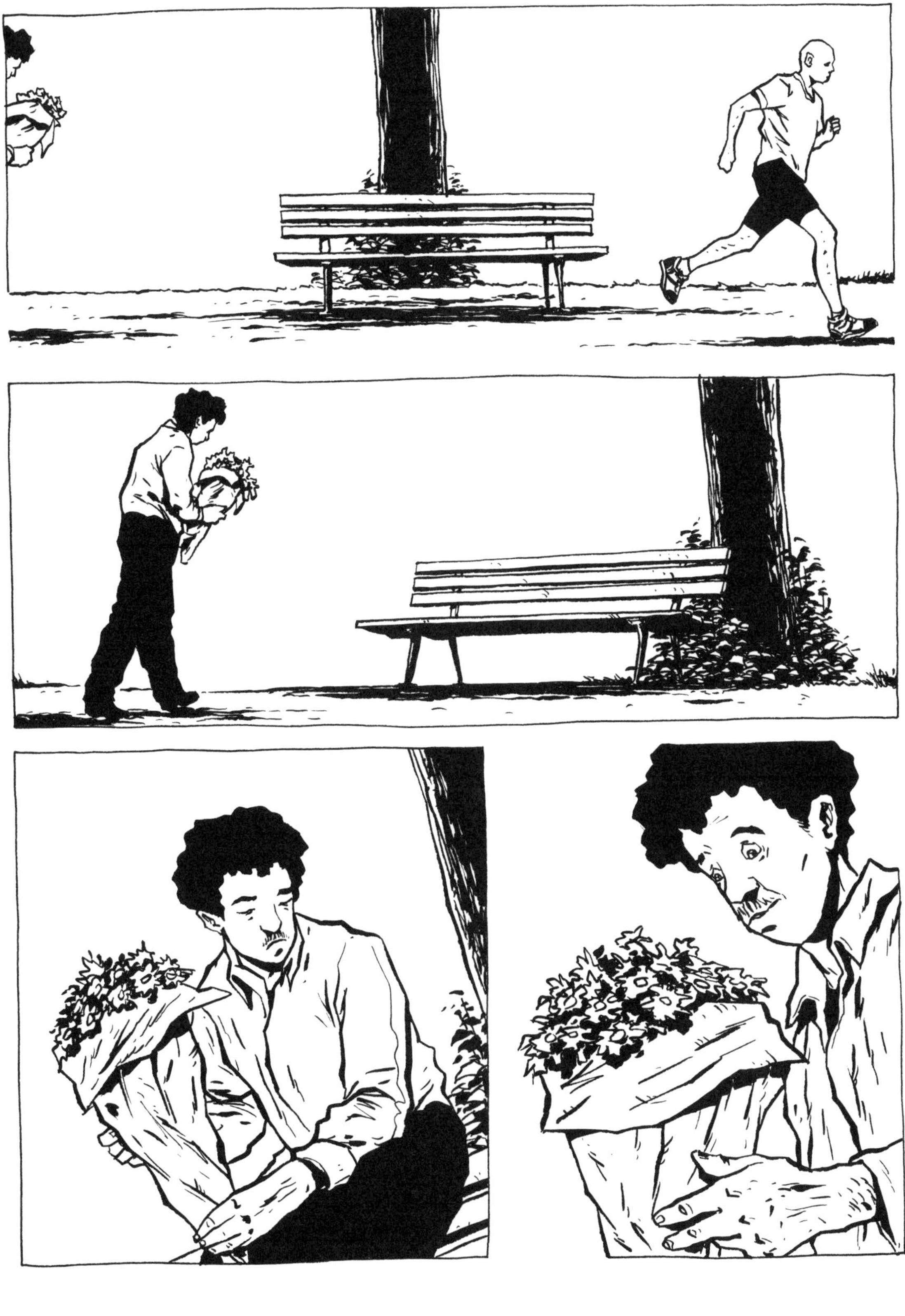

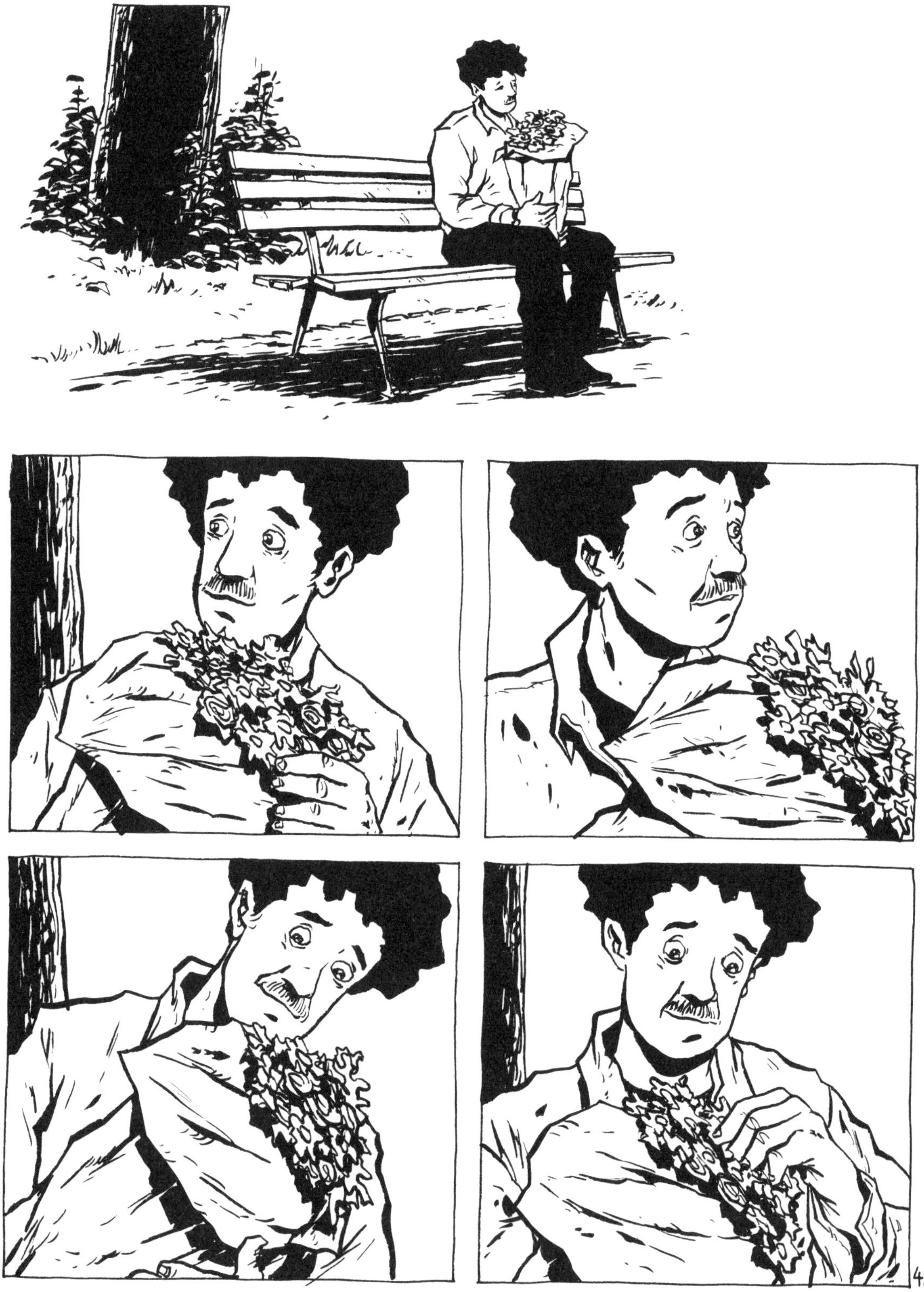

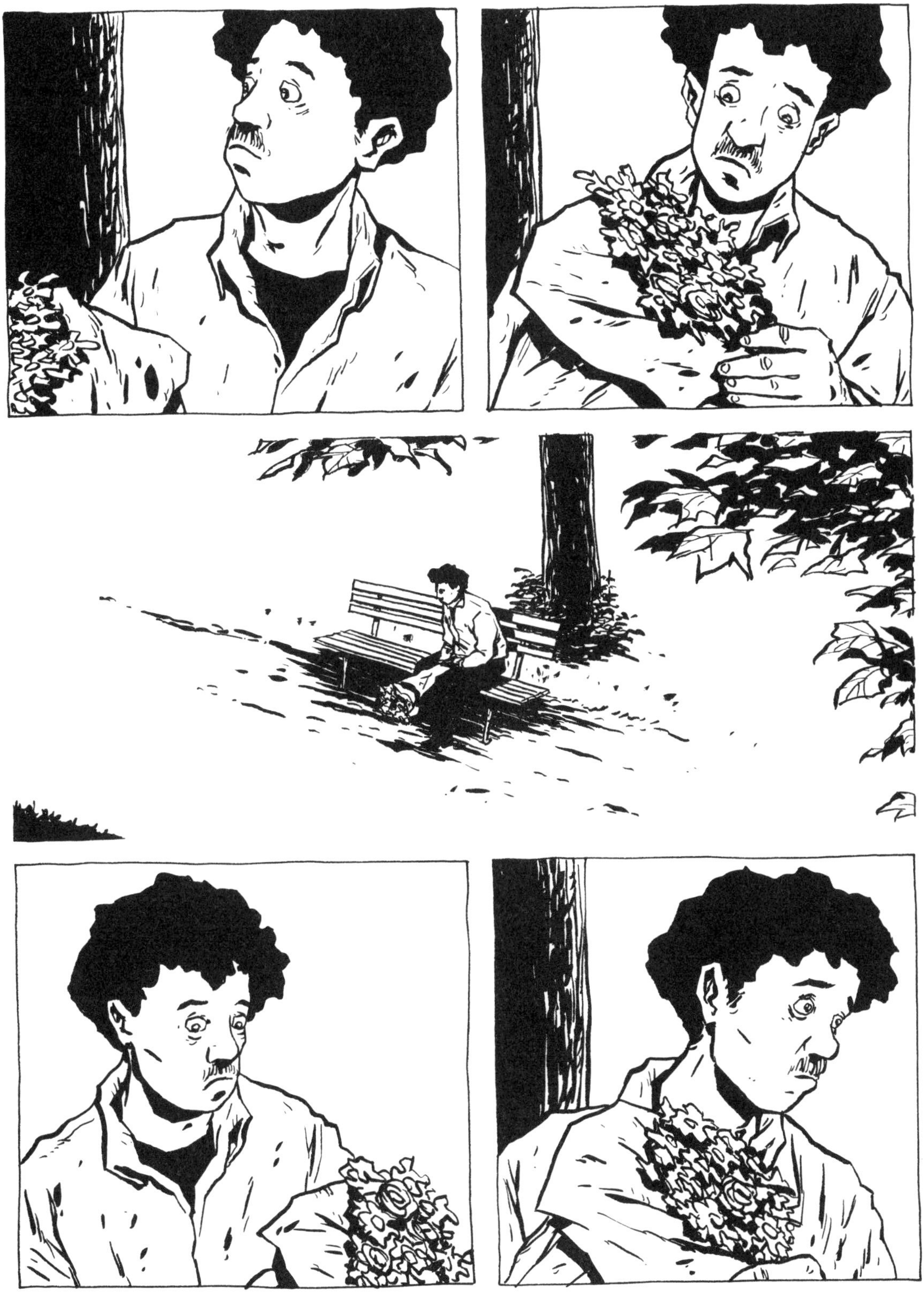

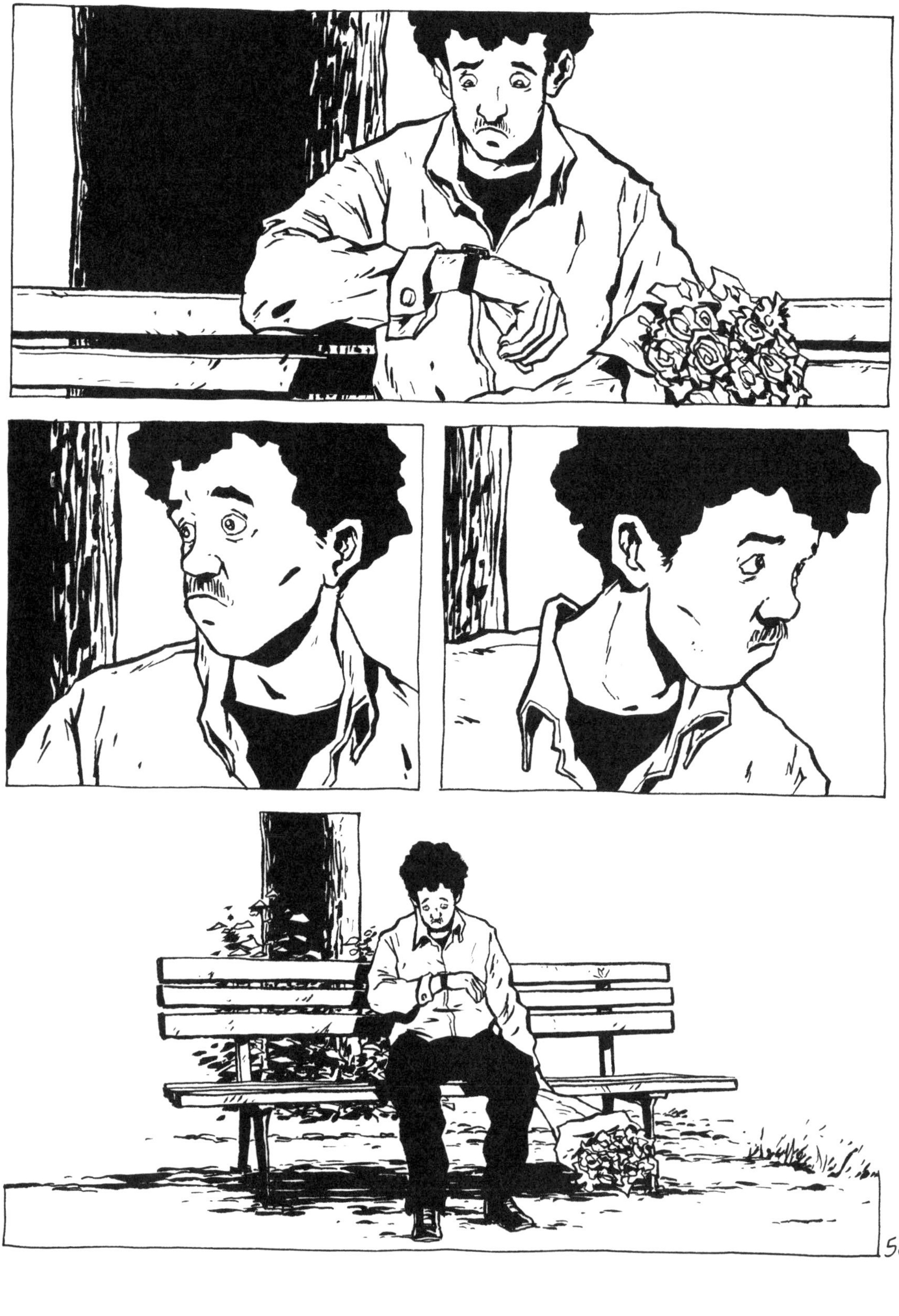

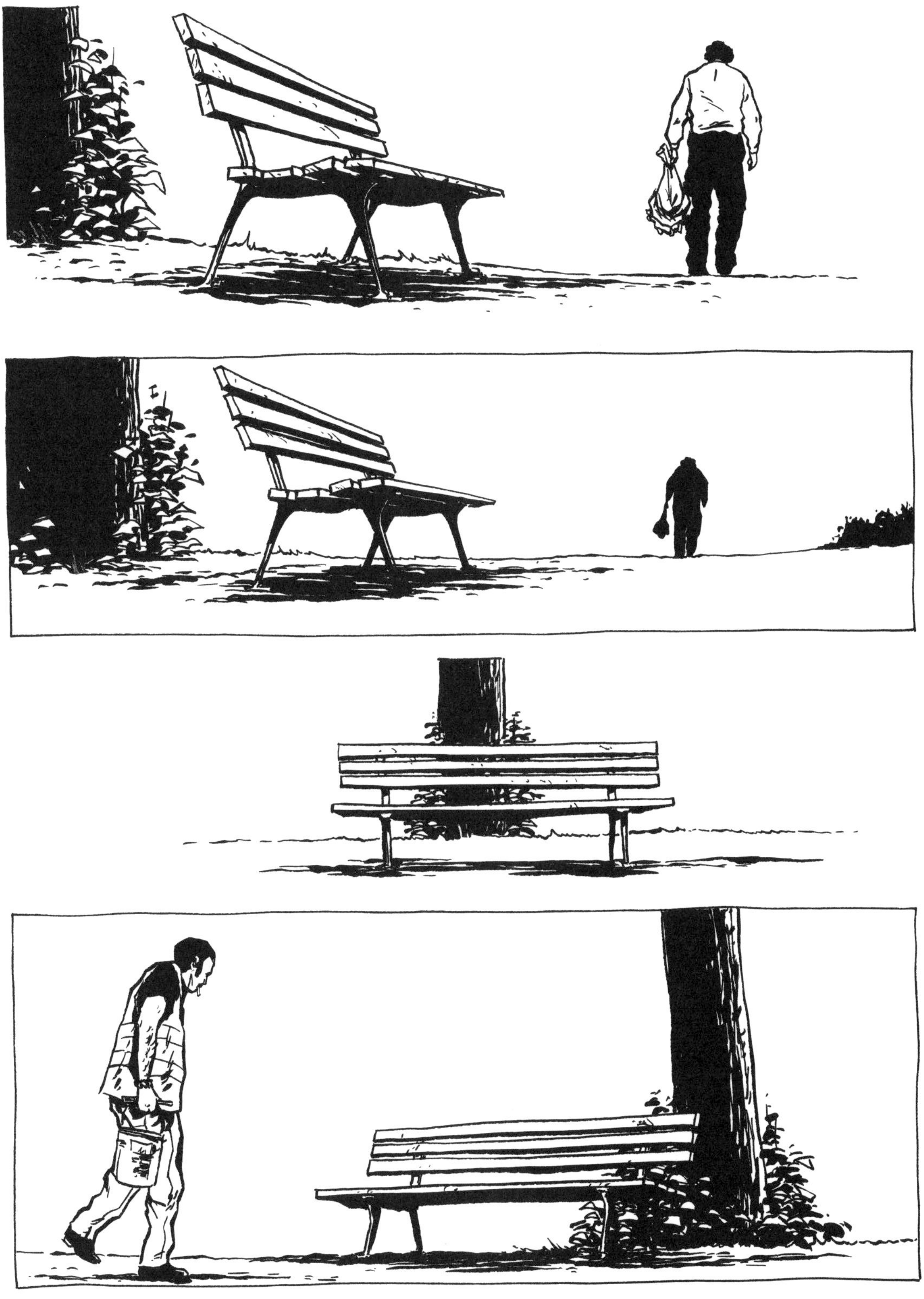

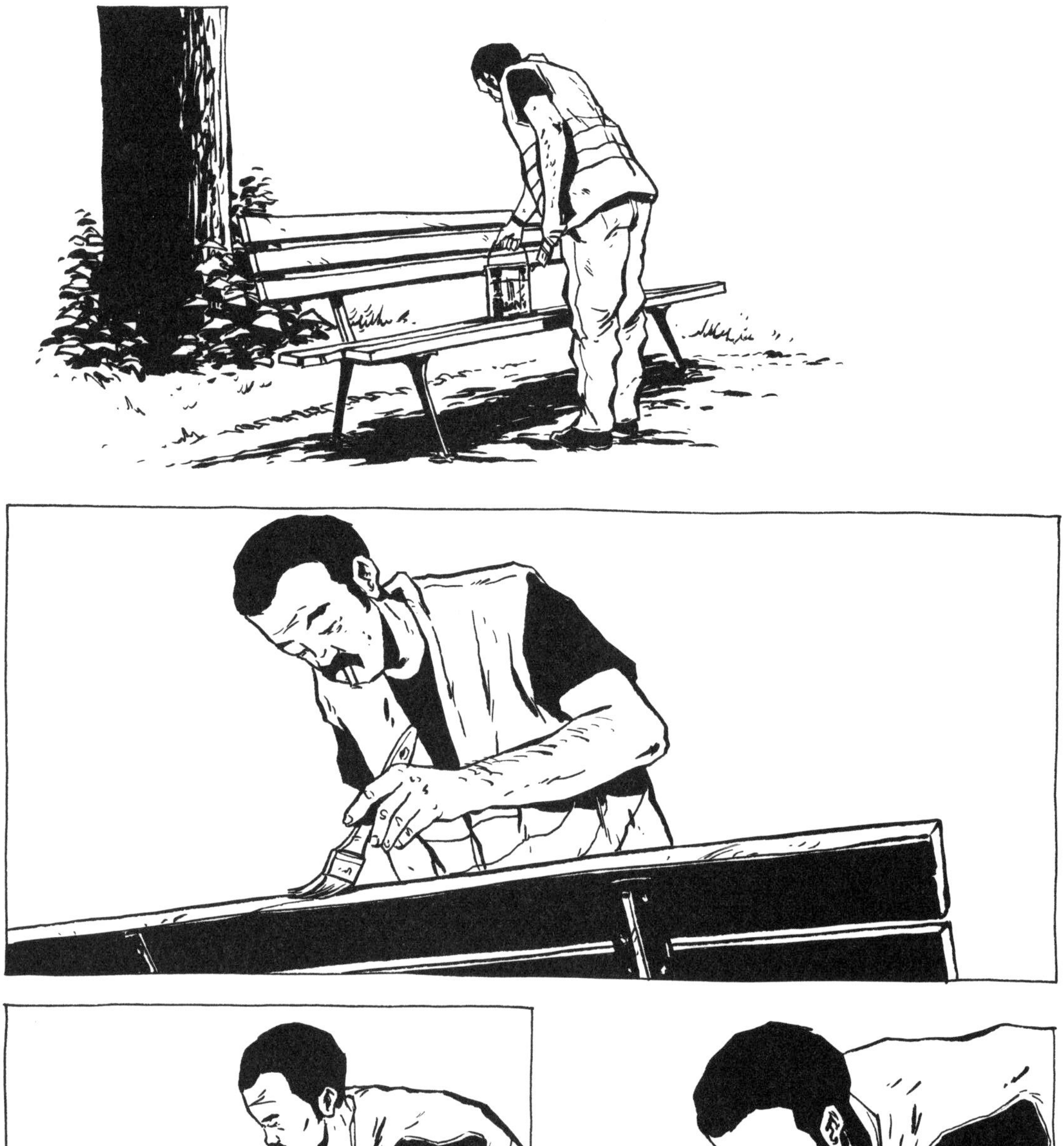

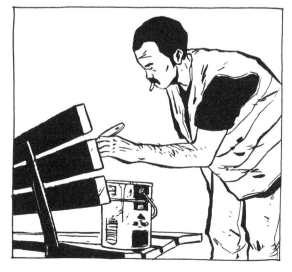

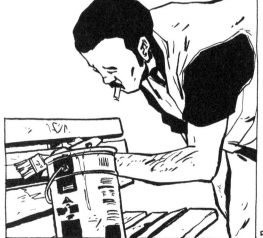

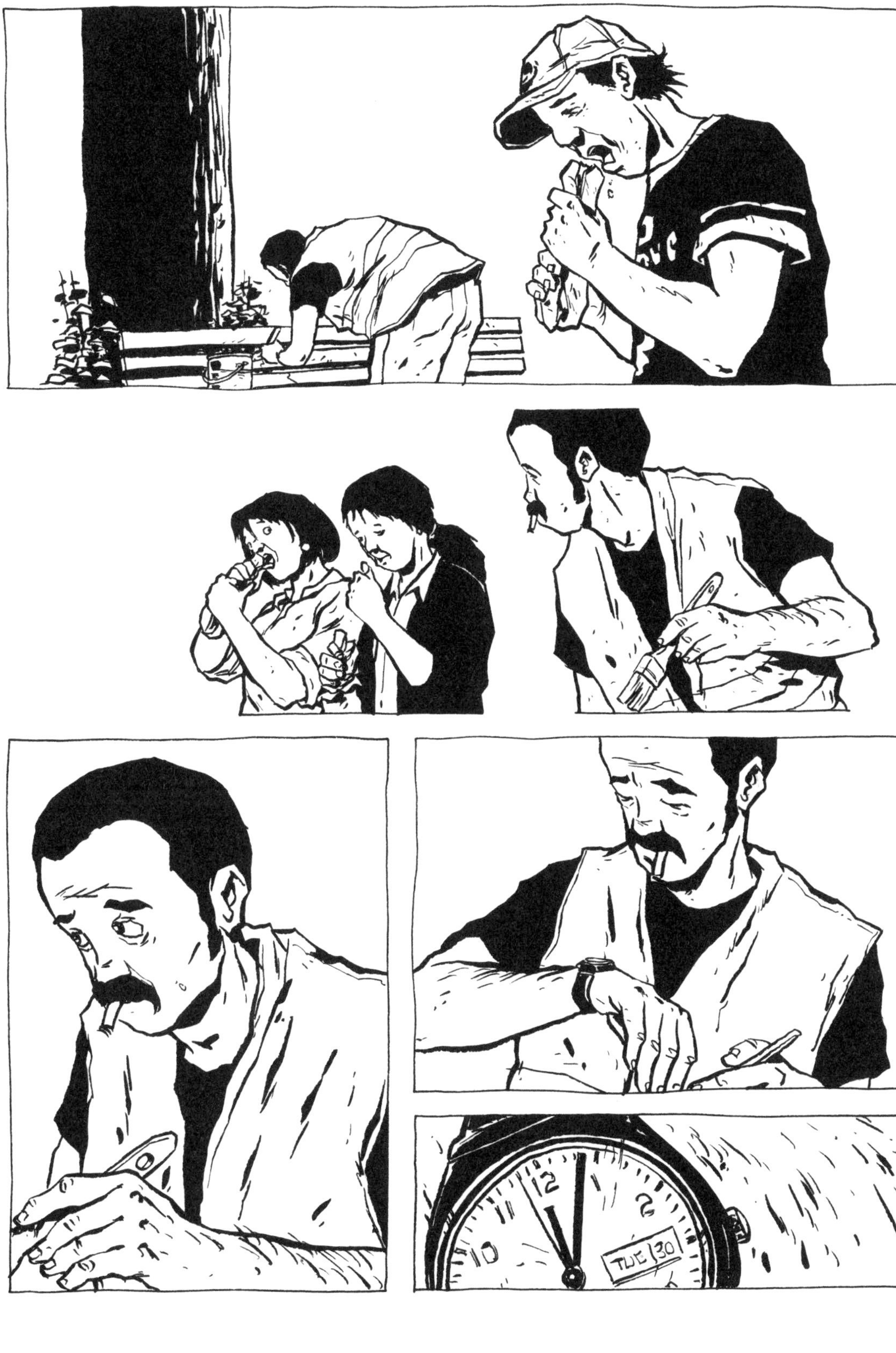
TUE 30

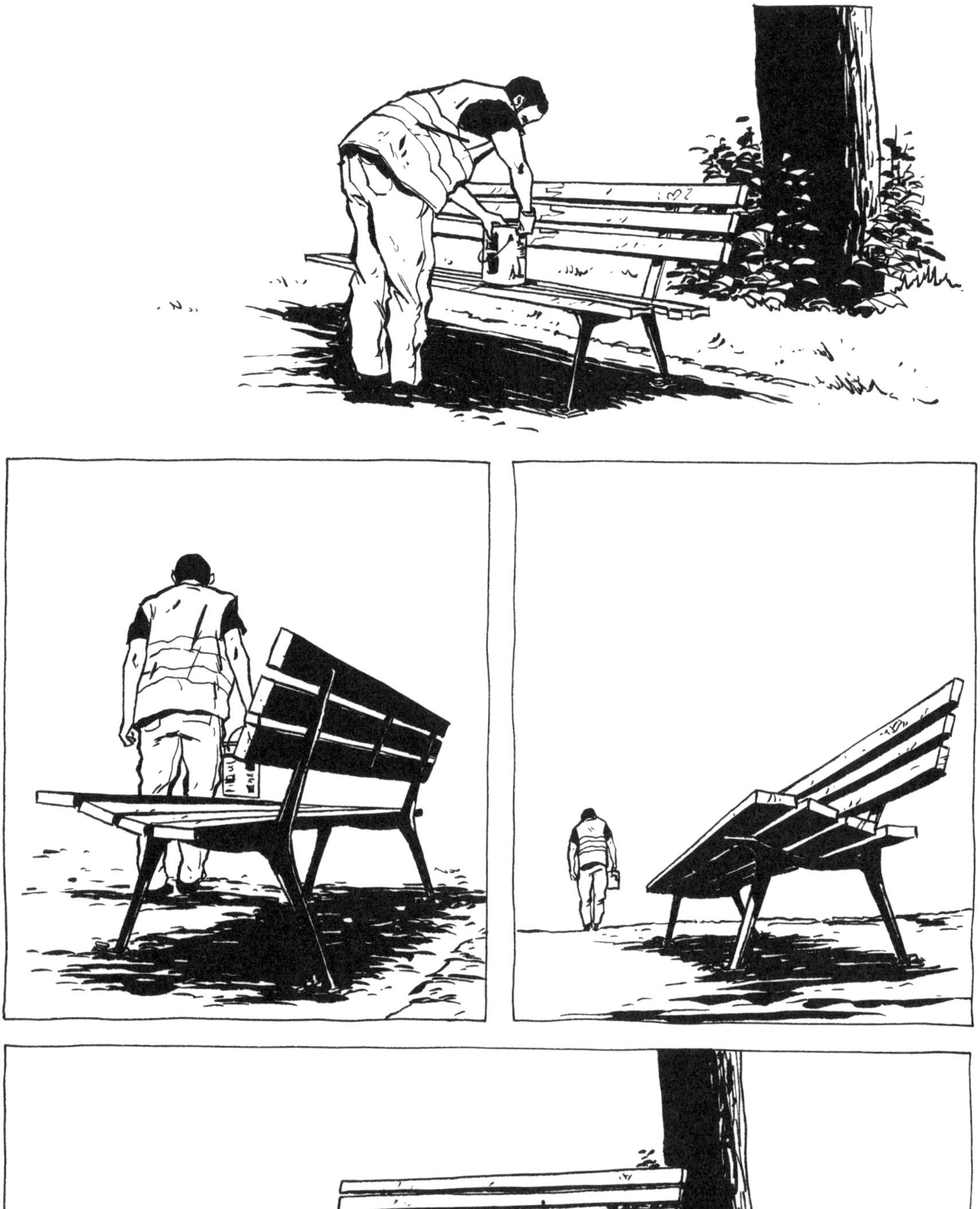

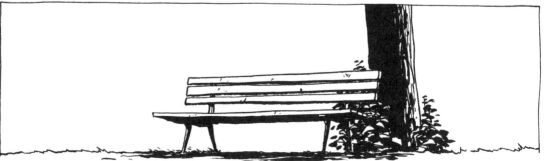

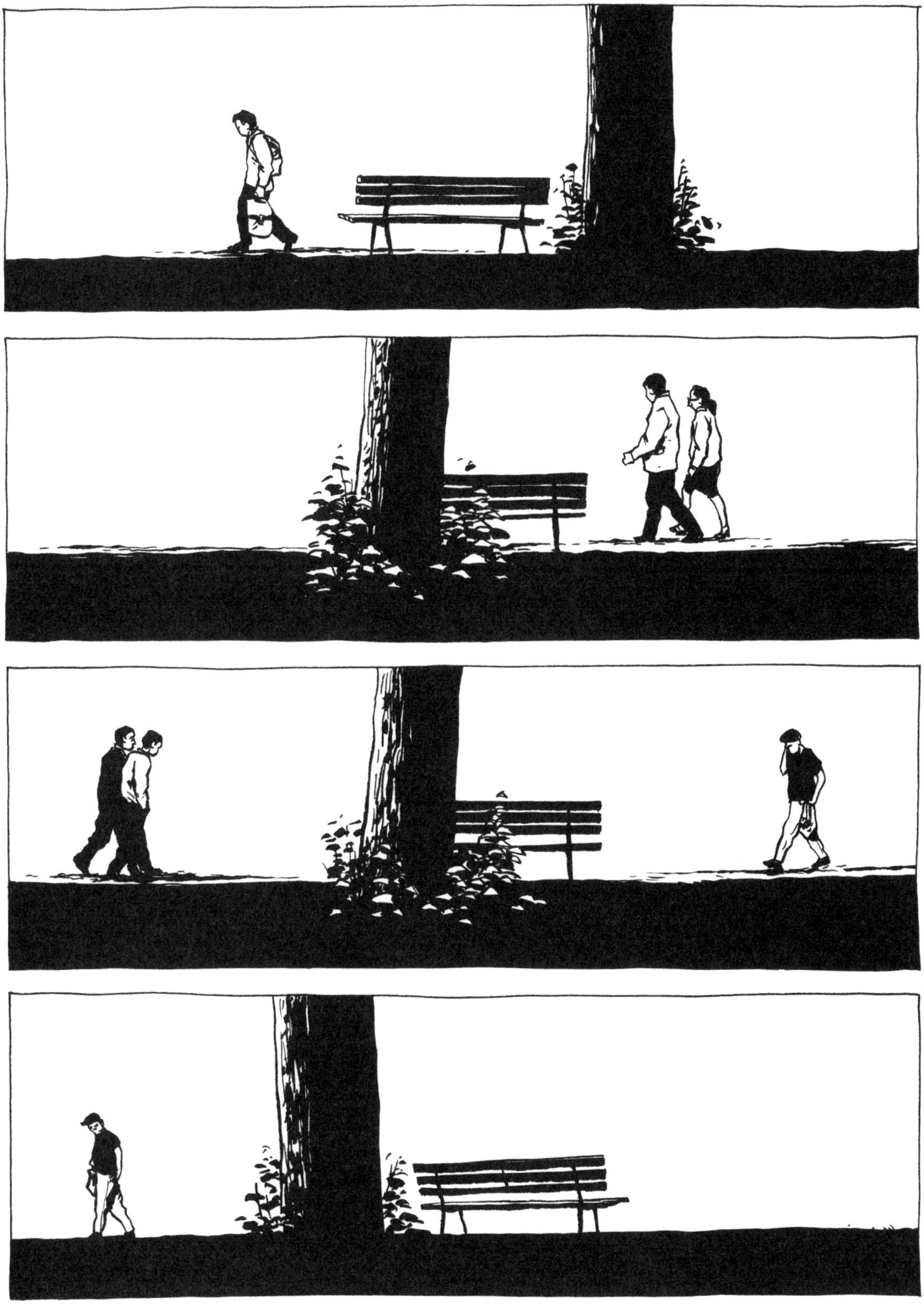

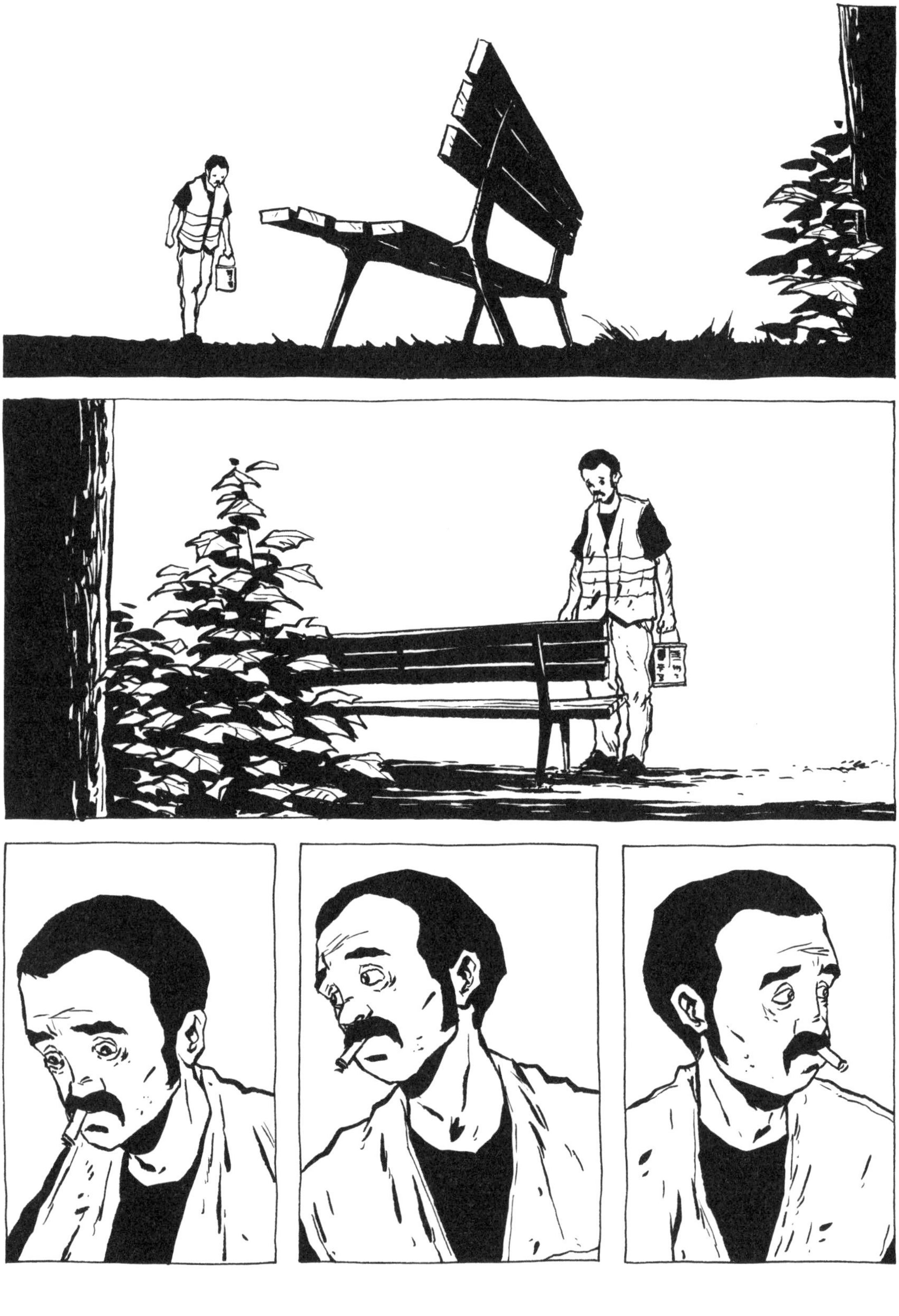

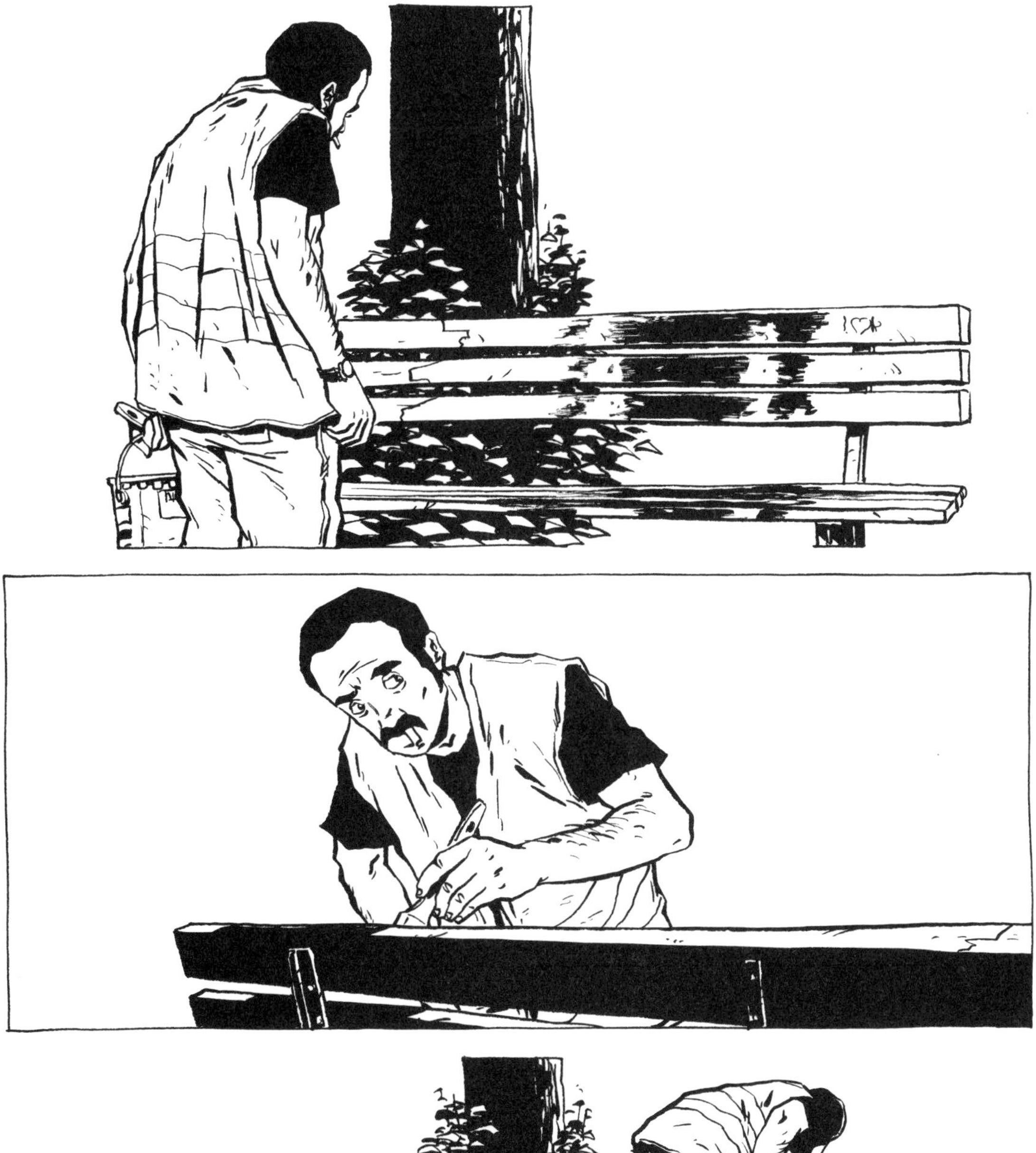

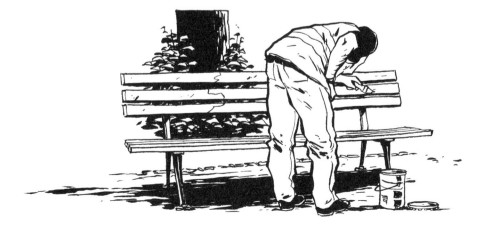

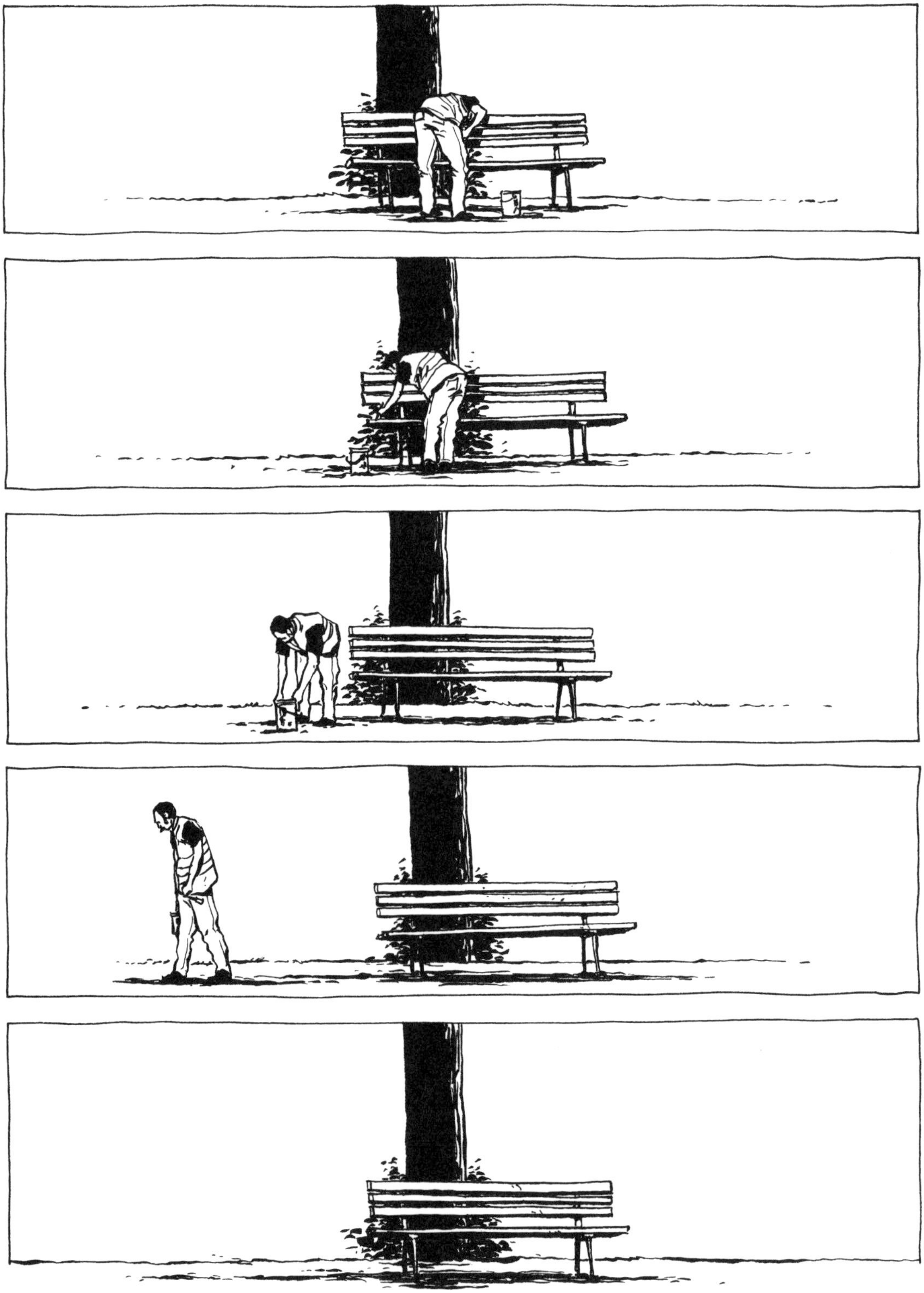

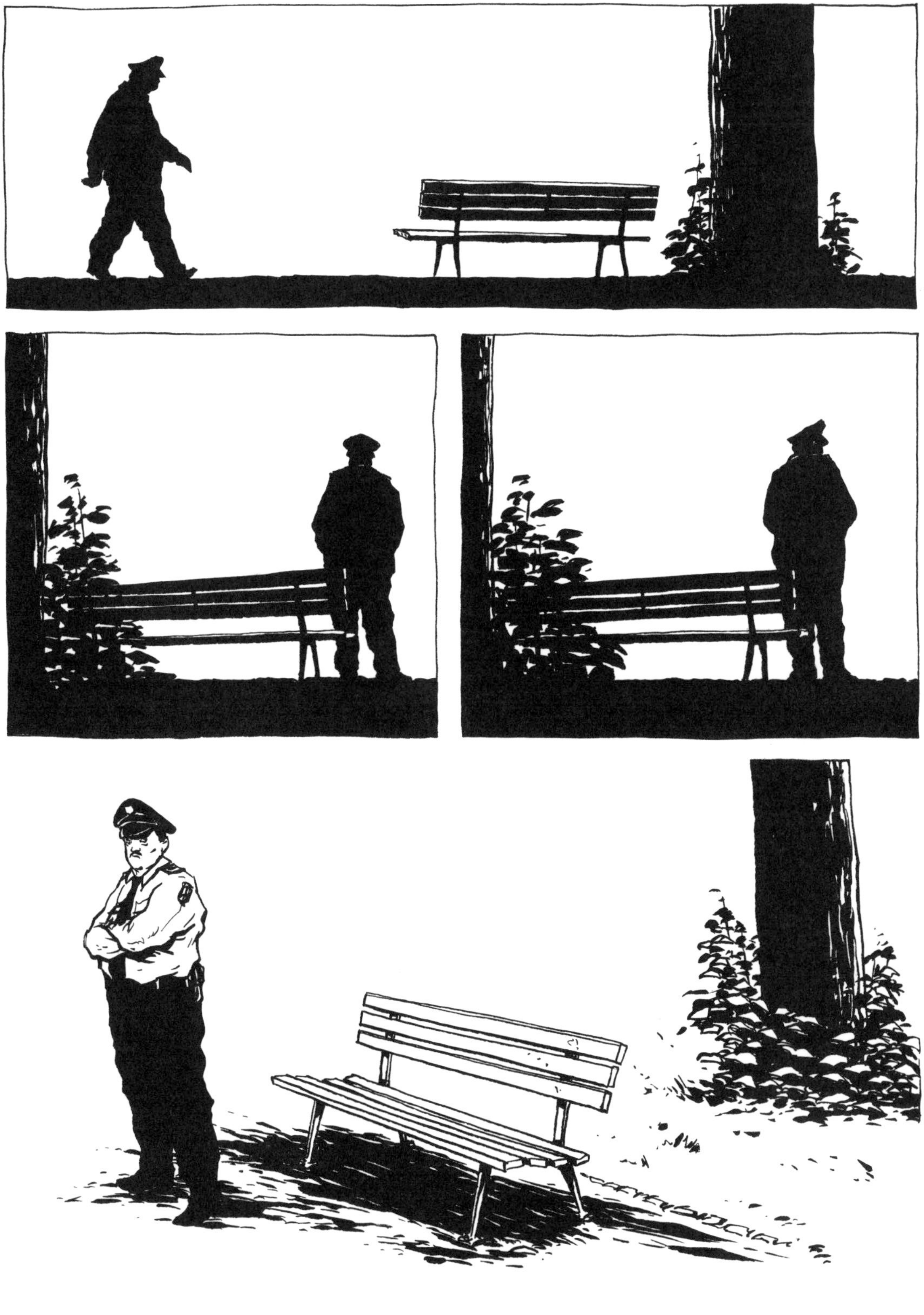

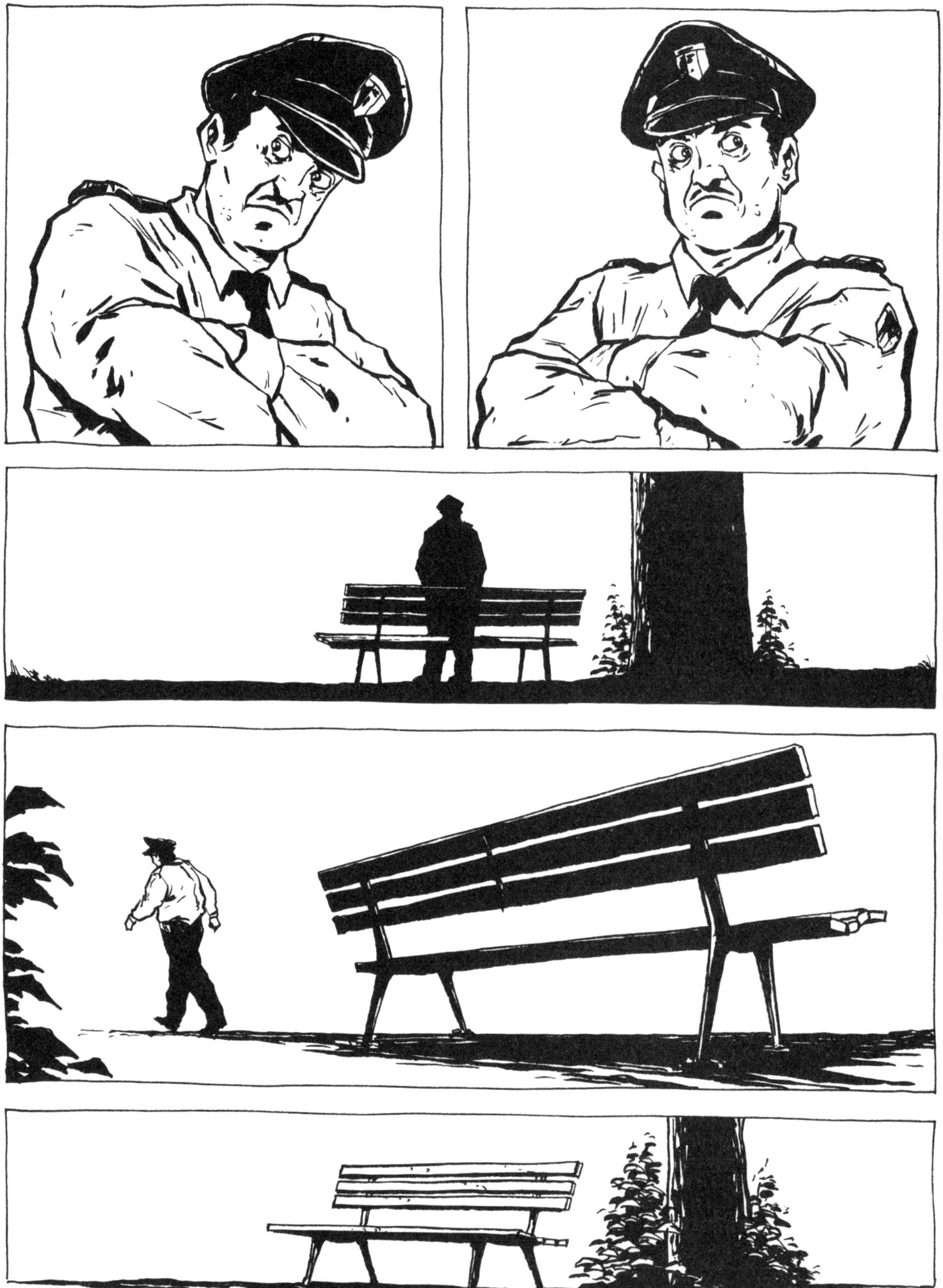

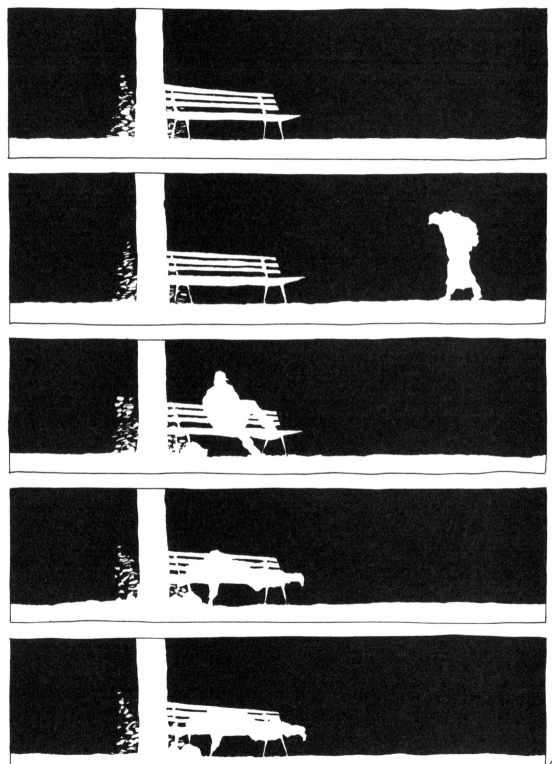

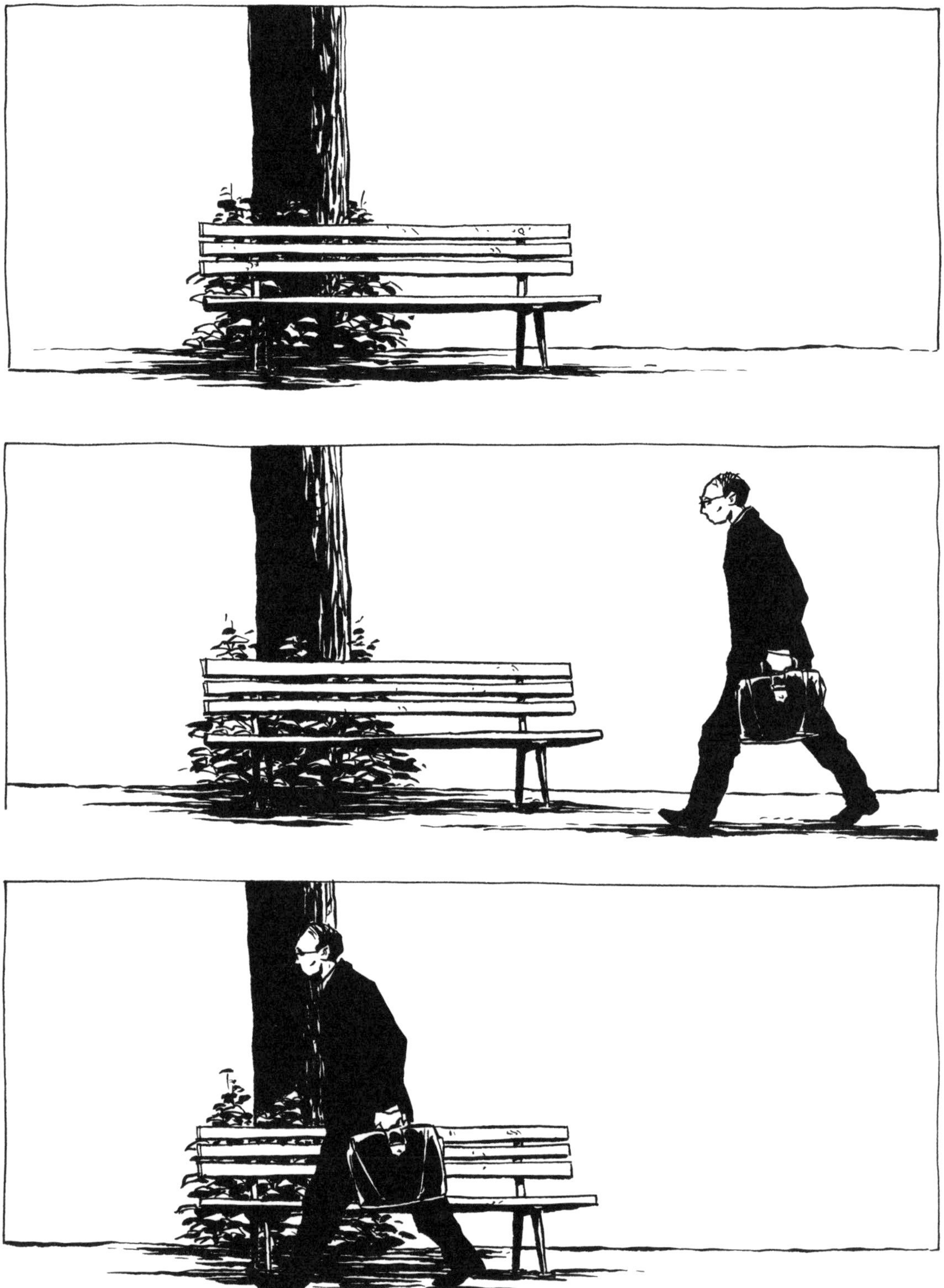

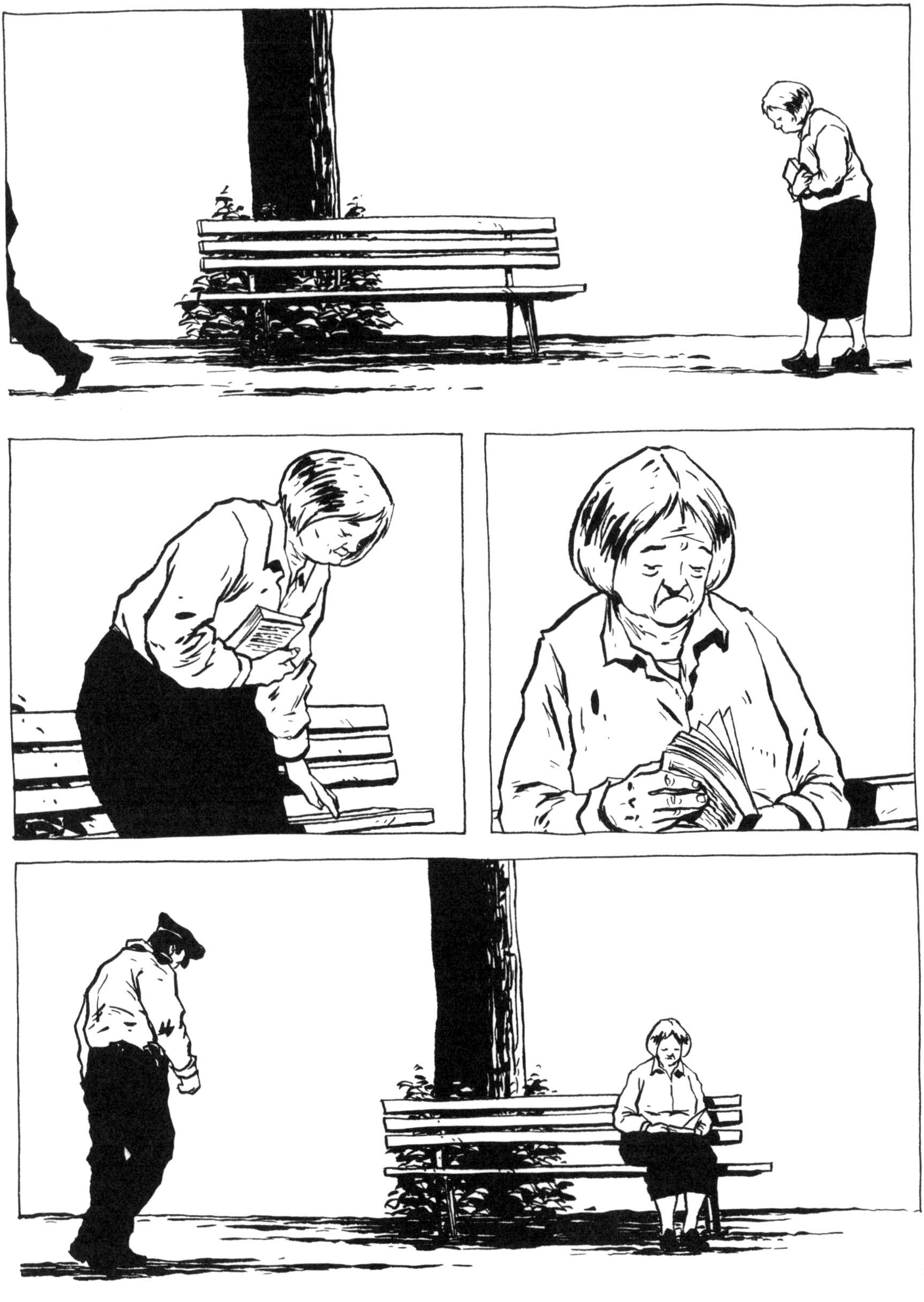

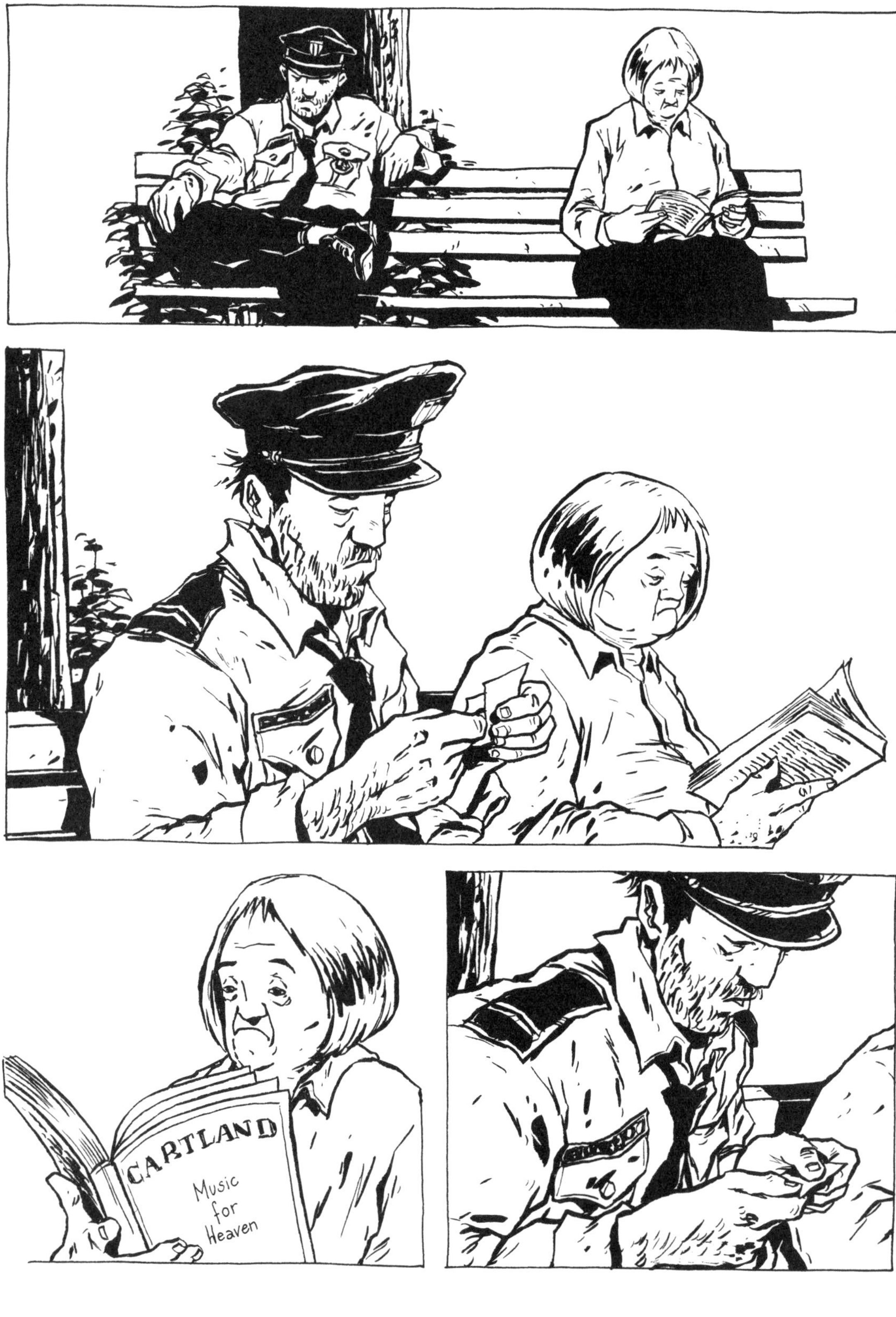
CARTLAND
Music for Heaven

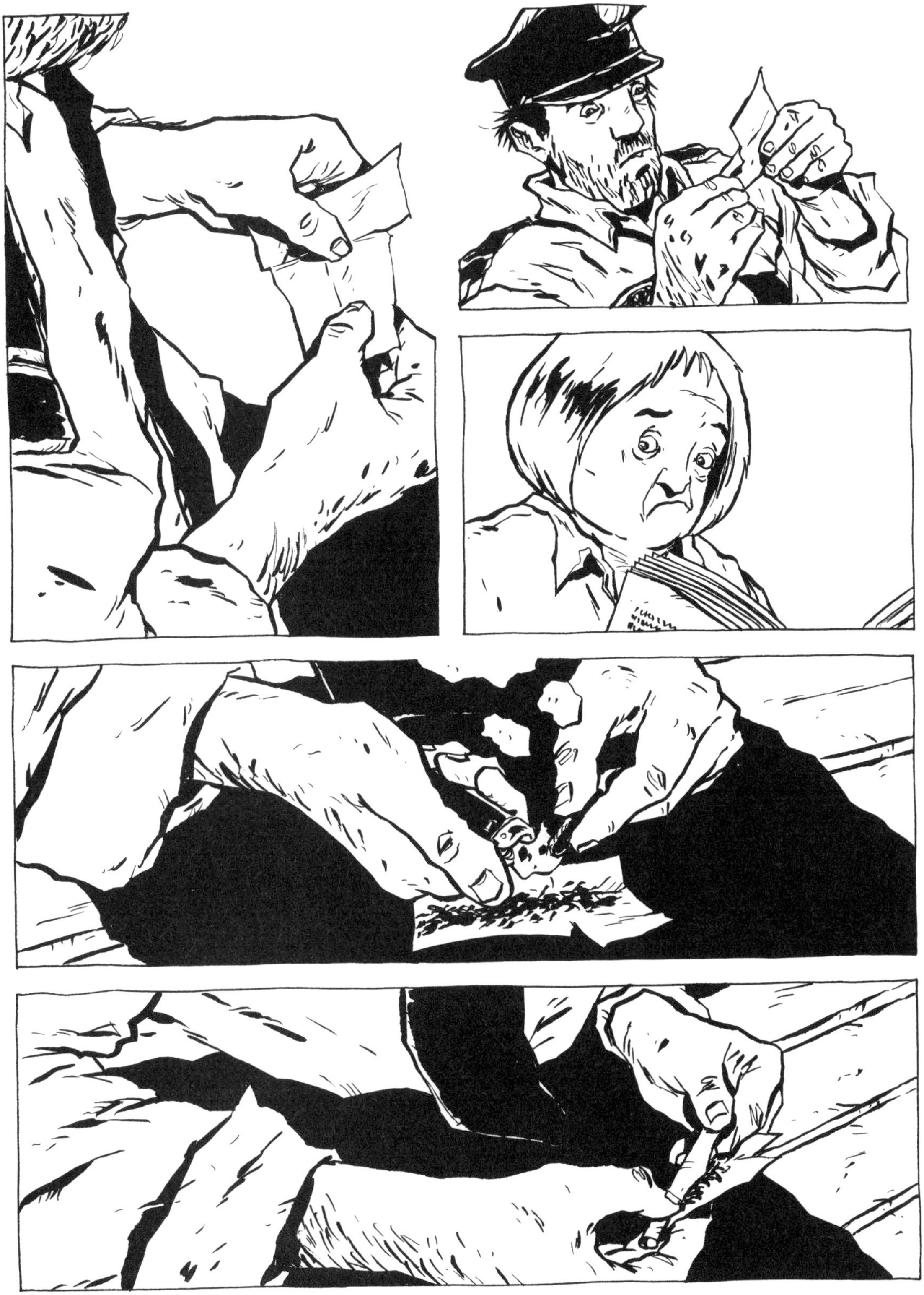

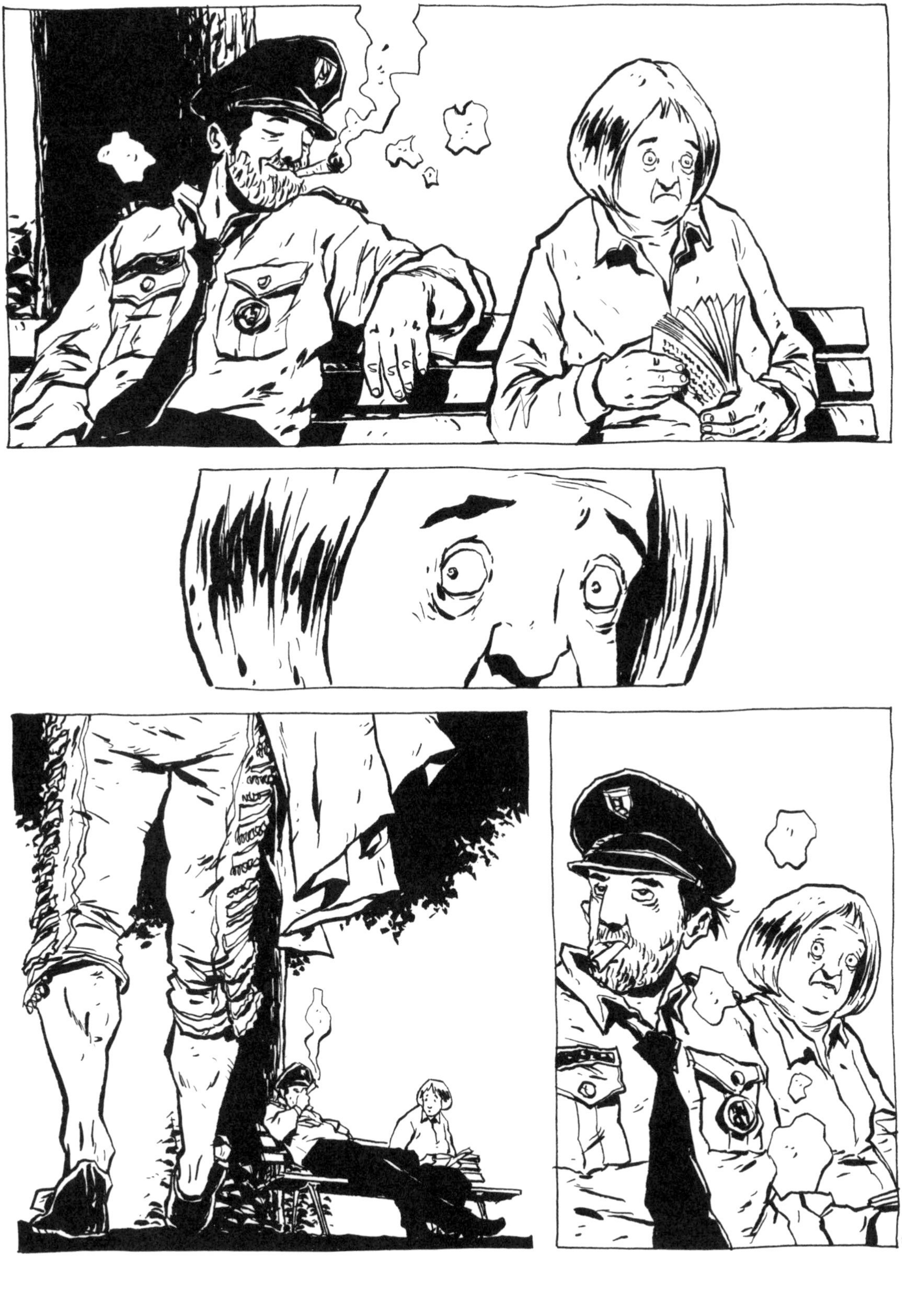

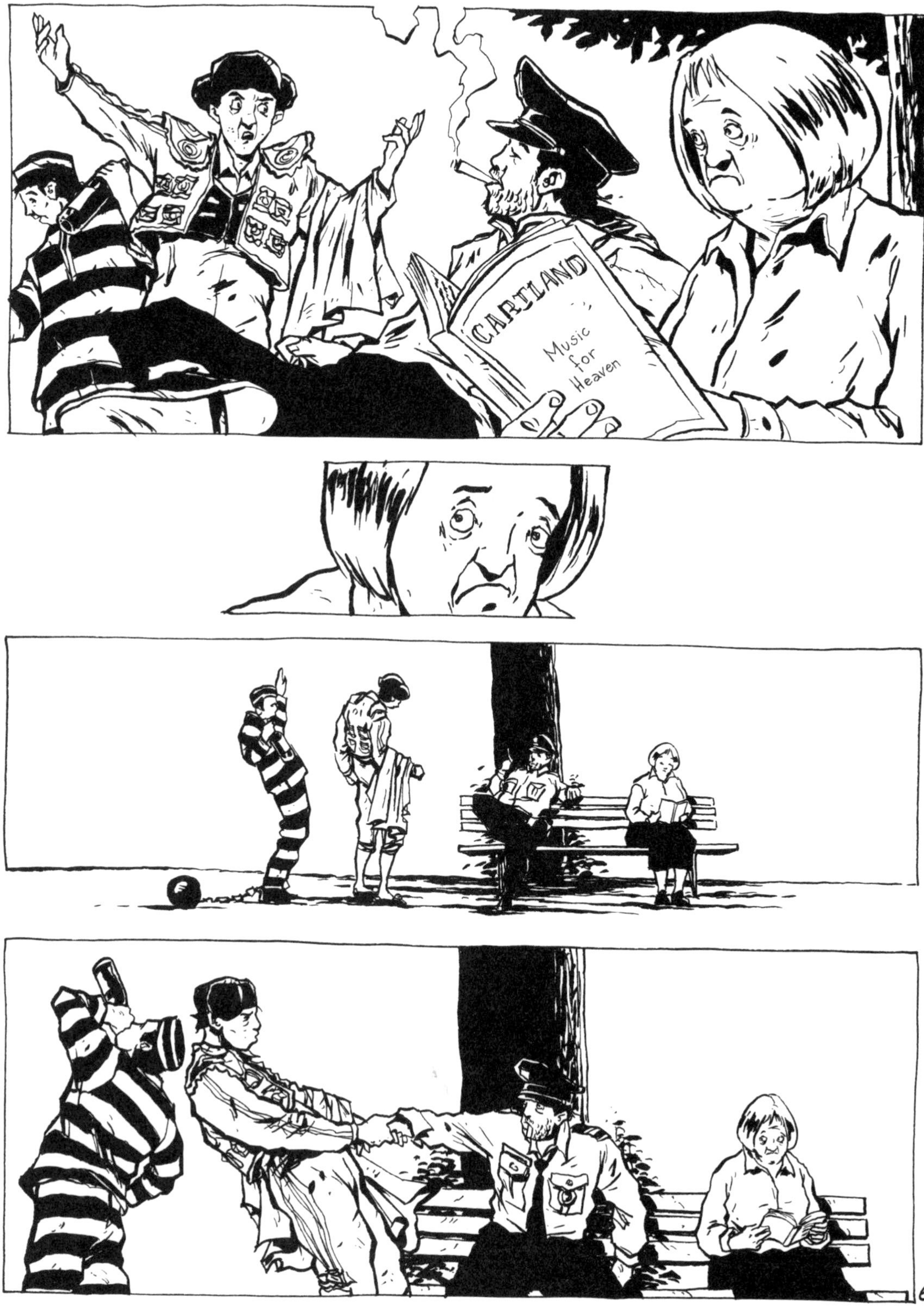
CARTLAND
Music for Heaven

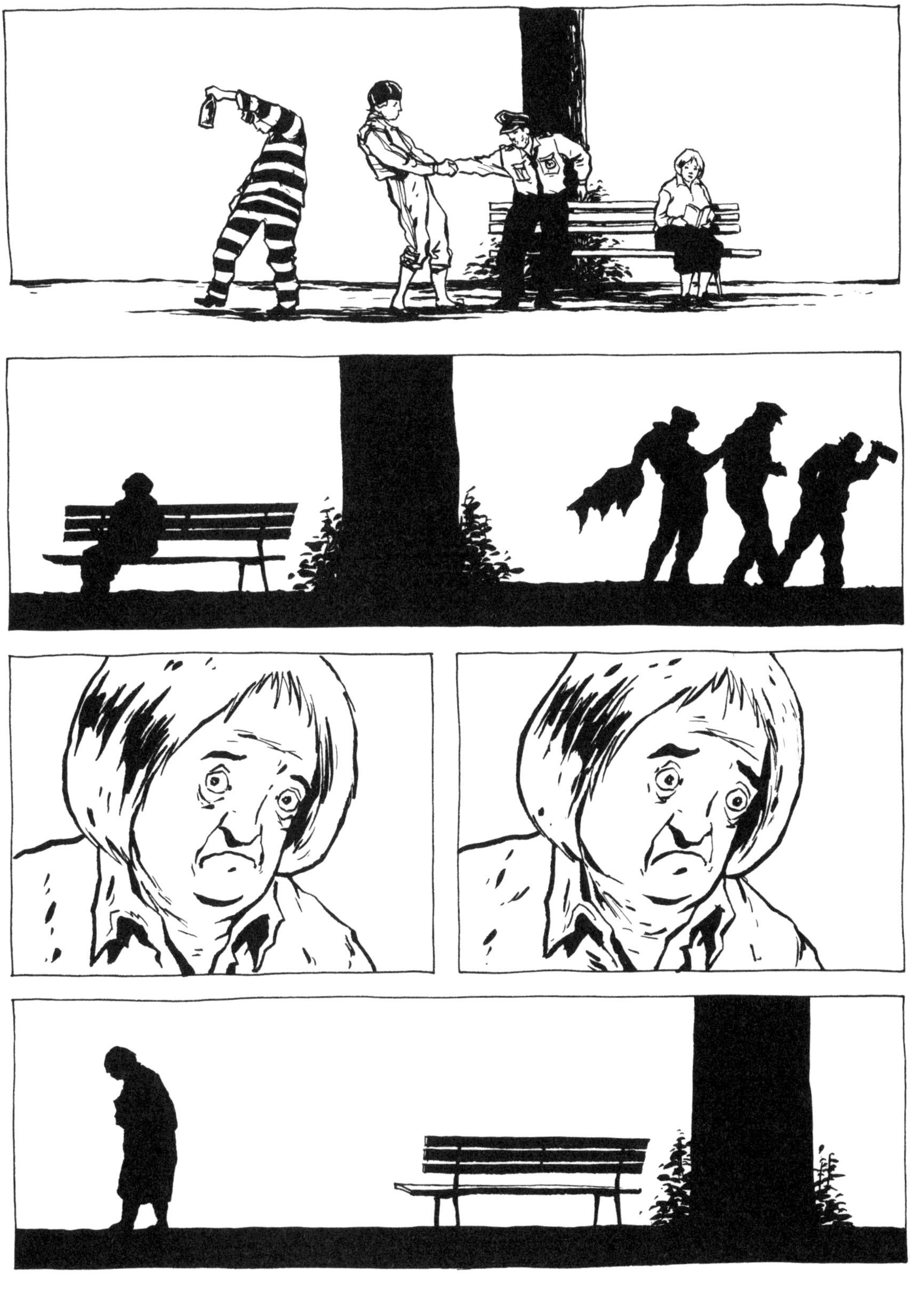

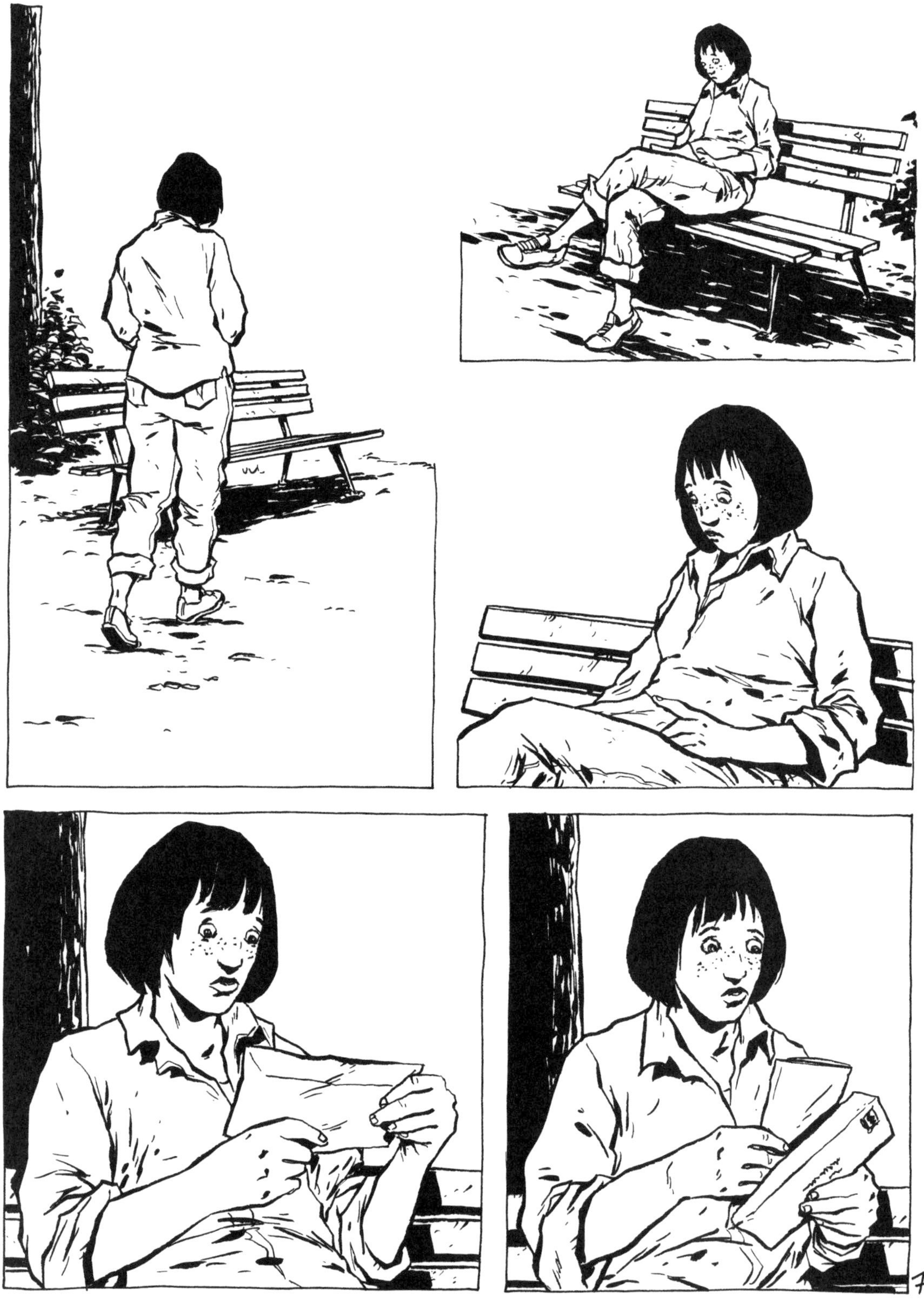

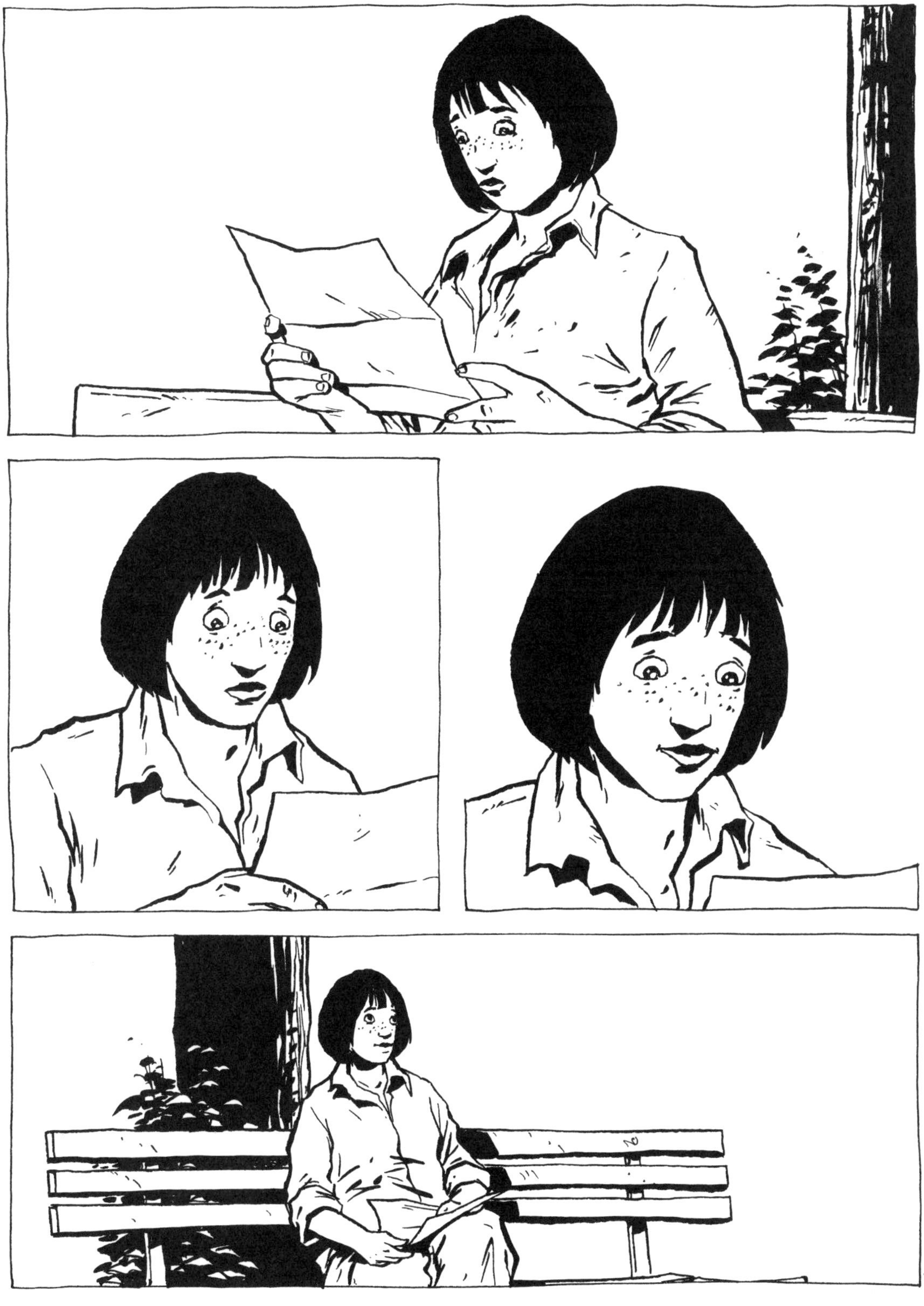

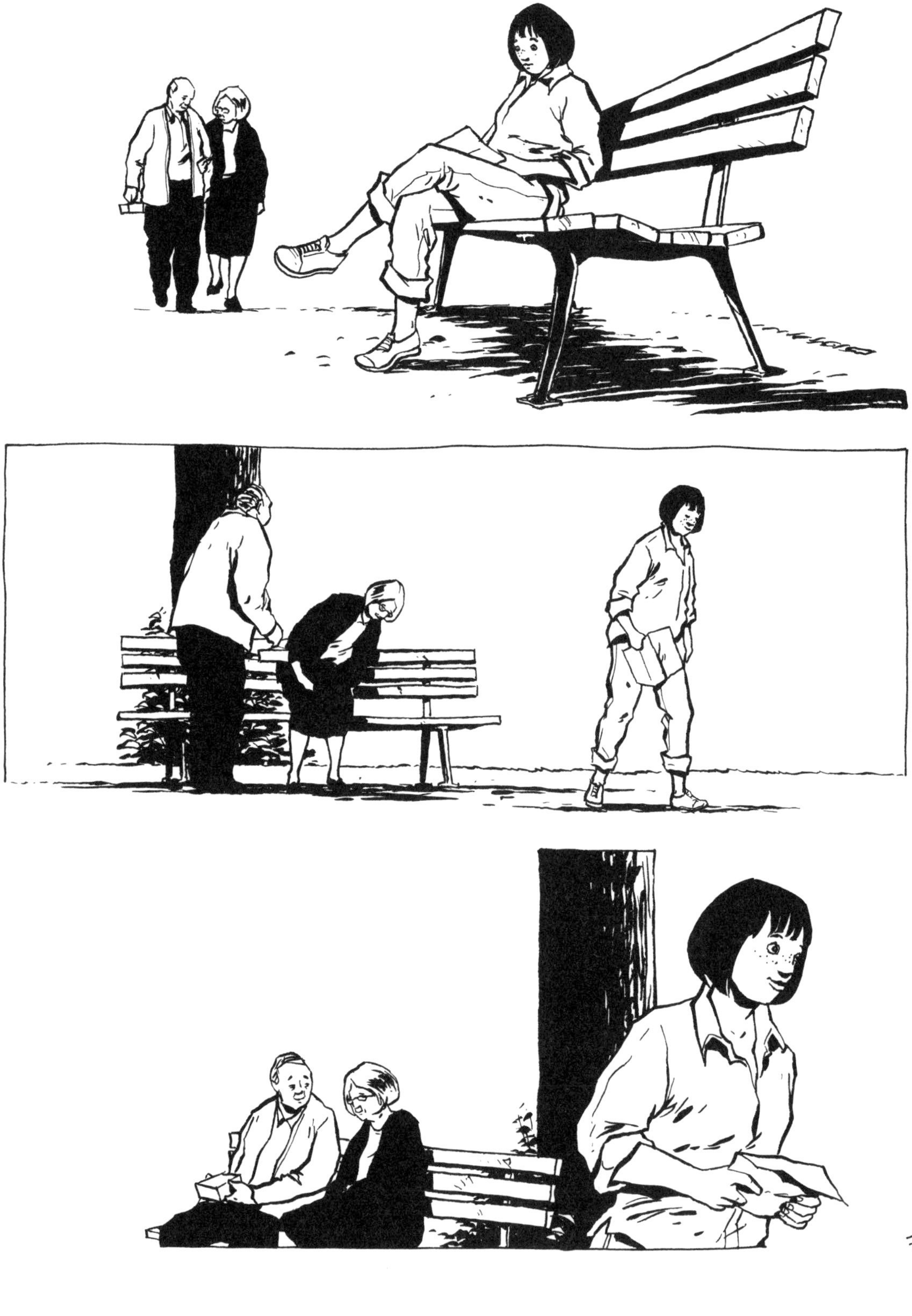

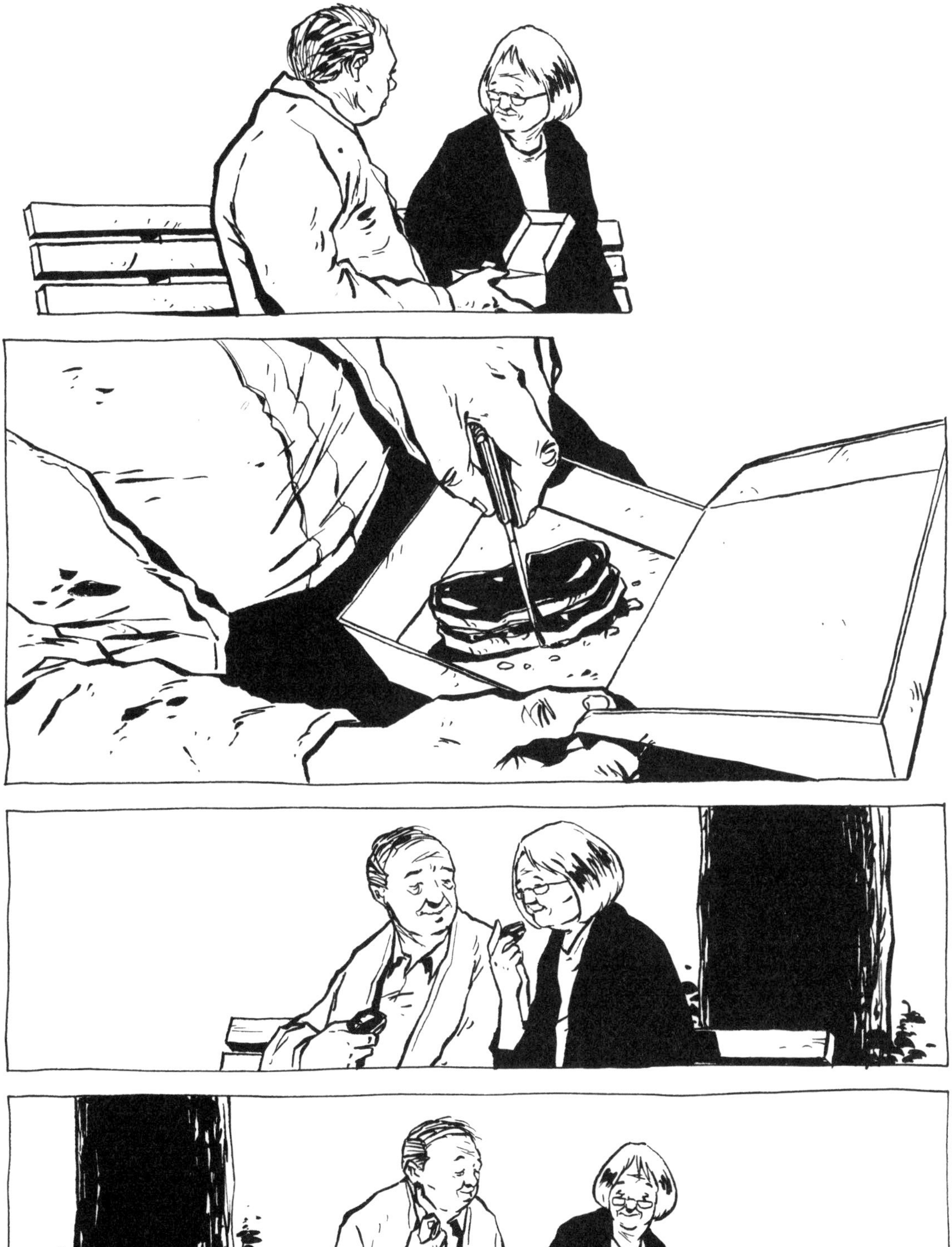

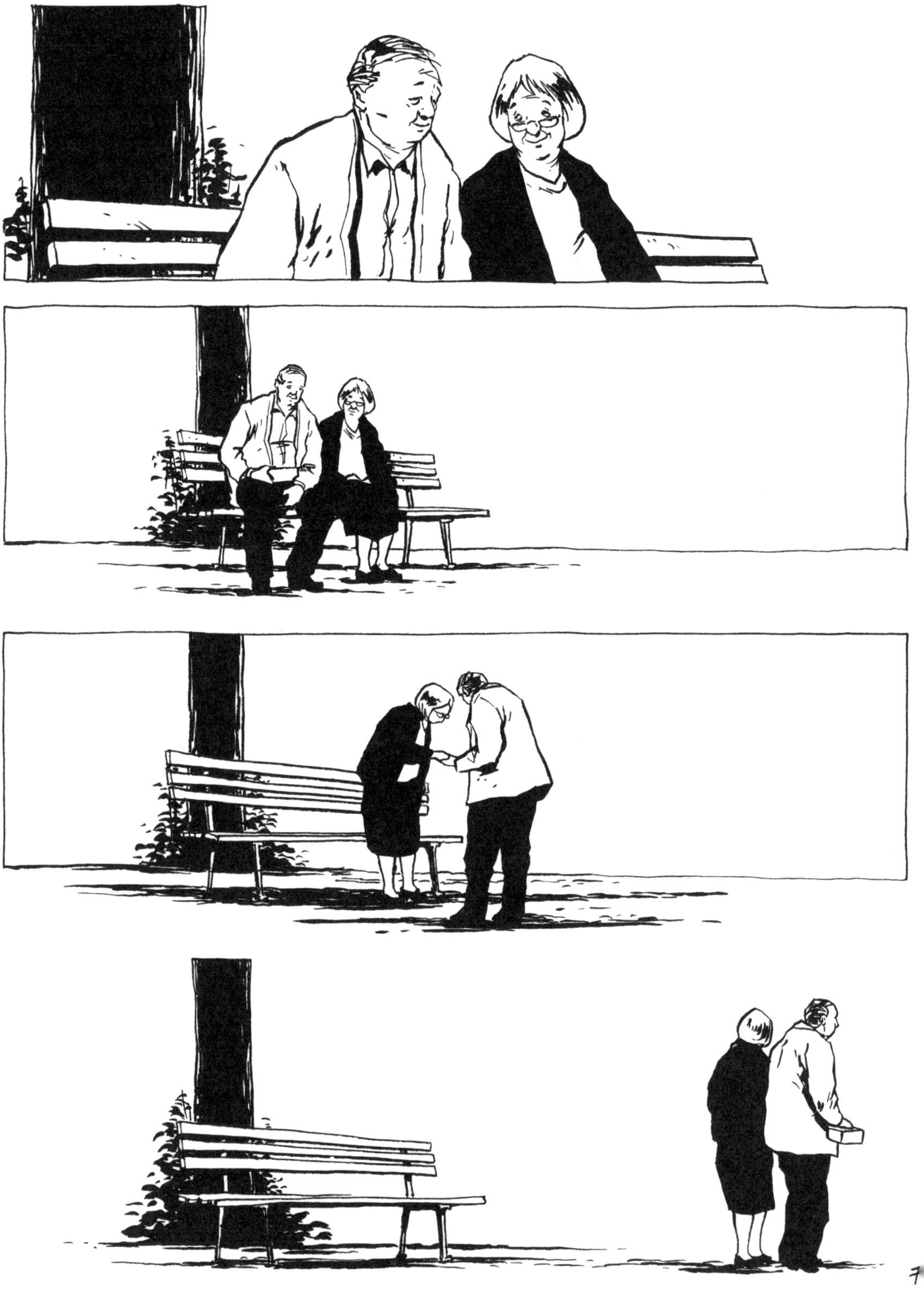
7

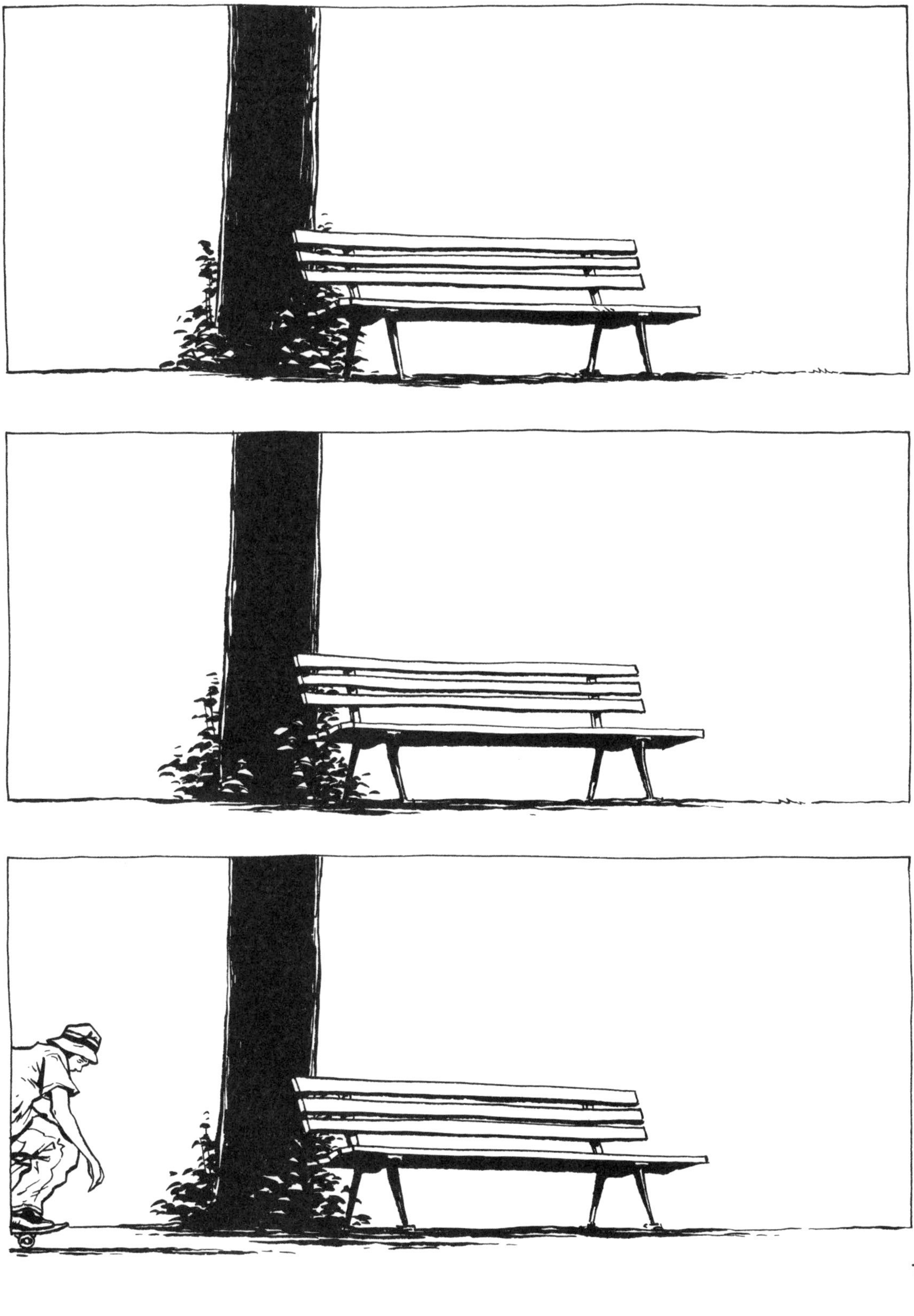

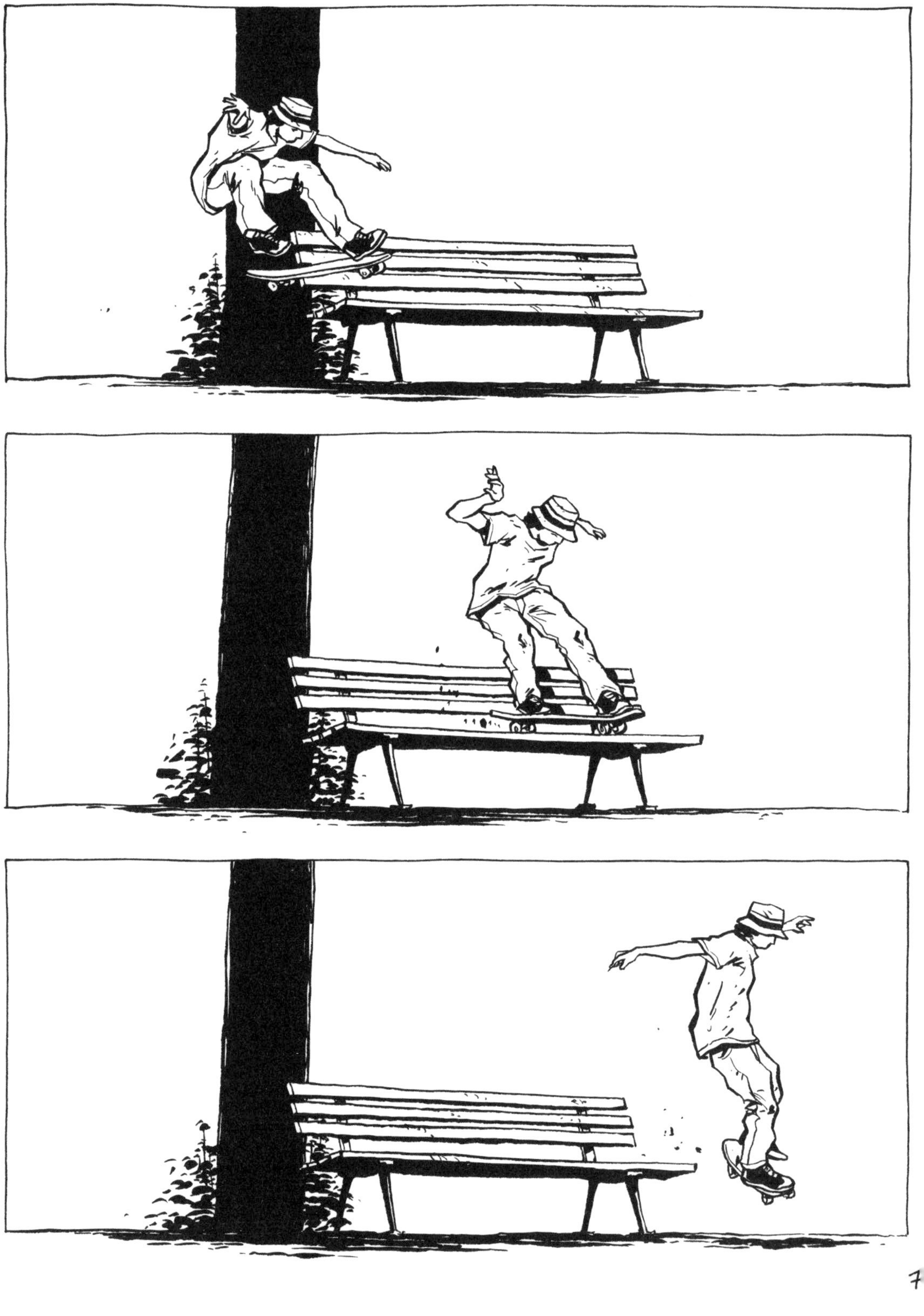

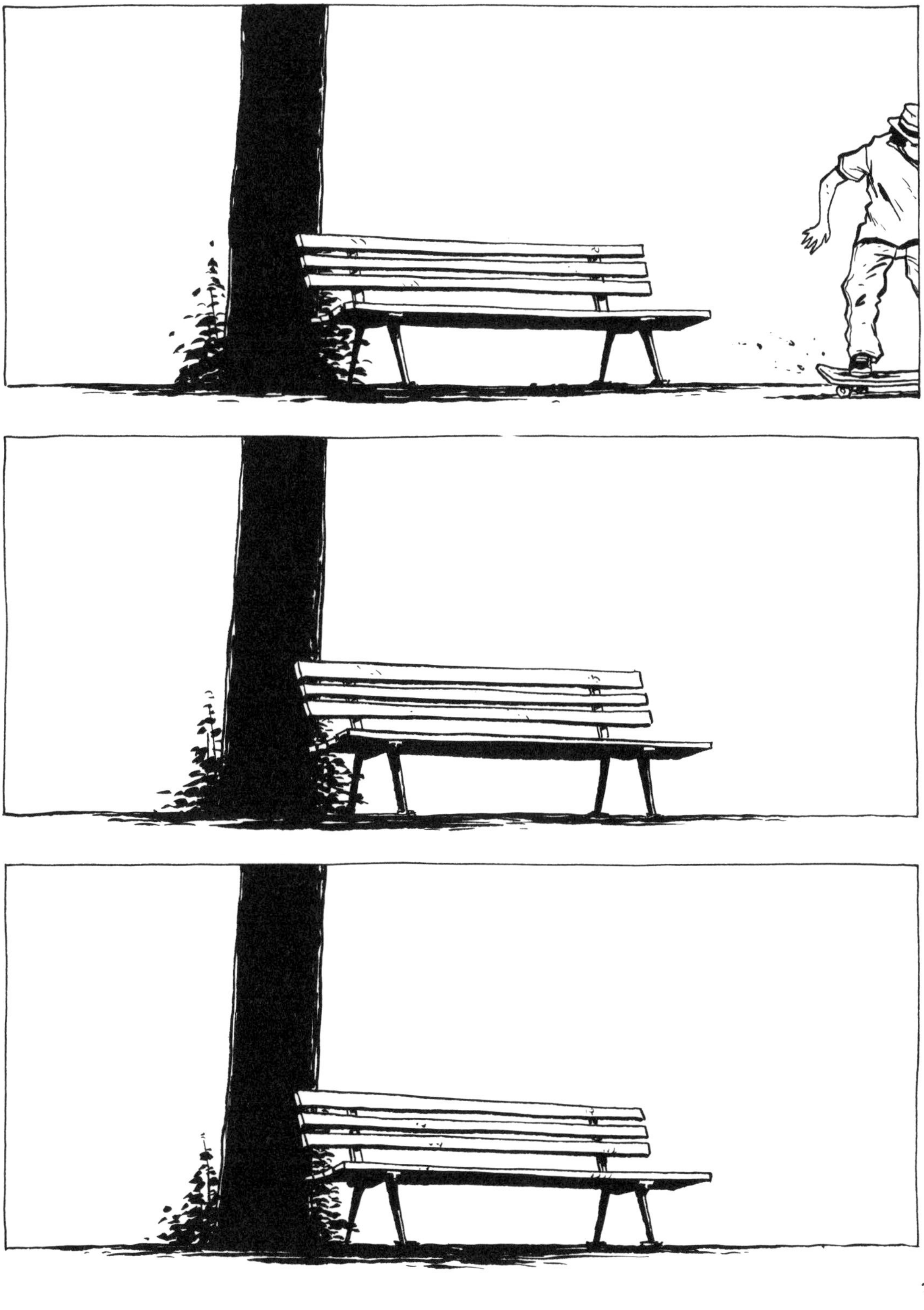

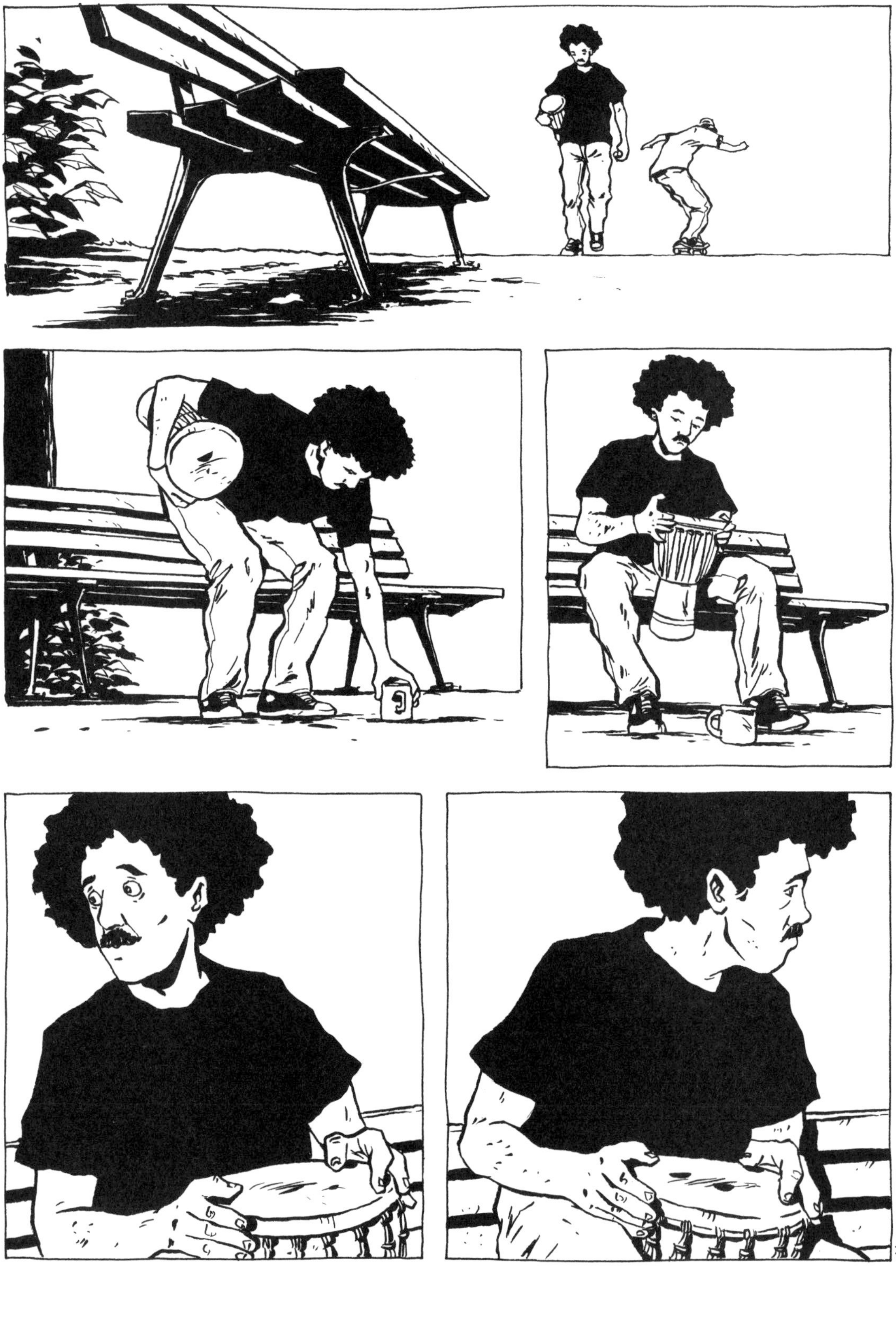

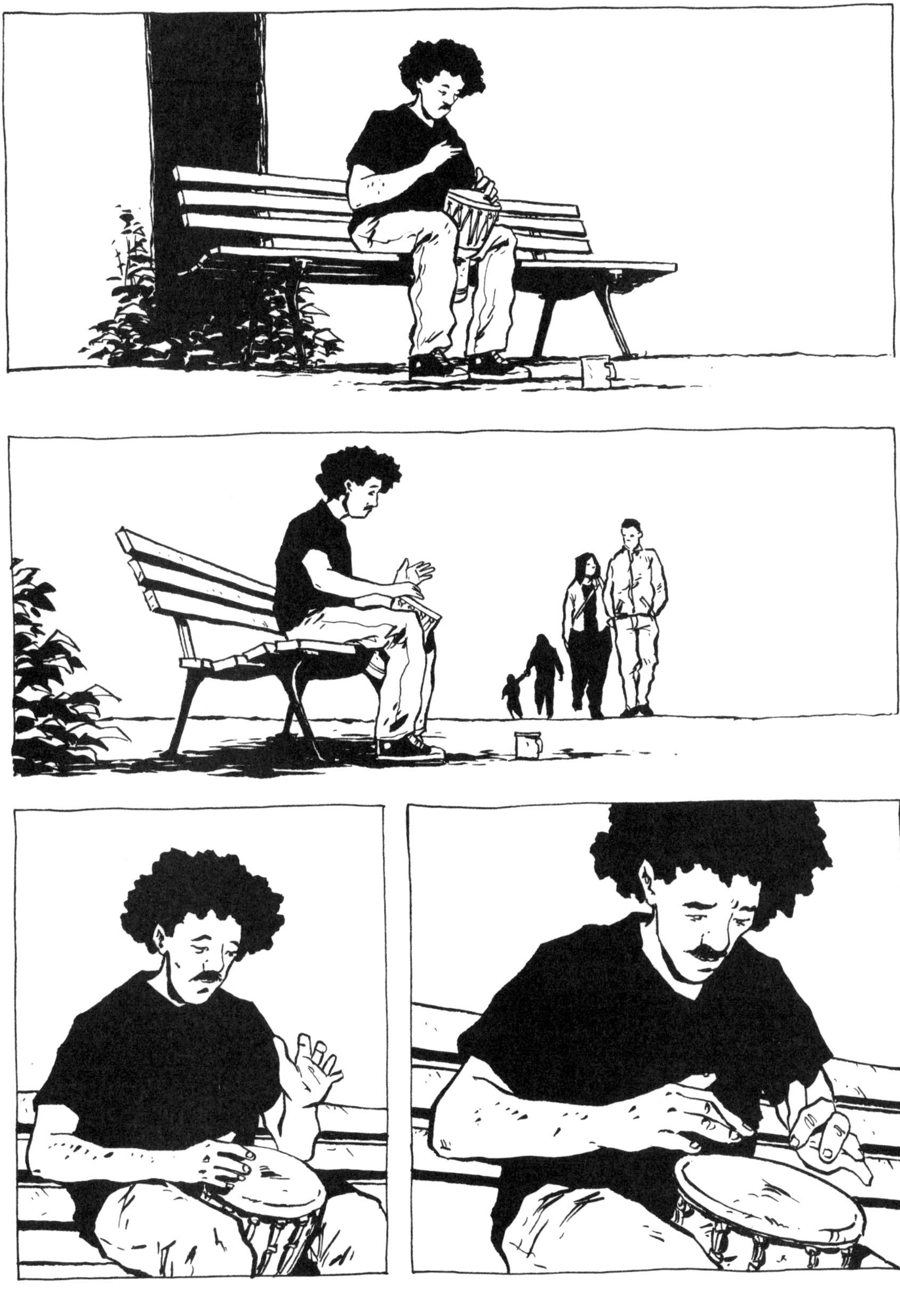

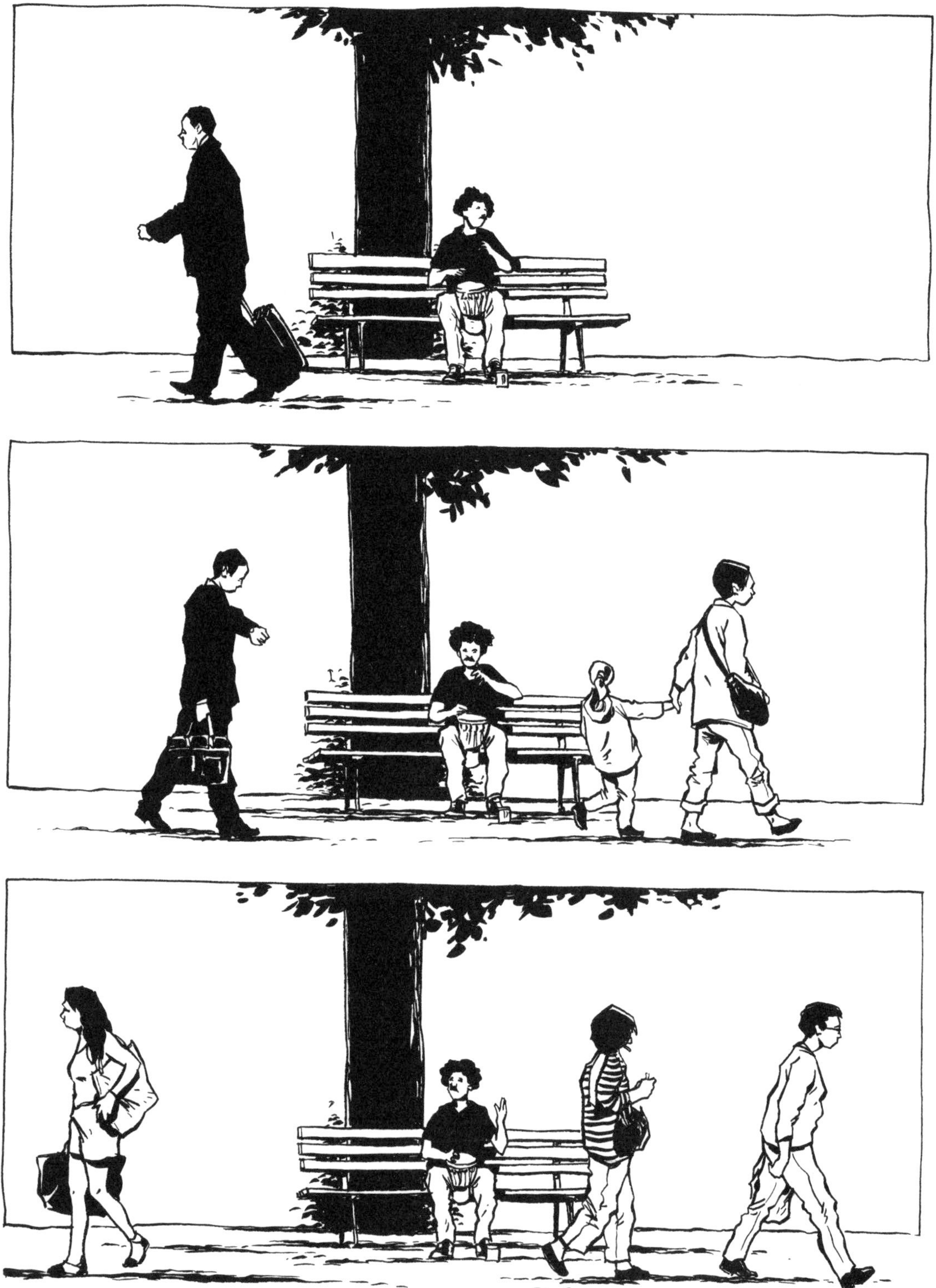

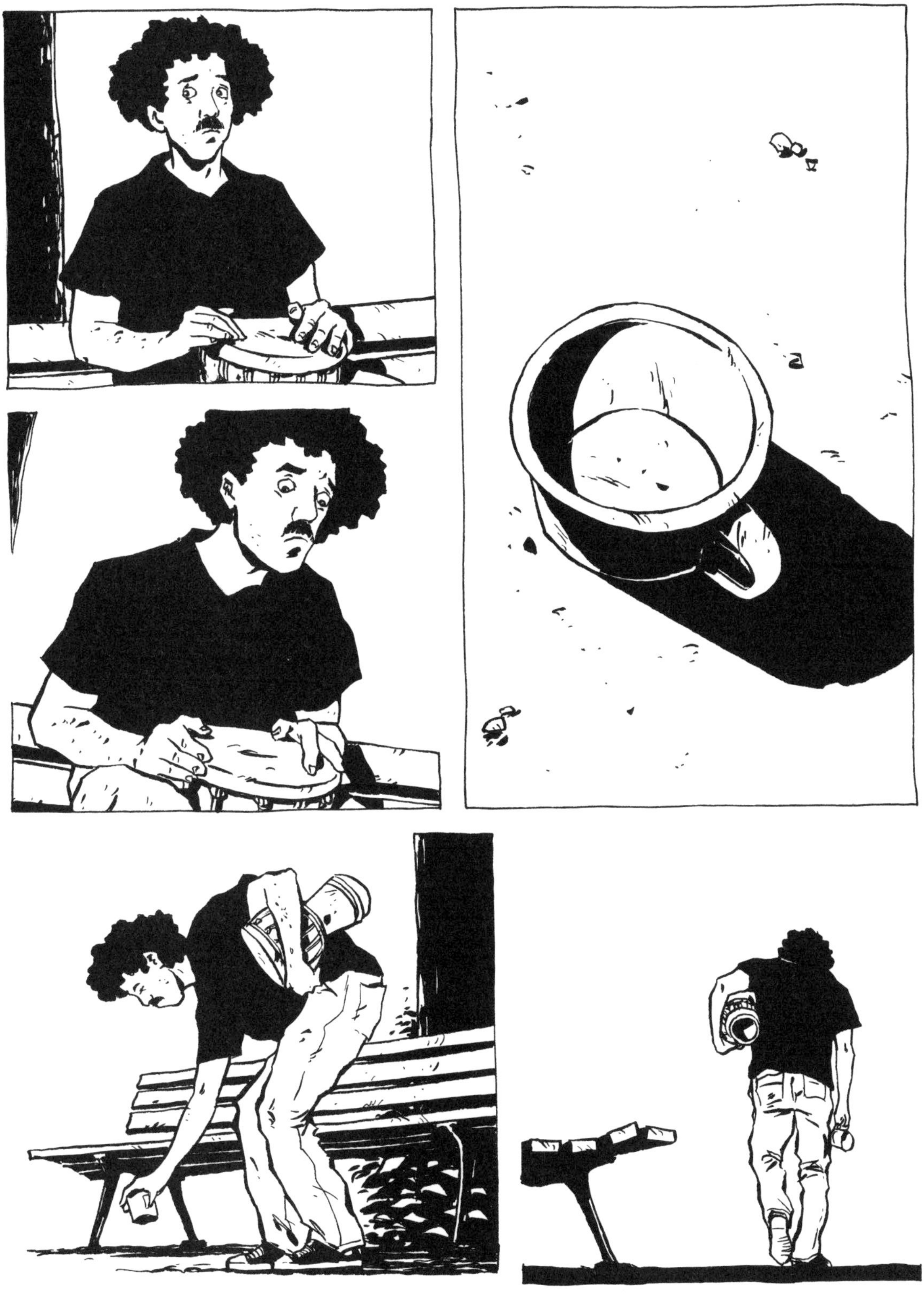

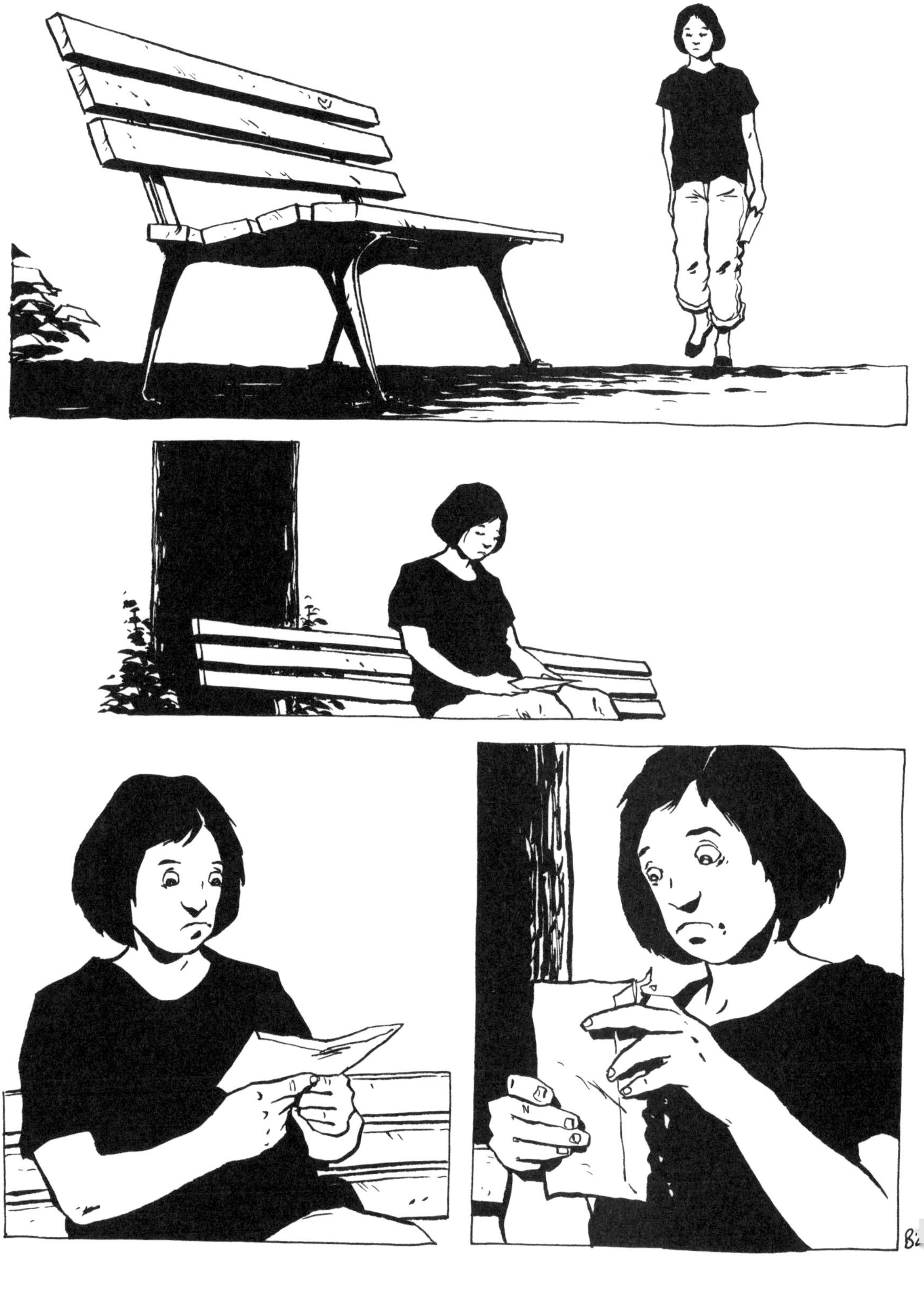

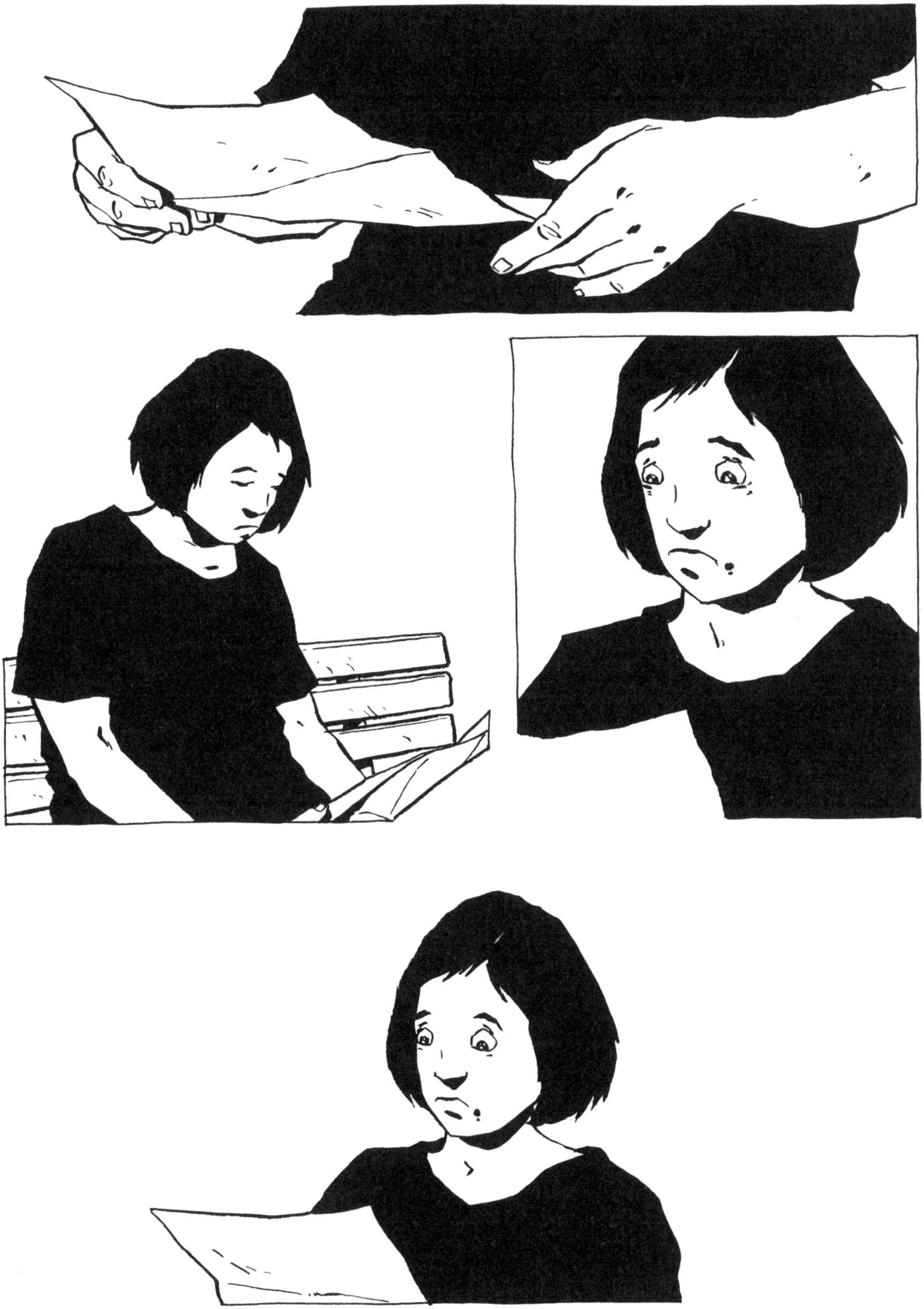

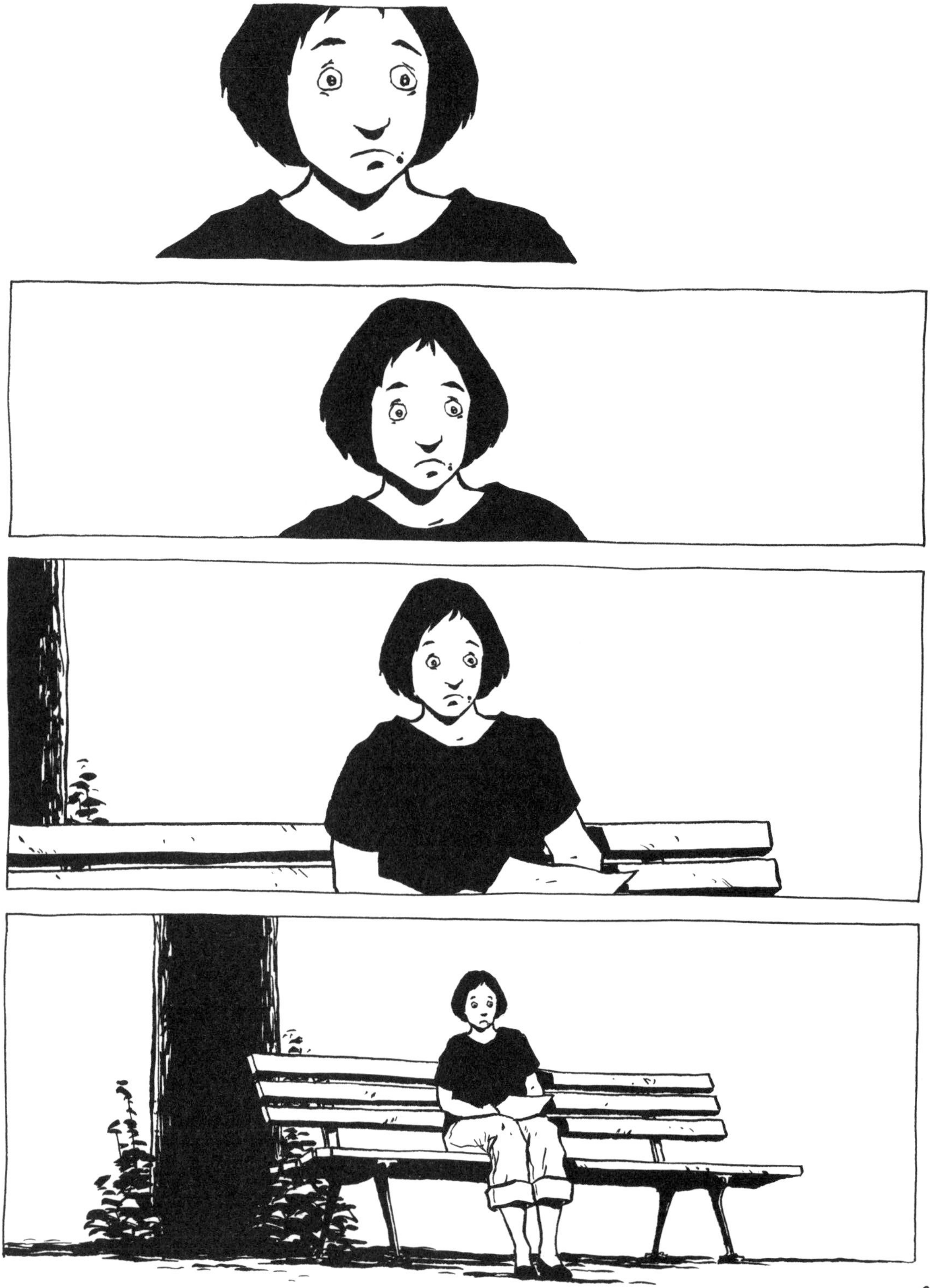

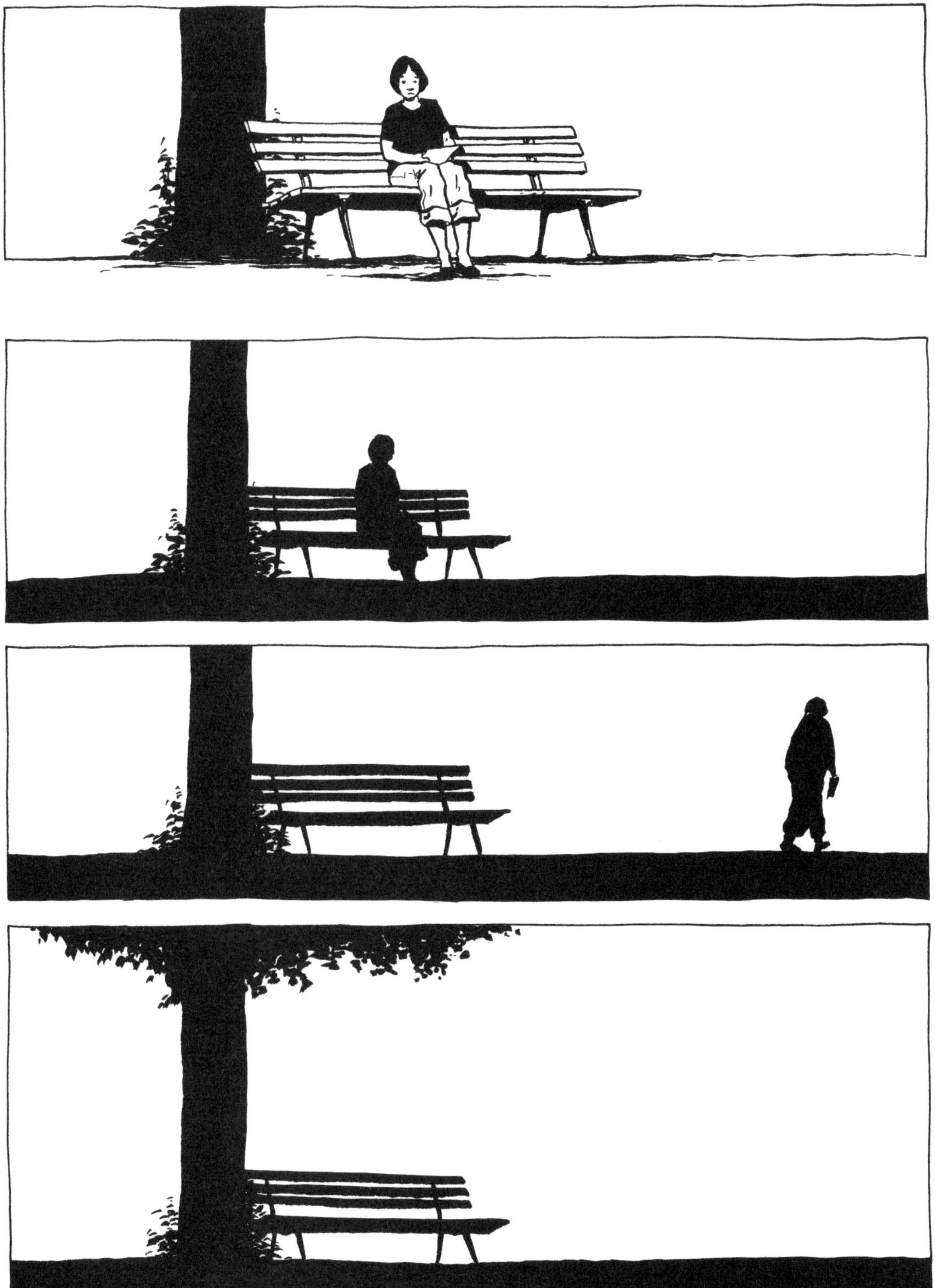

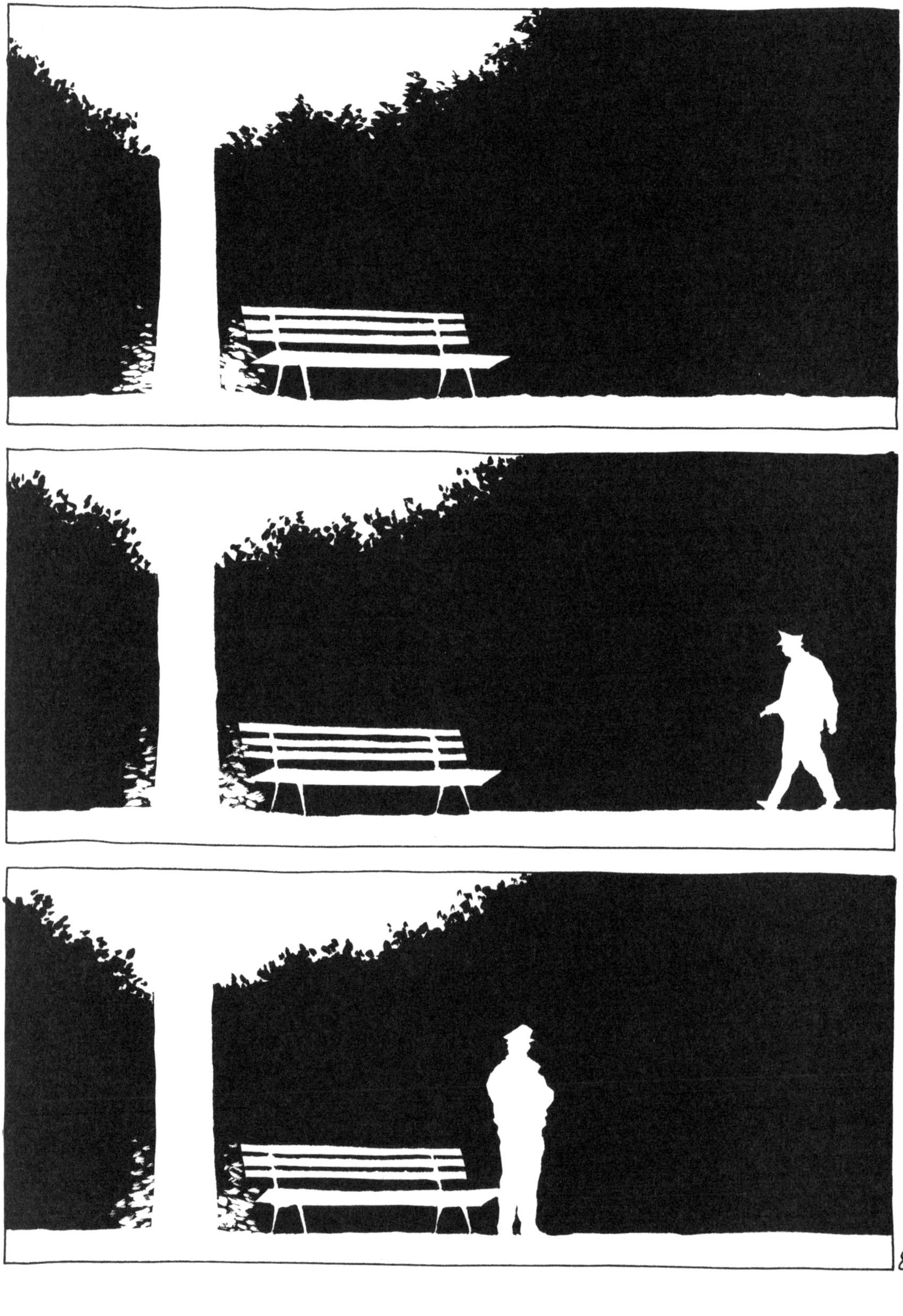

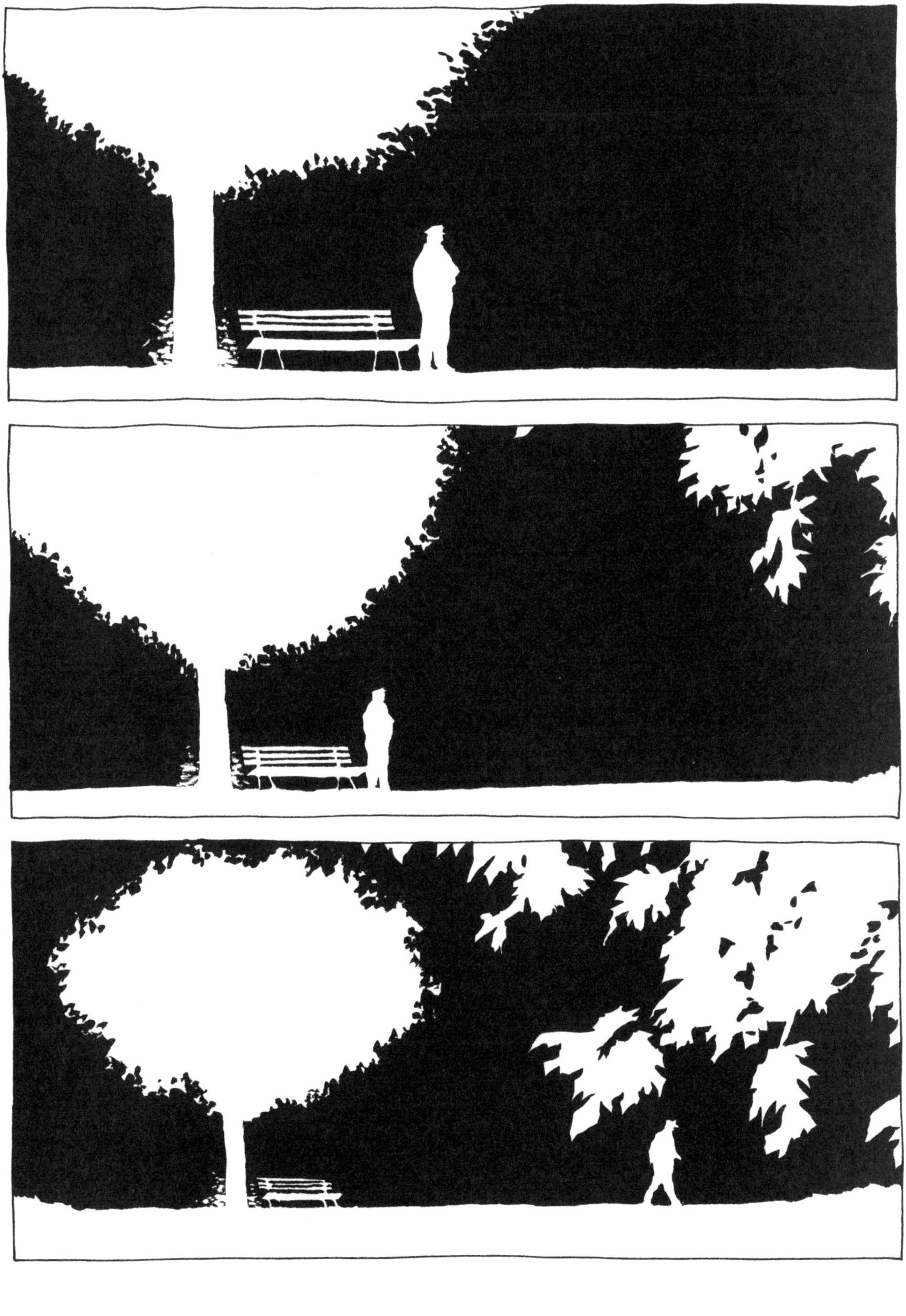

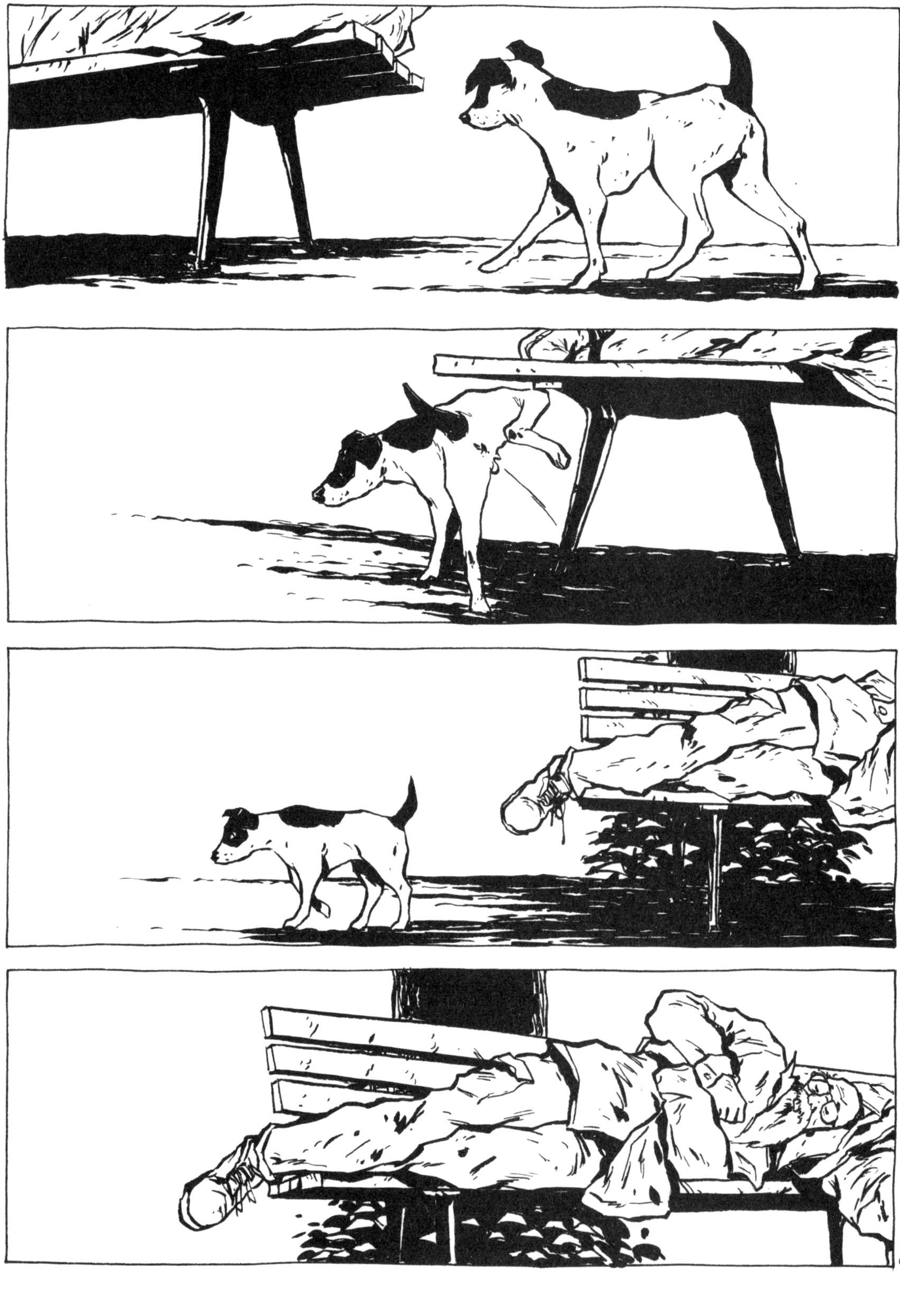

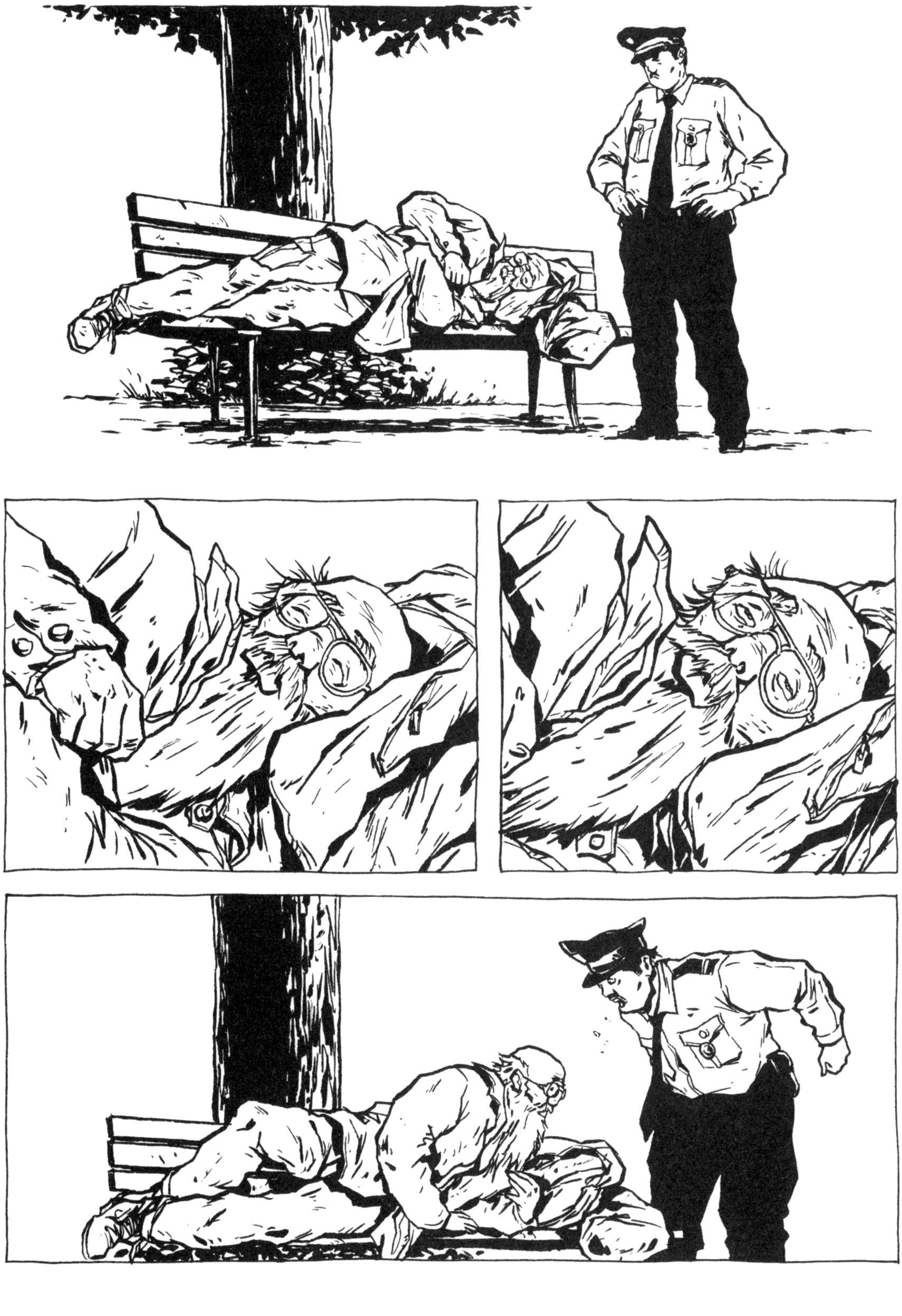

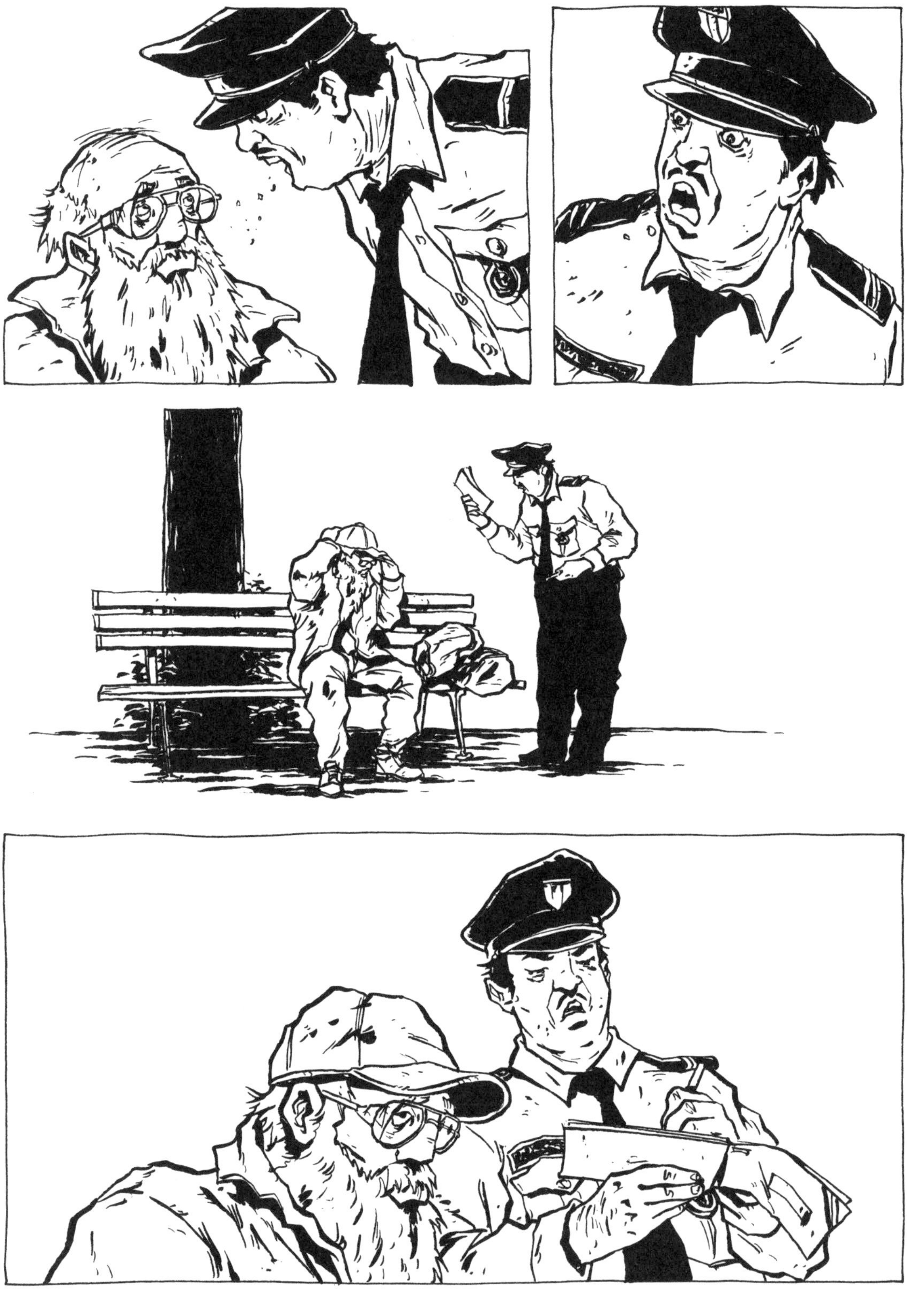

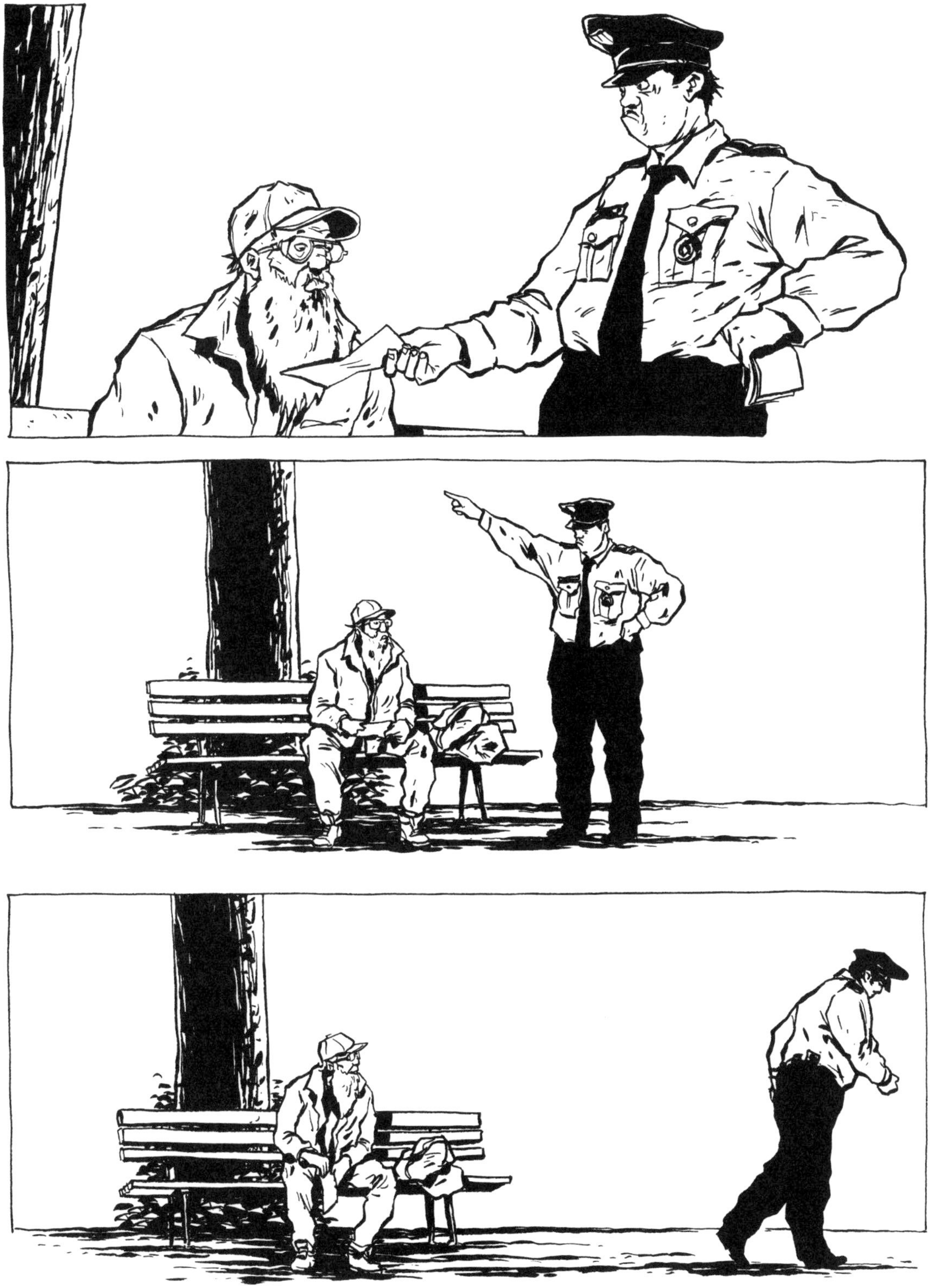

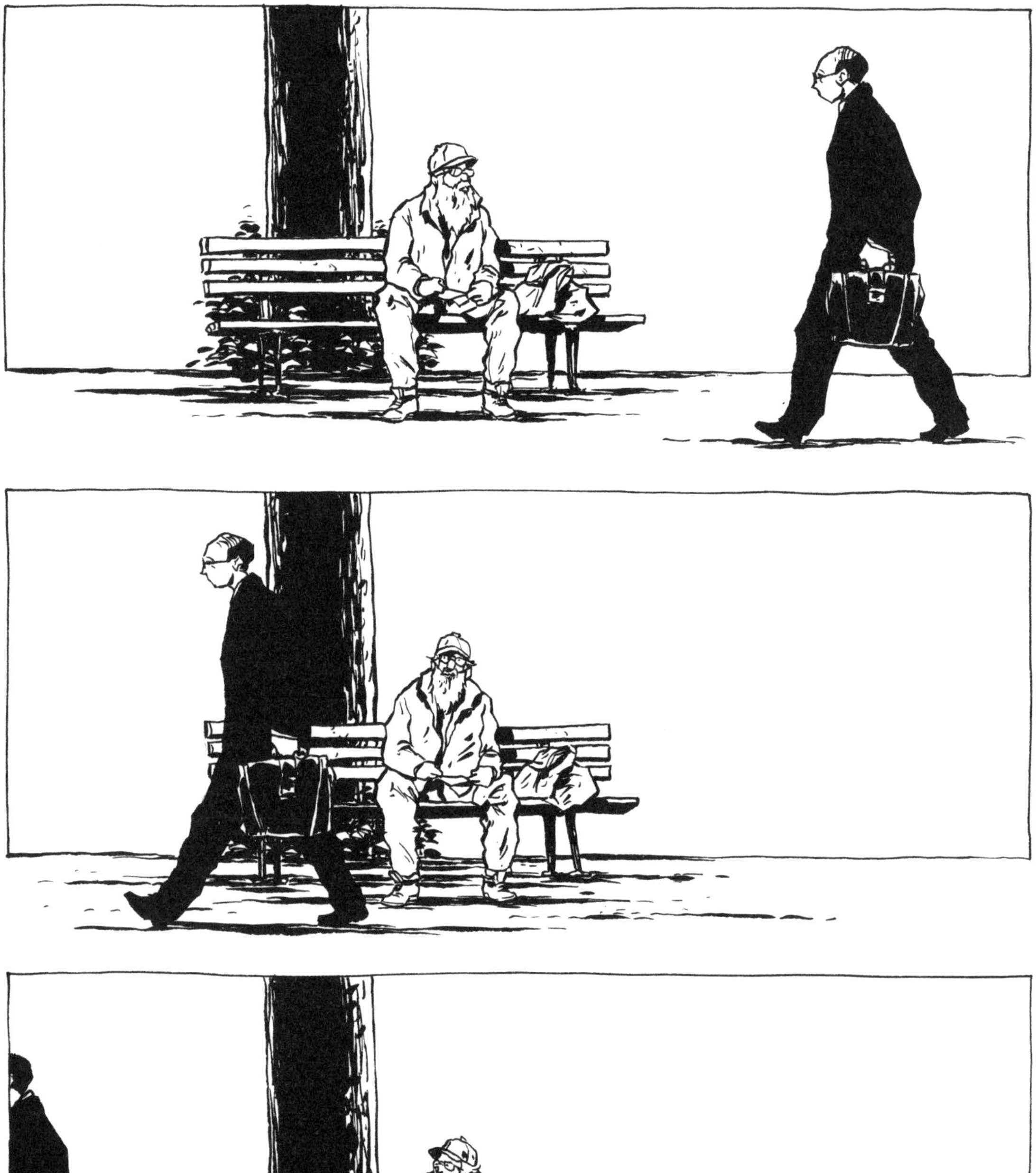

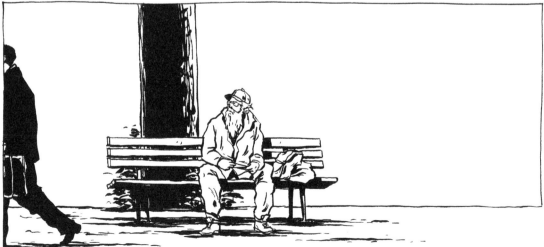

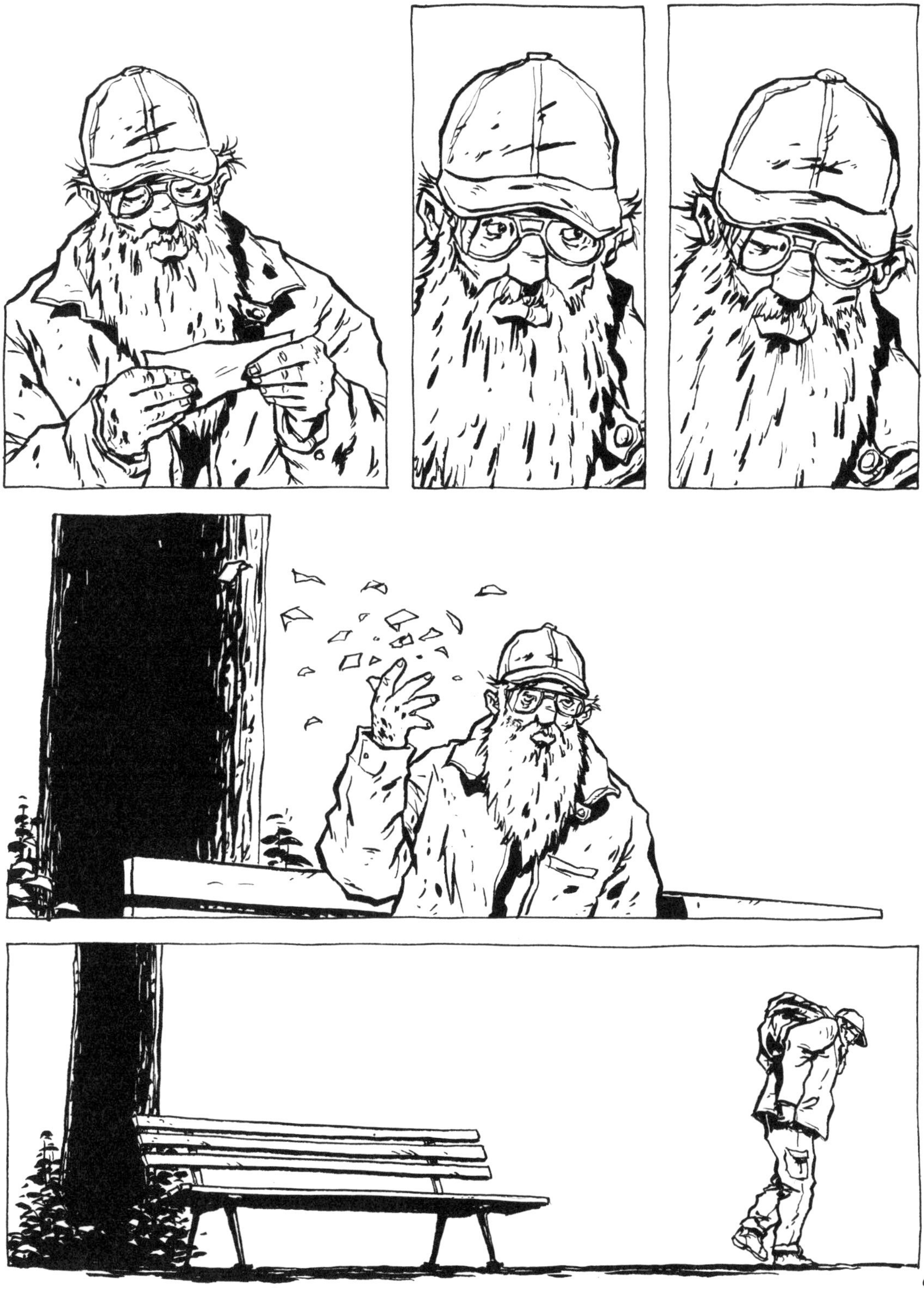

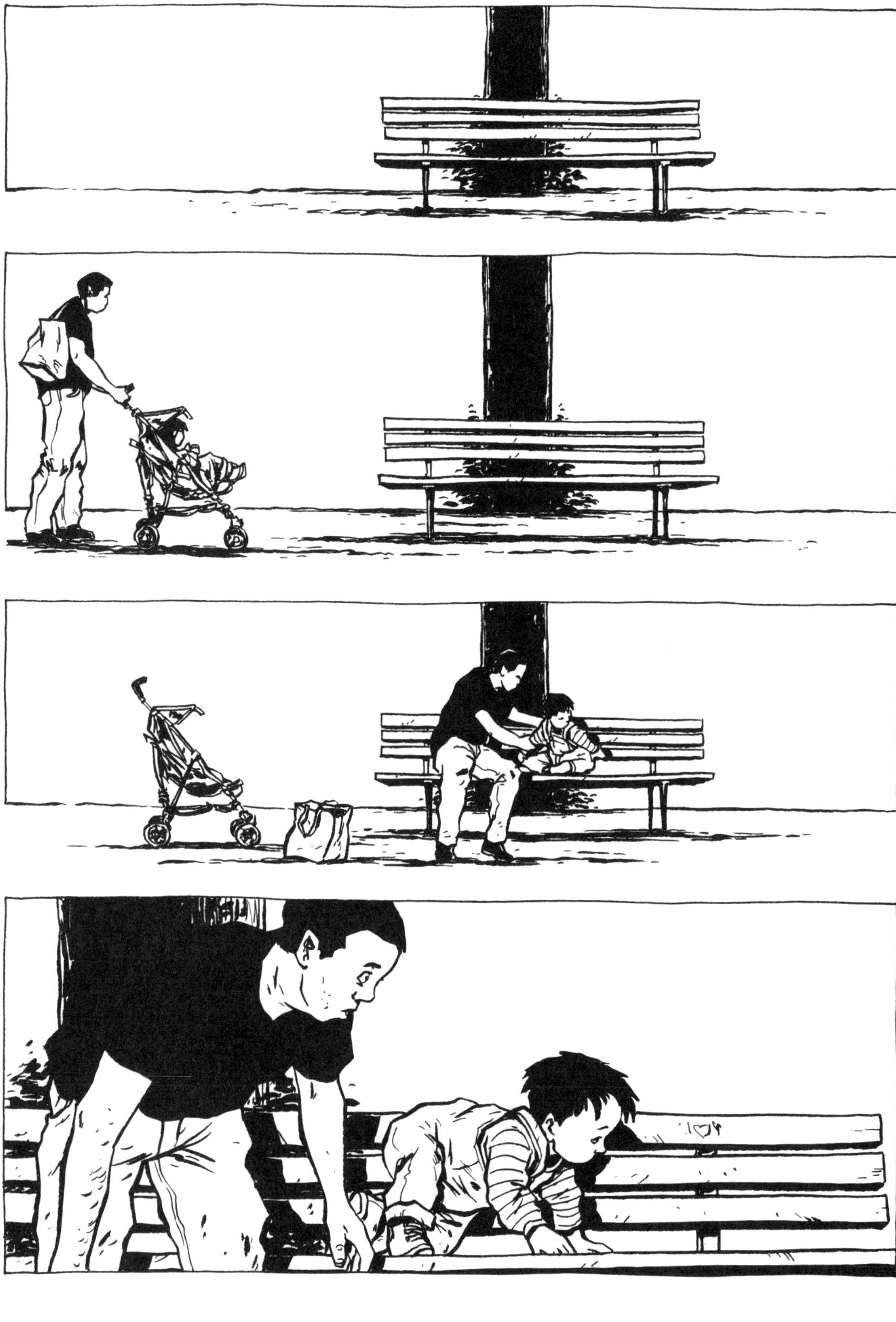

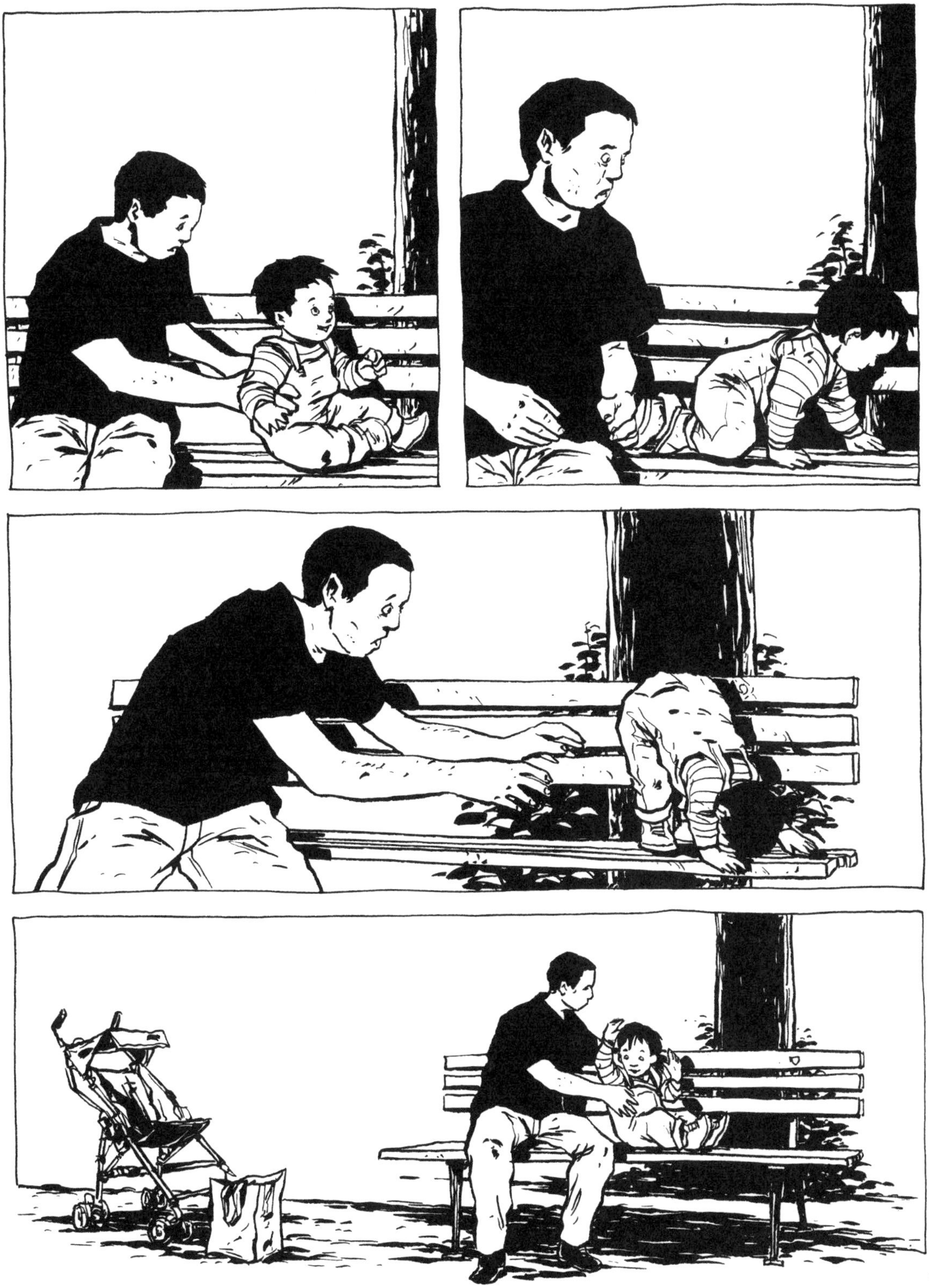

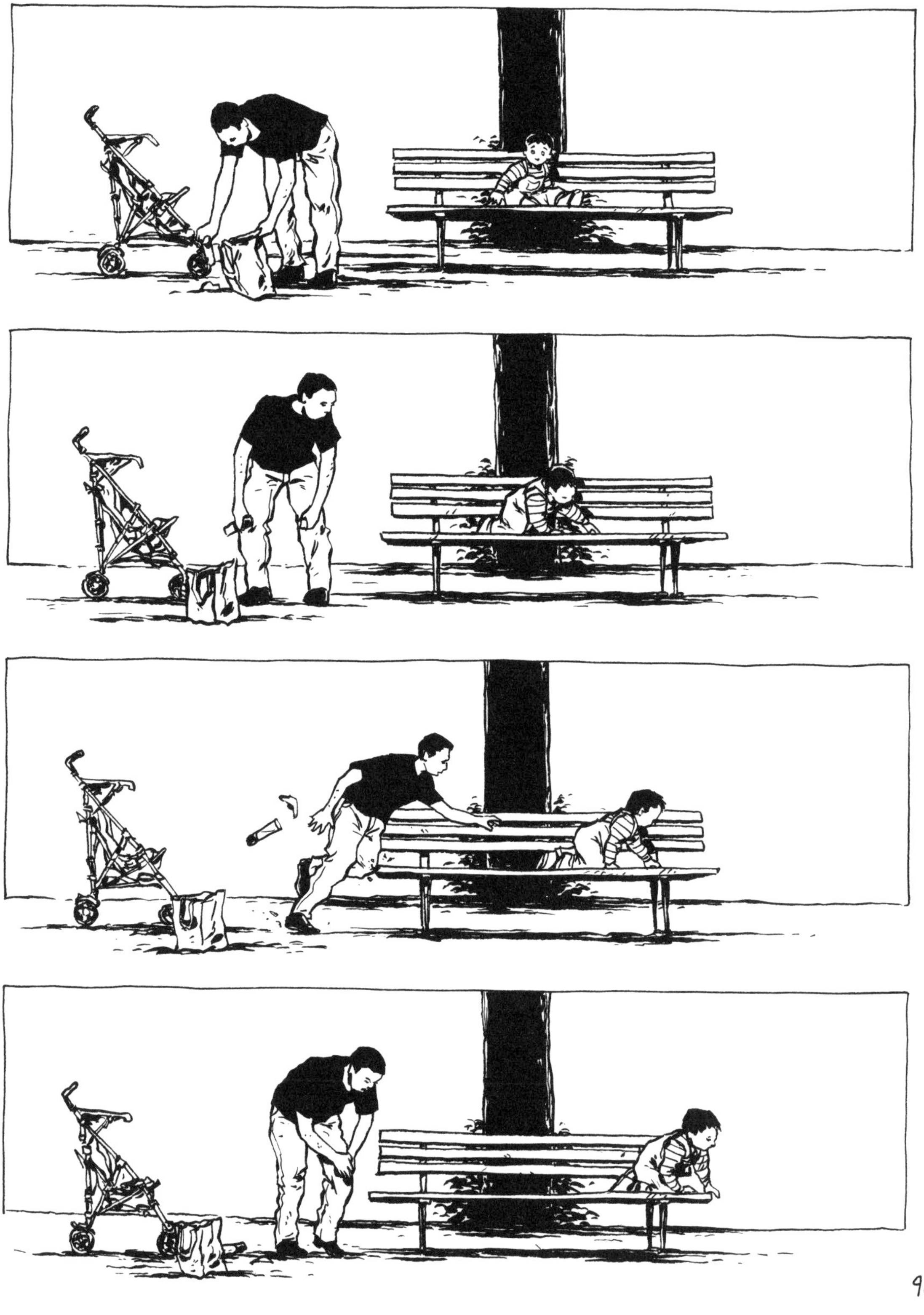

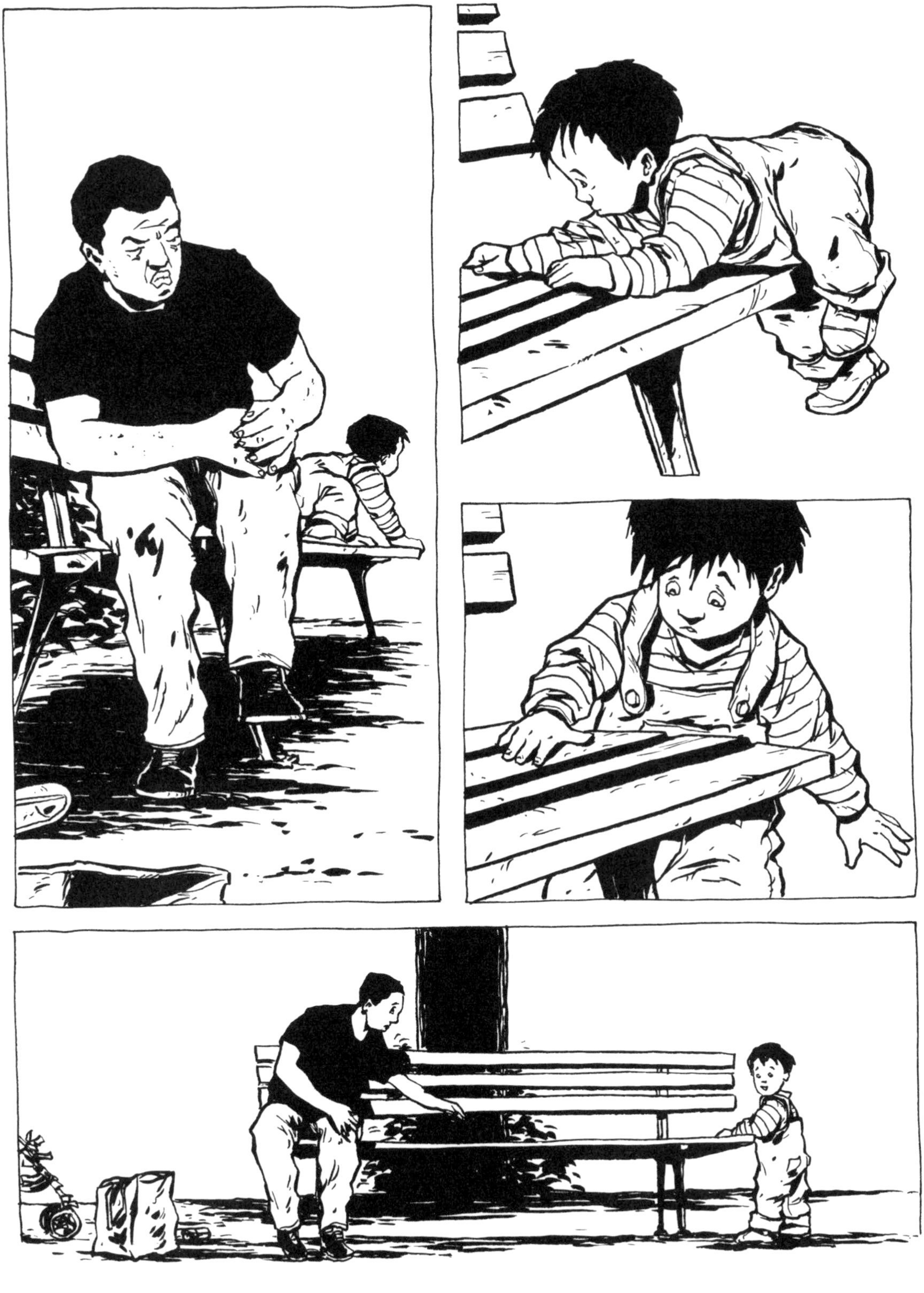

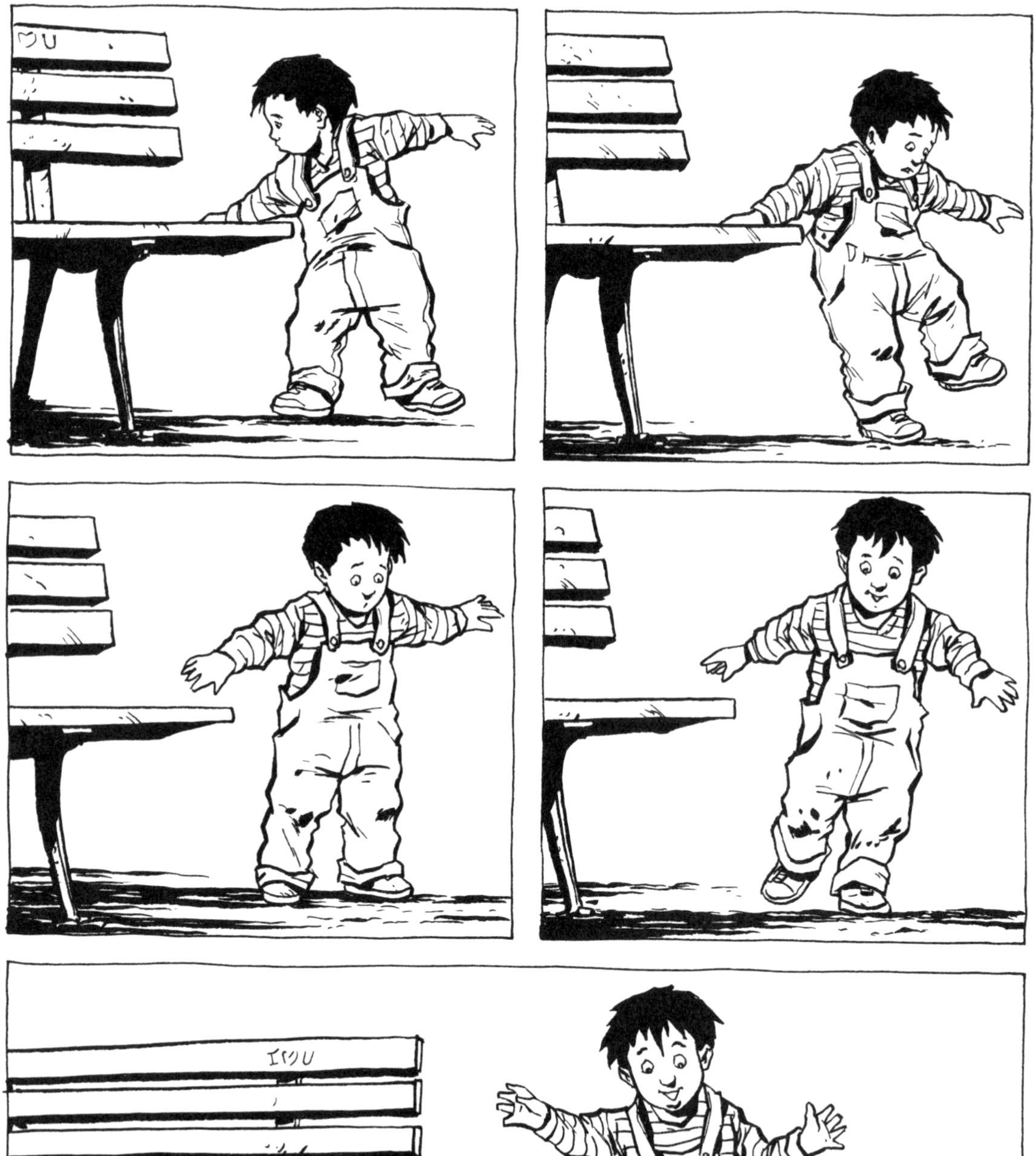
I♡U

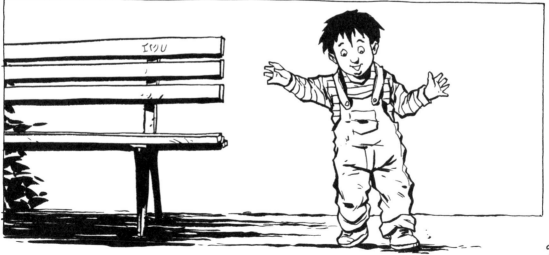

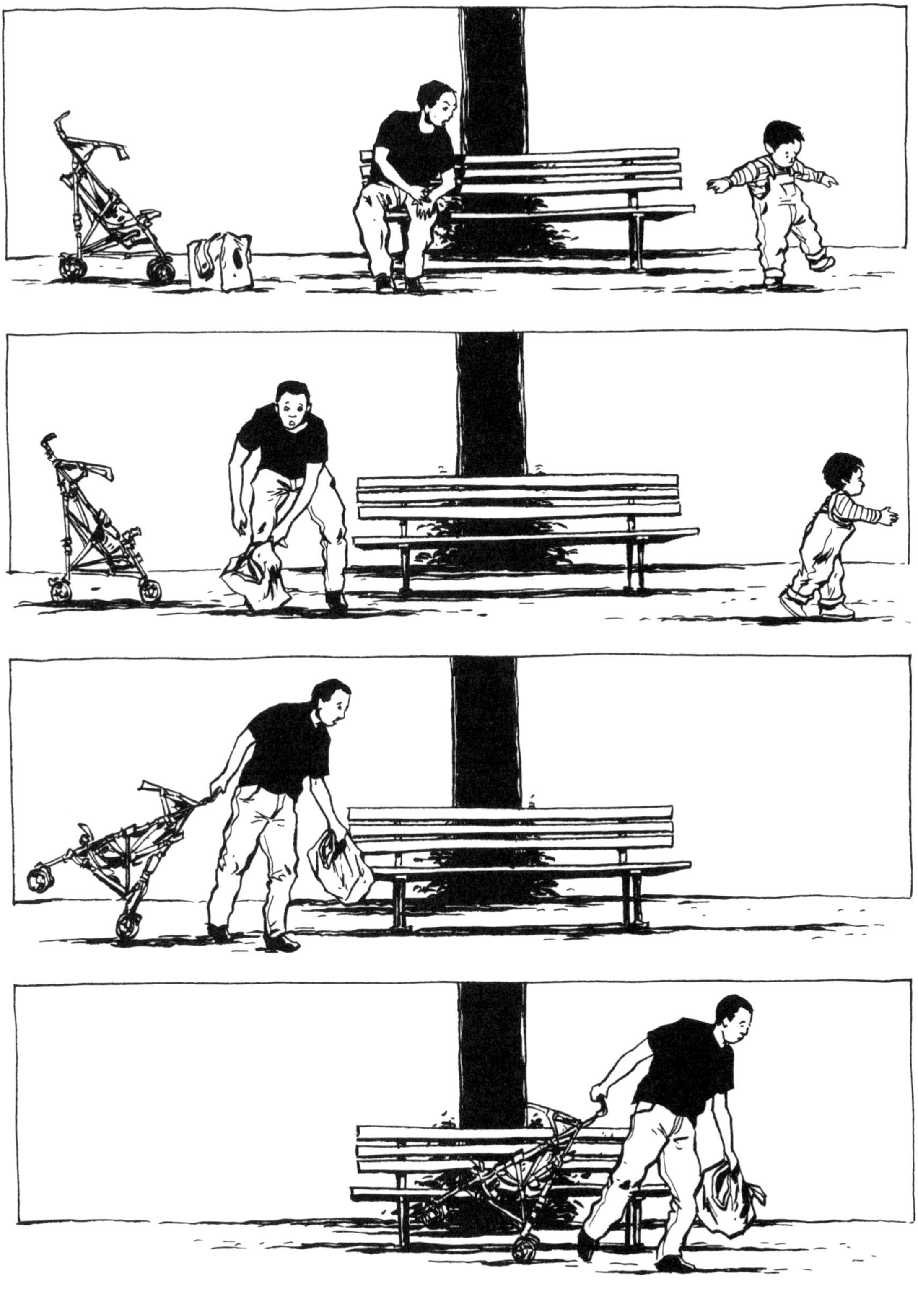

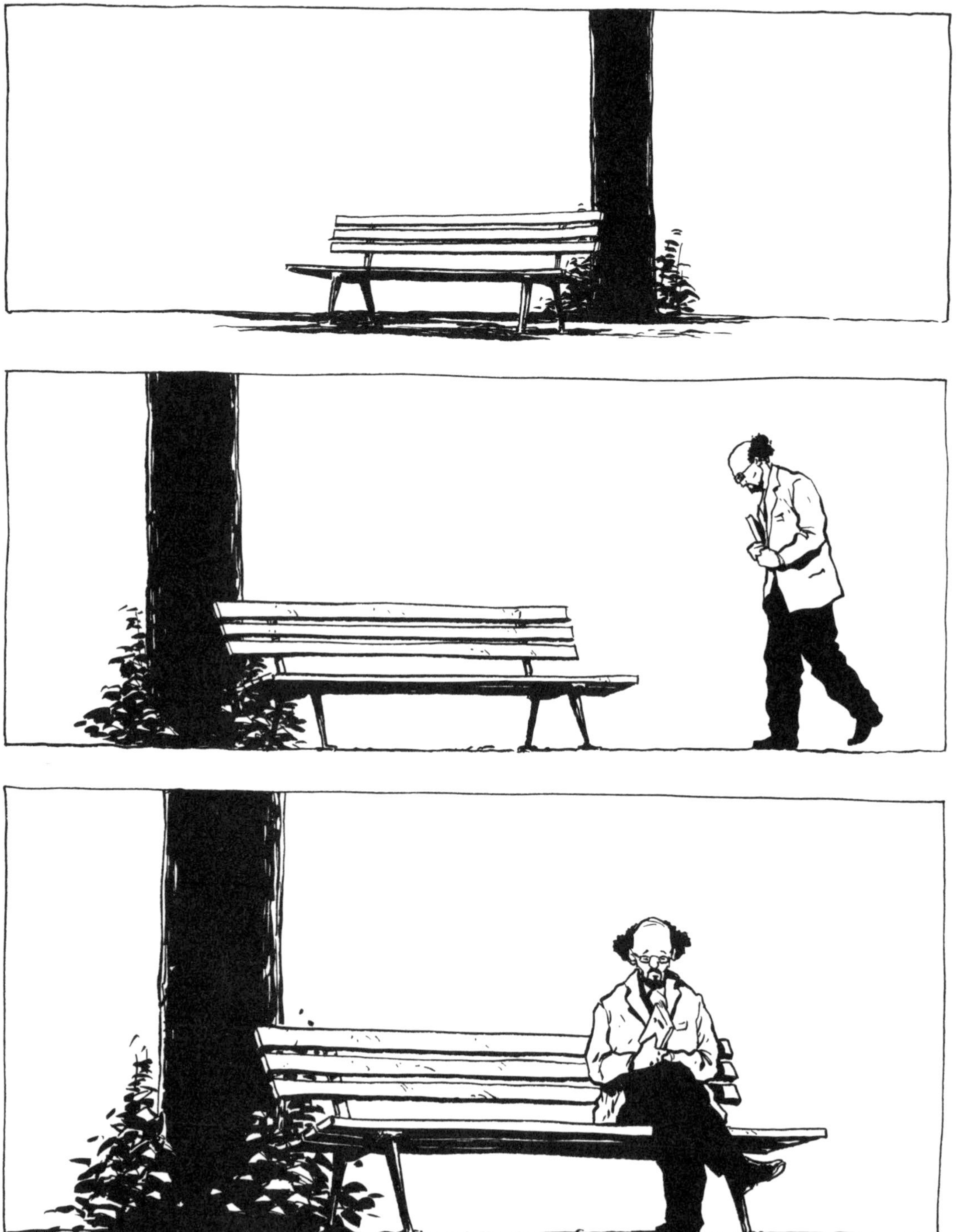

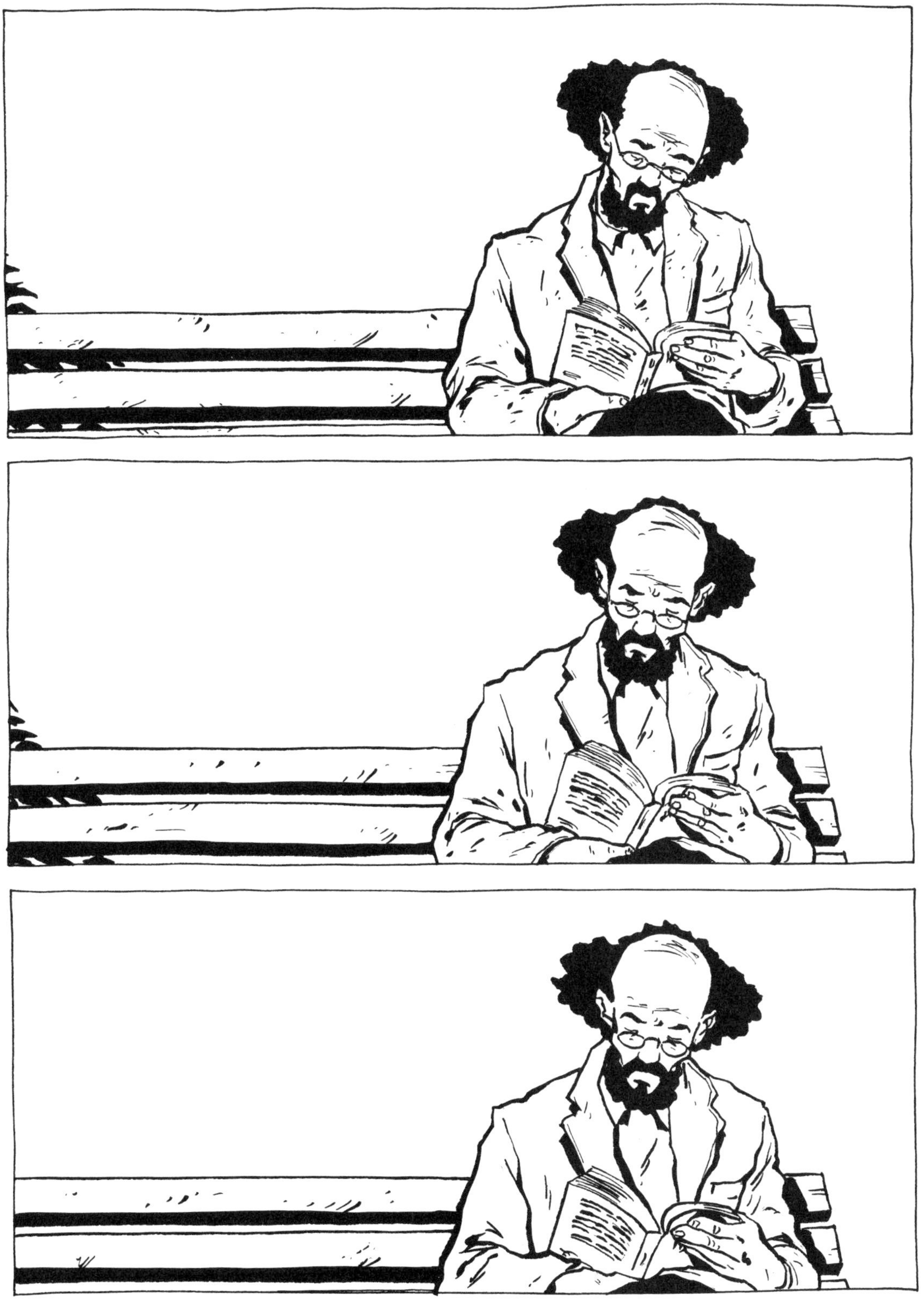

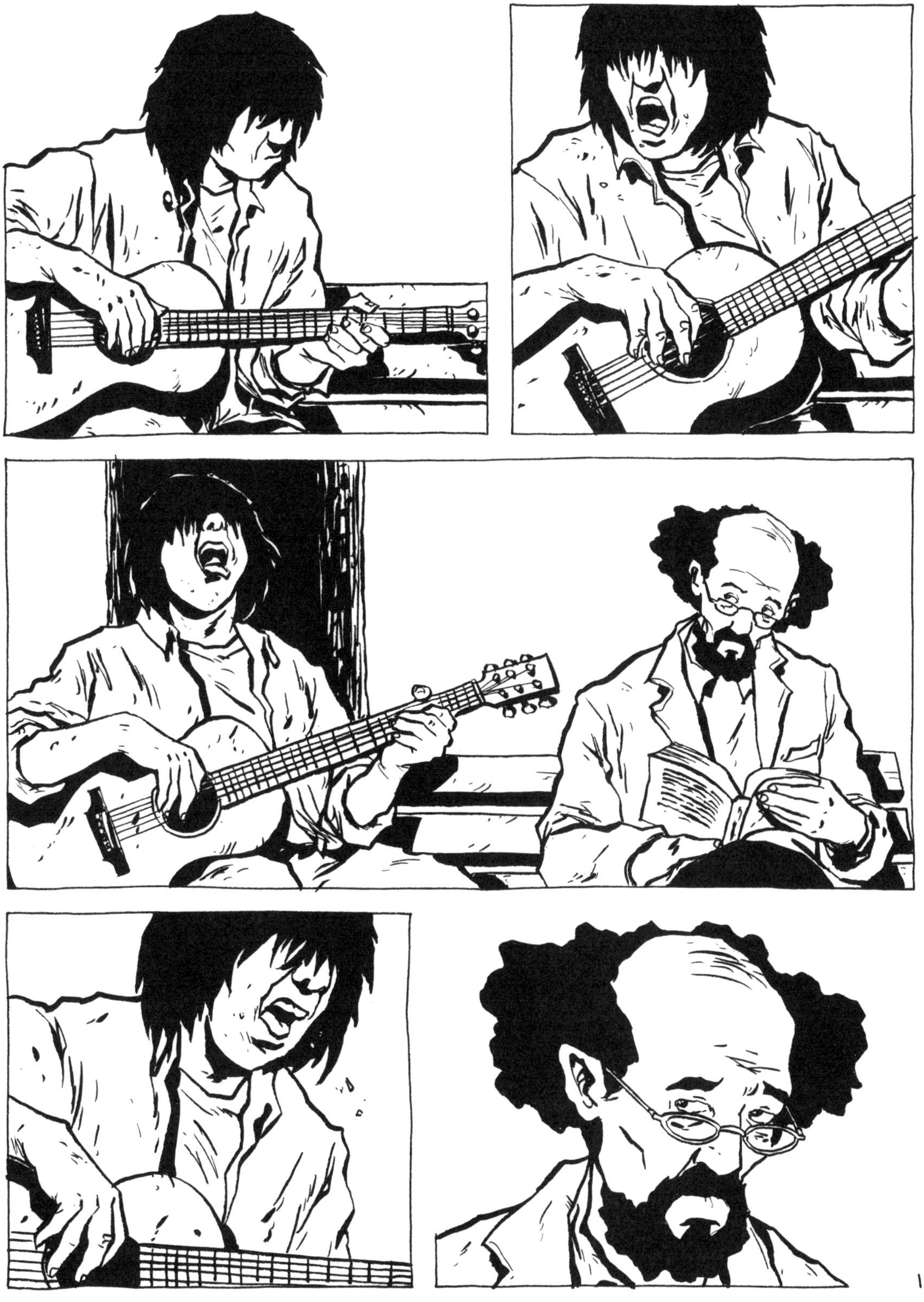

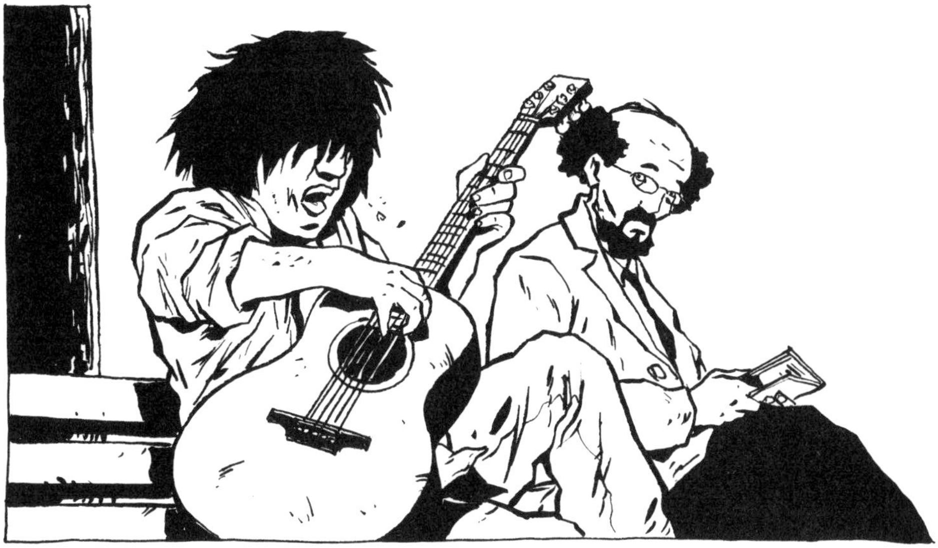
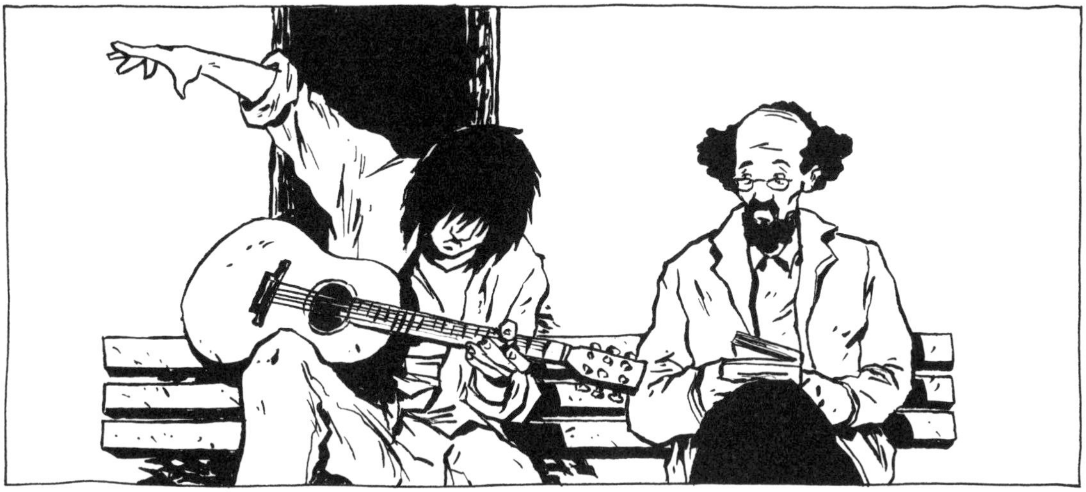
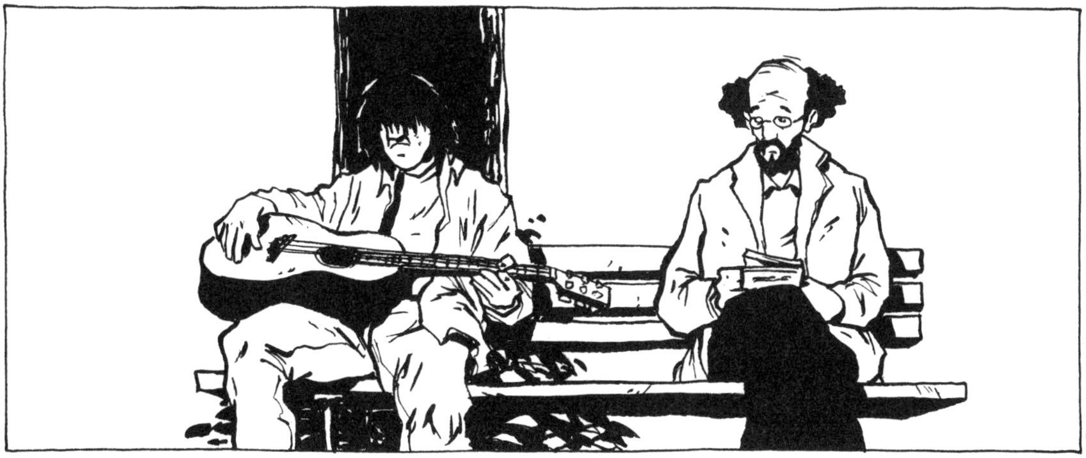

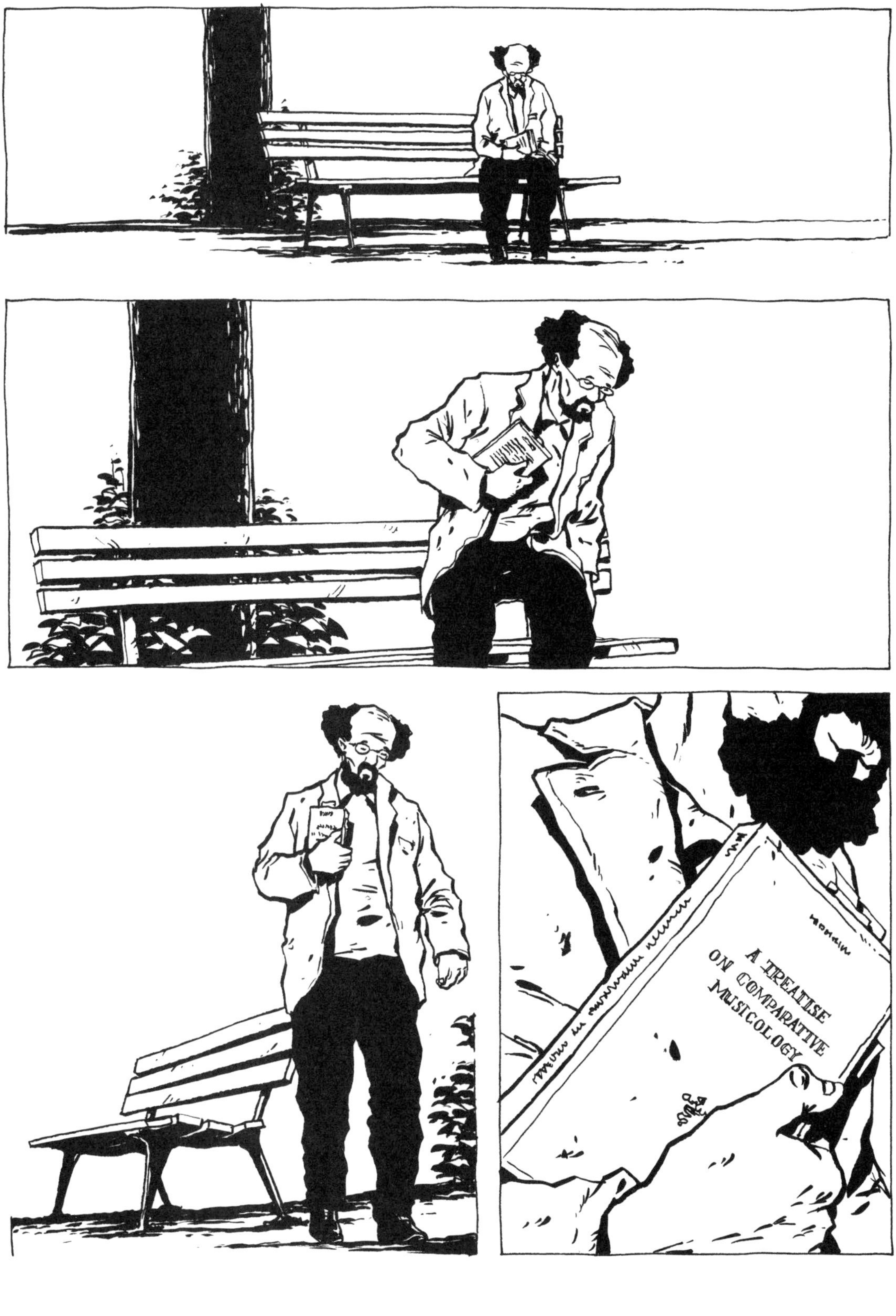
A TREATISE
ON COMPARATIVE
MUSICOLOGY

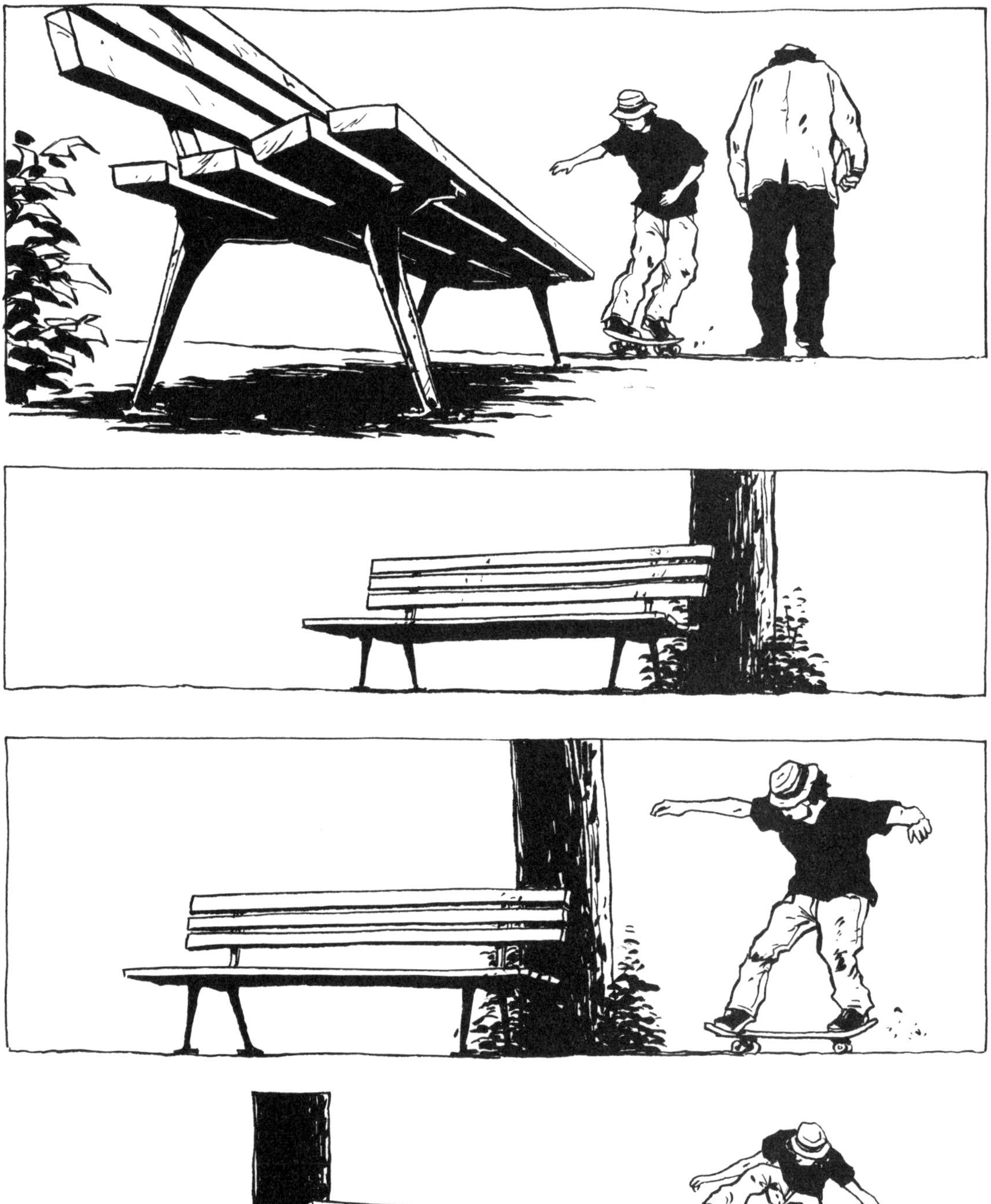

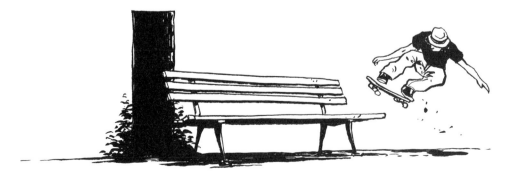

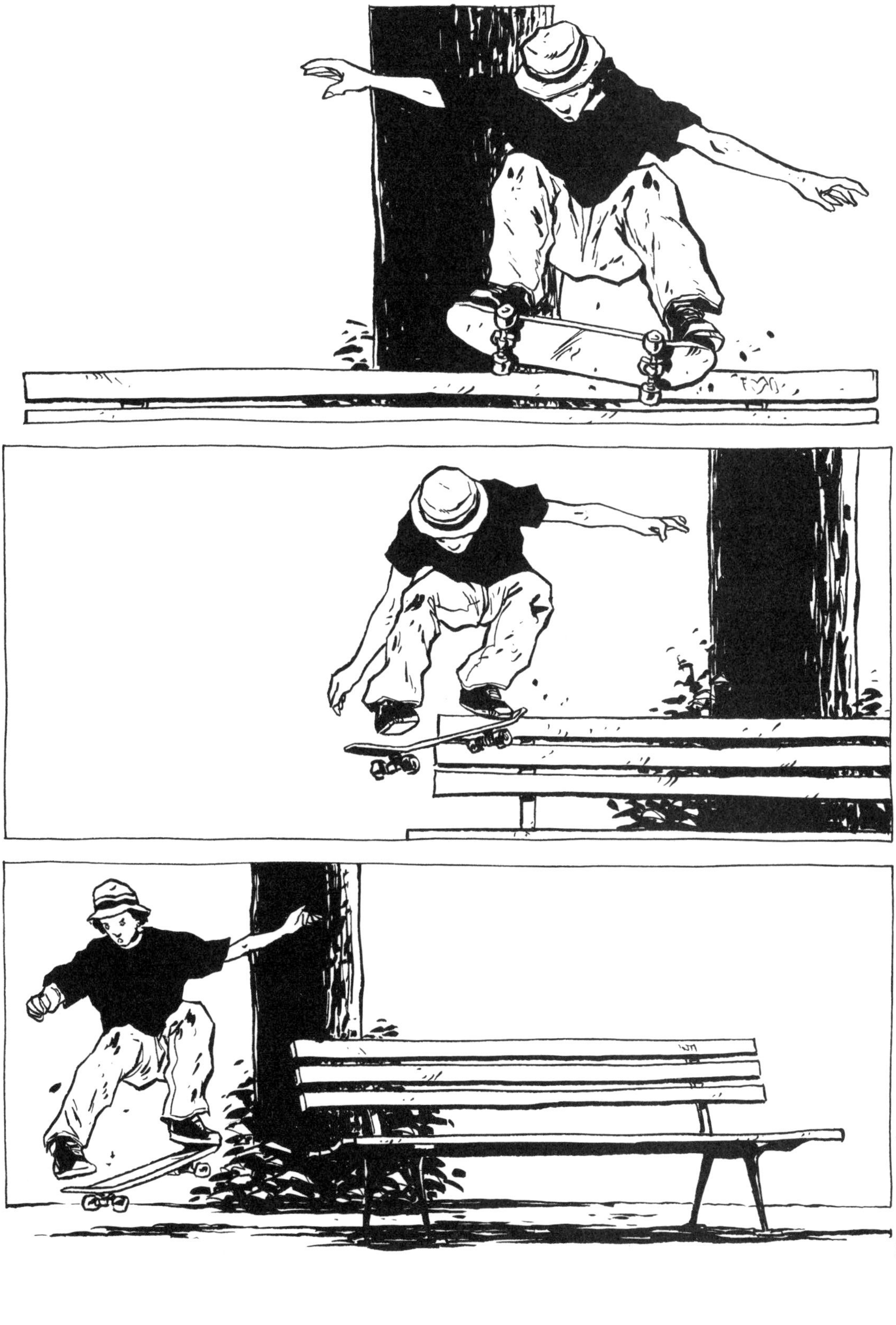

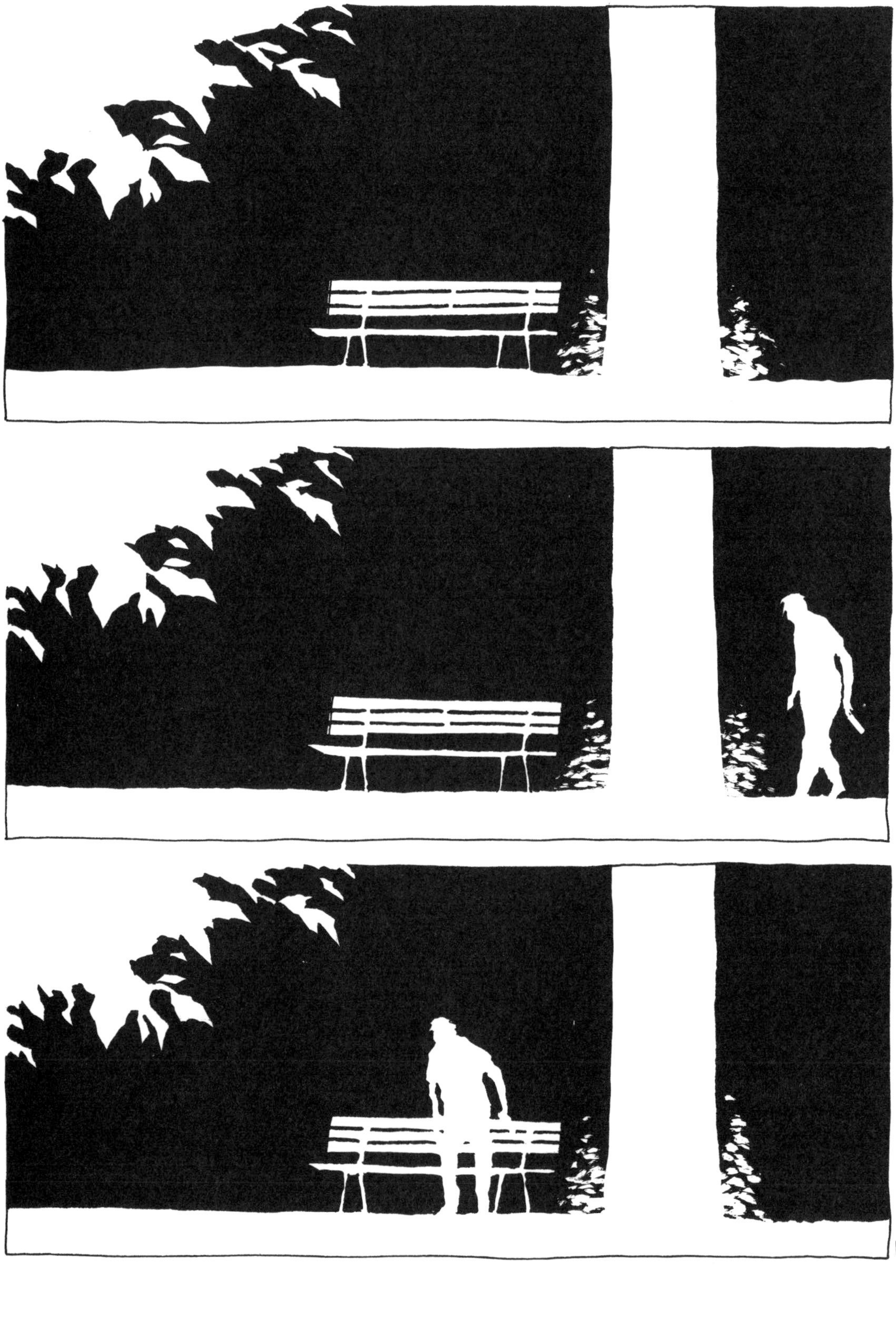

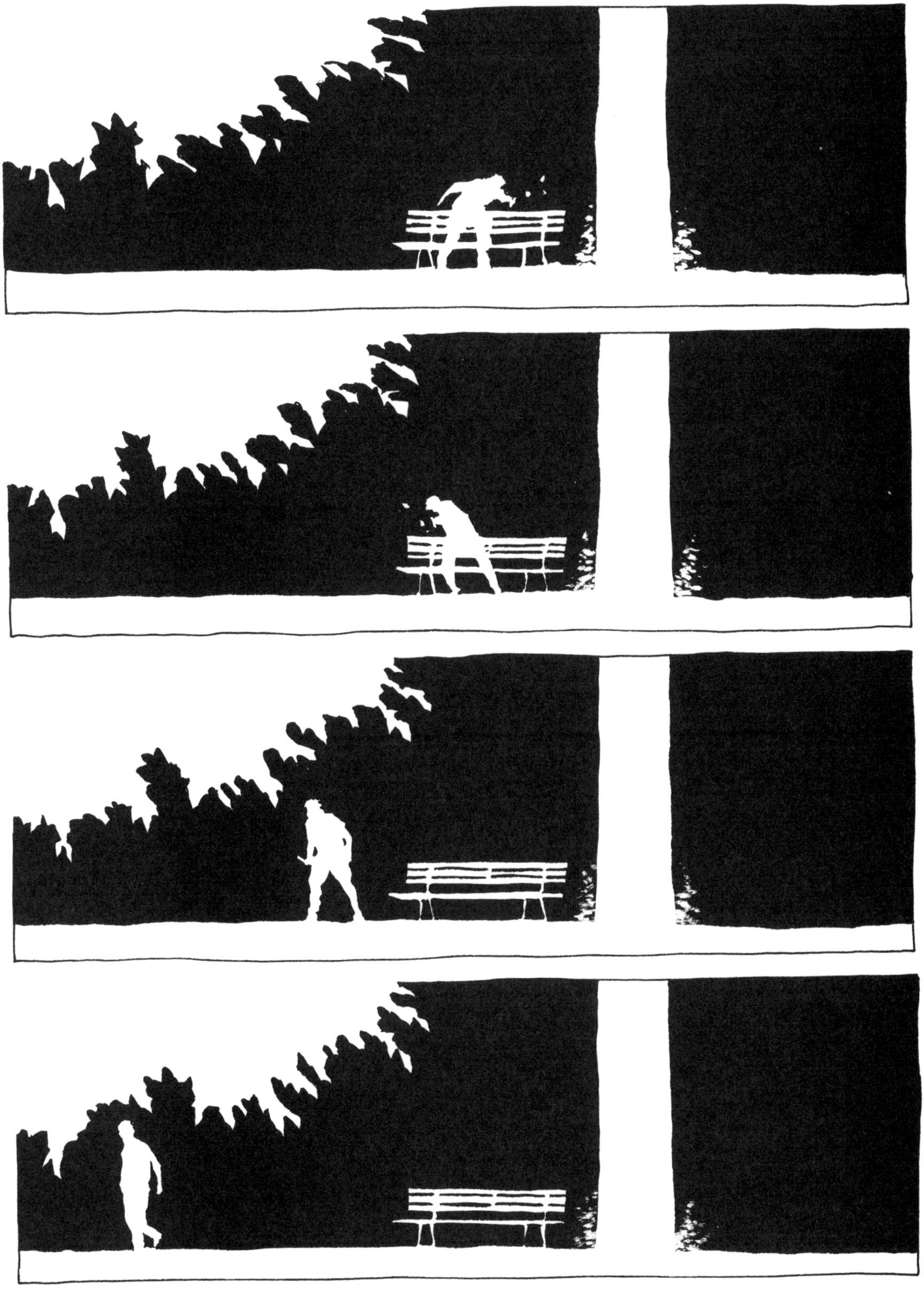

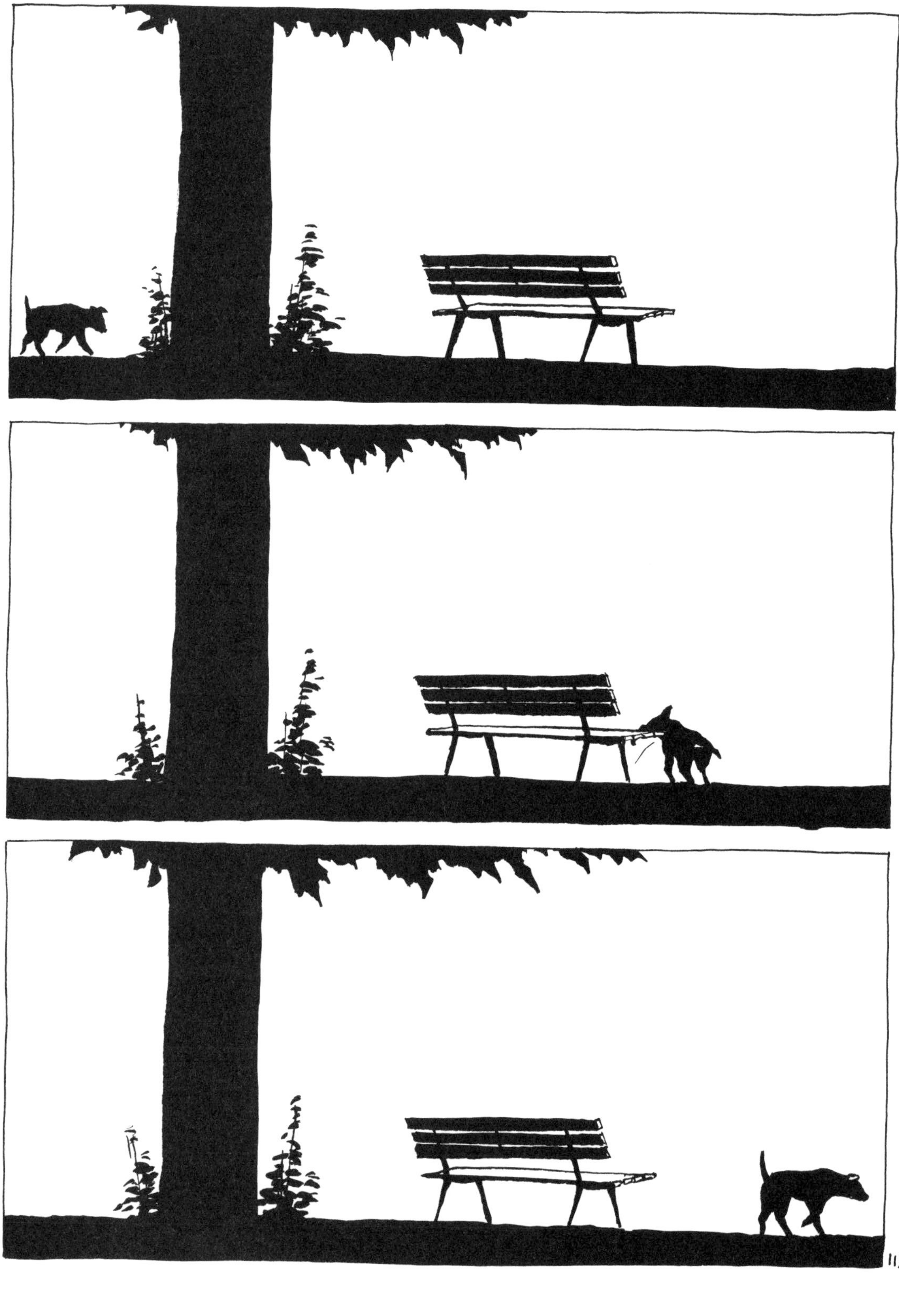

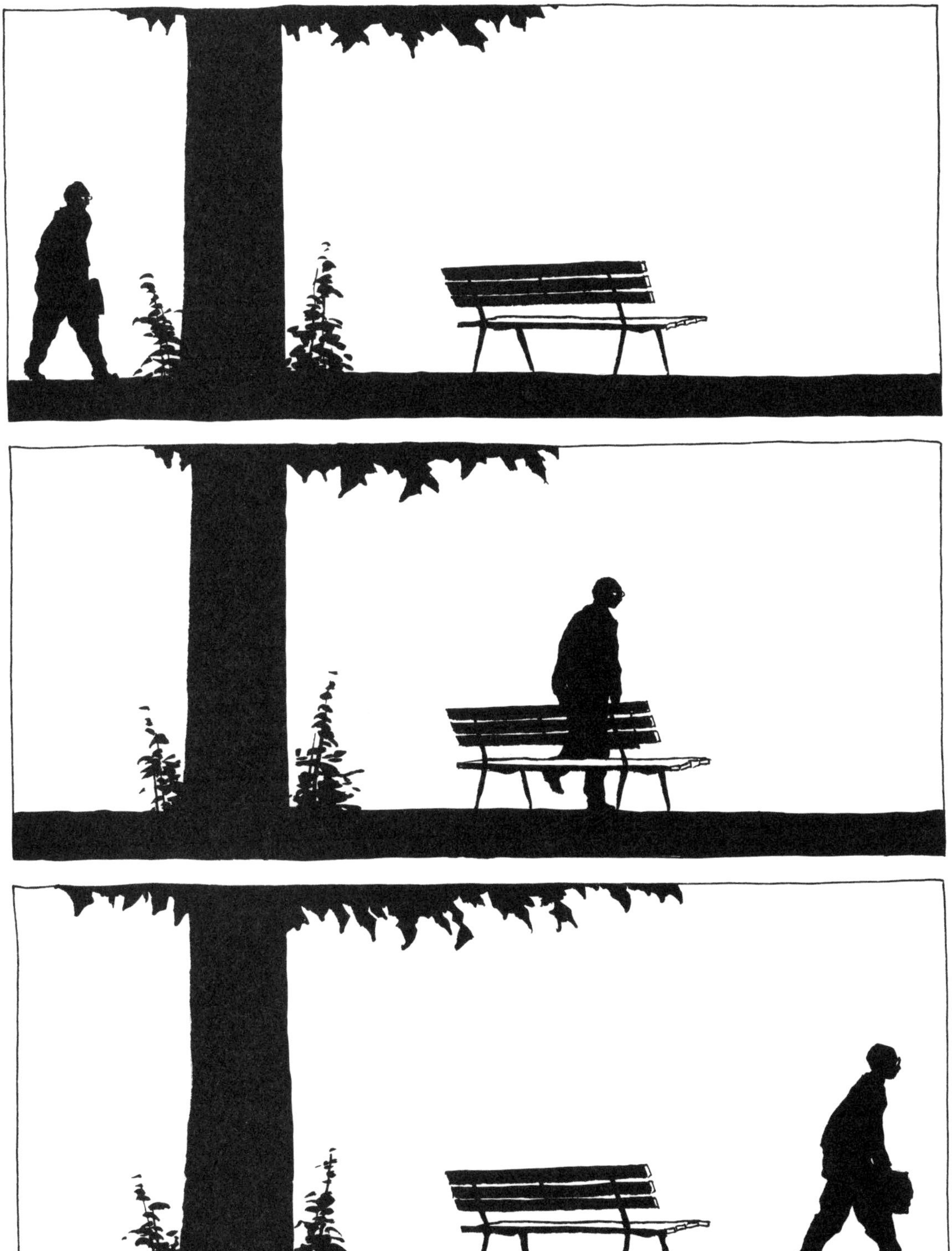

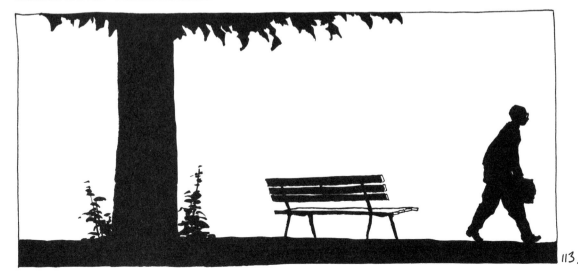

THE STUPIDITY IS UNENDING

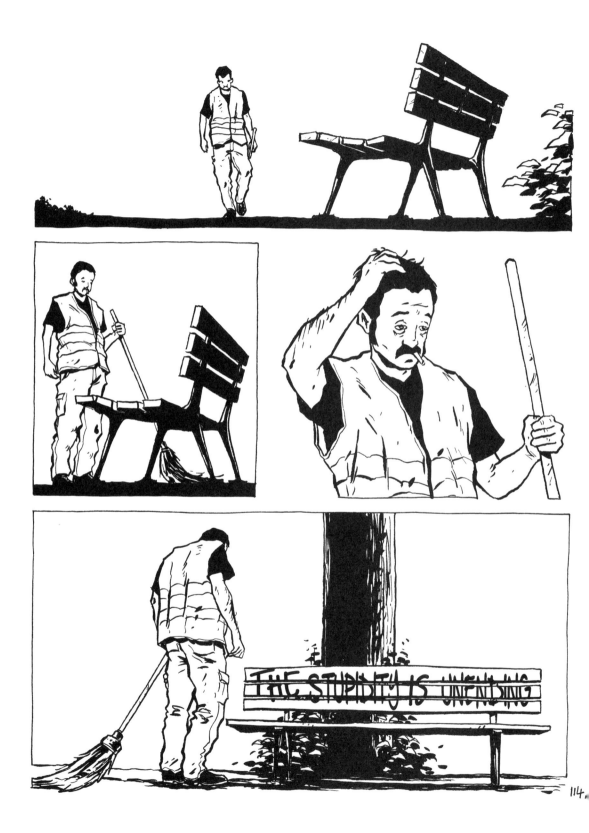

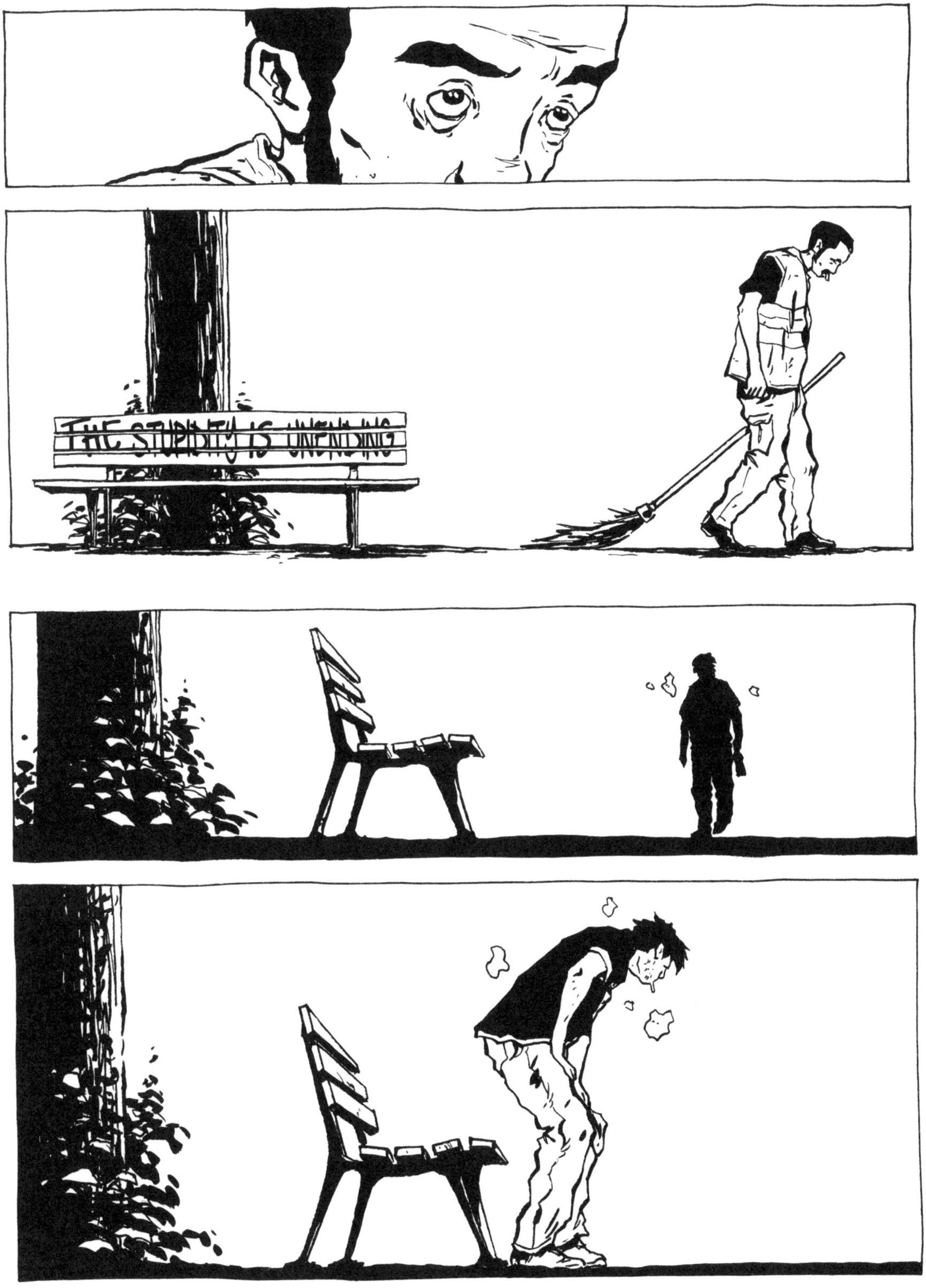
THE STUPIDITY IS UNENDING

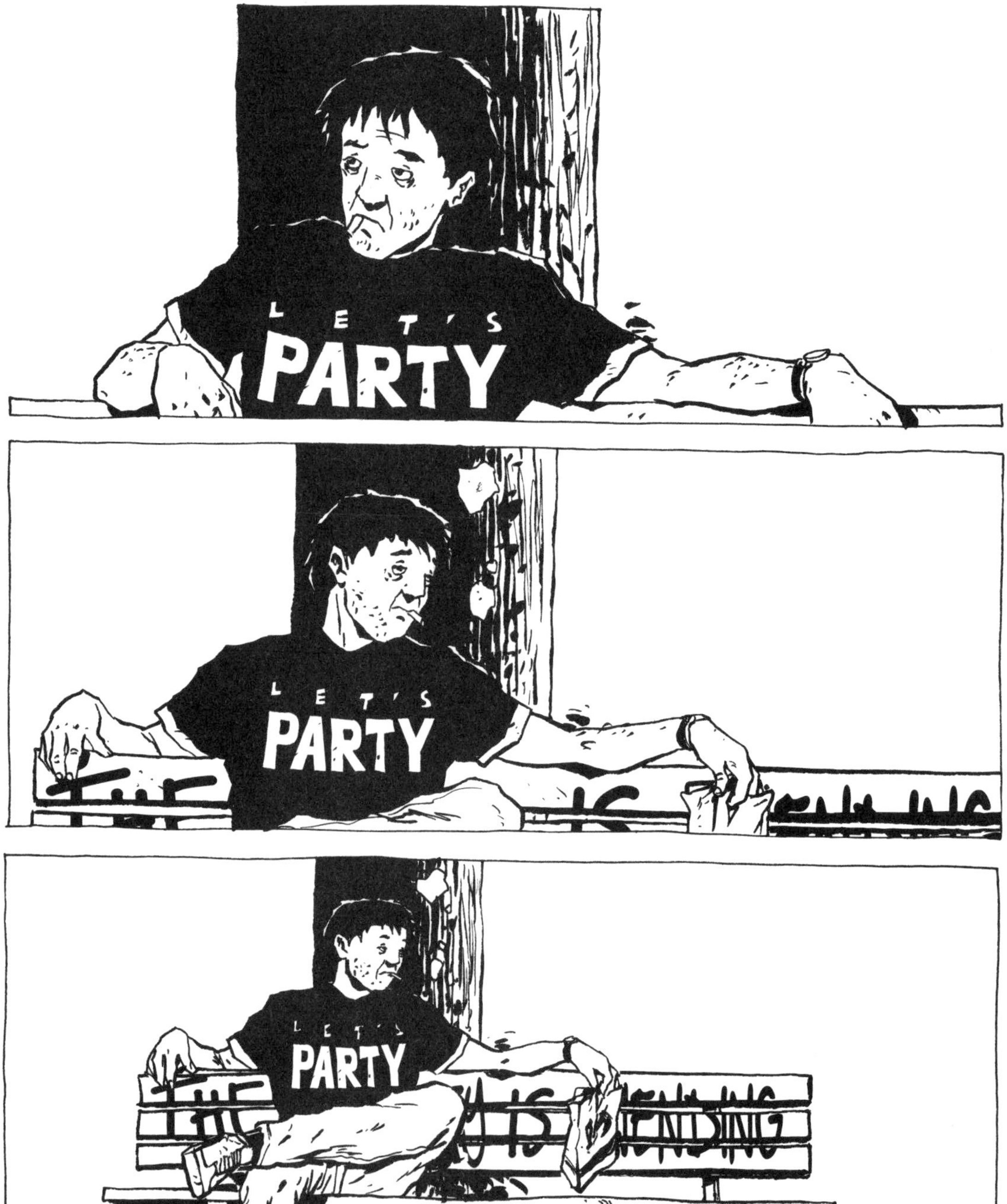
LET'S
PARTY
LET'S
PARTY
IS
LET'S
PARTY
IS

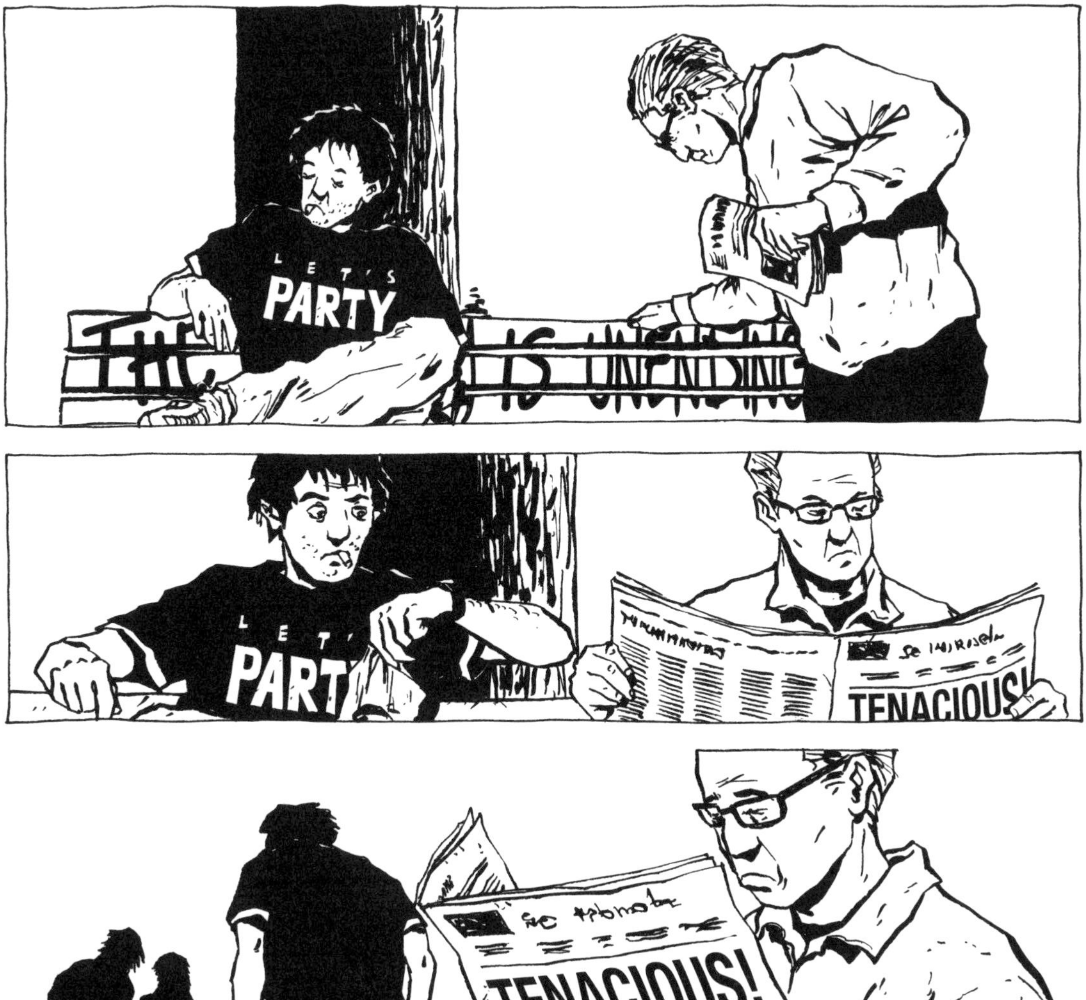
LET'S PARTY
TENACIOUS!
TENACIOUS!
THE STUPIDITY IS
TENACIOUS

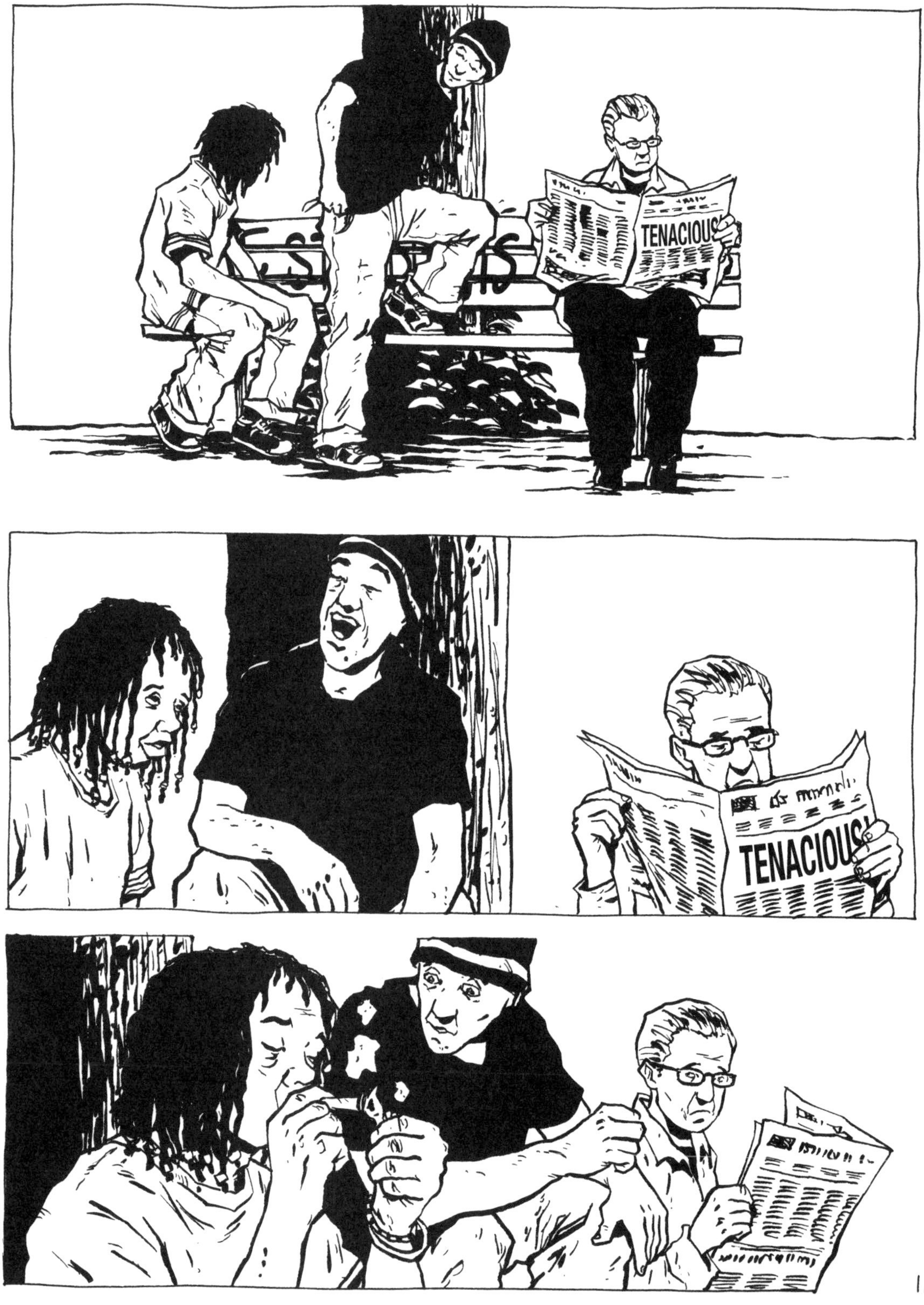
TENACIOUS!
TENACIOUS!

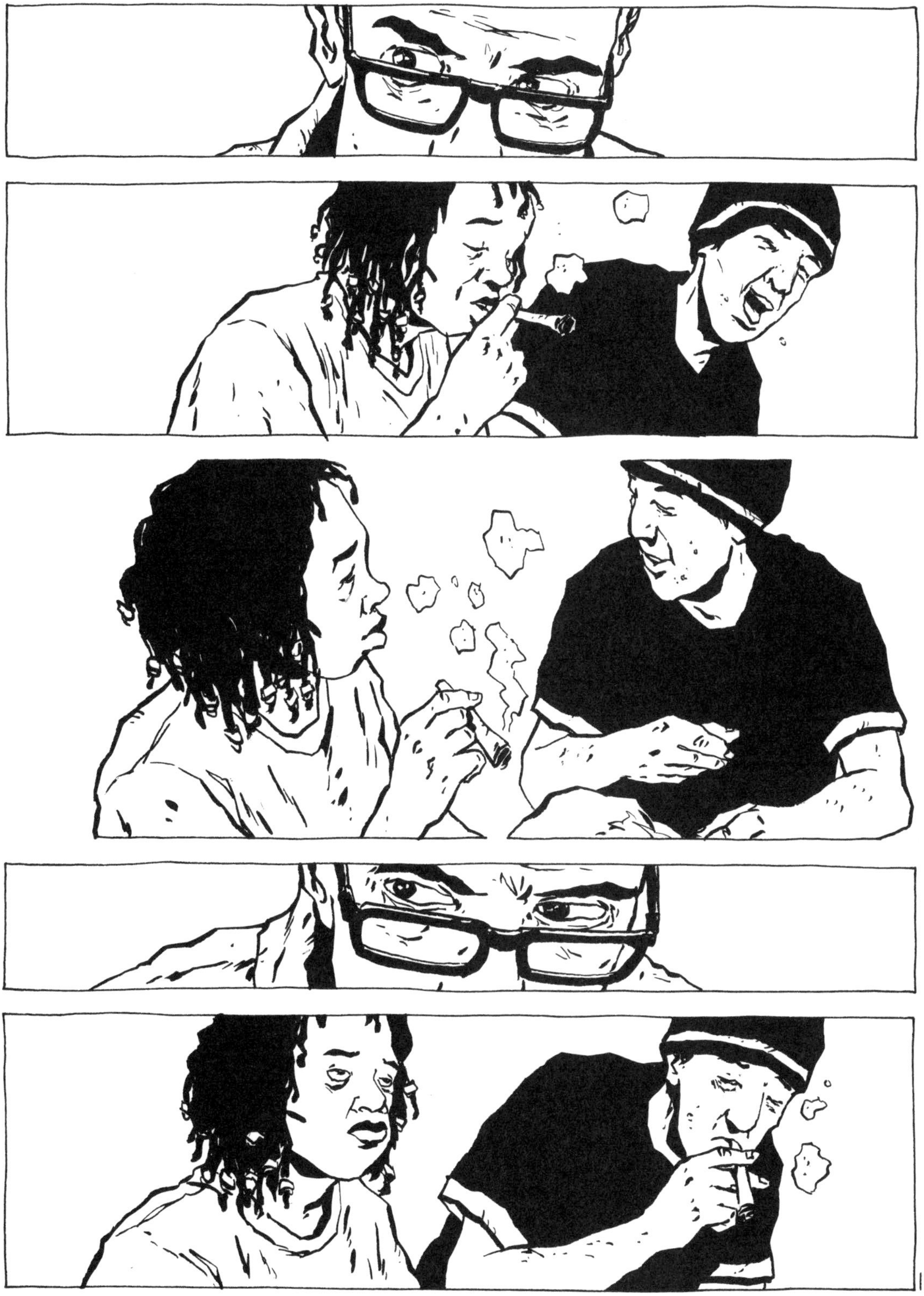

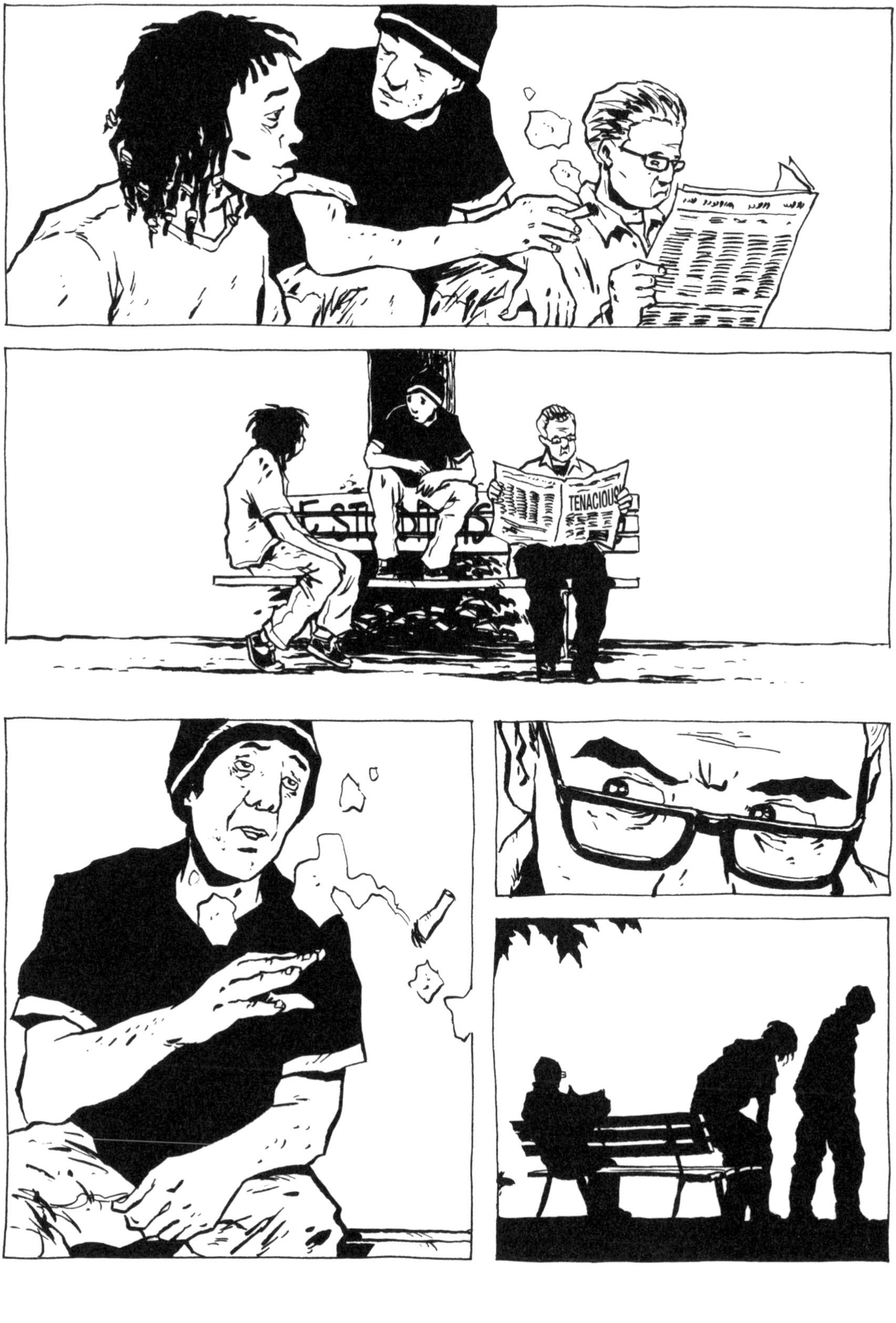
TENACIOUS

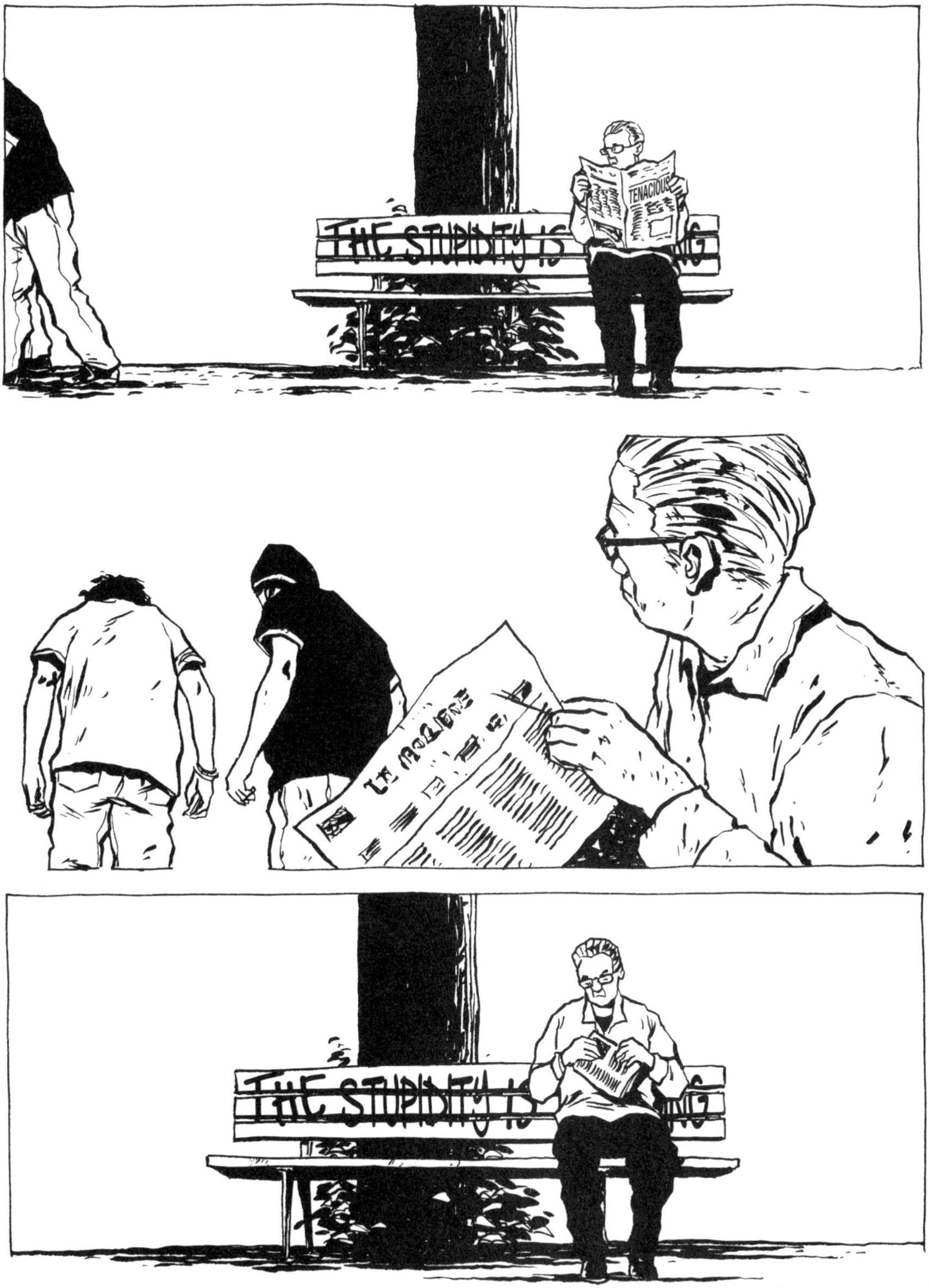
THE STUPIDITY IS
NG
TENACIOUS
THE STUPIDITY IS
NG

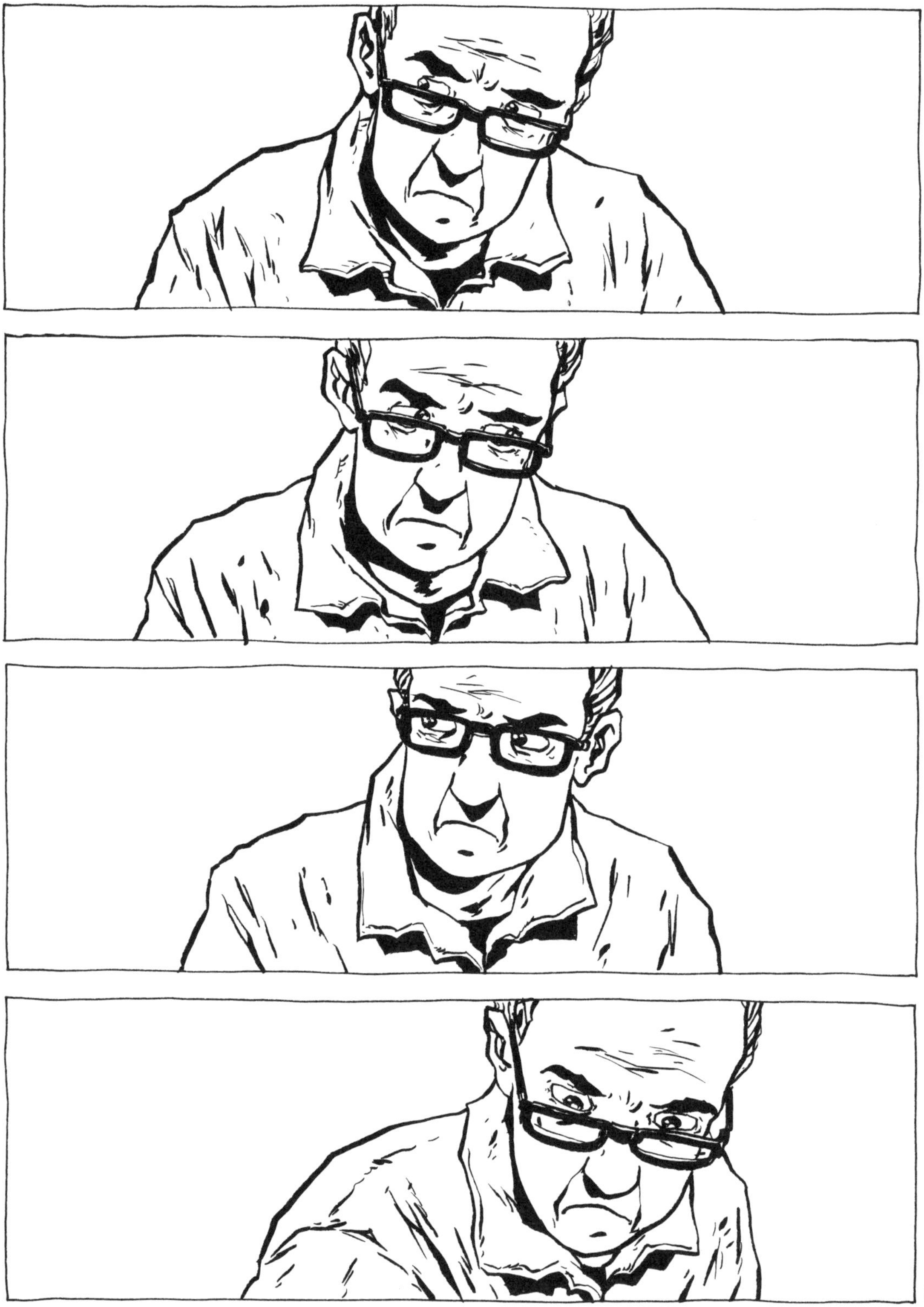

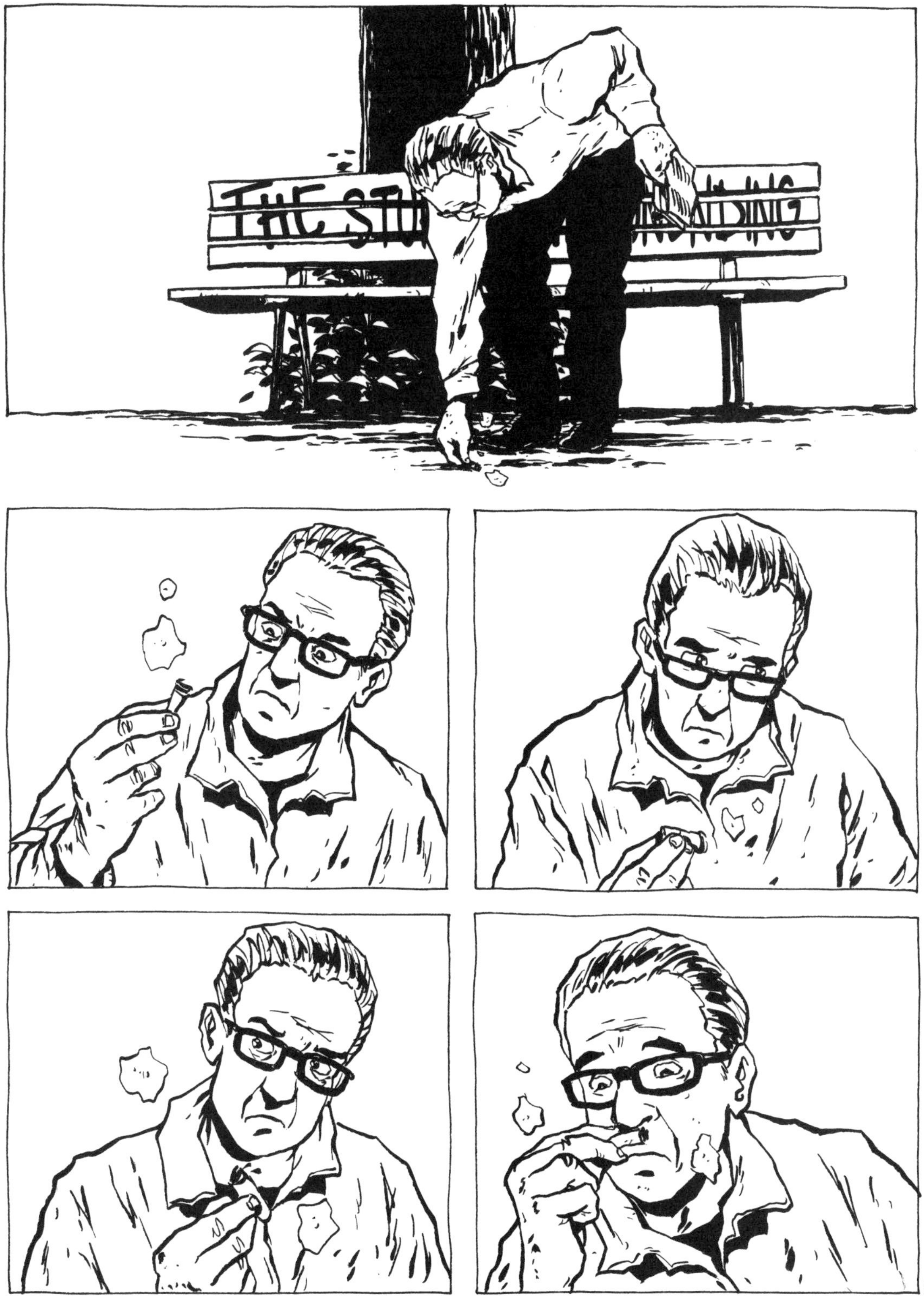

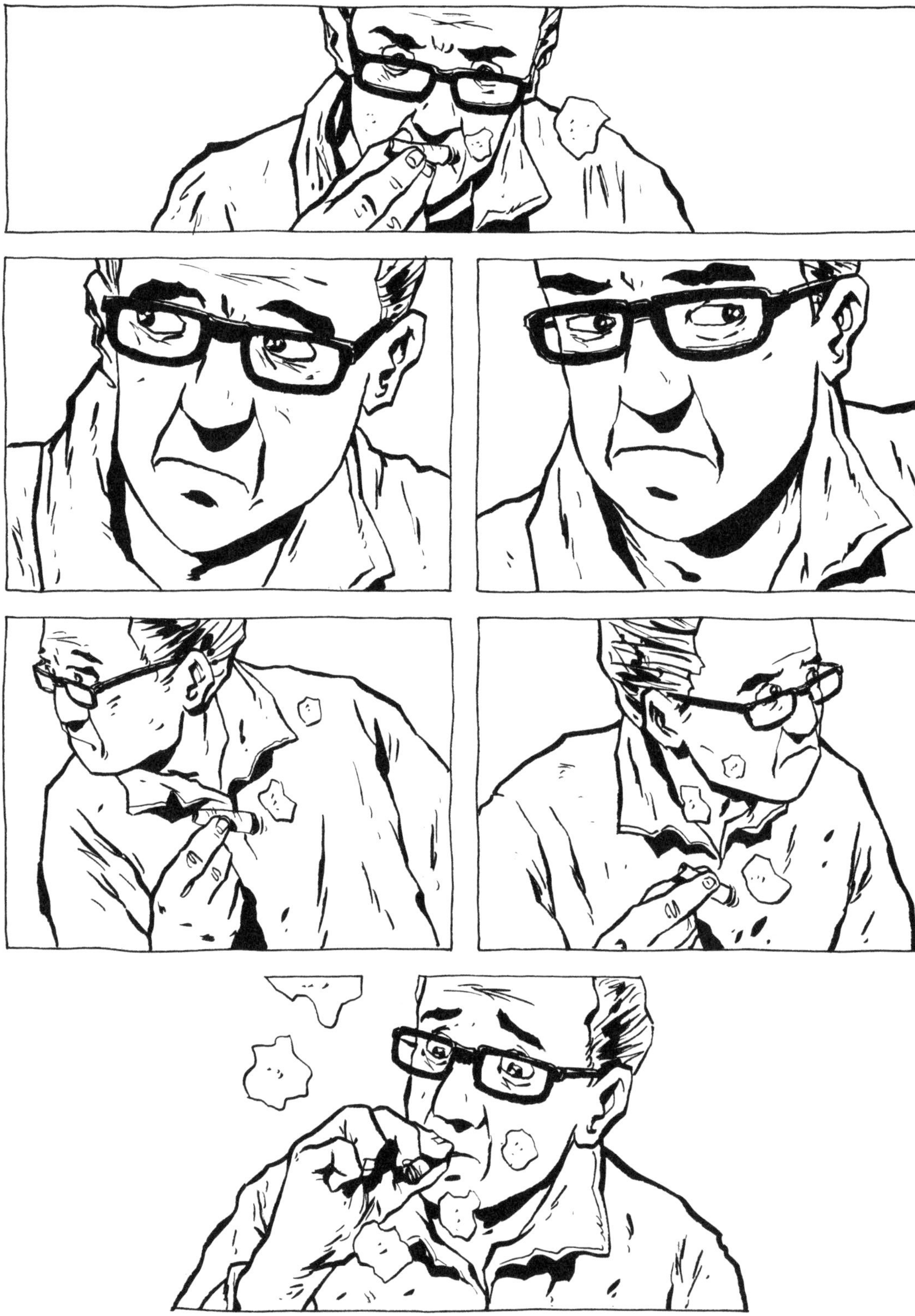

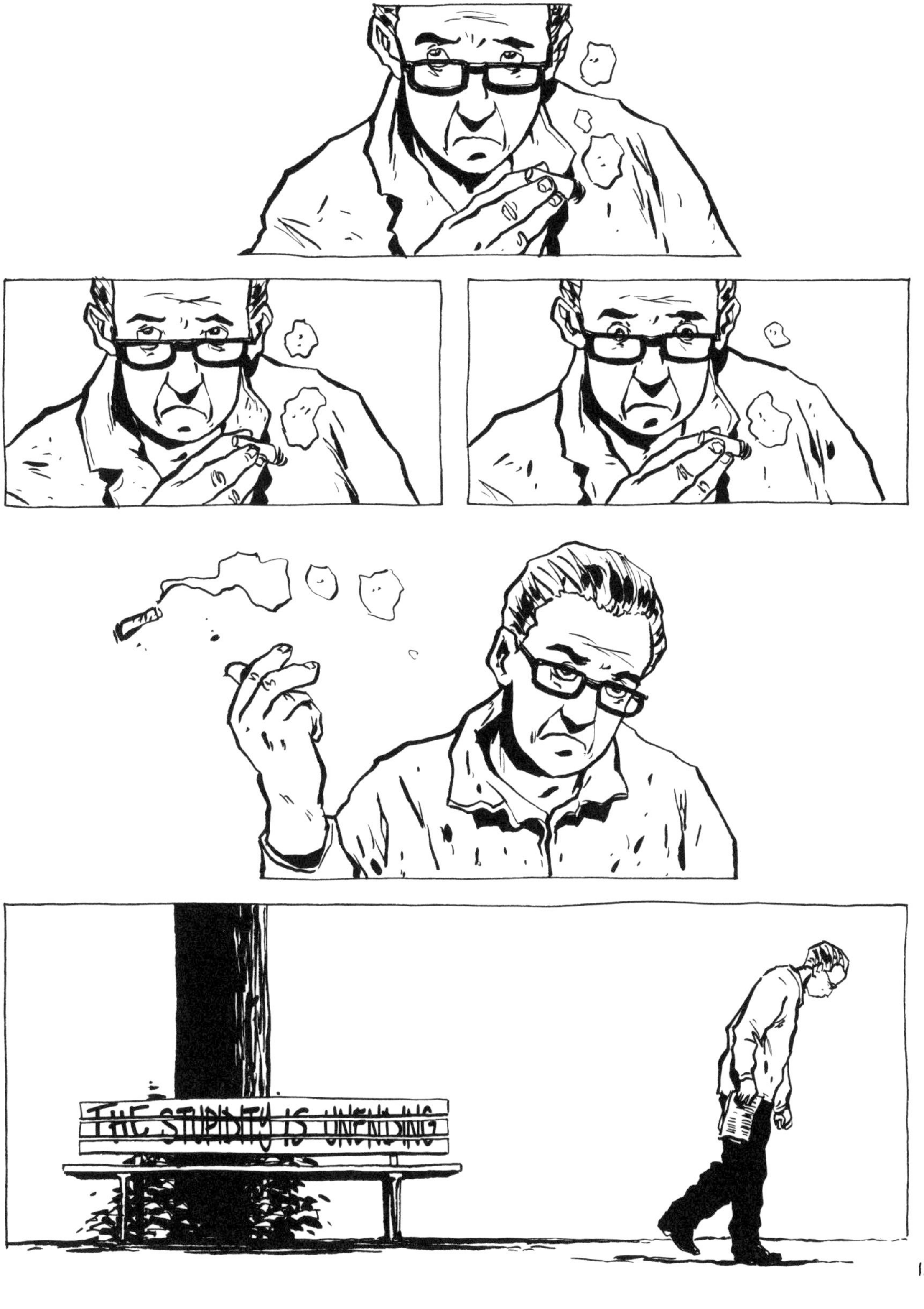
THE STUPIDITY IS UNENDING

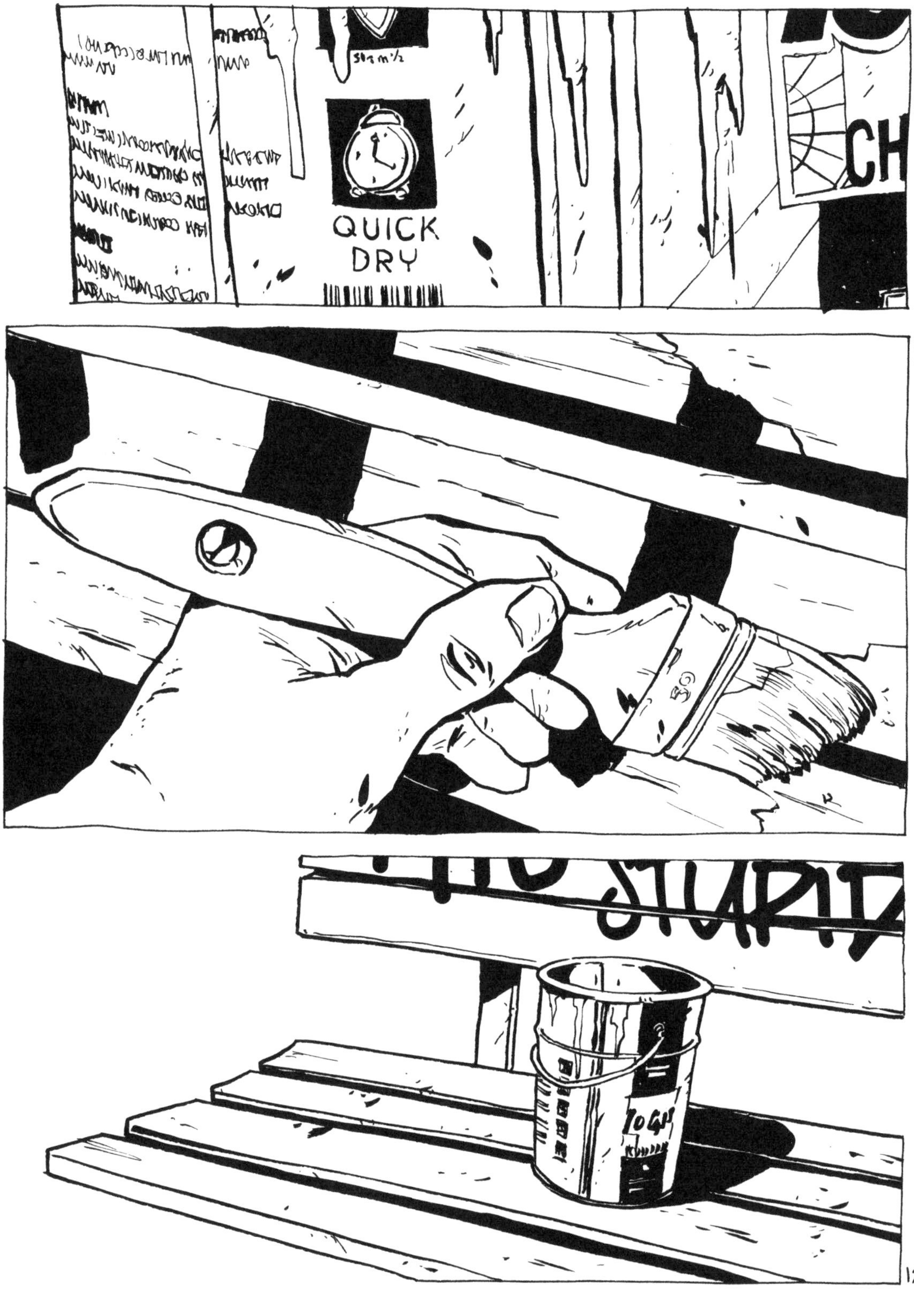
QUICK
DRY
CH

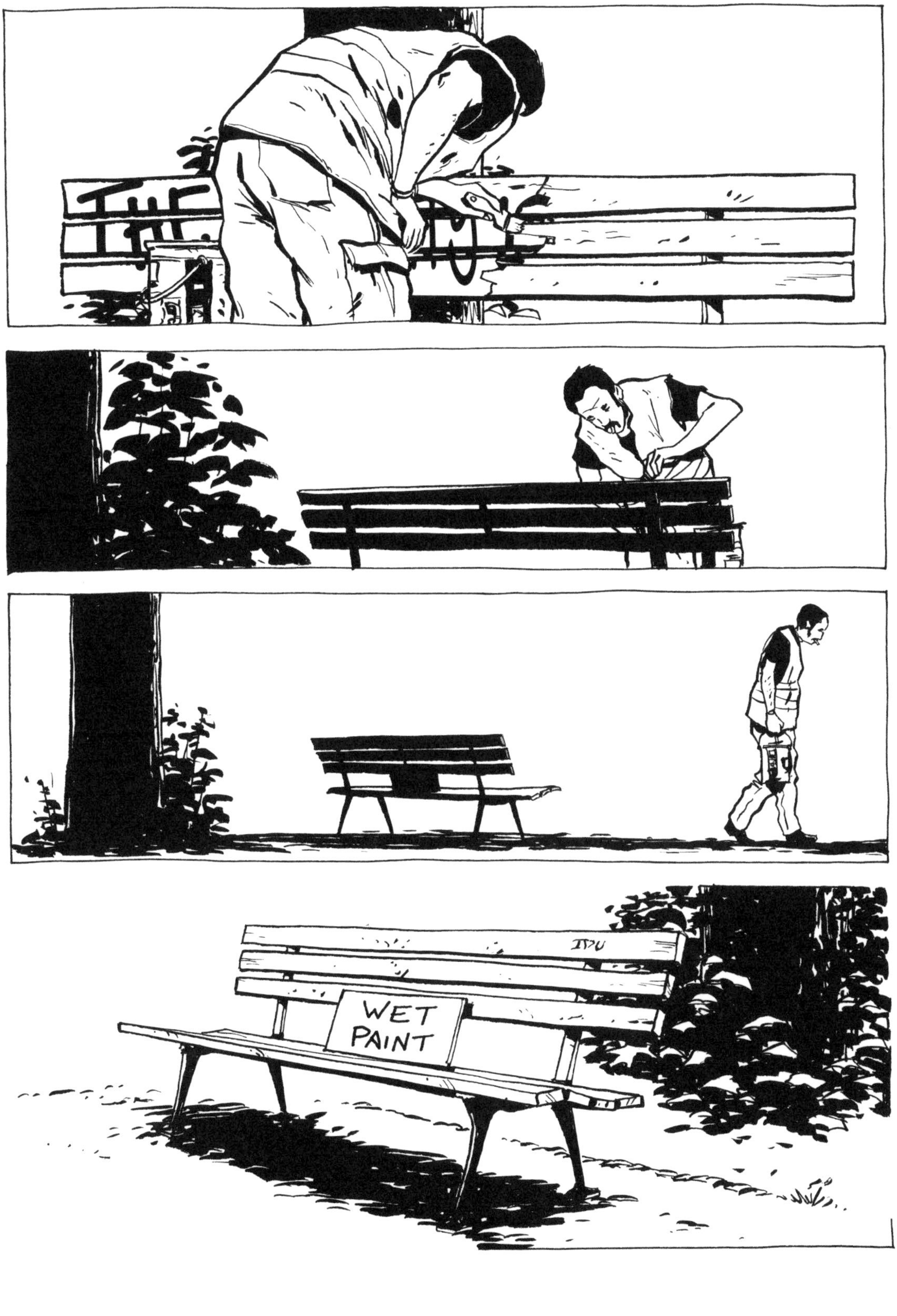
WET
PAINT

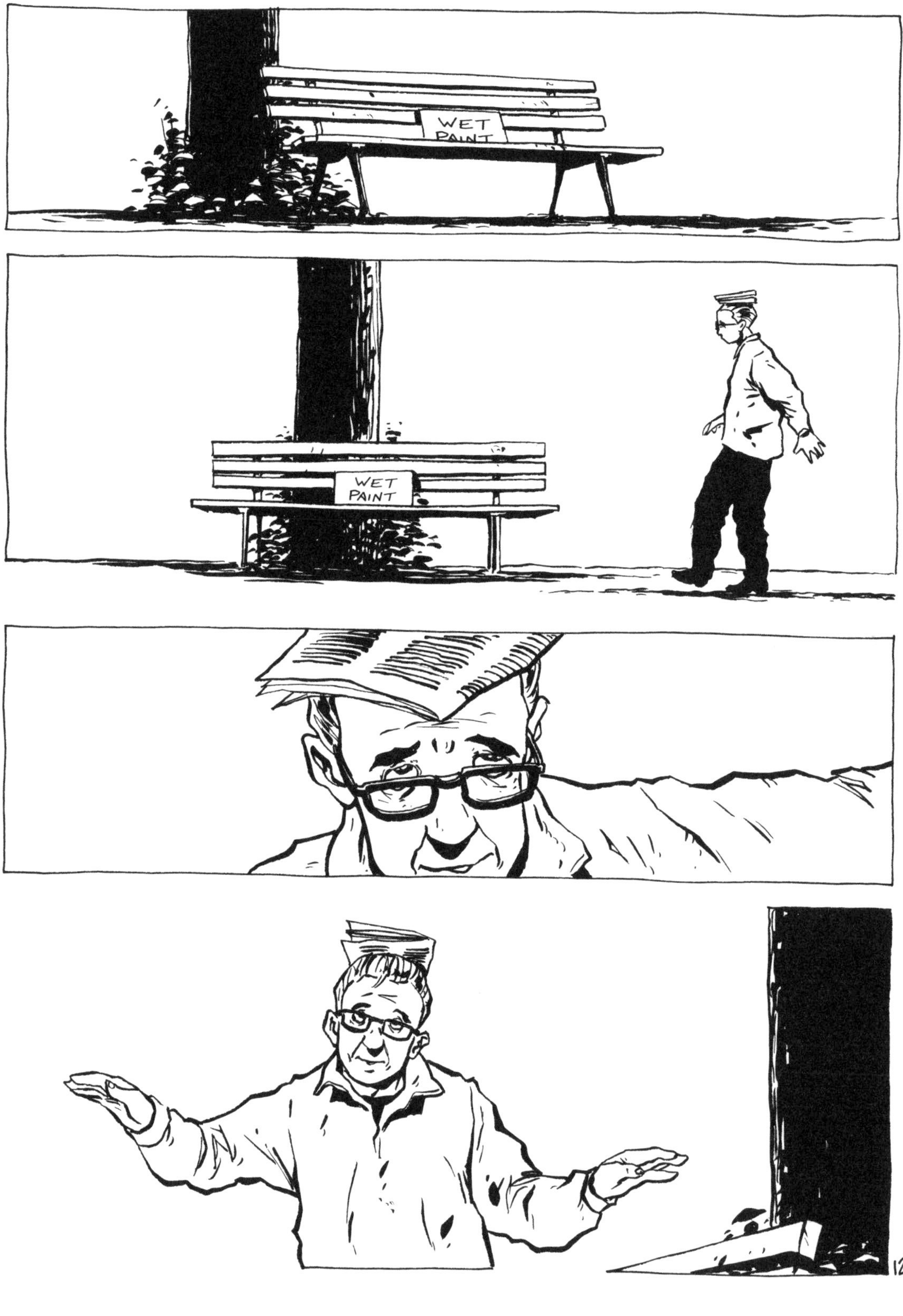
WET PAINT
WET PAINT

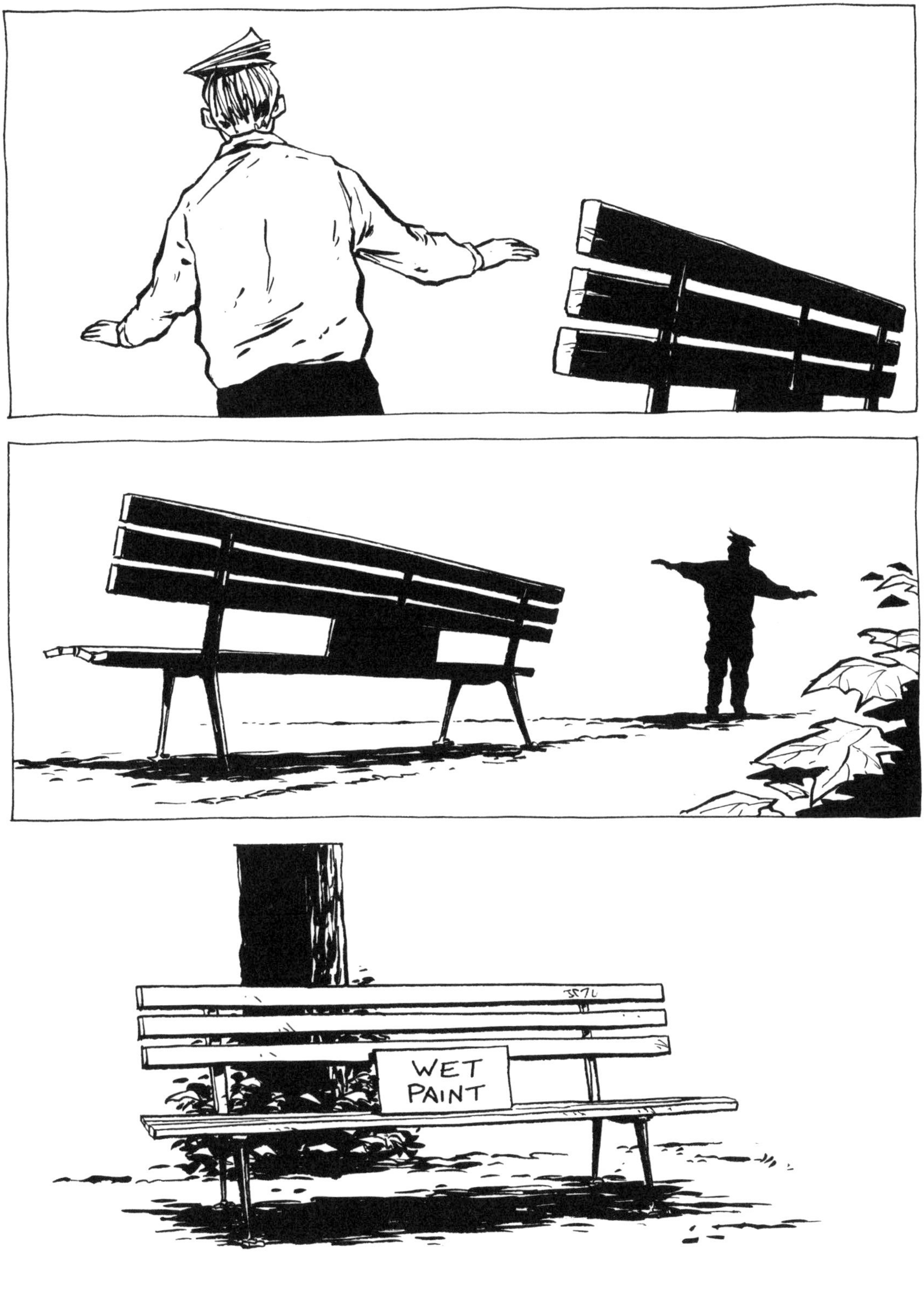
WET PAINT

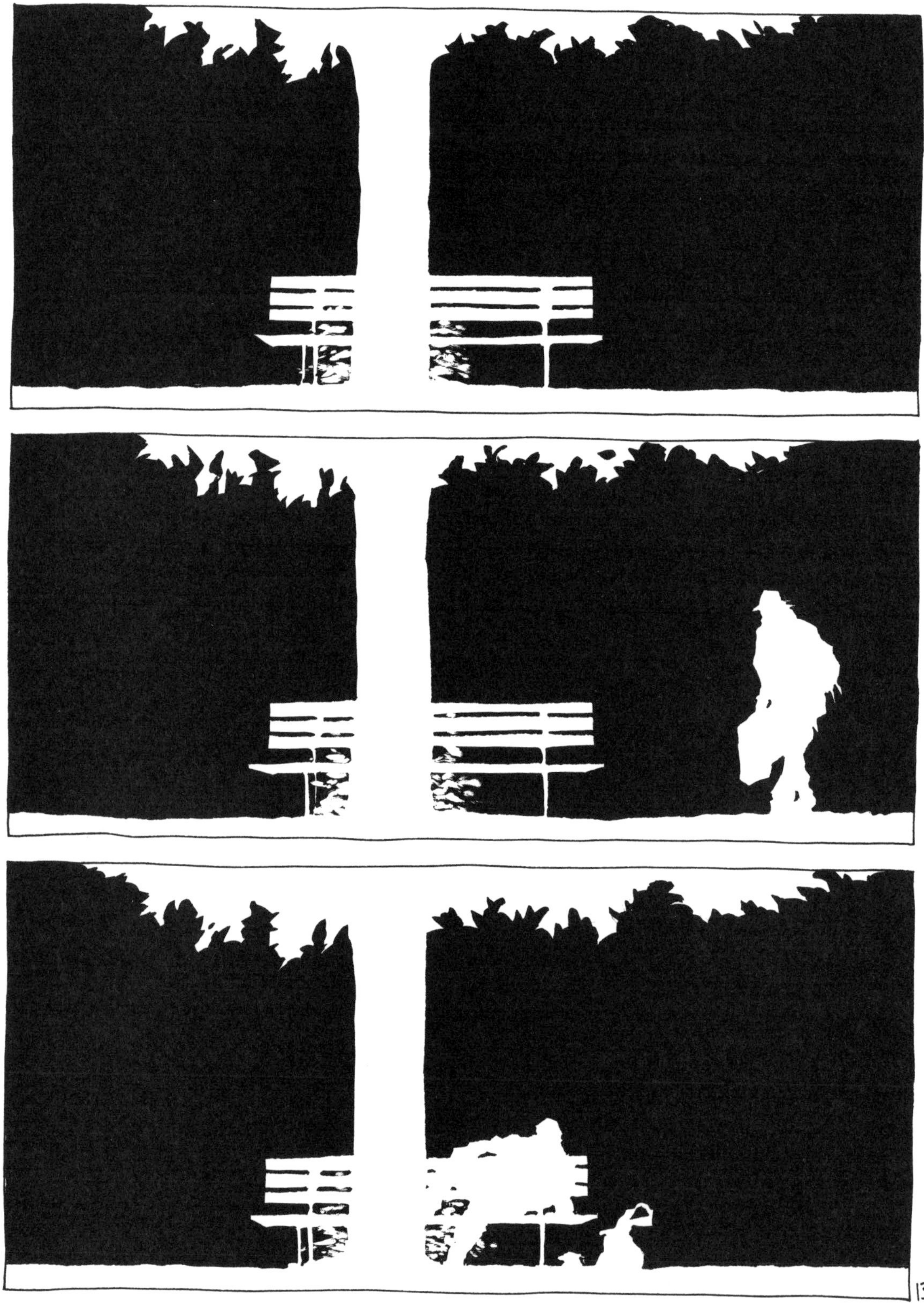

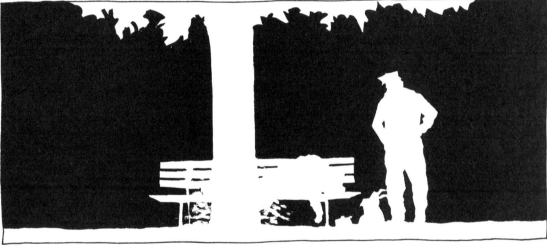

131,

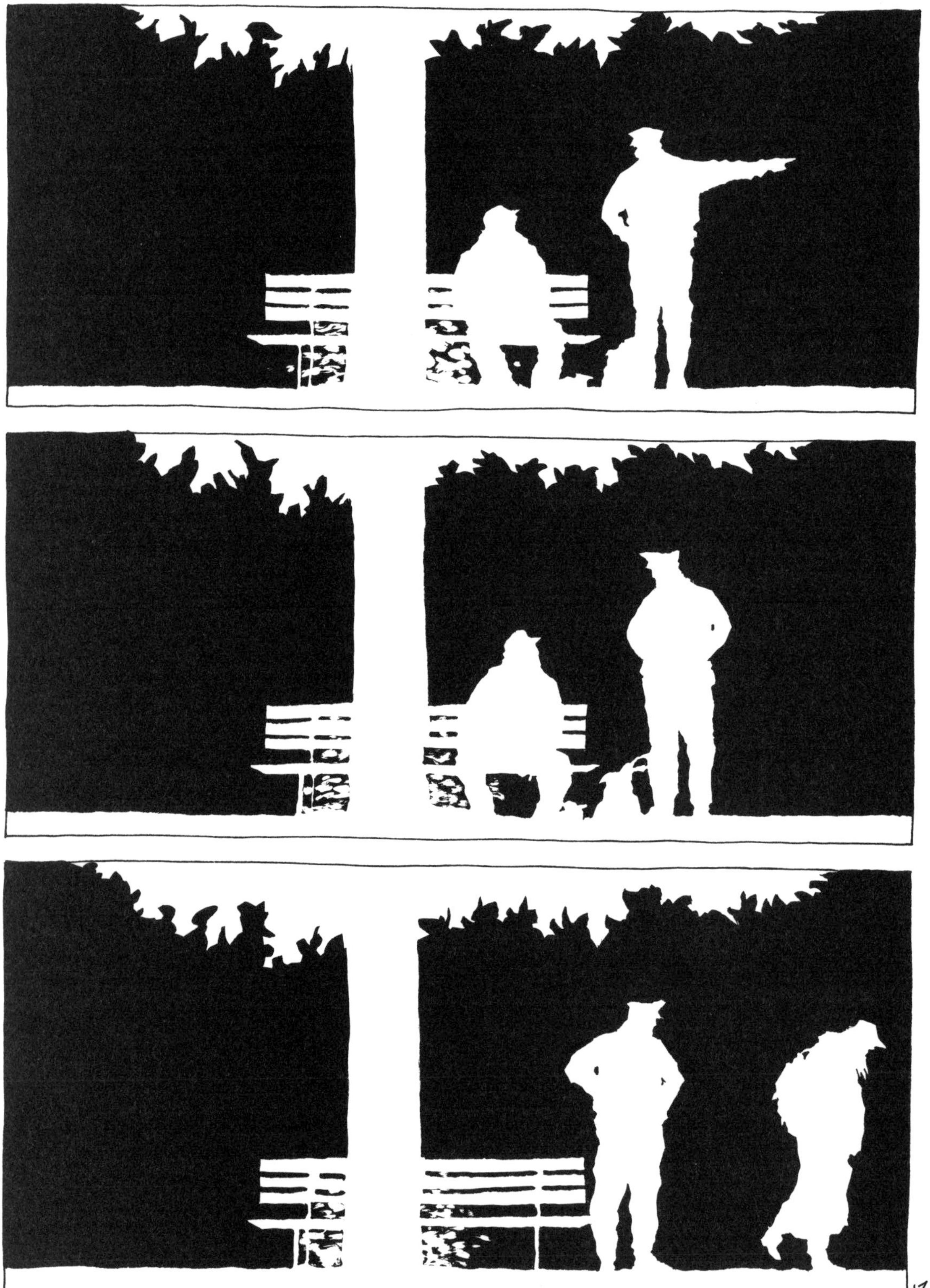

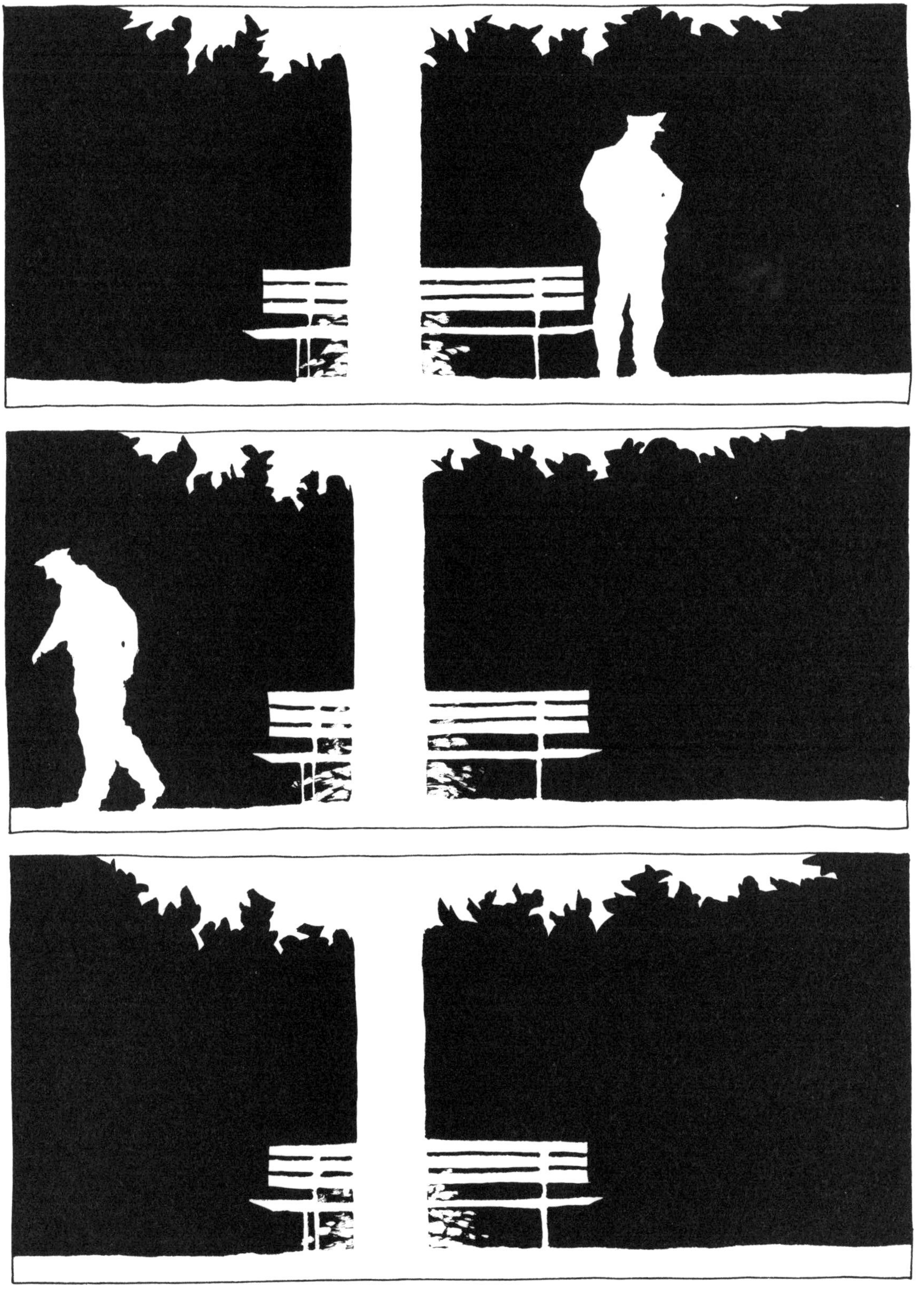

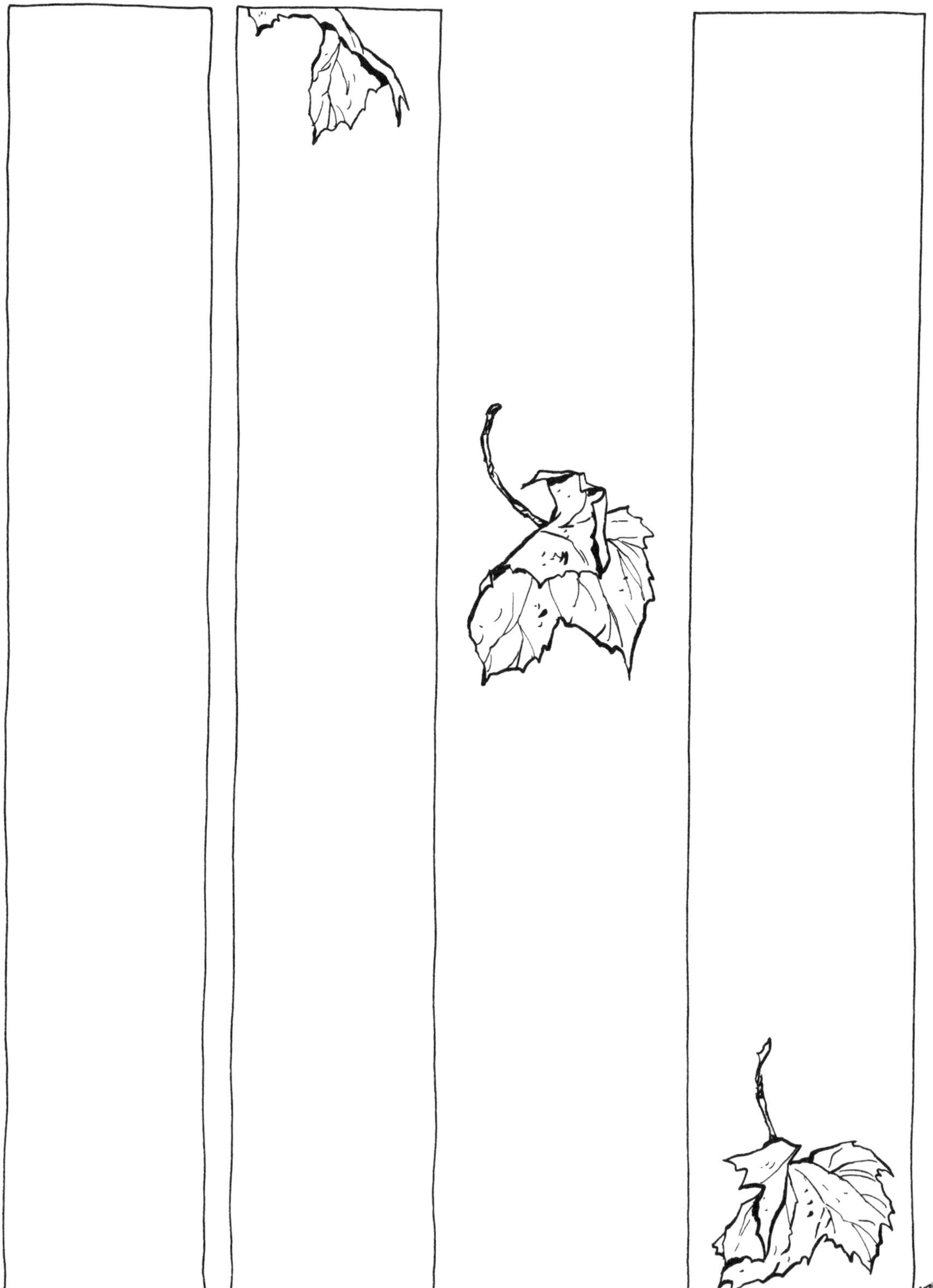

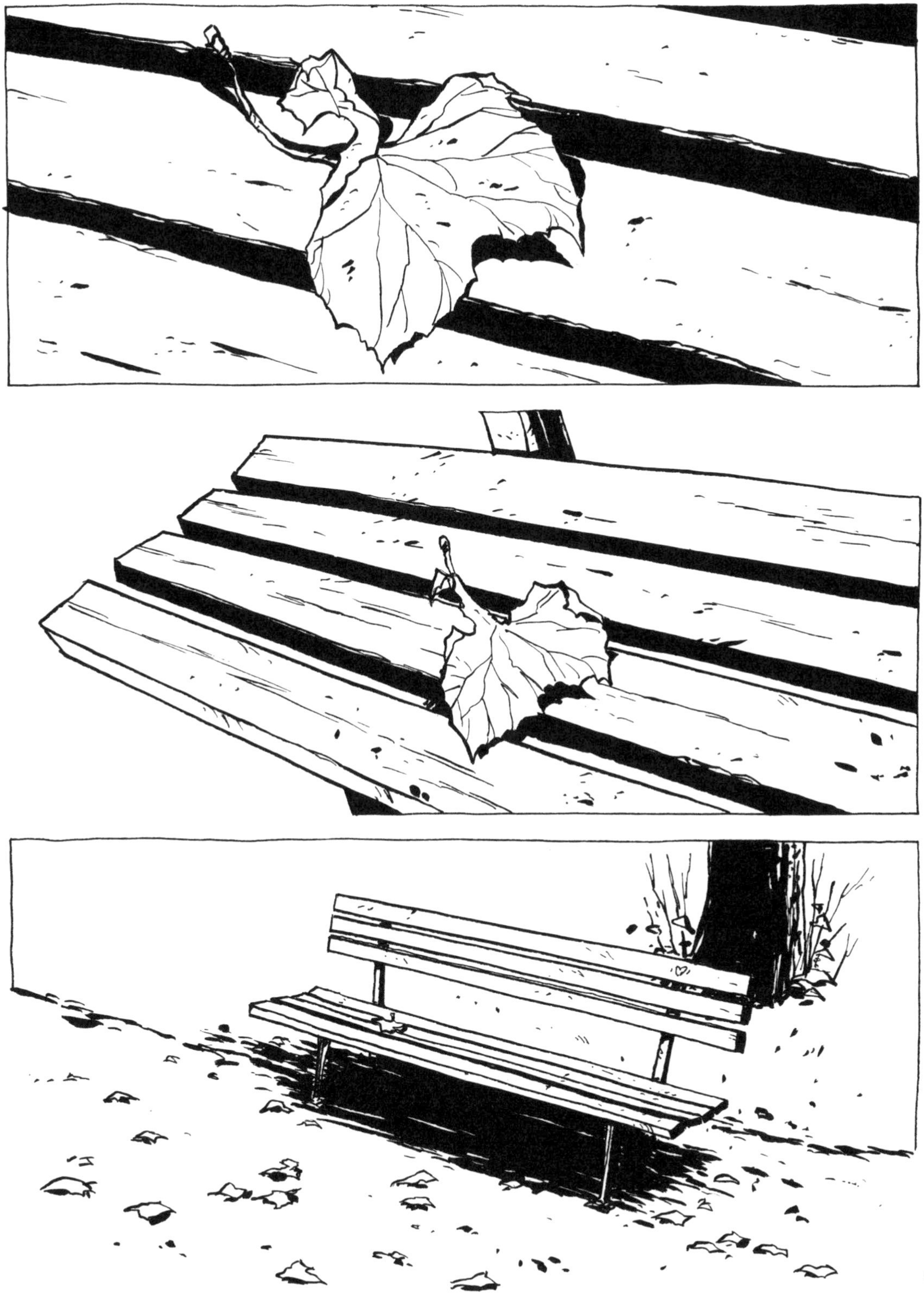

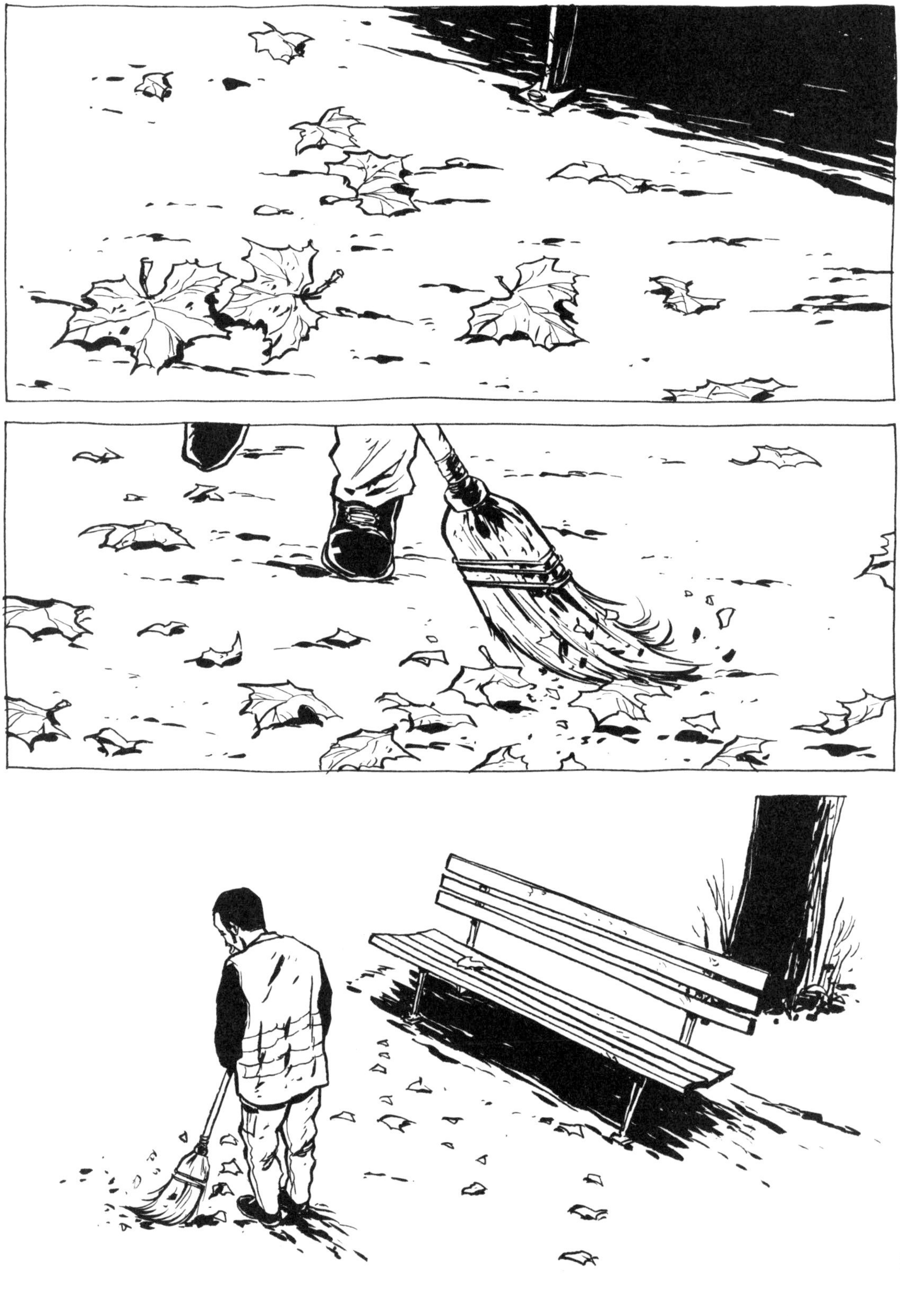

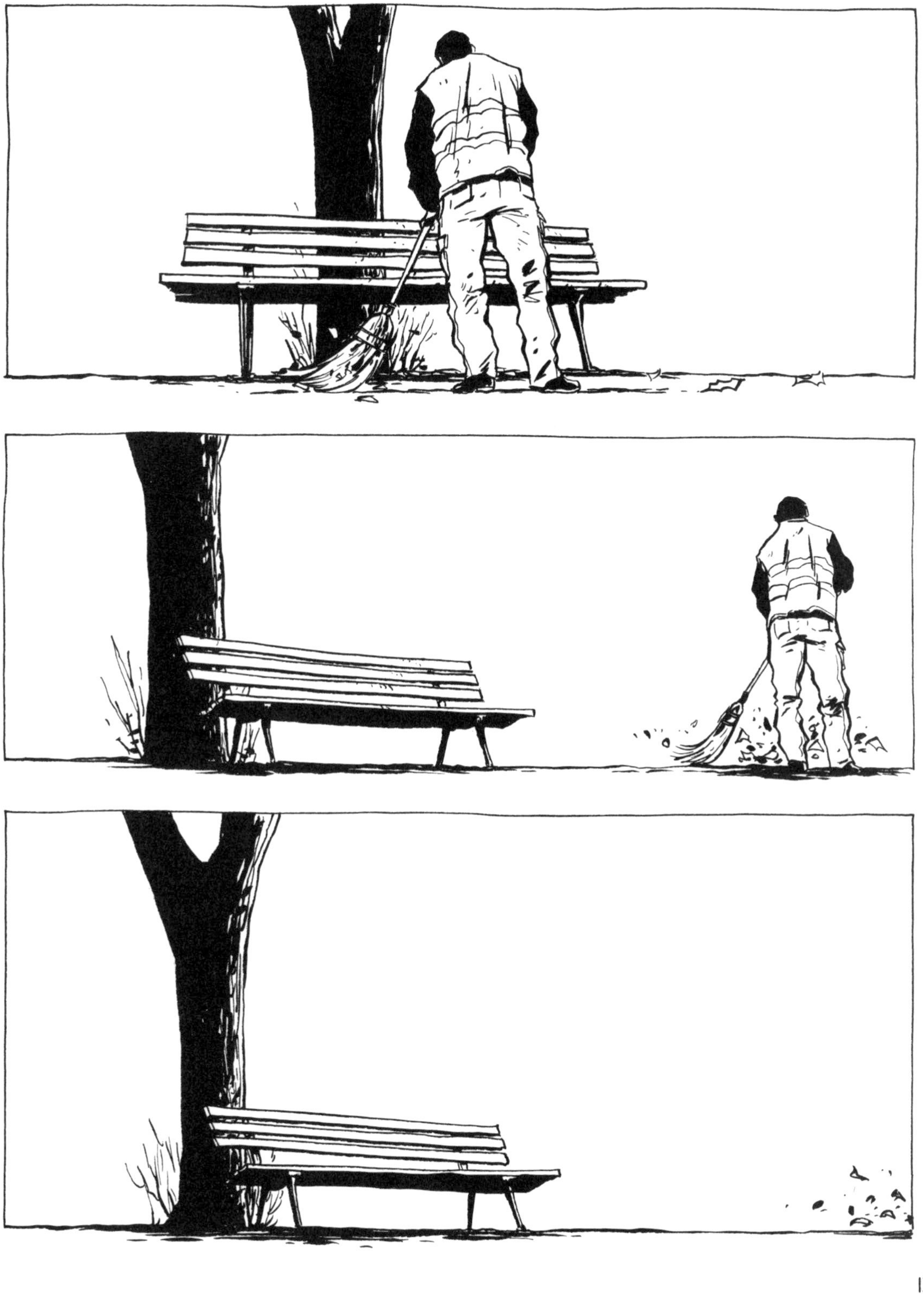

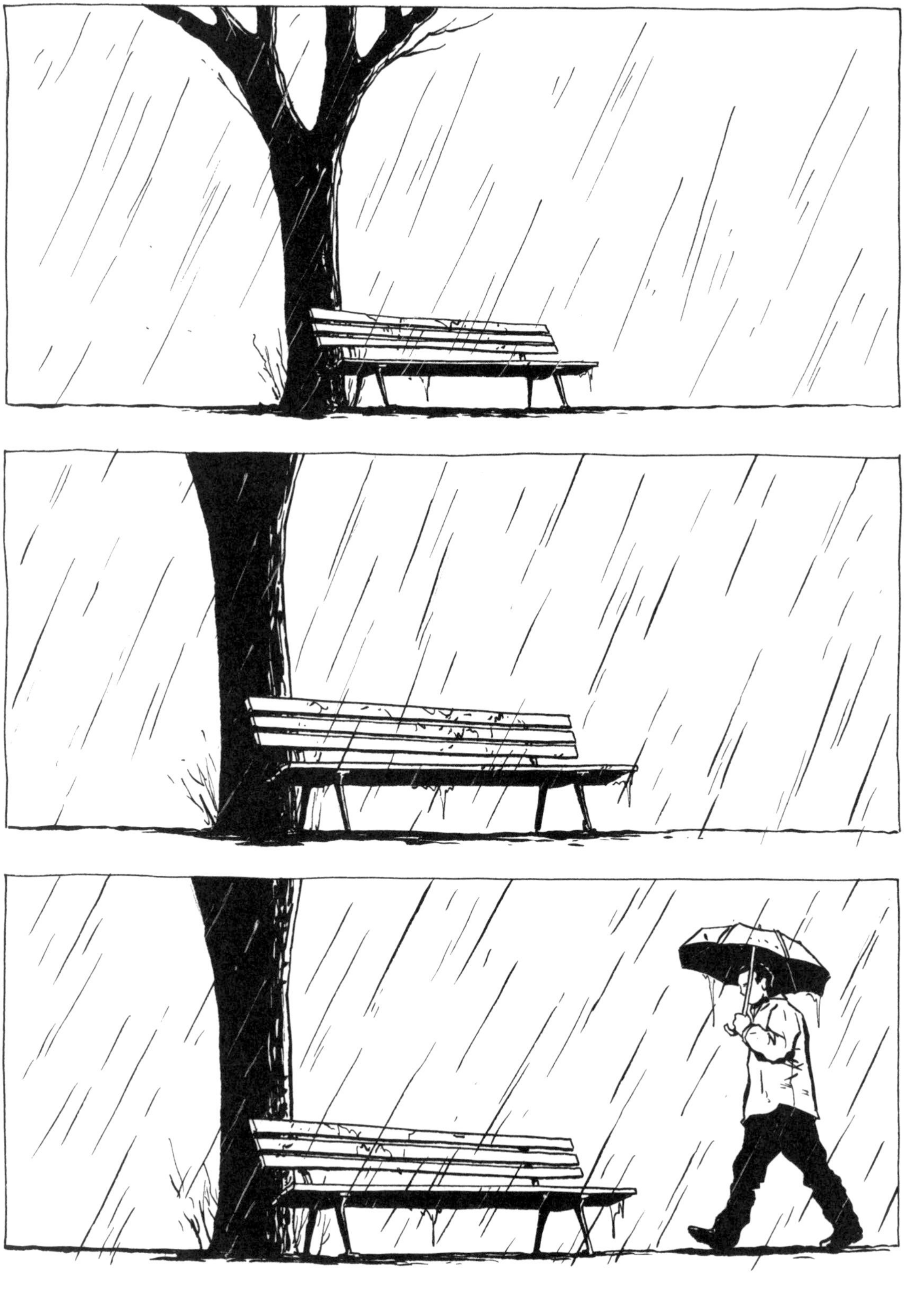

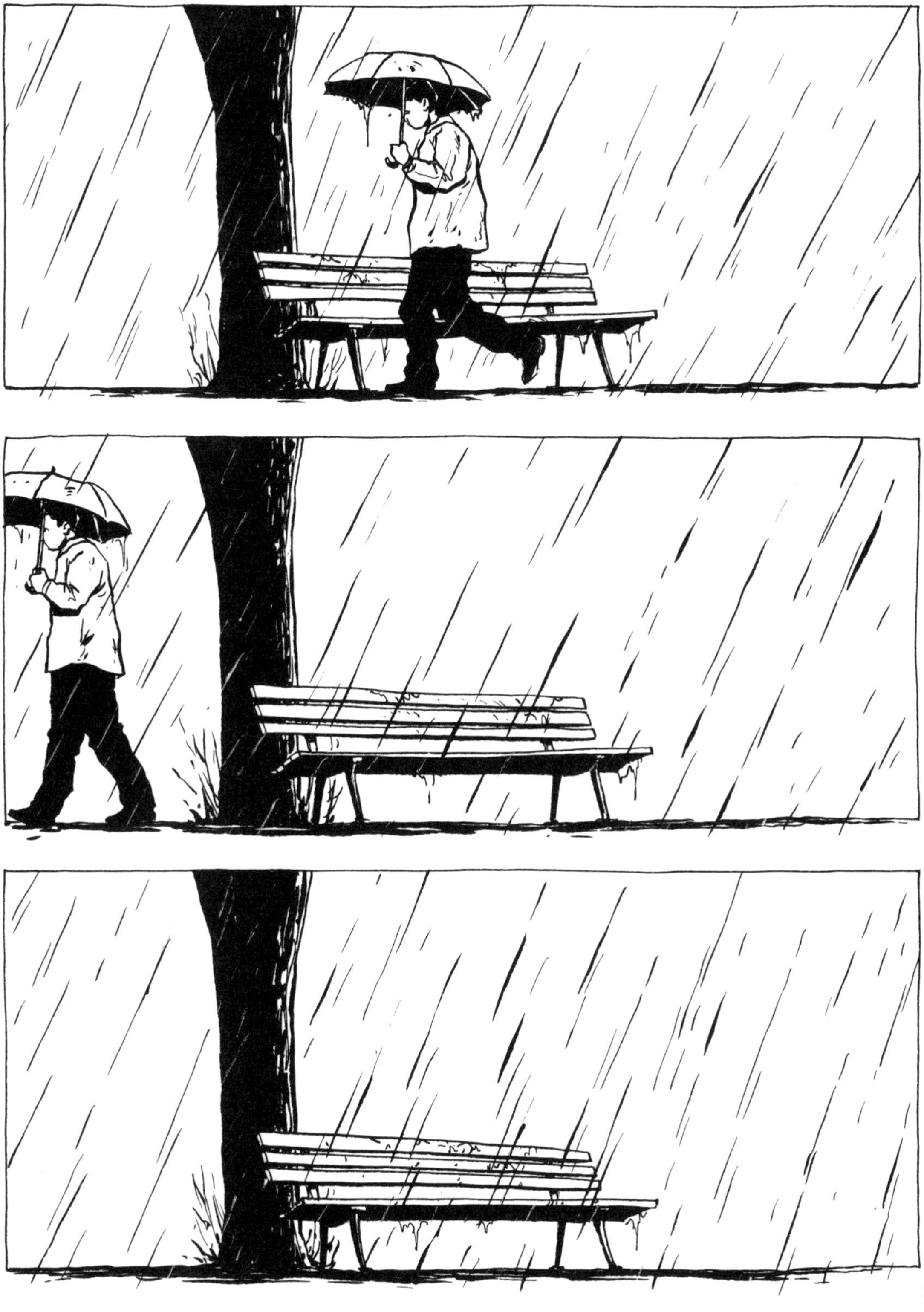

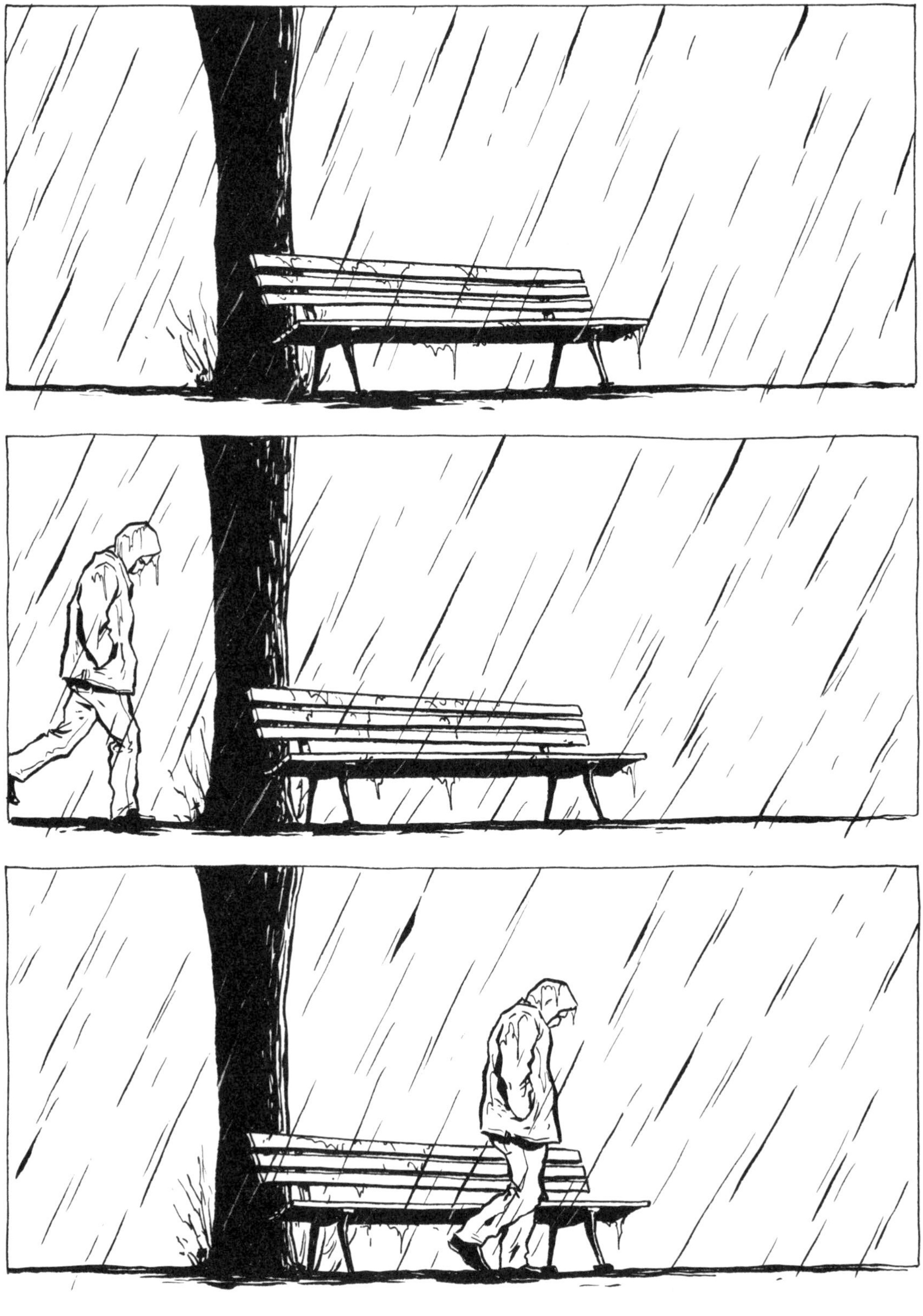

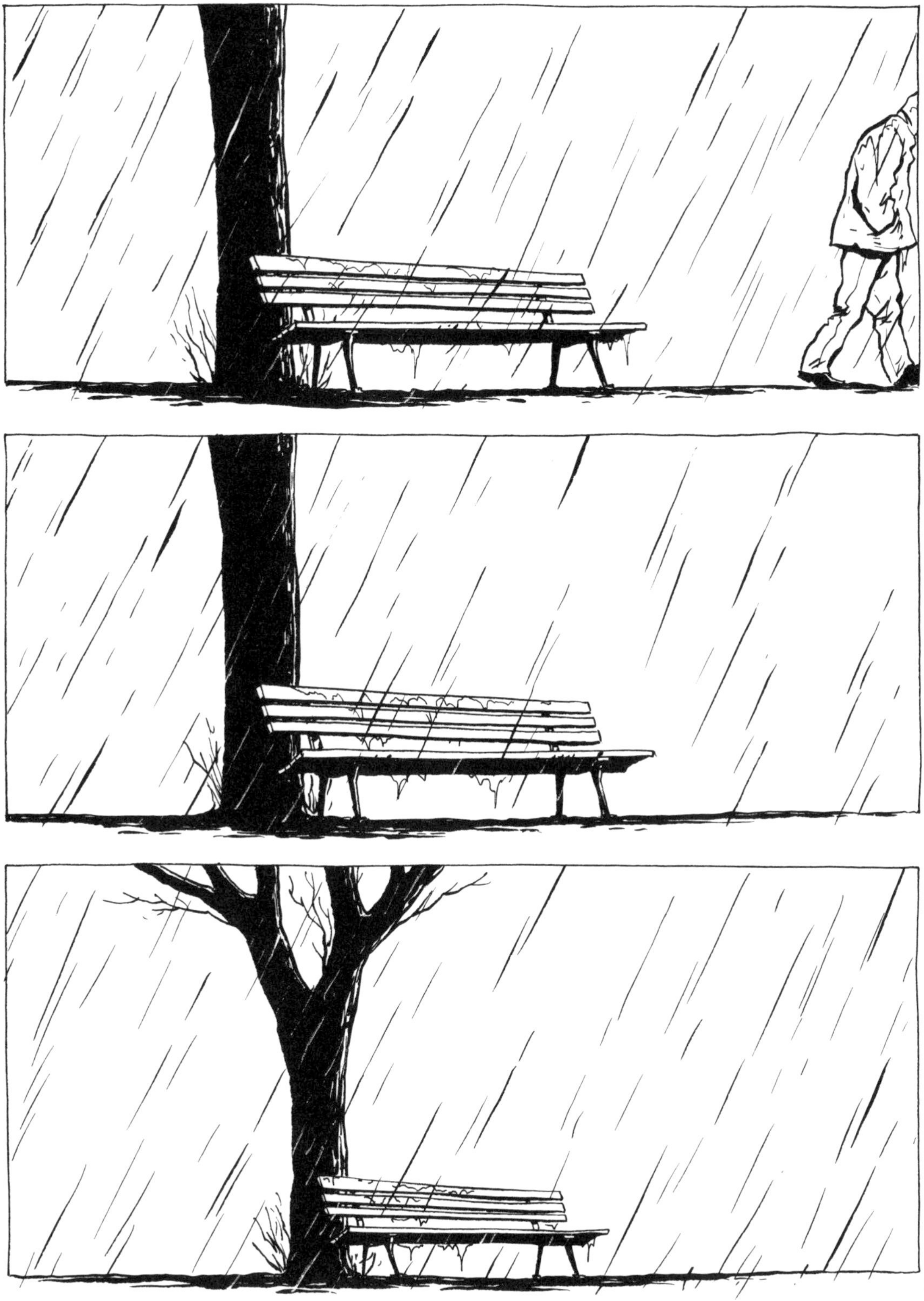

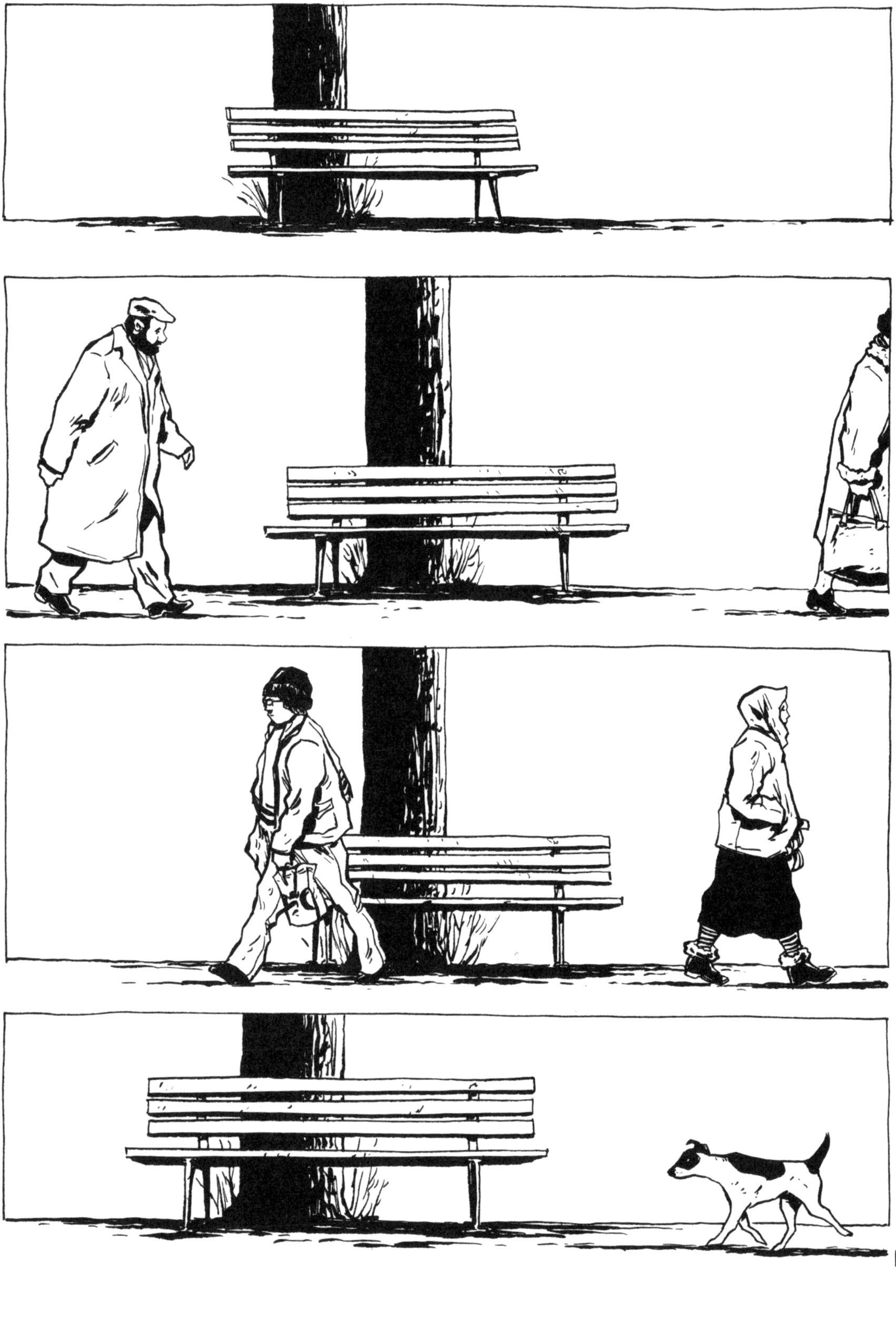

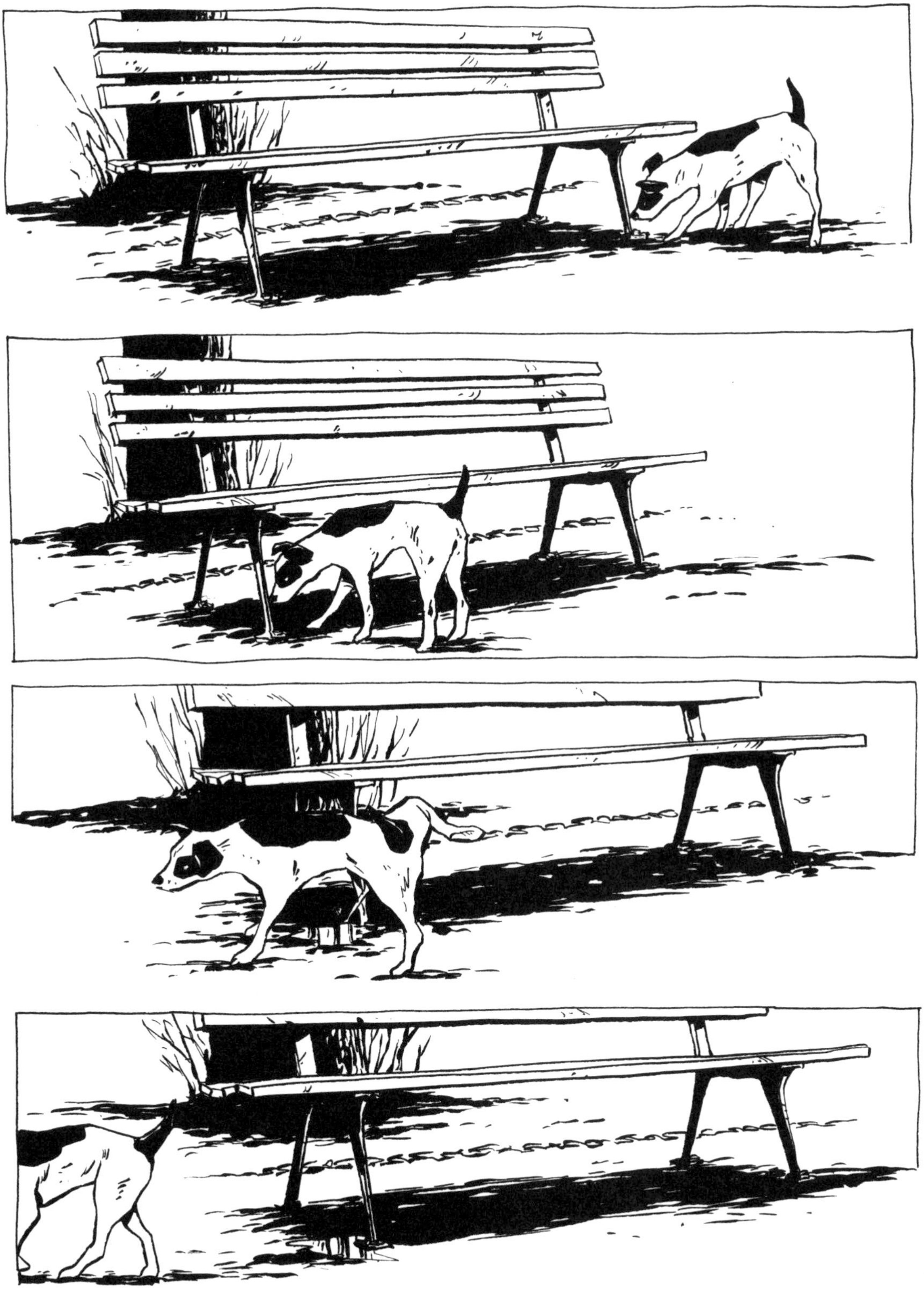

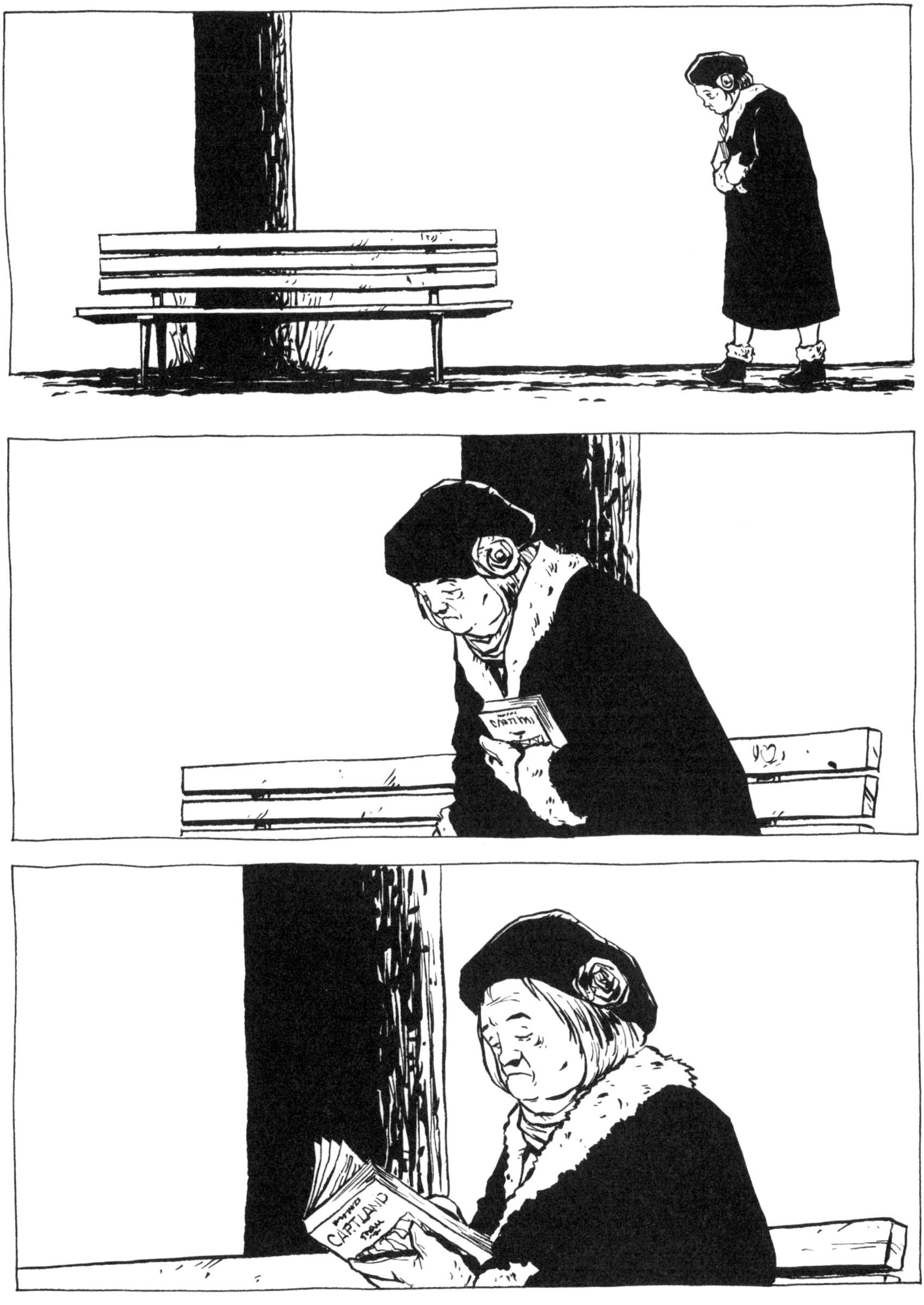
CAPTLAND

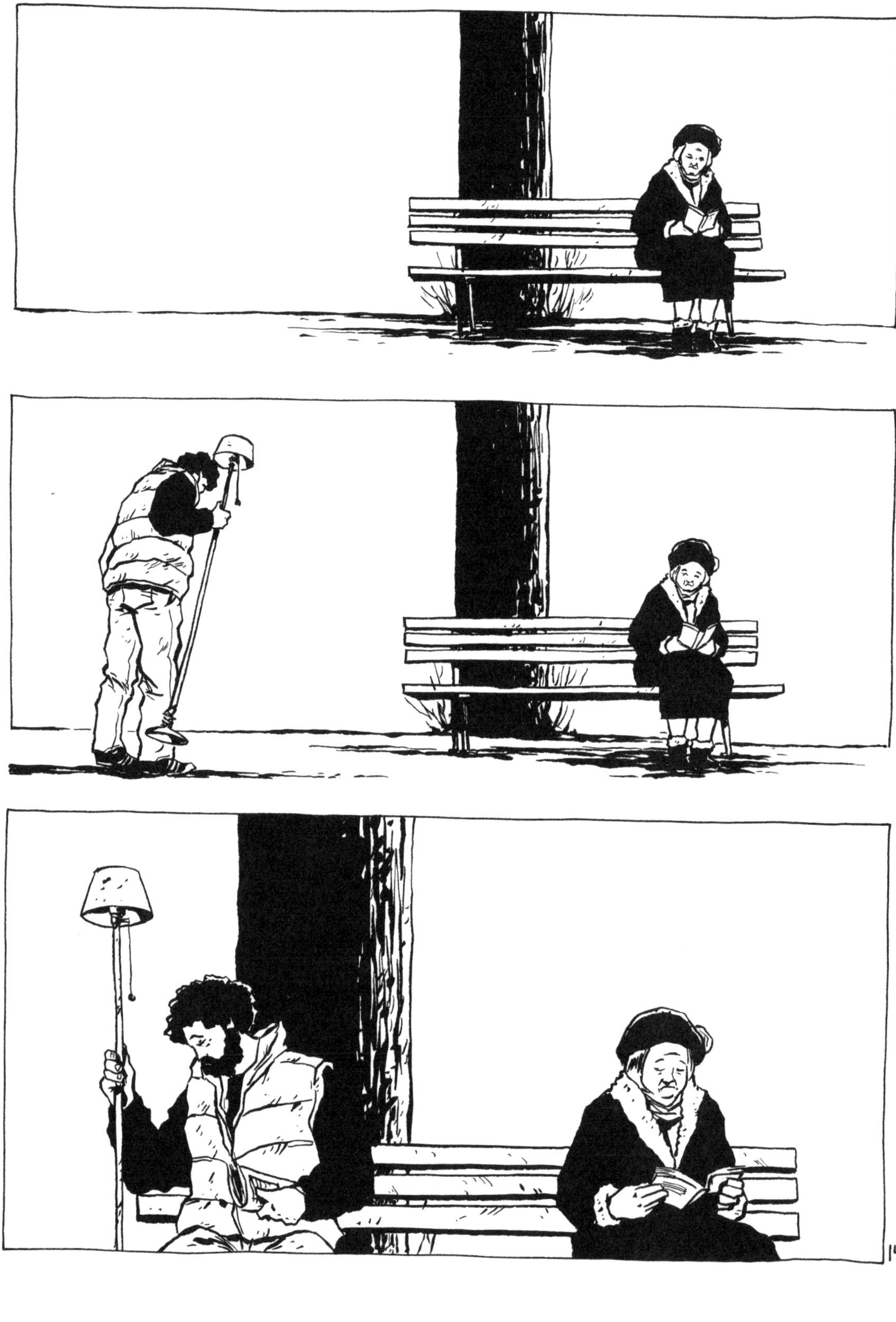

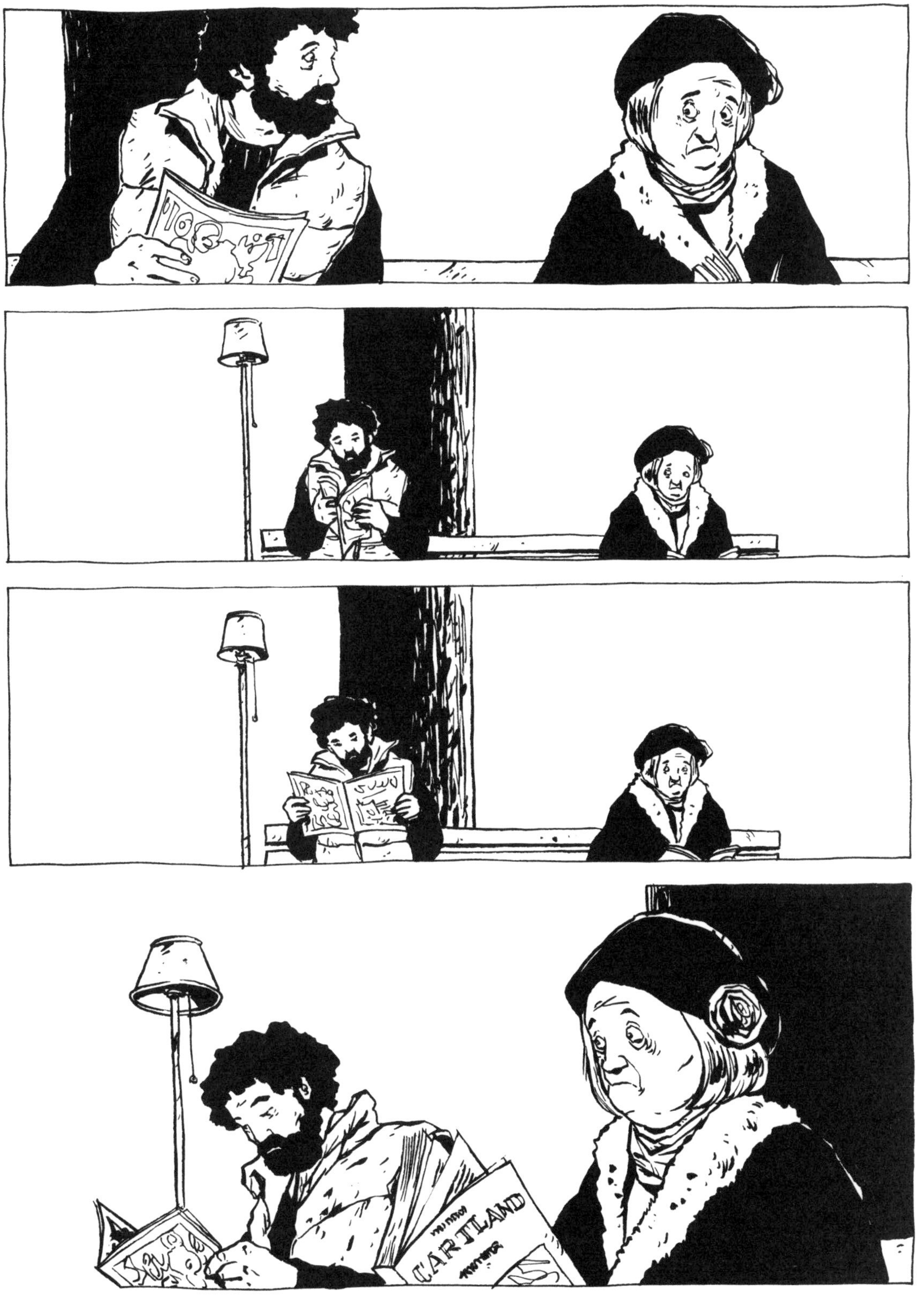
CARTLAND

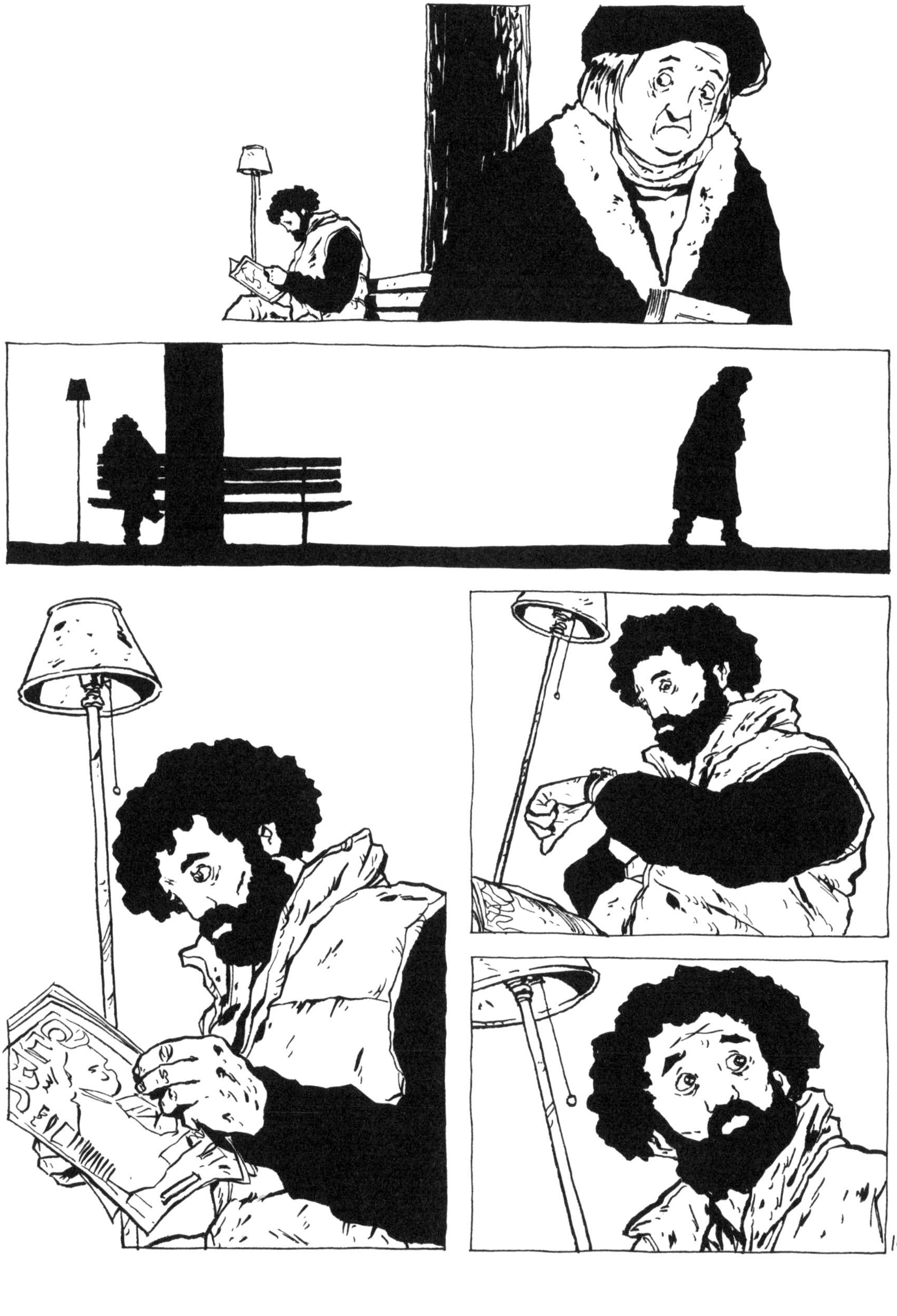

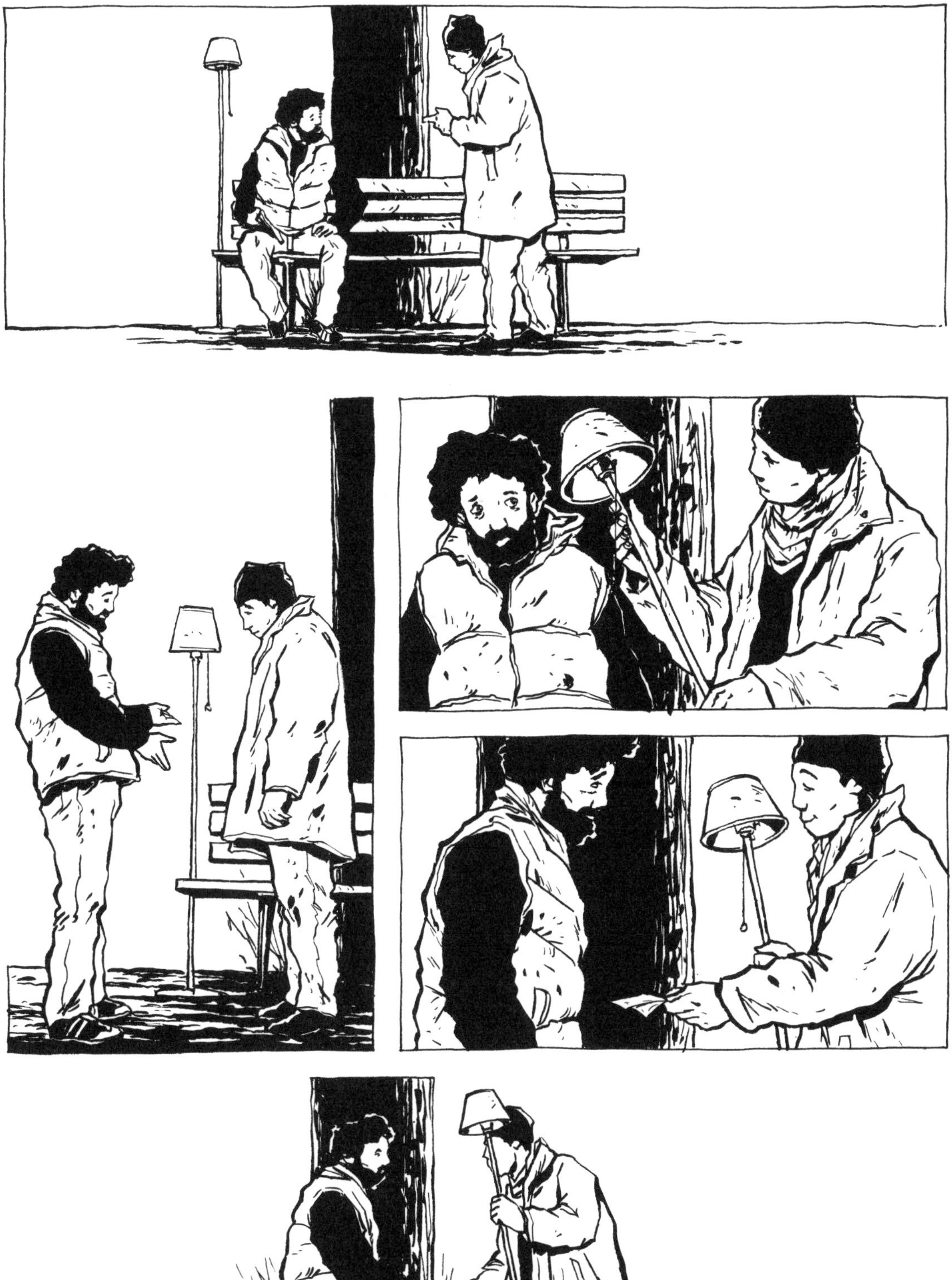

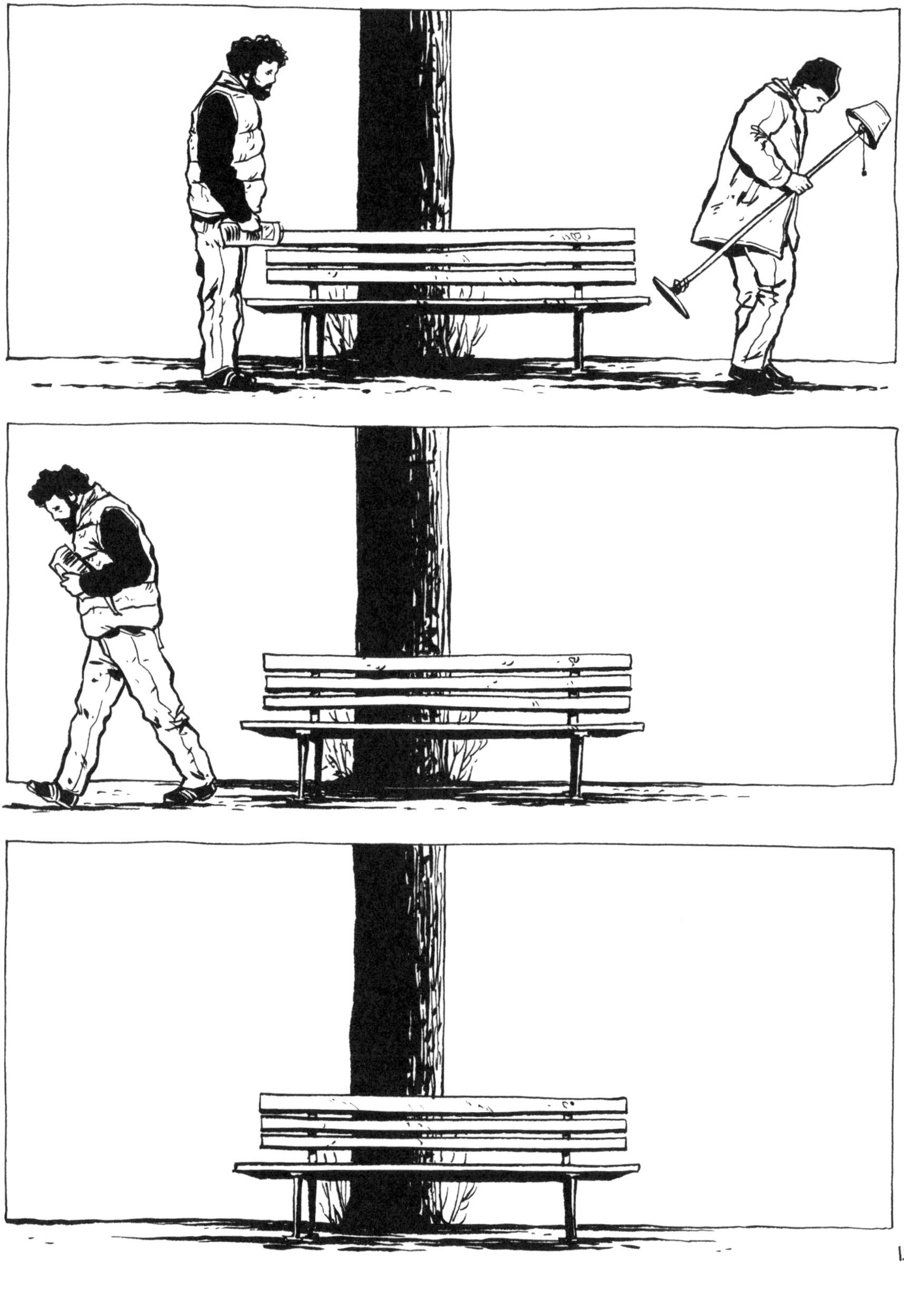

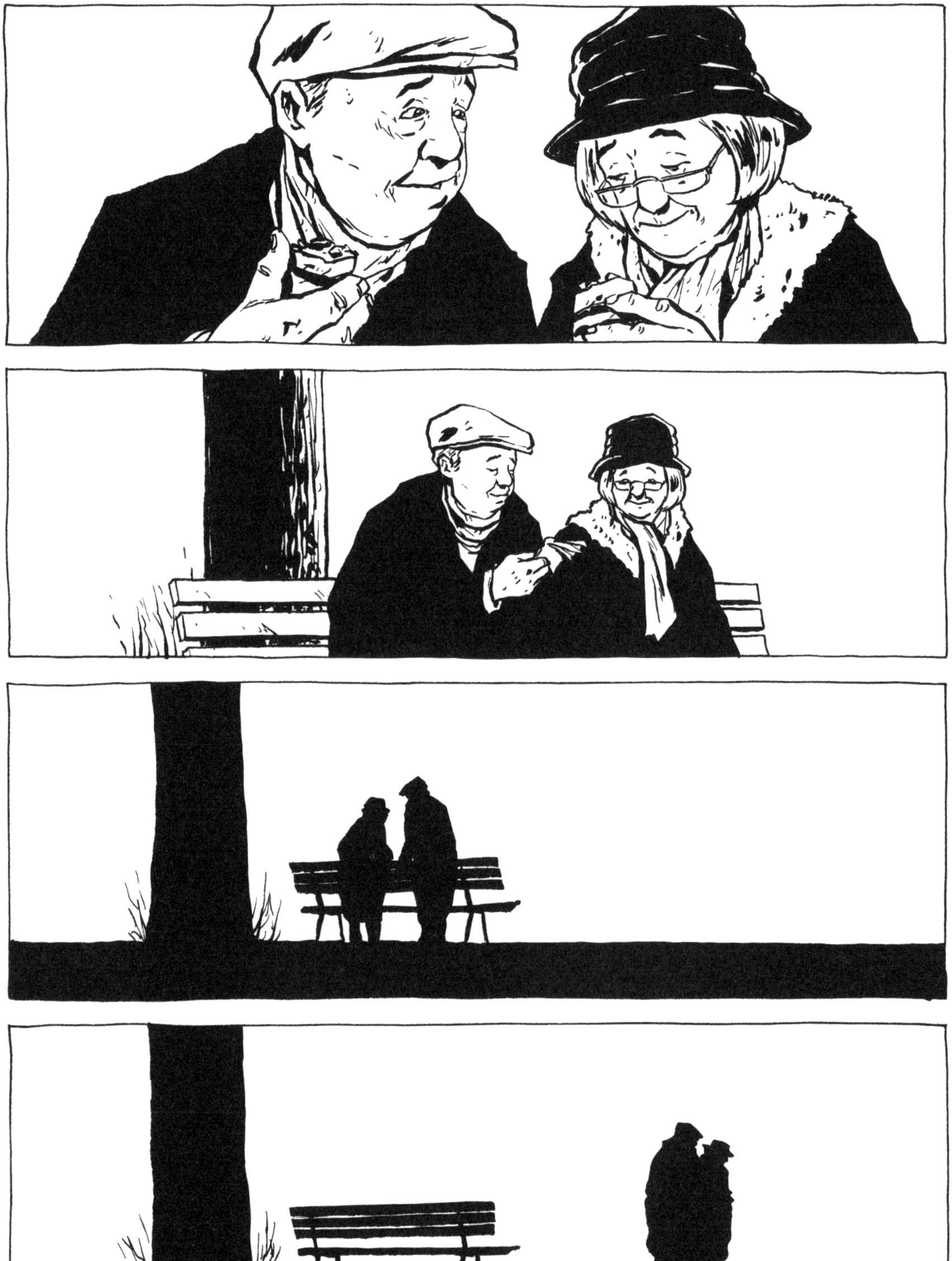

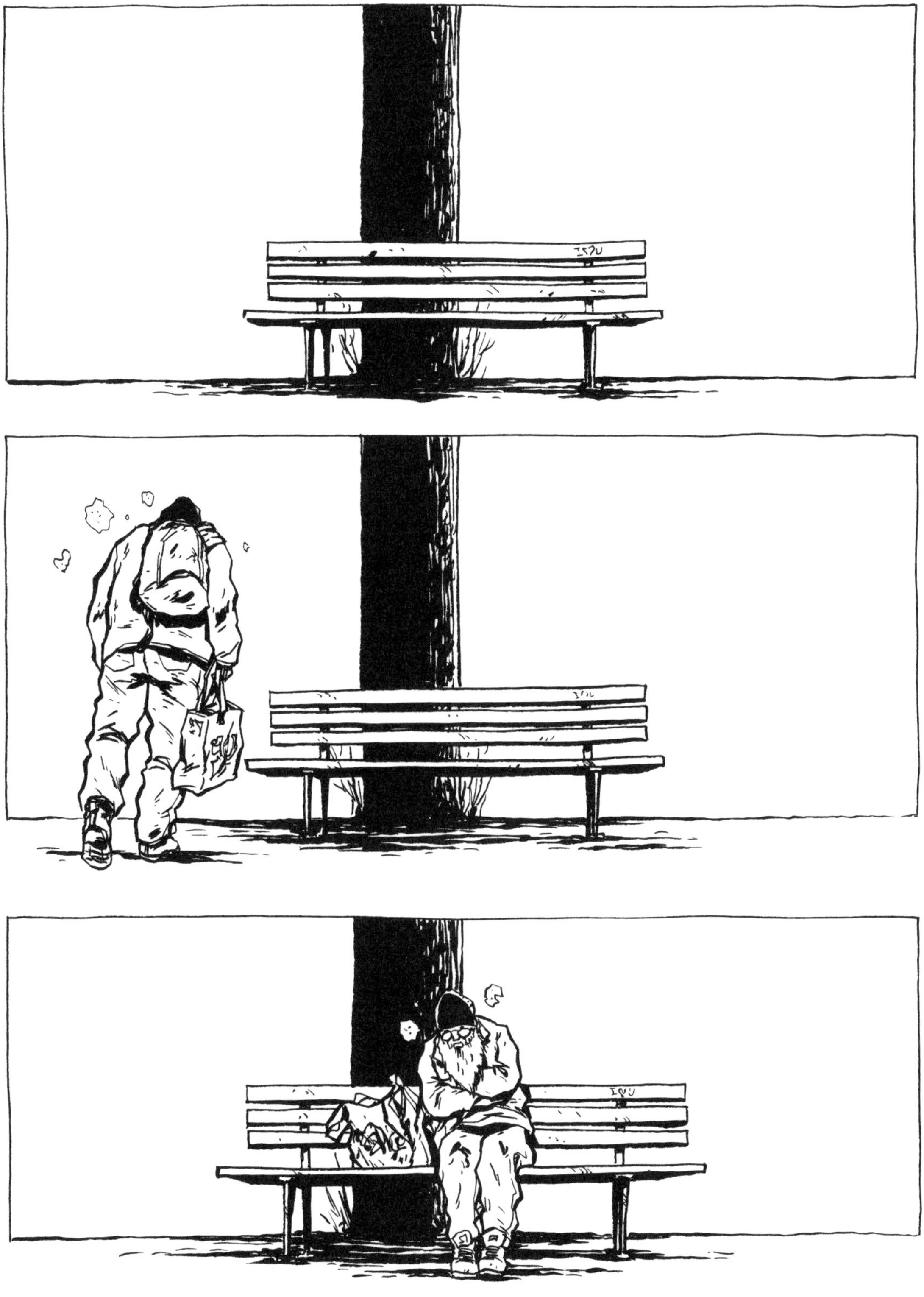

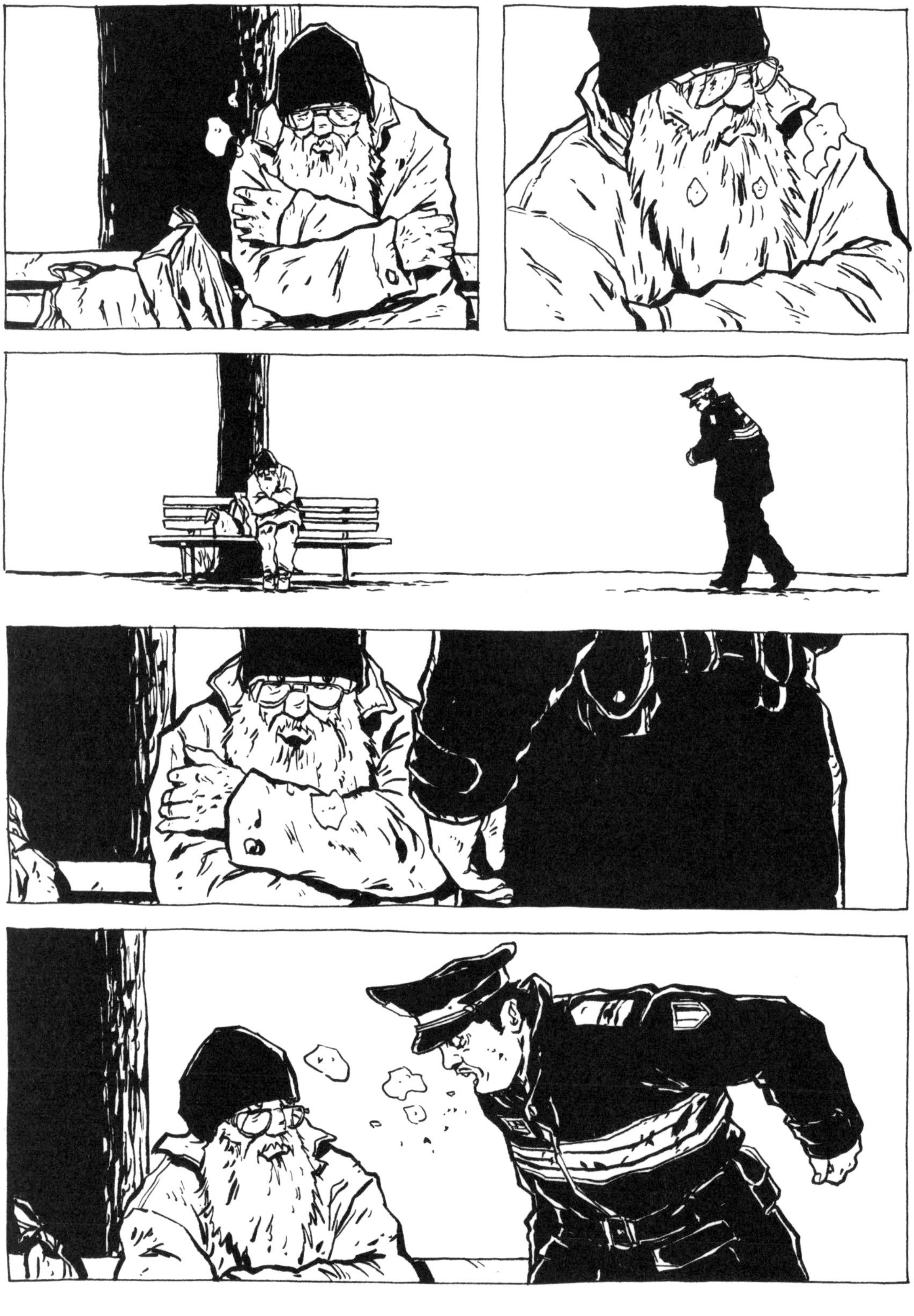

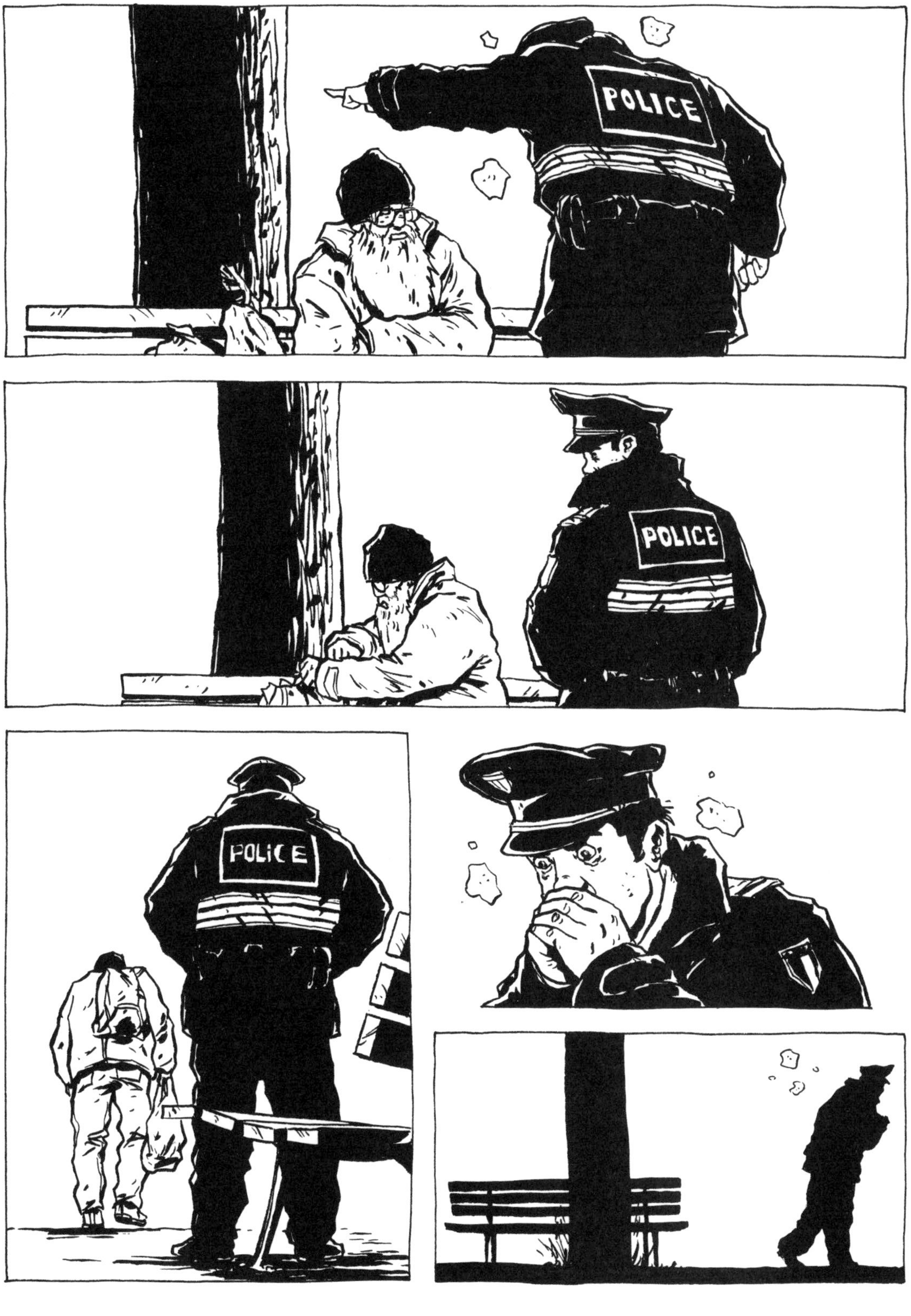
POLICE
POLICE
POLICE

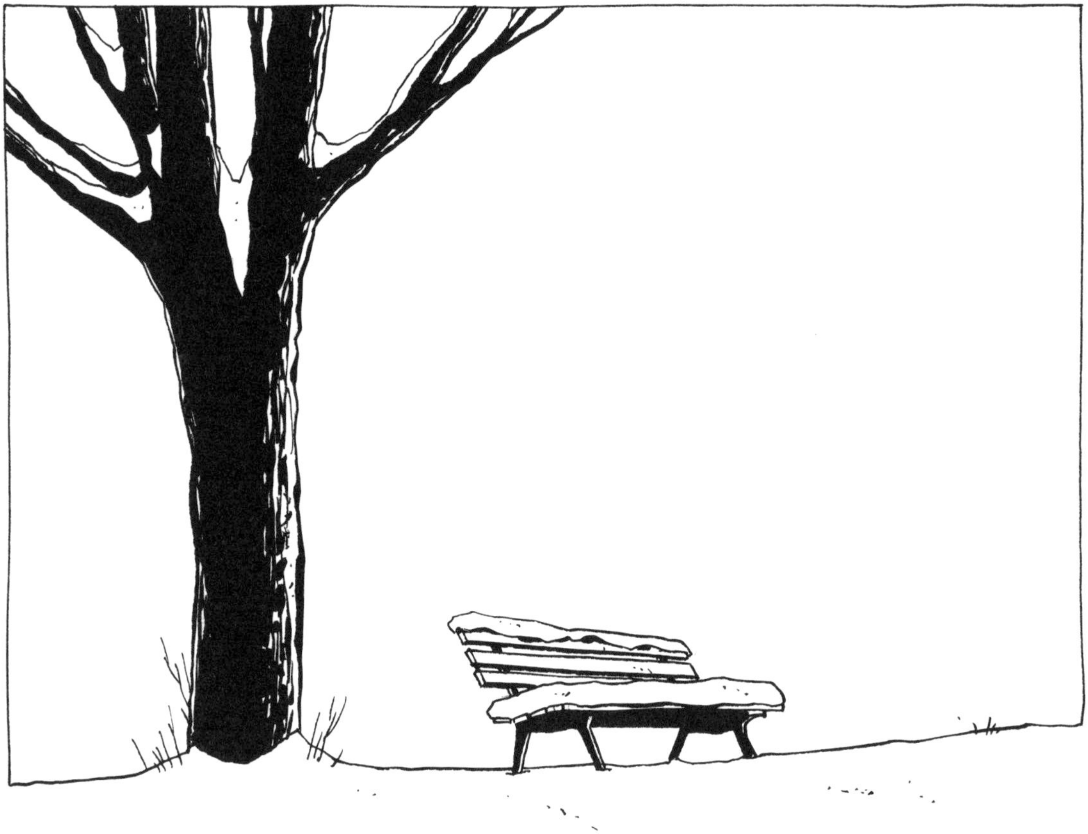

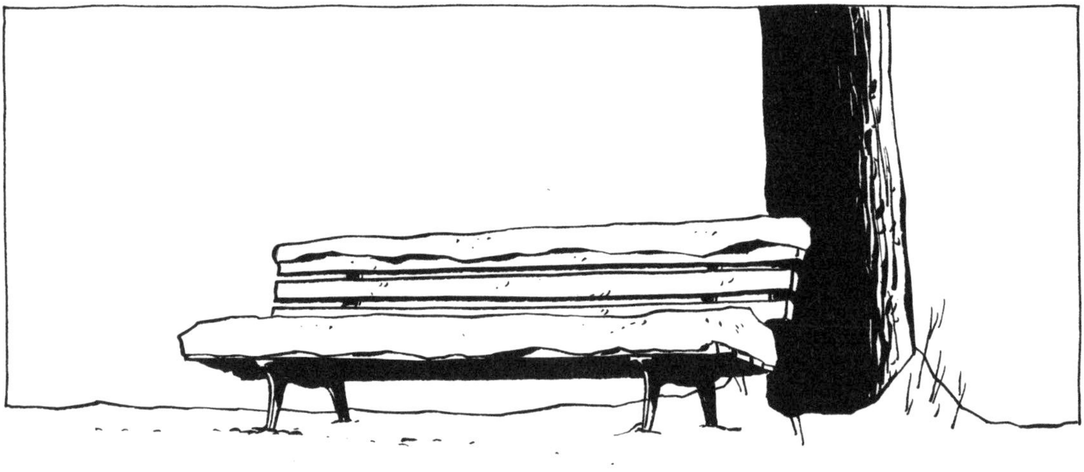

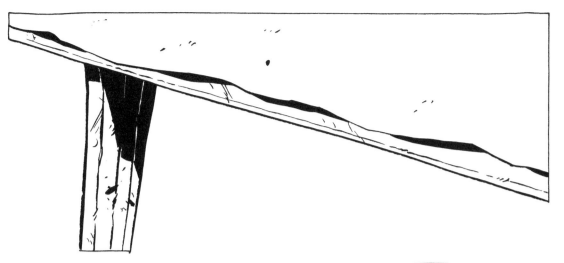

157.

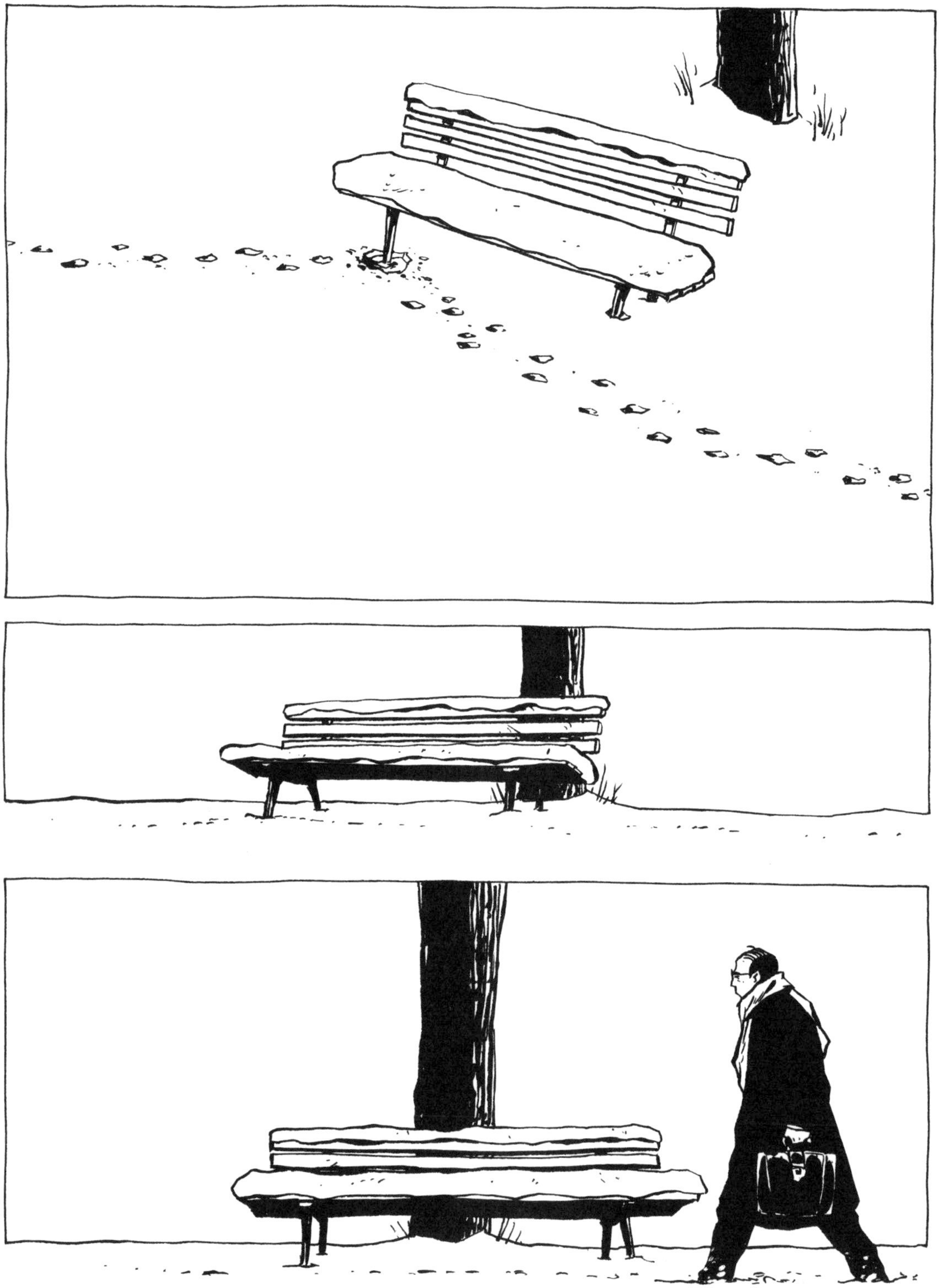

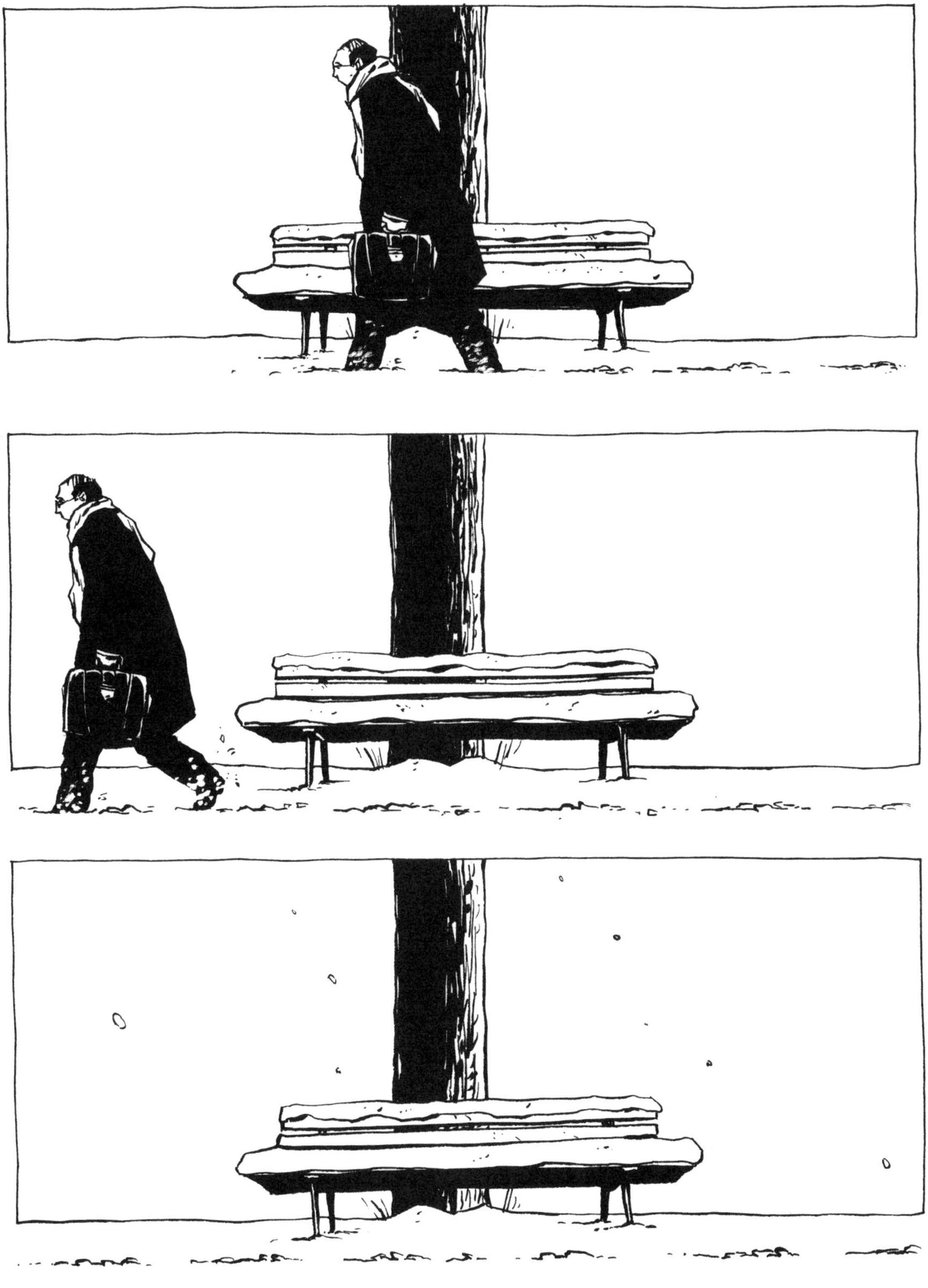

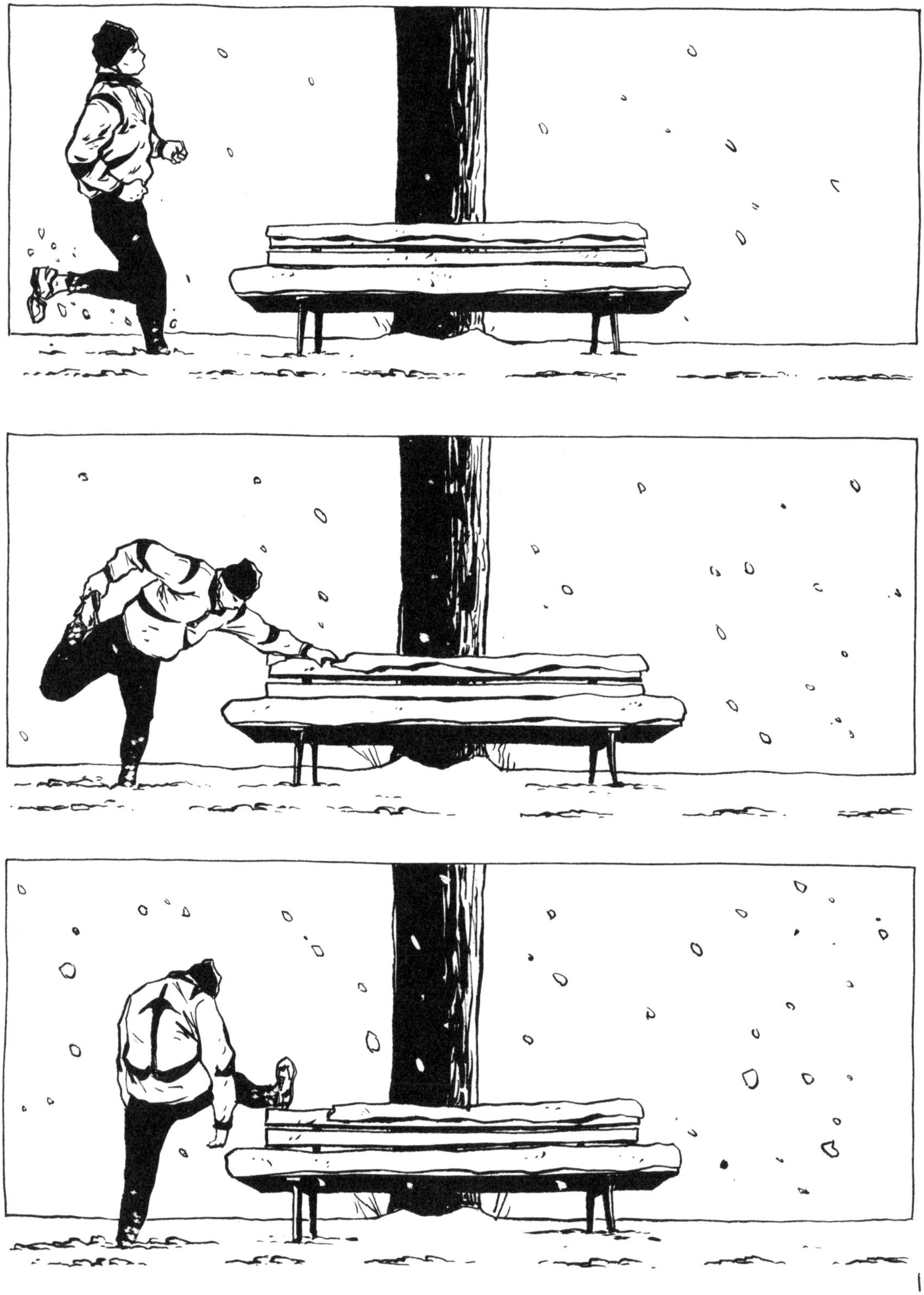

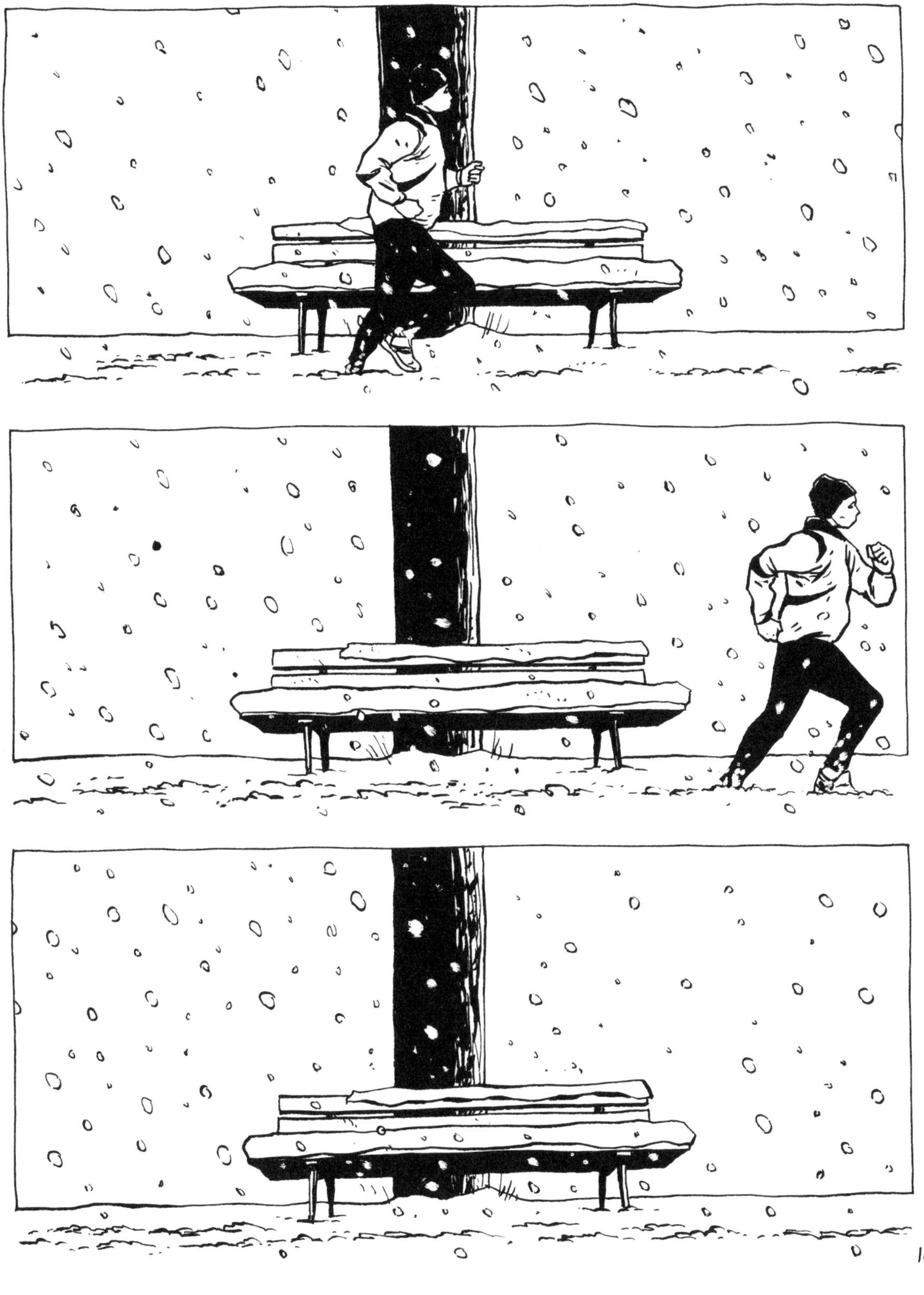

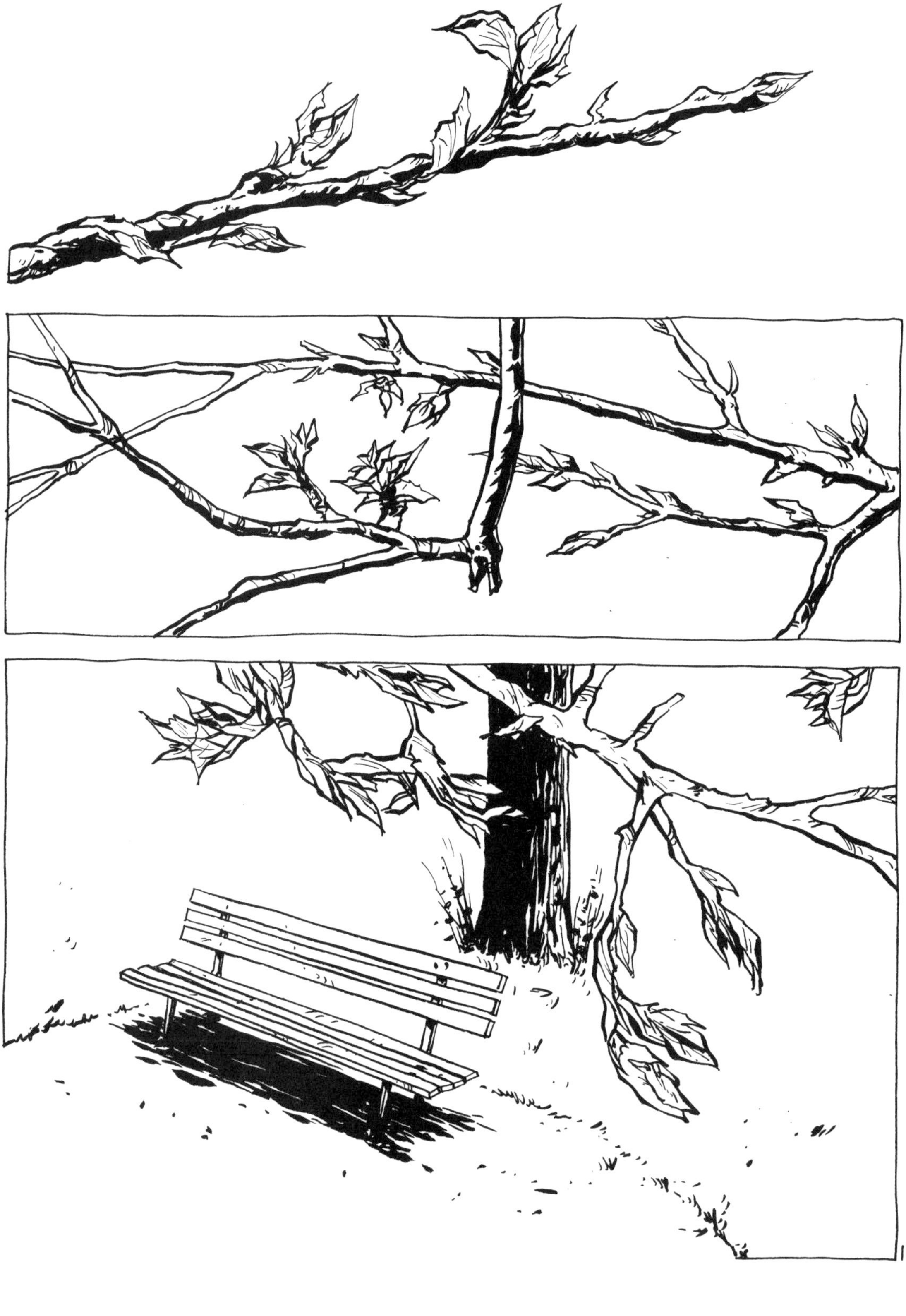

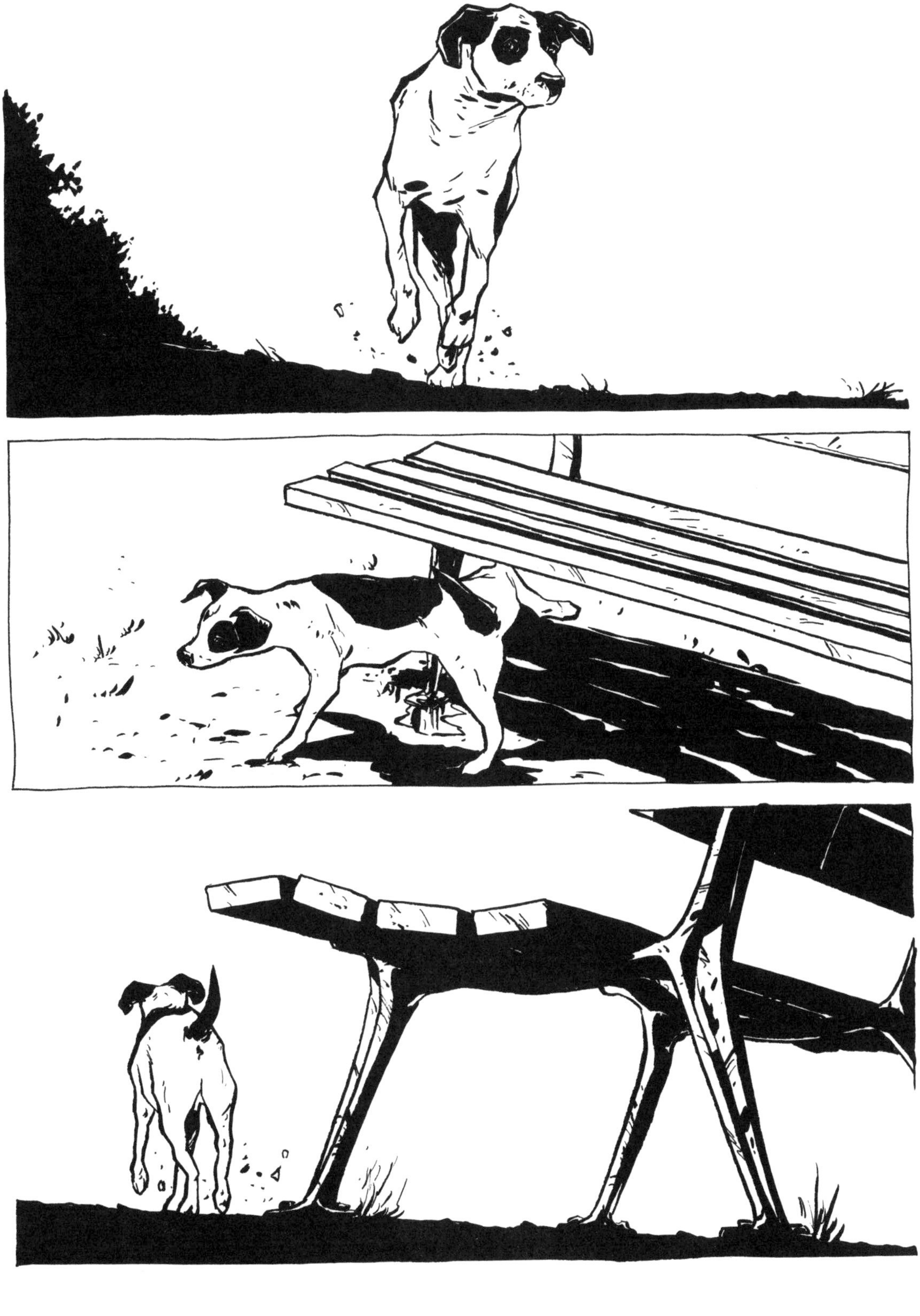

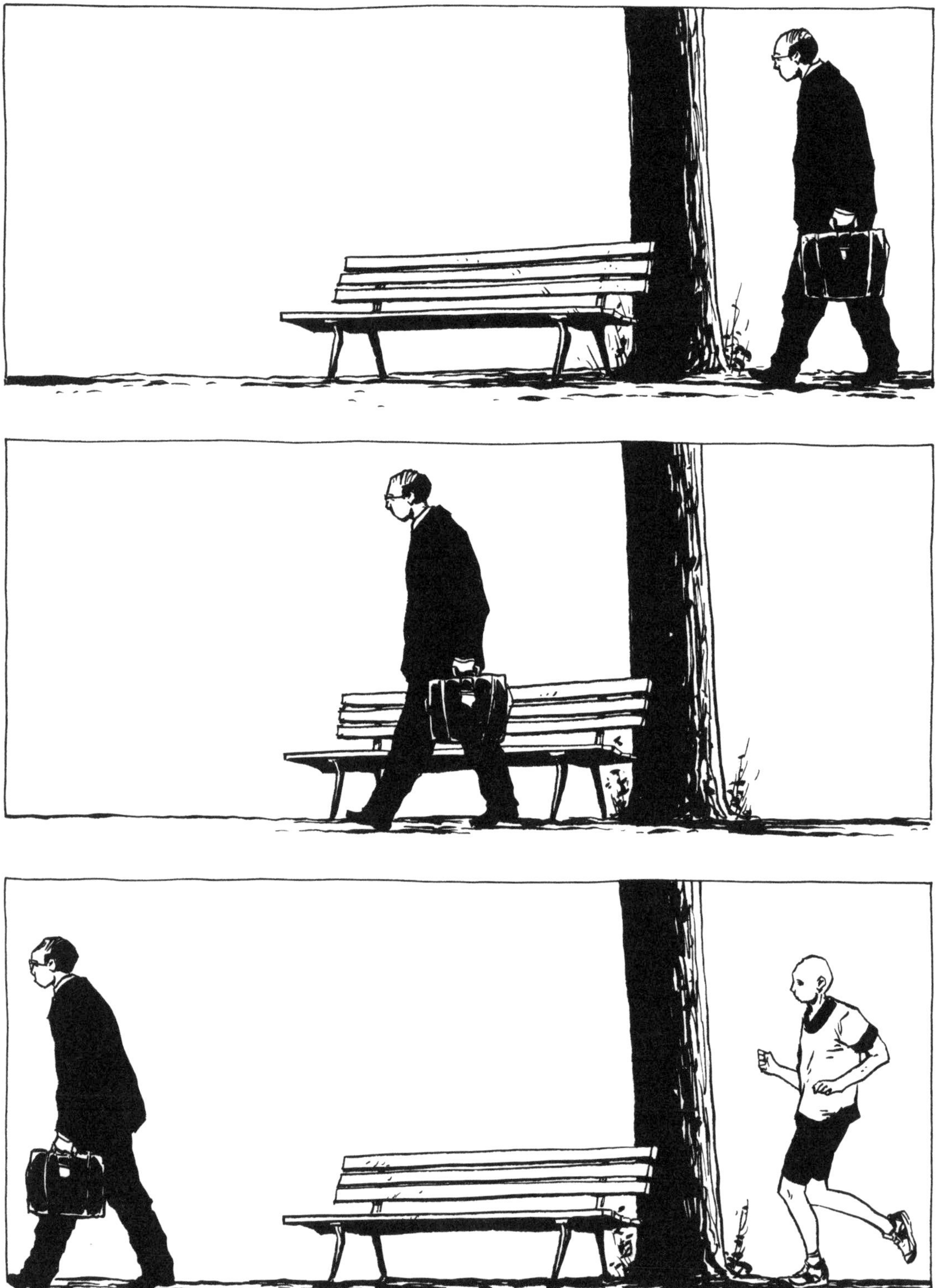

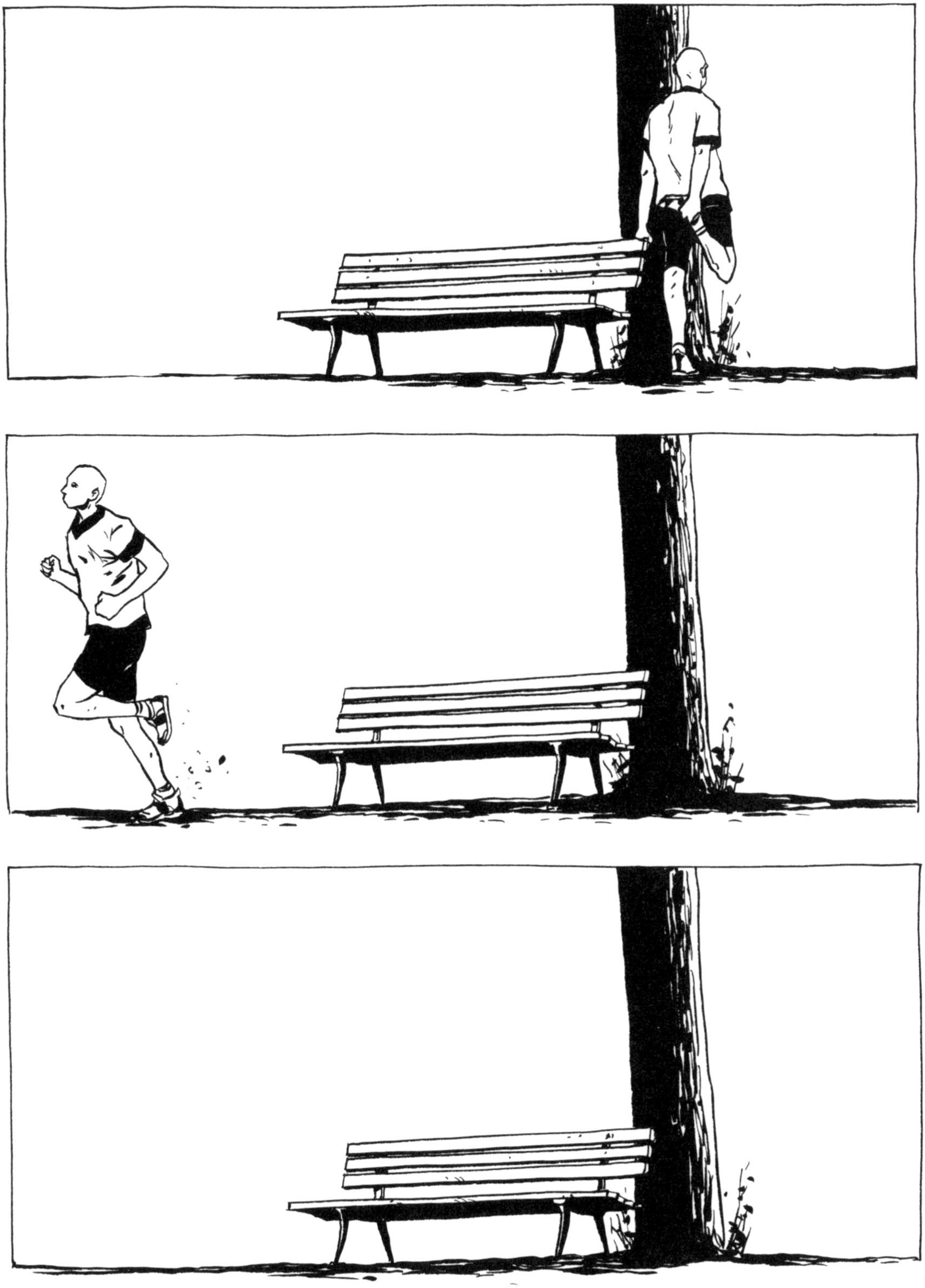

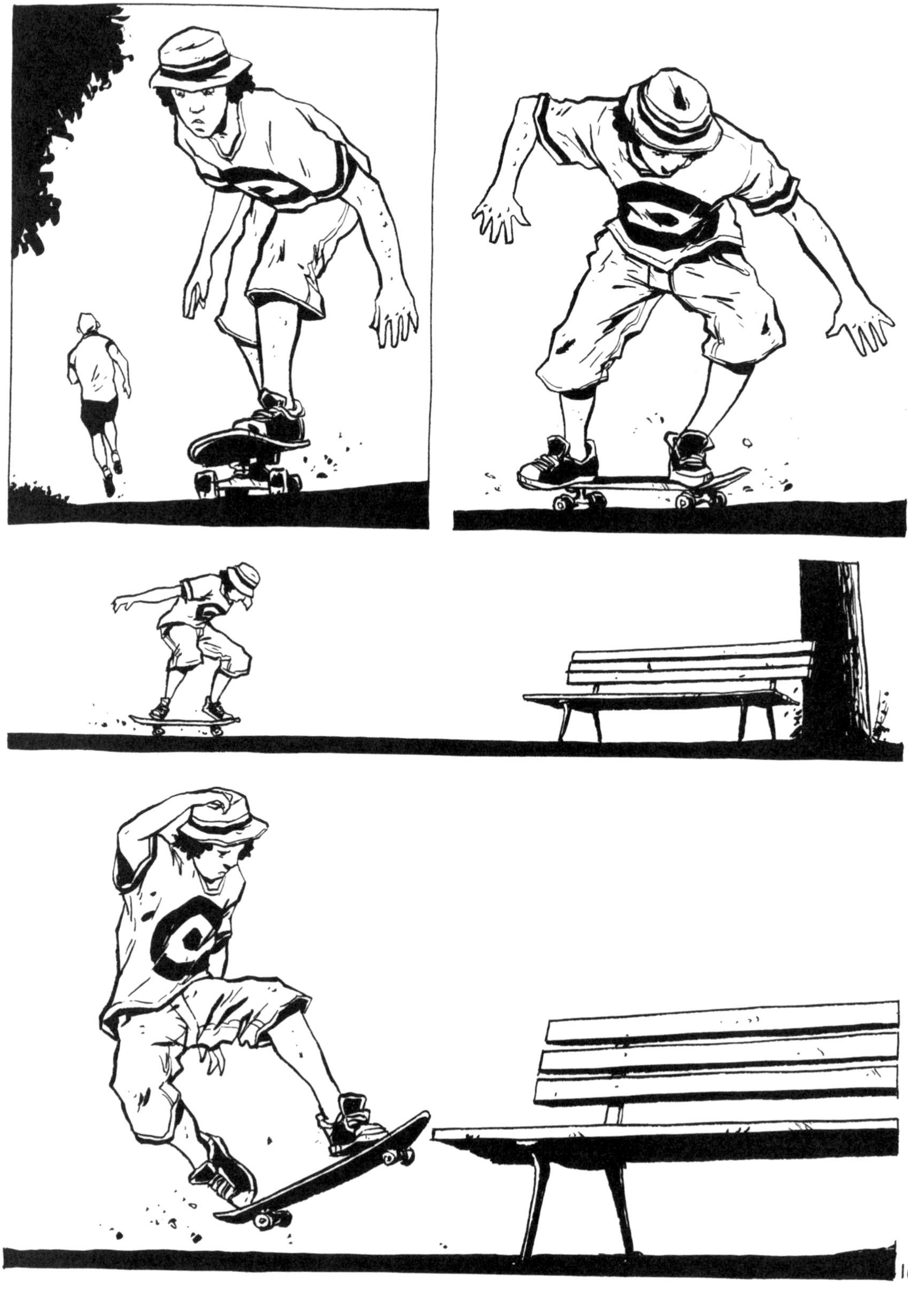

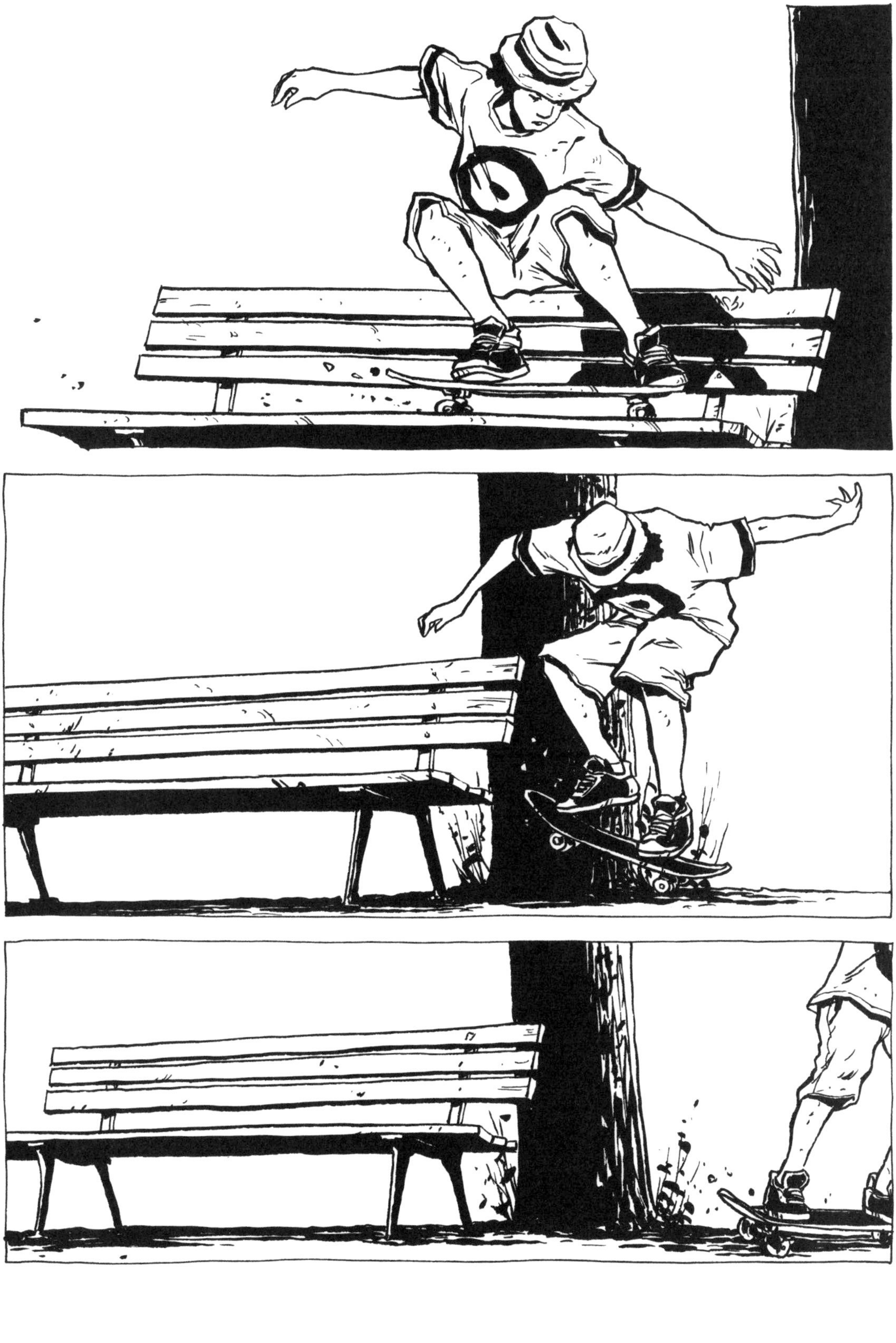

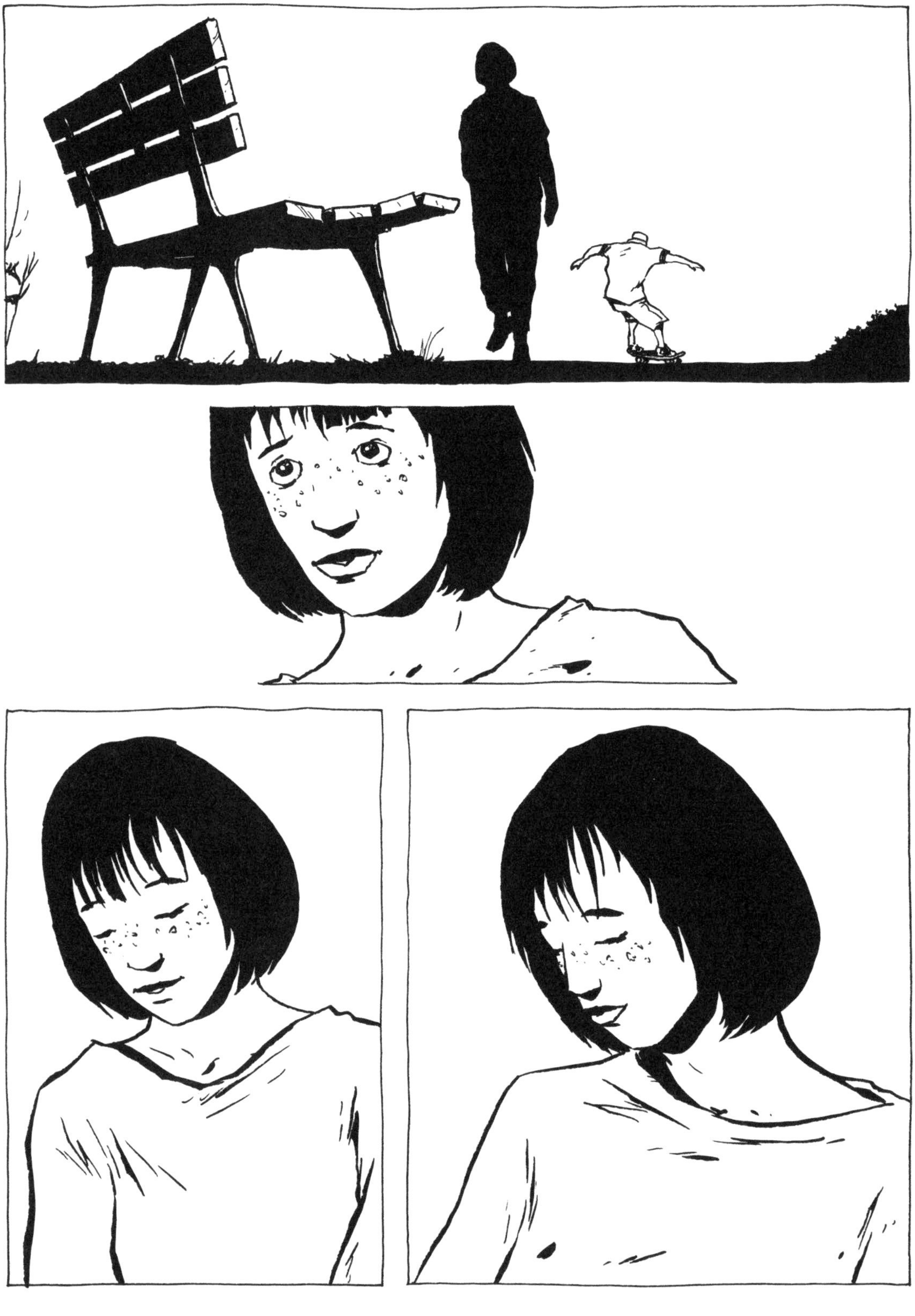

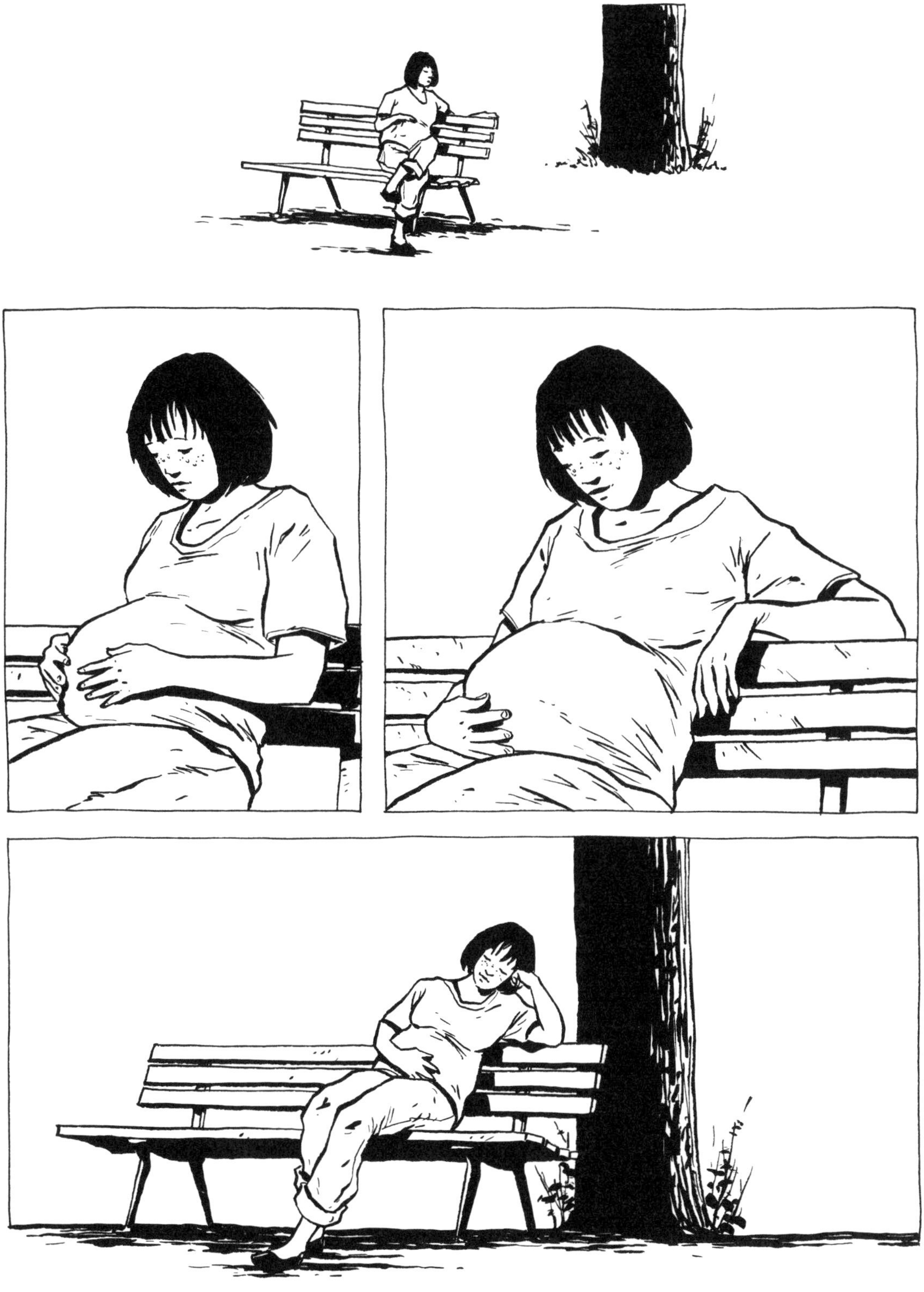

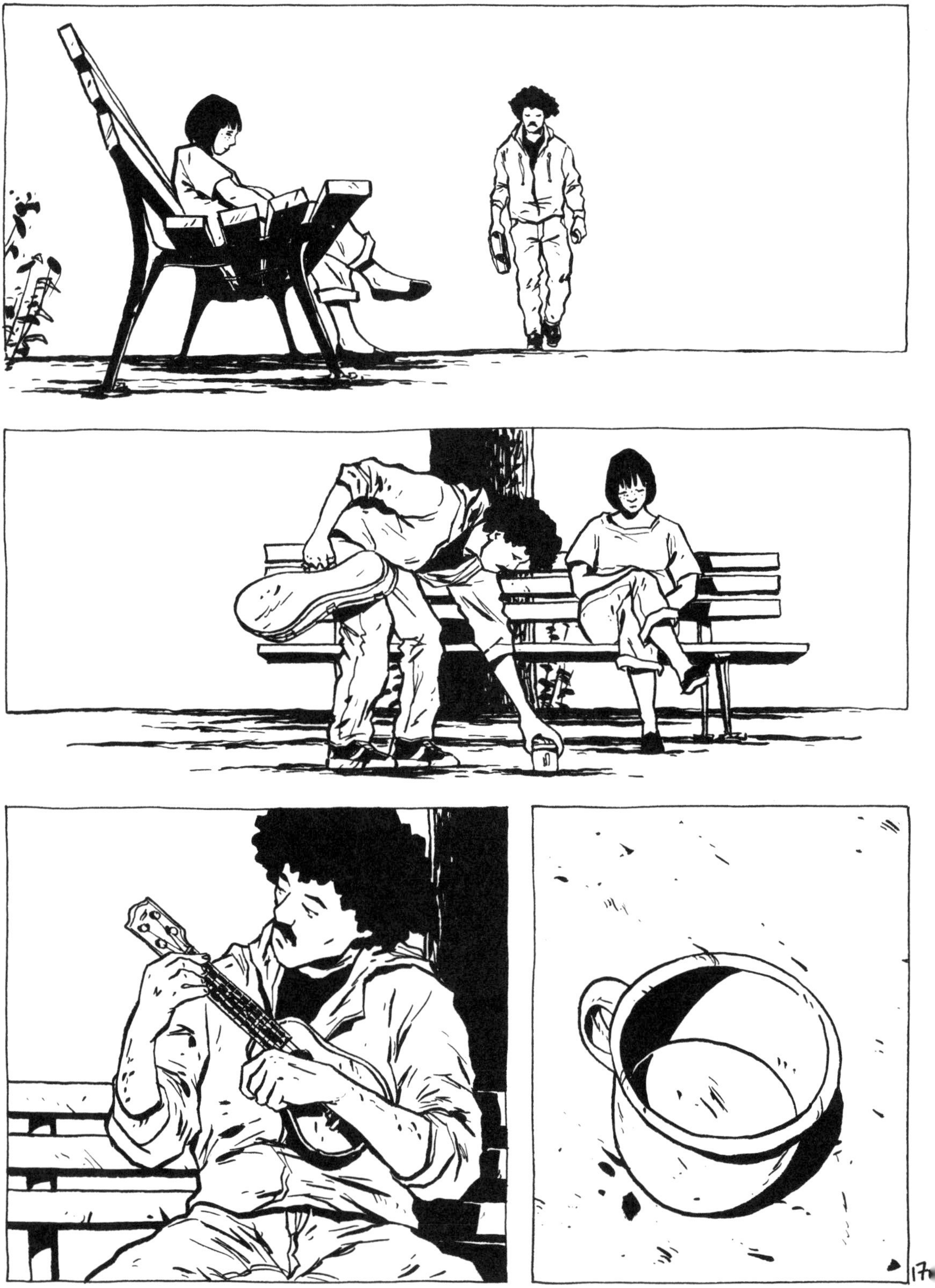
17

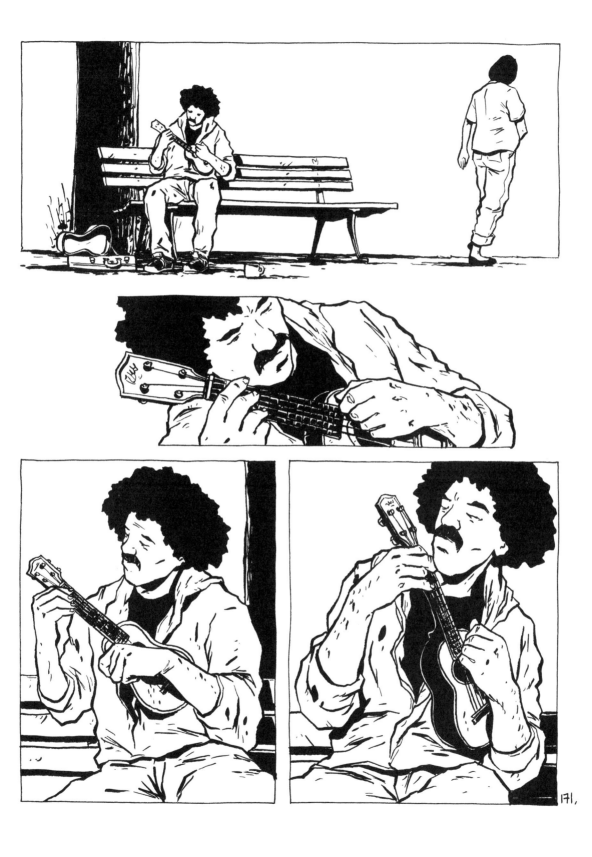

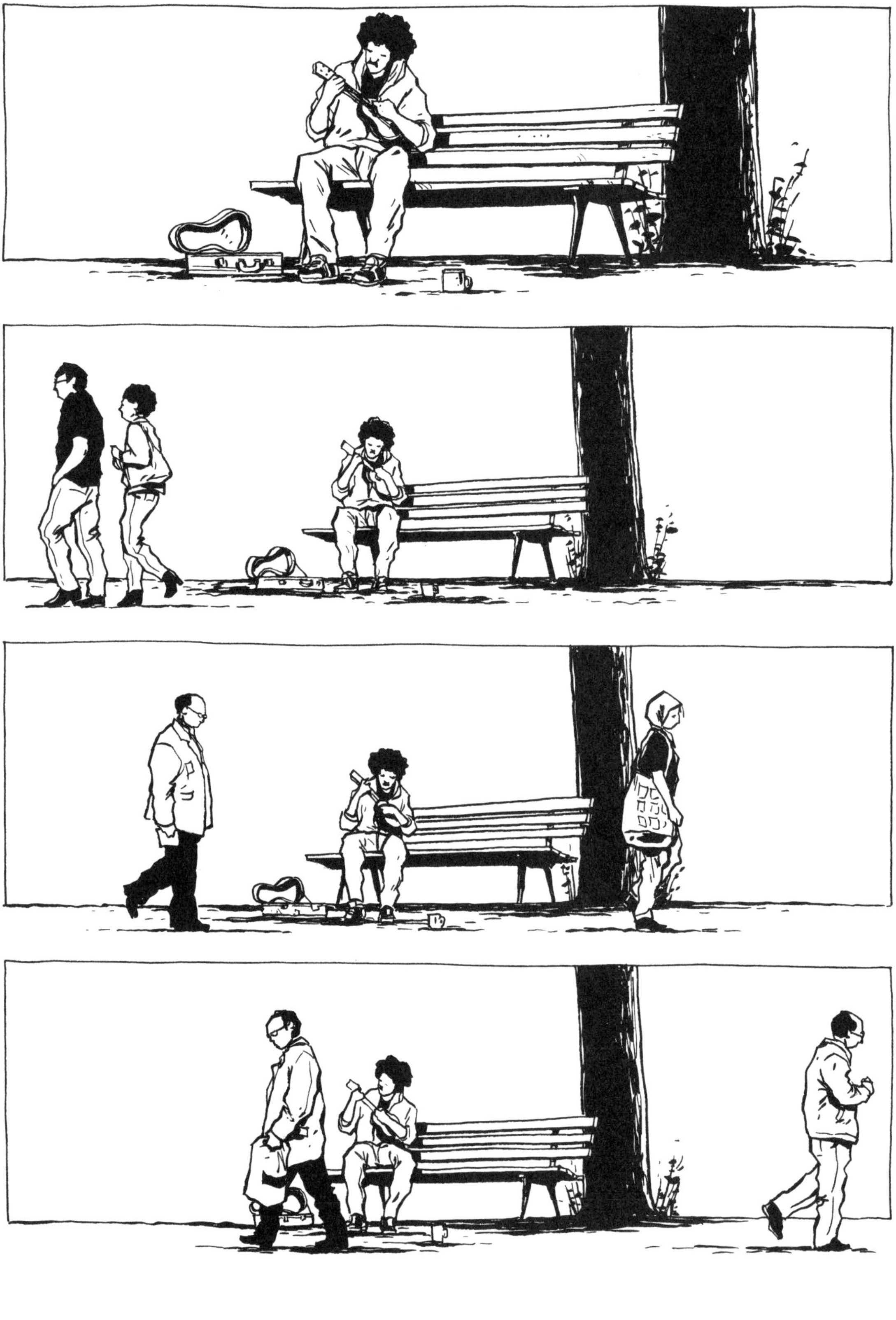

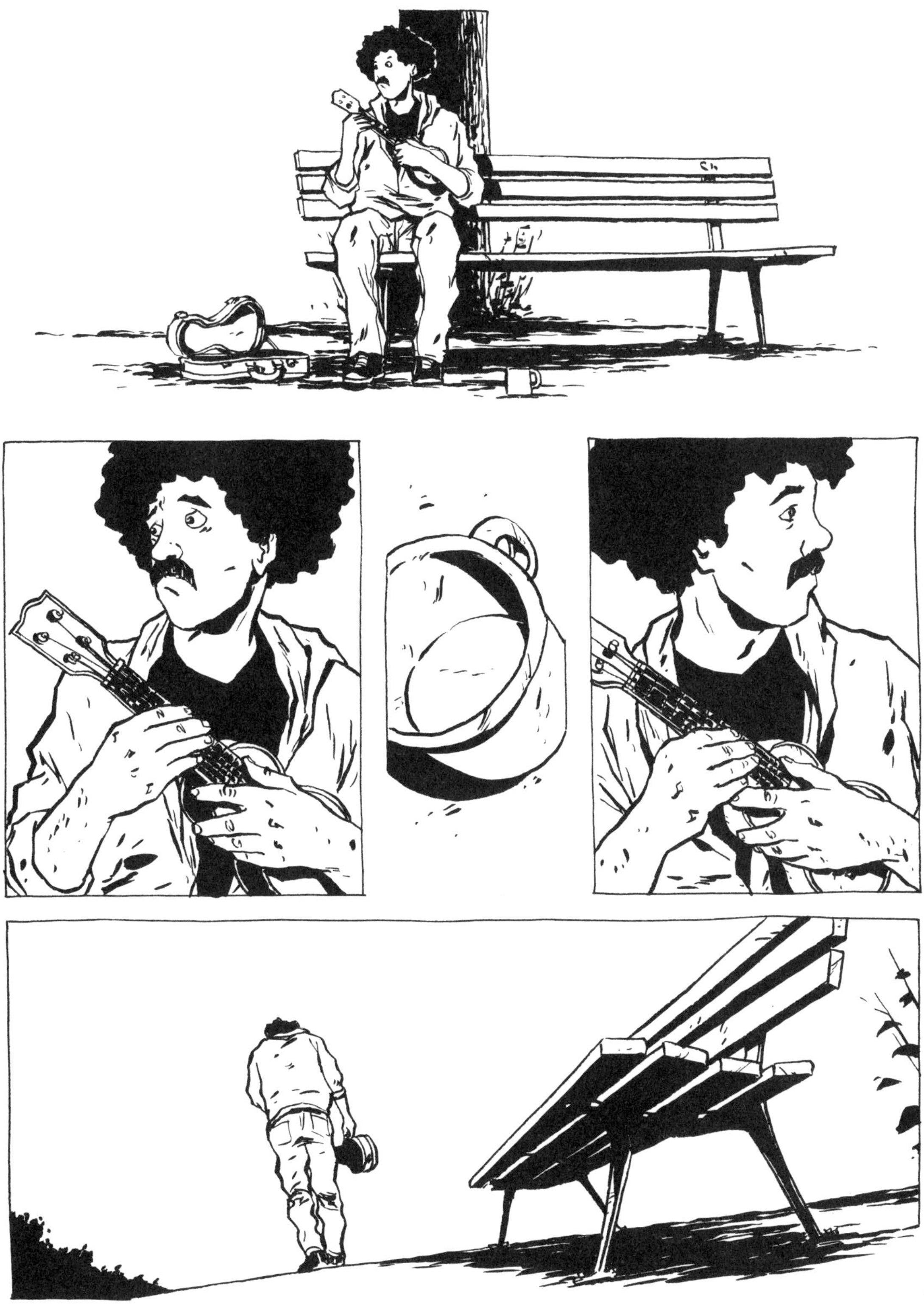

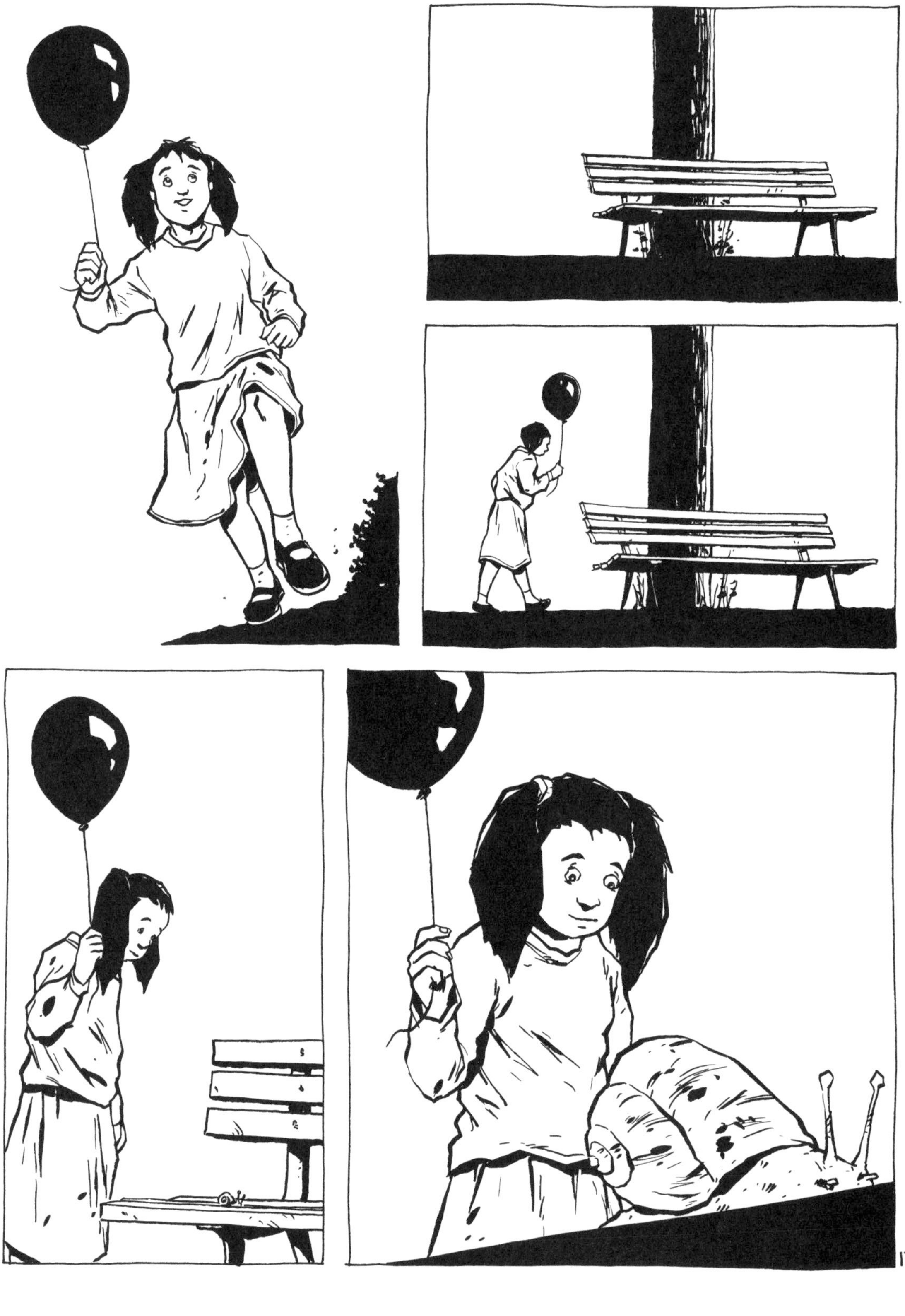

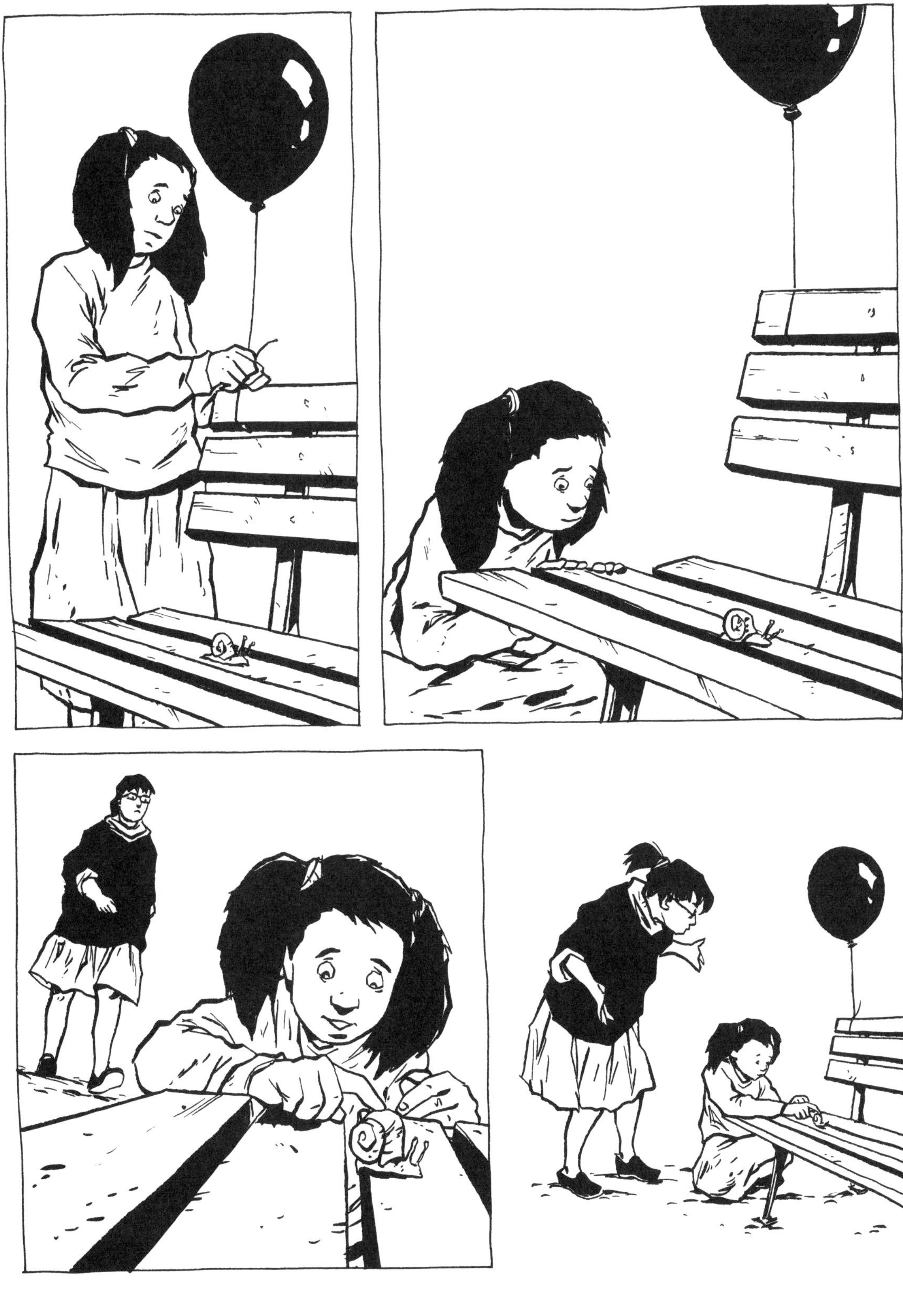

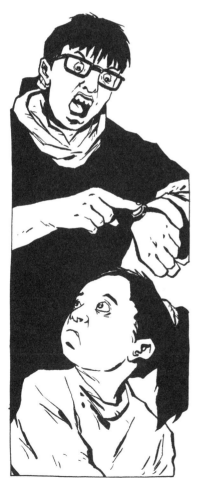

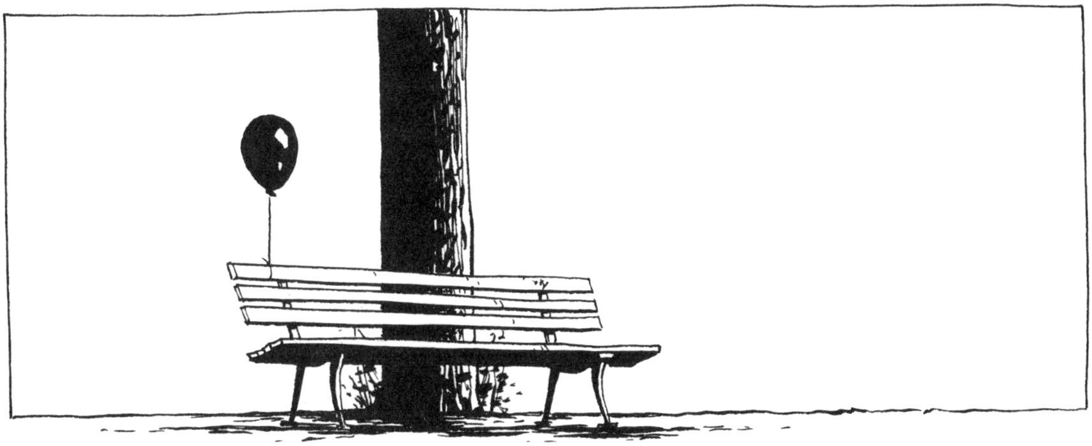
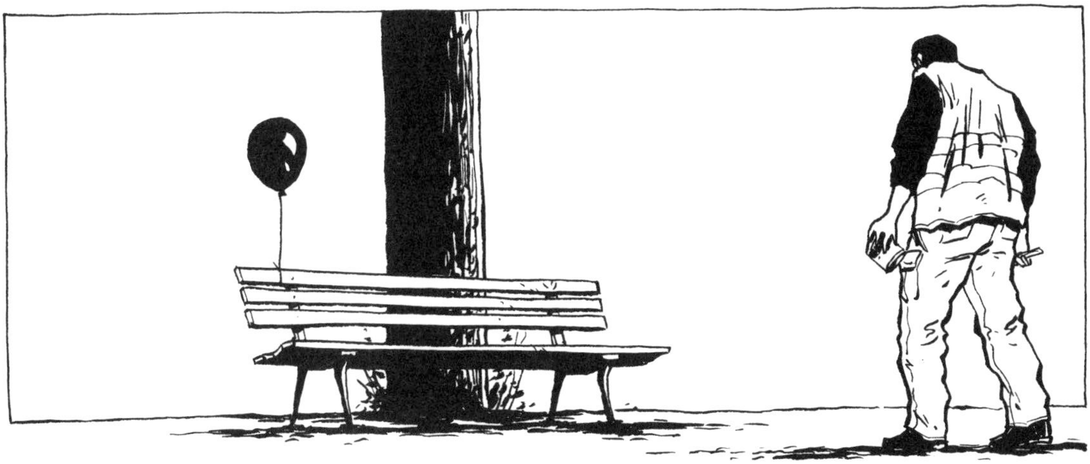
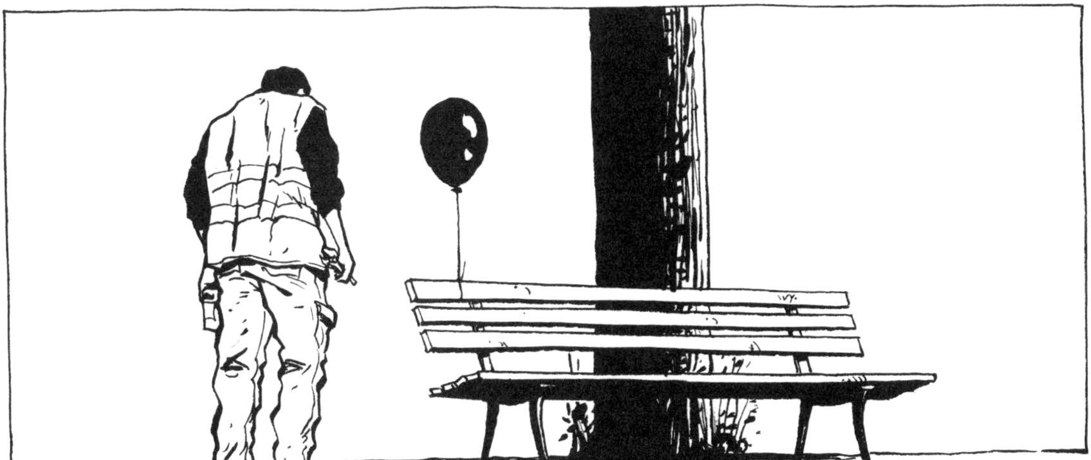

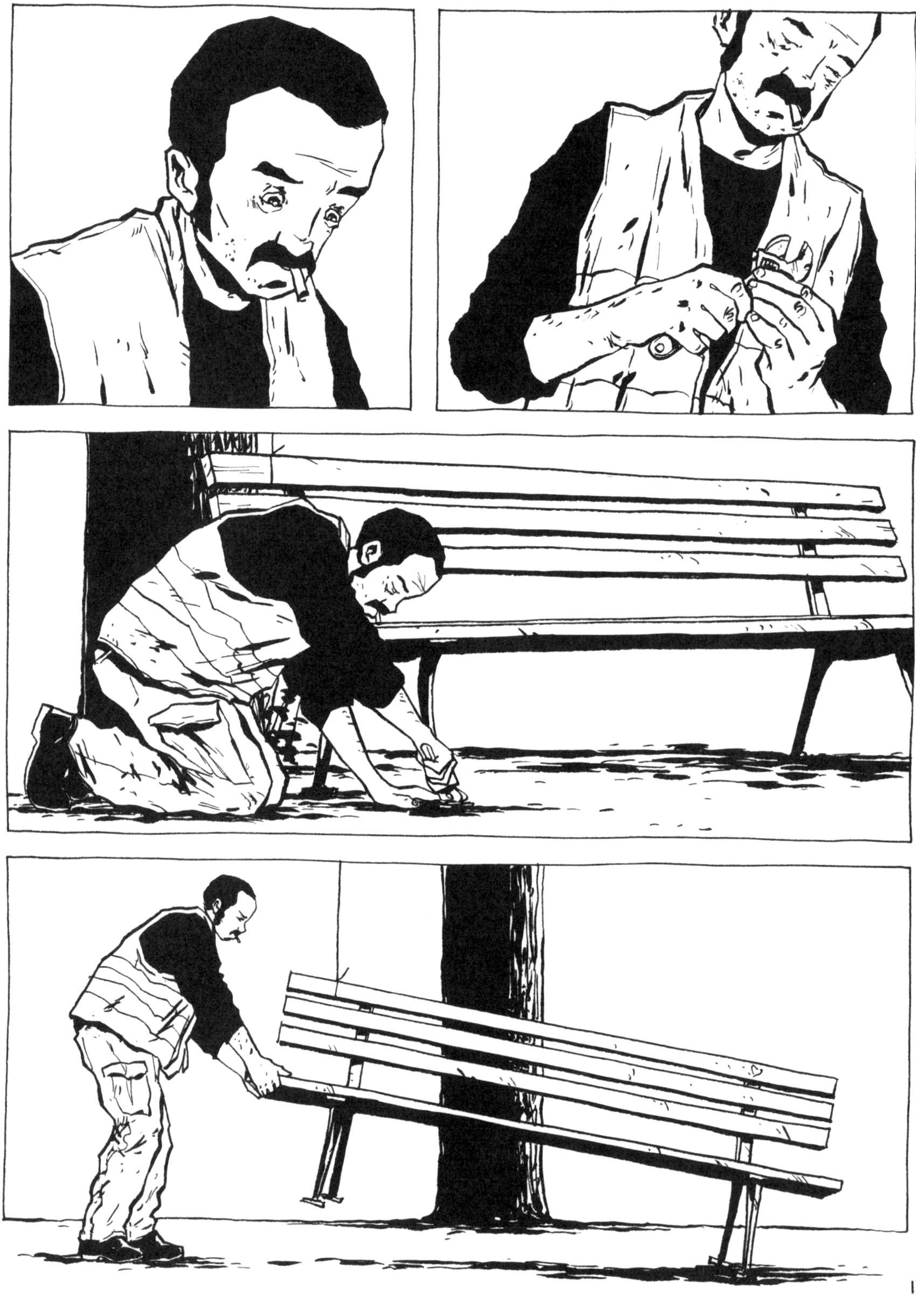

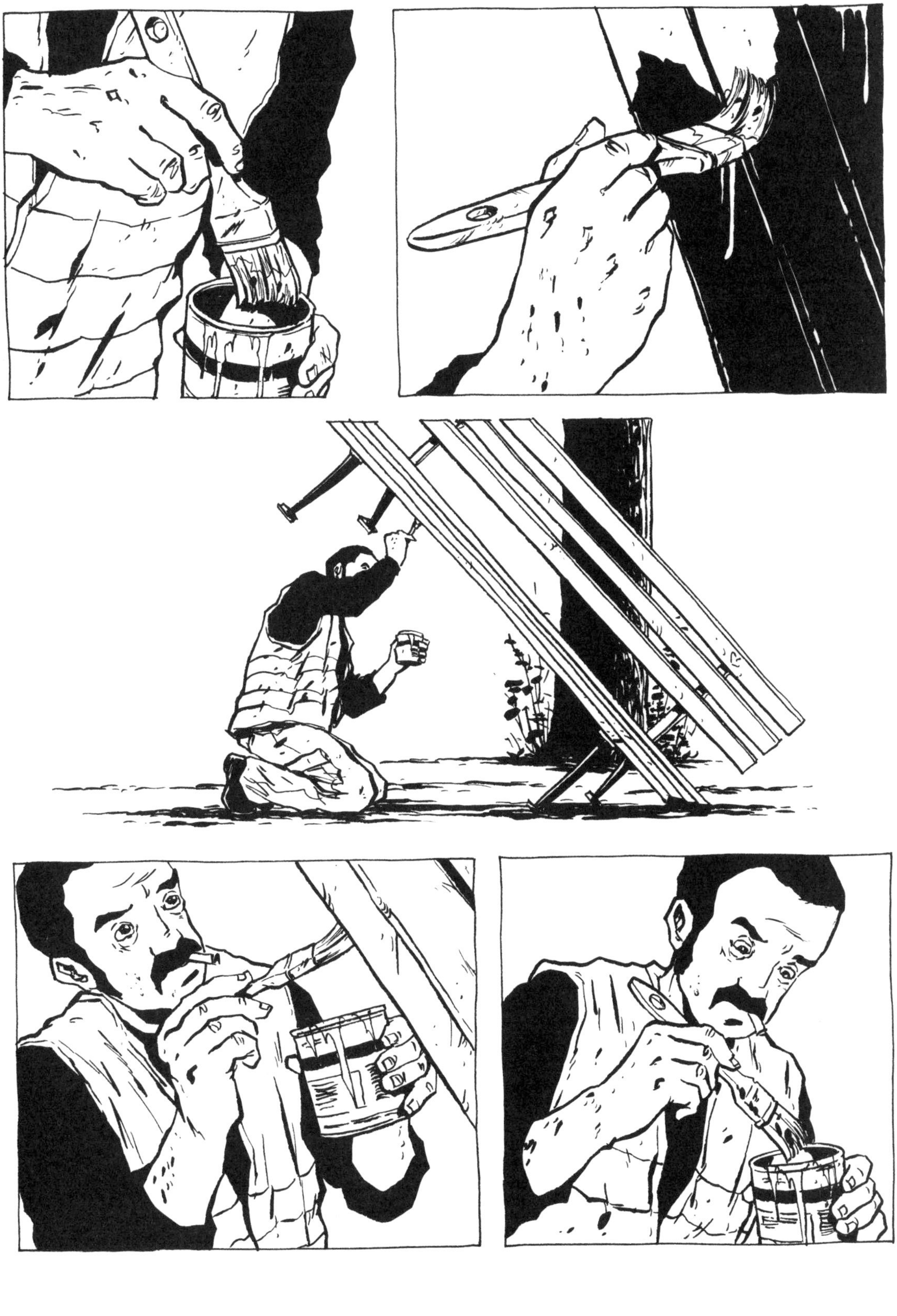

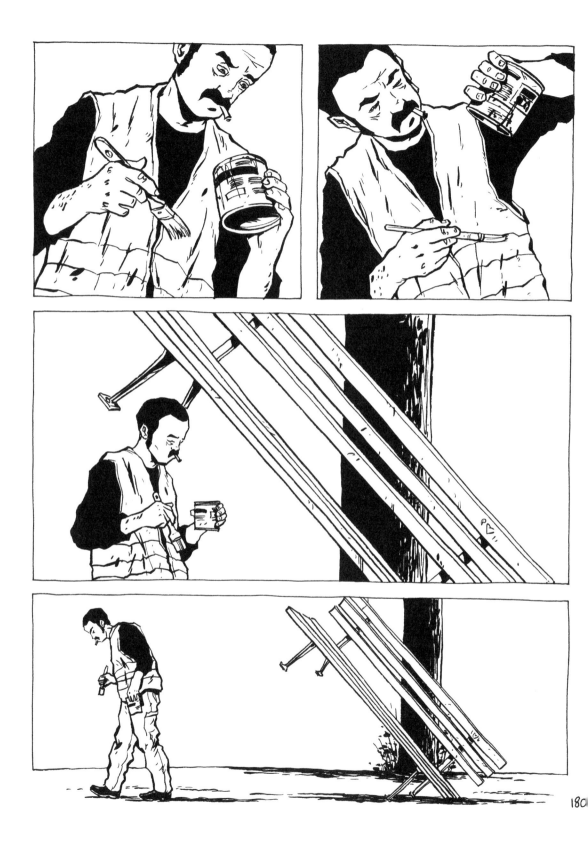

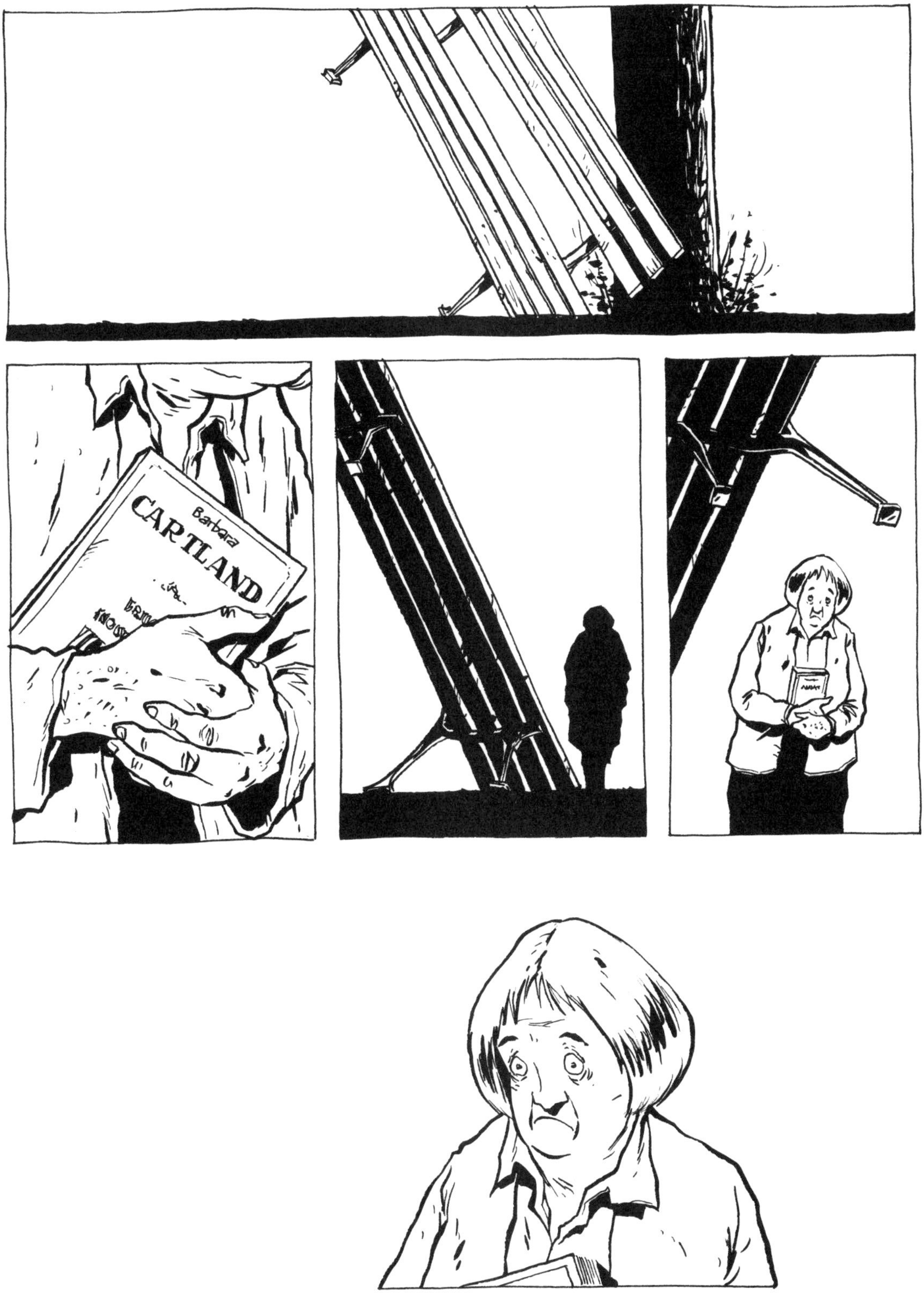
Barbara
CARTLAND

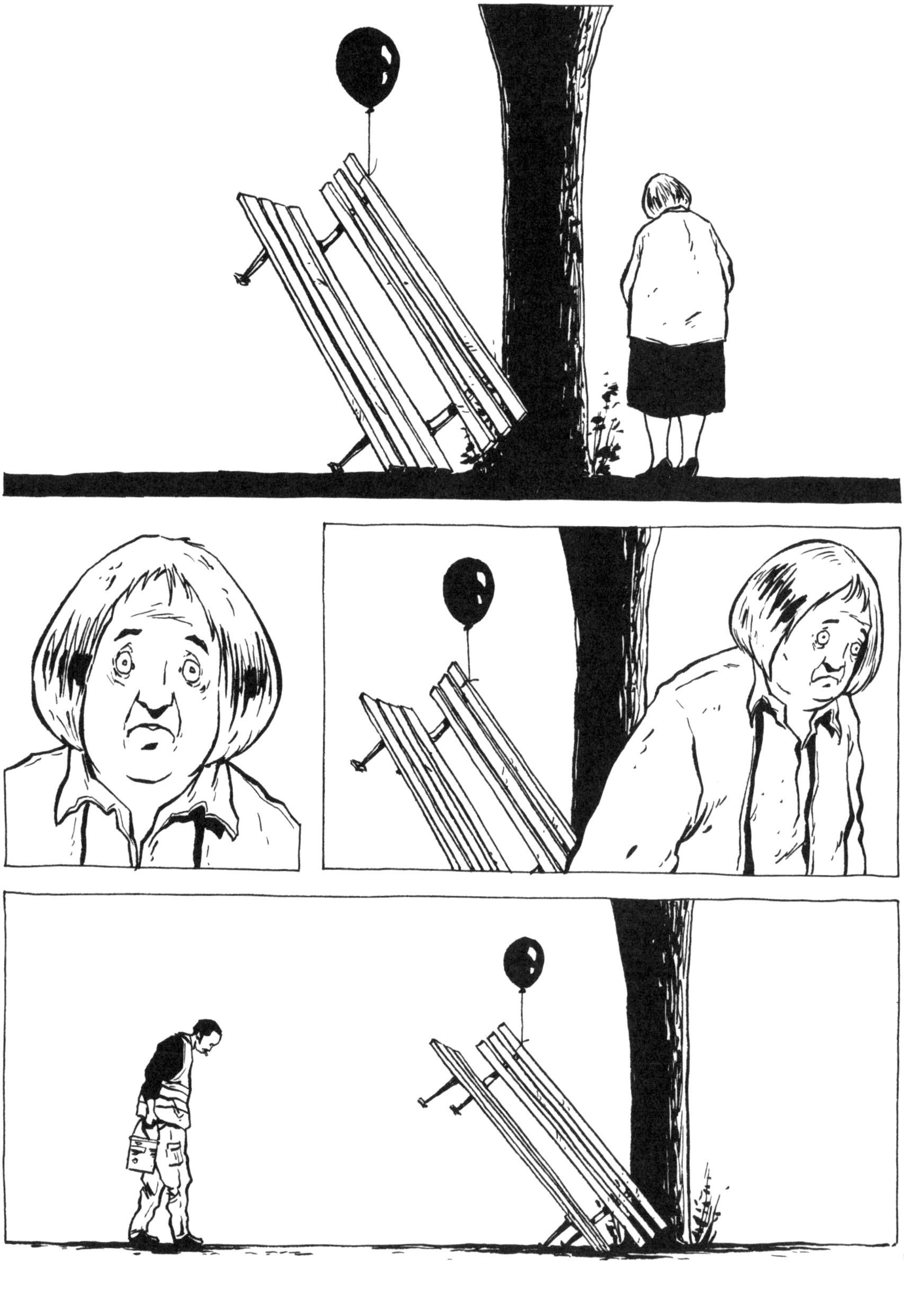

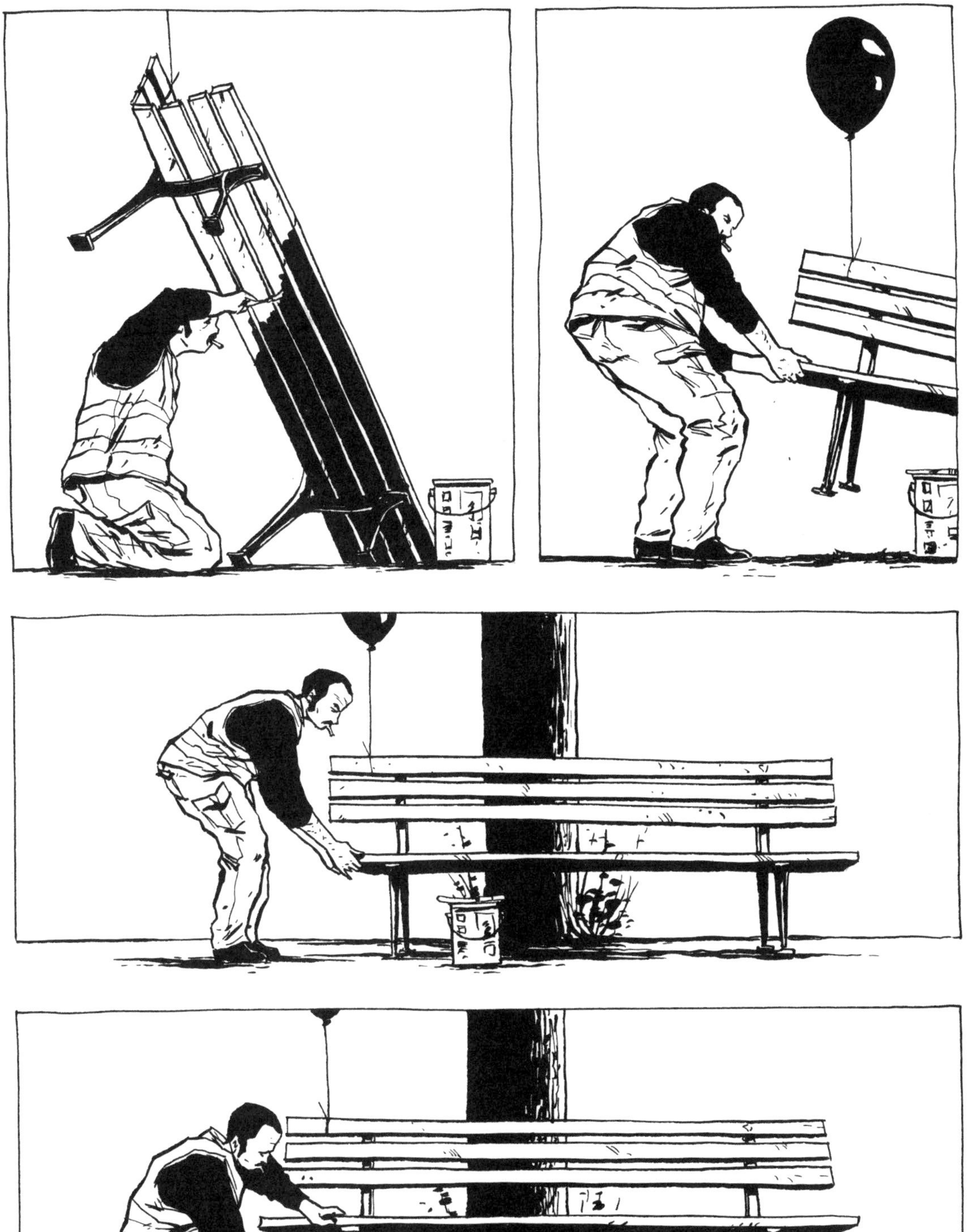

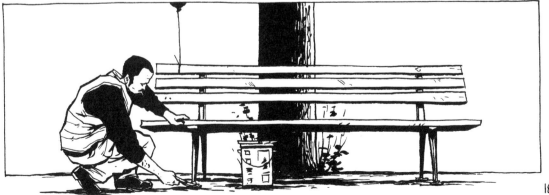

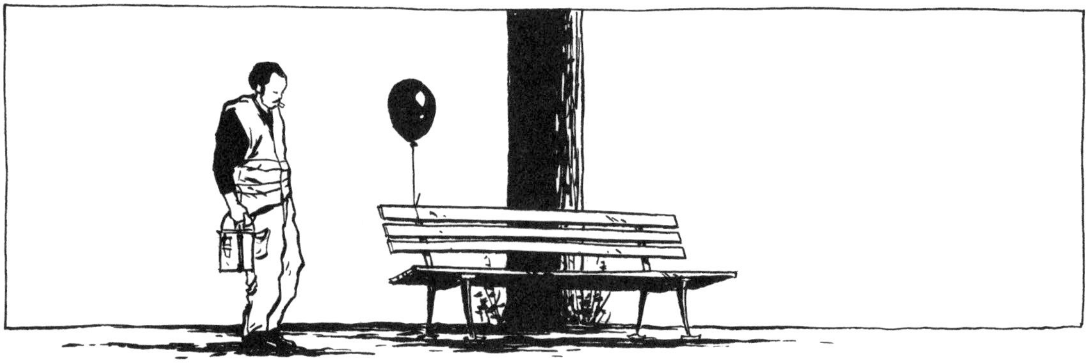

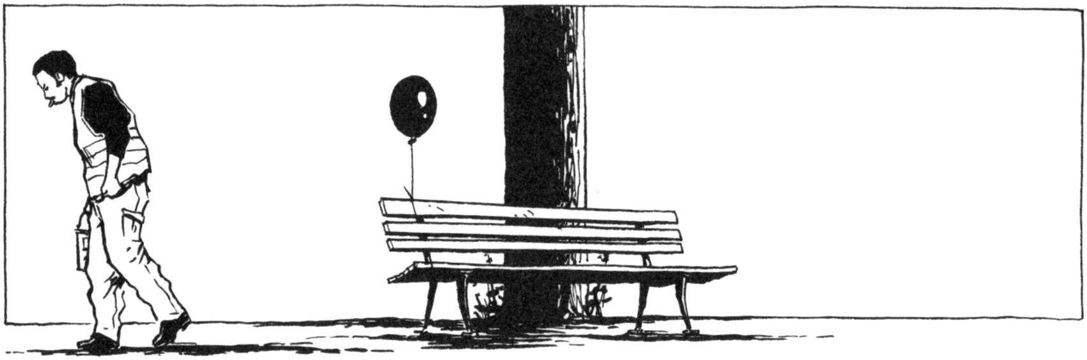

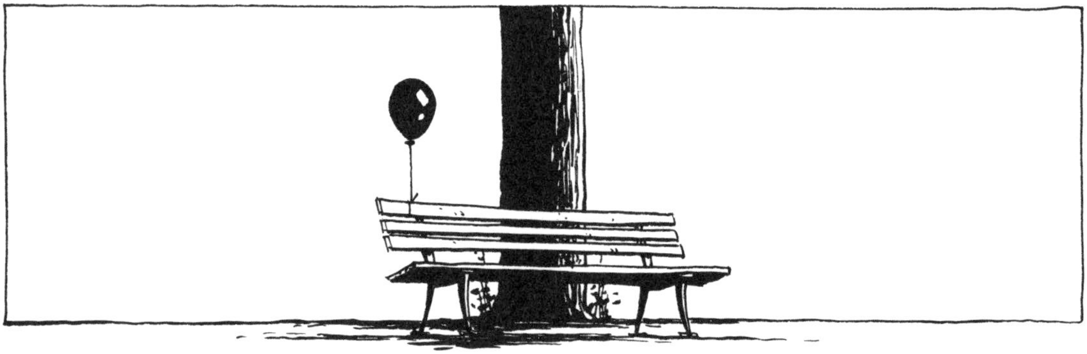

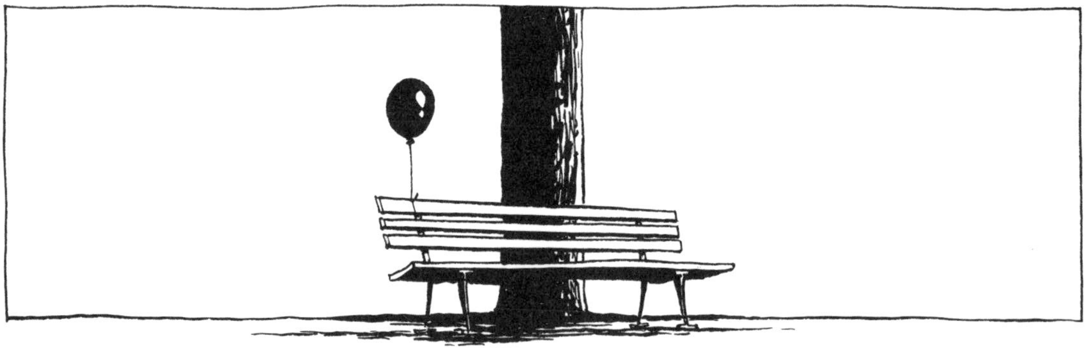

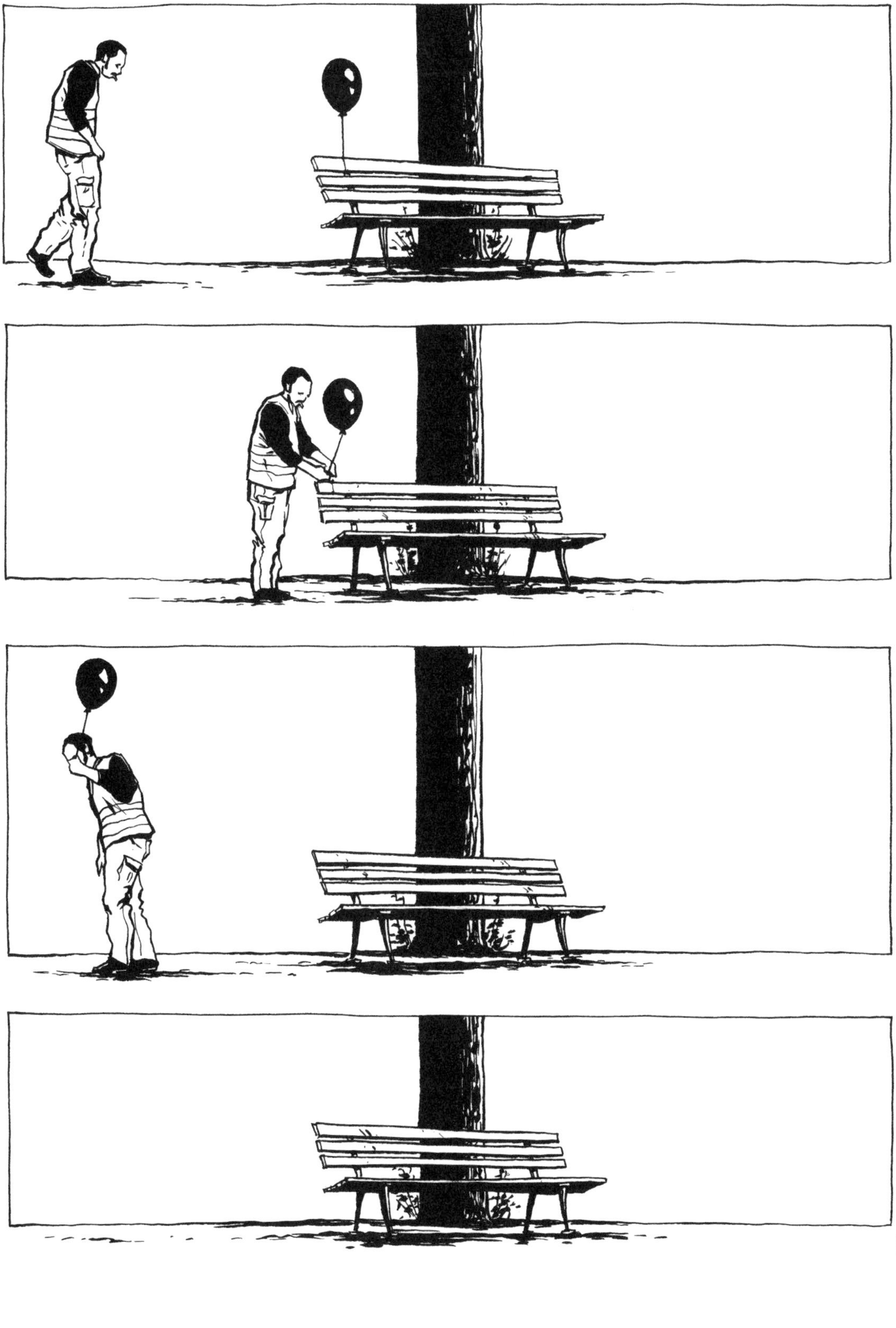

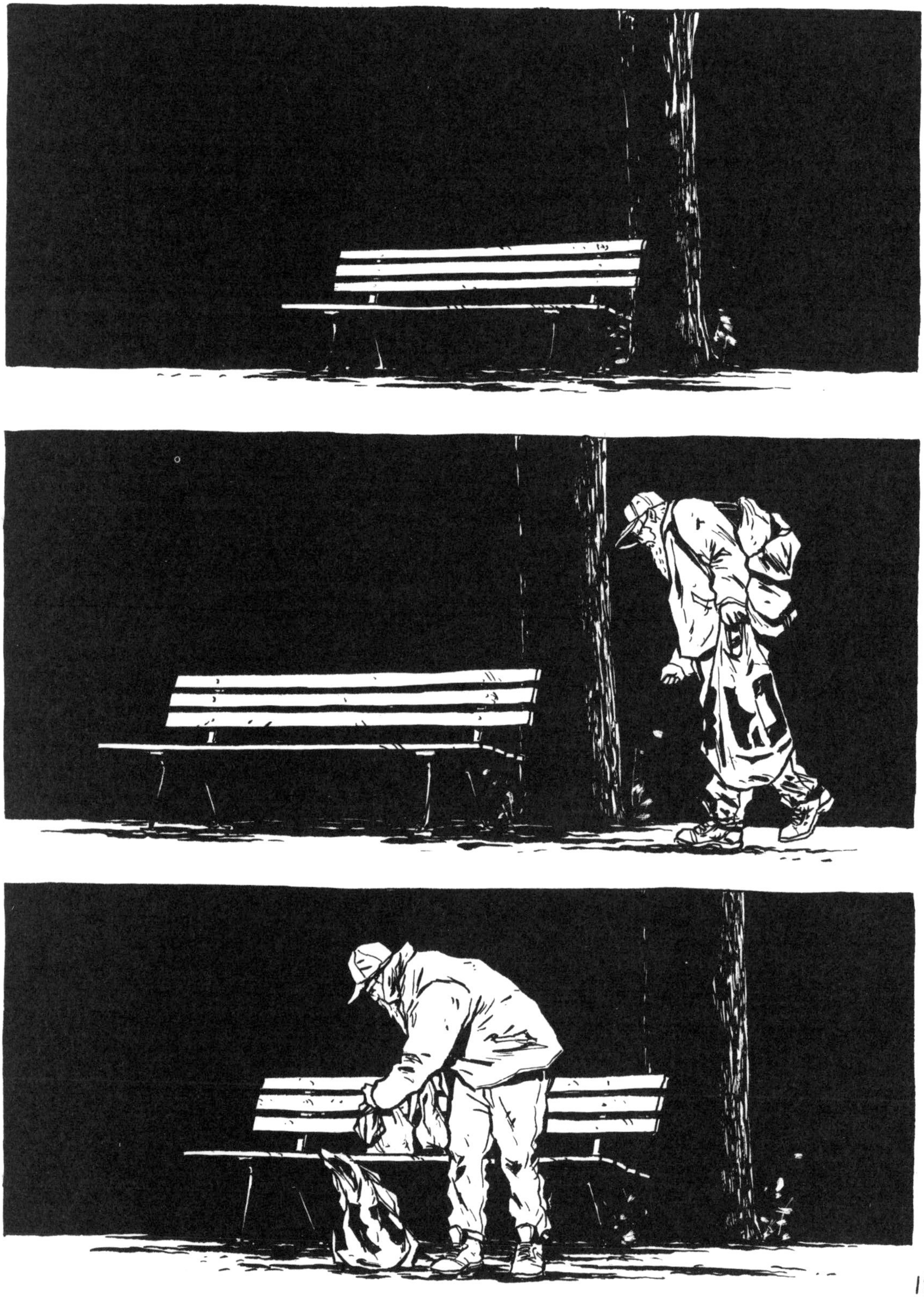

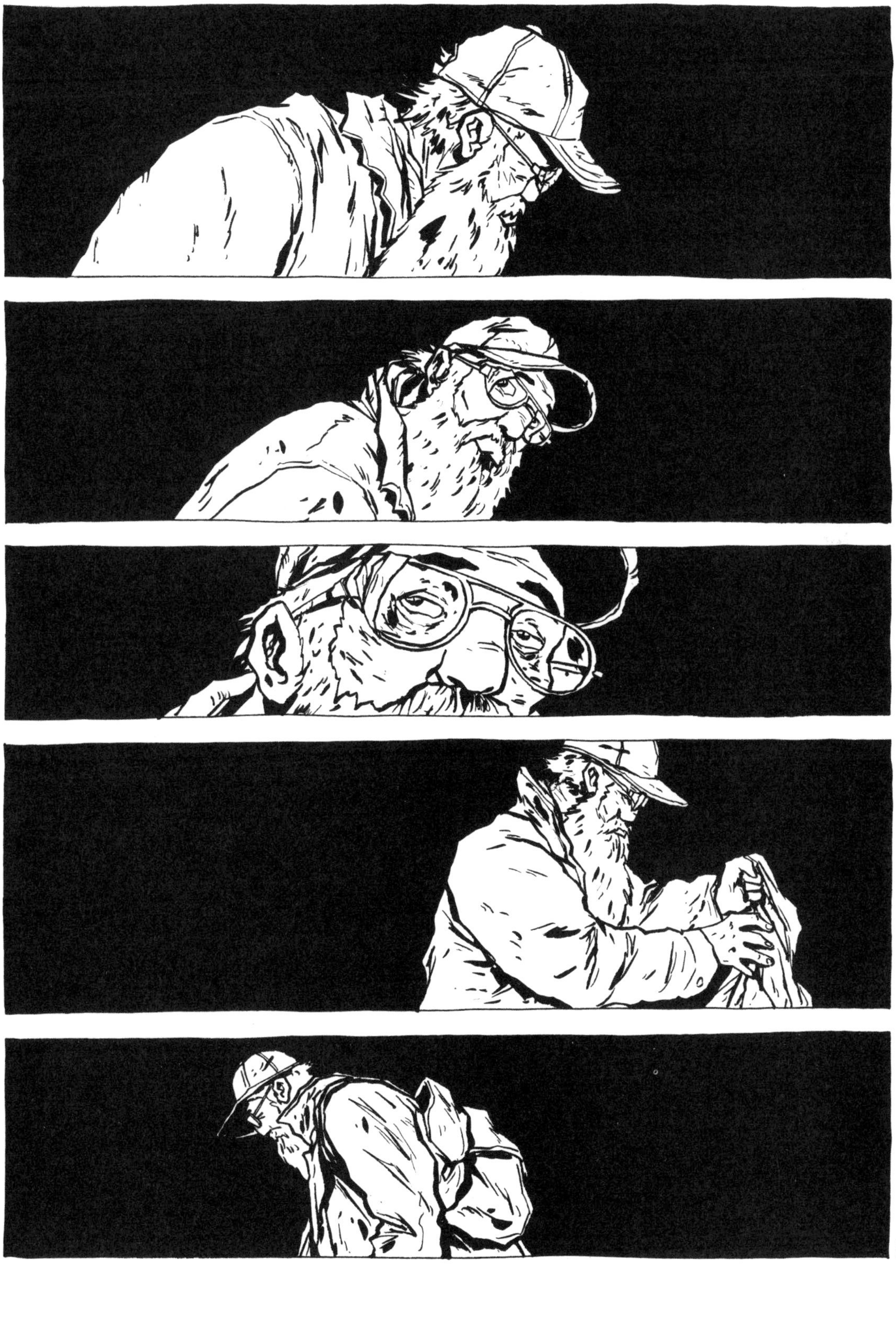

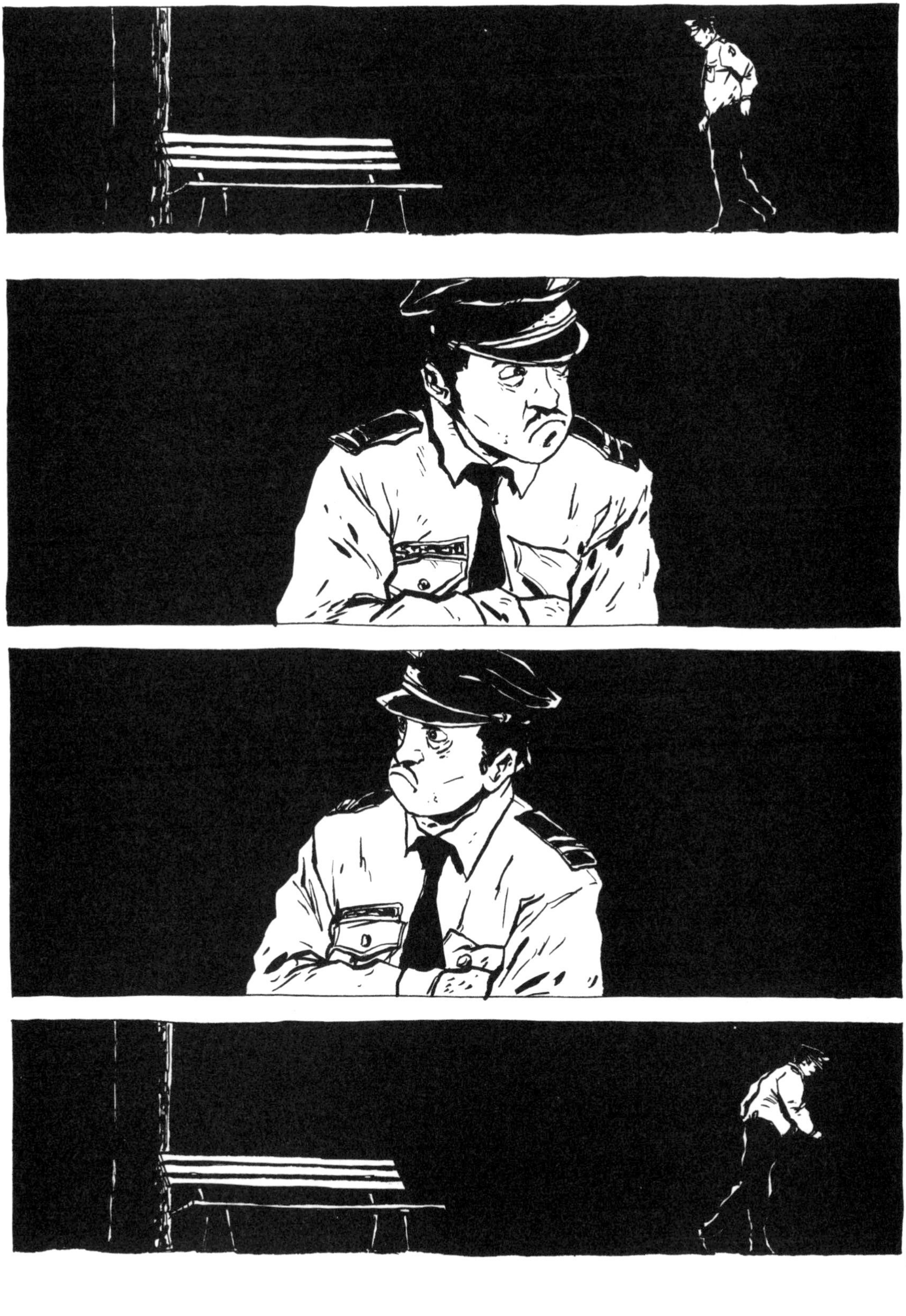

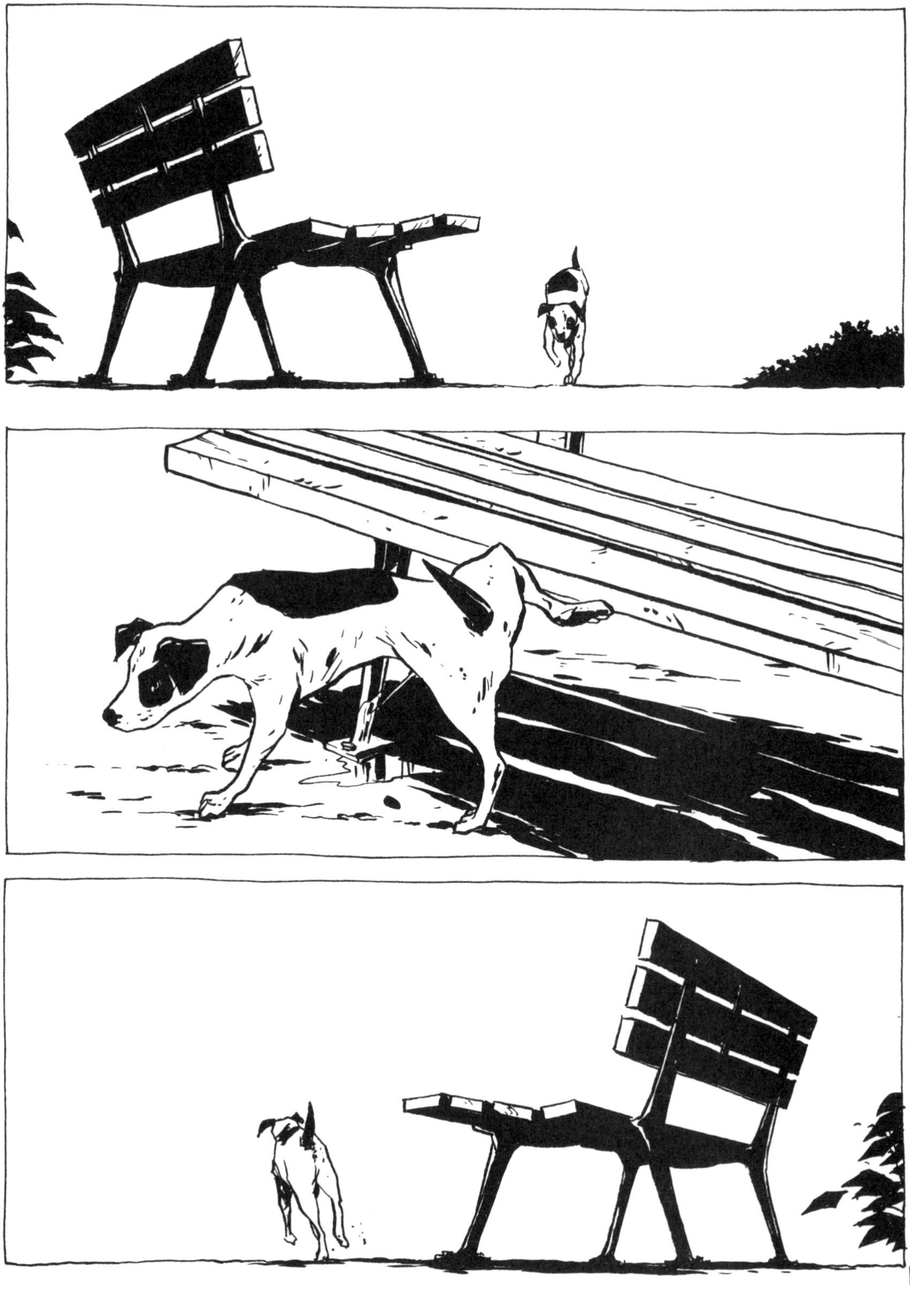

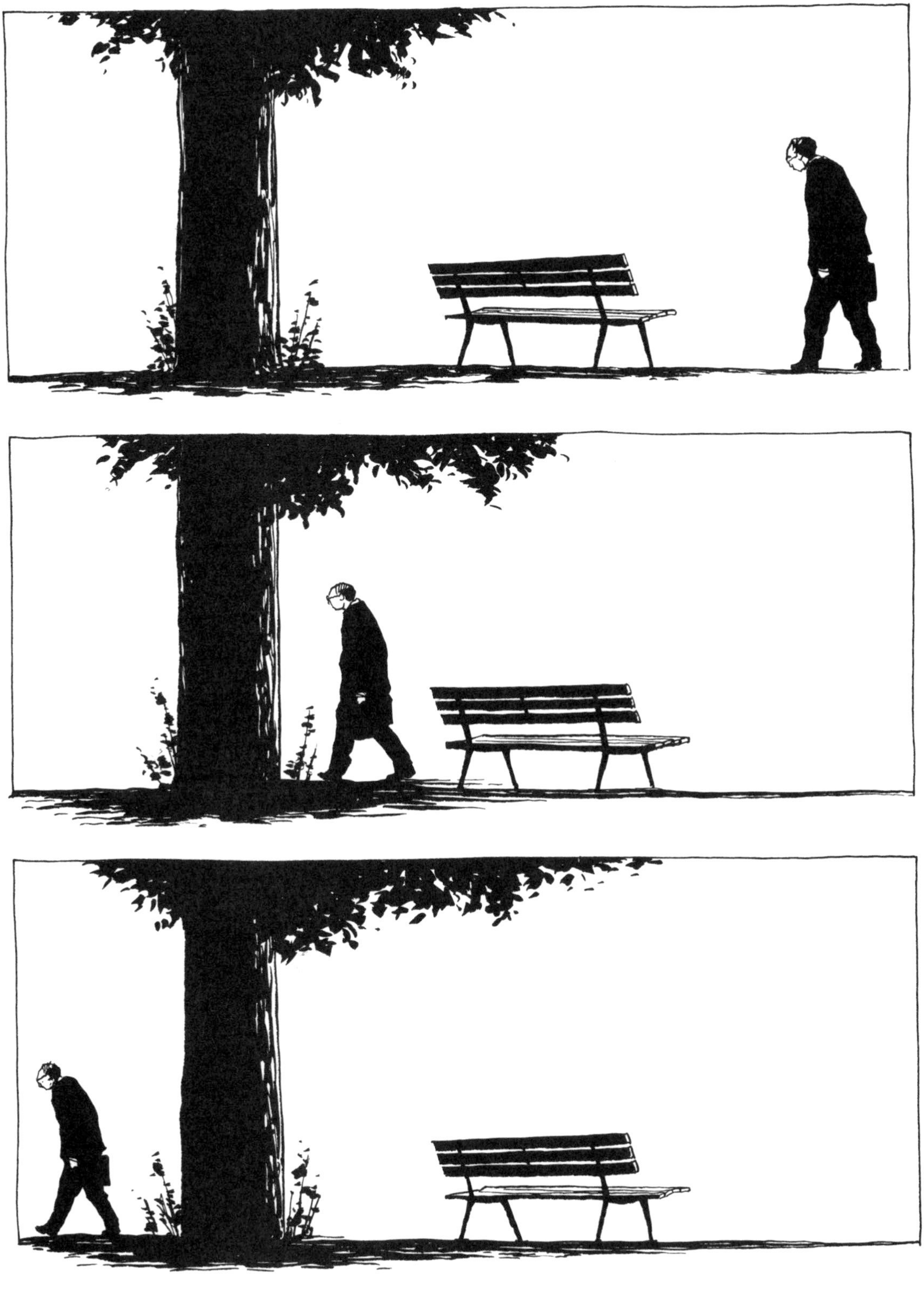

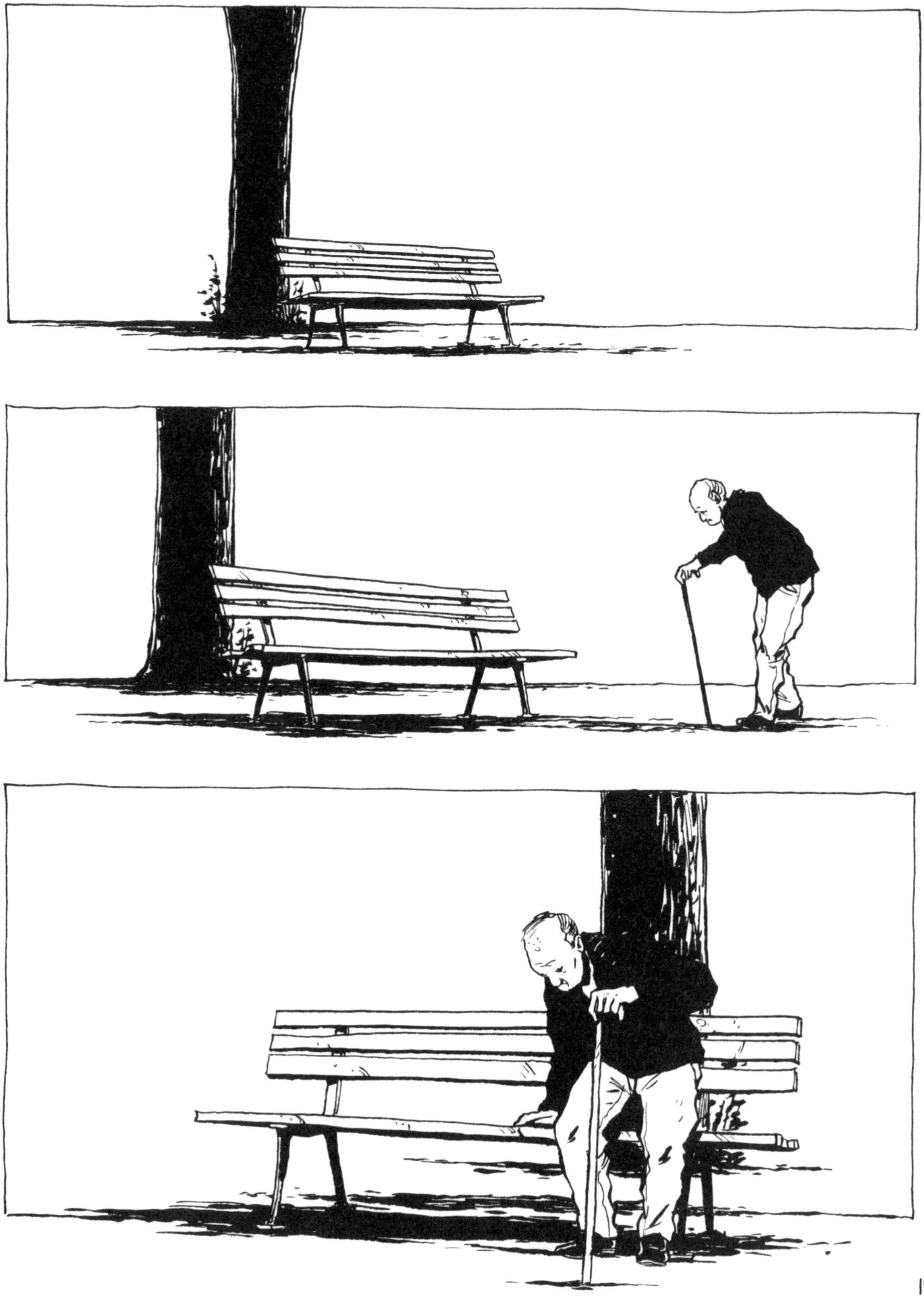

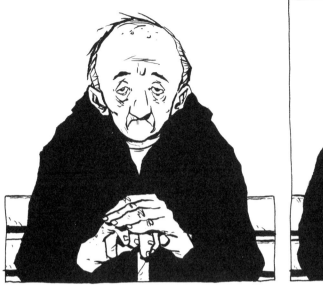

193.

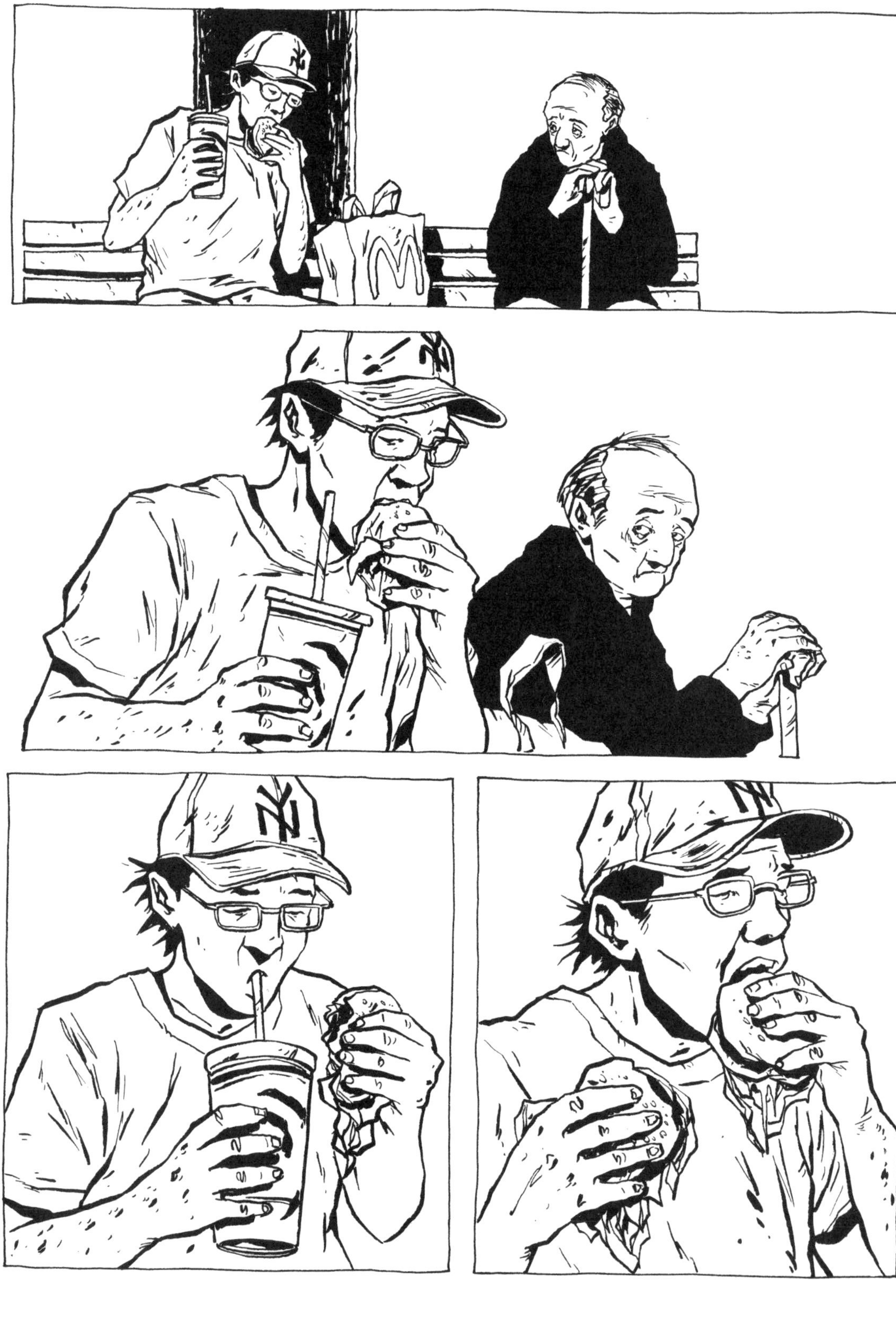

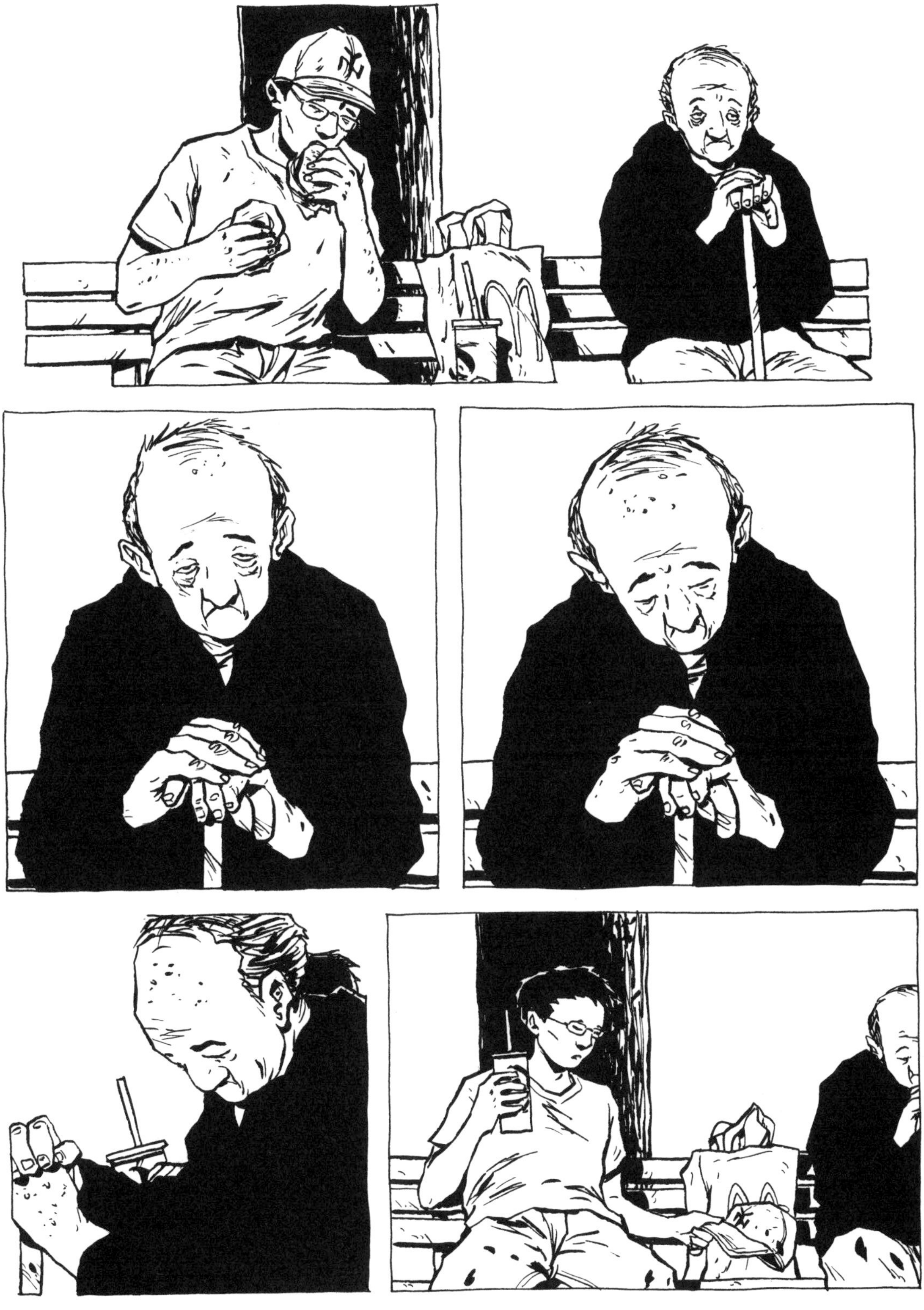

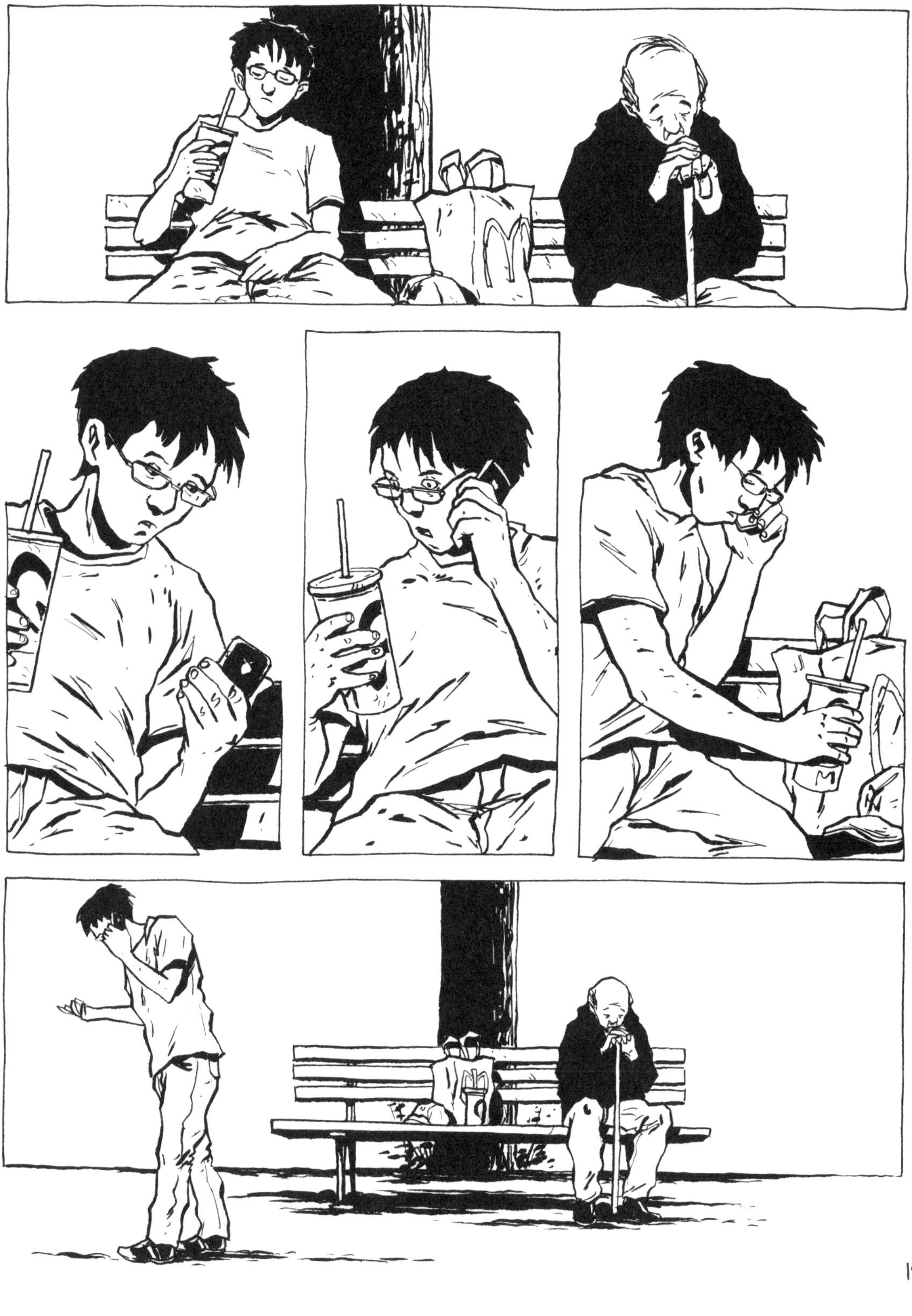

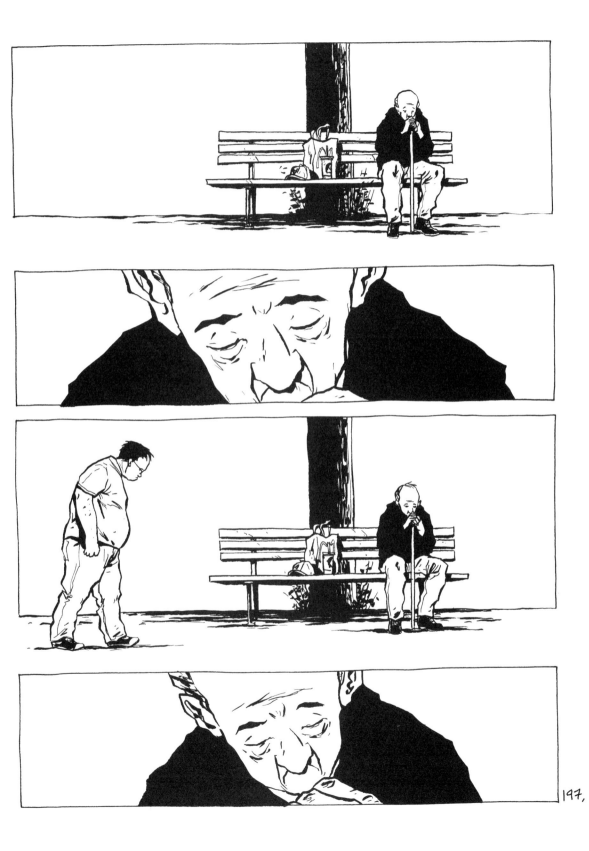

197,

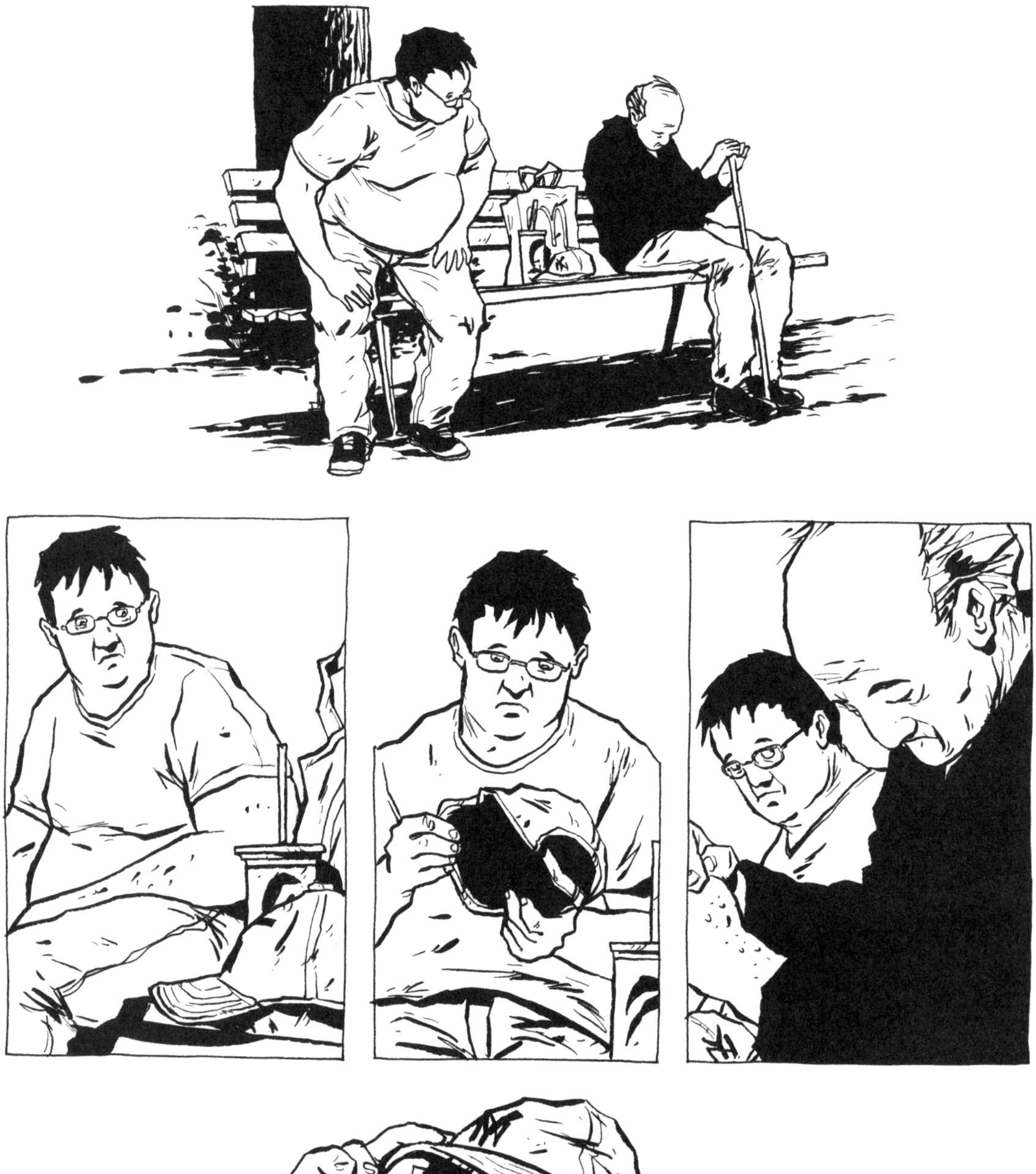

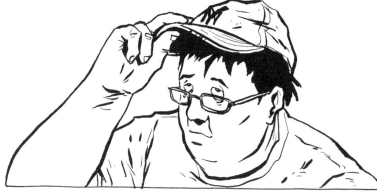

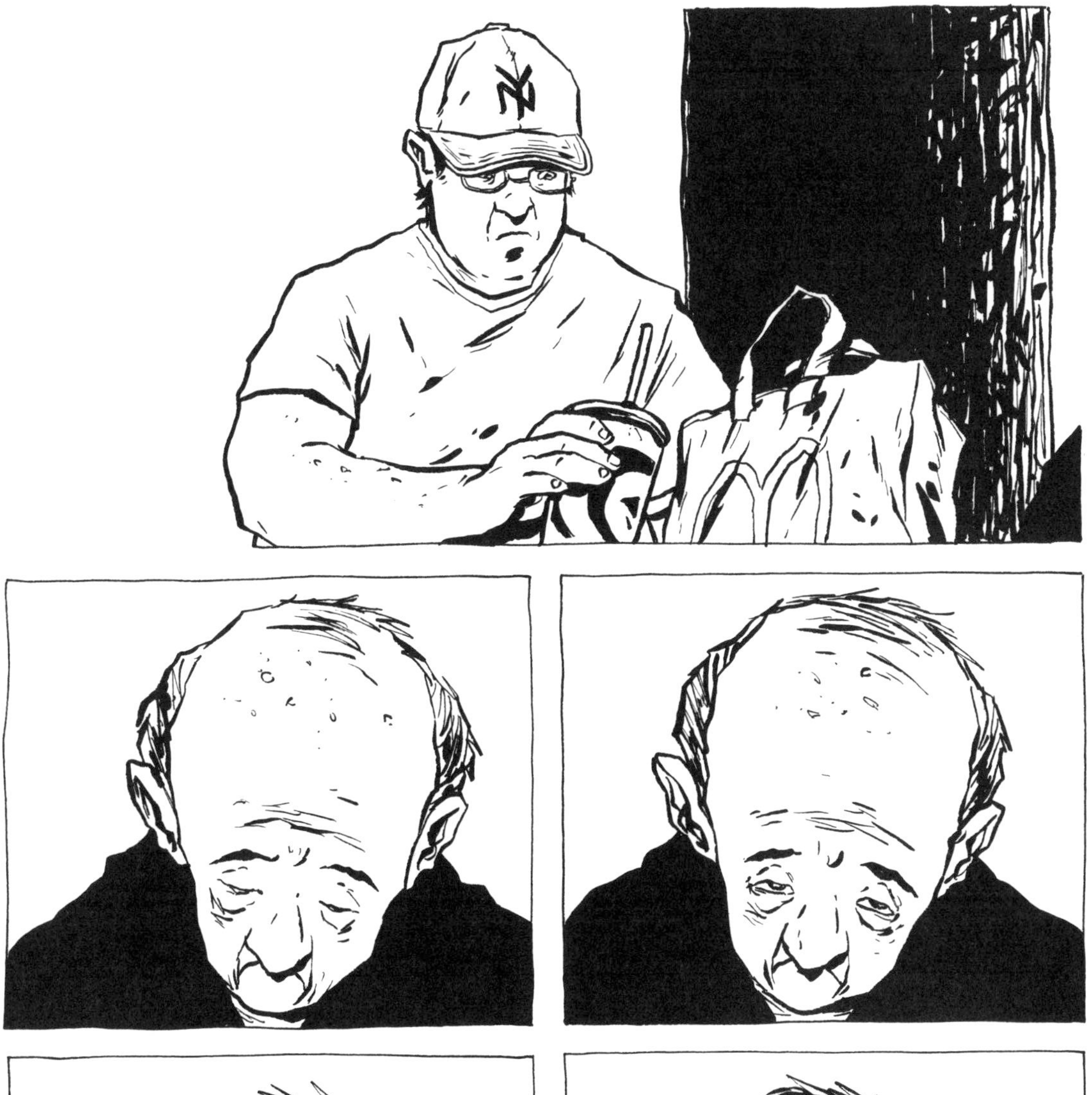
NY

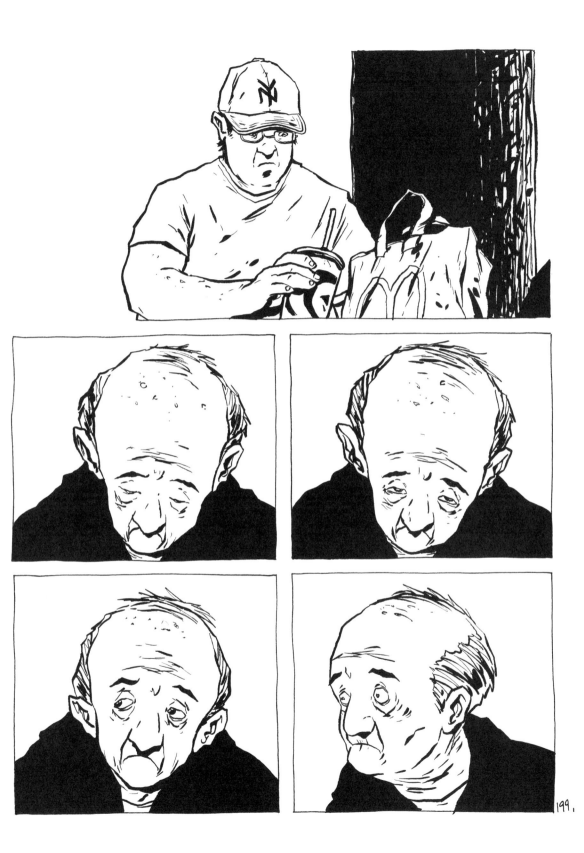

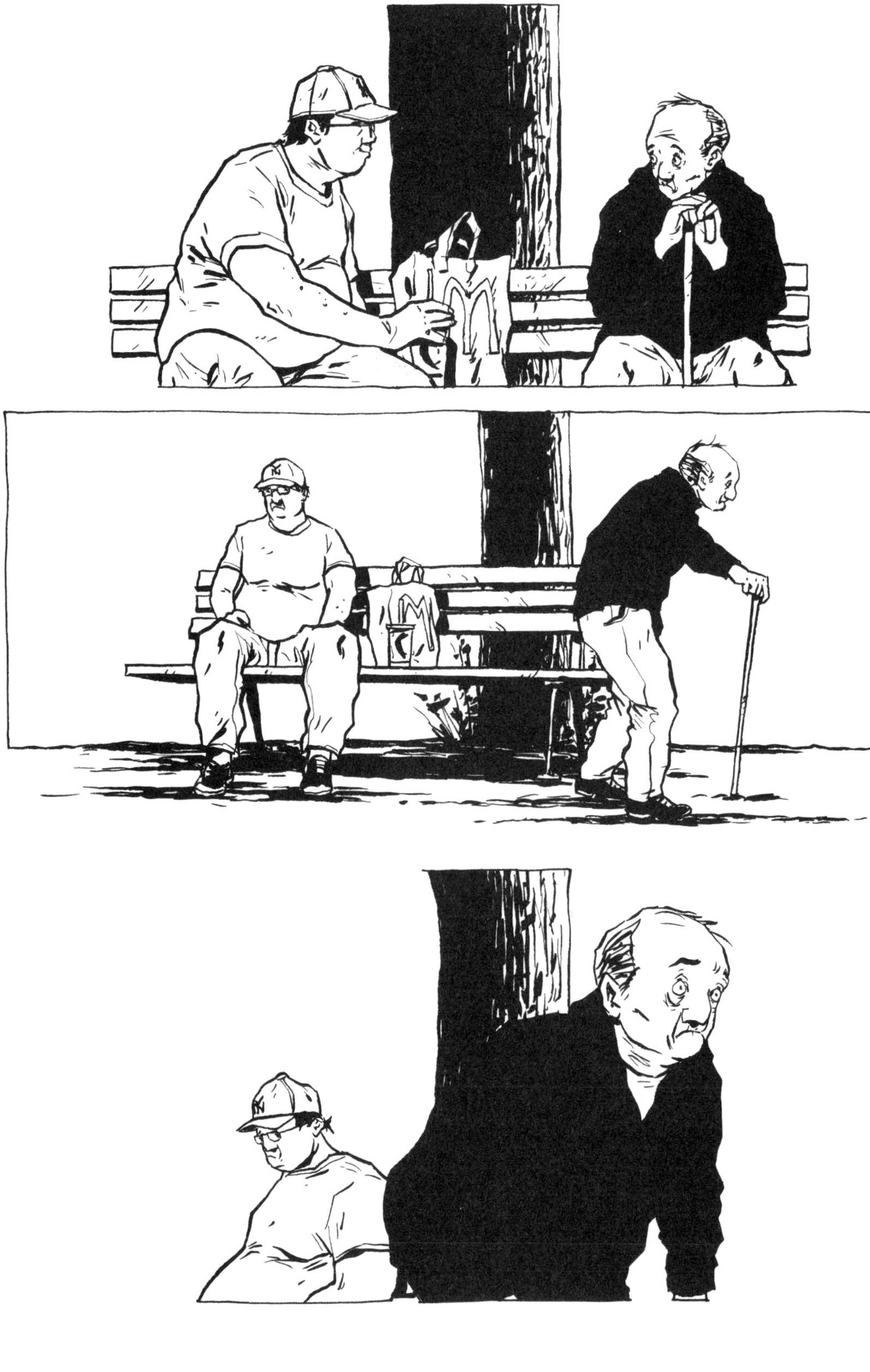

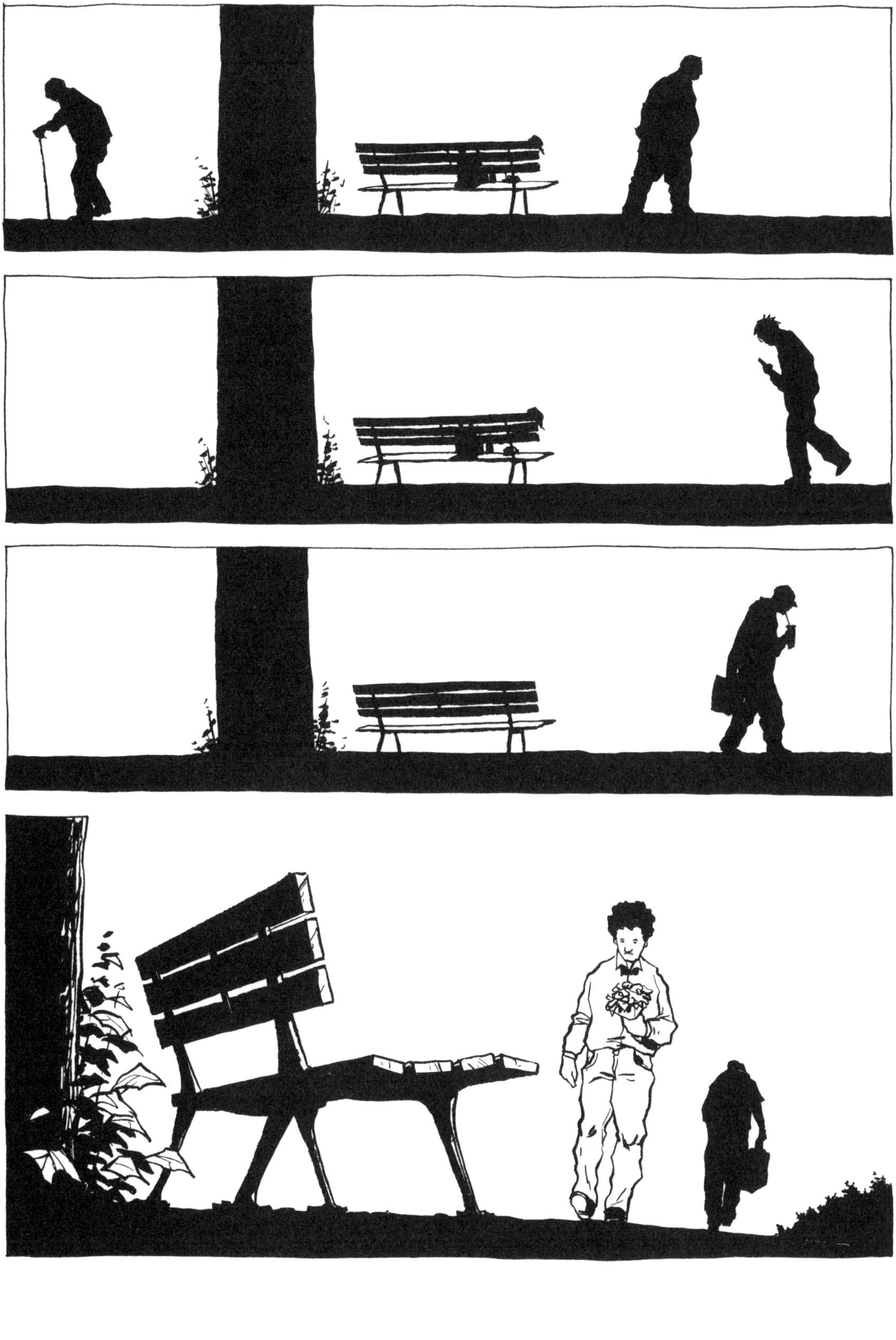

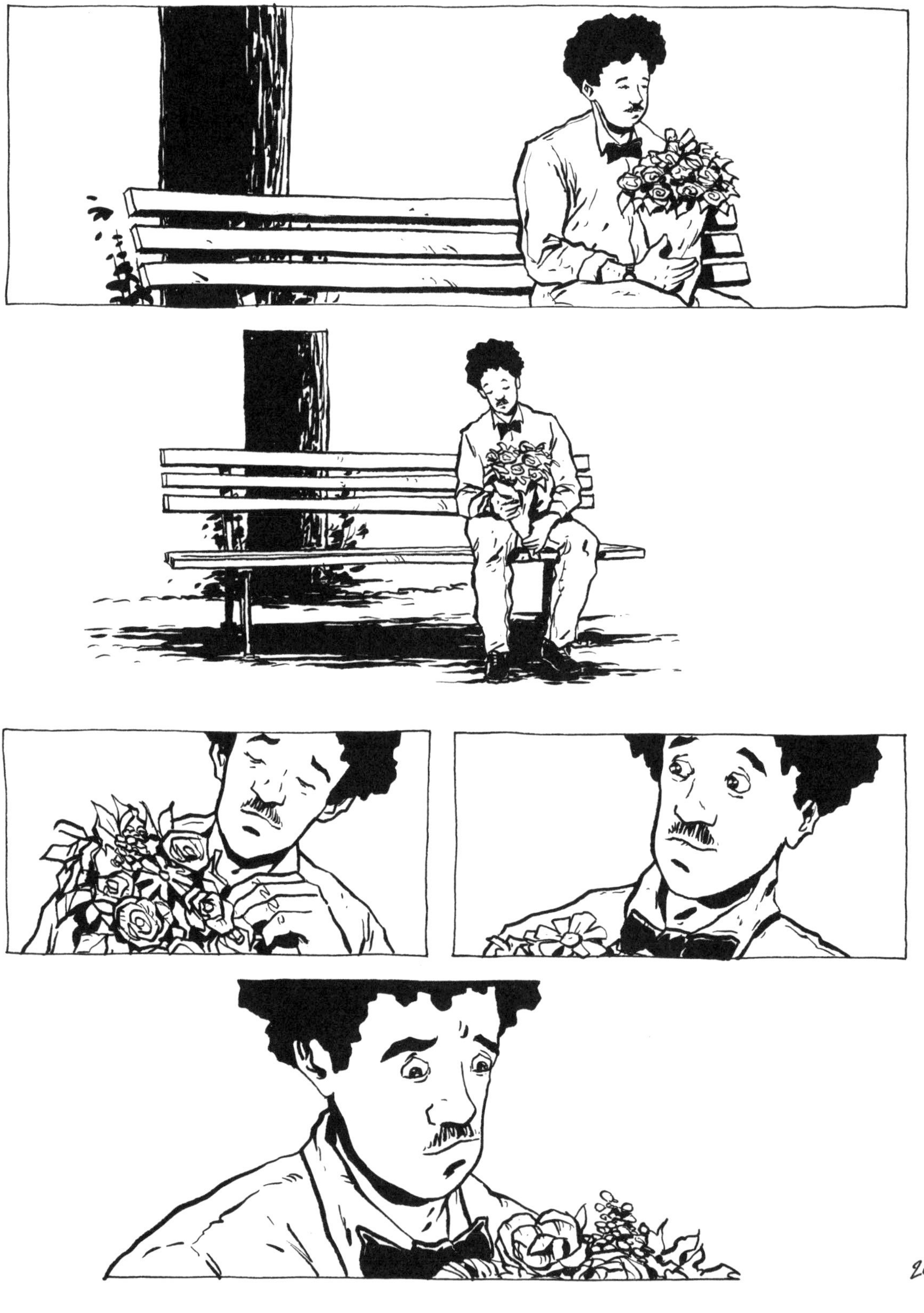

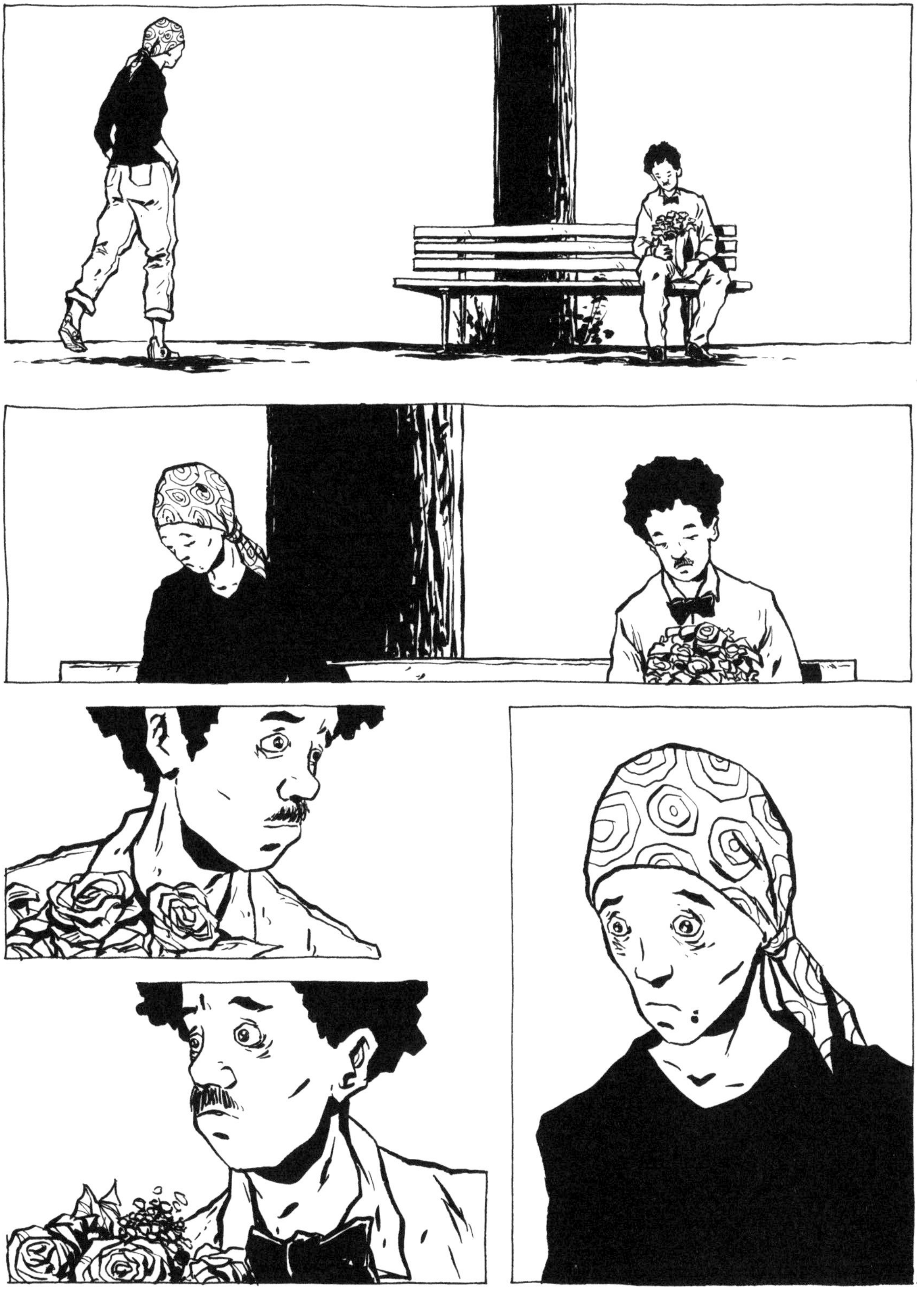

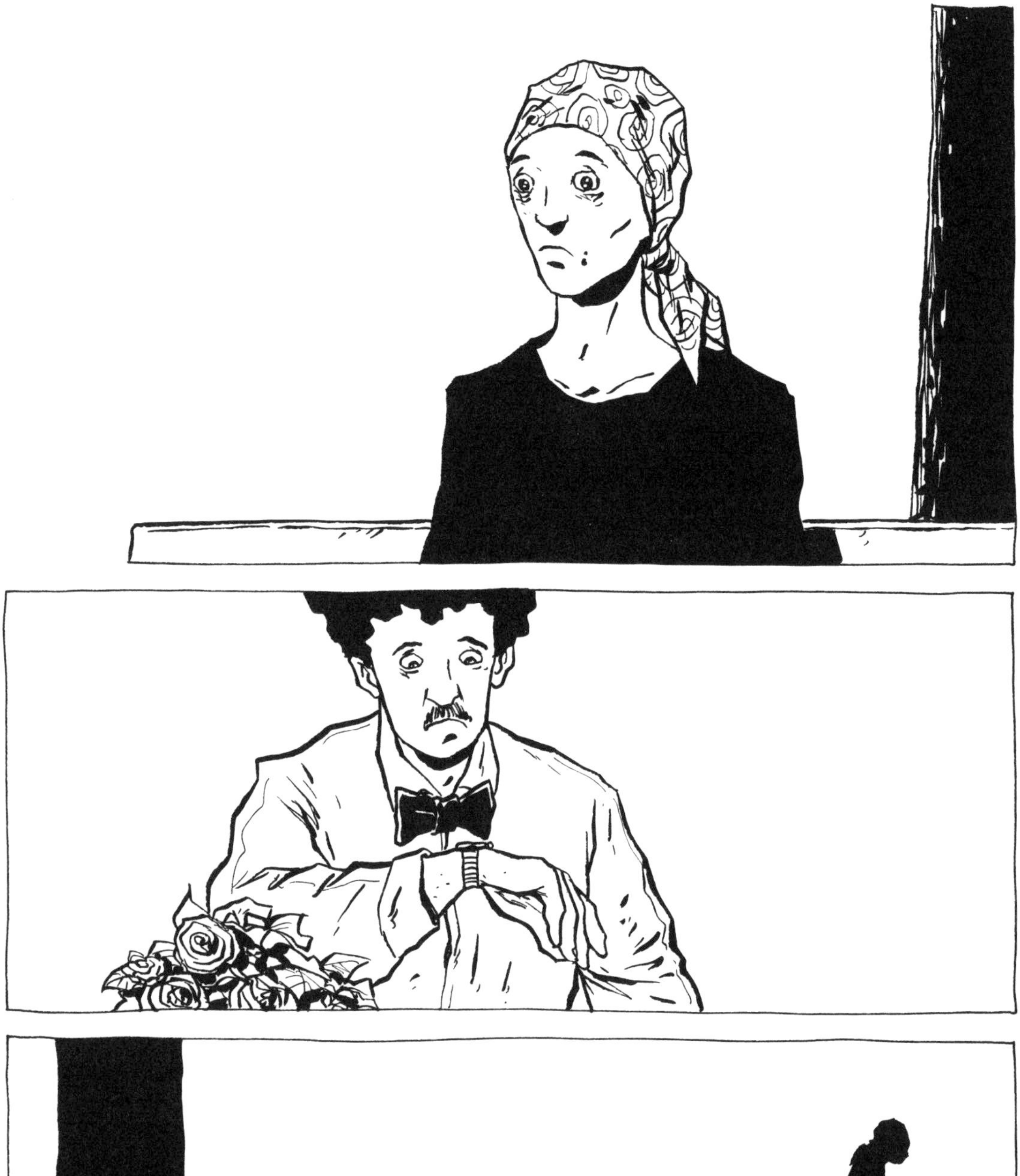

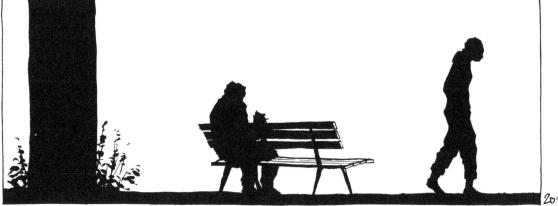

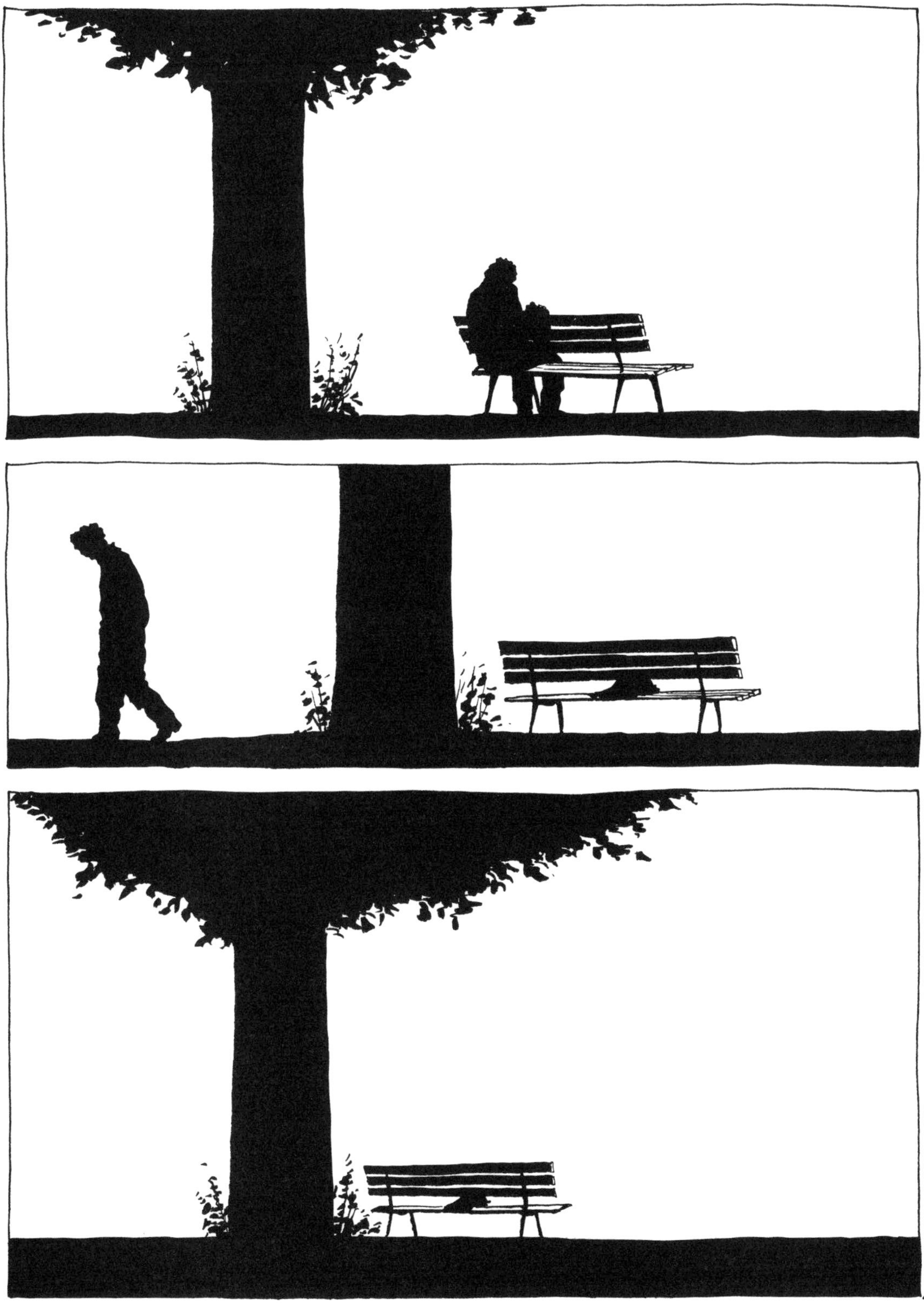

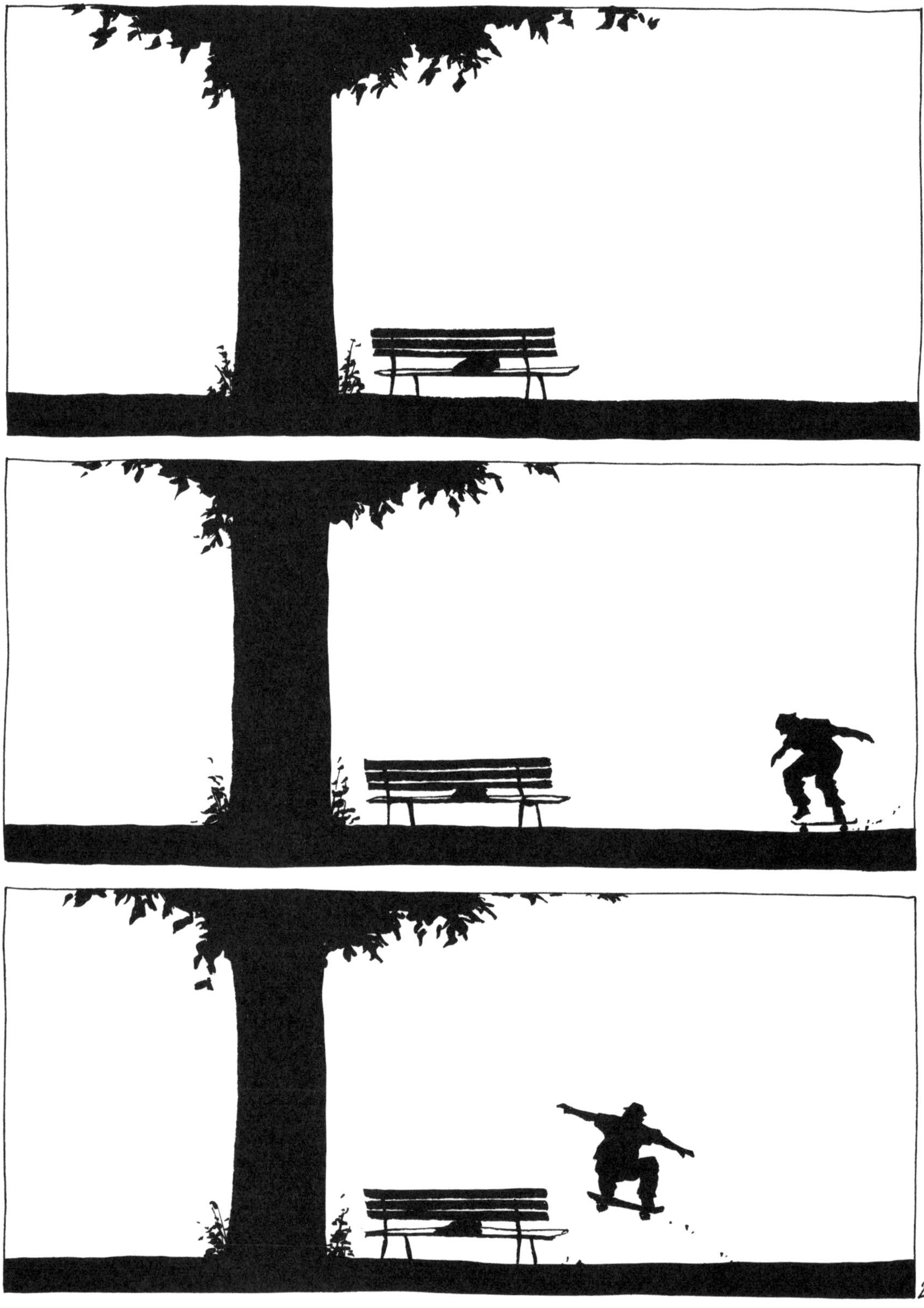

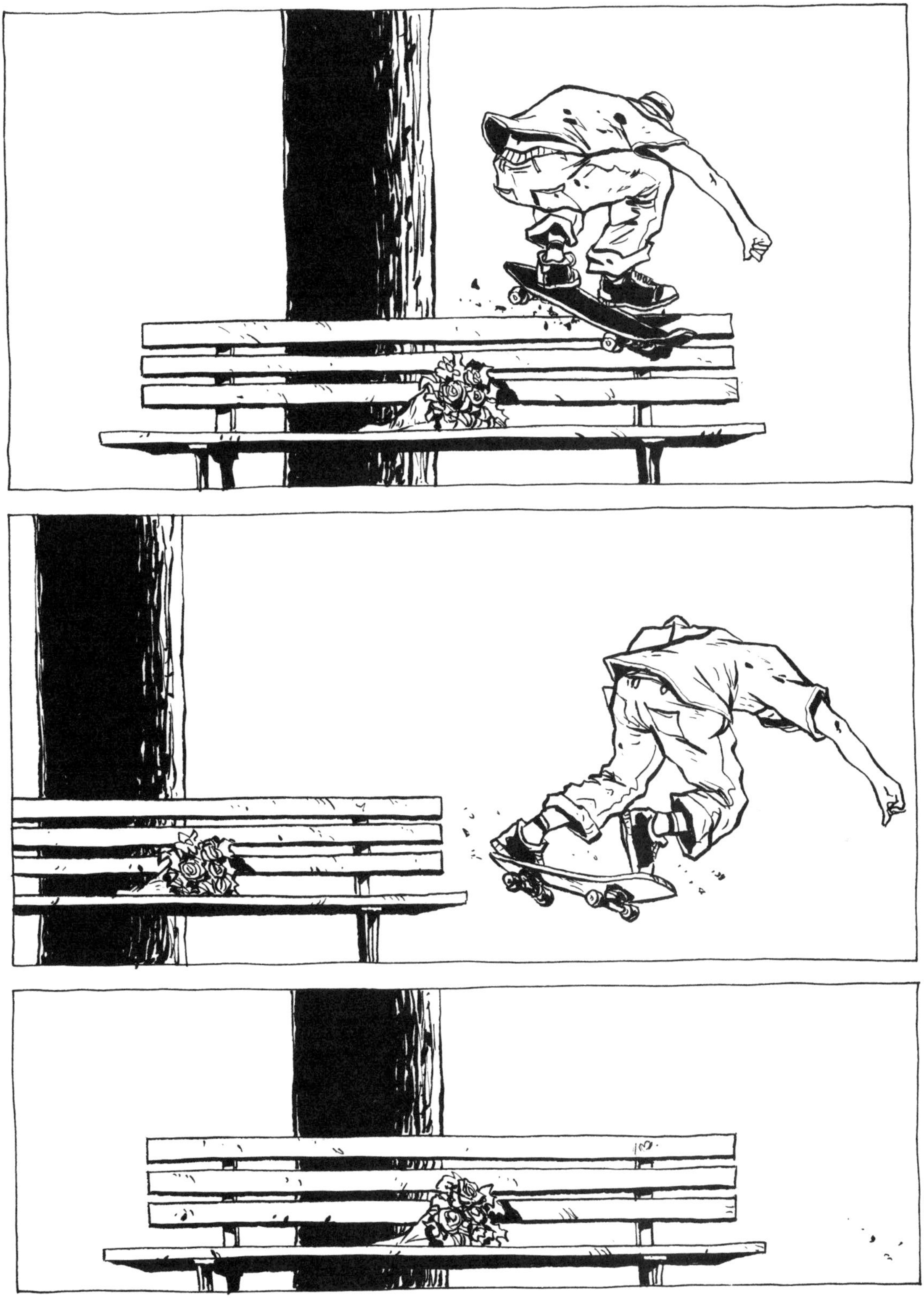

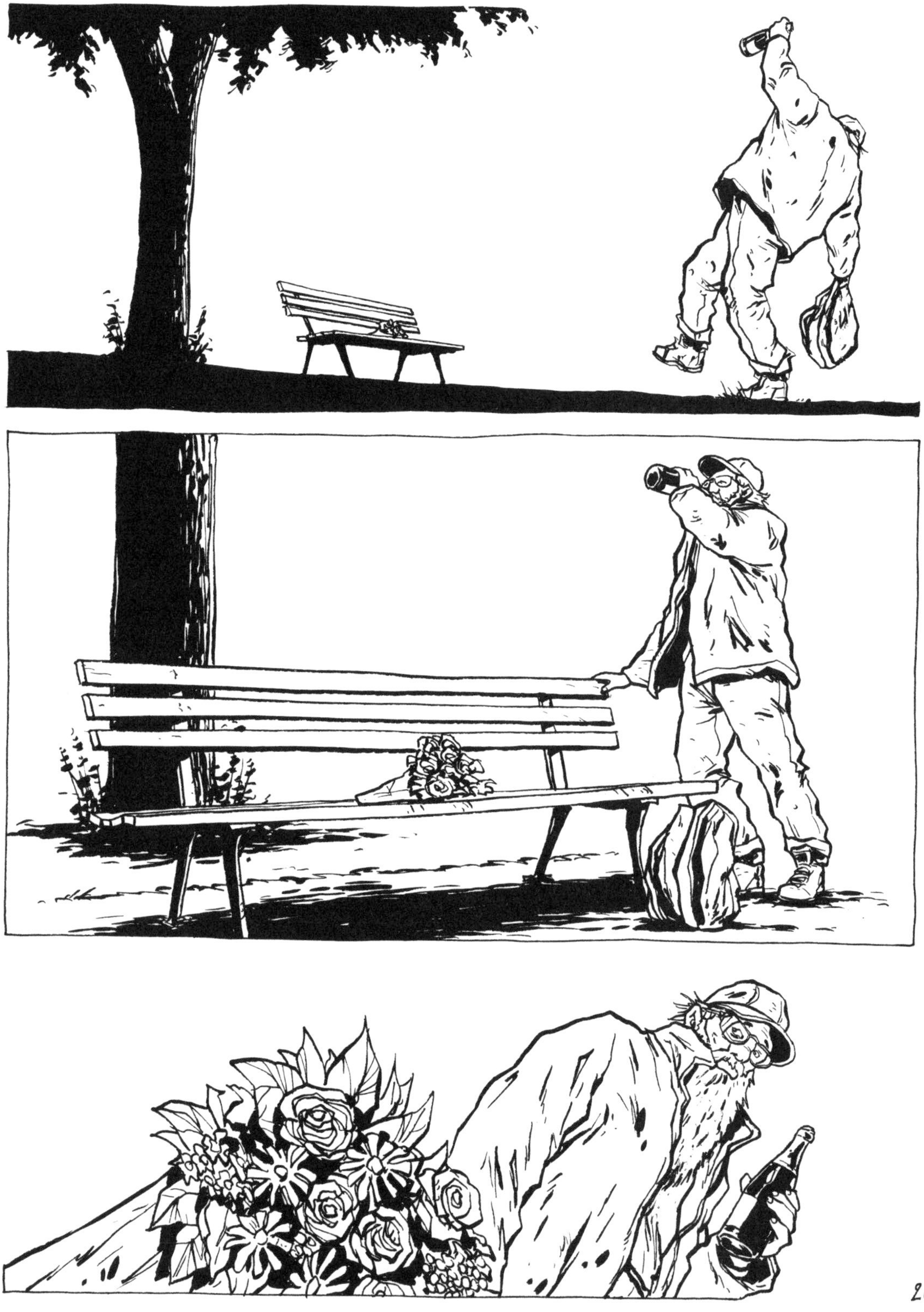

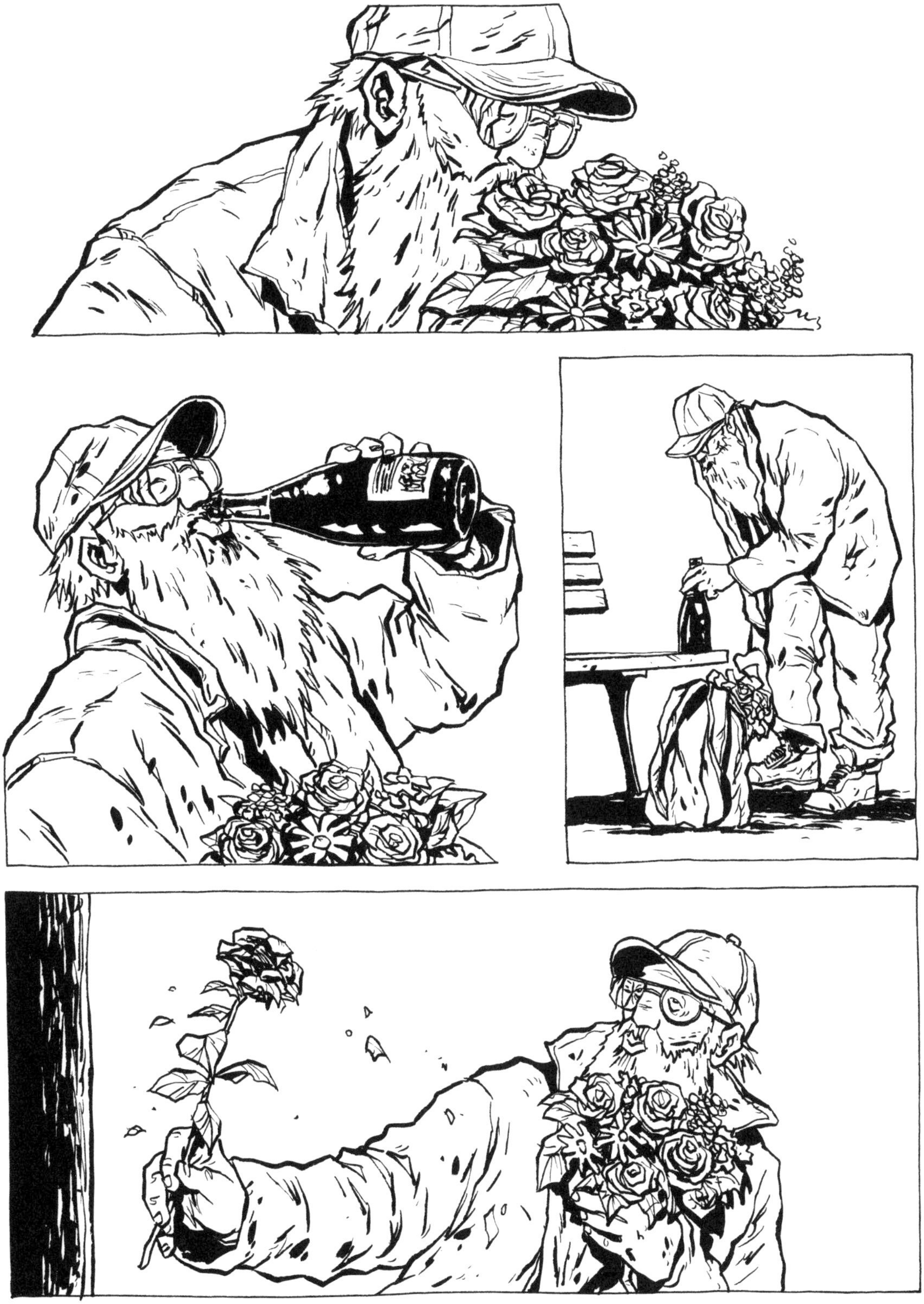

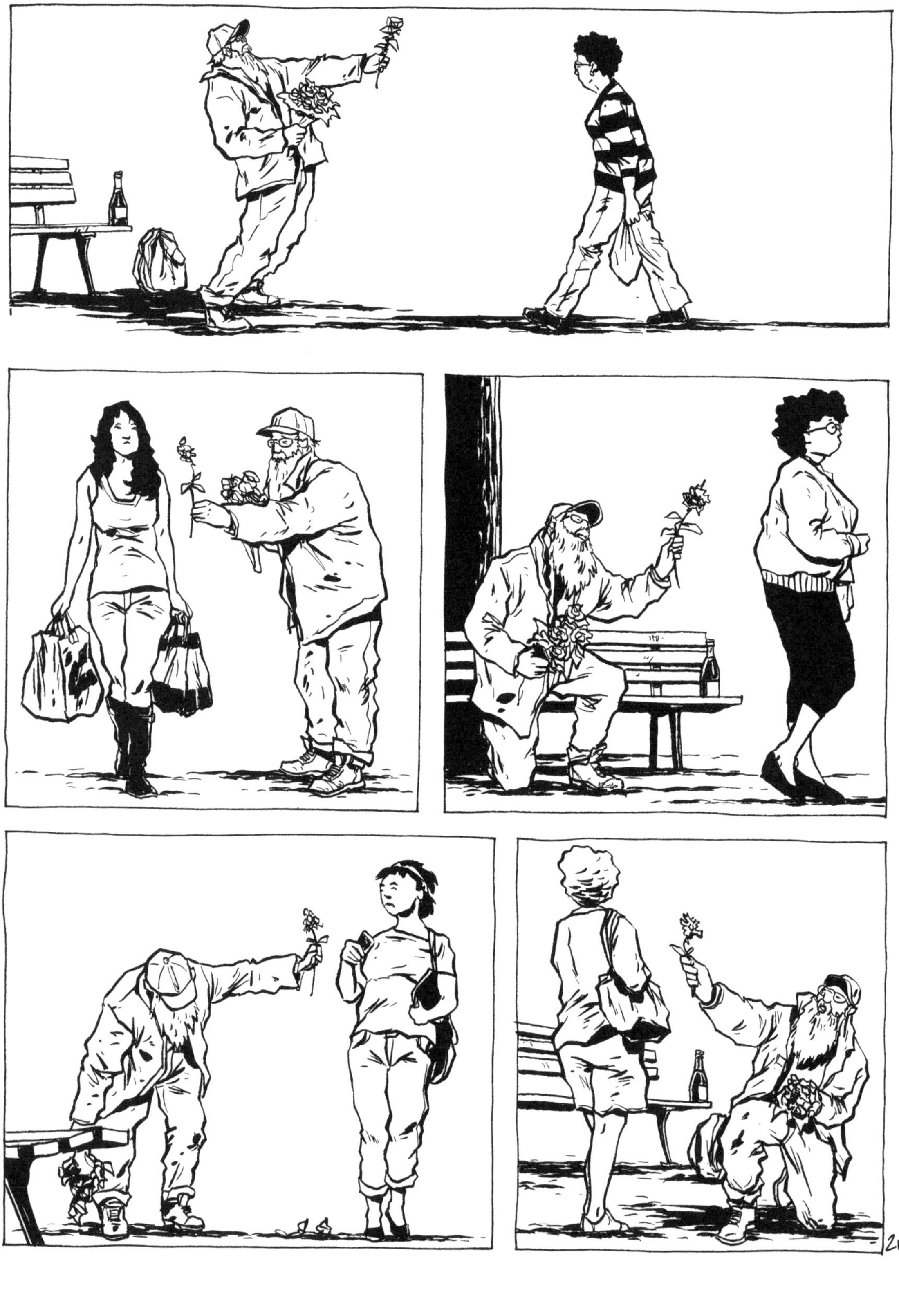

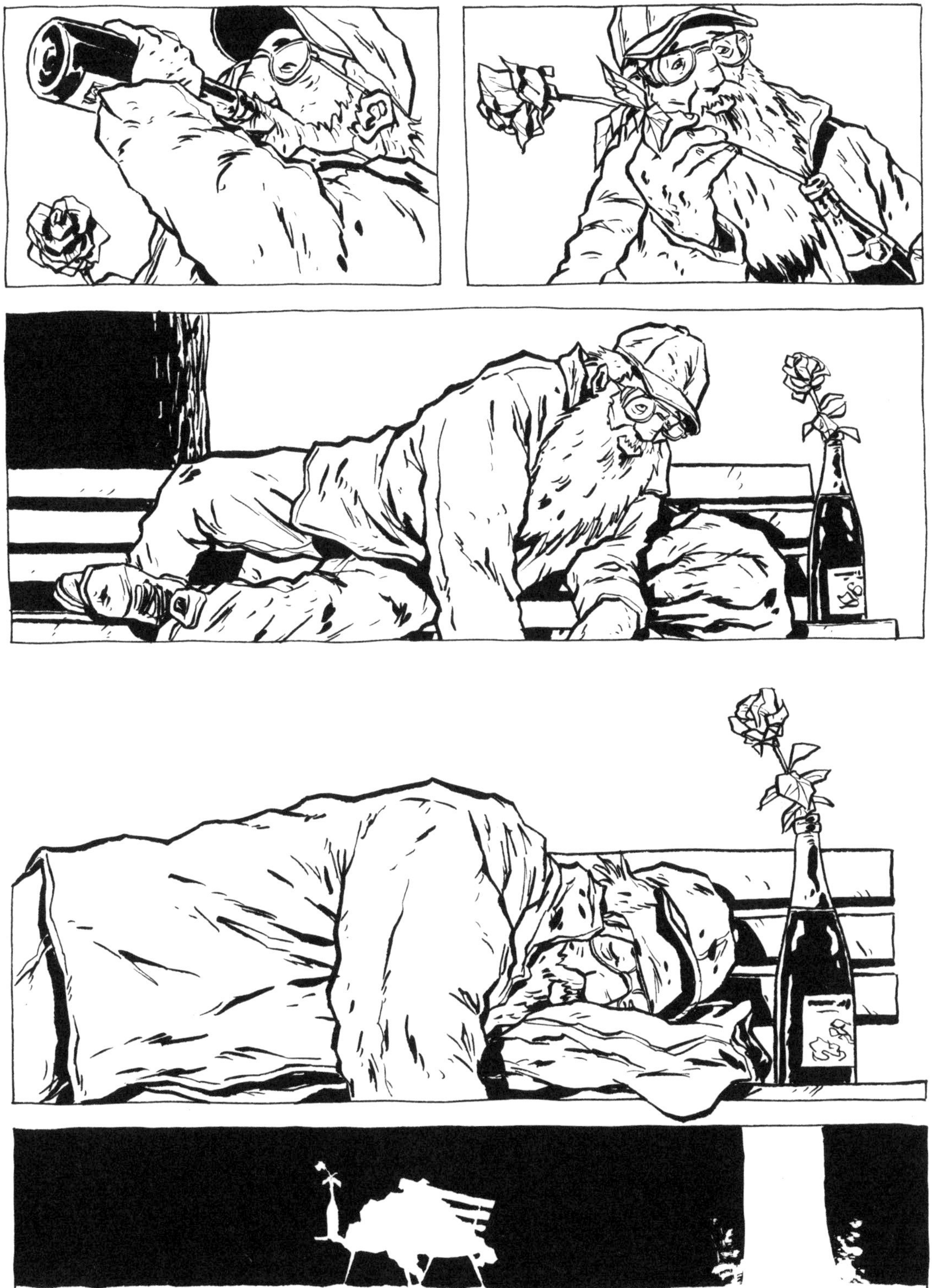

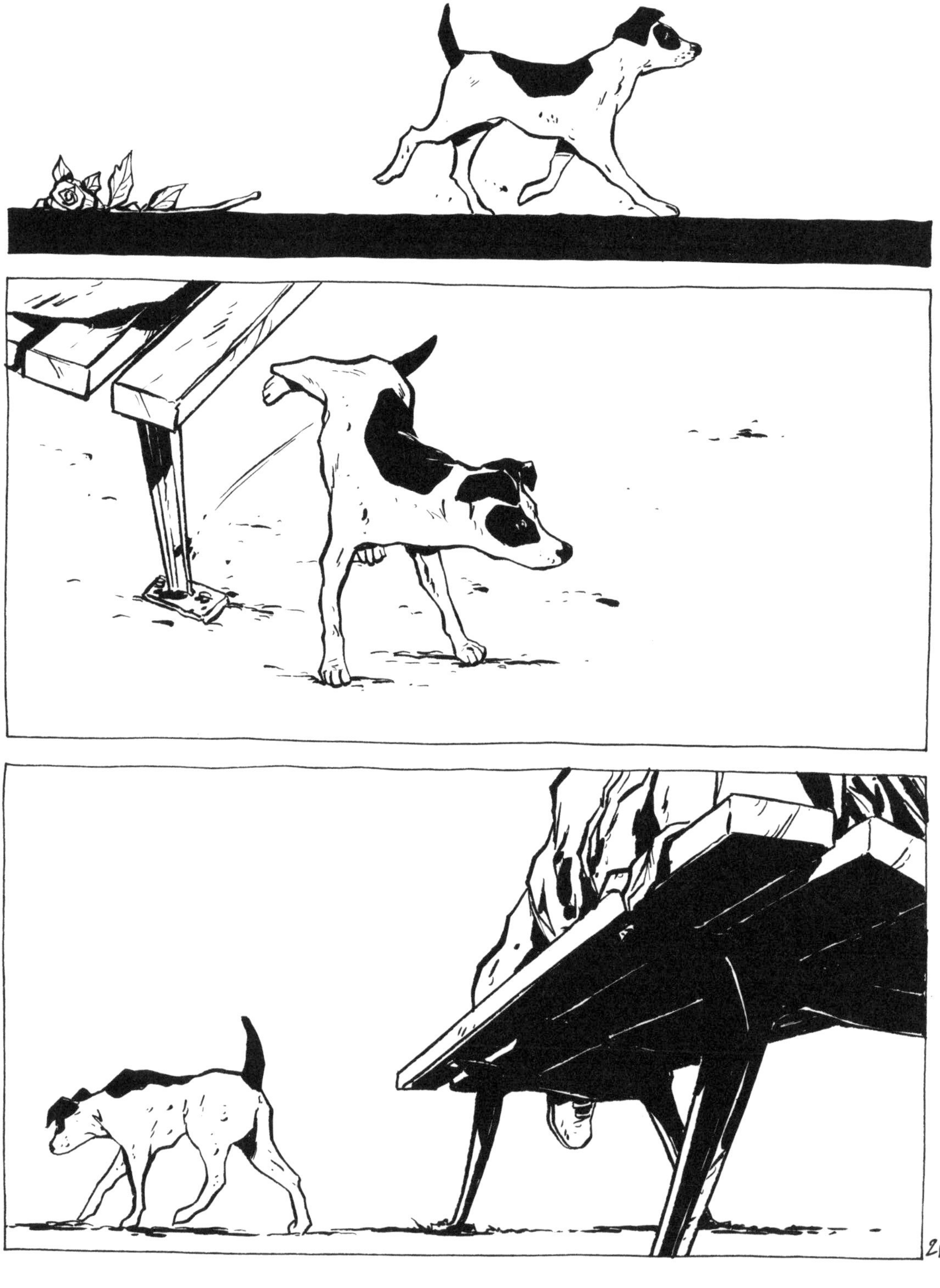

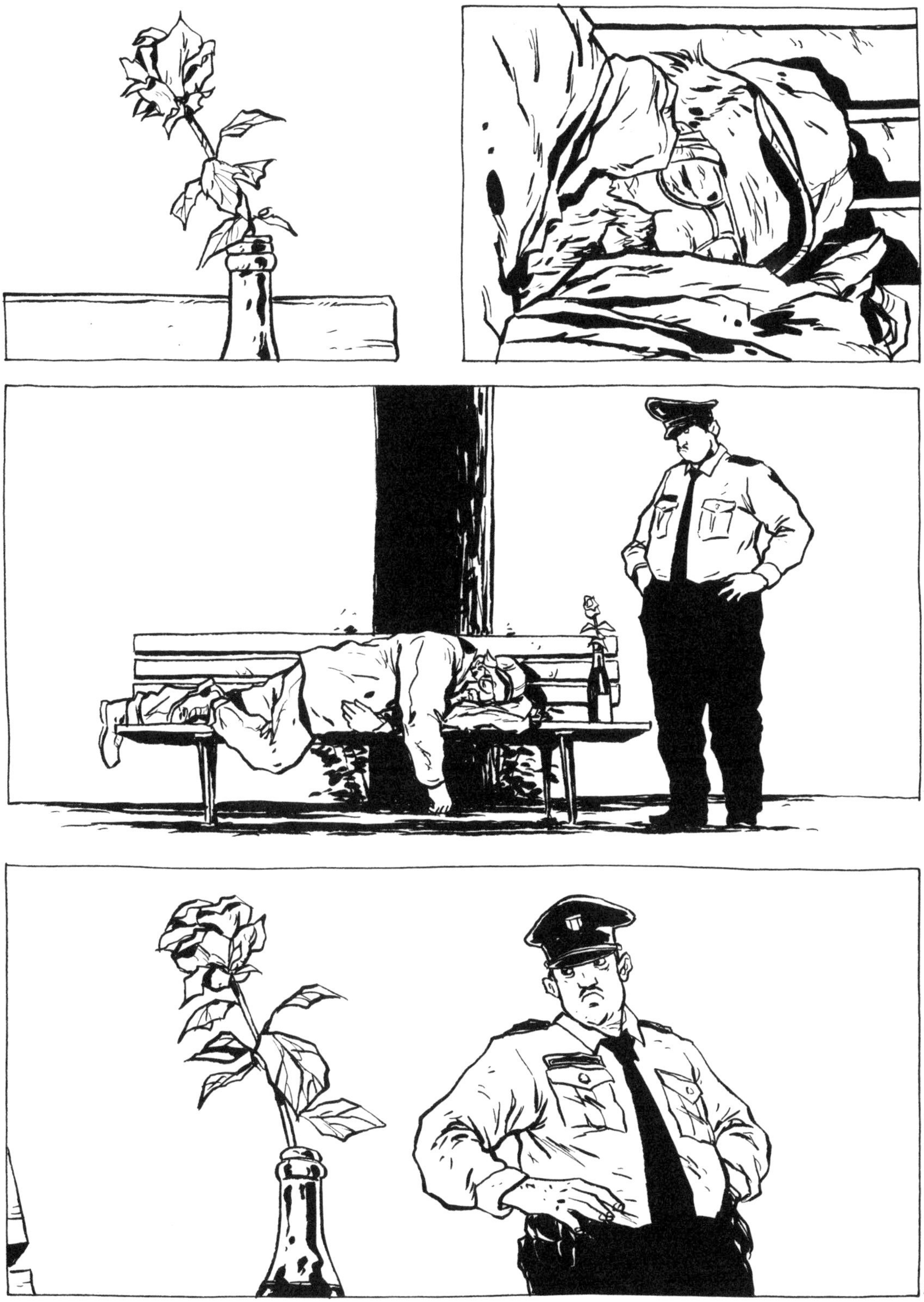

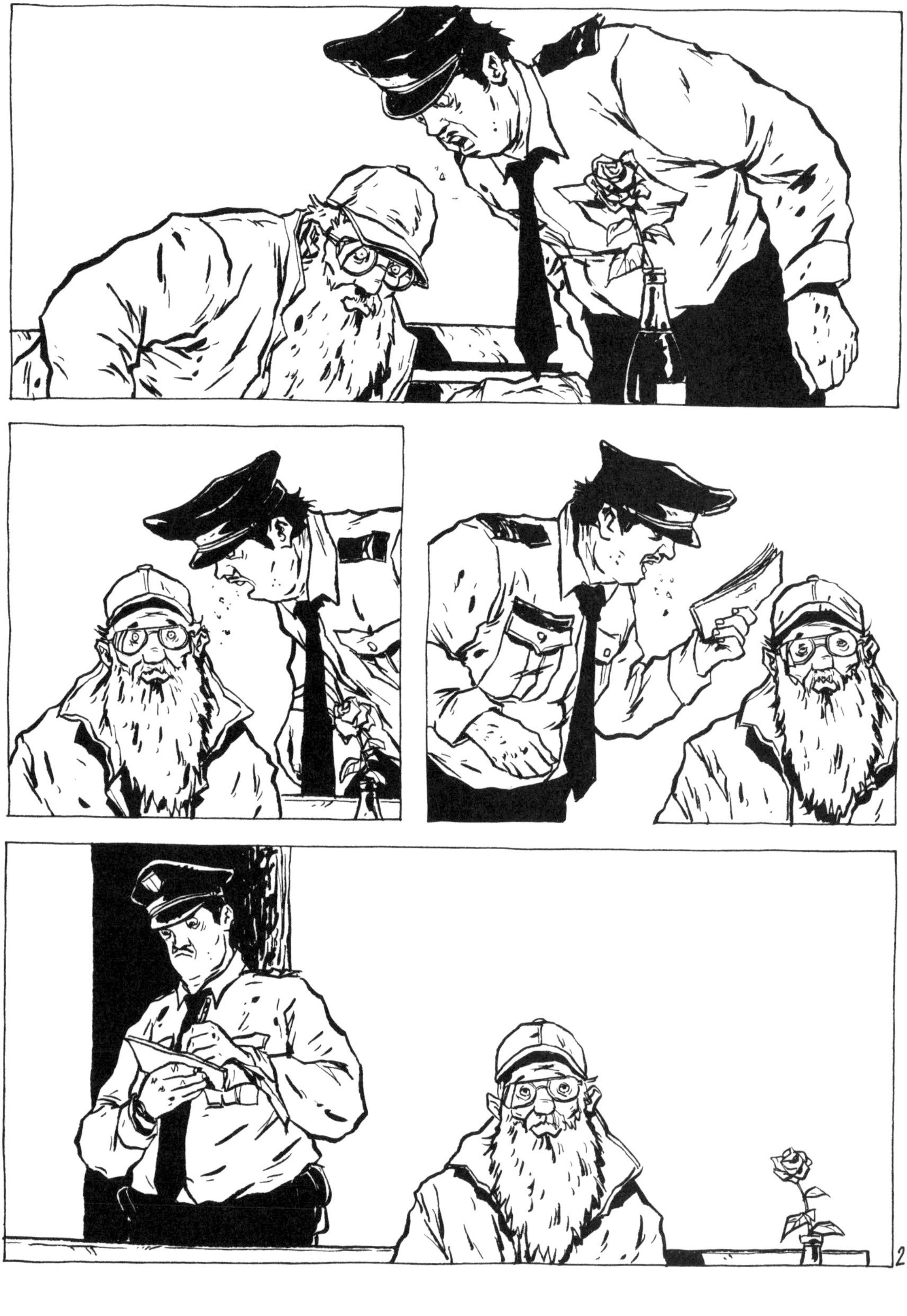

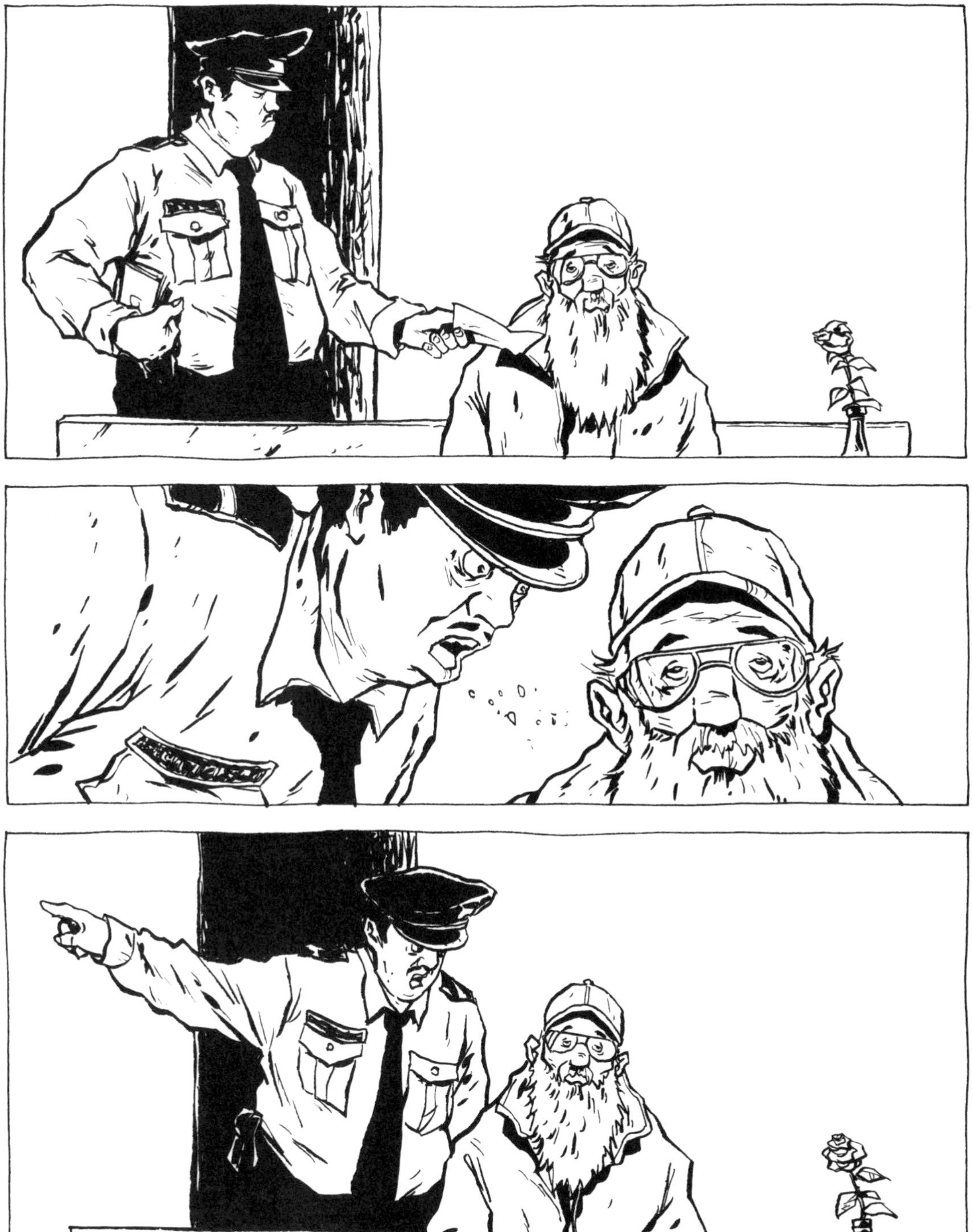

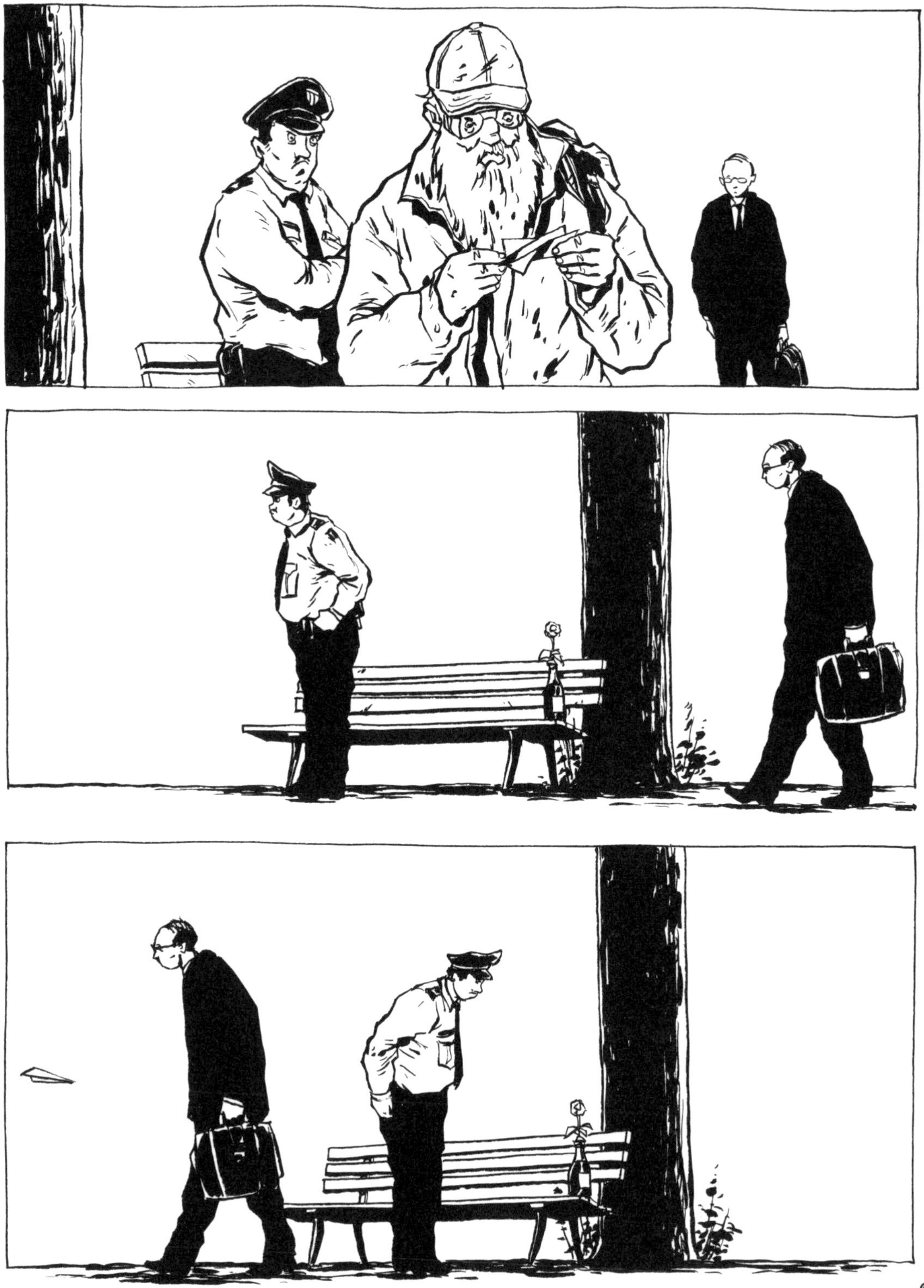

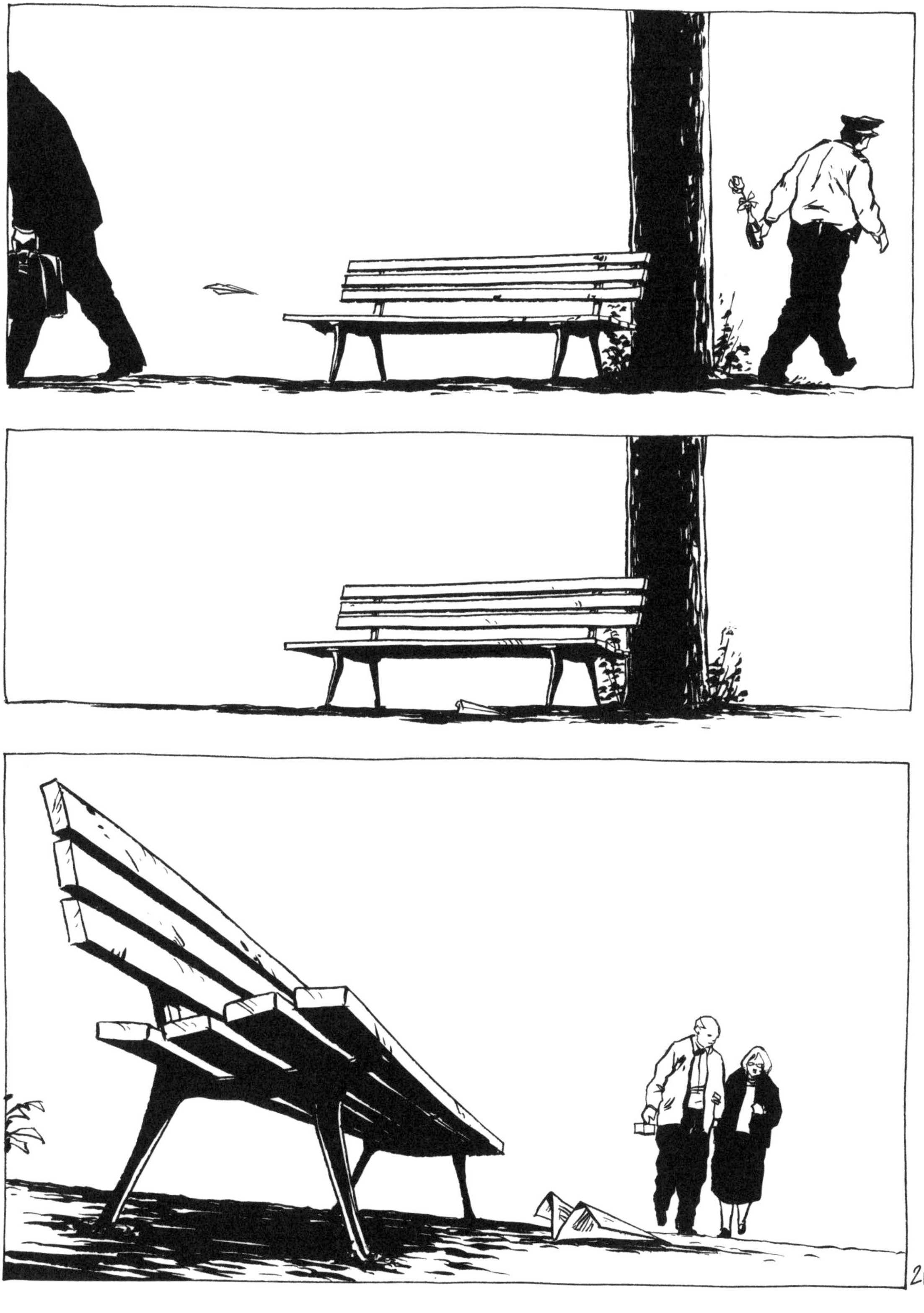

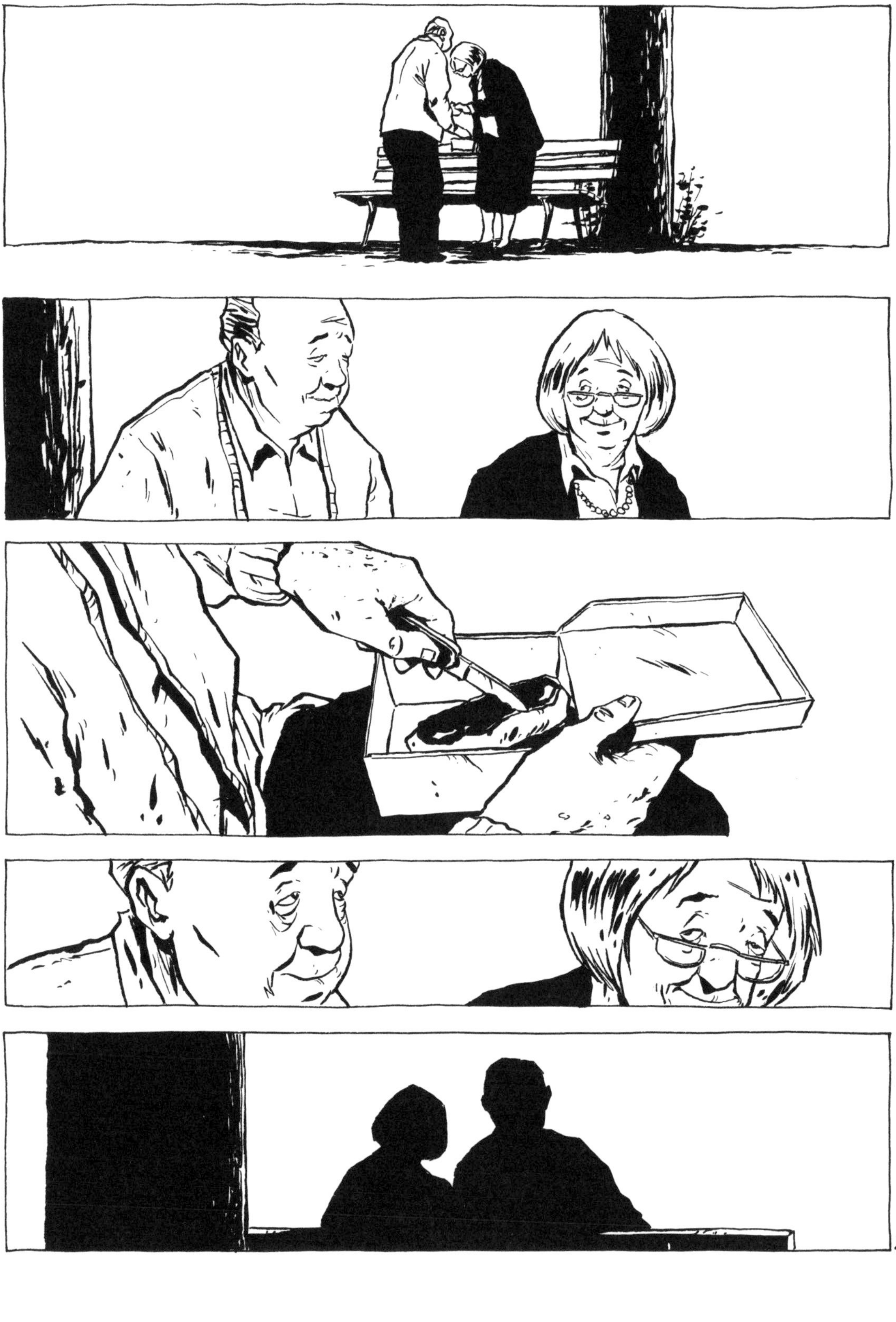

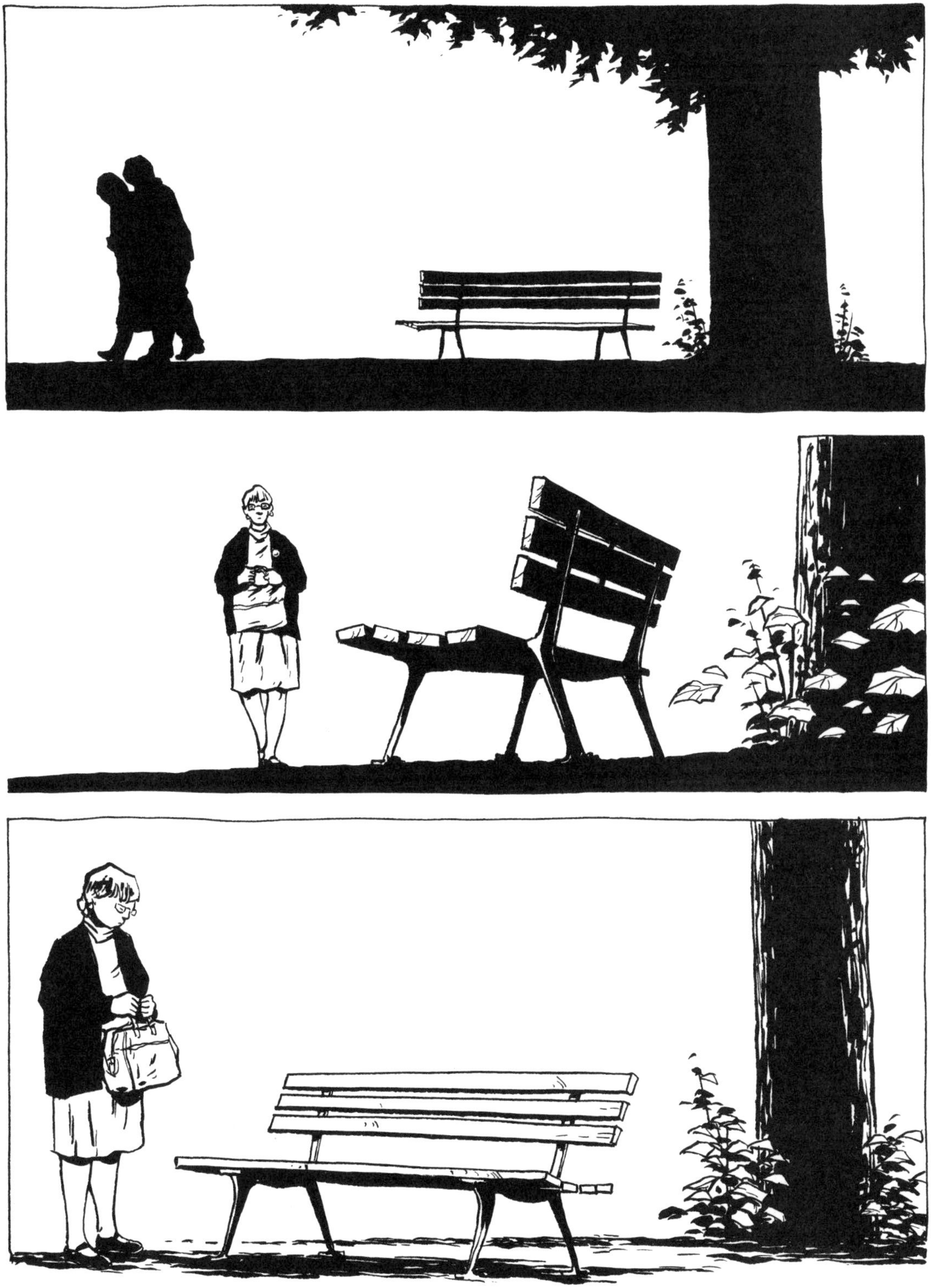

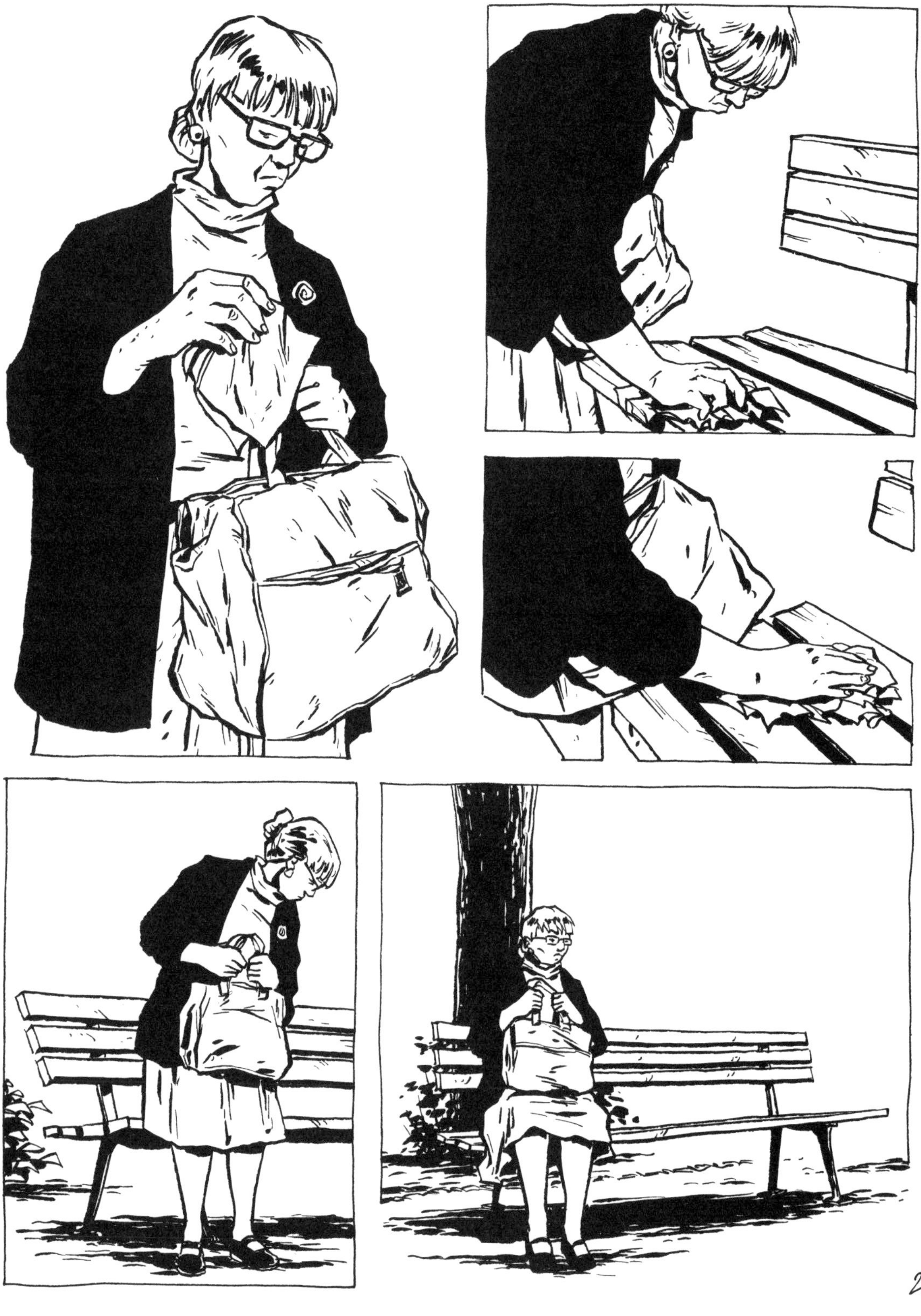

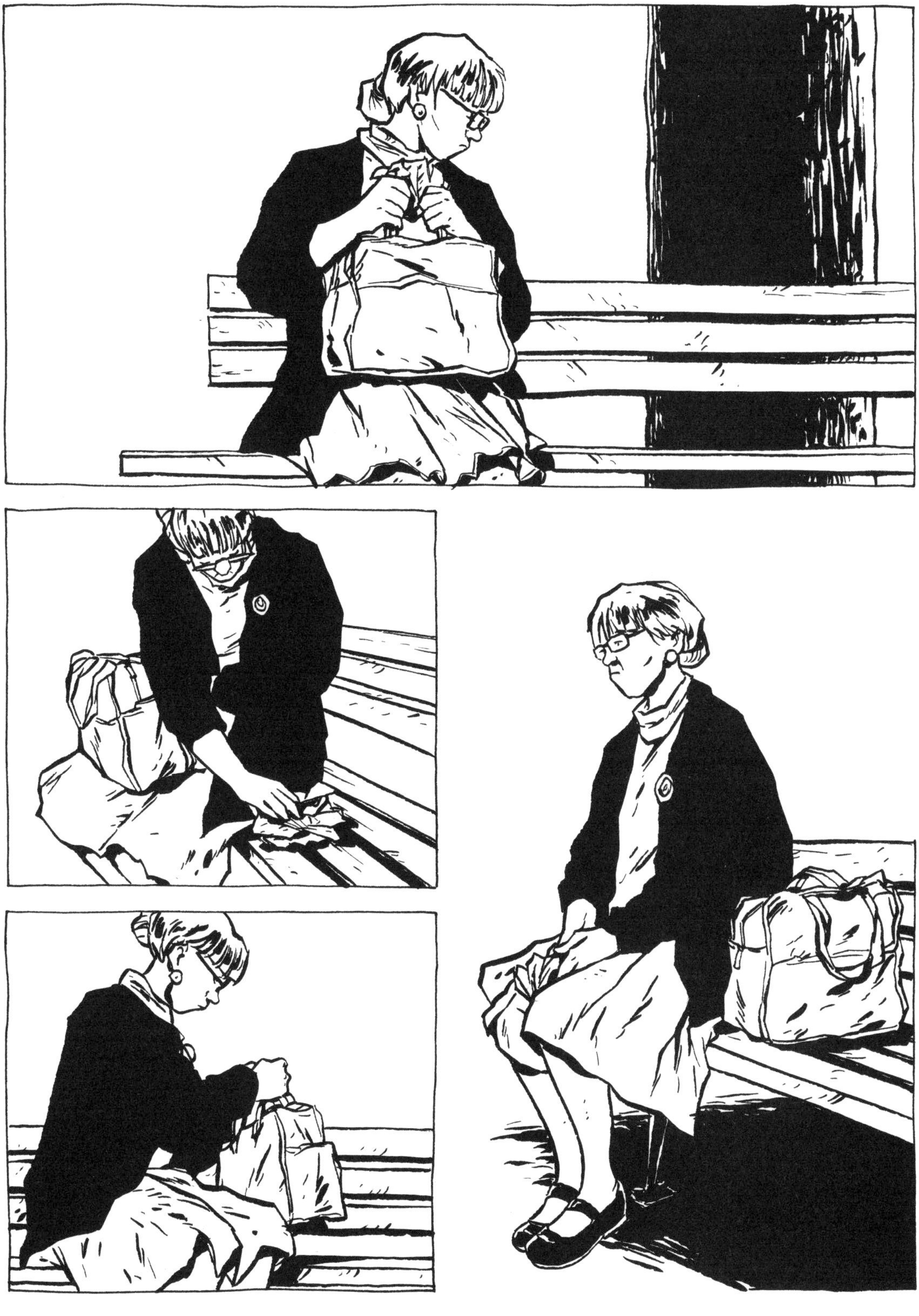

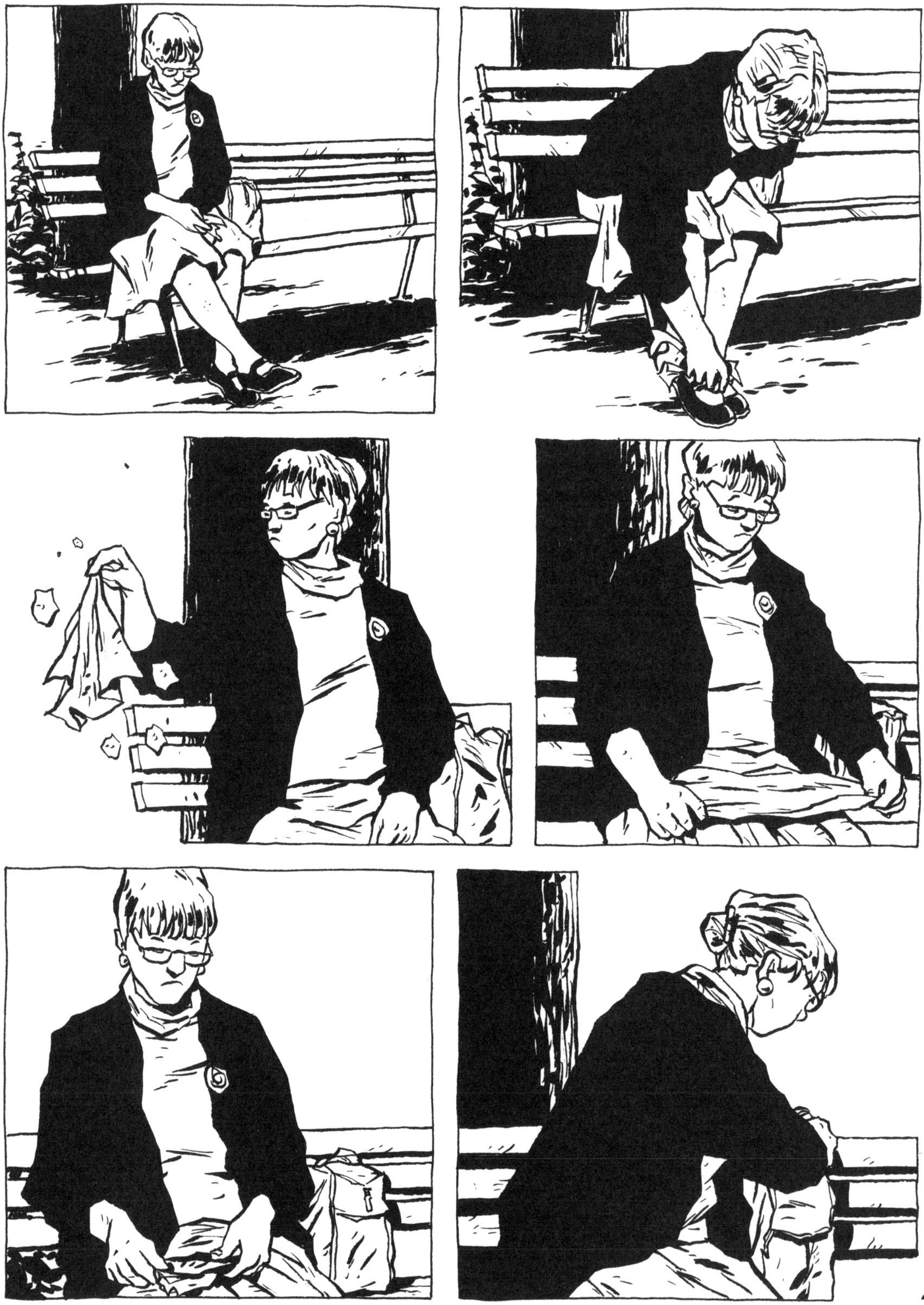

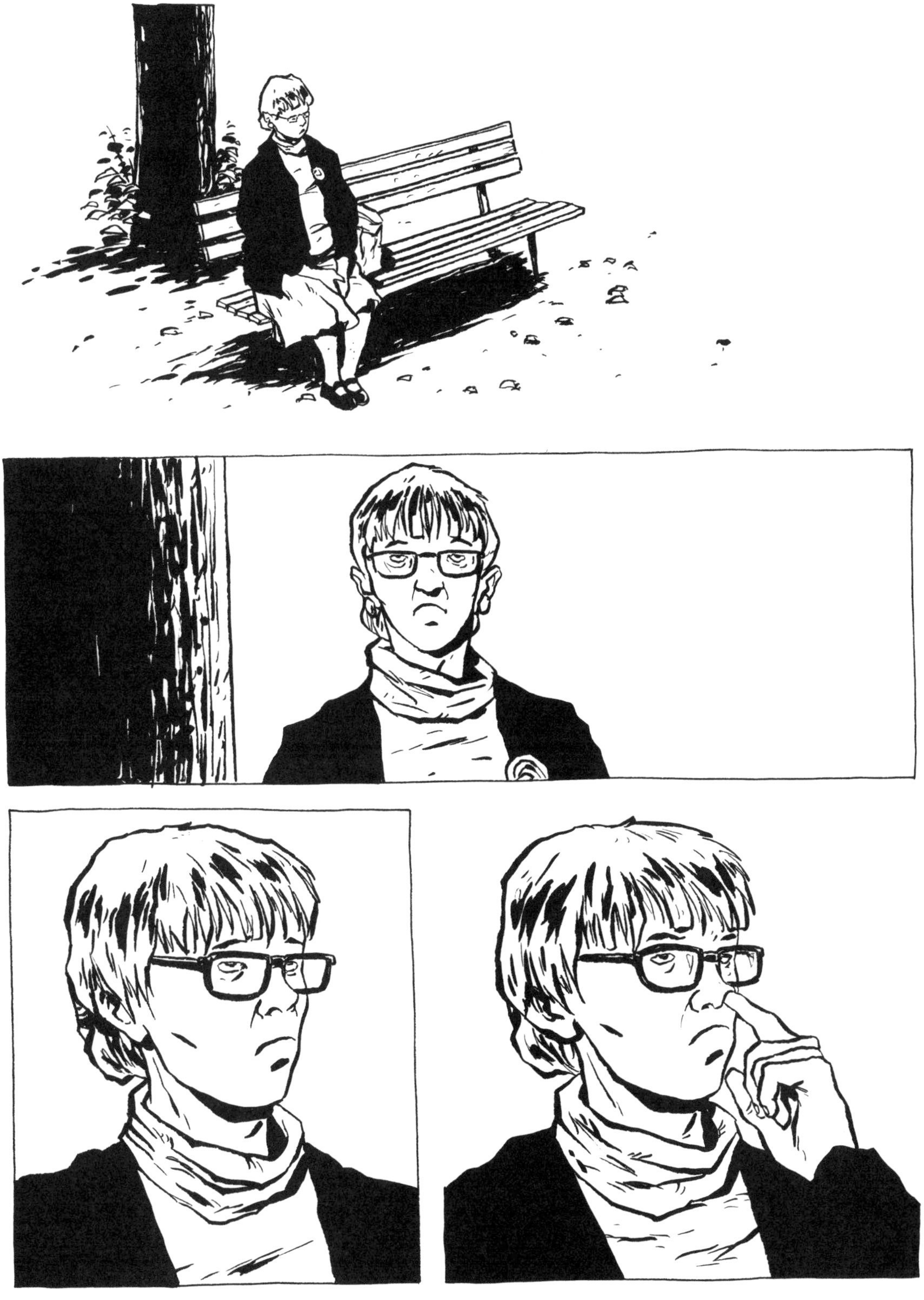

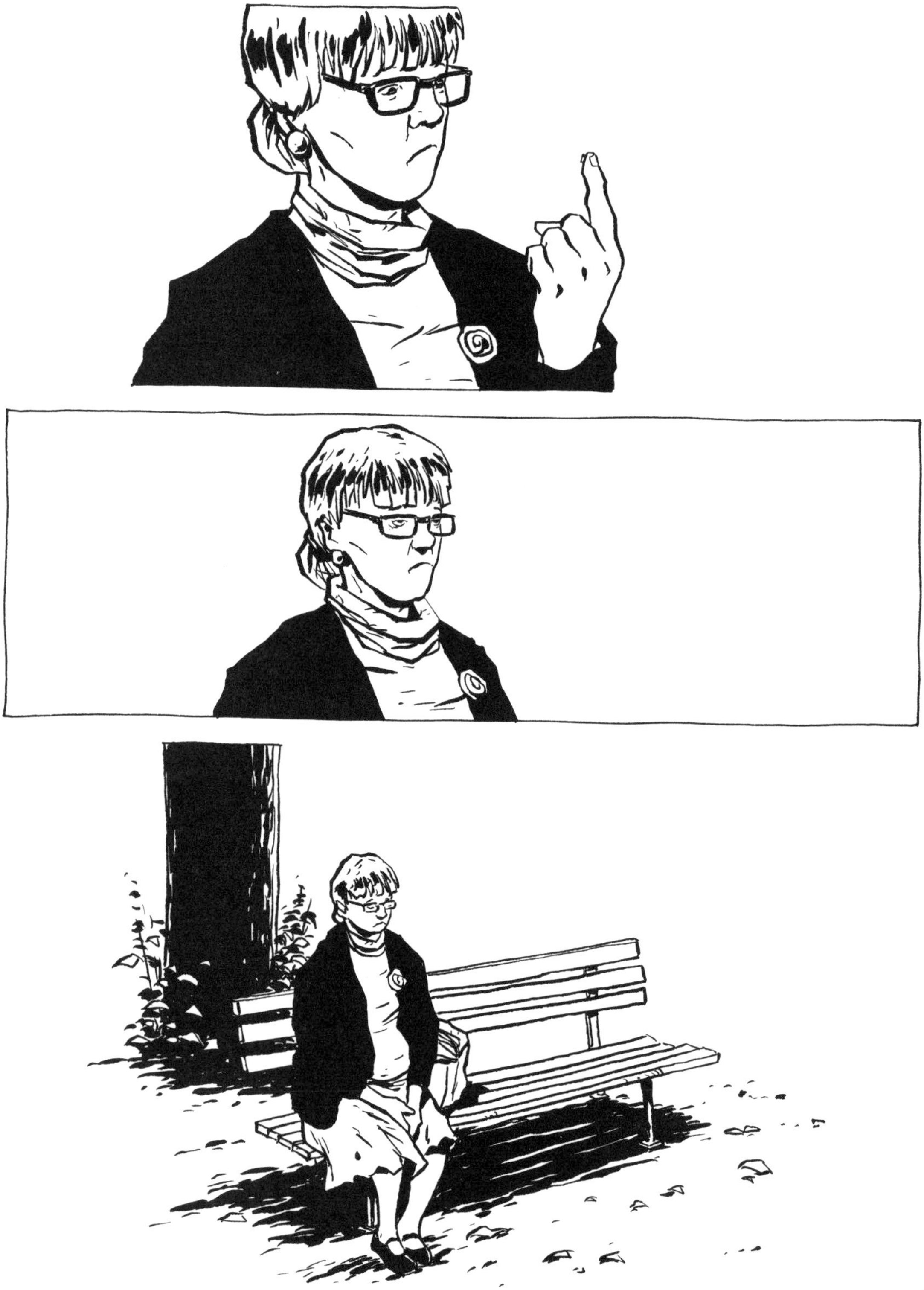

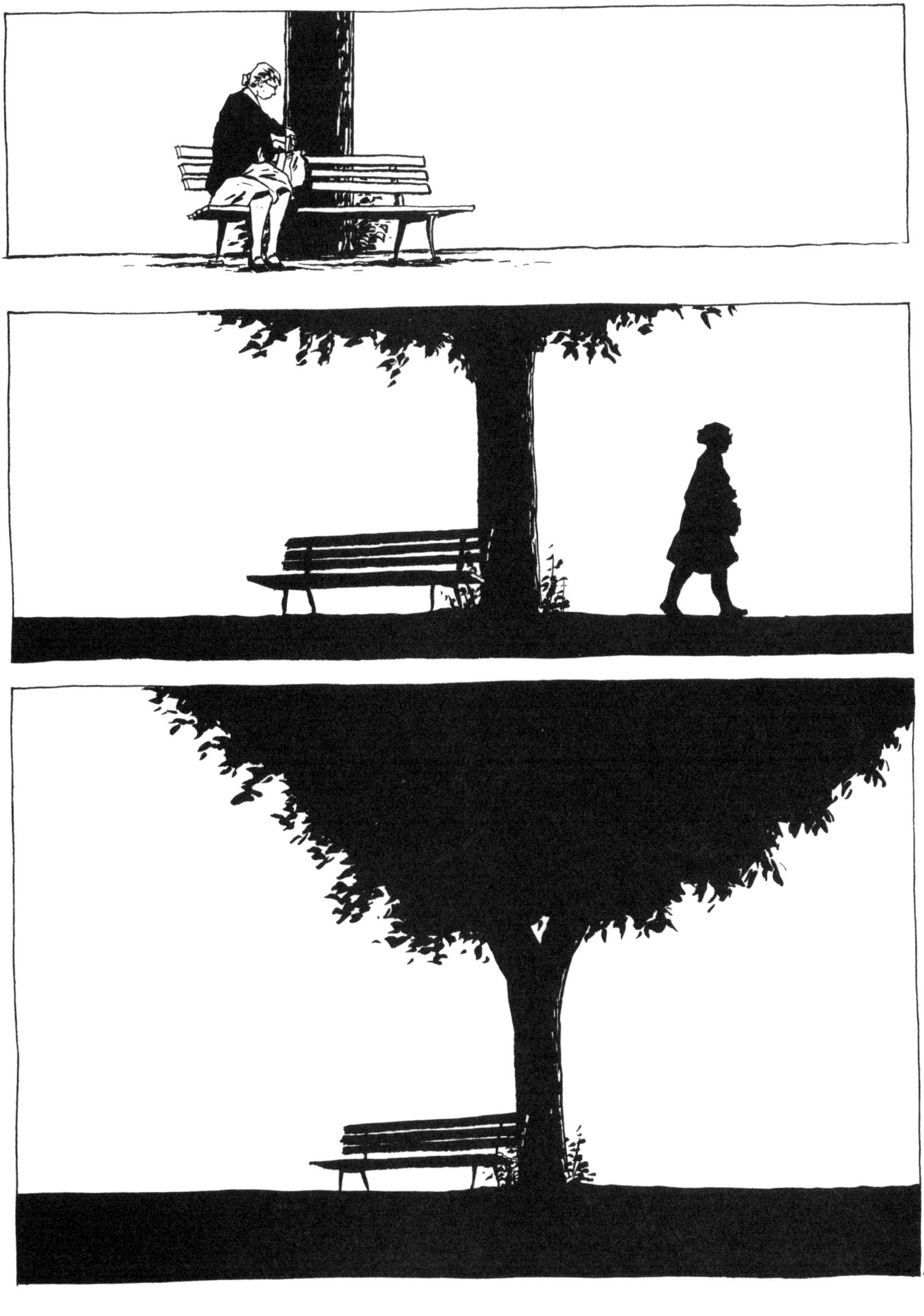

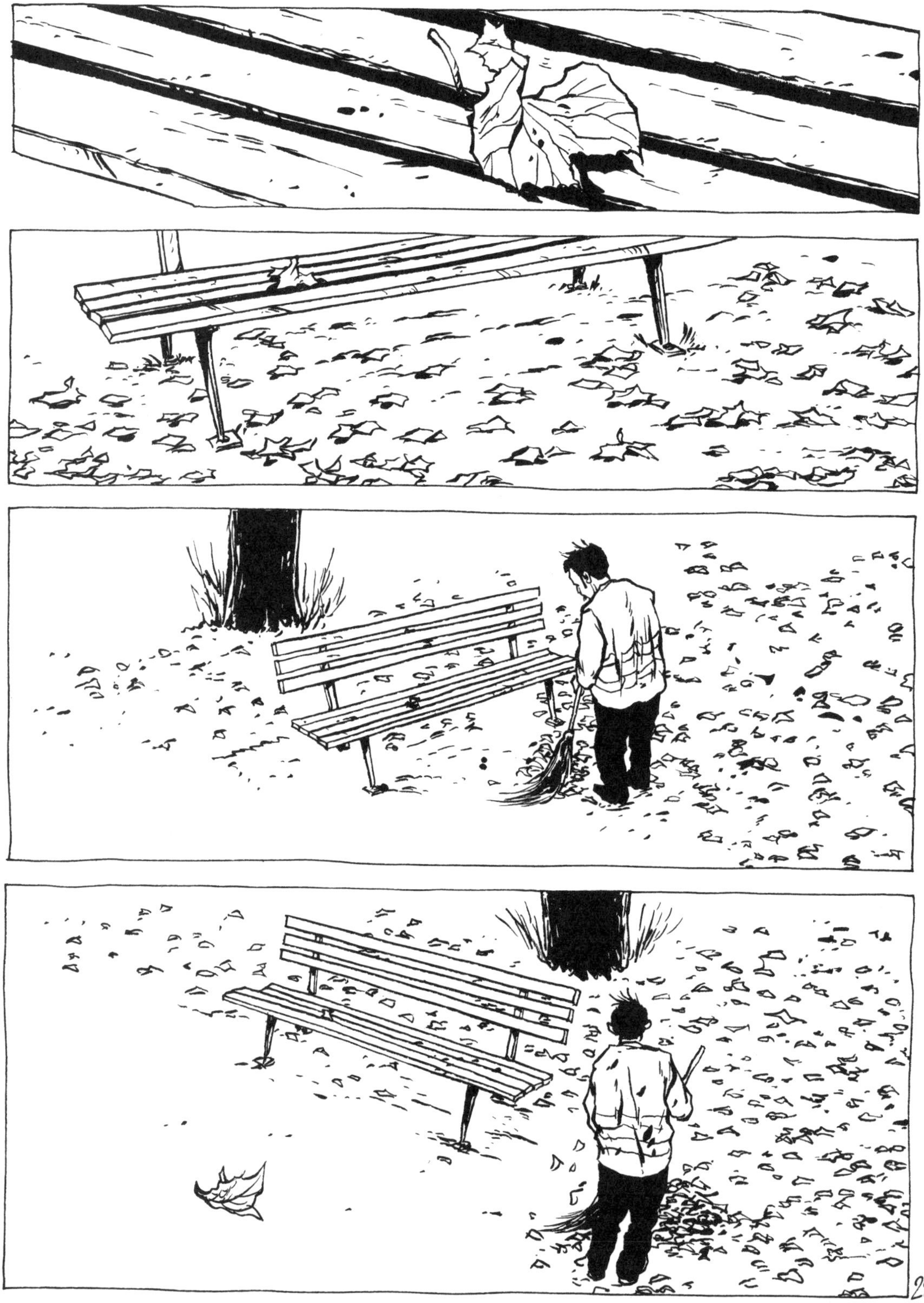

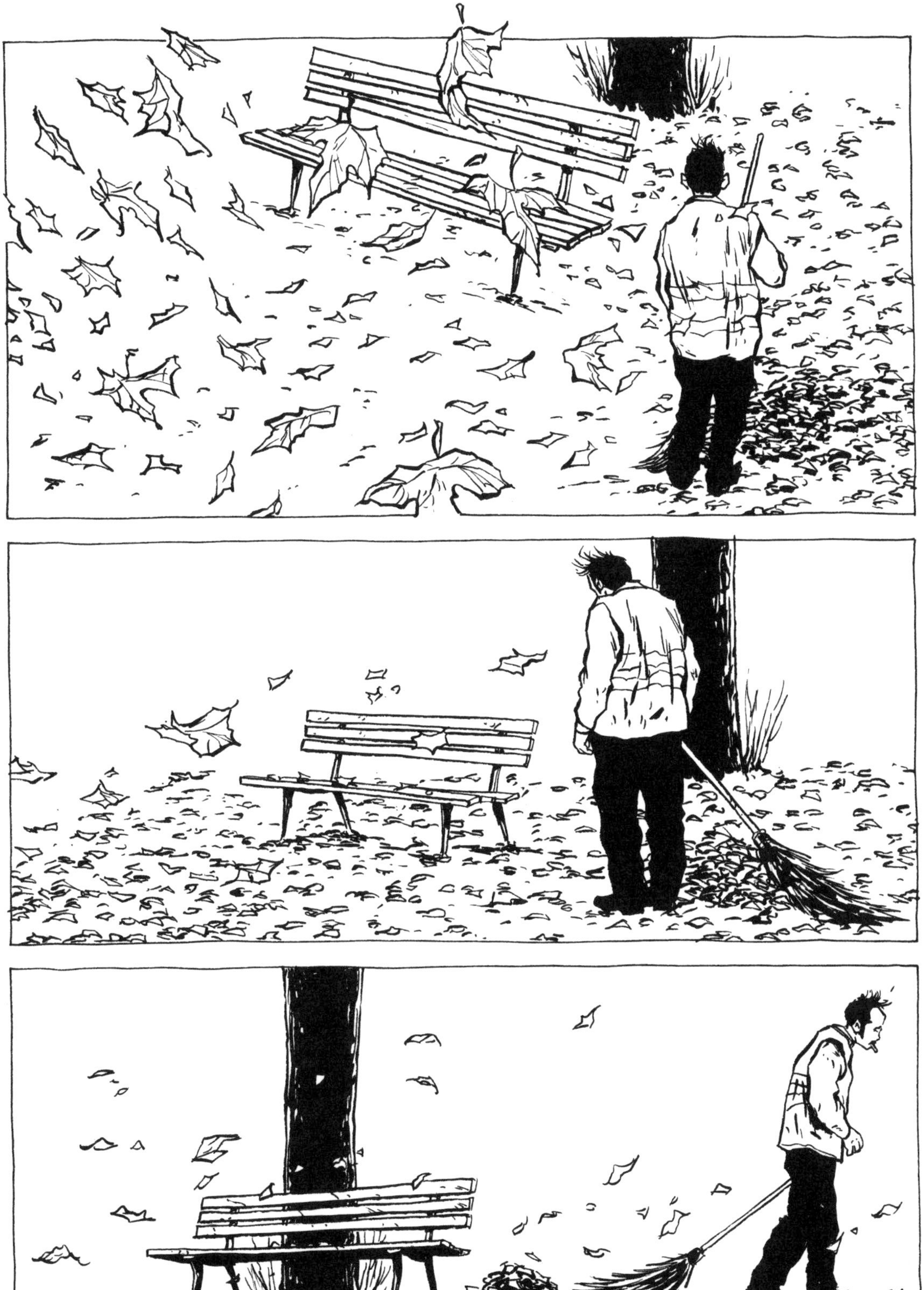

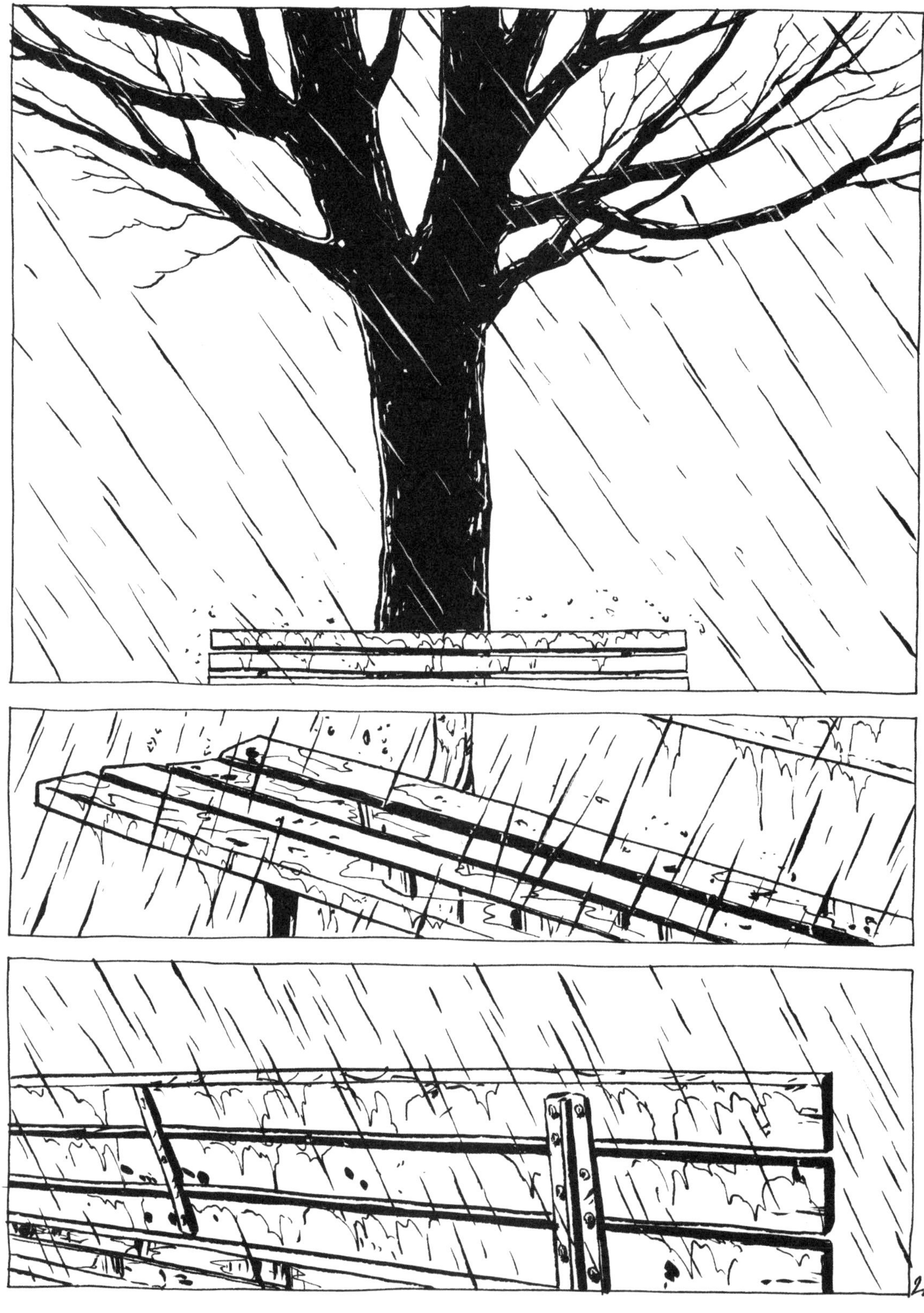

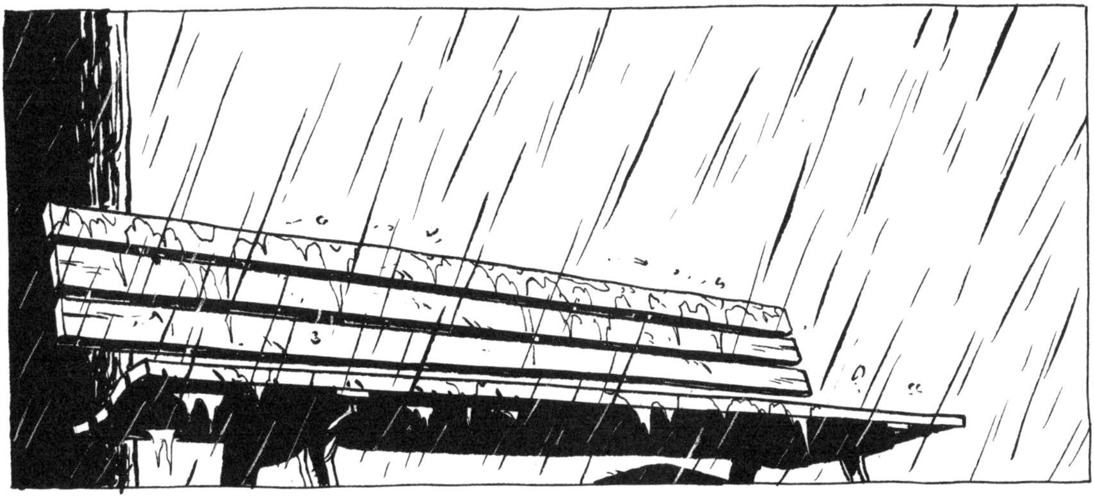

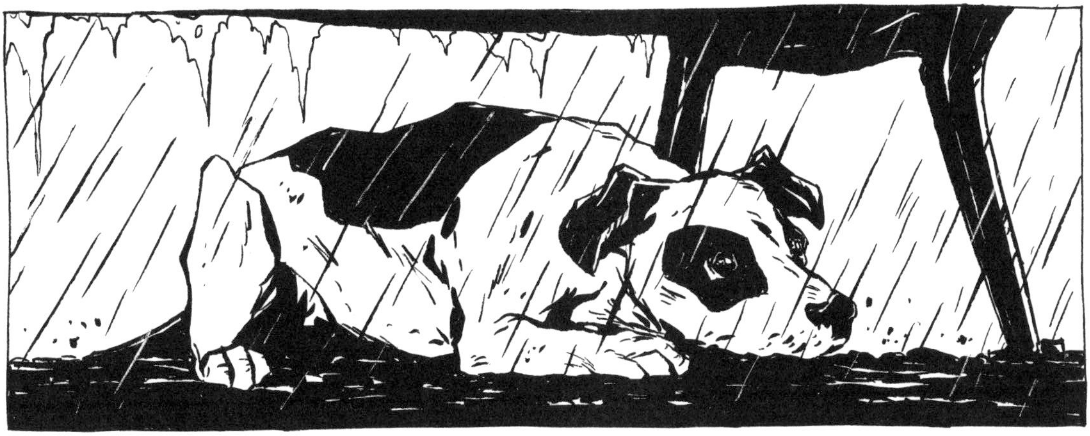

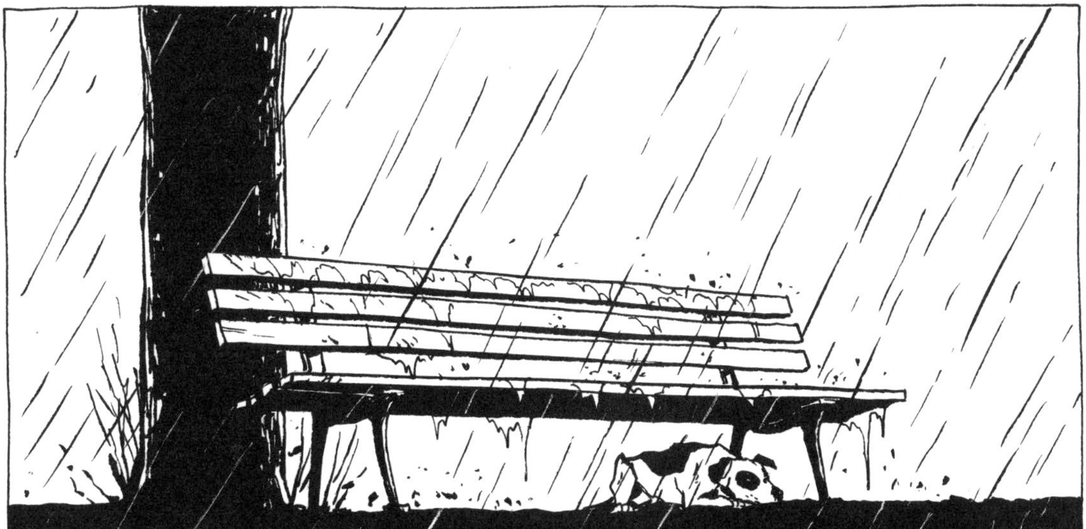

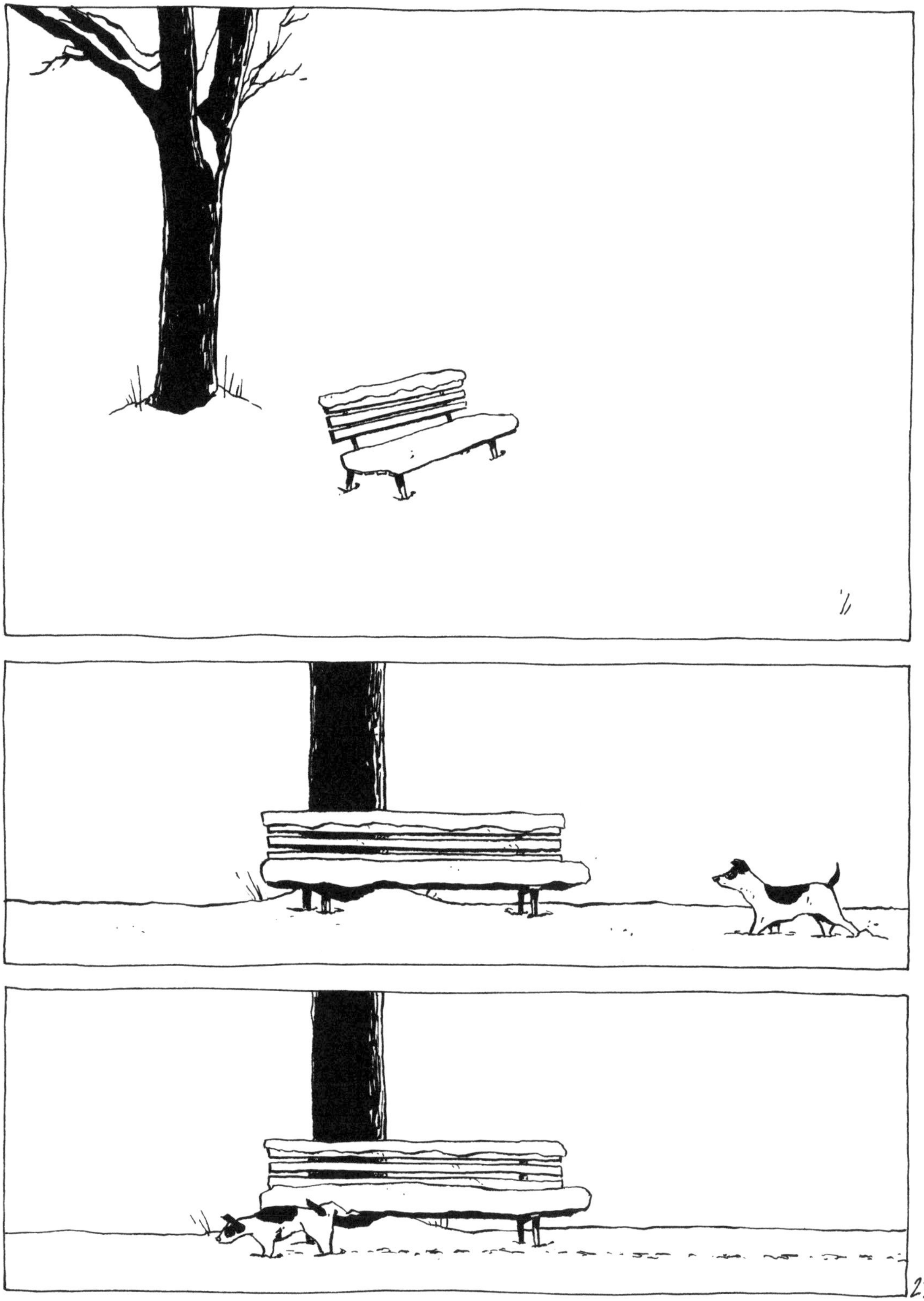

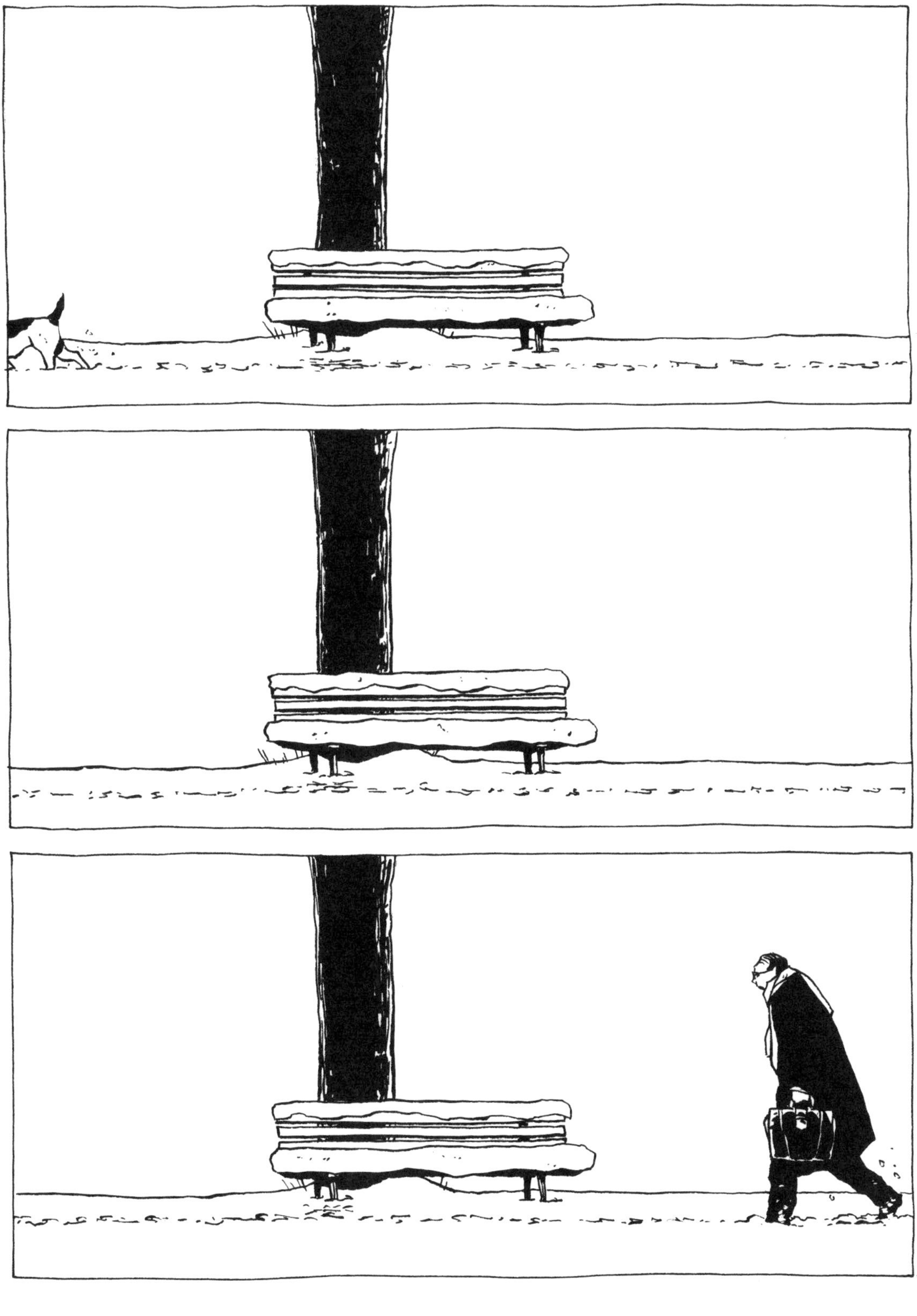

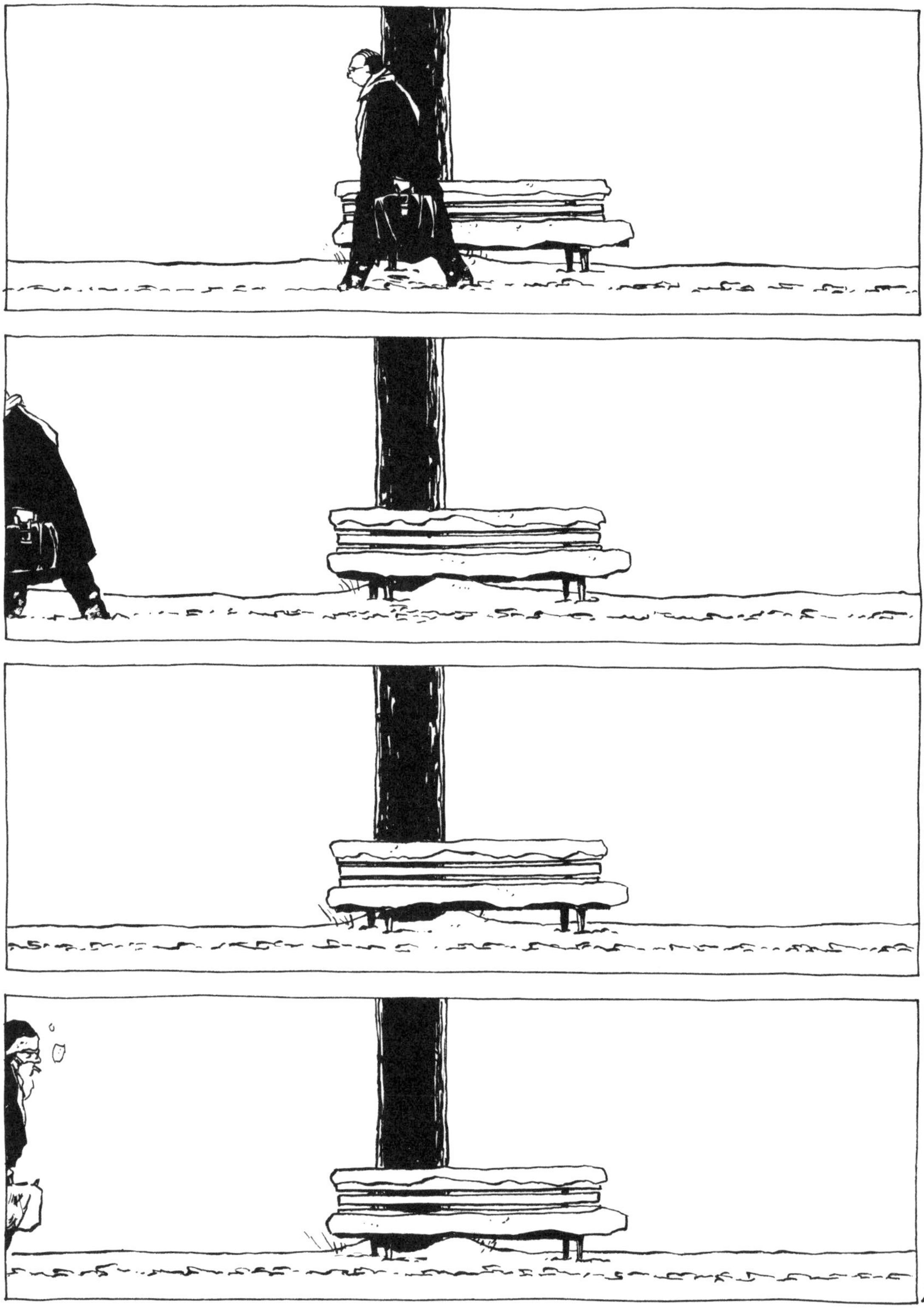

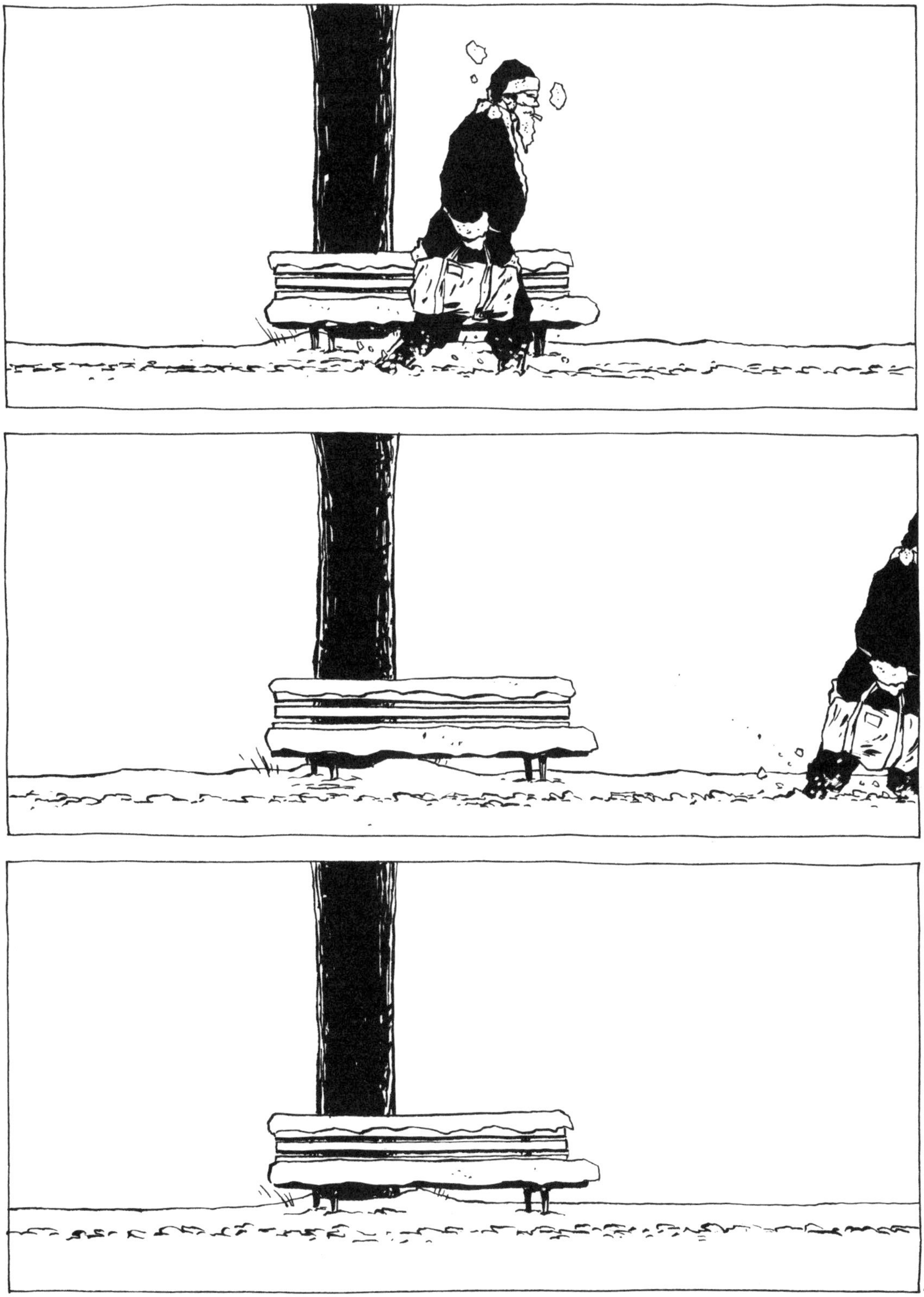

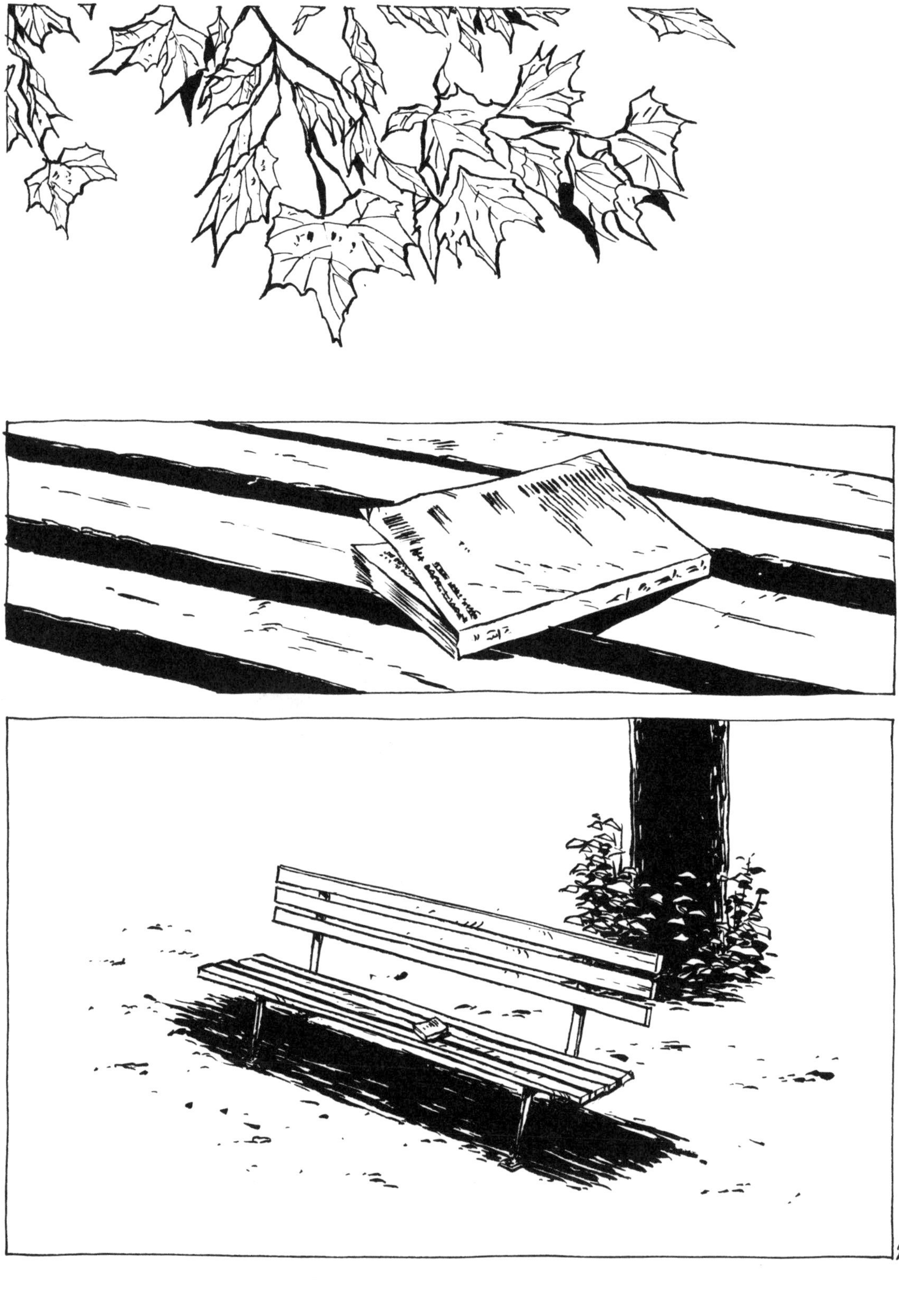

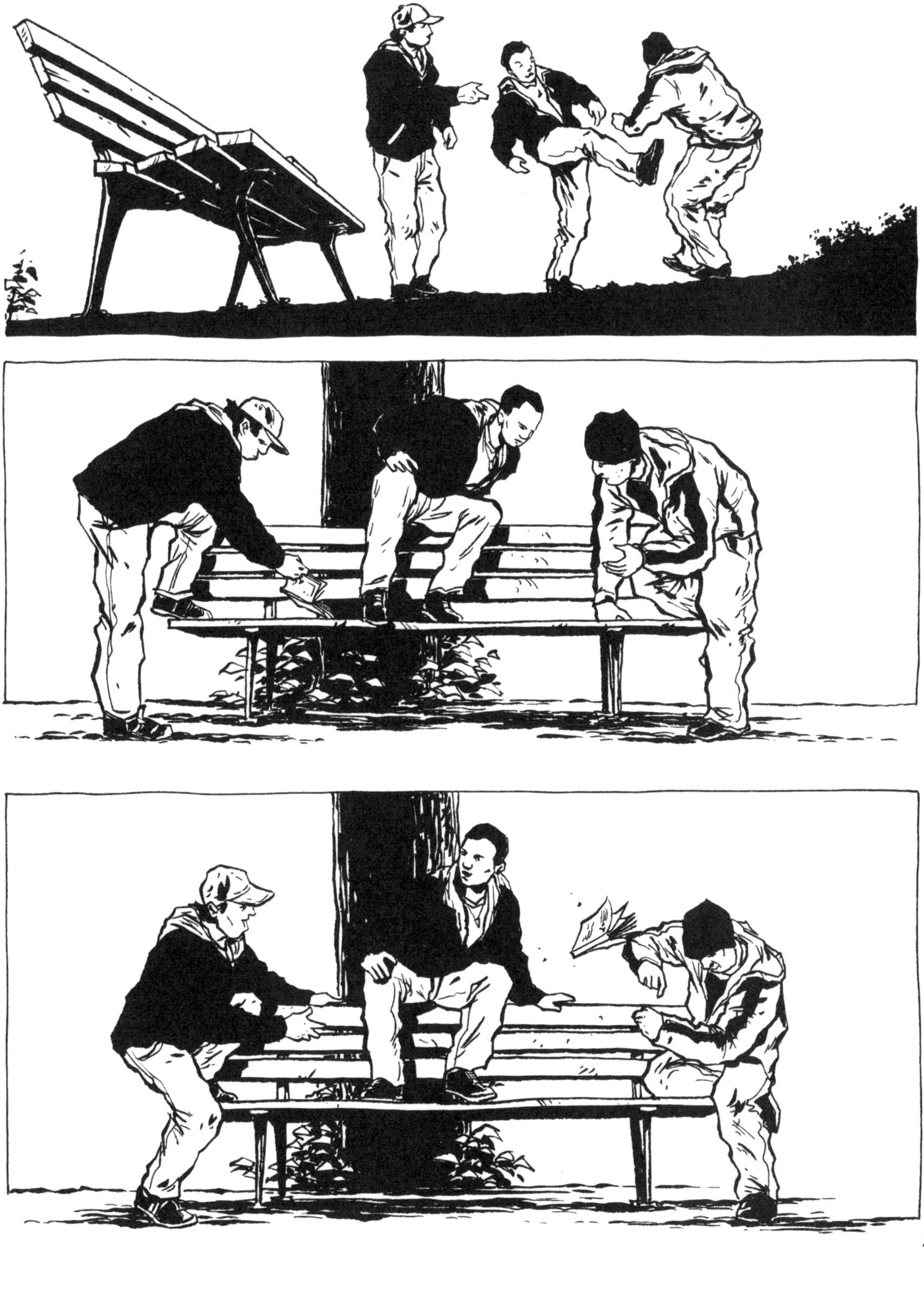

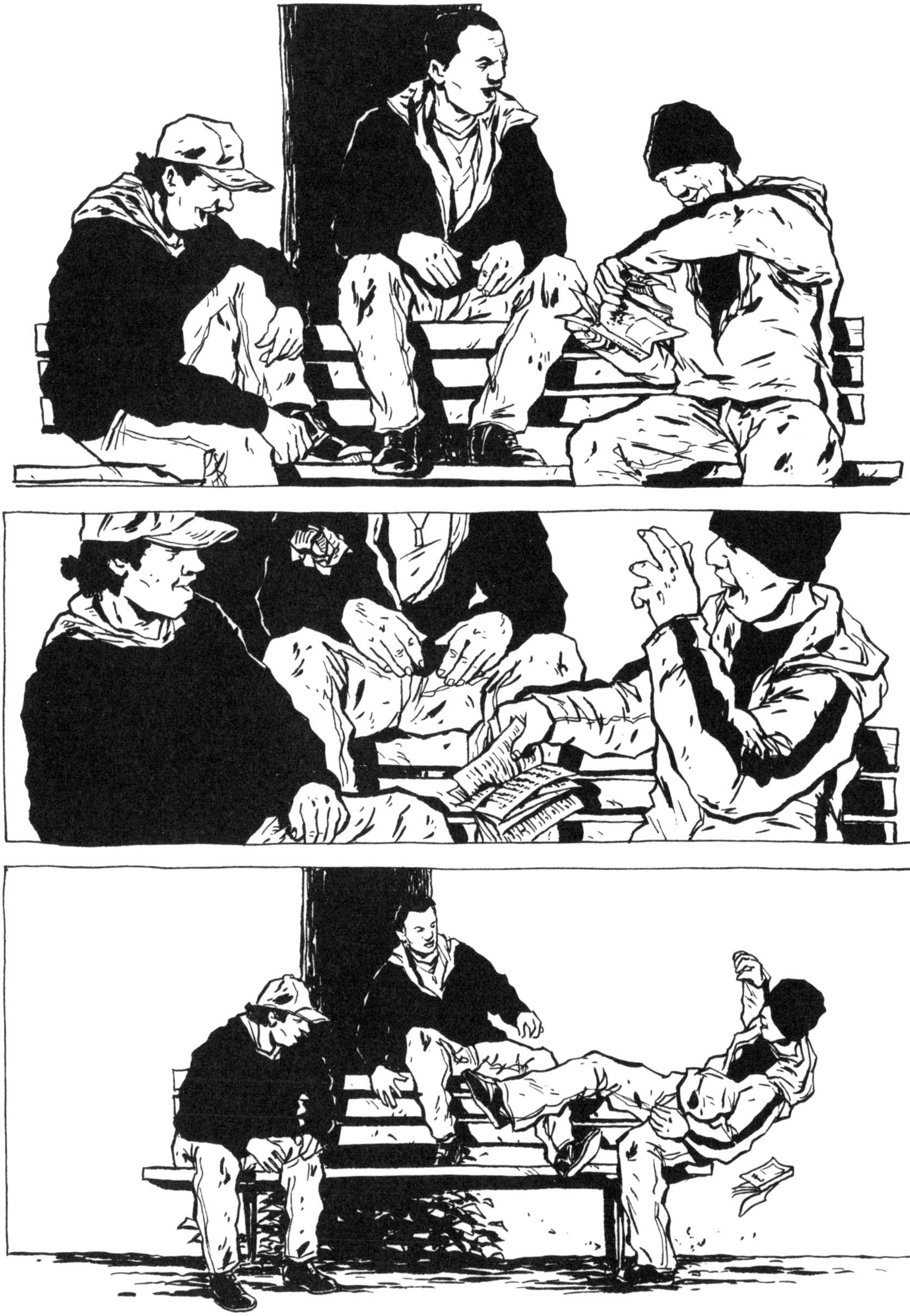

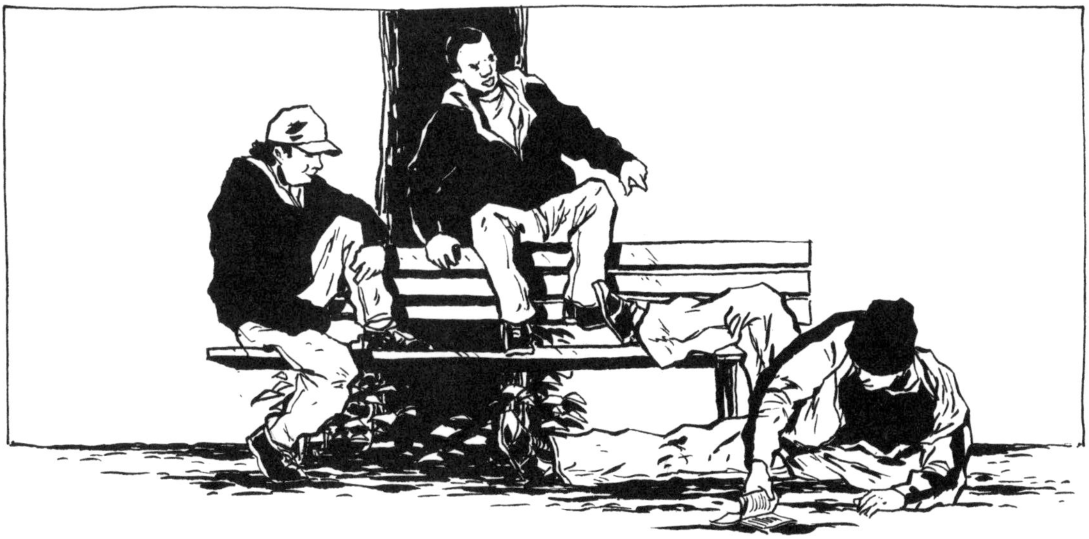

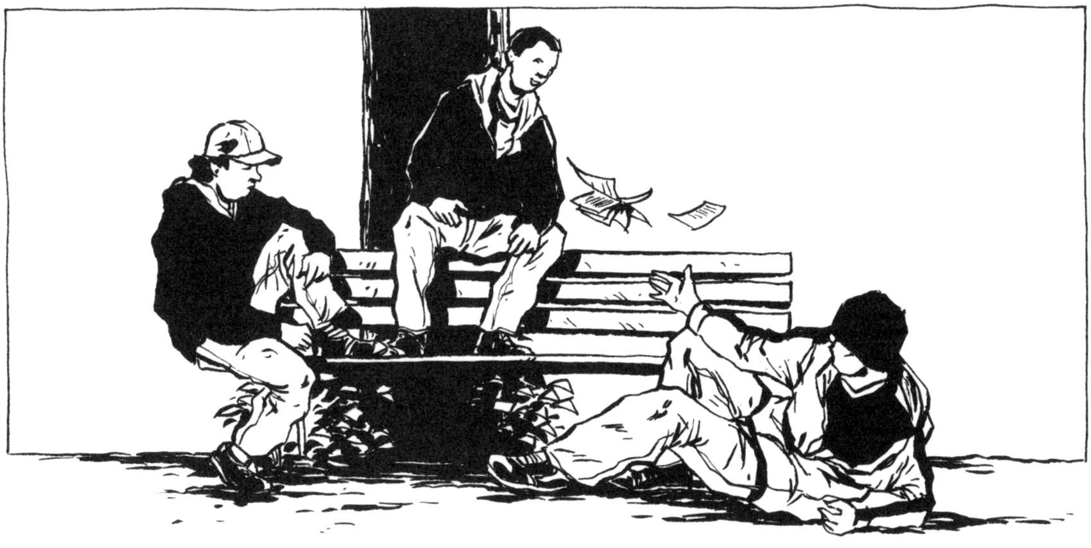

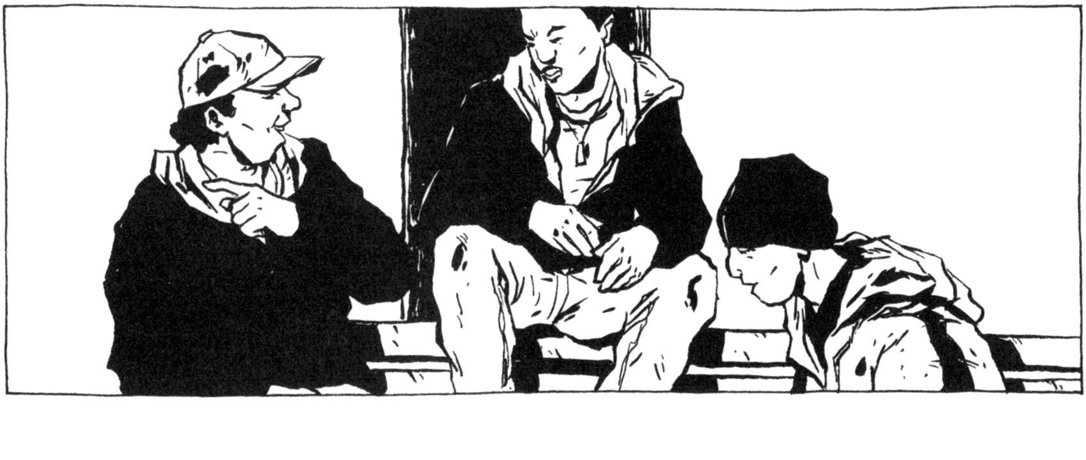

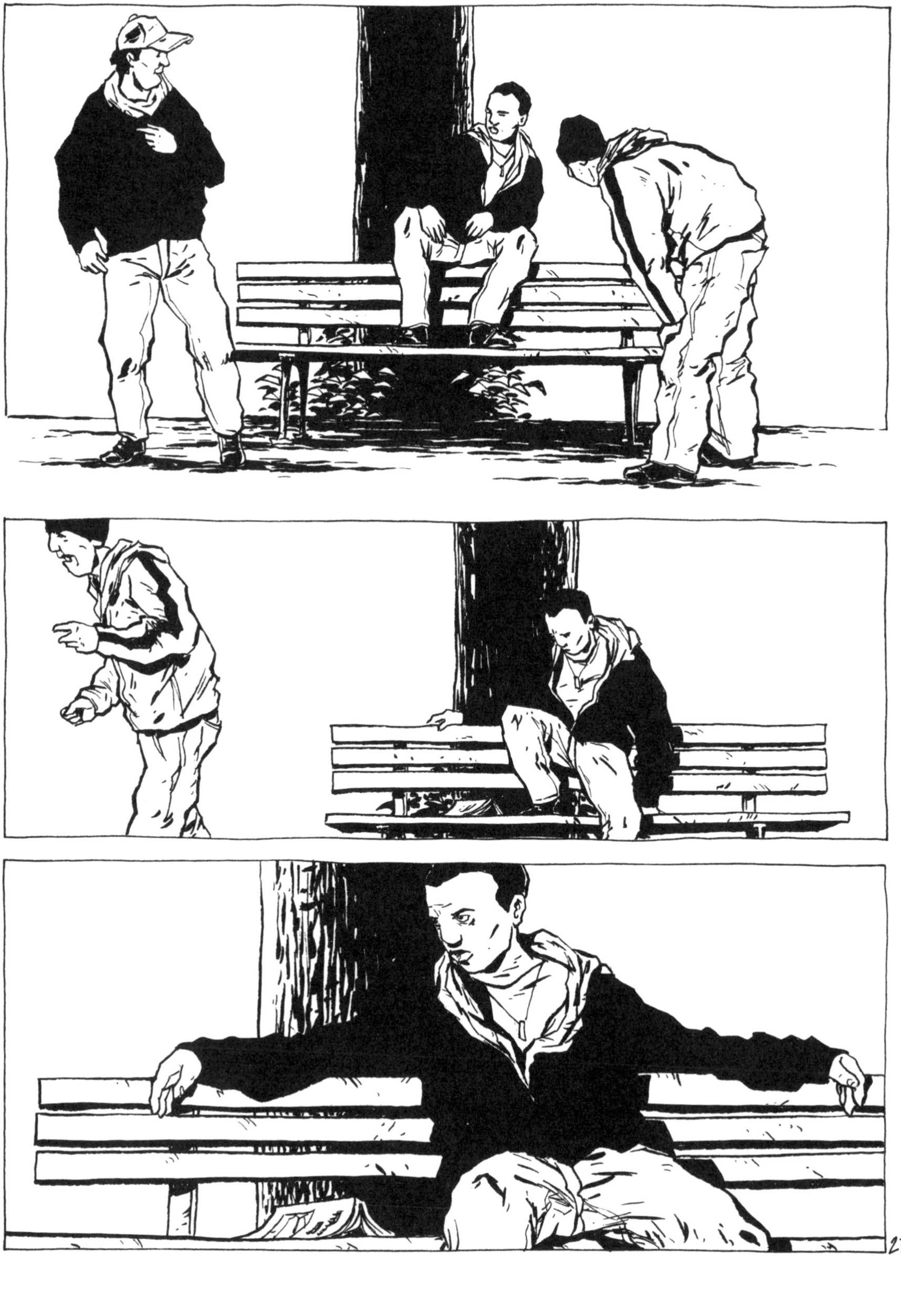

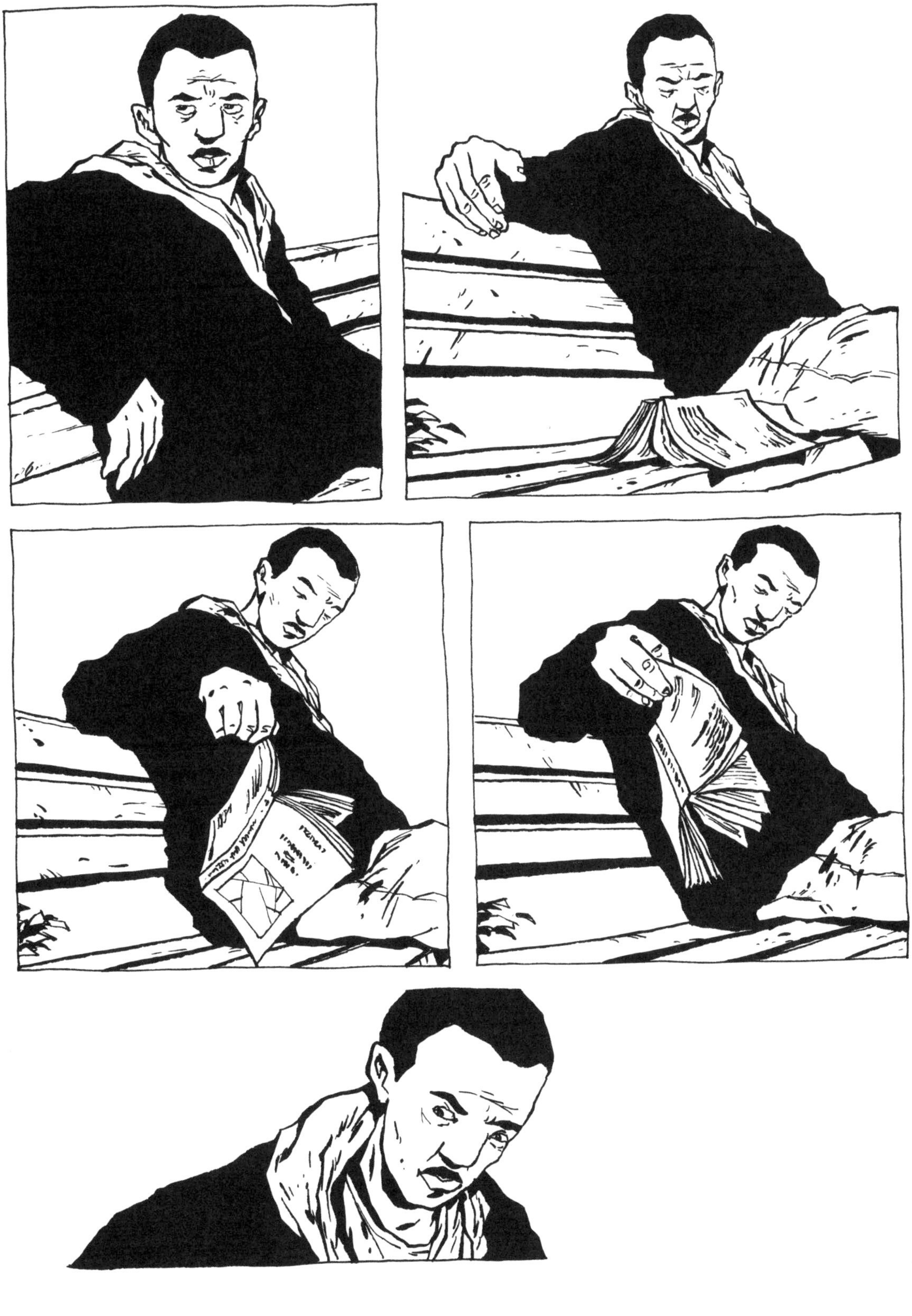

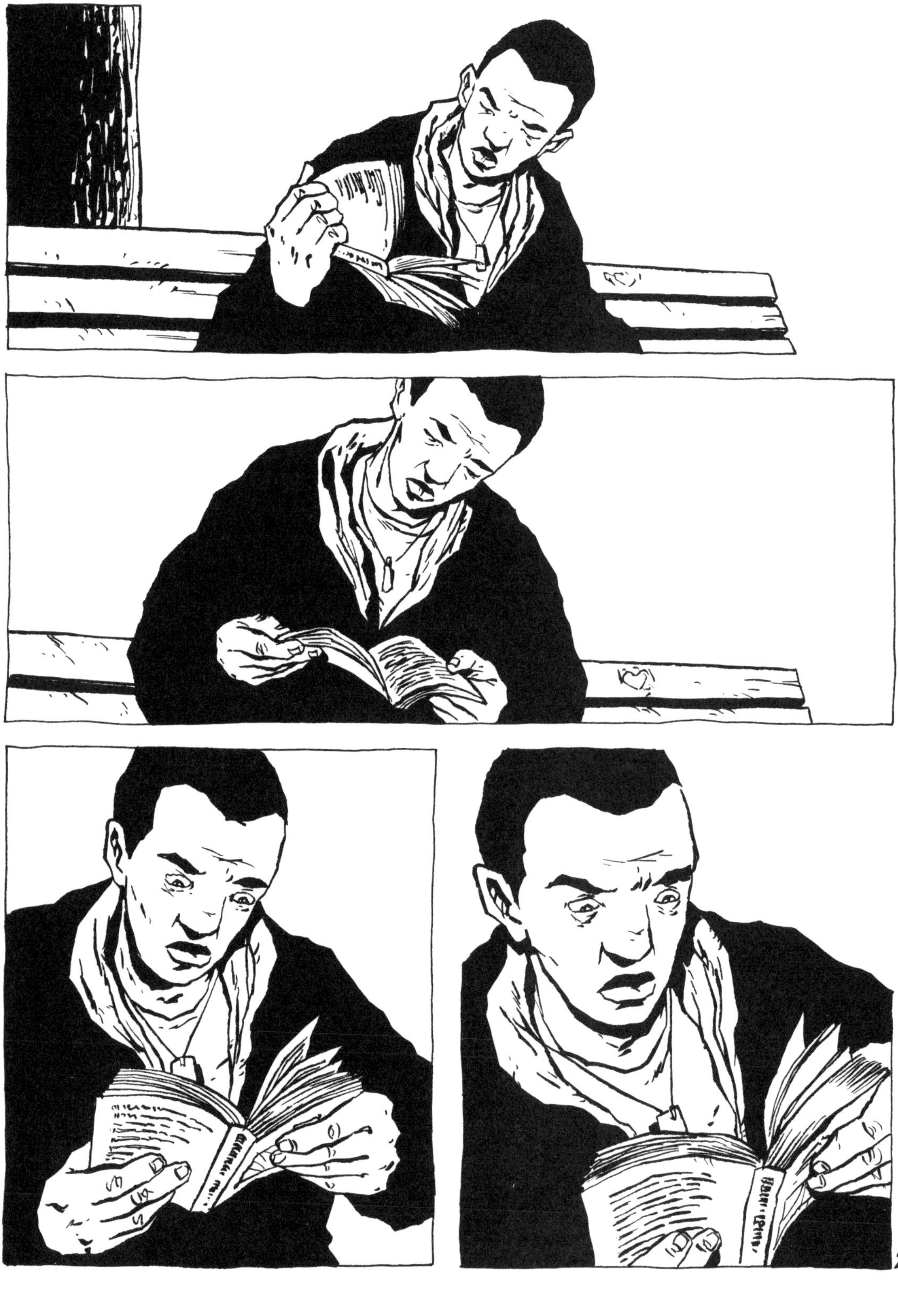

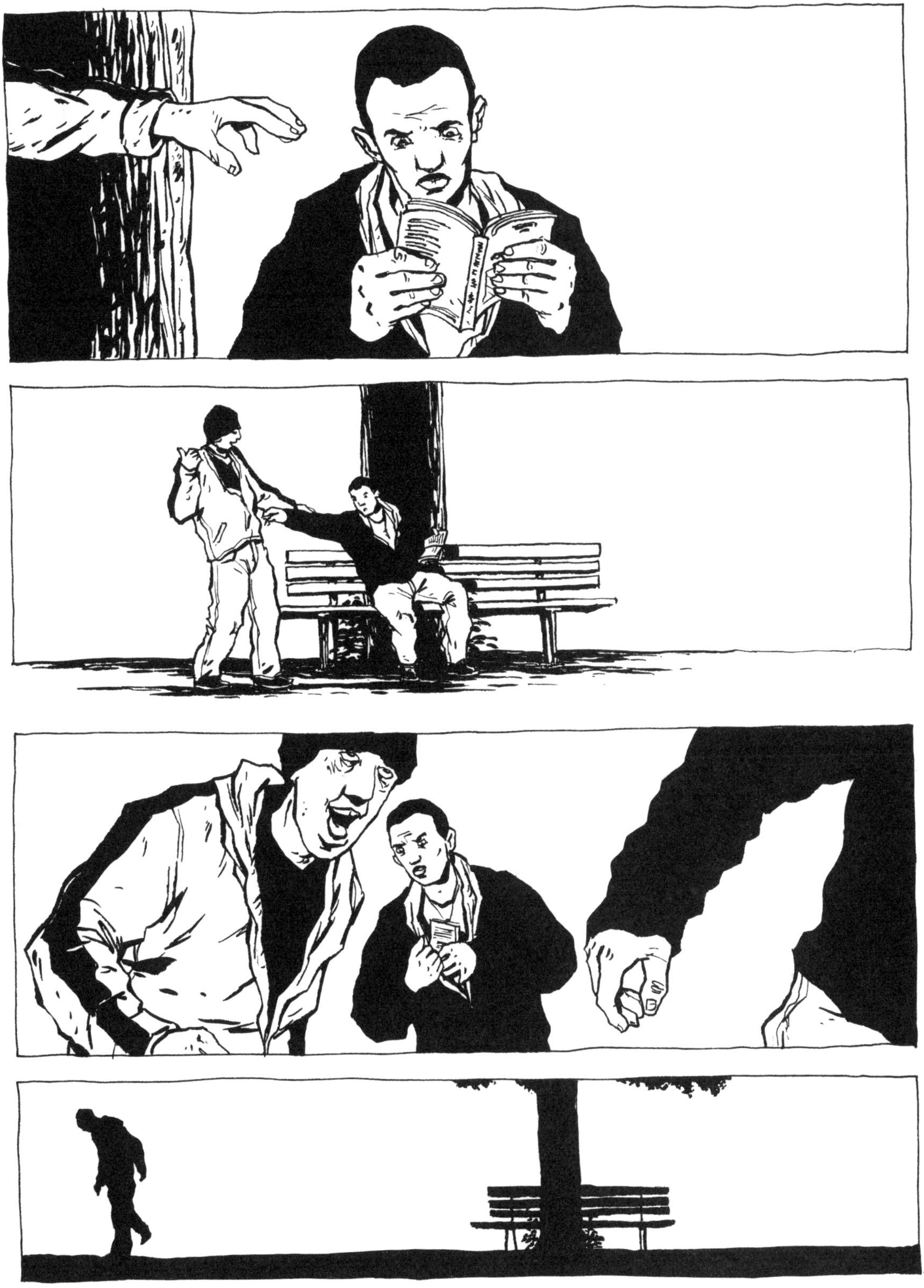

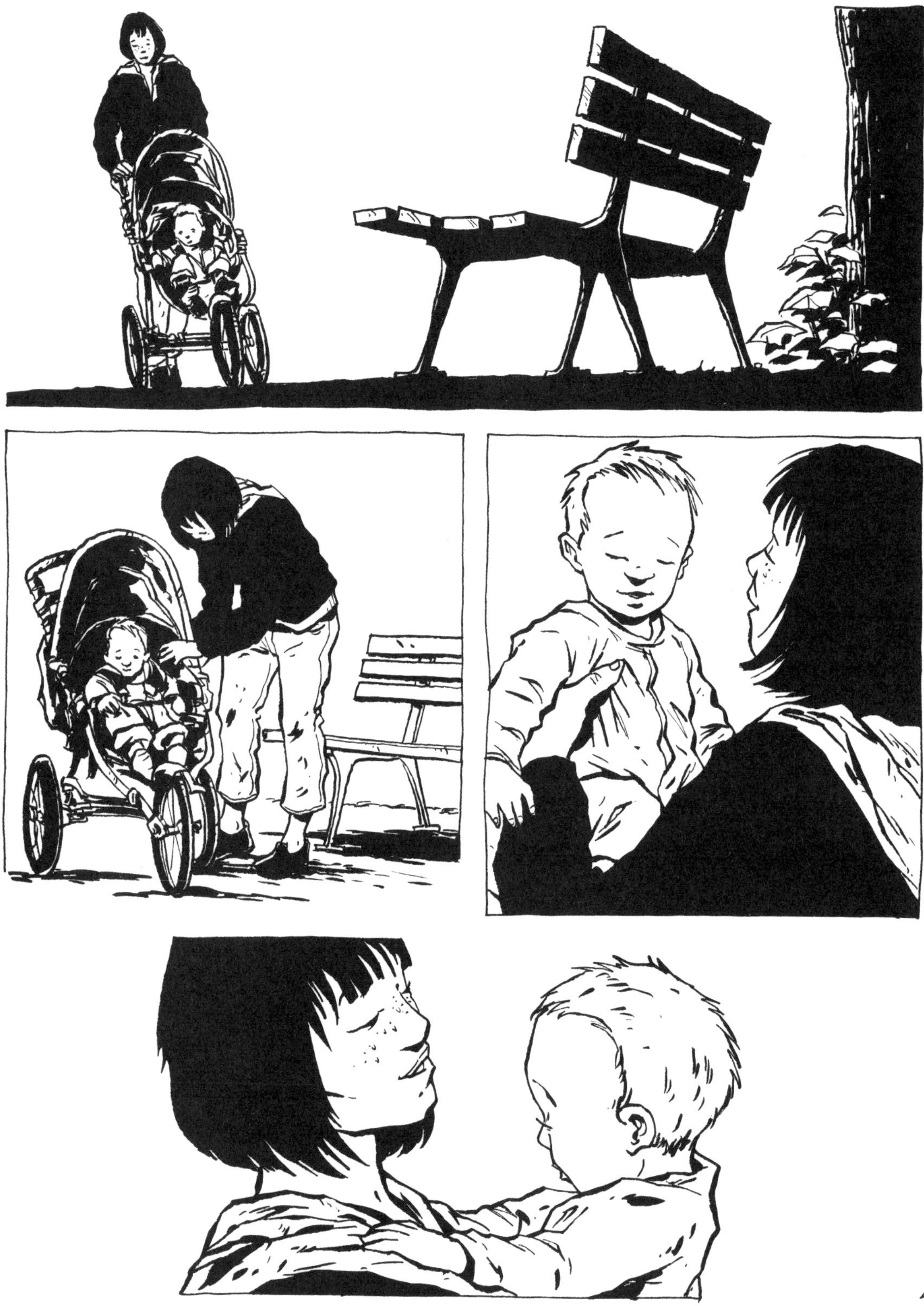

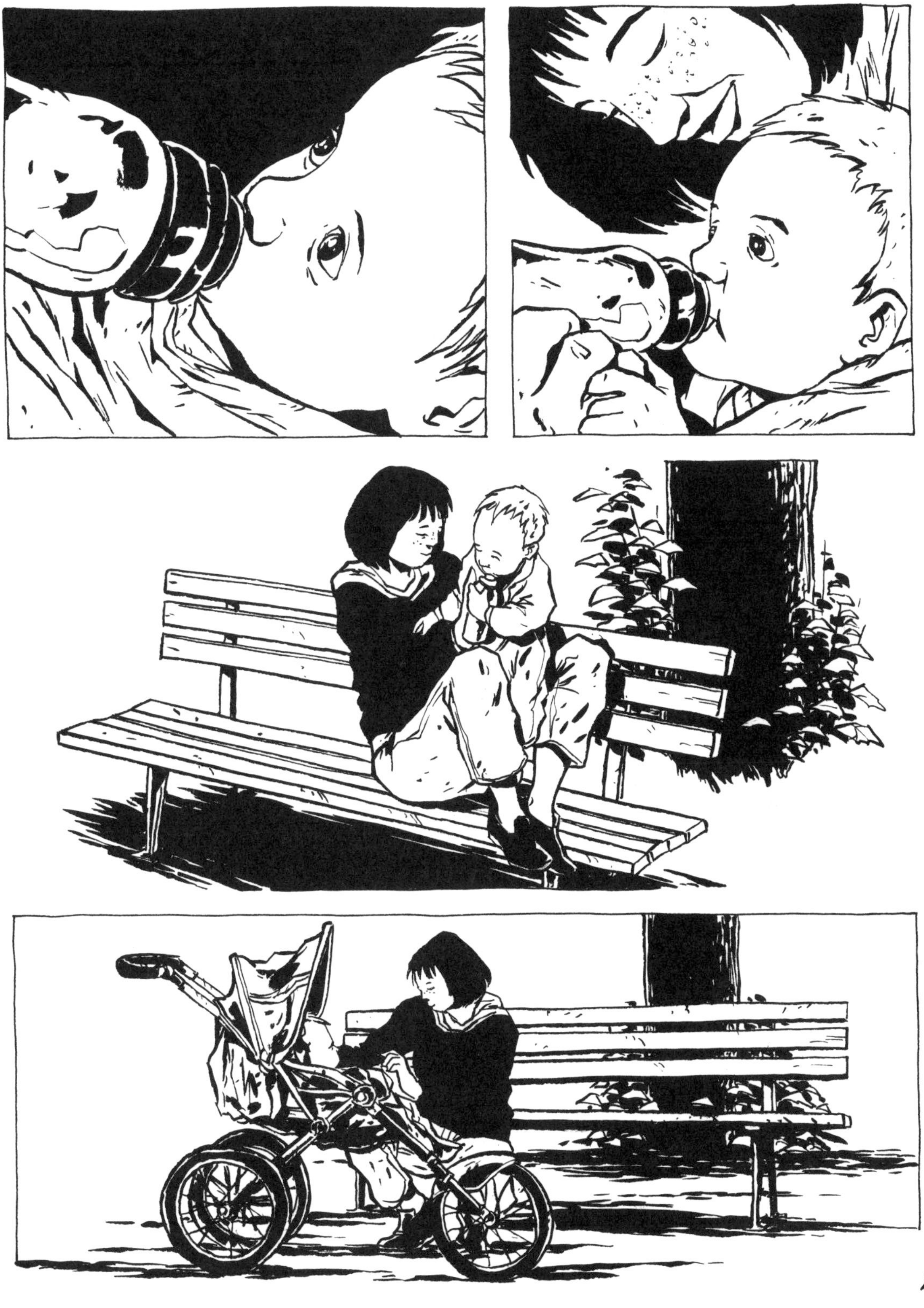

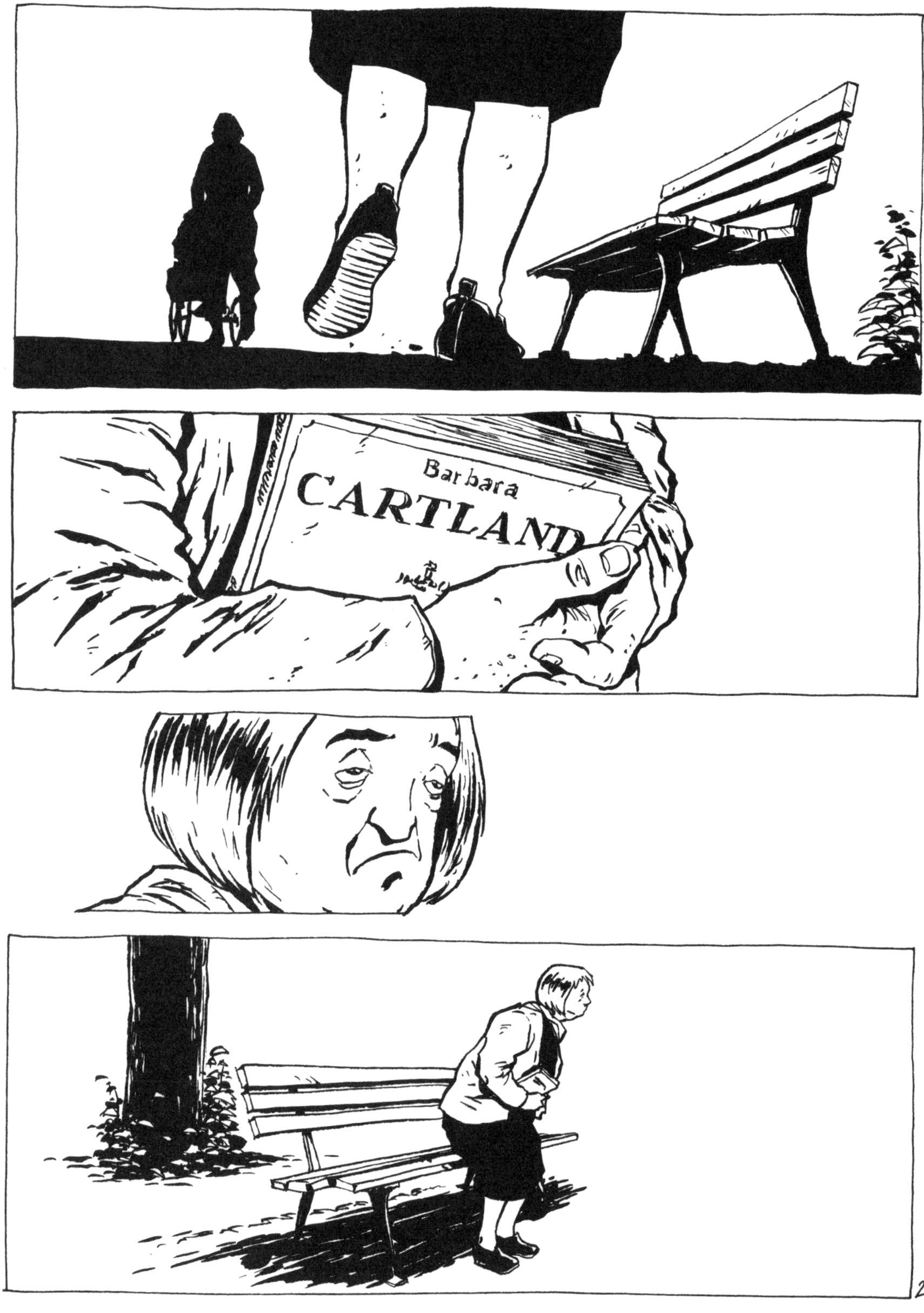
Barbara
CARTLAND

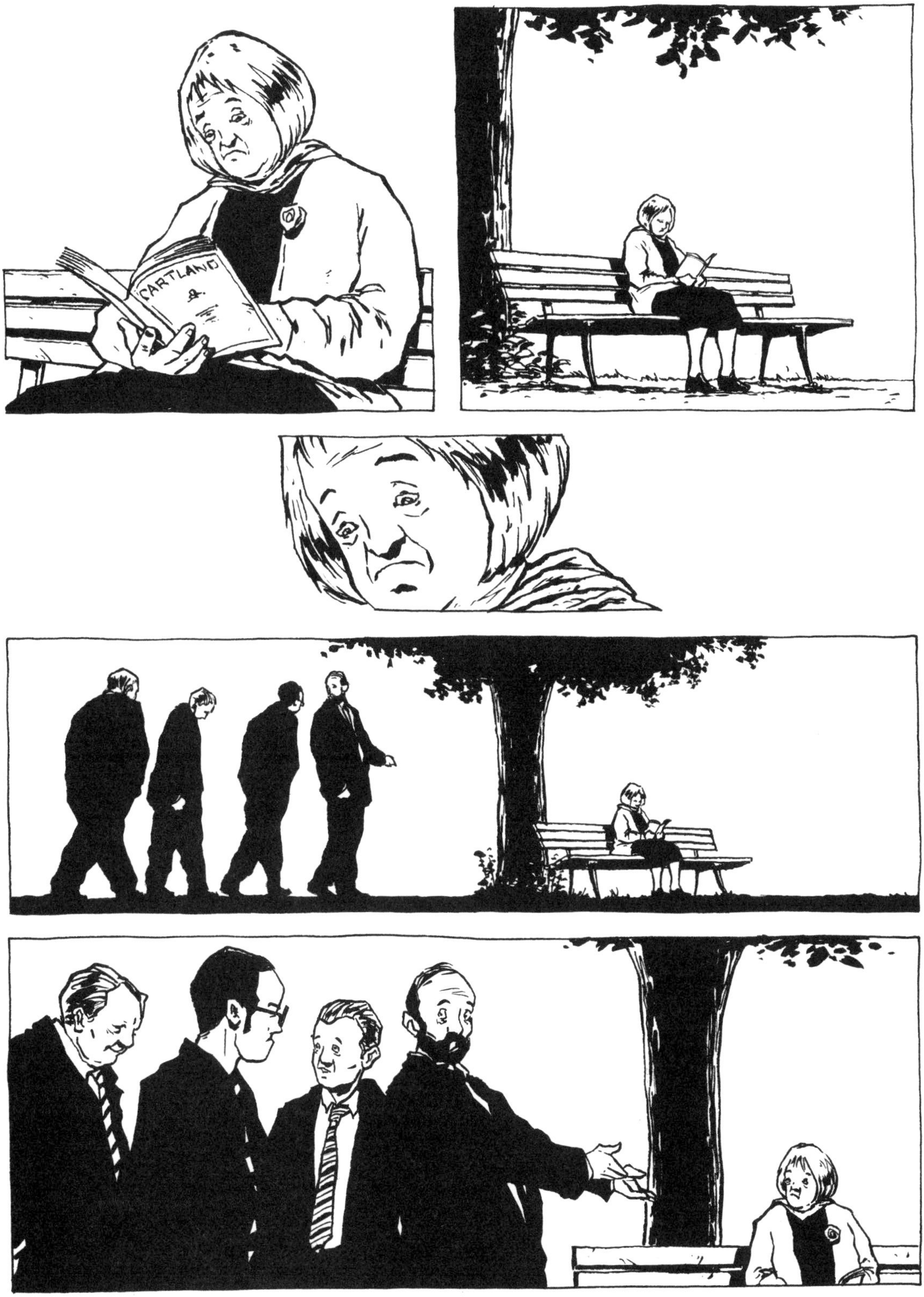
CARTLAND

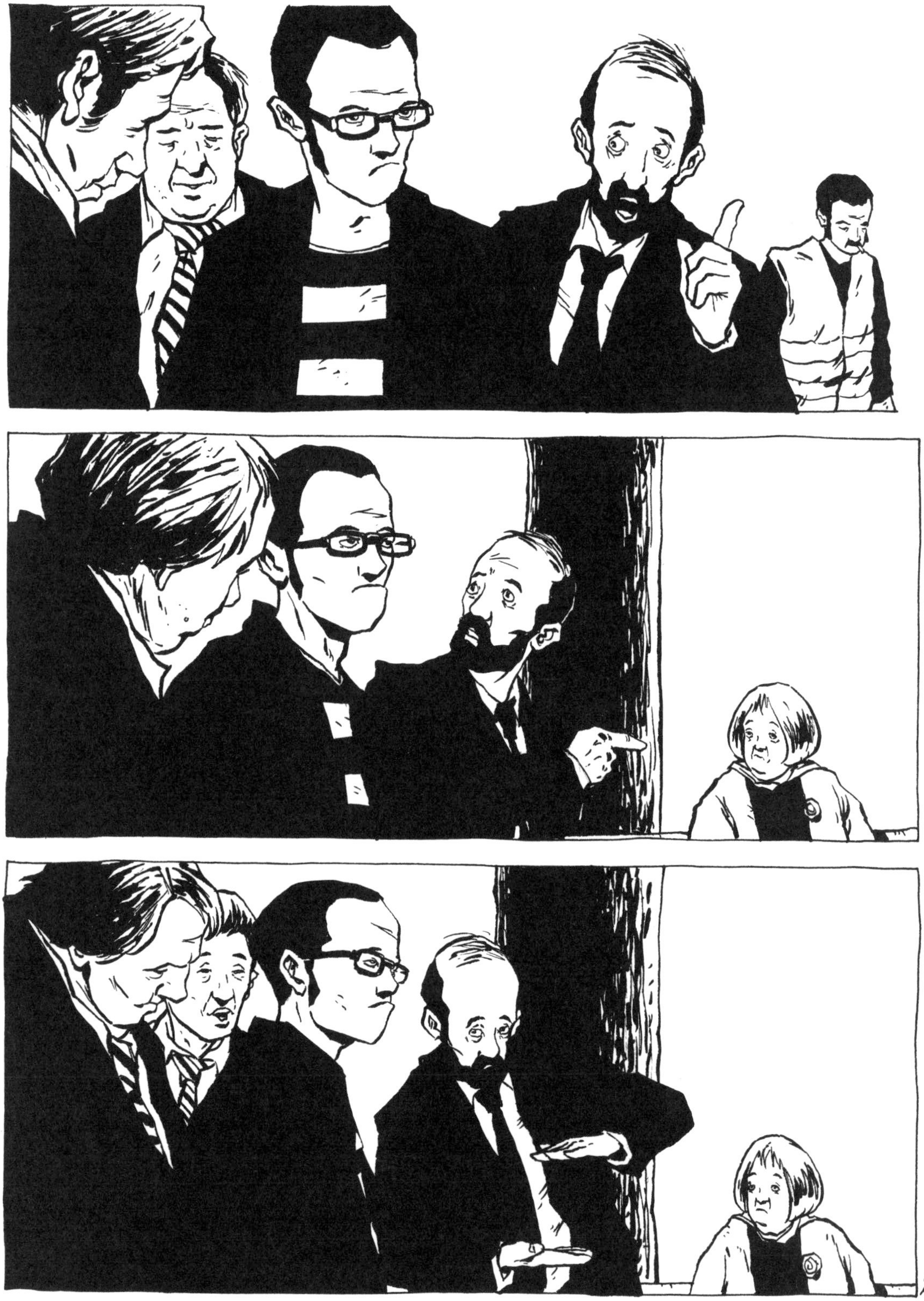

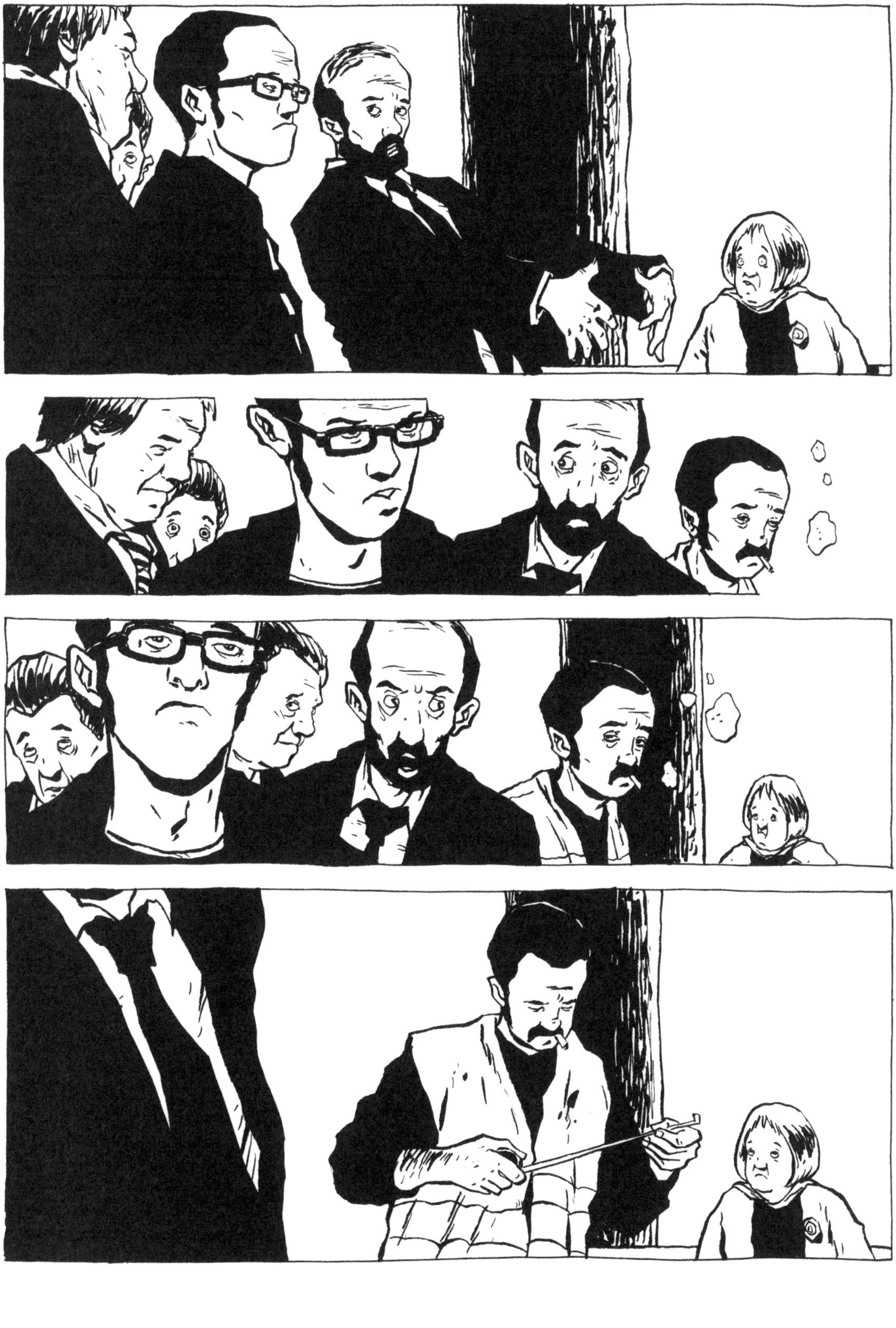

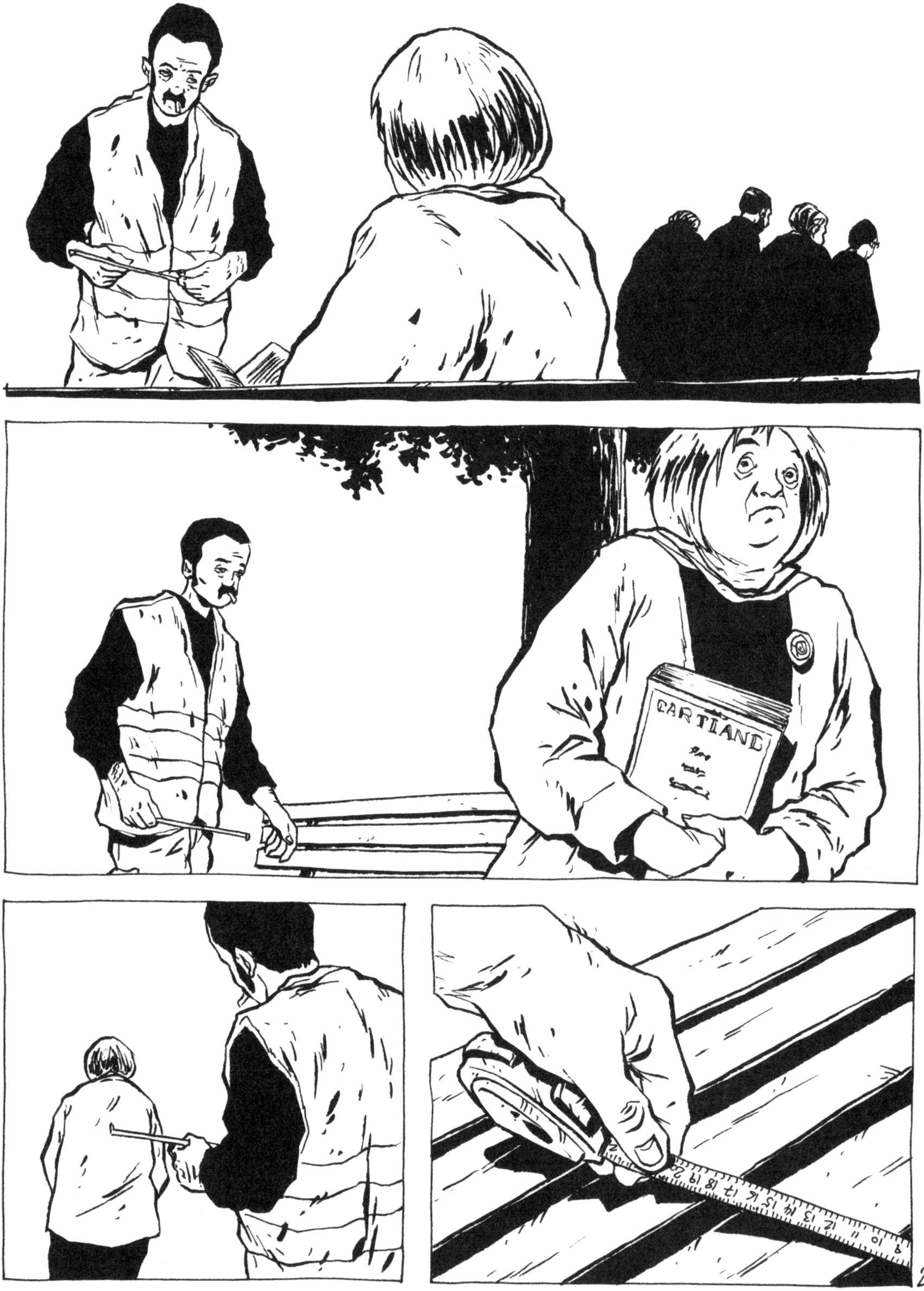
CARTIAND

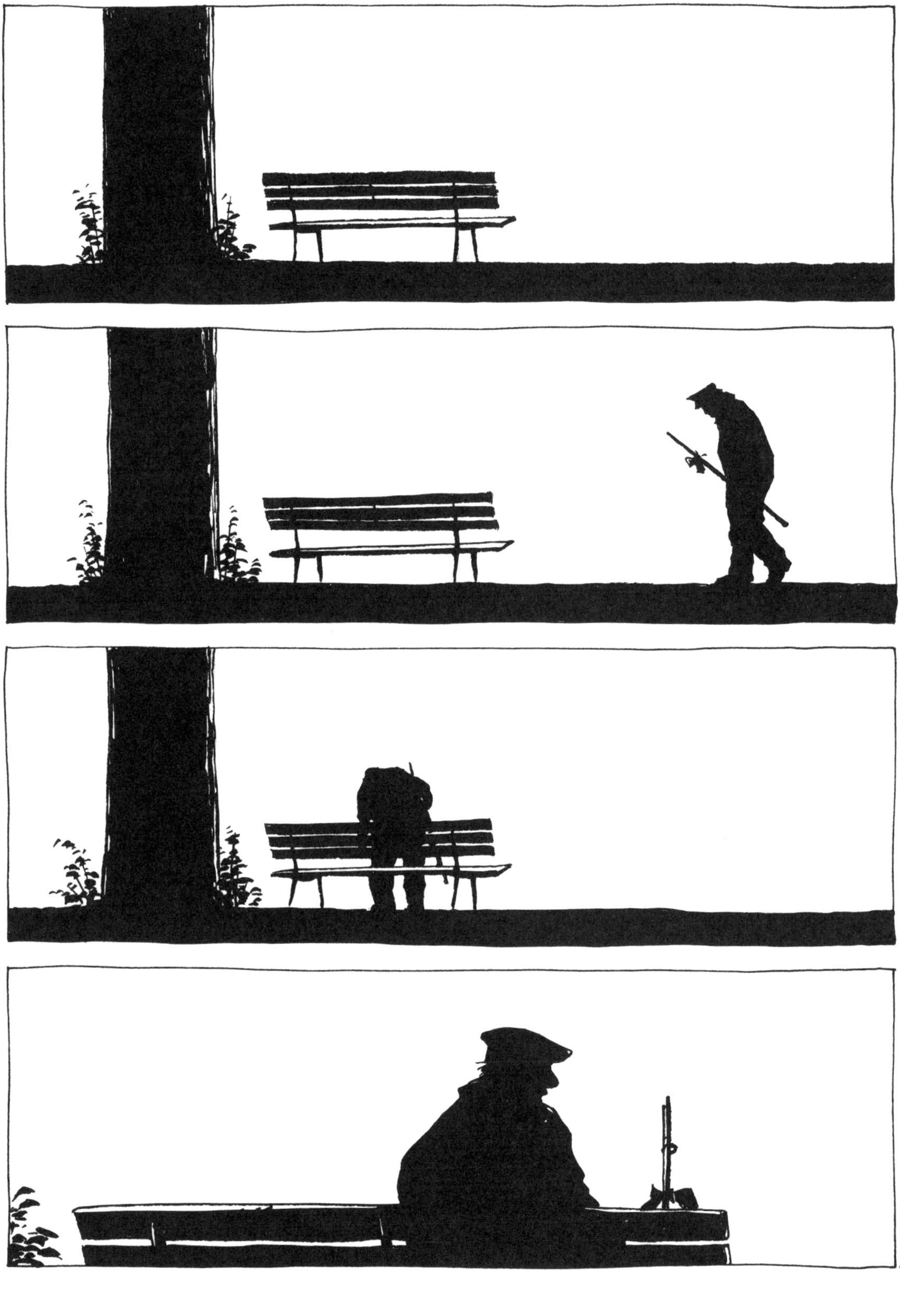

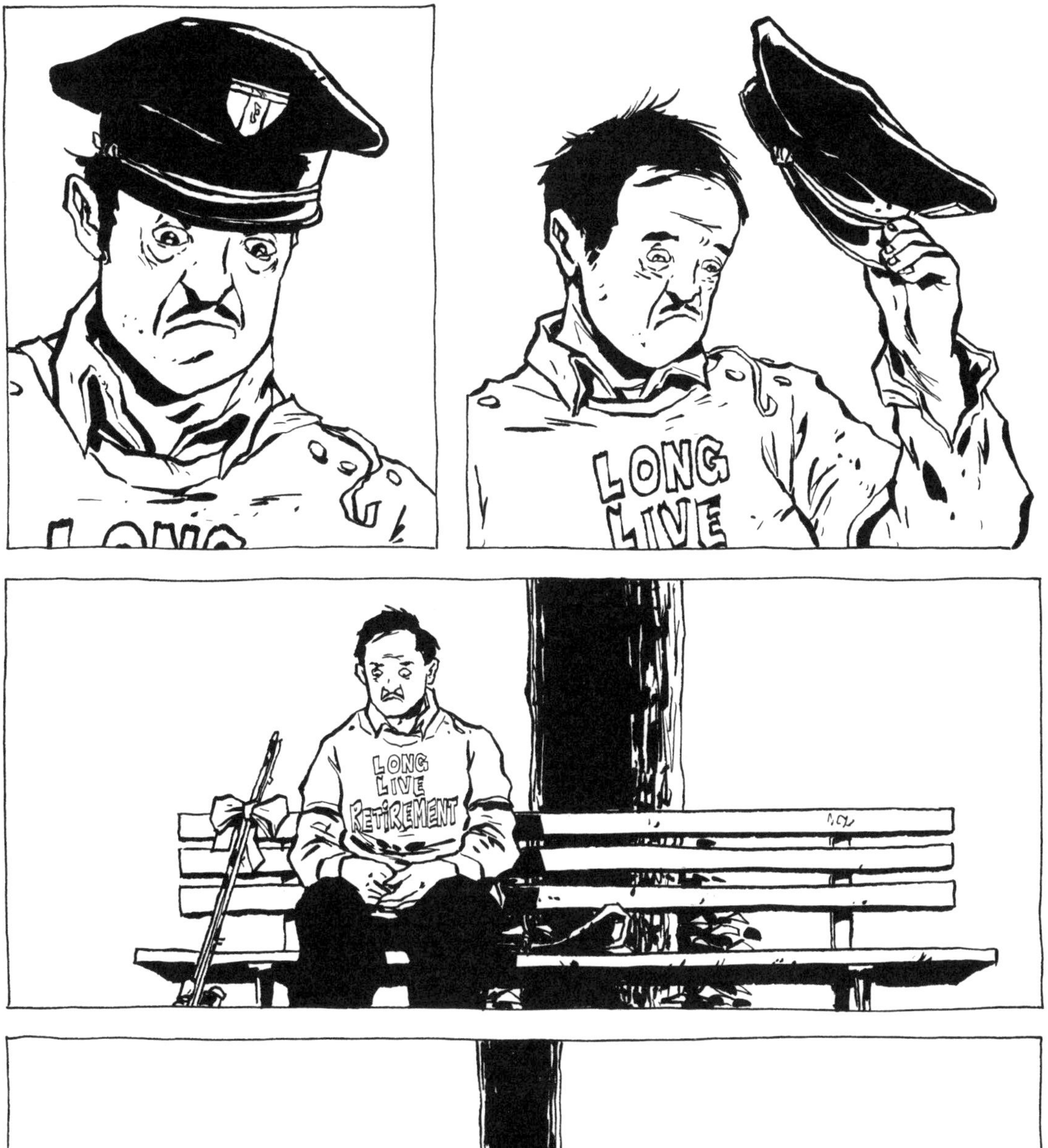
LONG LIVE
LONG LIVE RETIREMENT
LONG LIVE RETIREMENT

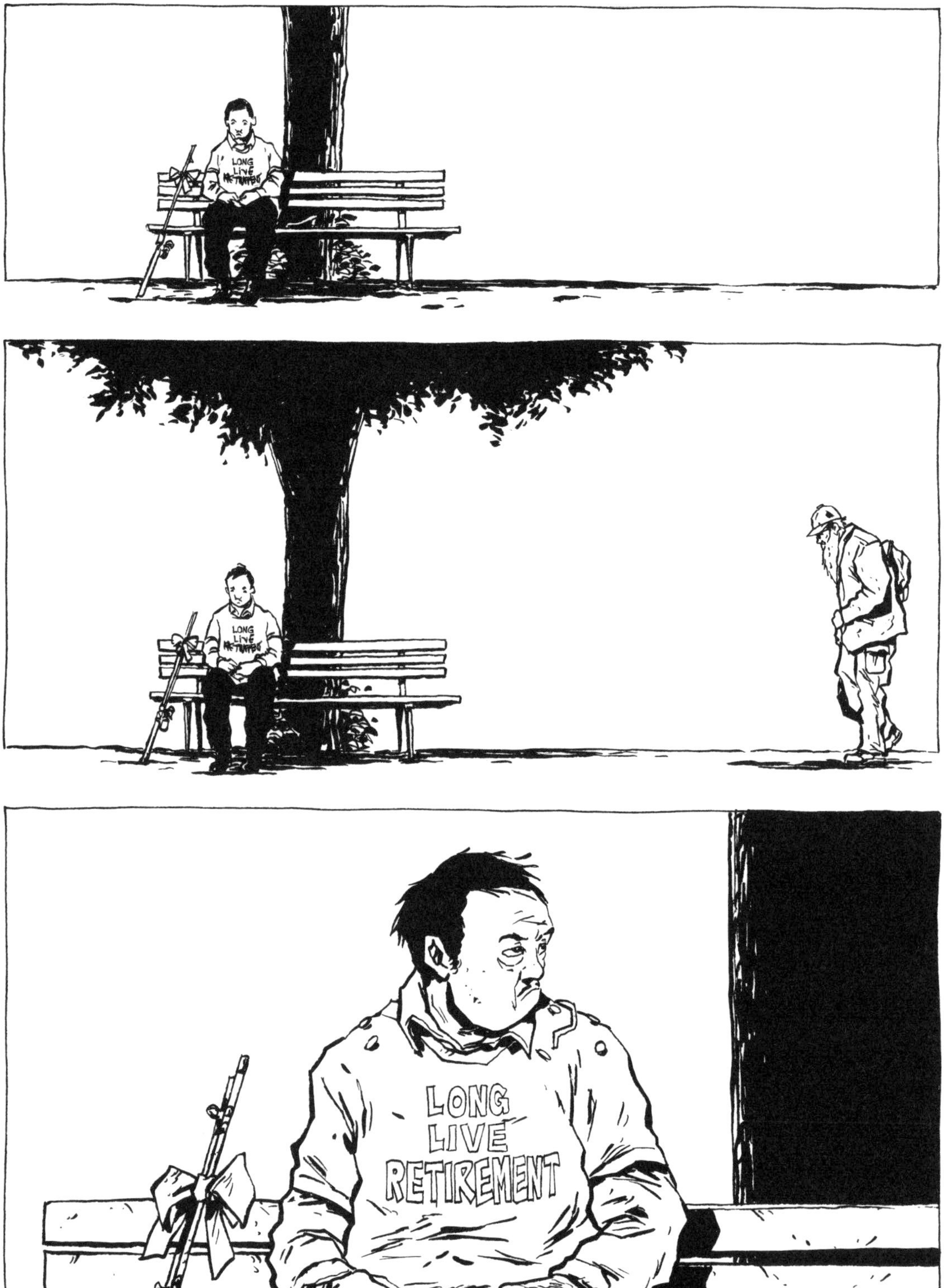
LONG
LIVE
RETIREMENT

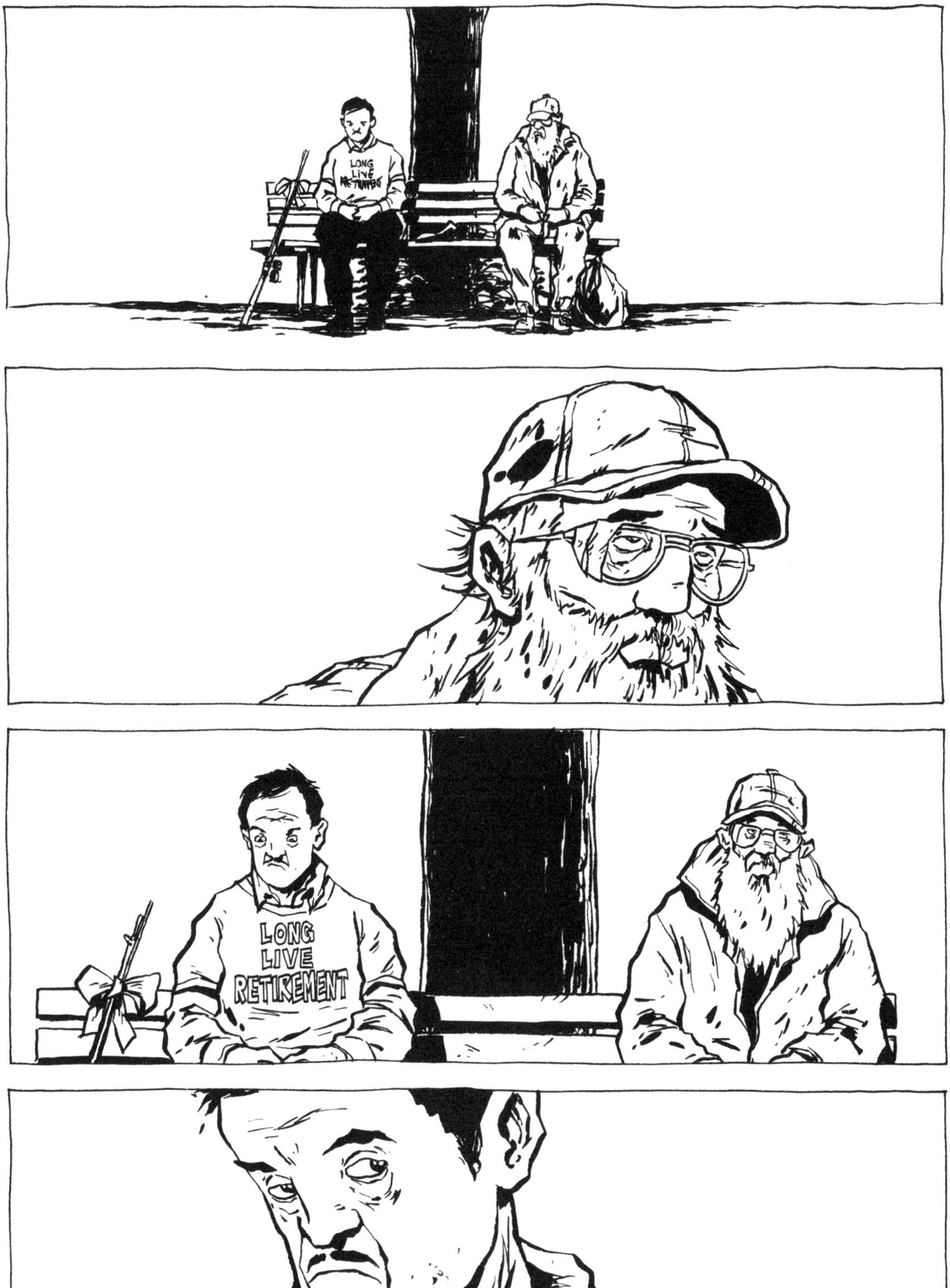
LONG
LIVE
RETIREMENT

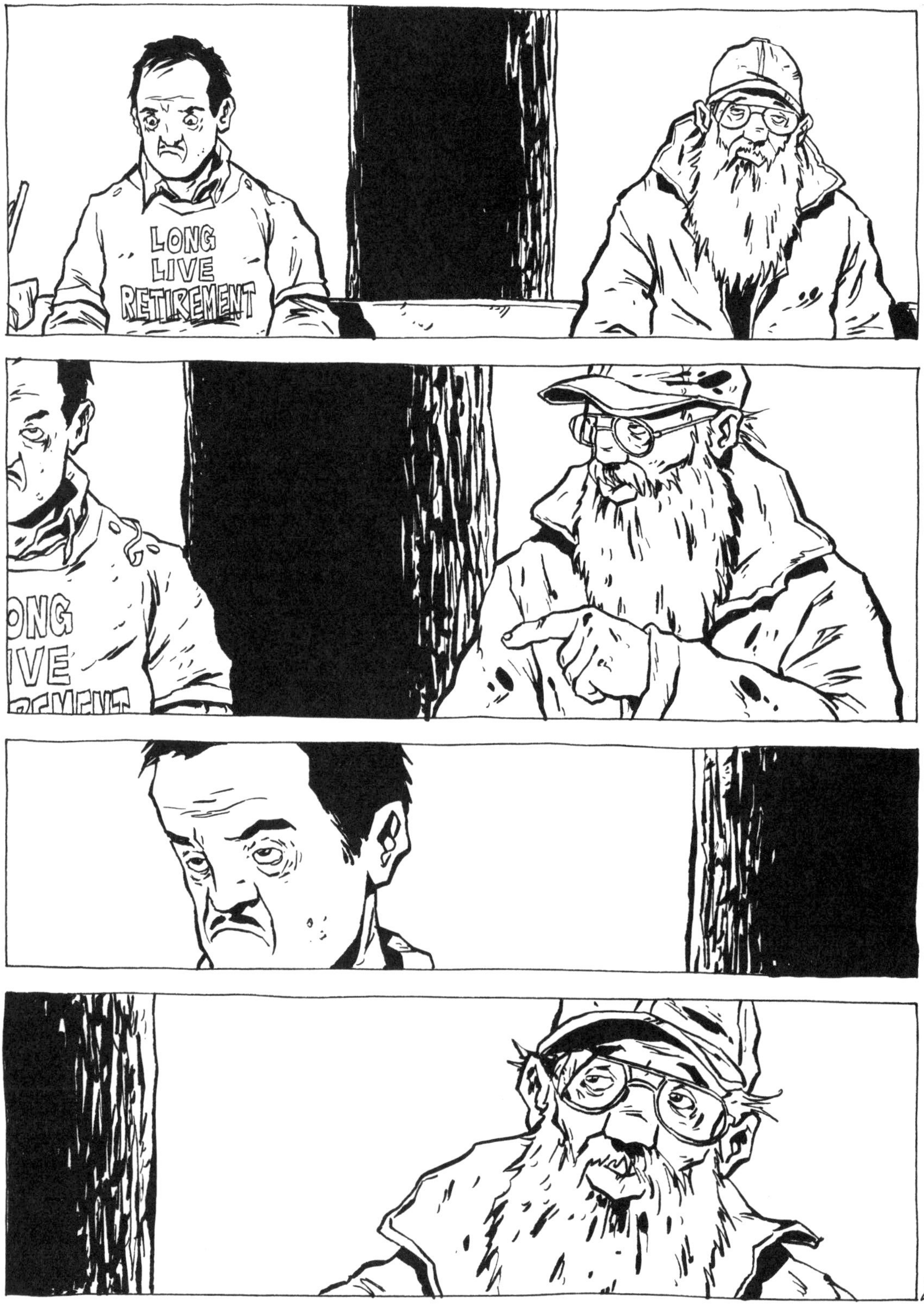
LONG
LIVE
RETIREMENT

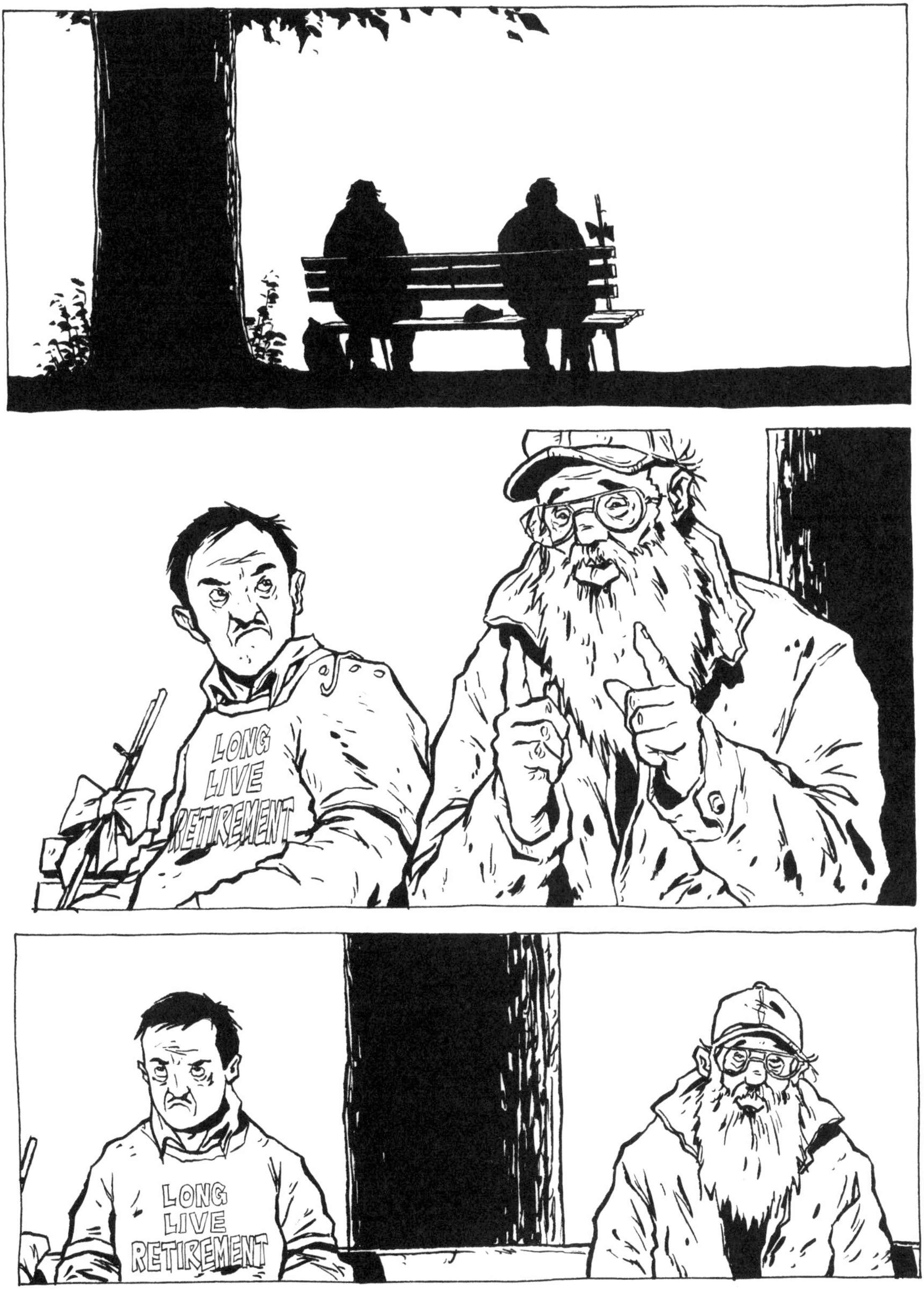
LONG LIVE RETIREMENT
LONG LIVE RETIREMENT

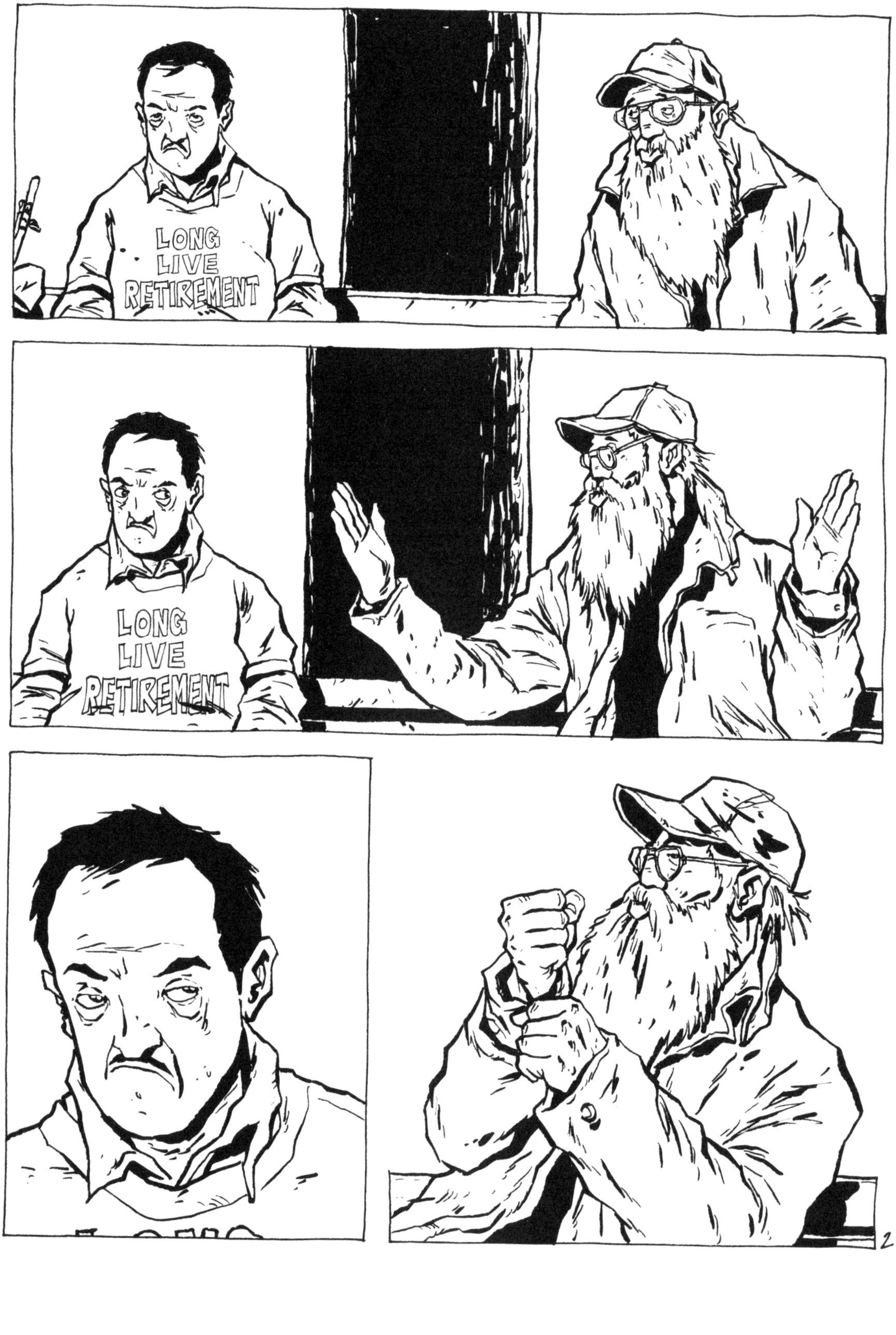
LONG
LIVE
RETIREMENT
LONG
LIVE
RETIREMENT

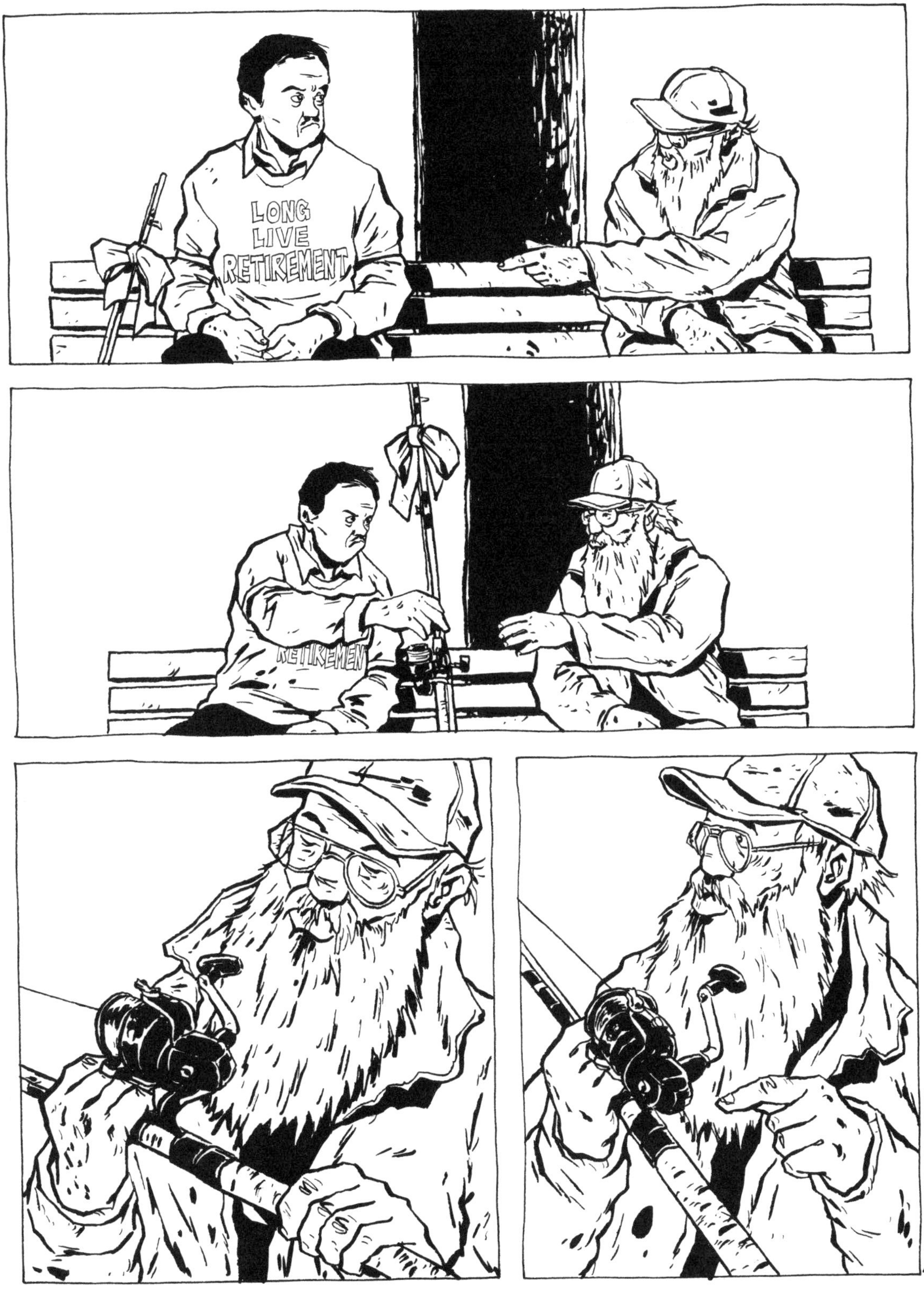
LONG
LIVE
RETIREMENT
RETIREMENT

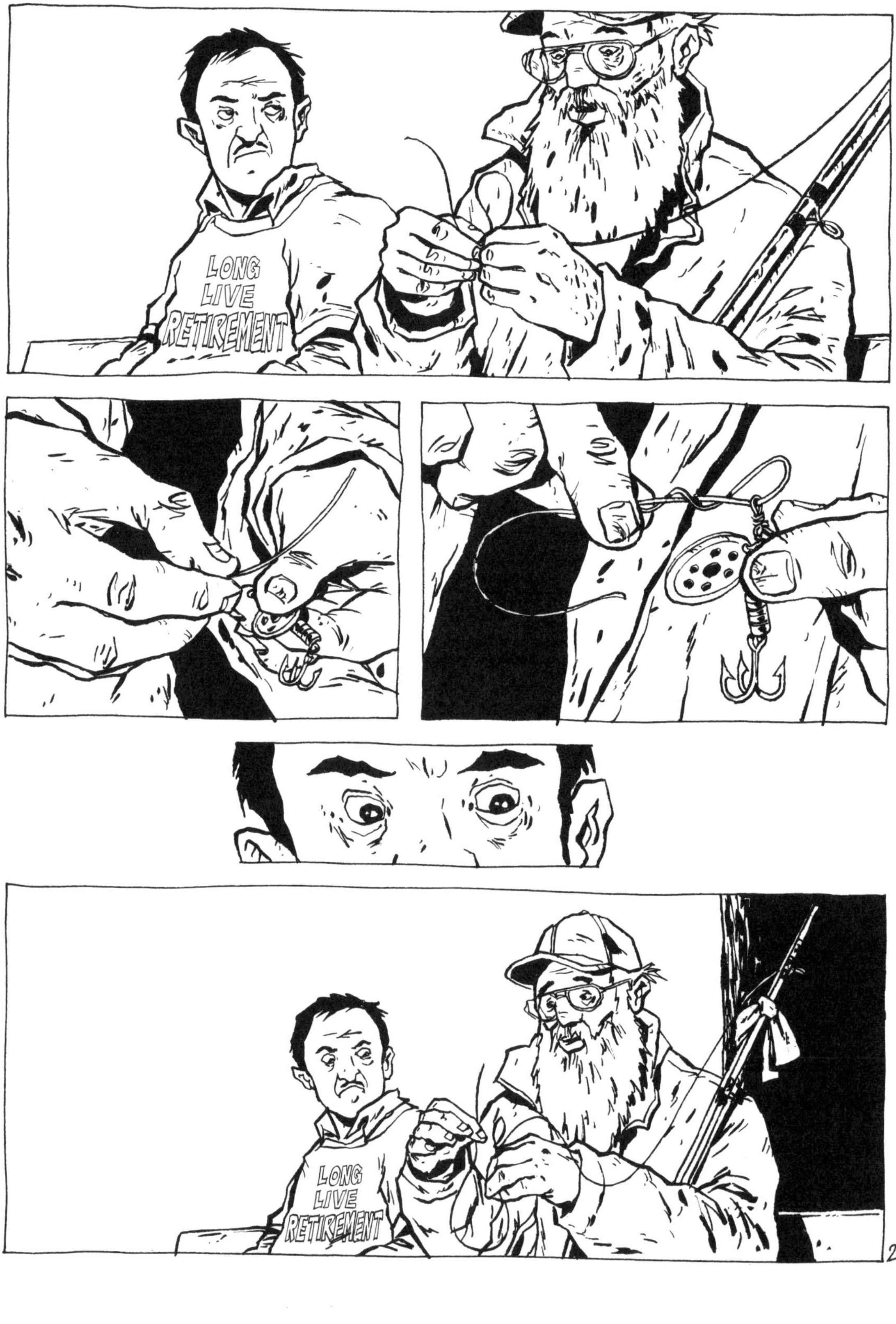
LONG
LIVE
RETIREMENT
LONG
LIVE
RETIREMENT

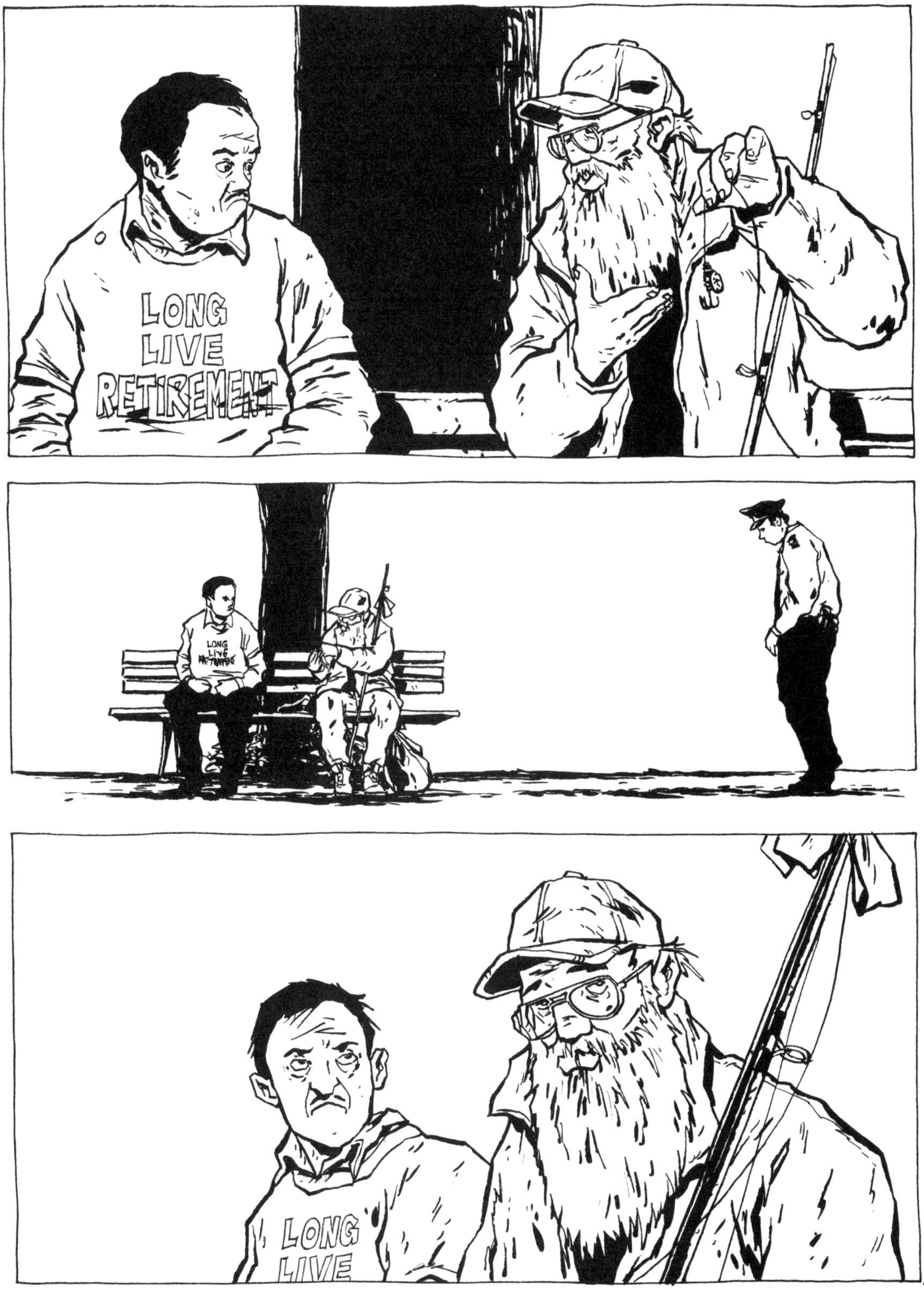
LONG
LIVE
RETIREMENT
LONG
LIVE
LONG
LIVE

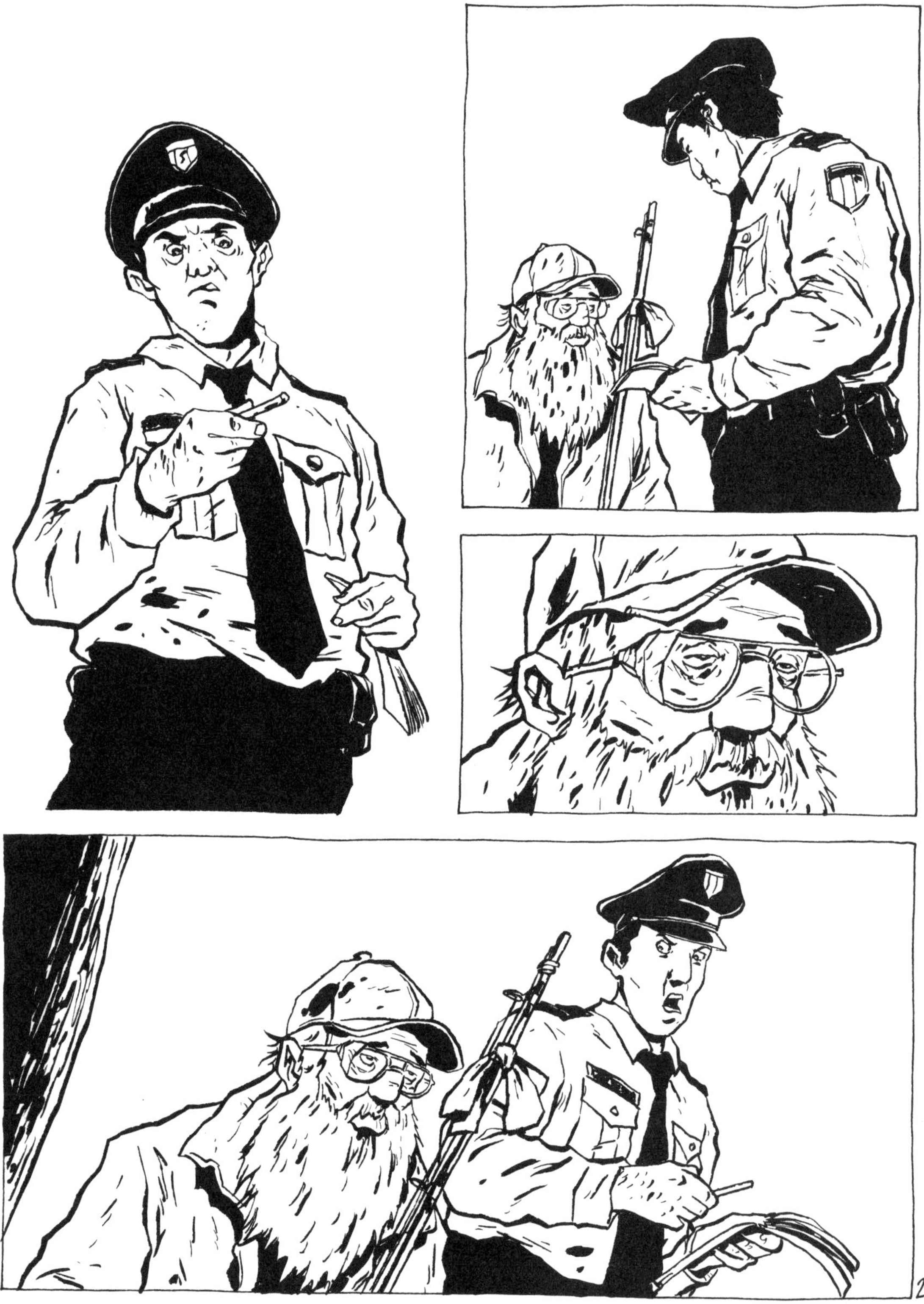

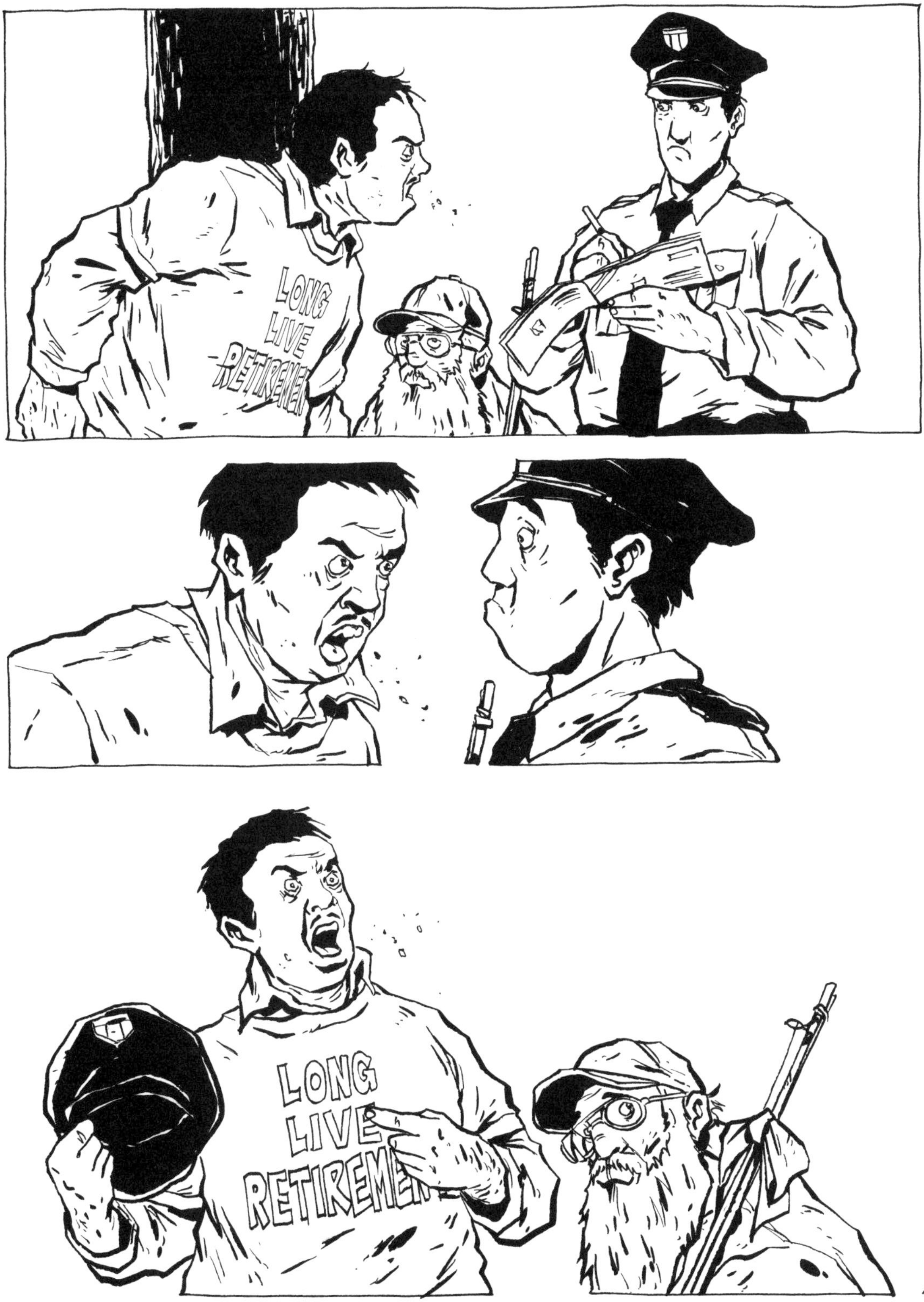
LONG
LIVE
RETIREMEN
LONG
LIVE
RETIREMEN

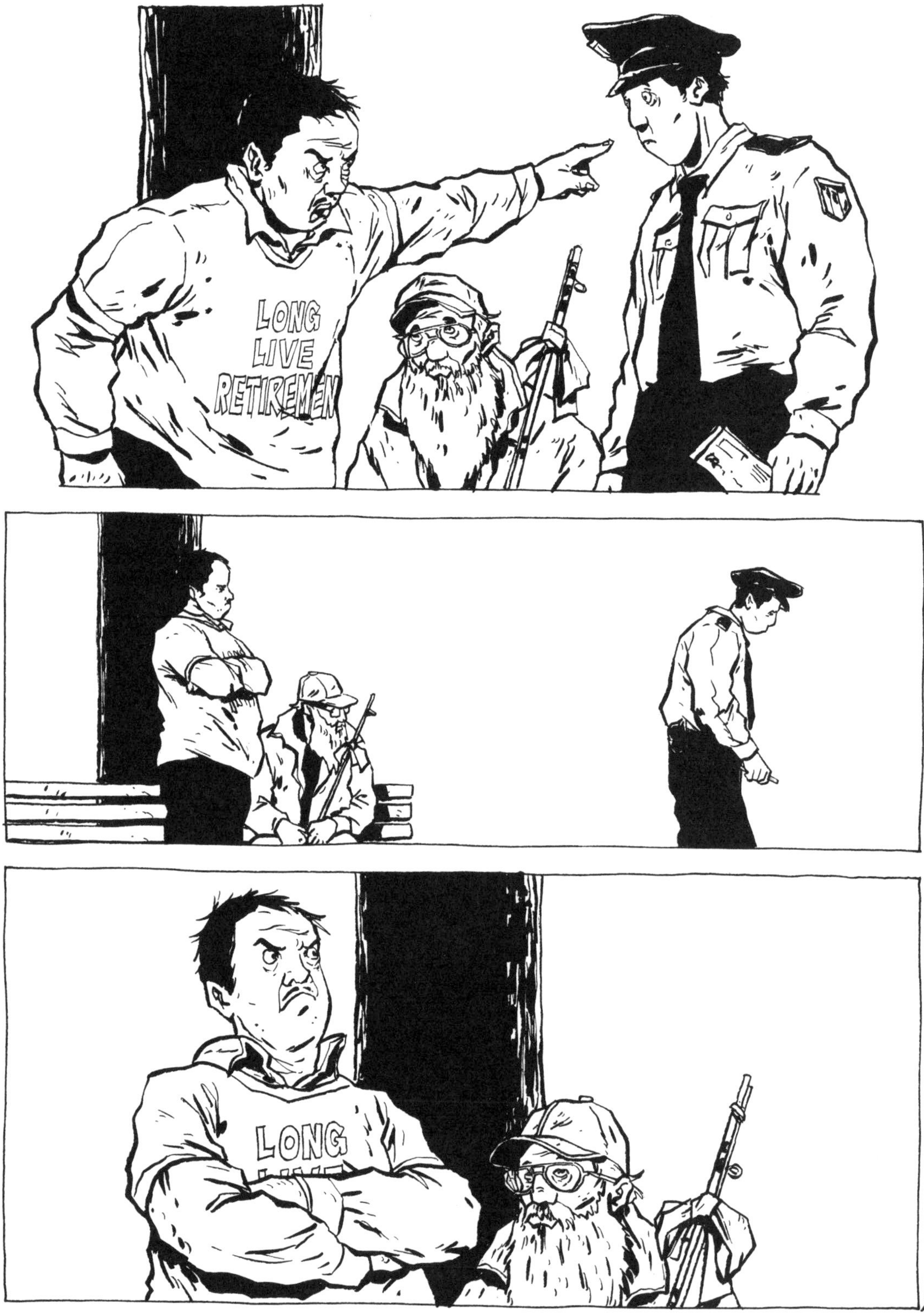
LONG
LIVE
RETIREMEN
LONG

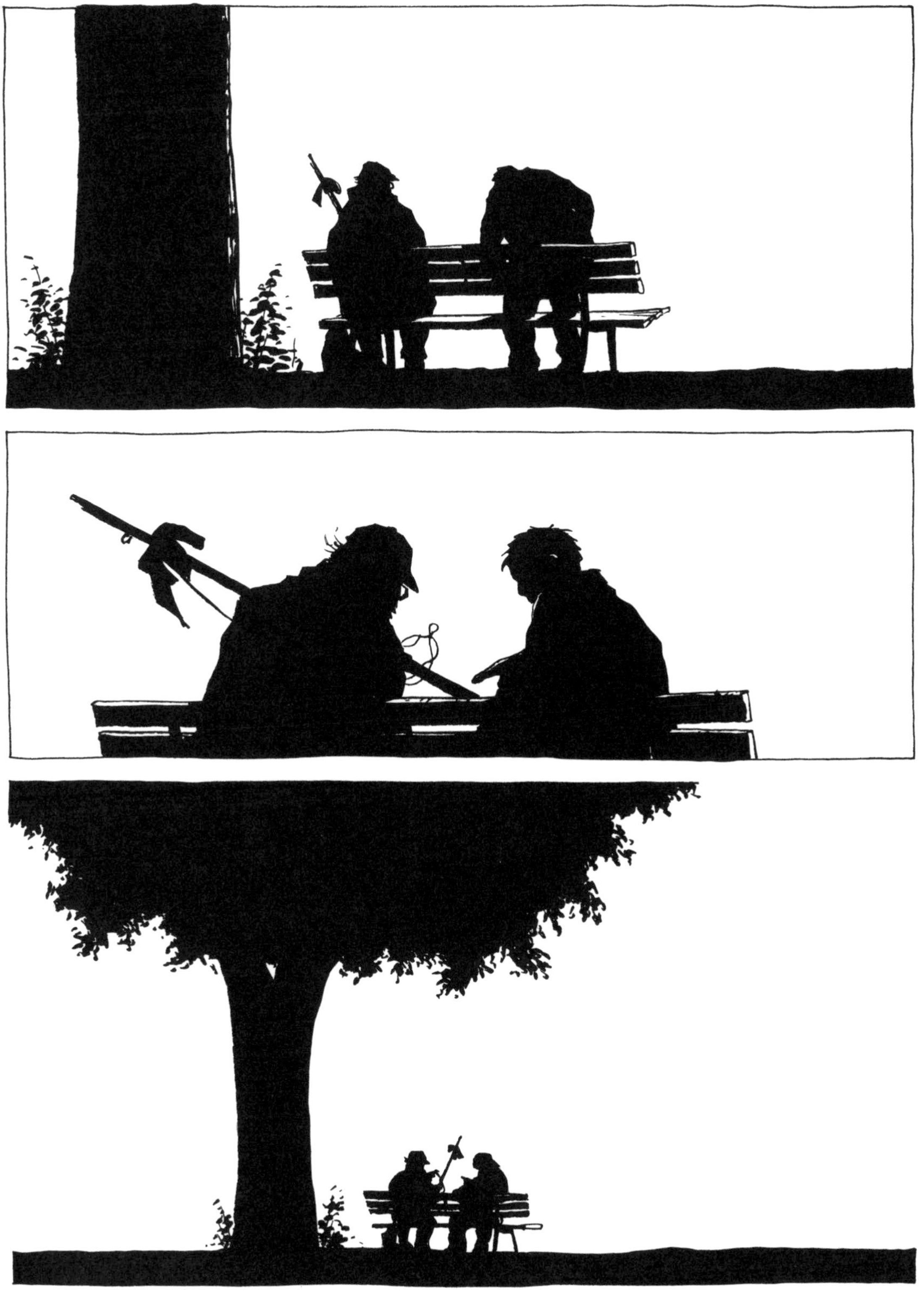

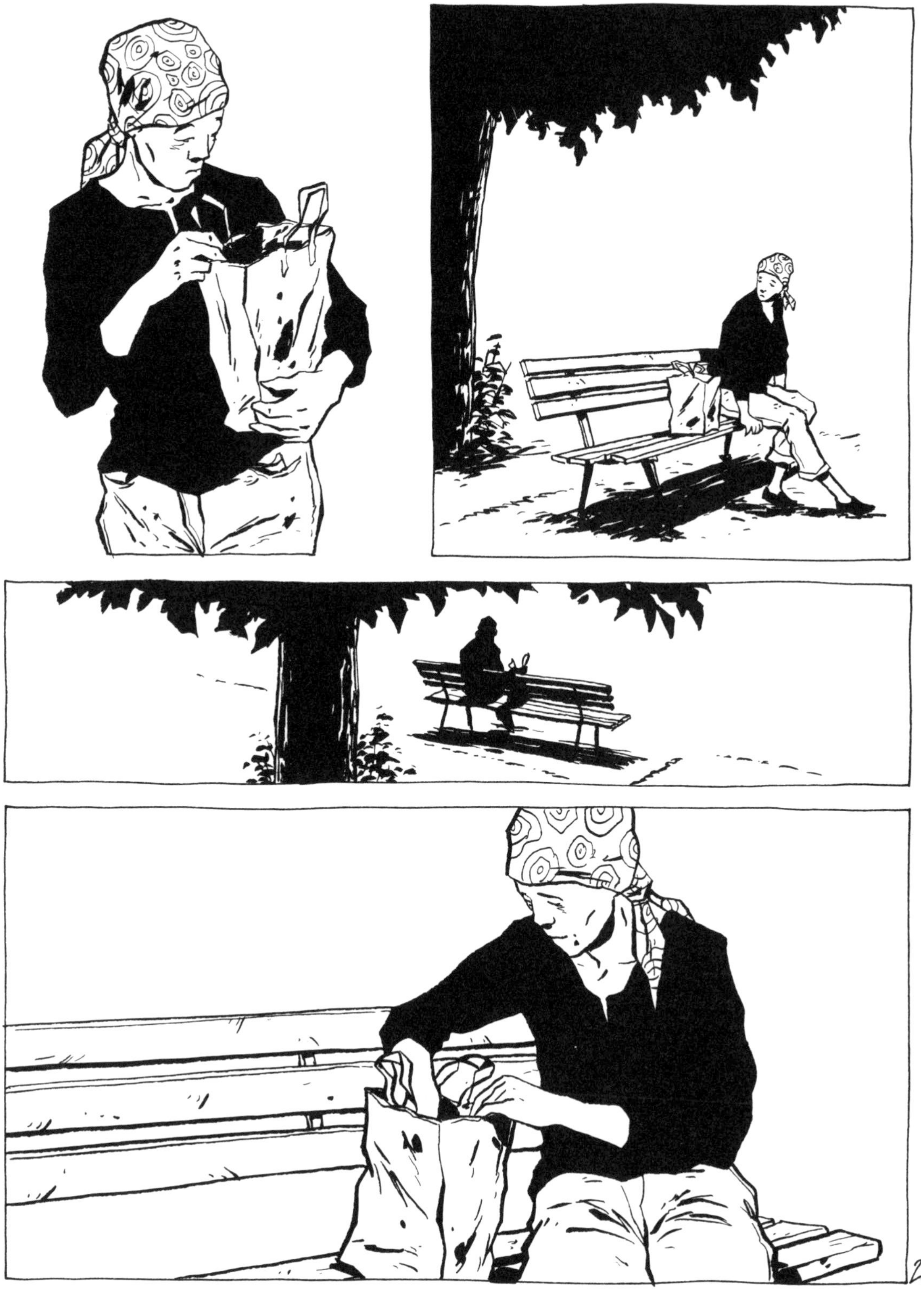

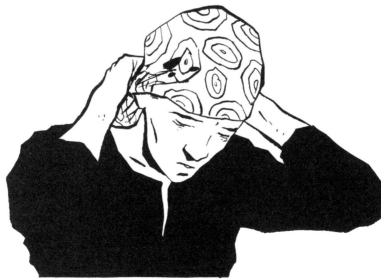

265.

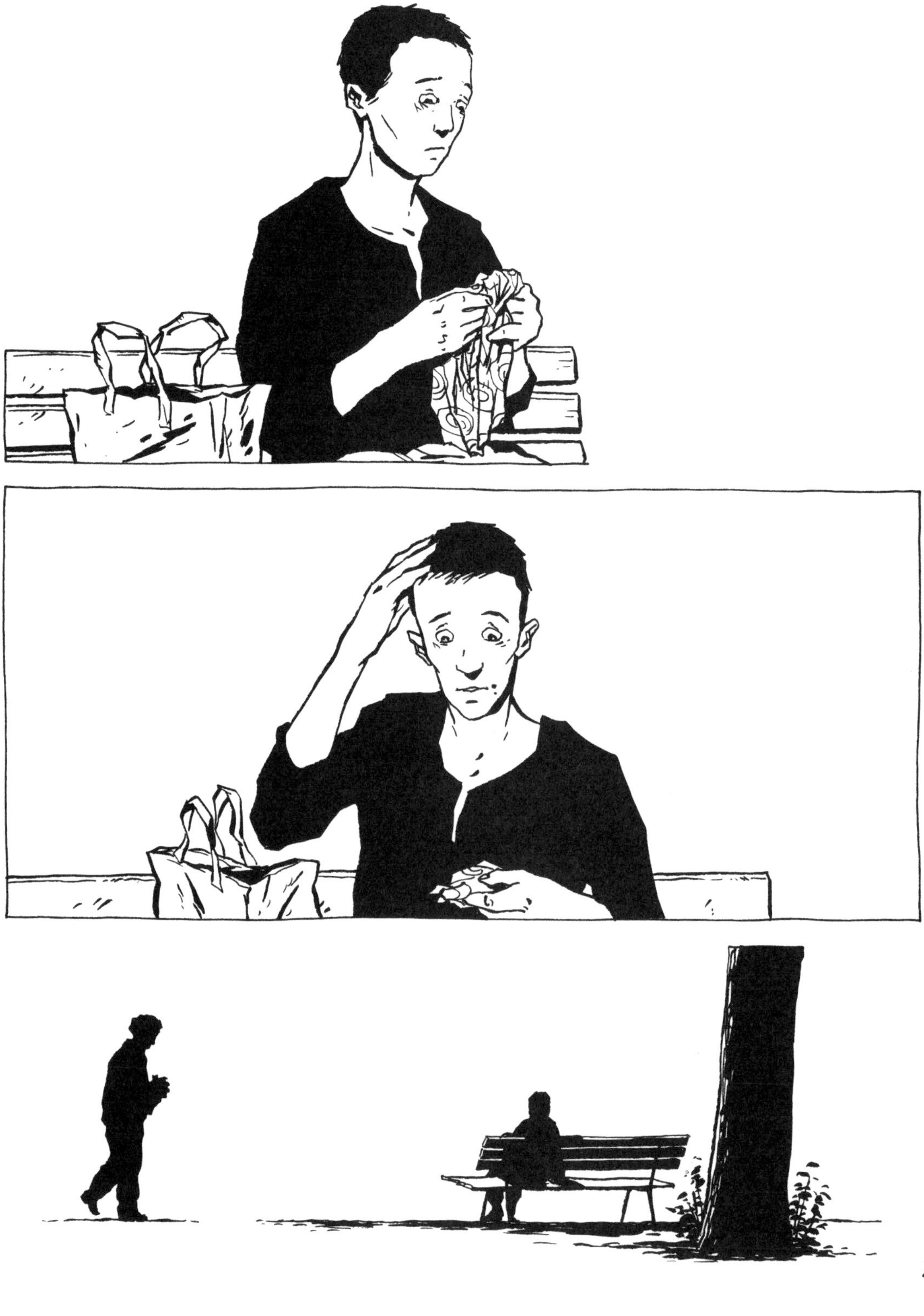

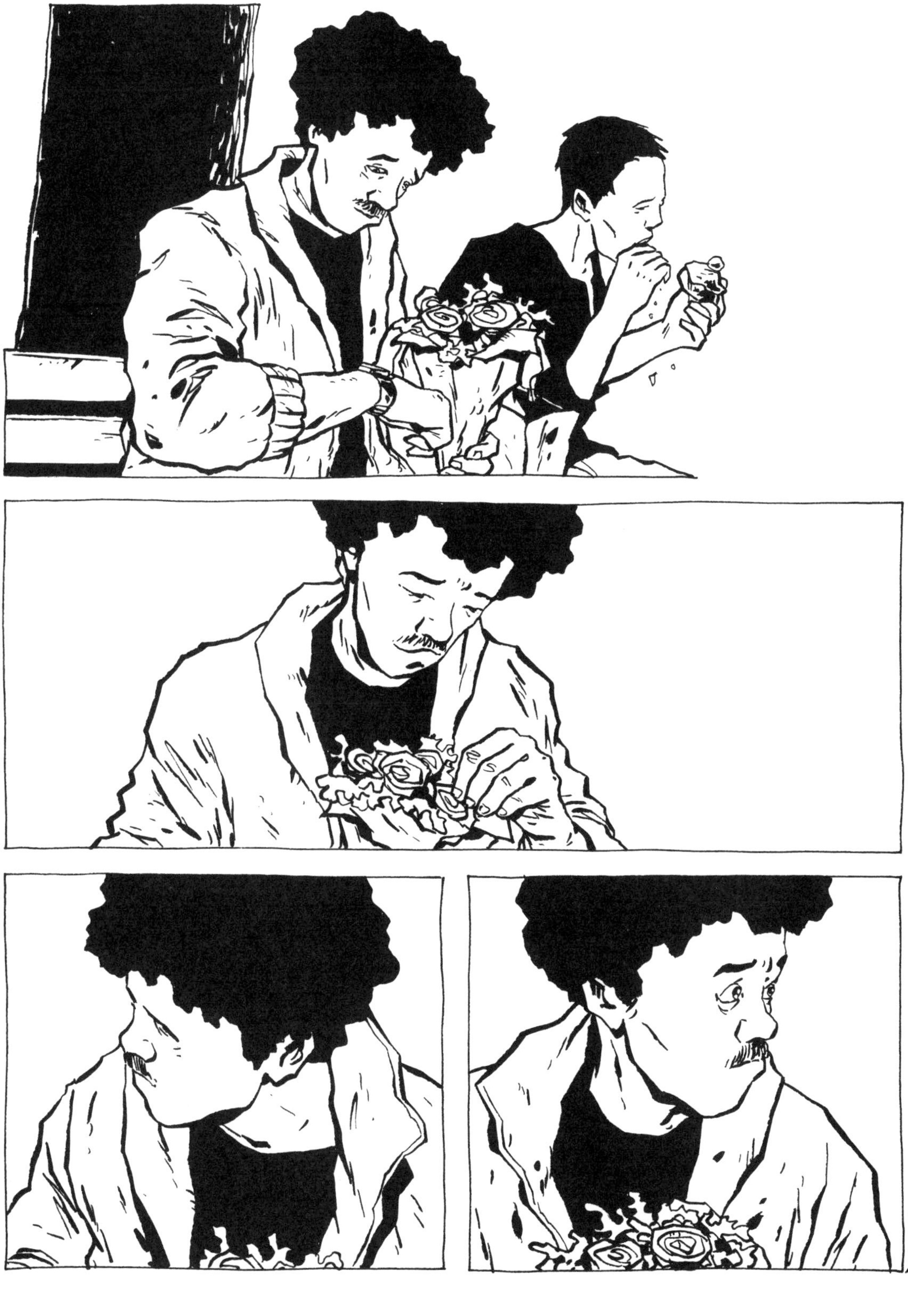

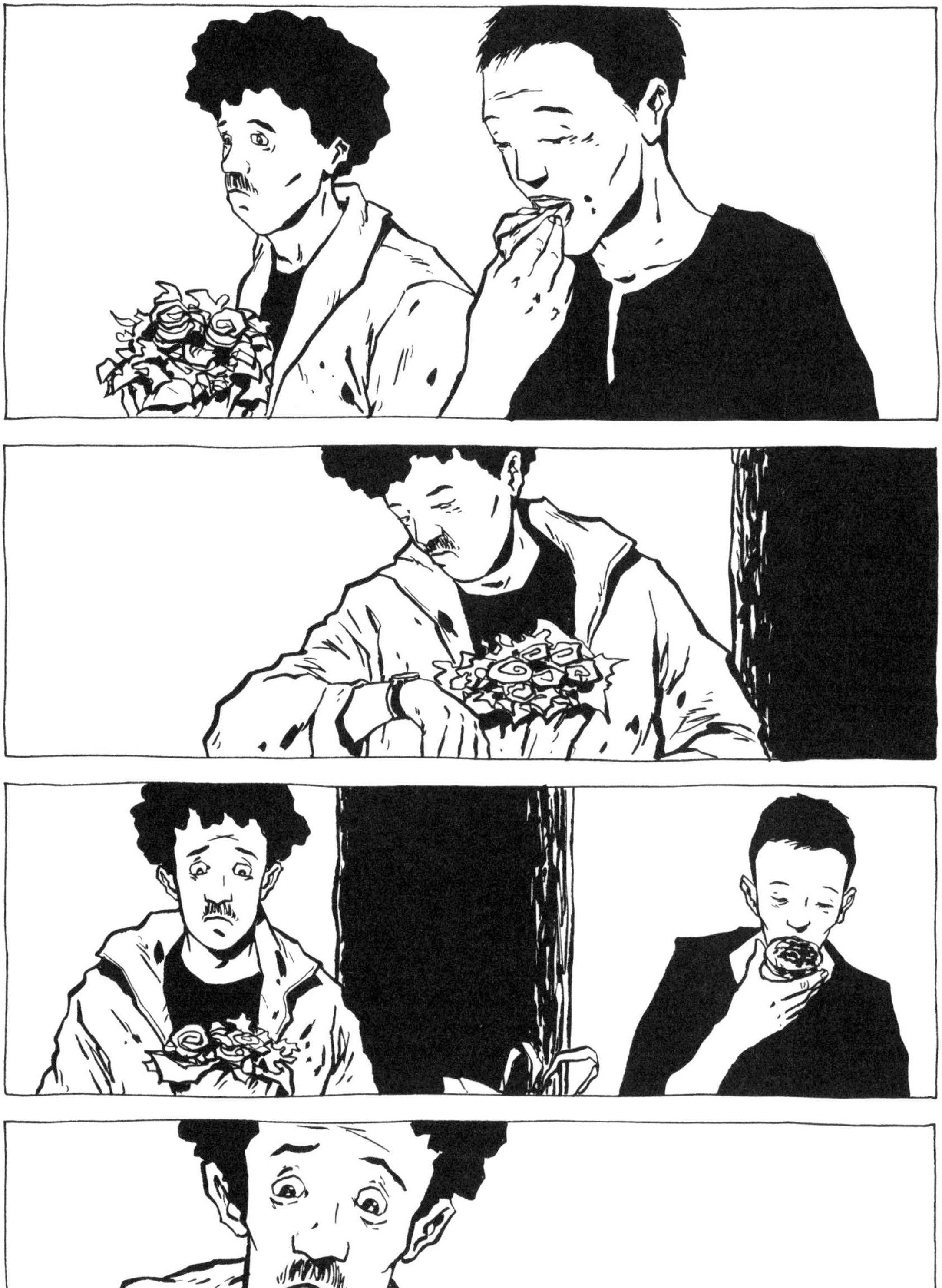

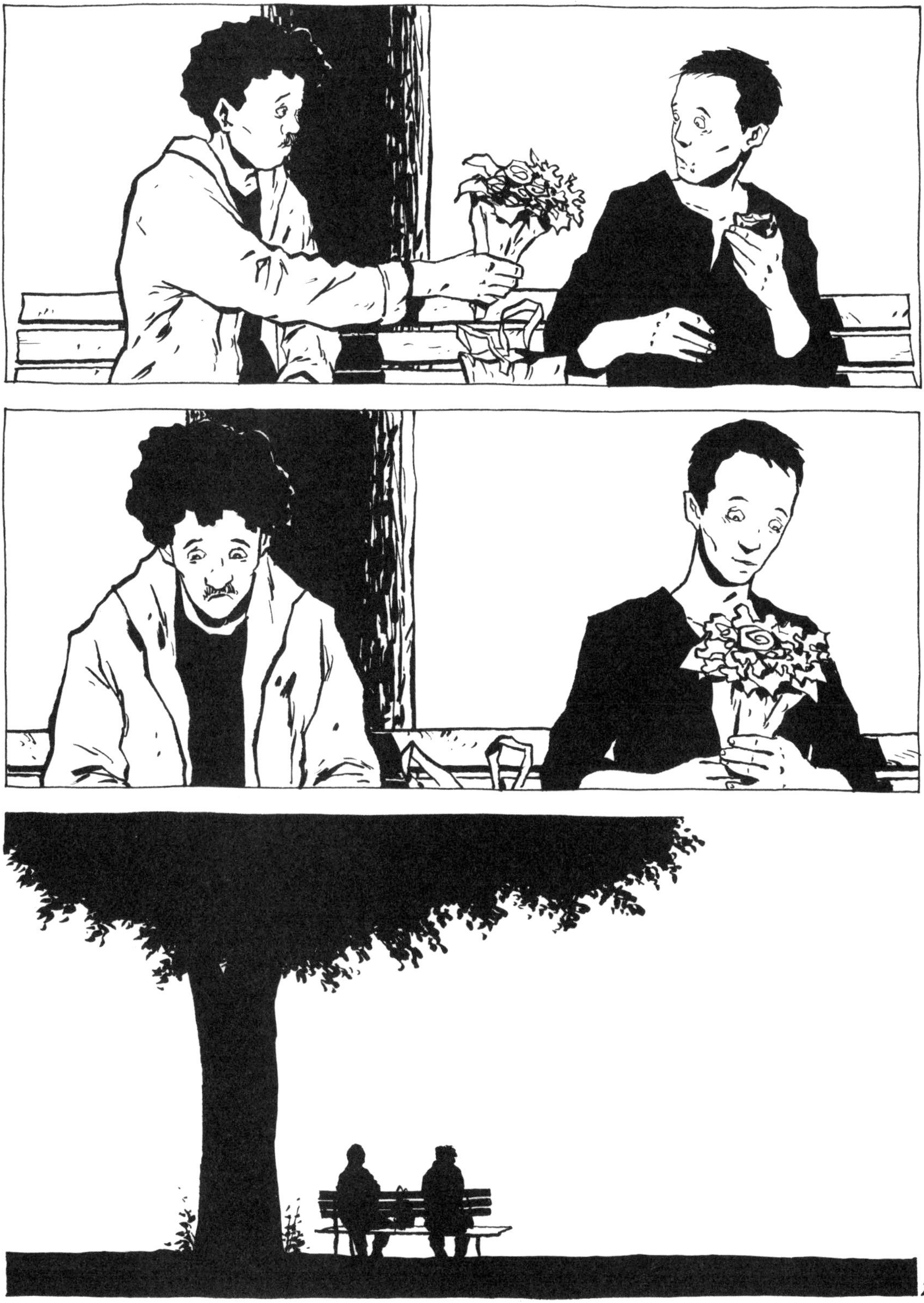

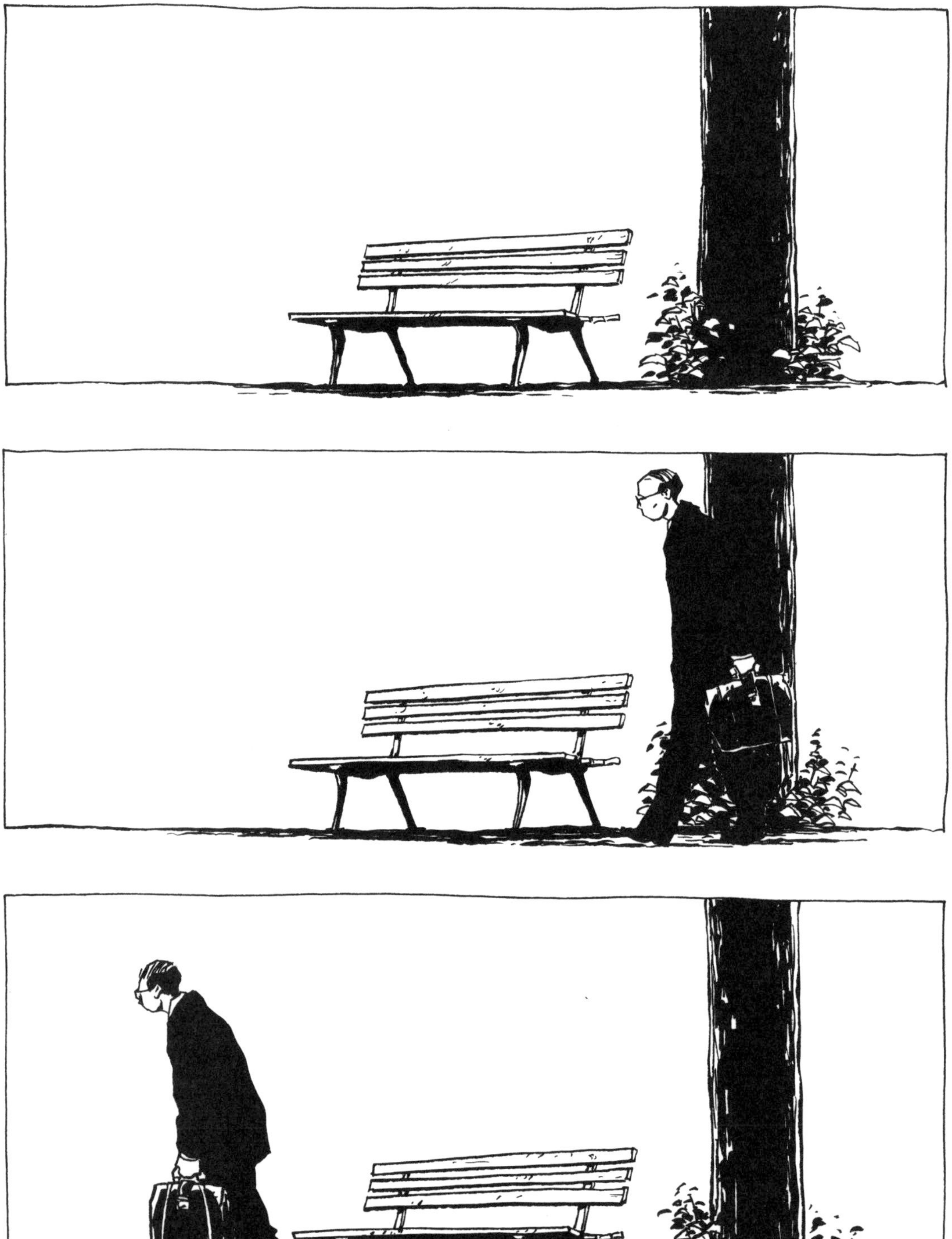

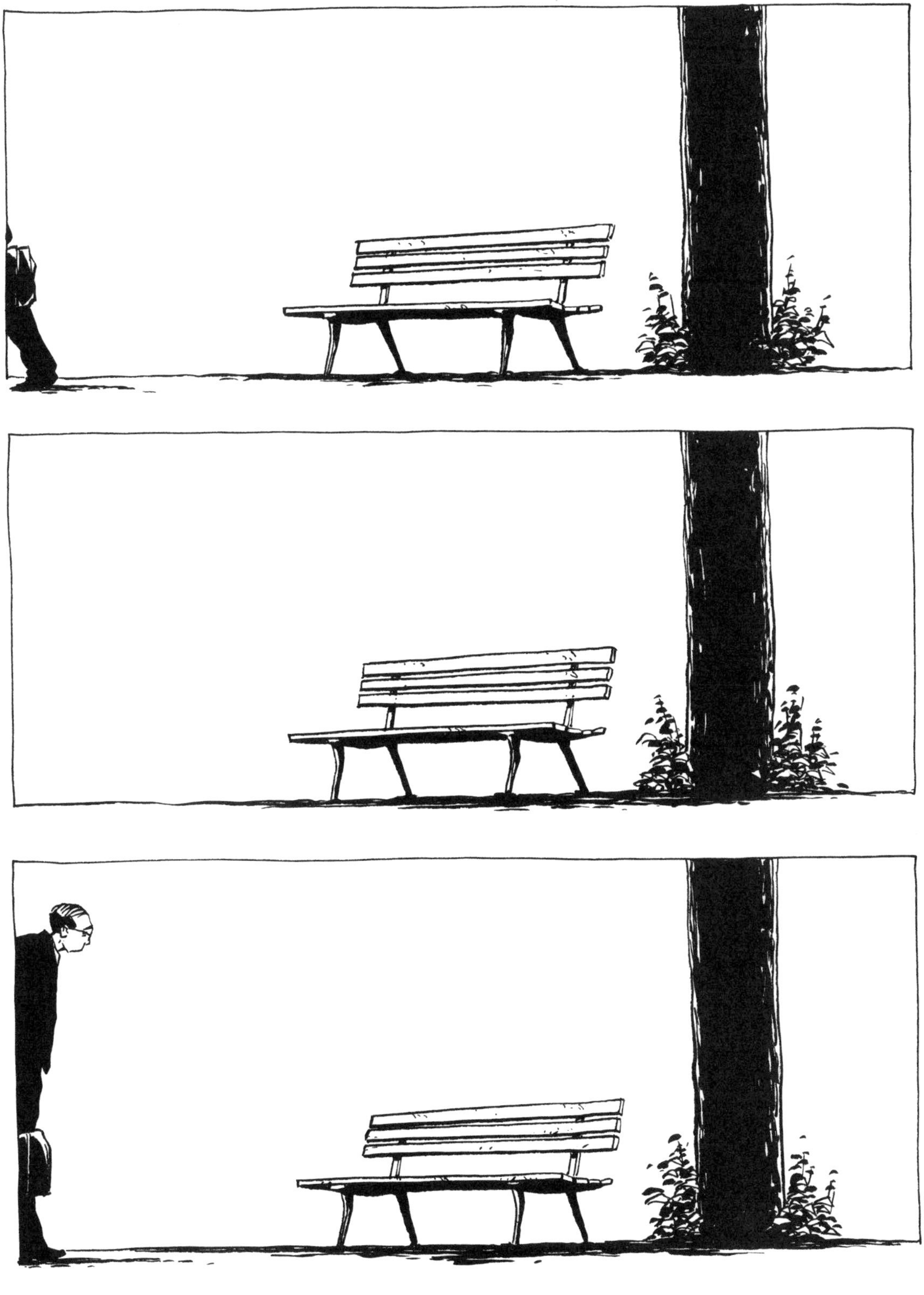

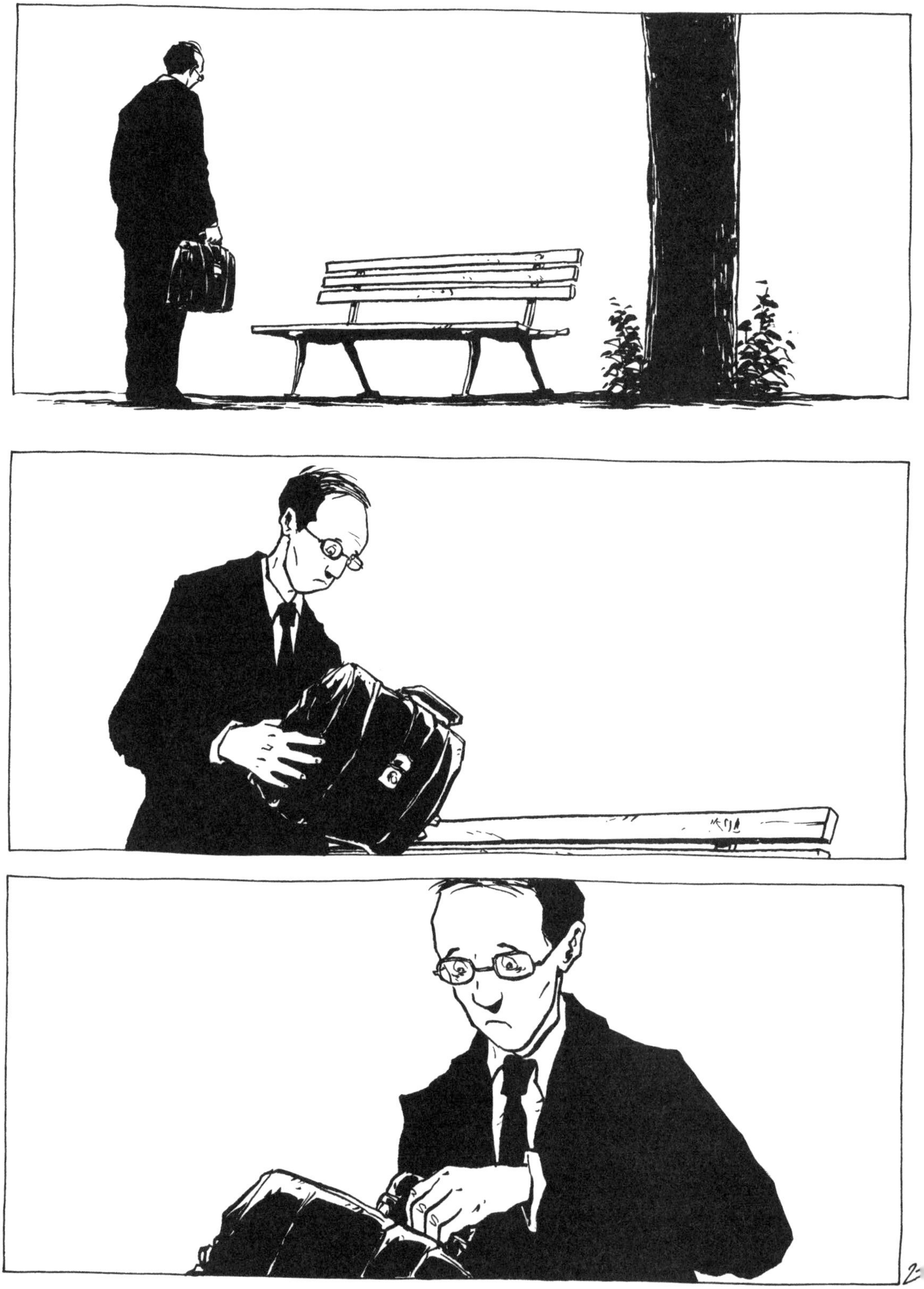

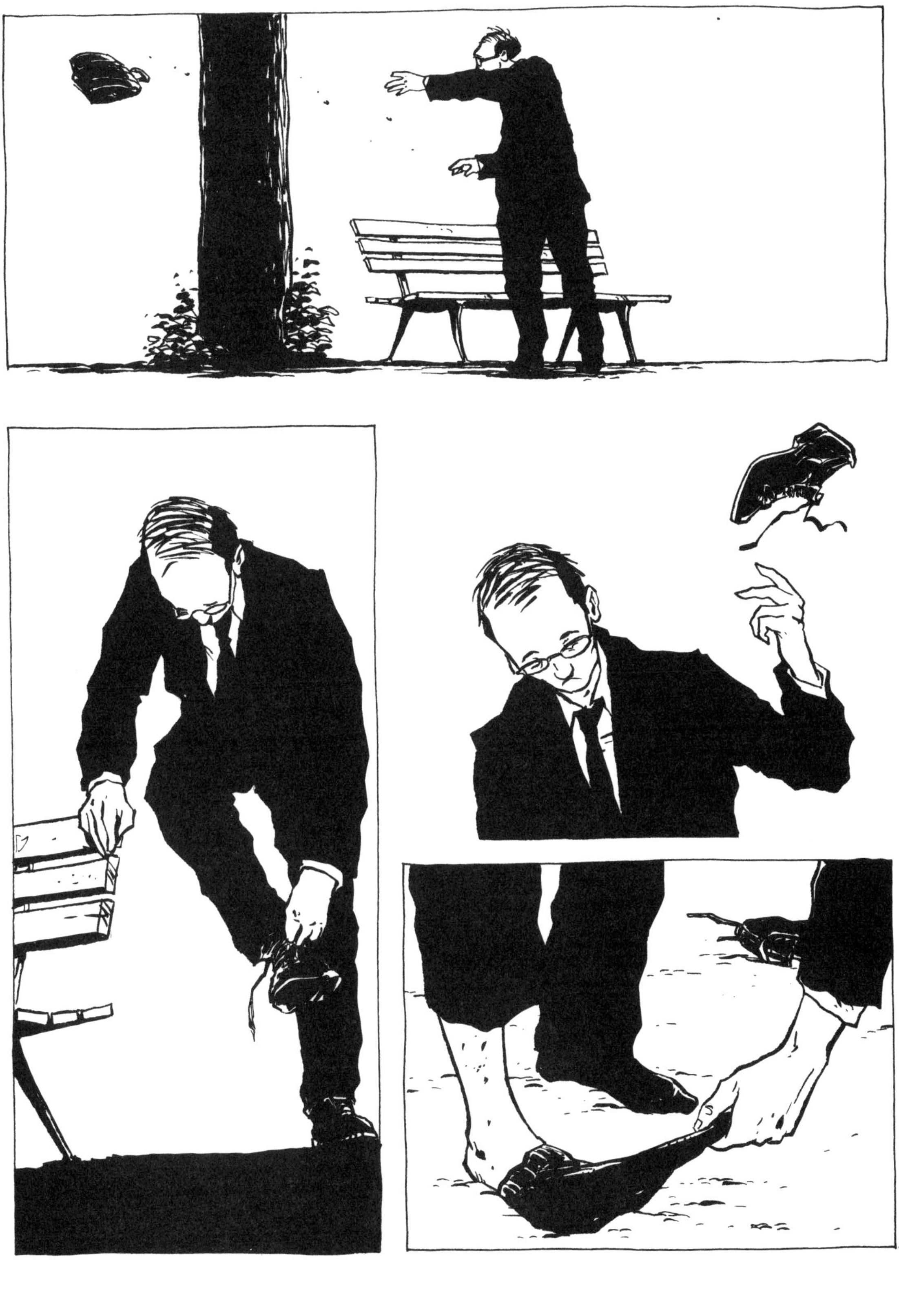

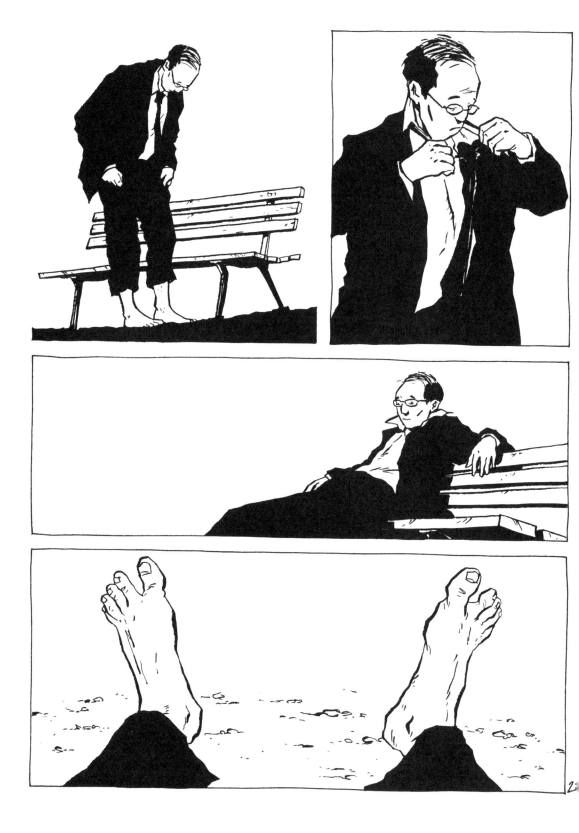

21

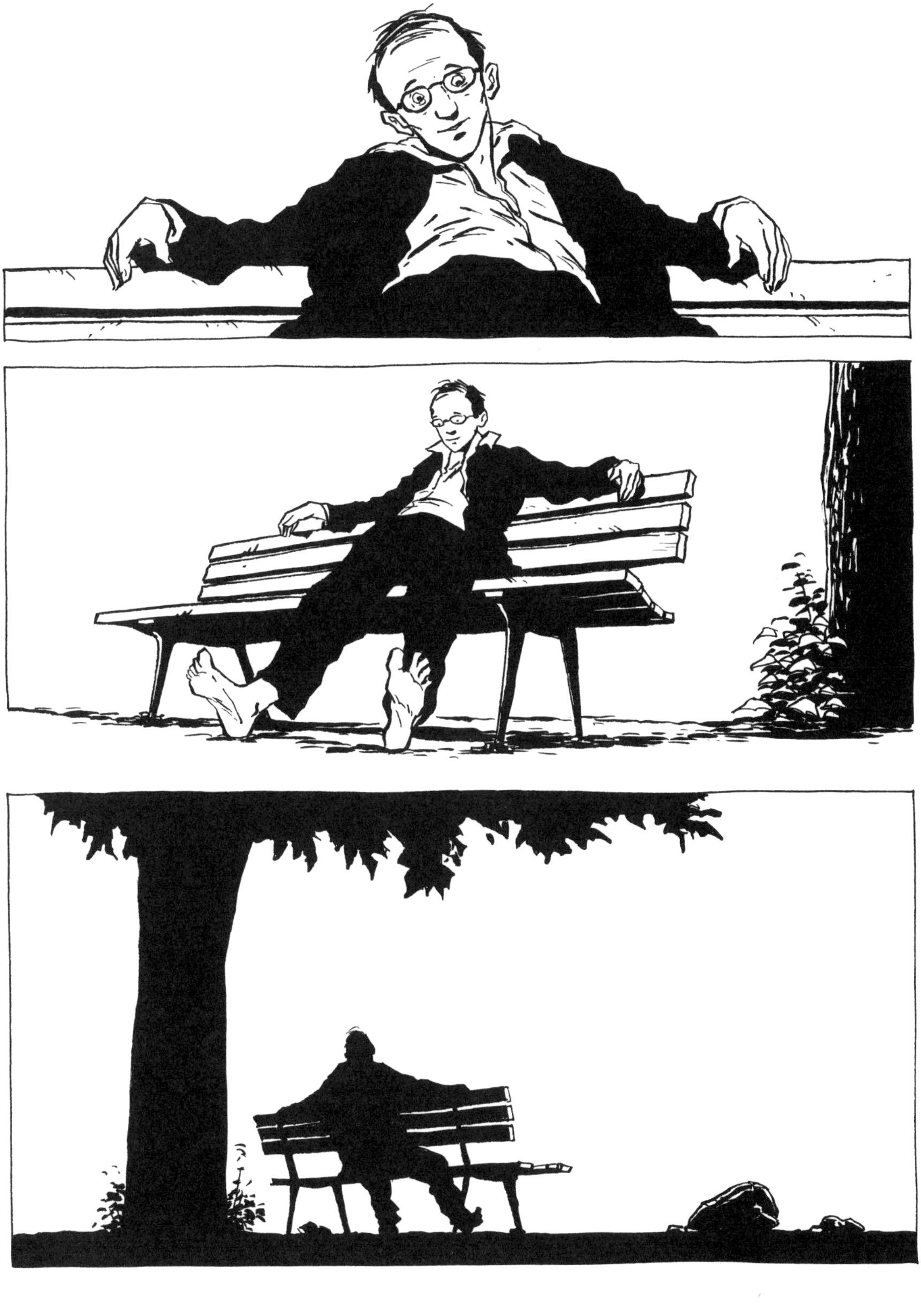

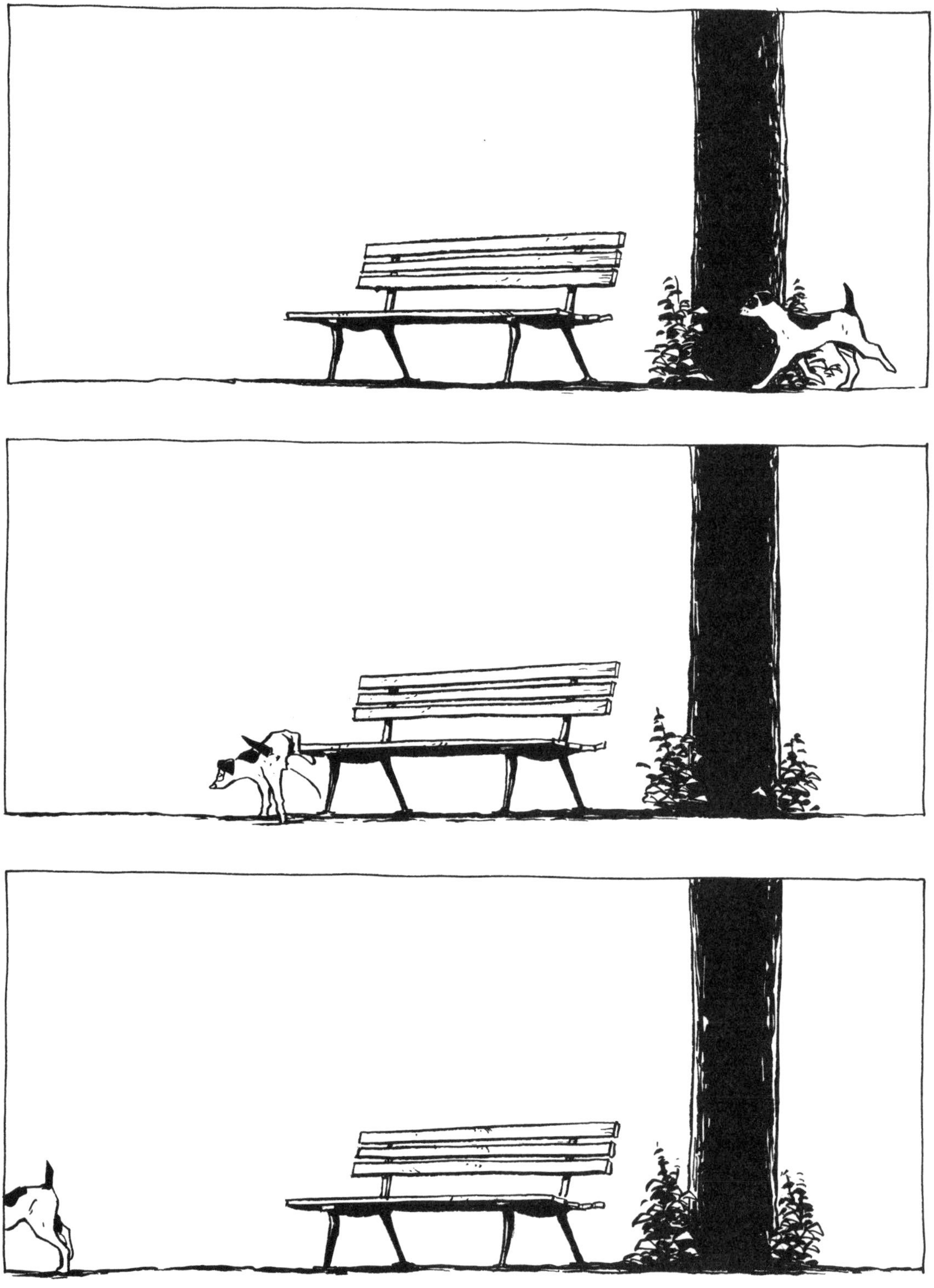

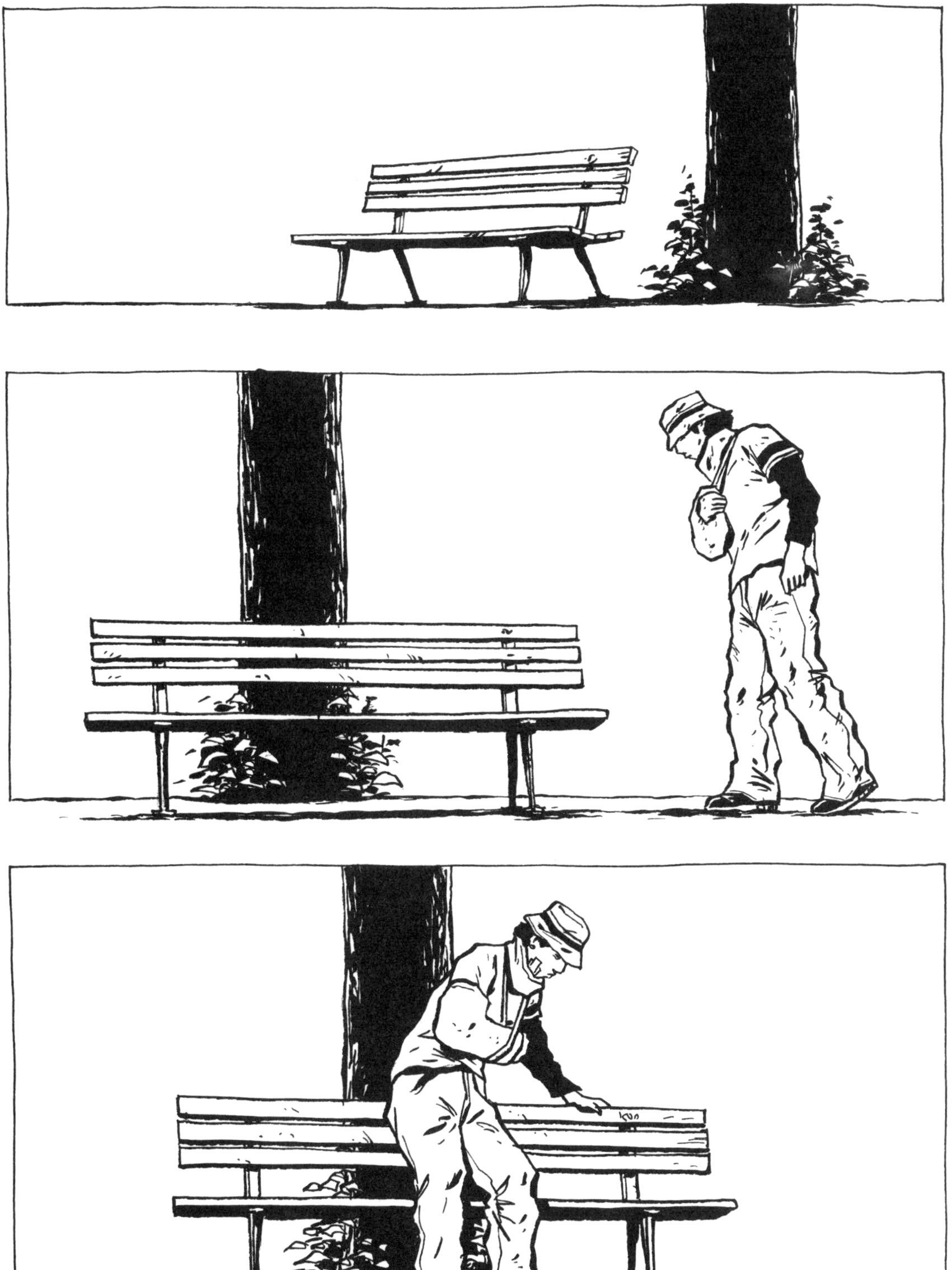

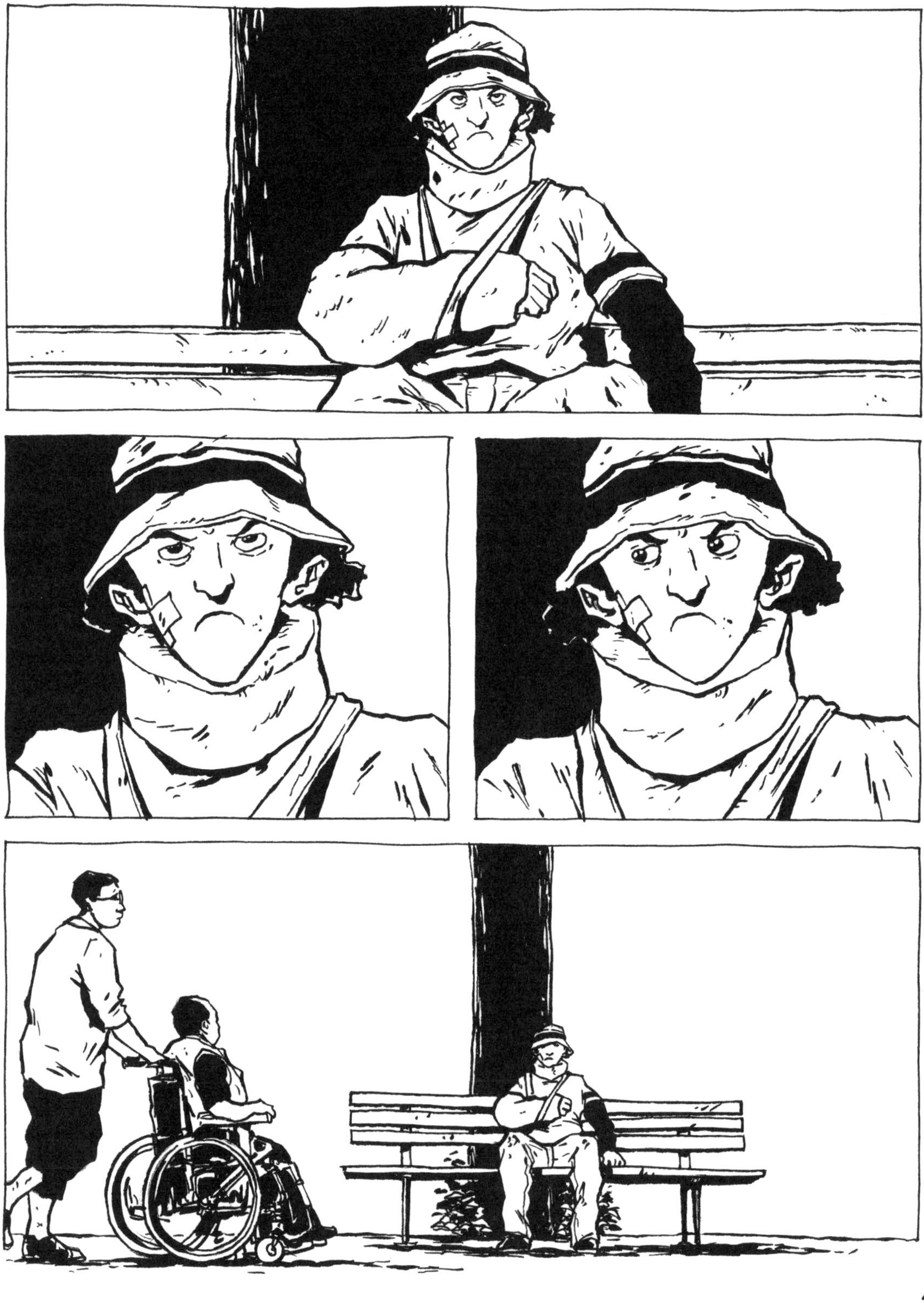

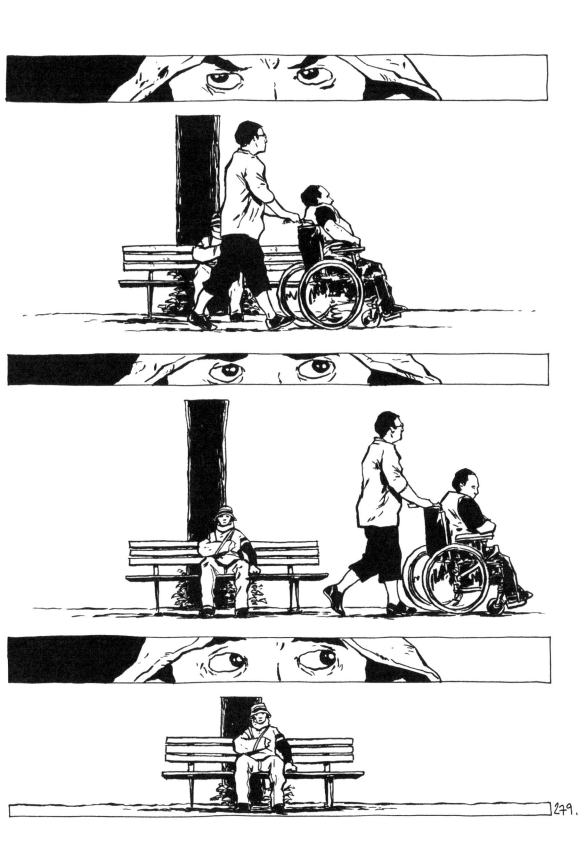

279.

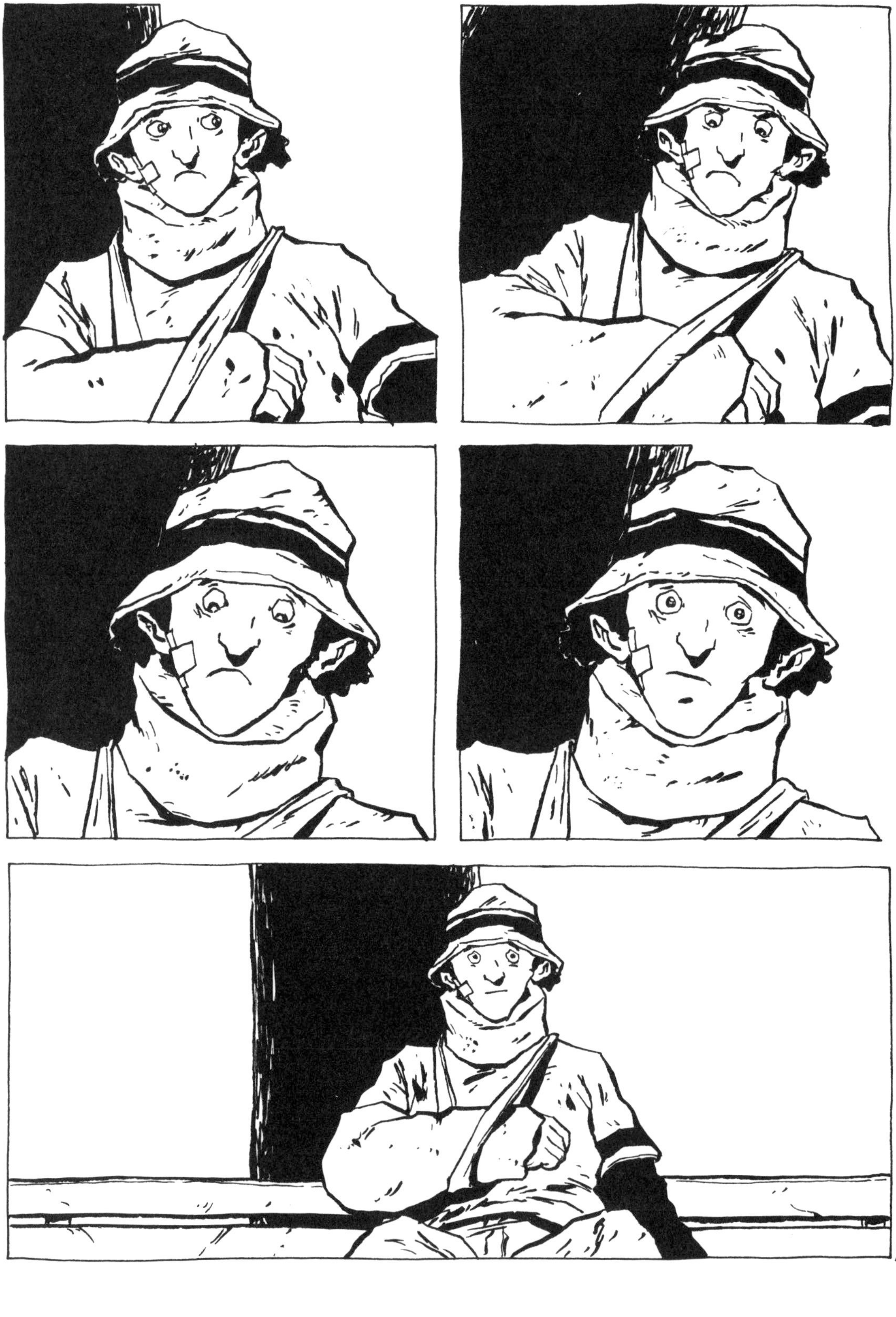

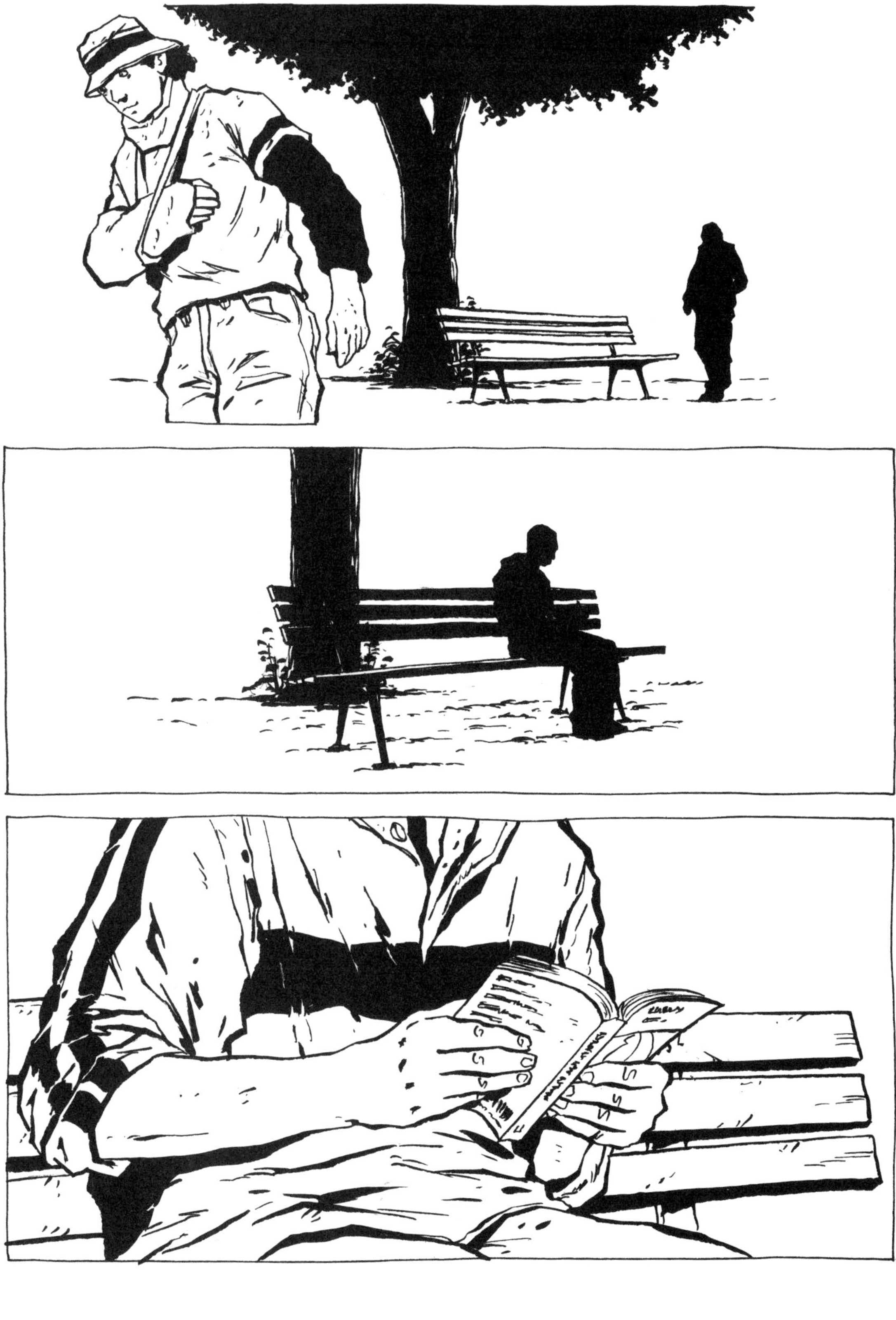

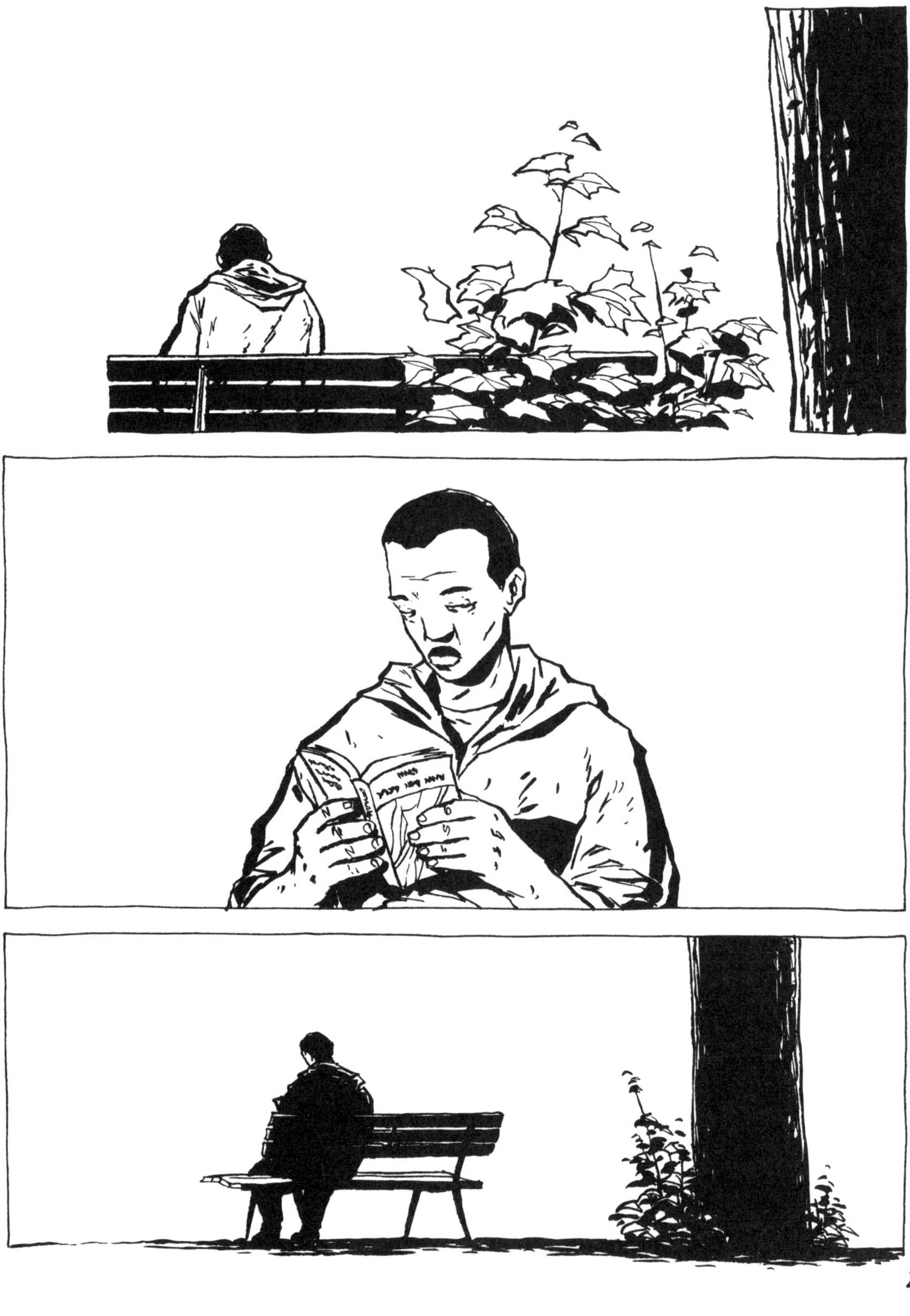

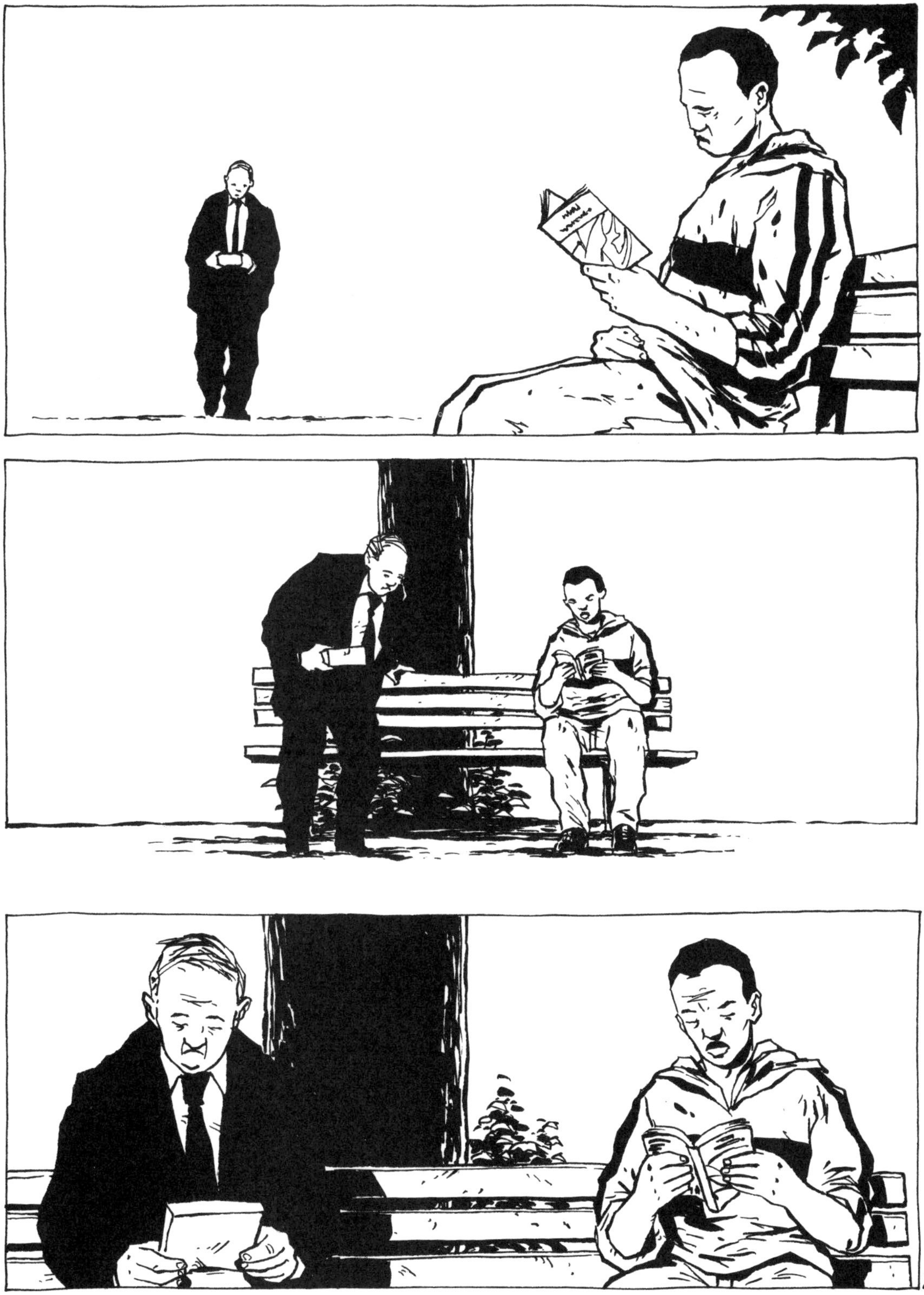

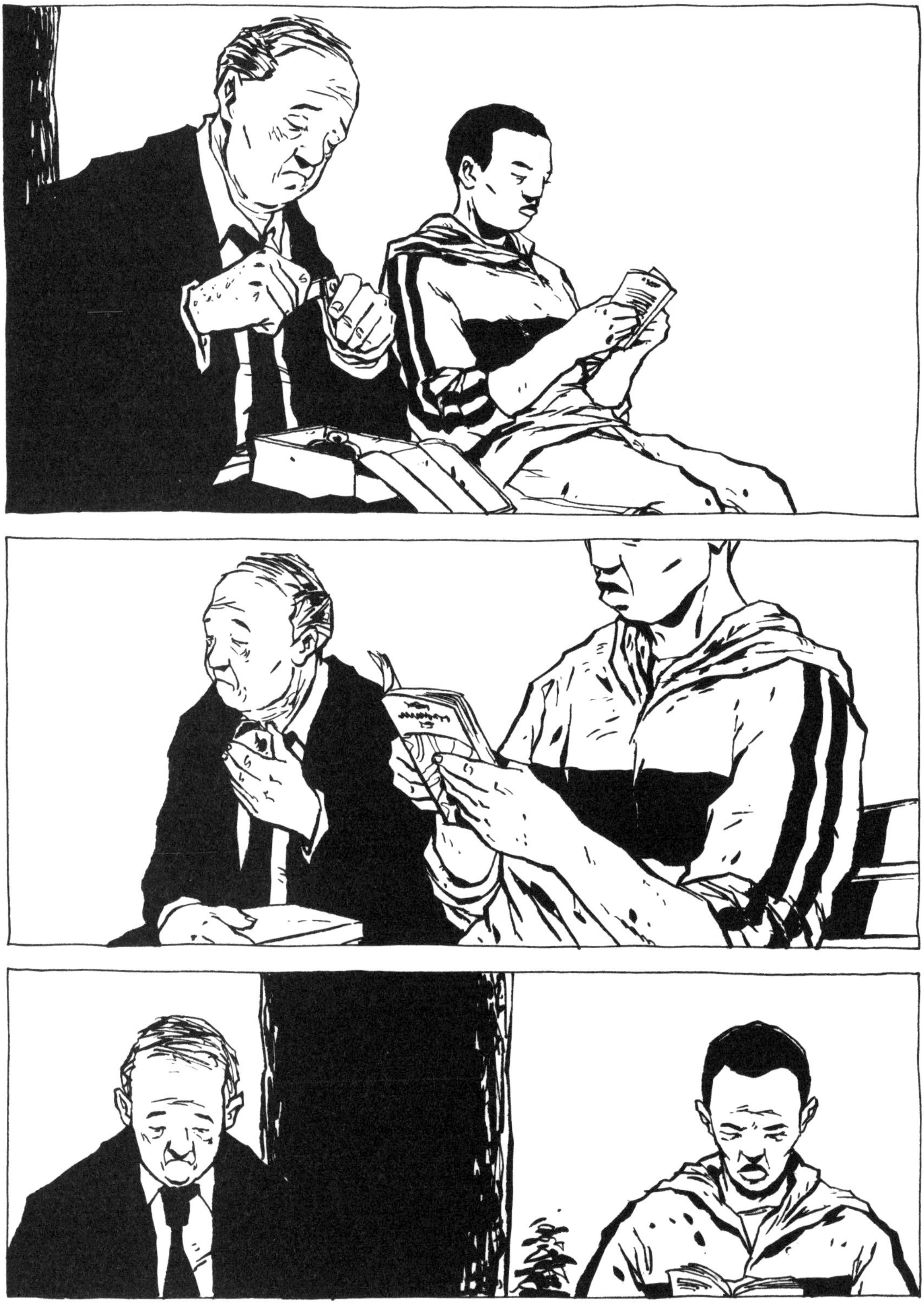

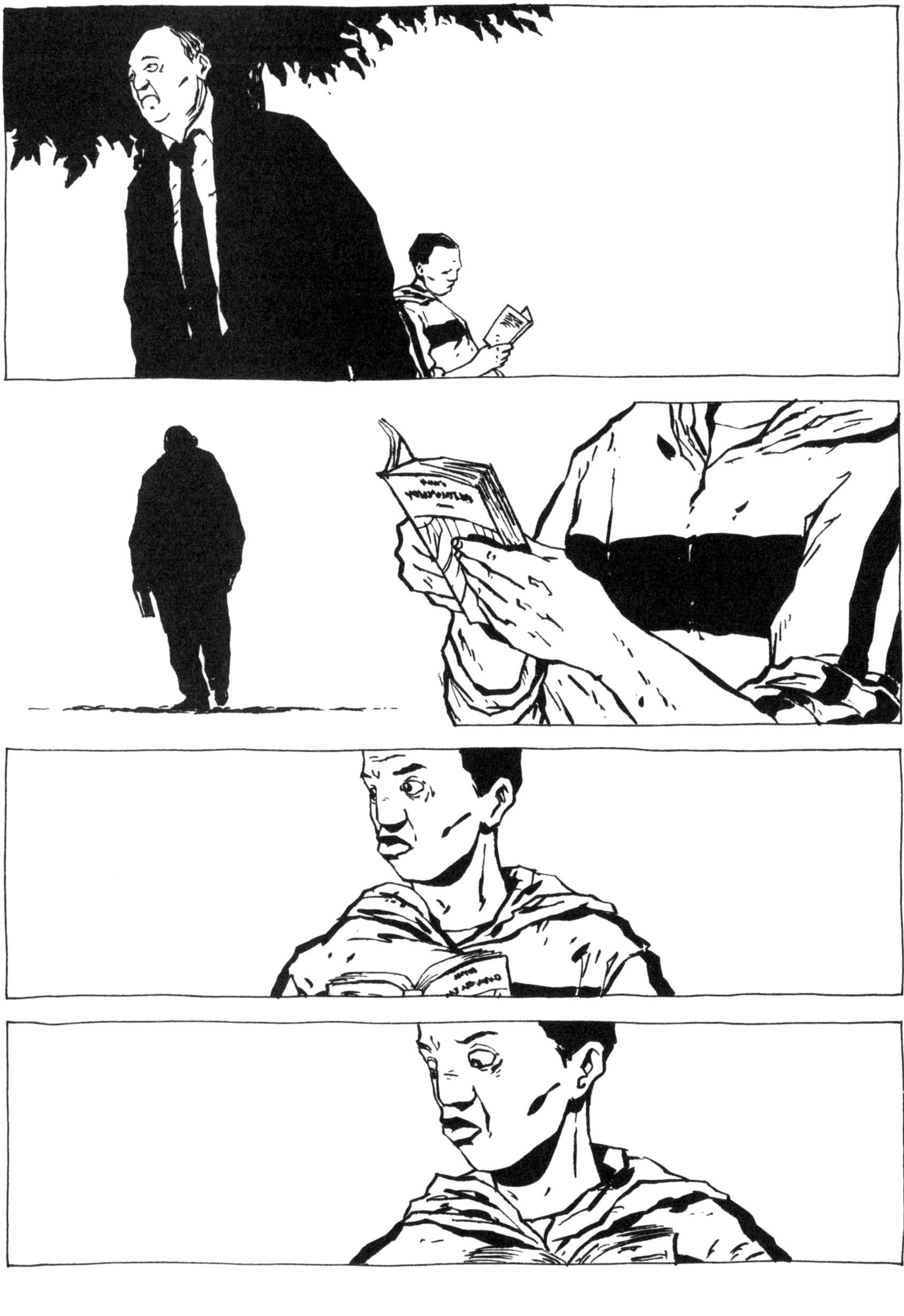

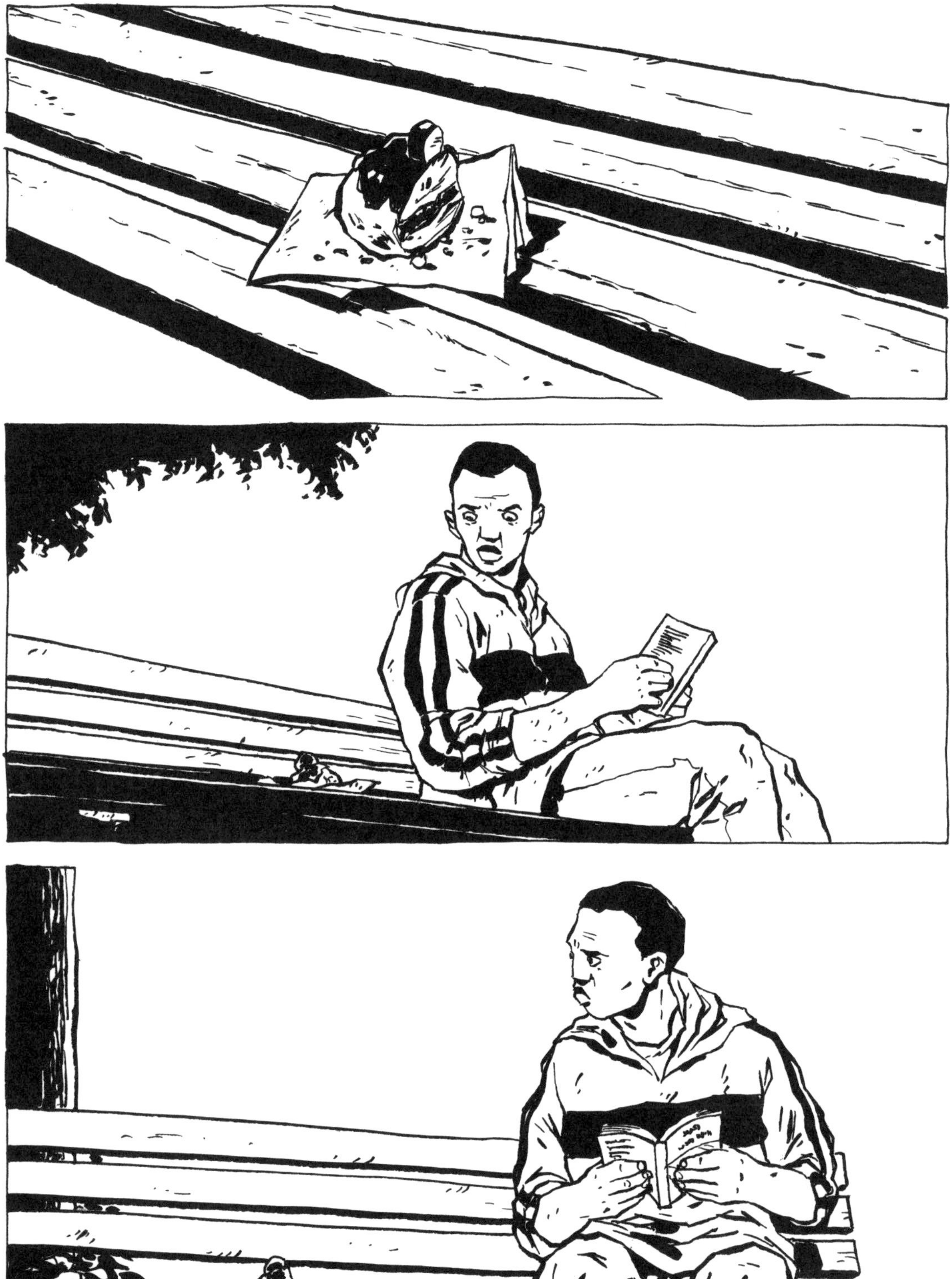

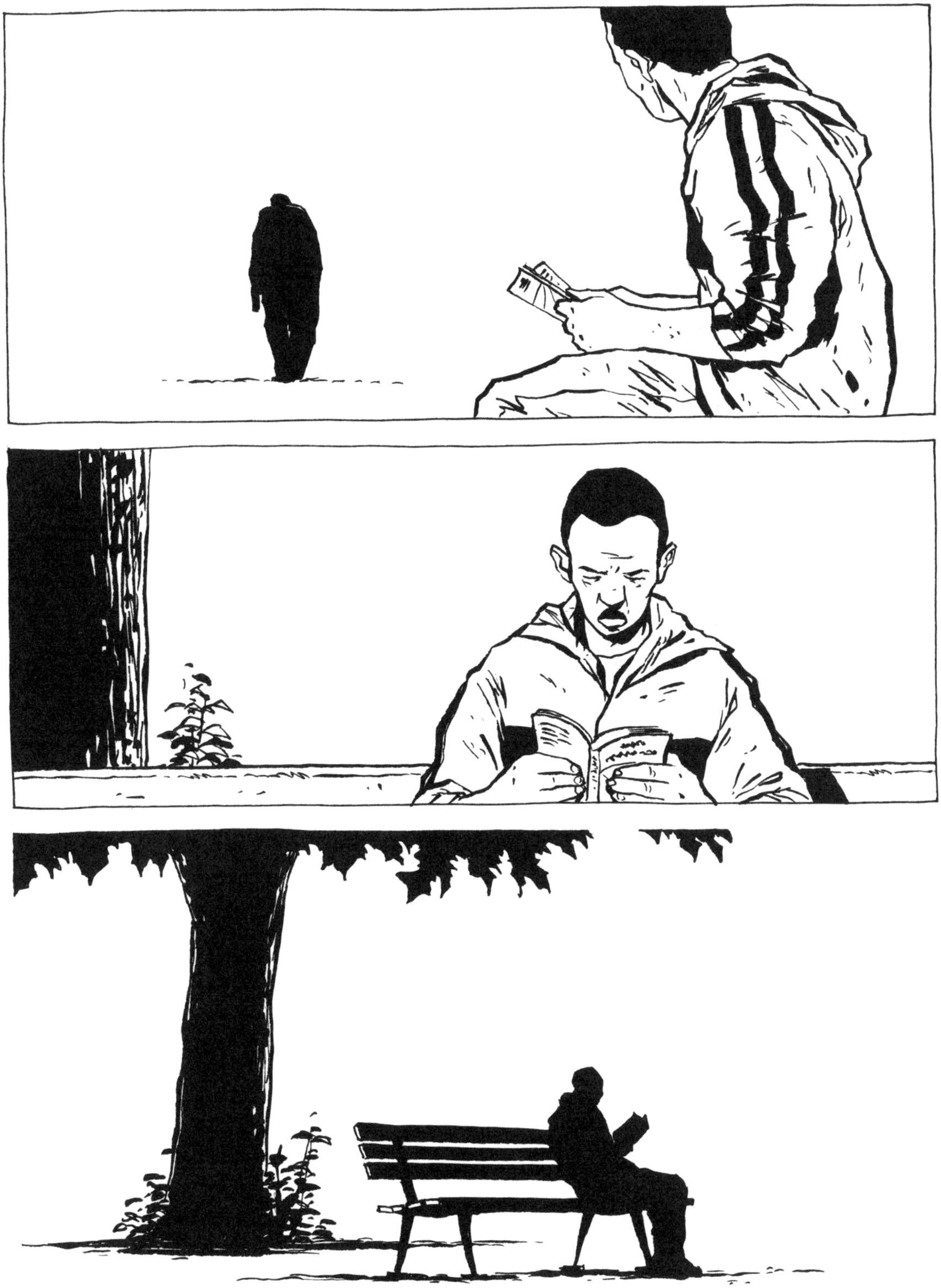

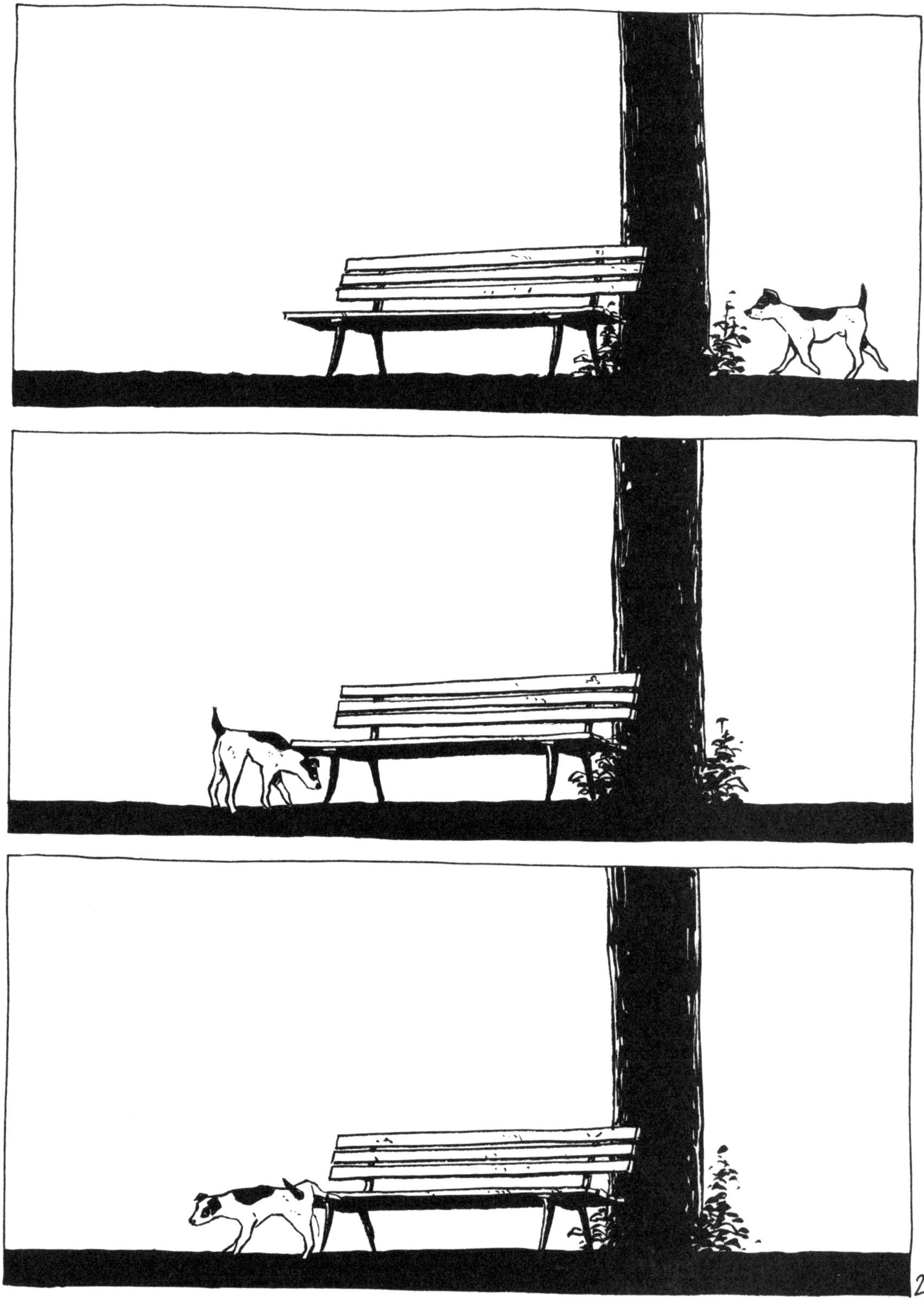

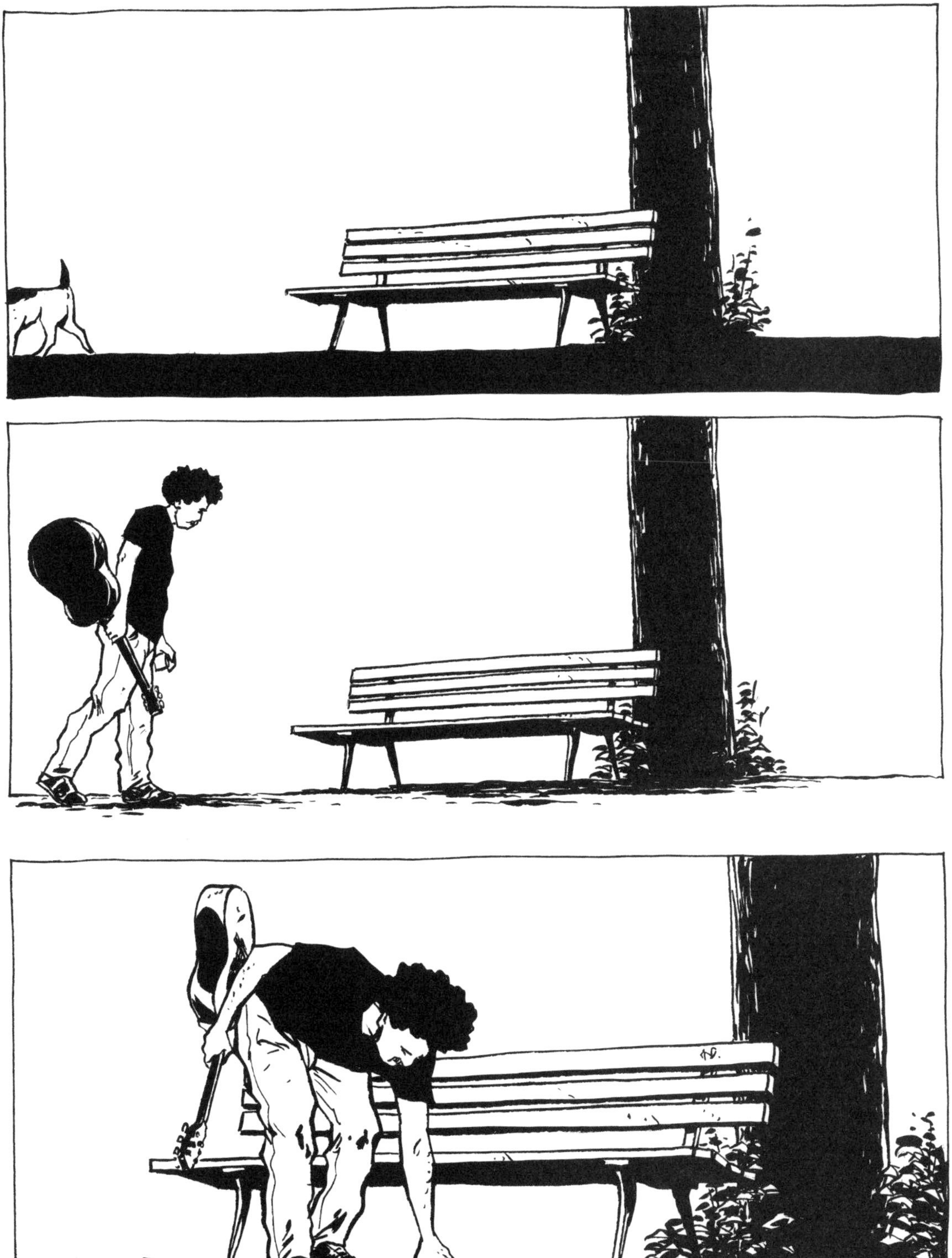

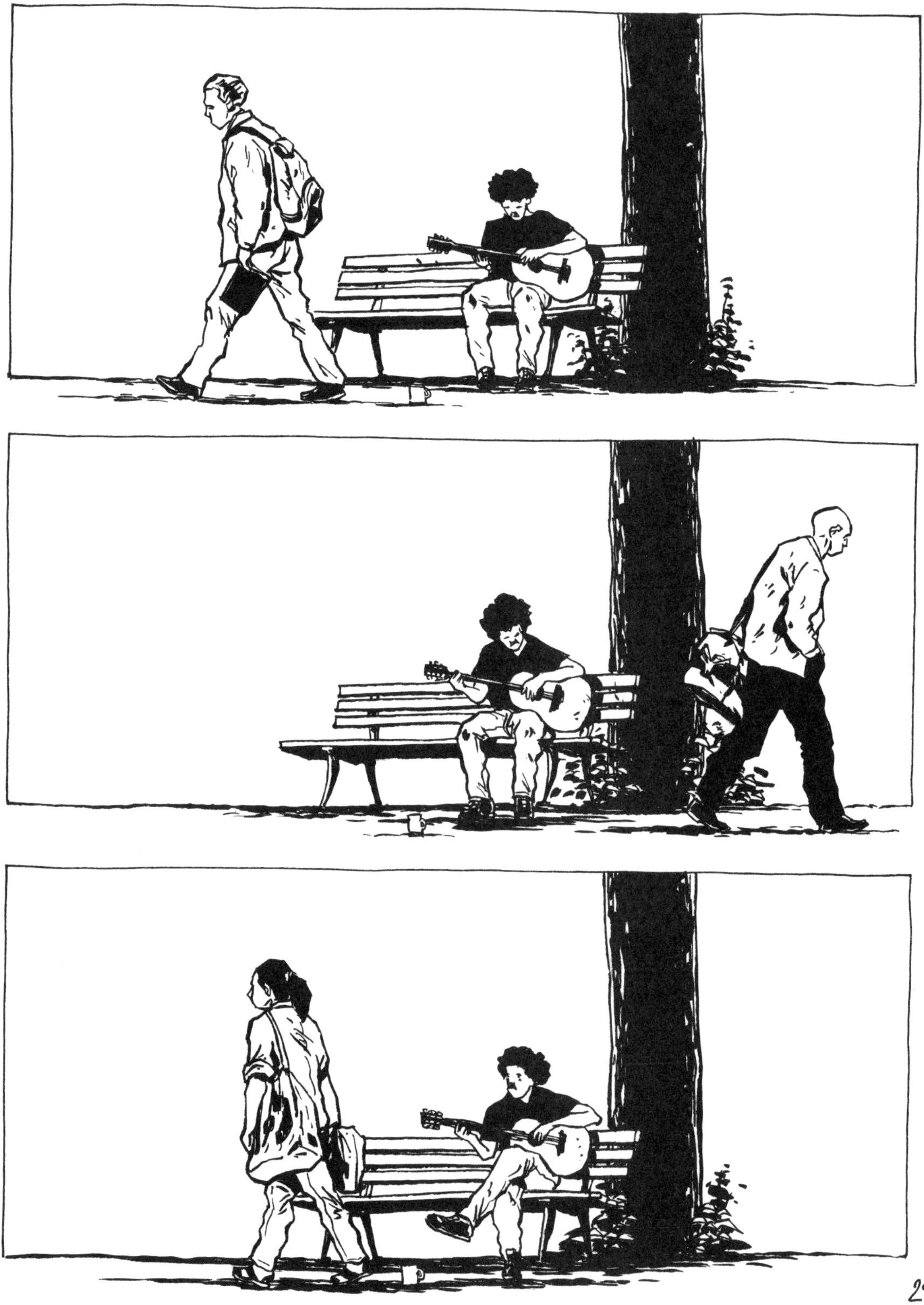

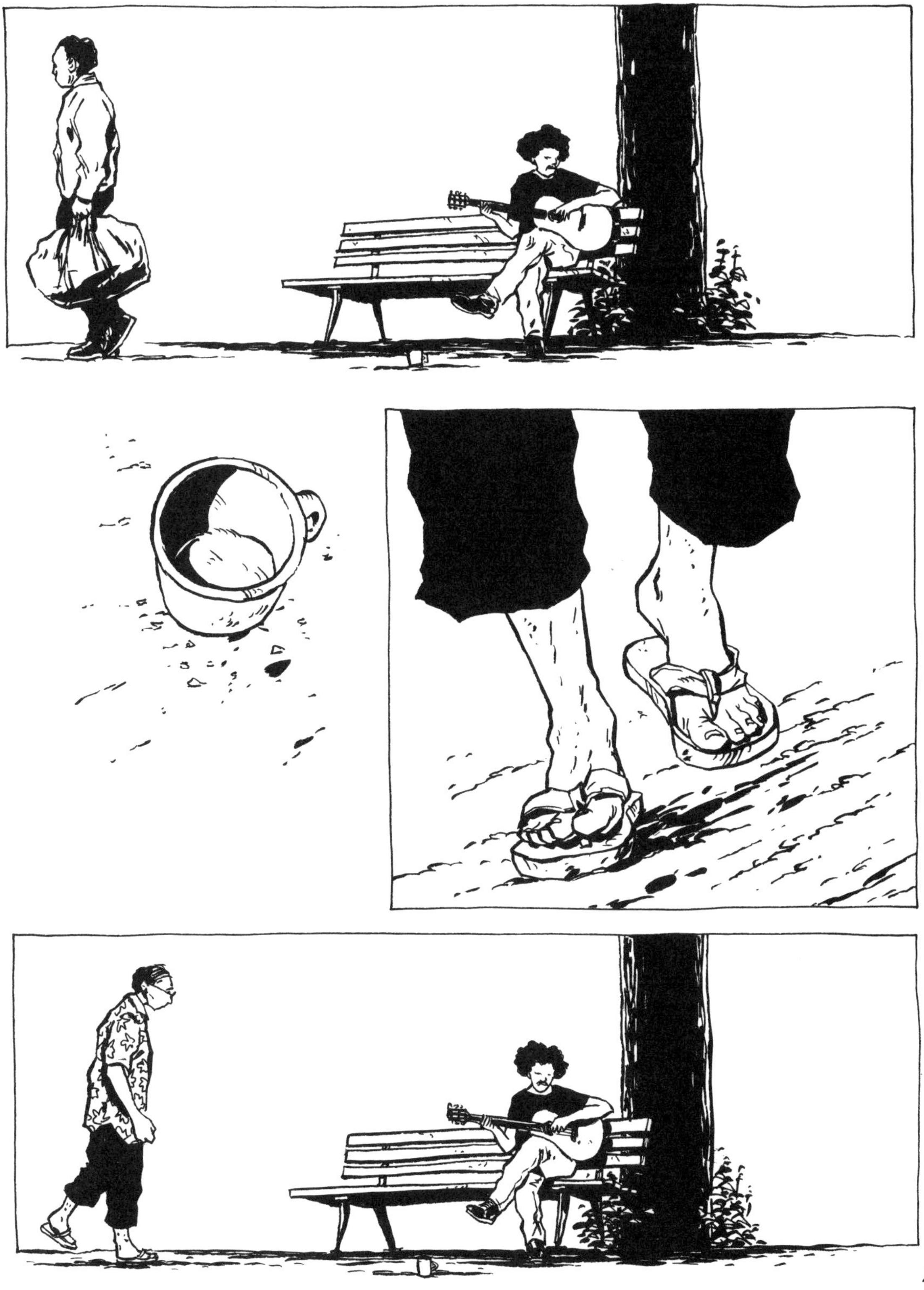

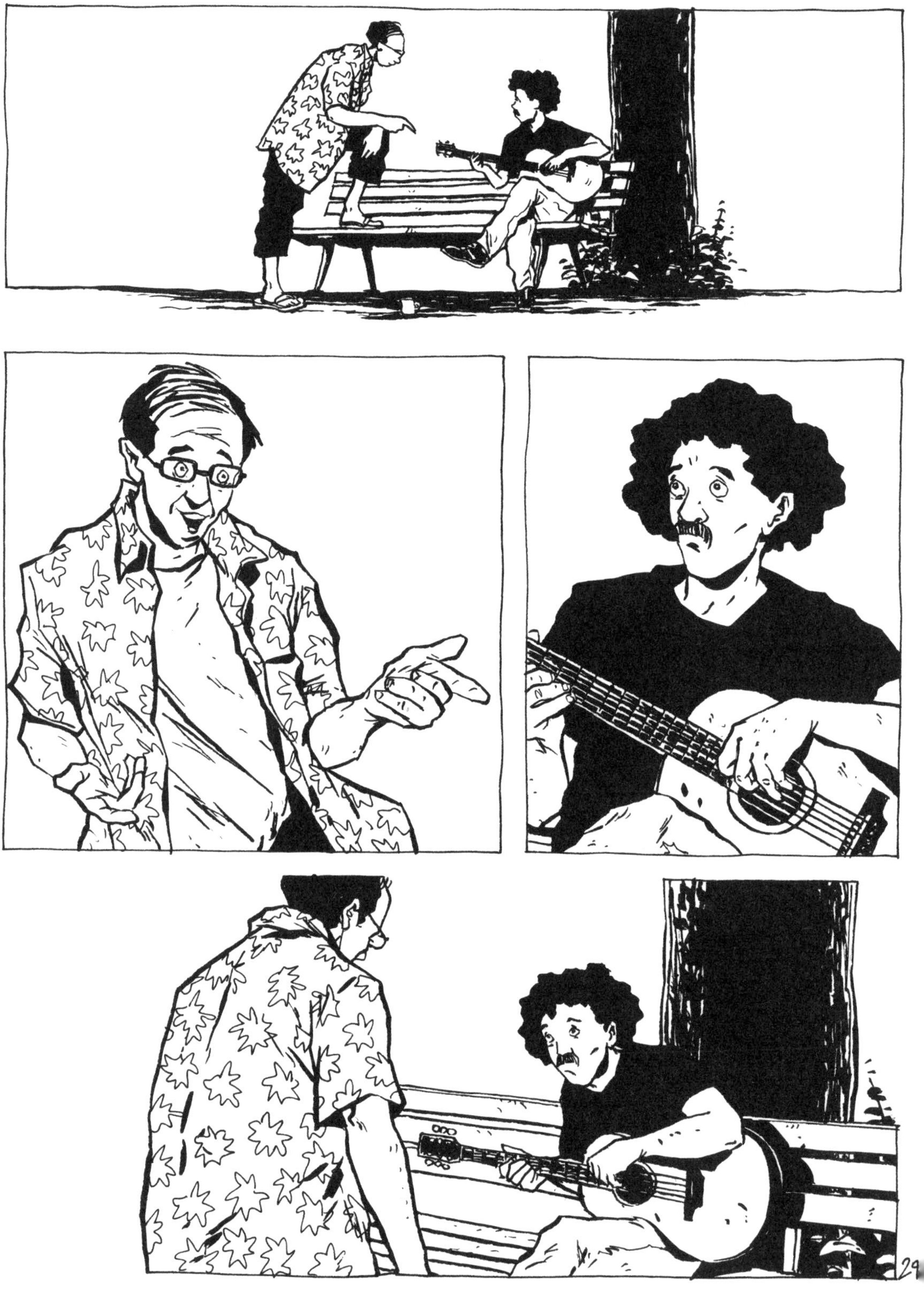

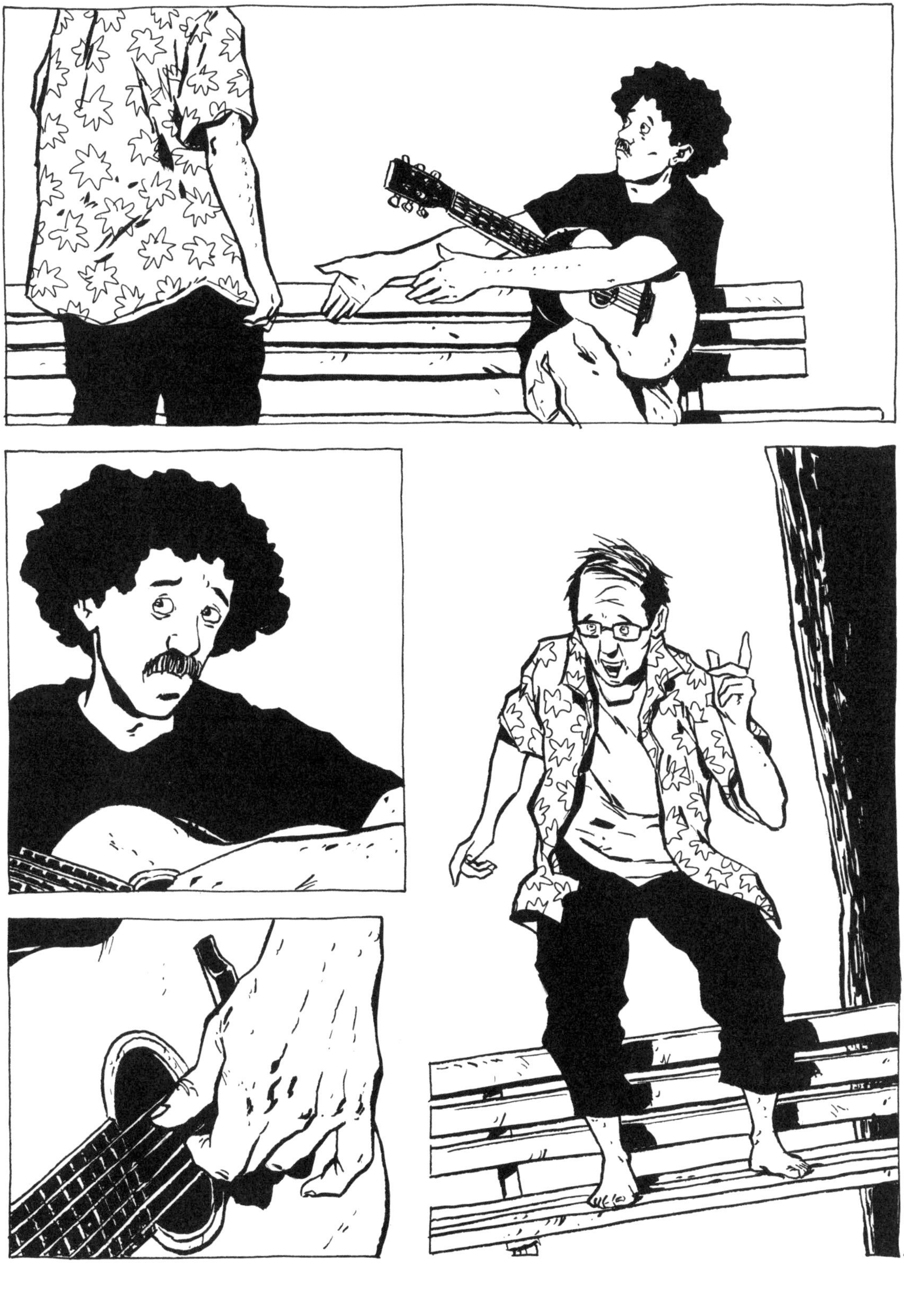

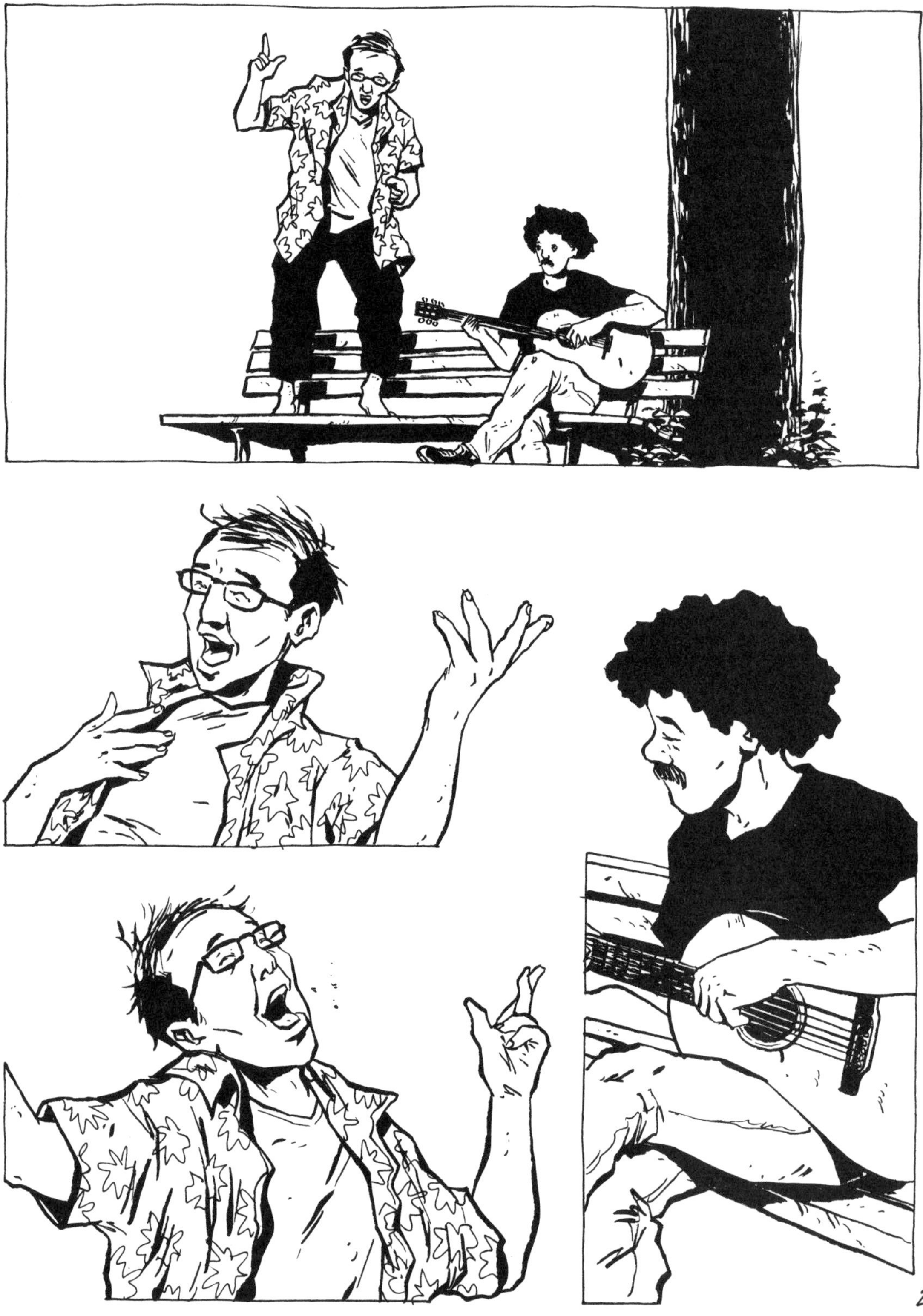

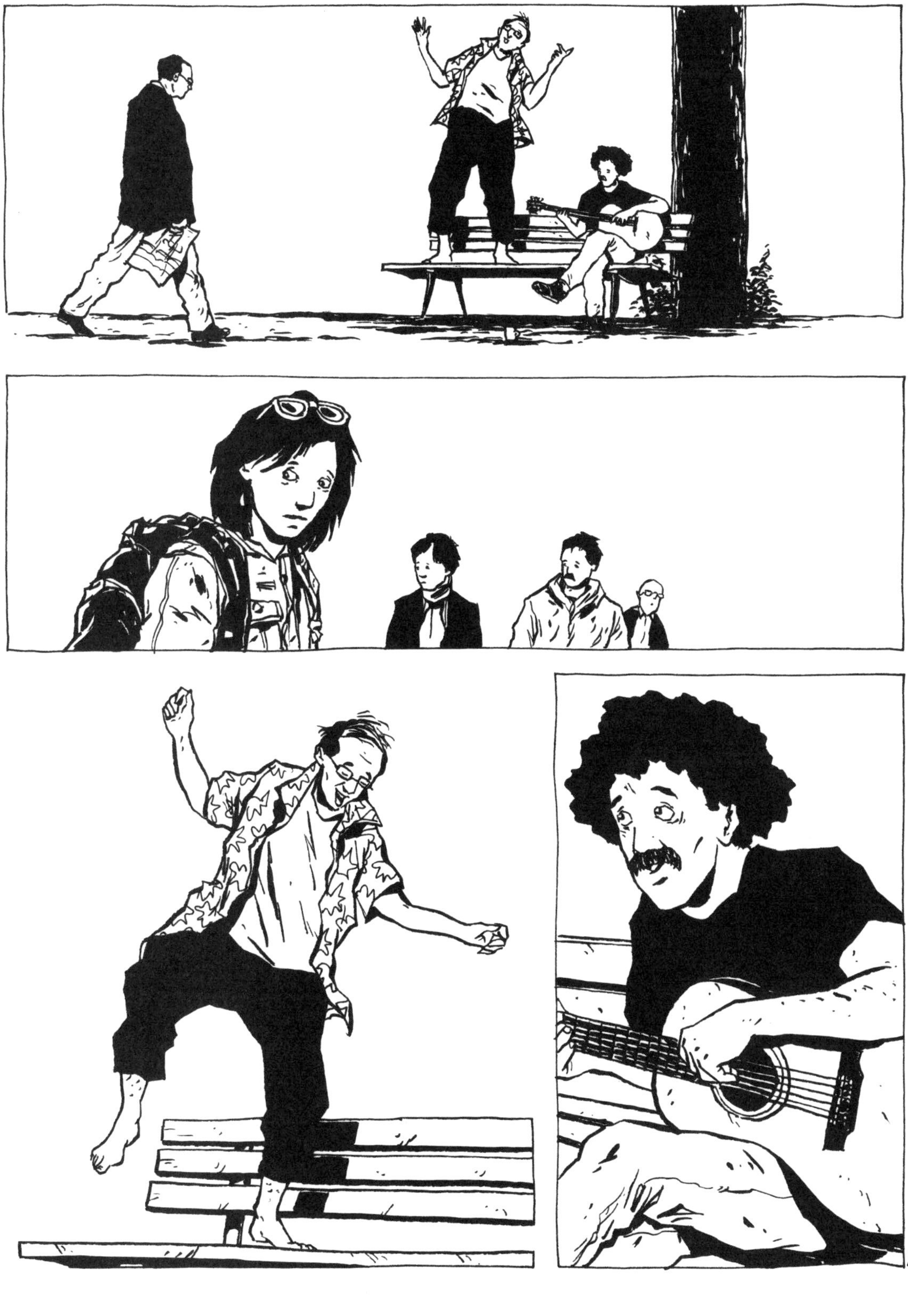

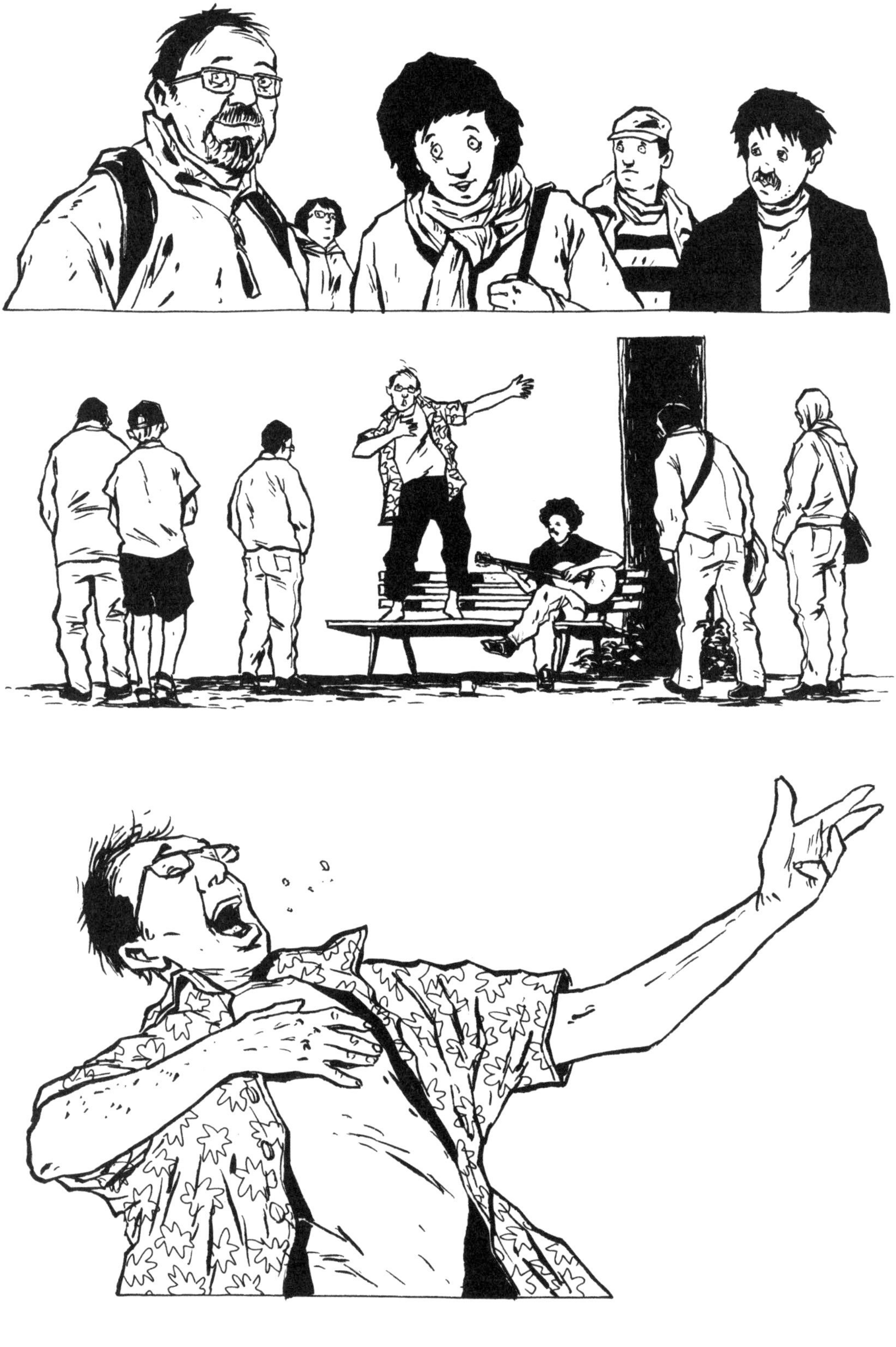

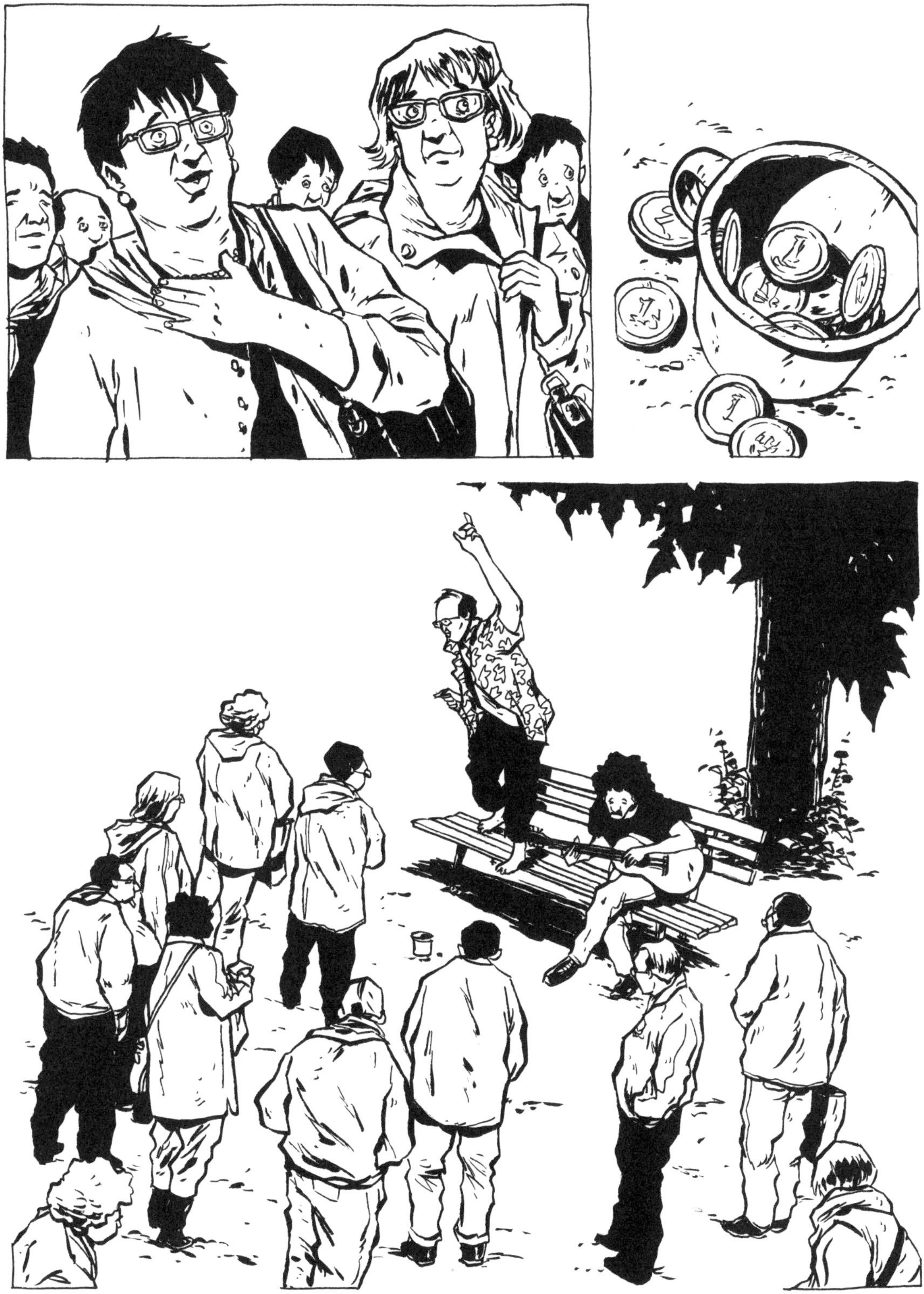

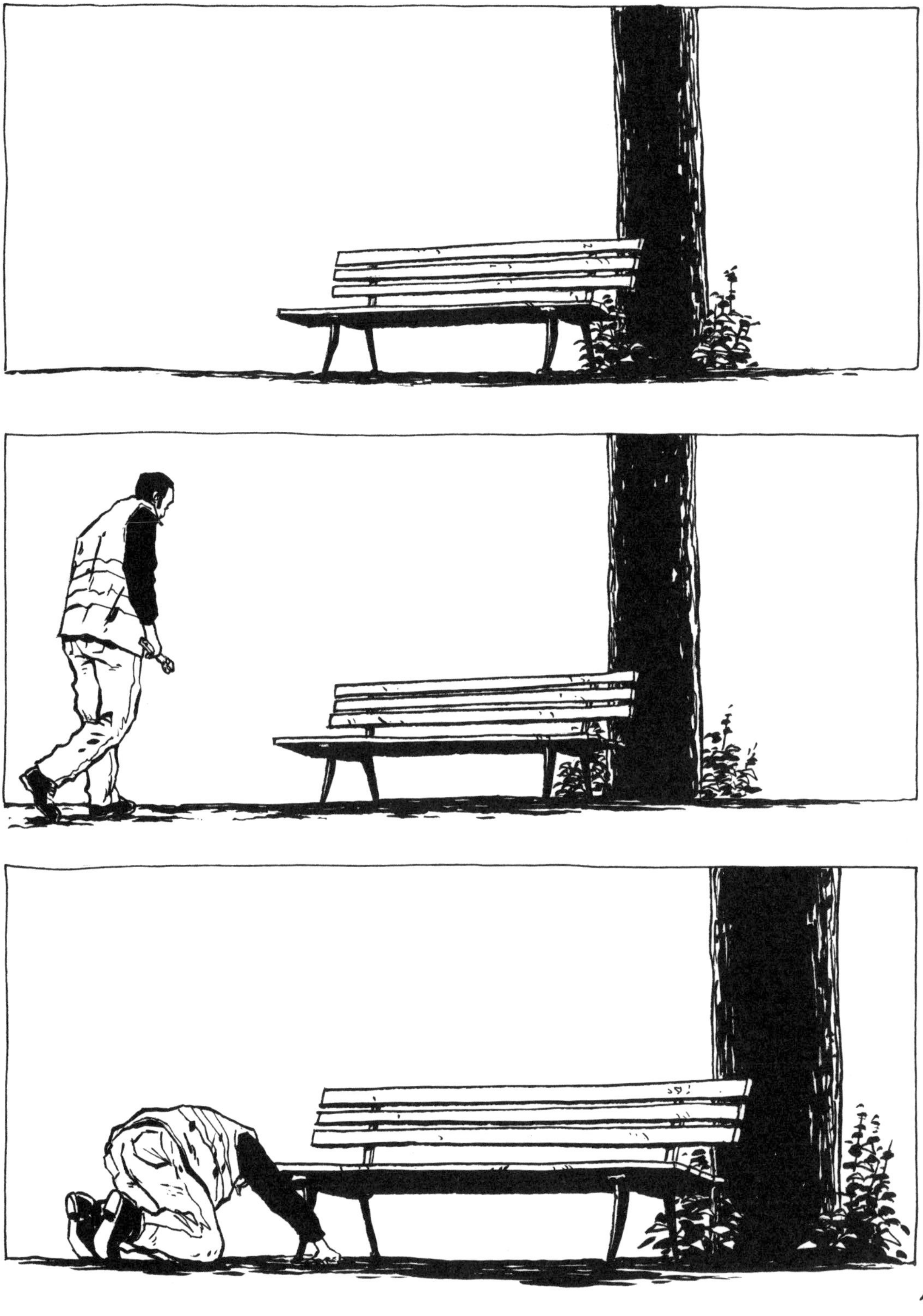

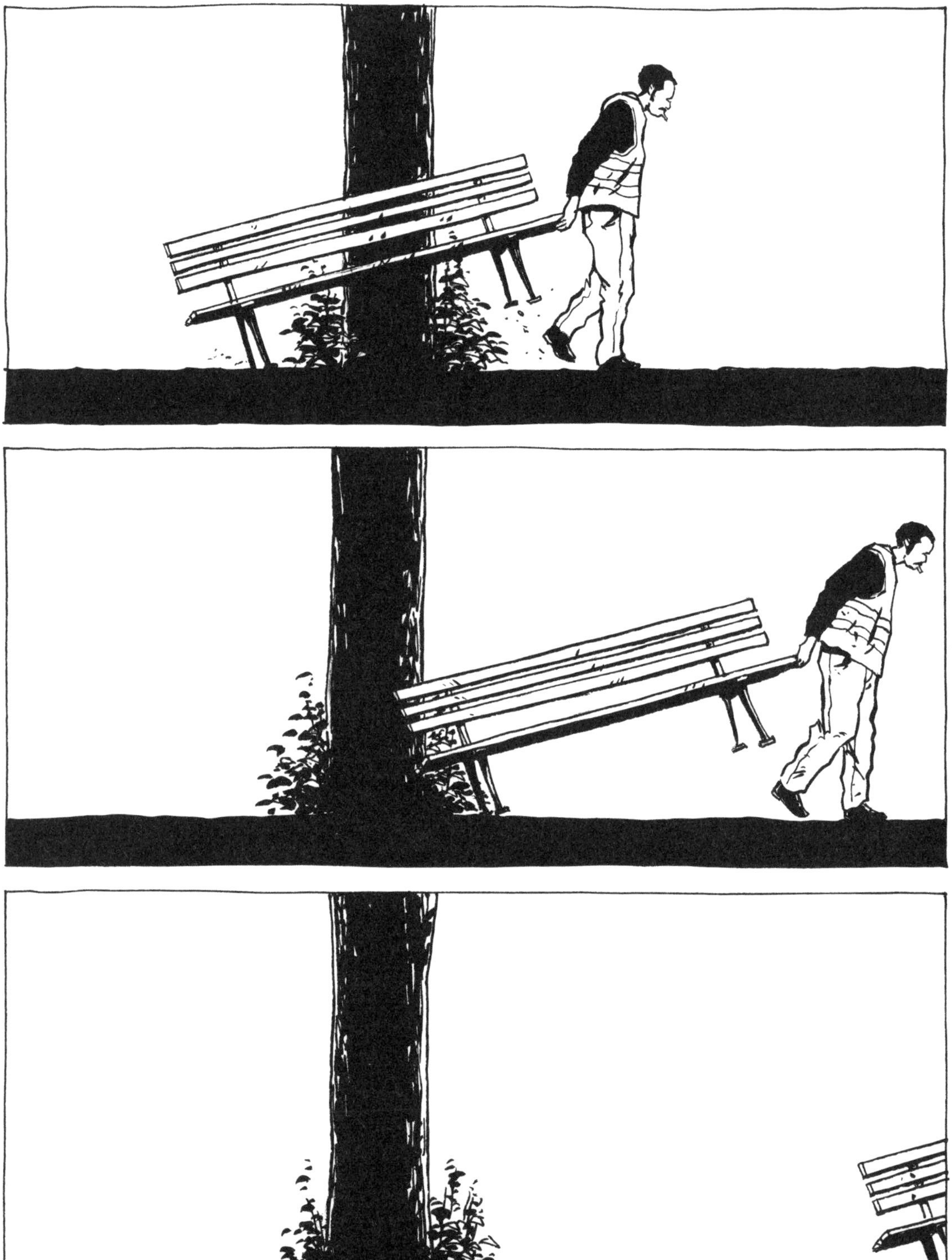

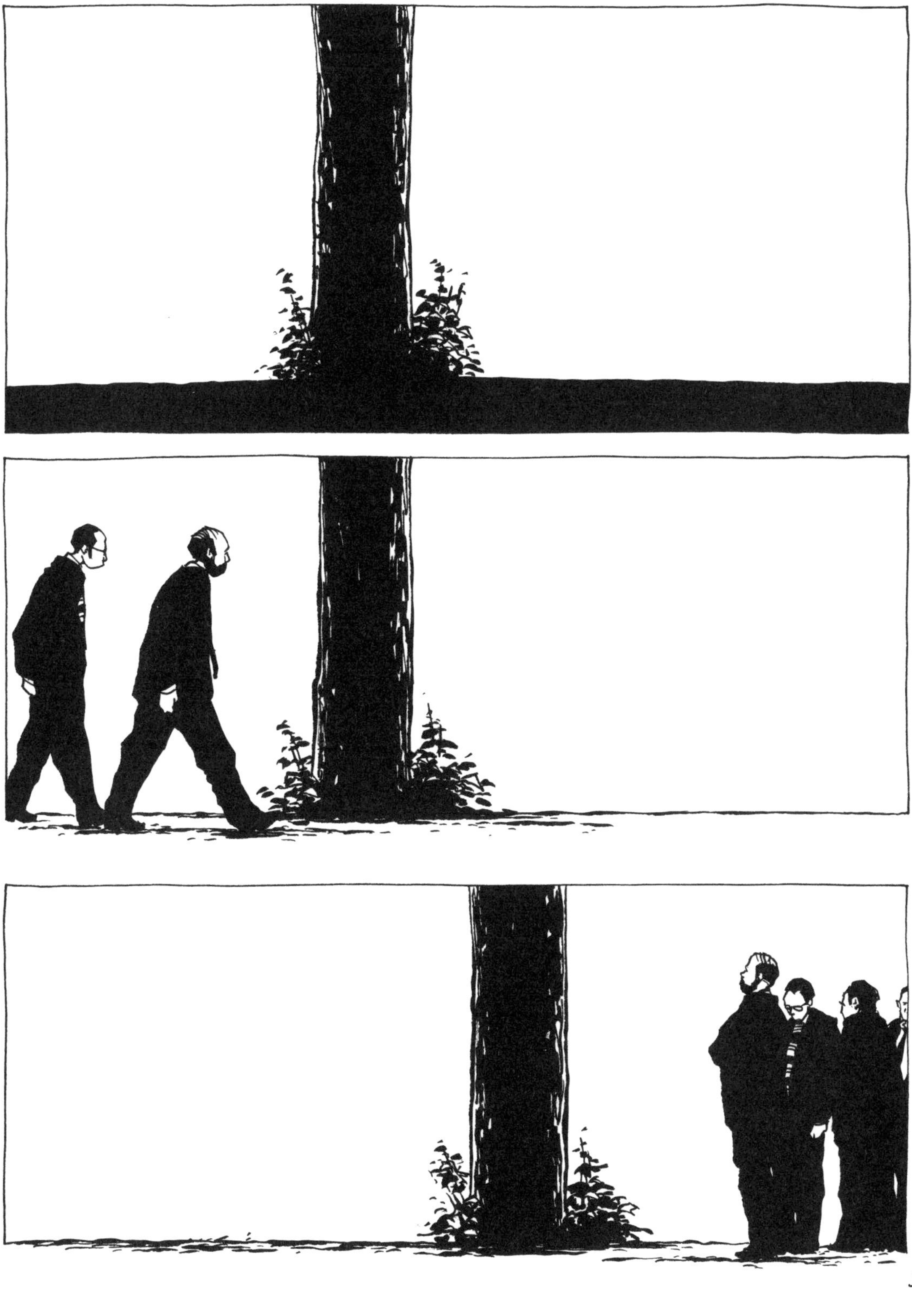

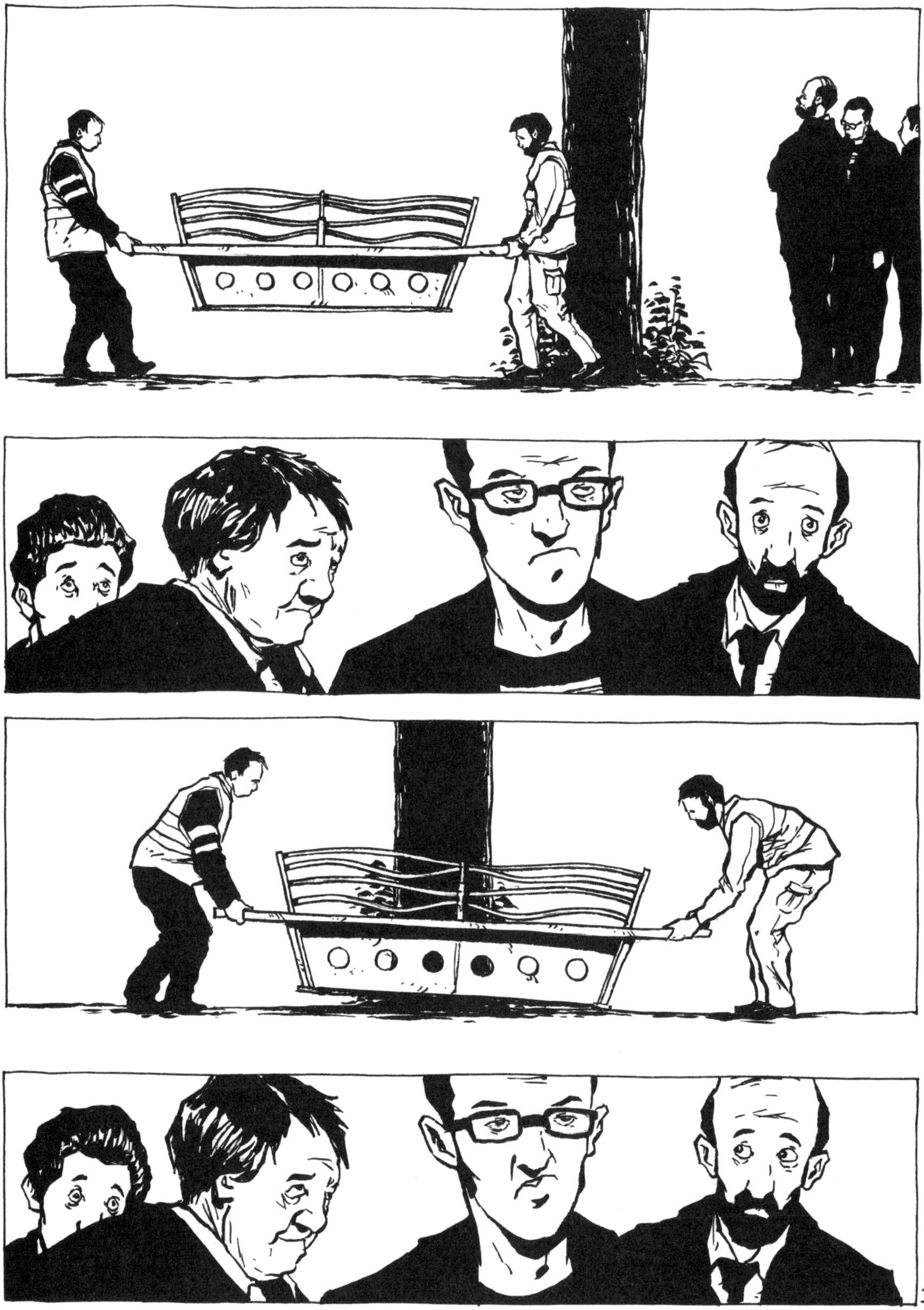

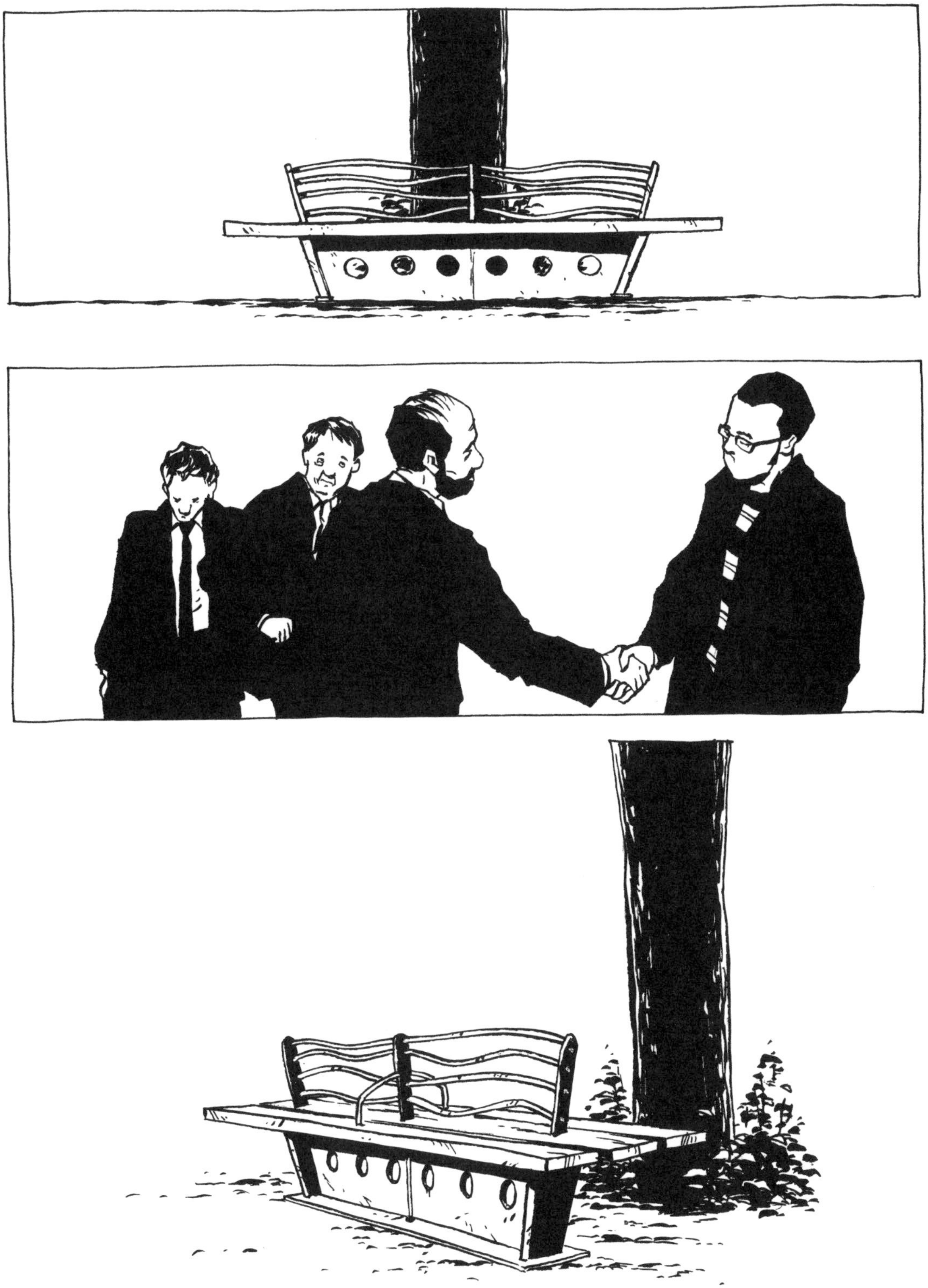

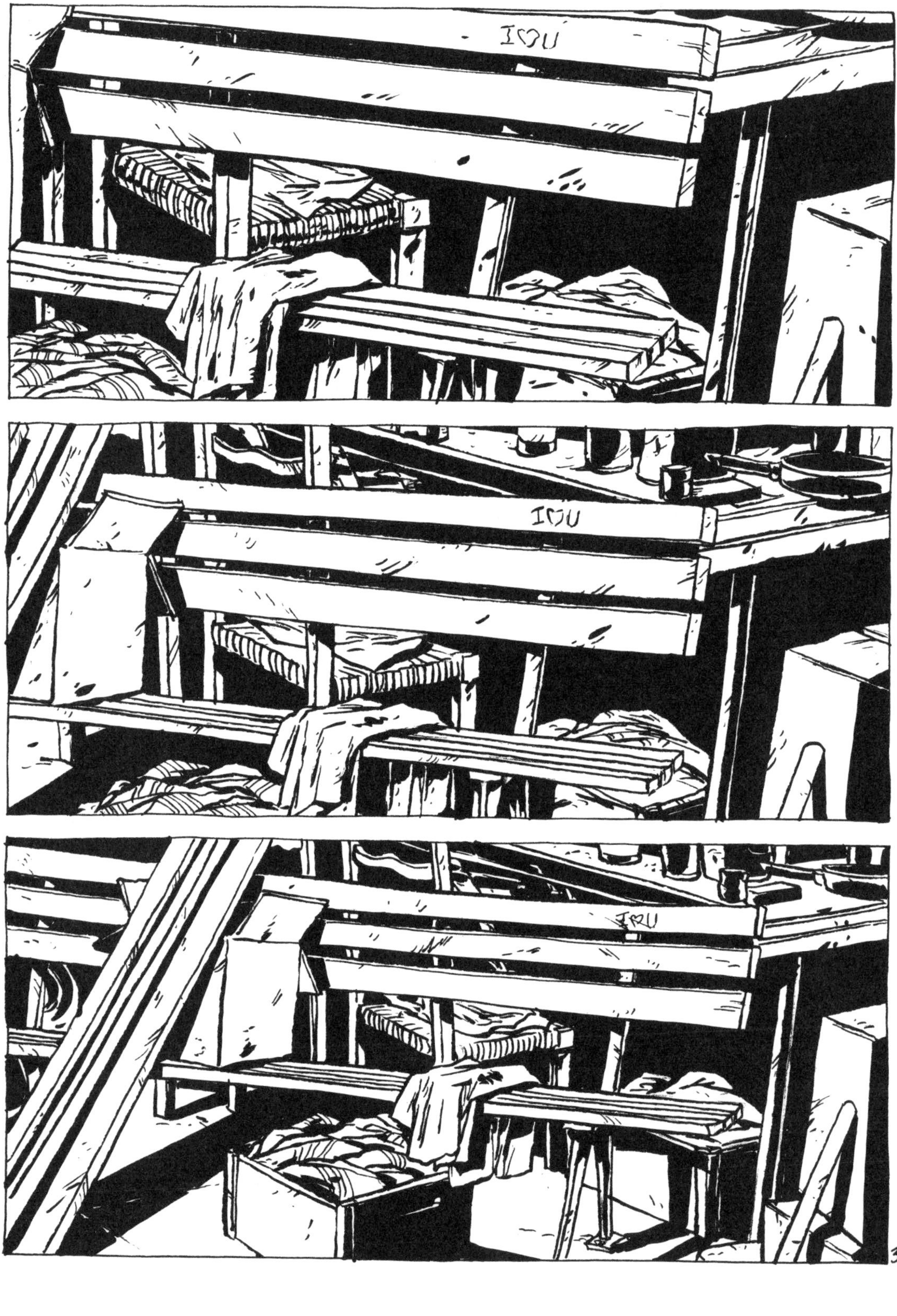
I♡U
I♡U
I♡U

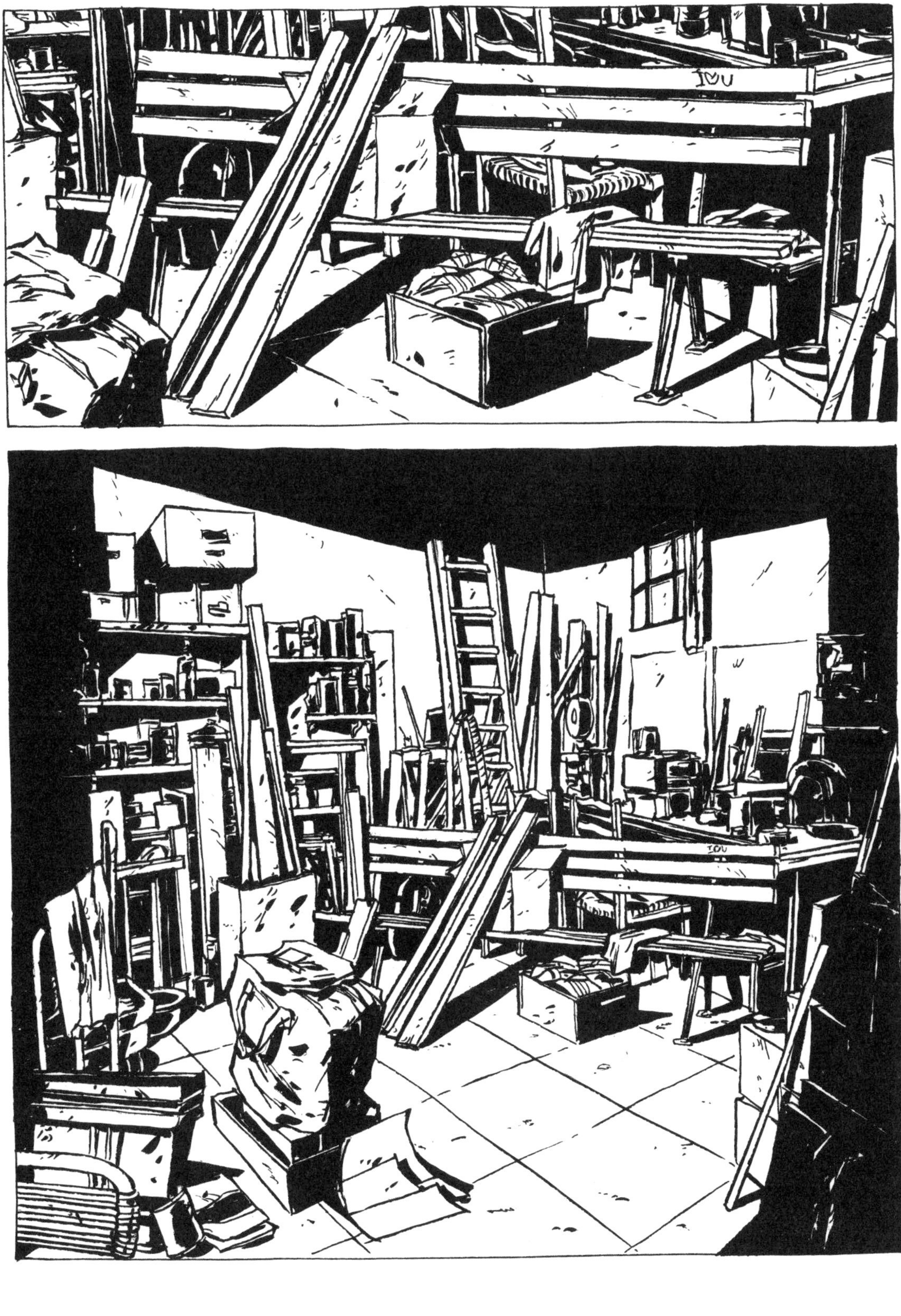

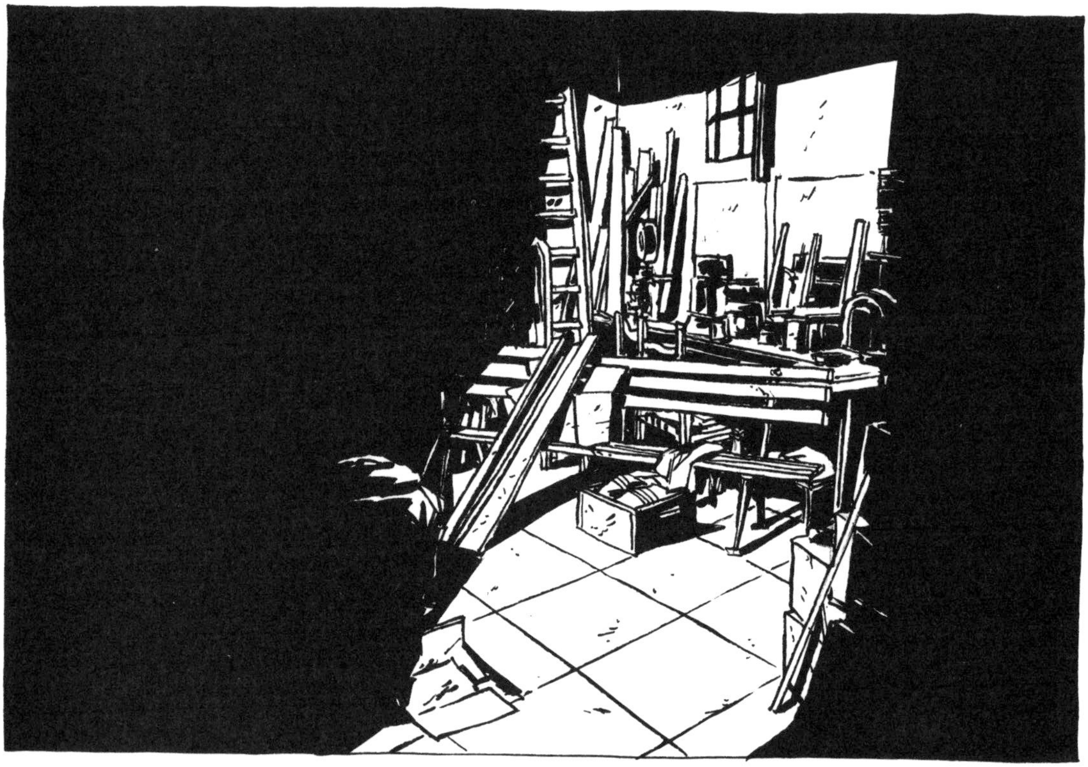

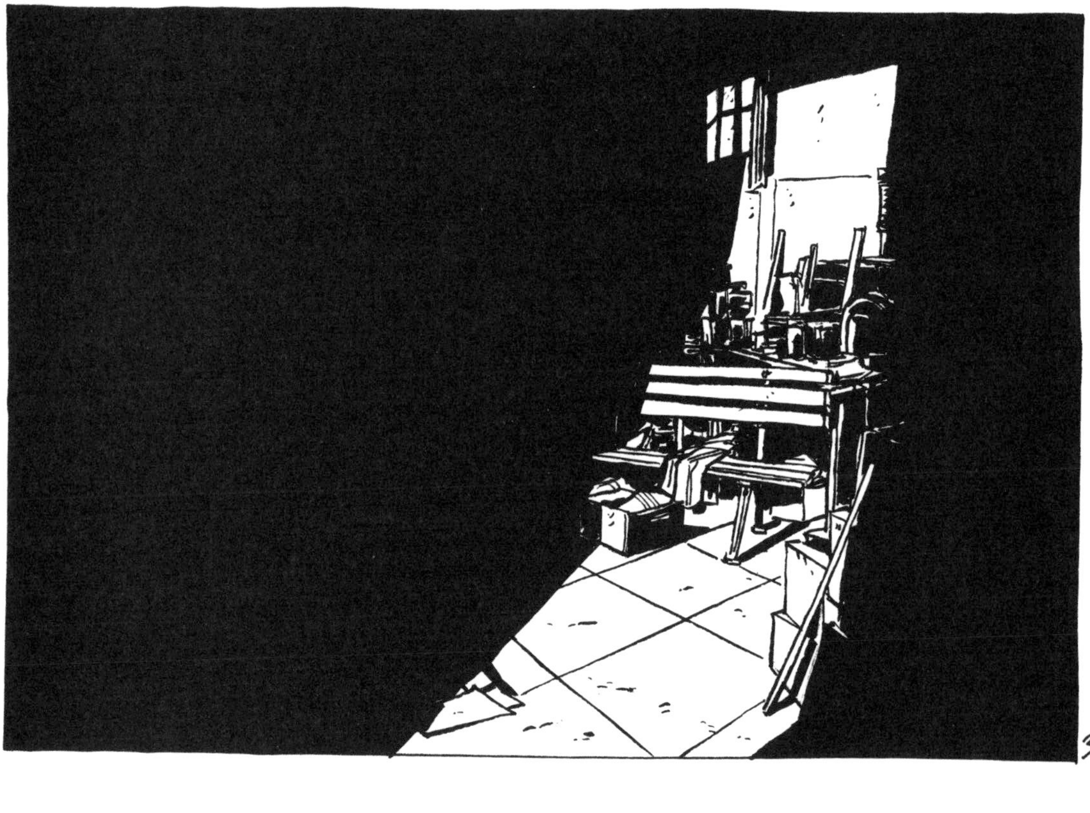

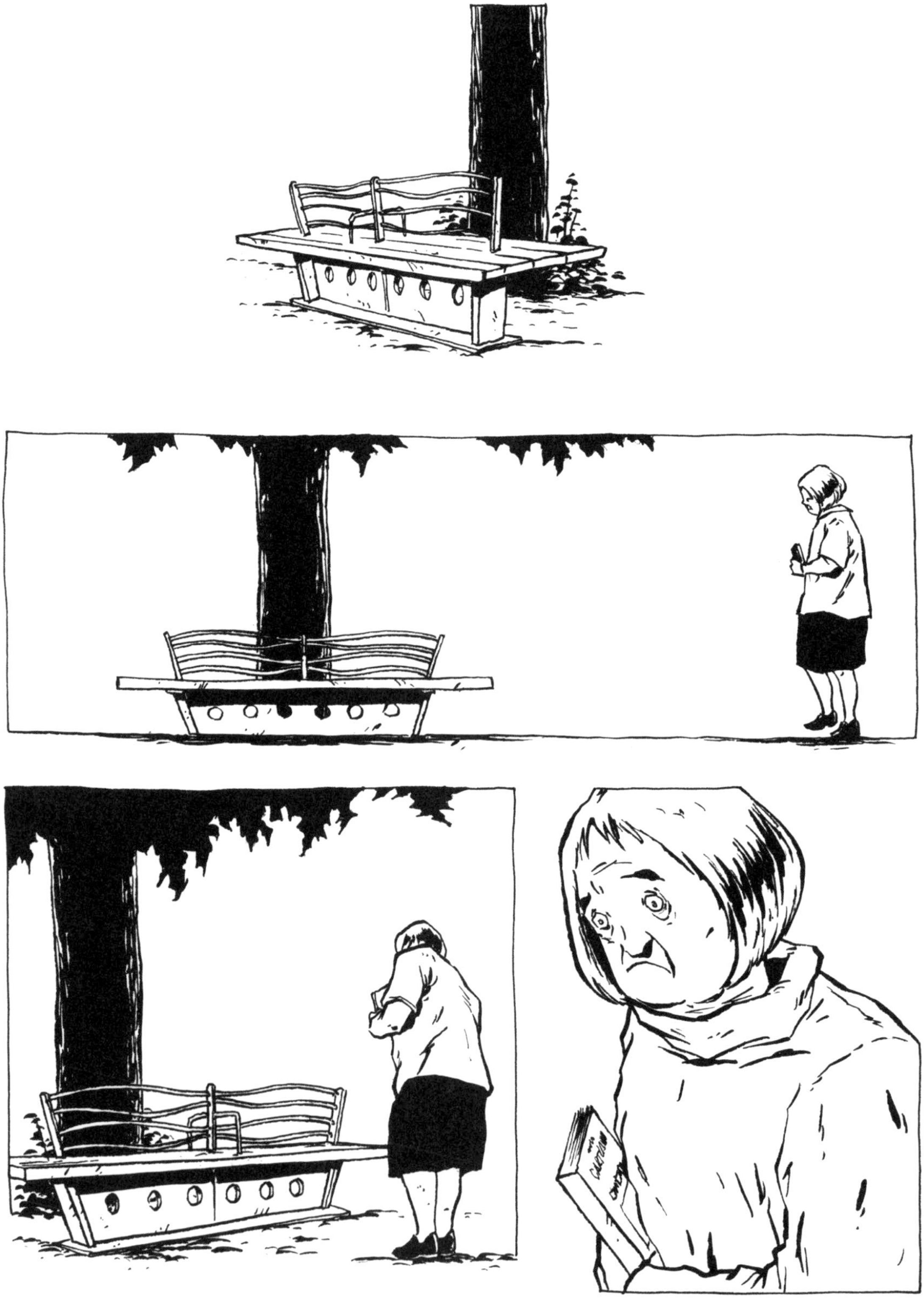

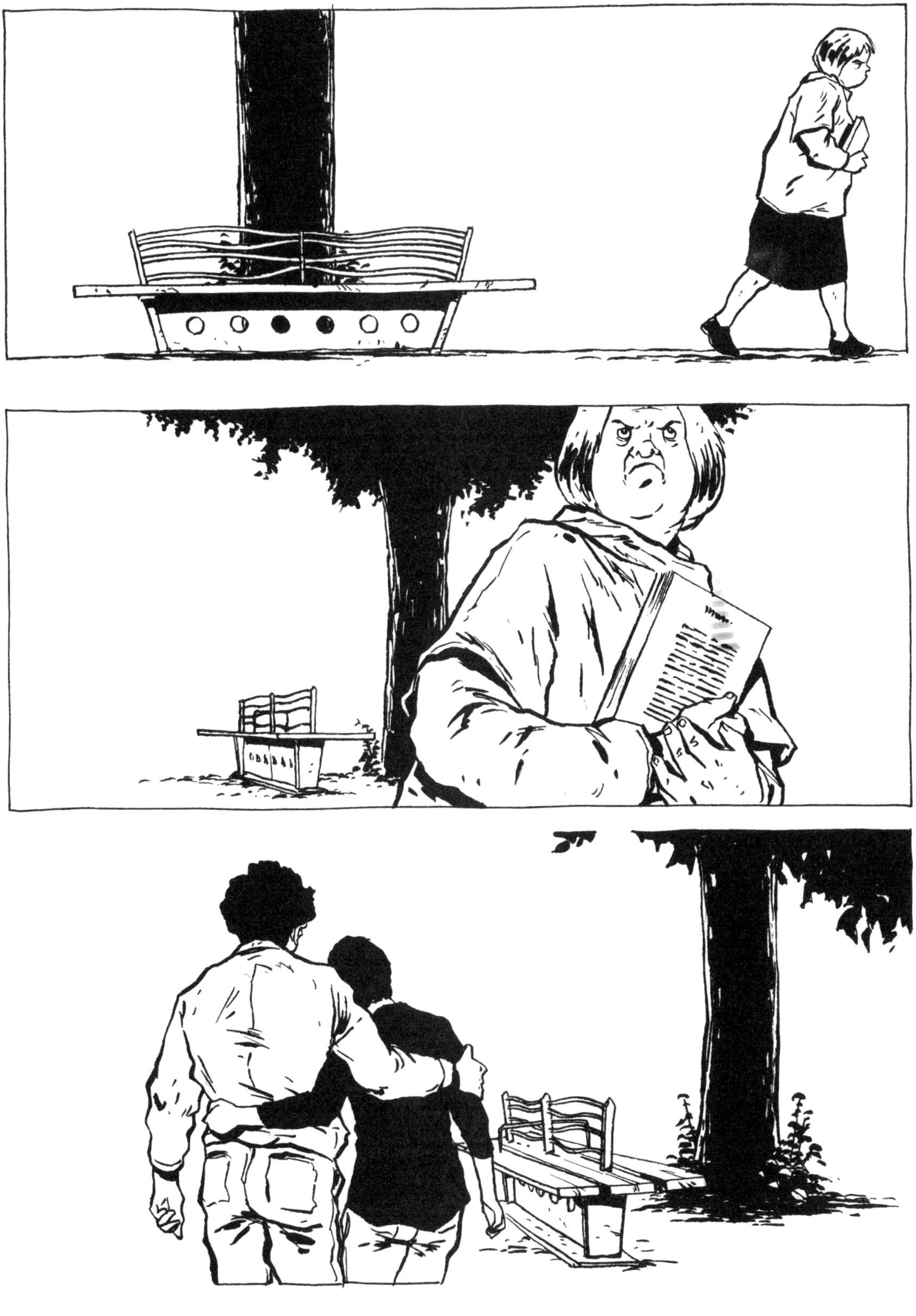

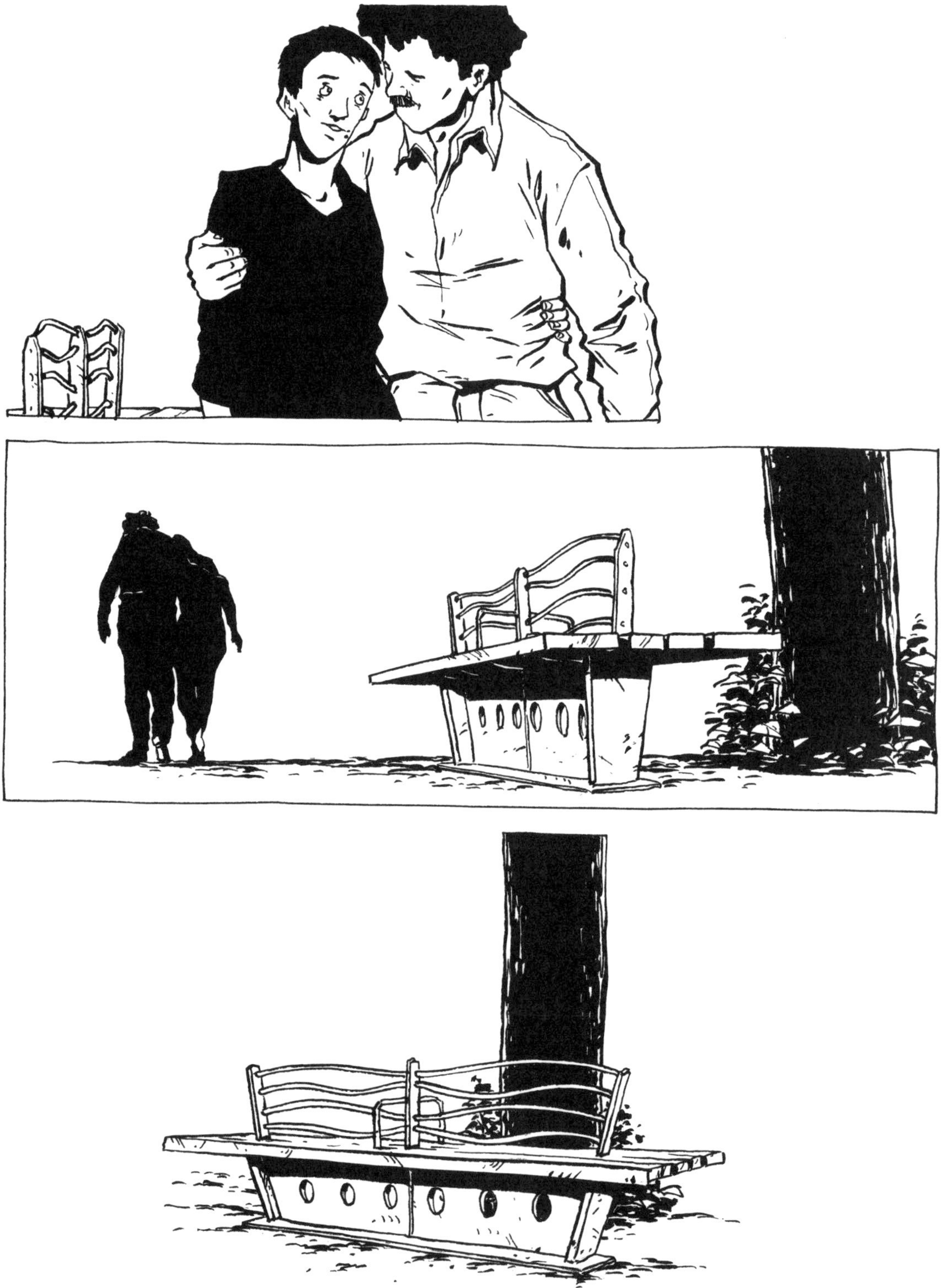

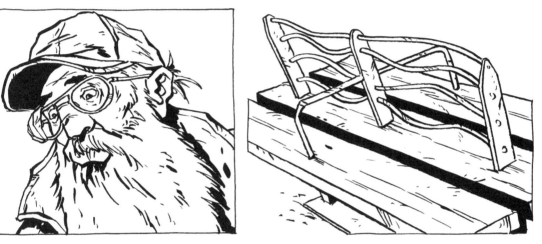

311.

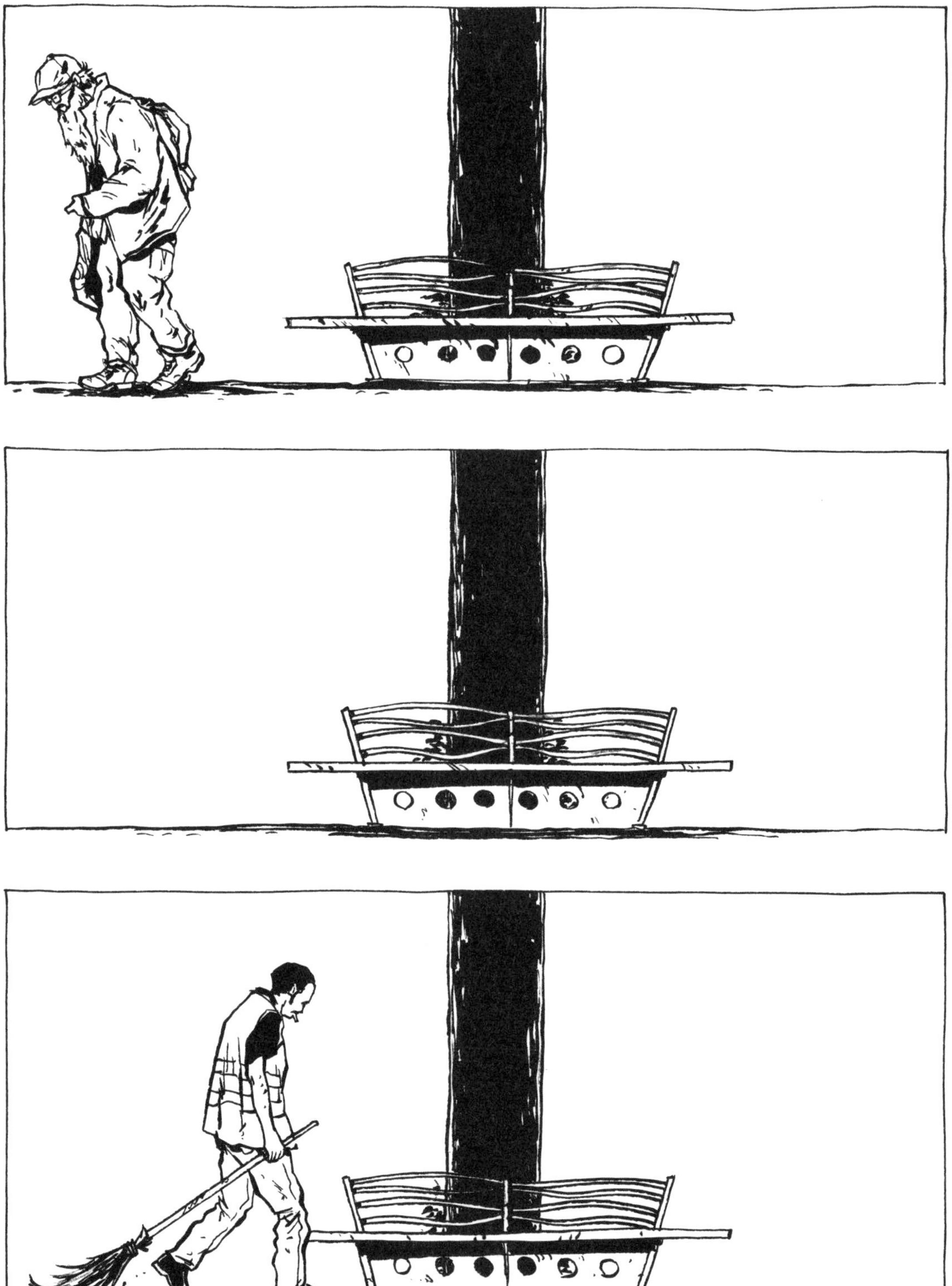

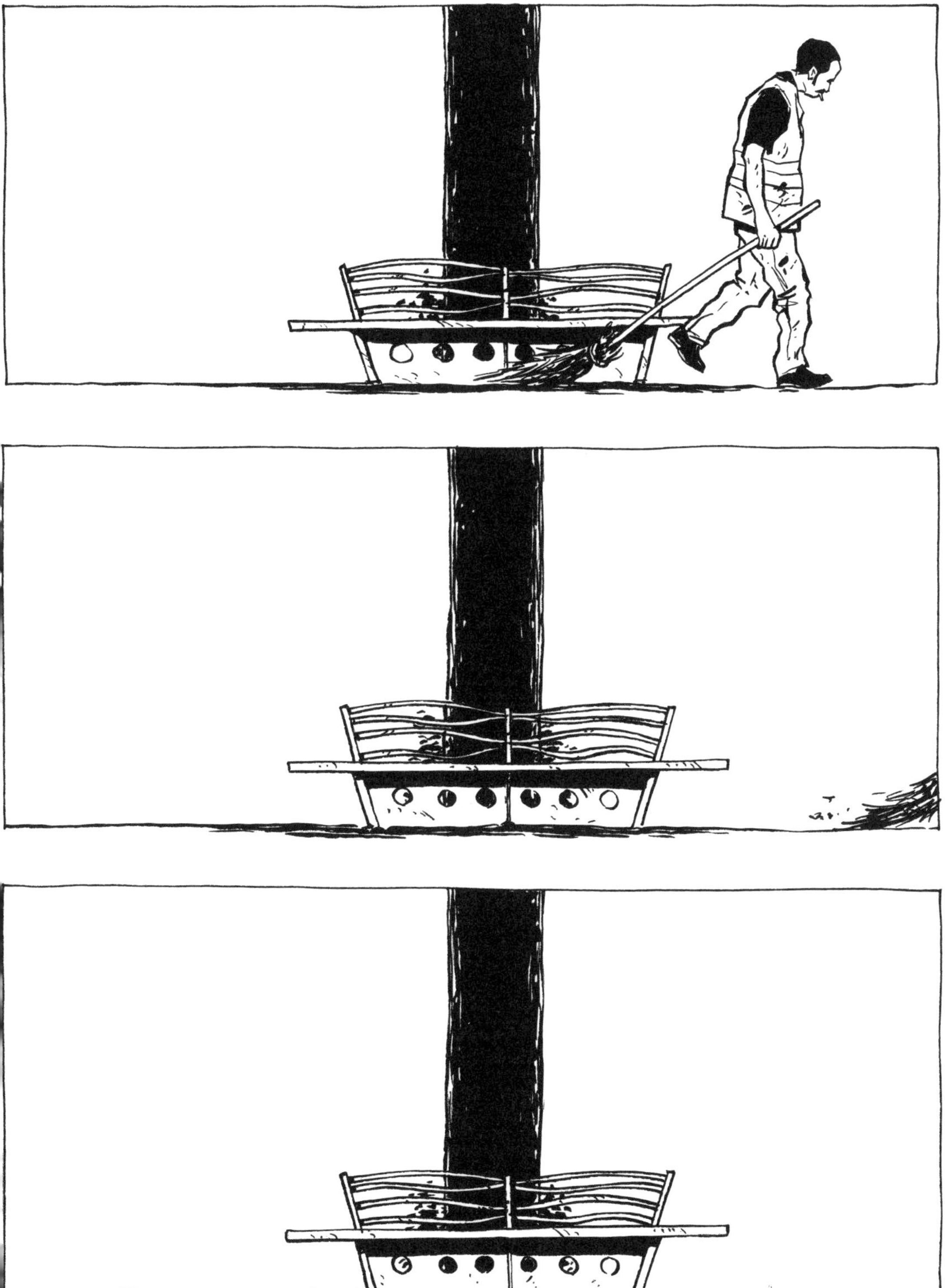

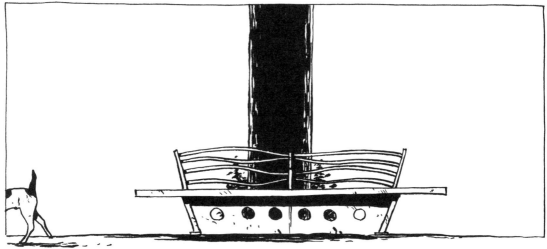

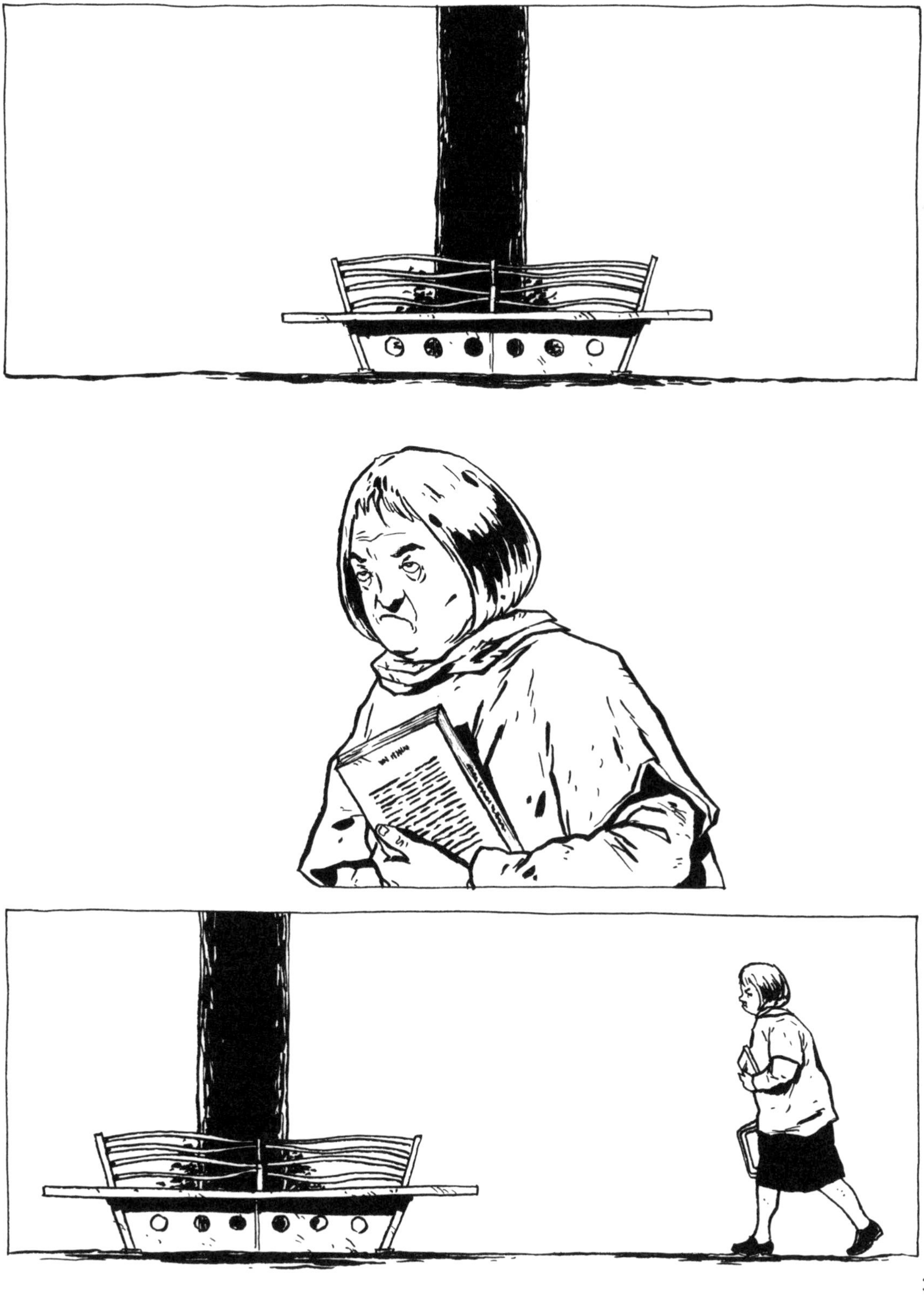

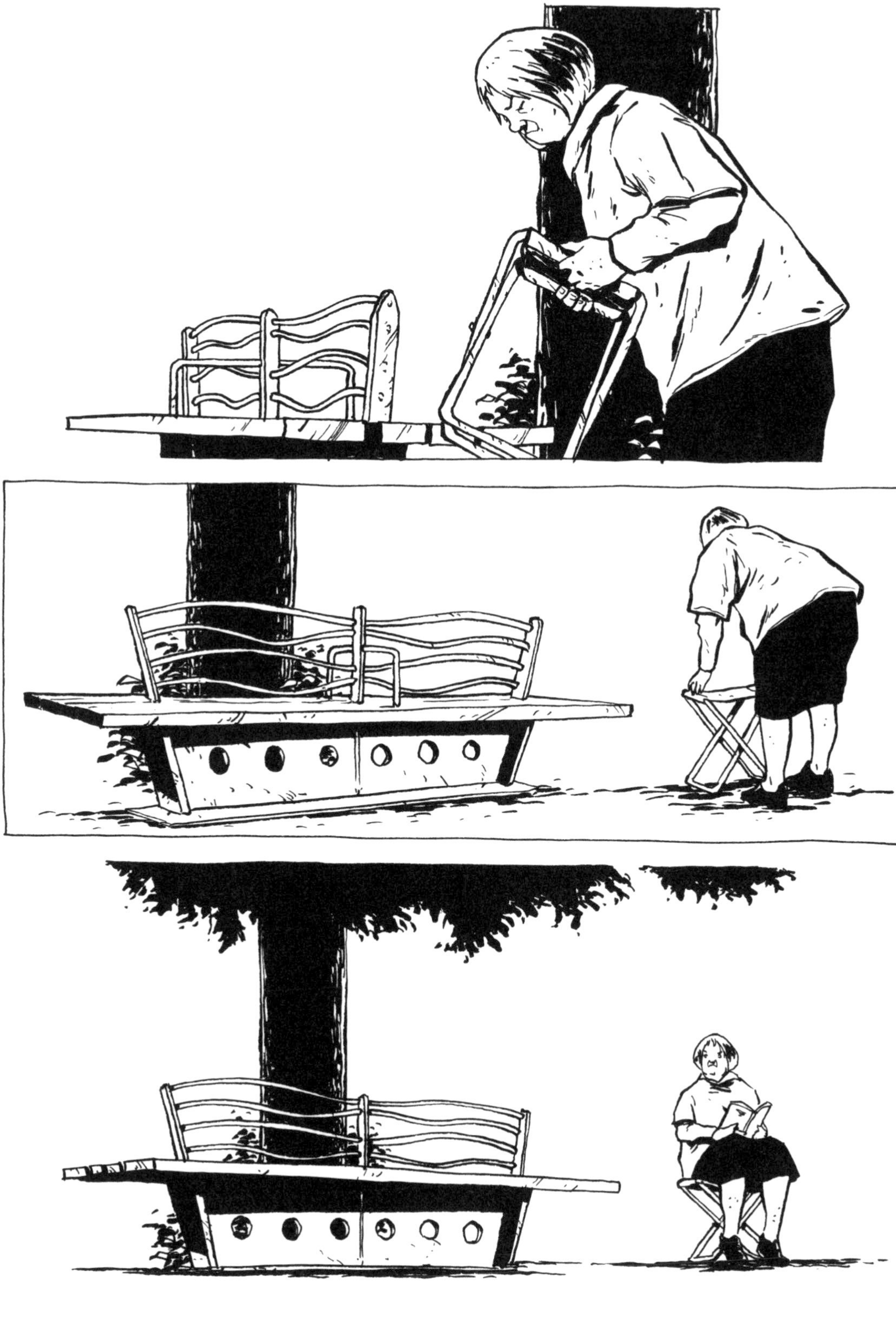

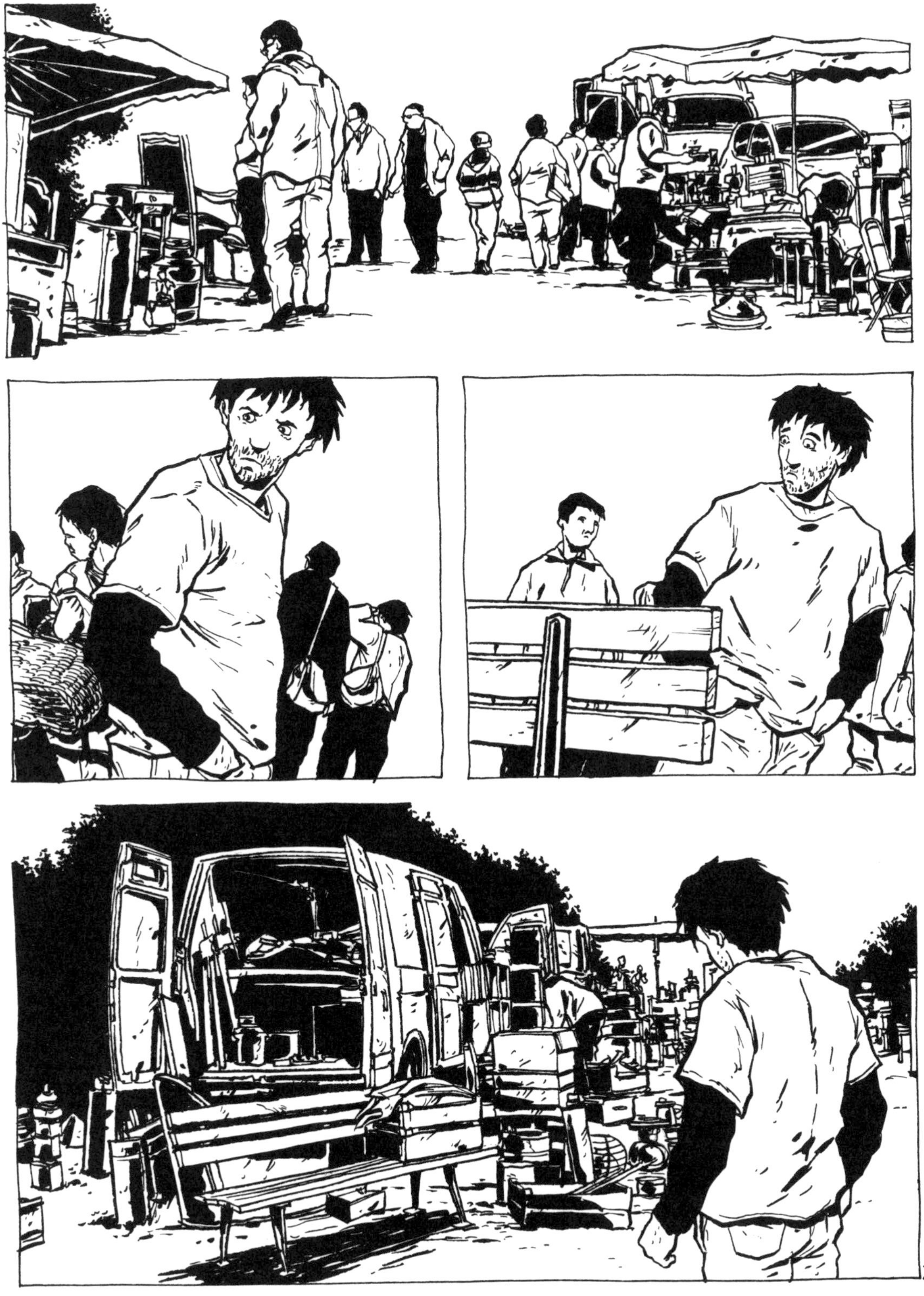

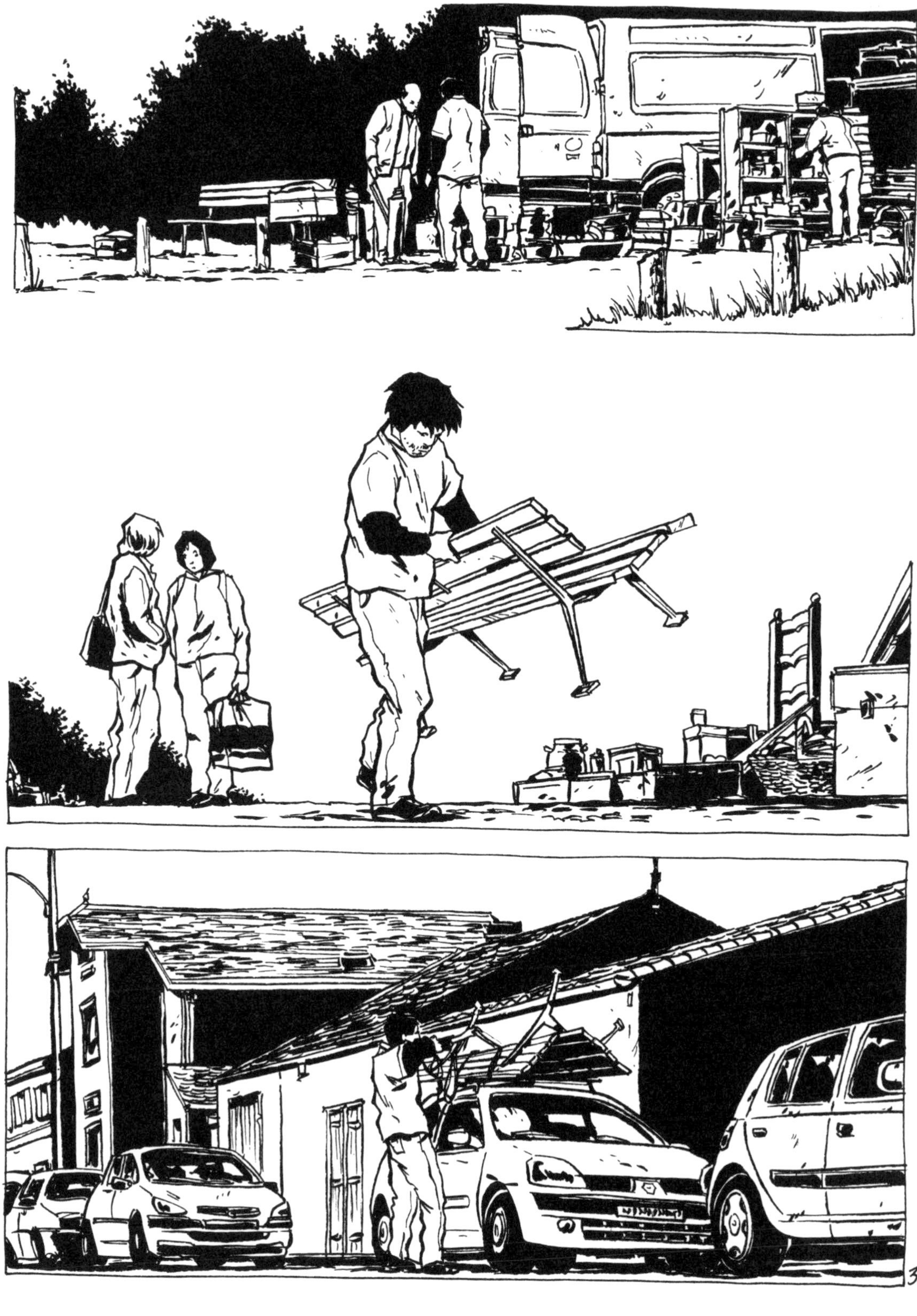

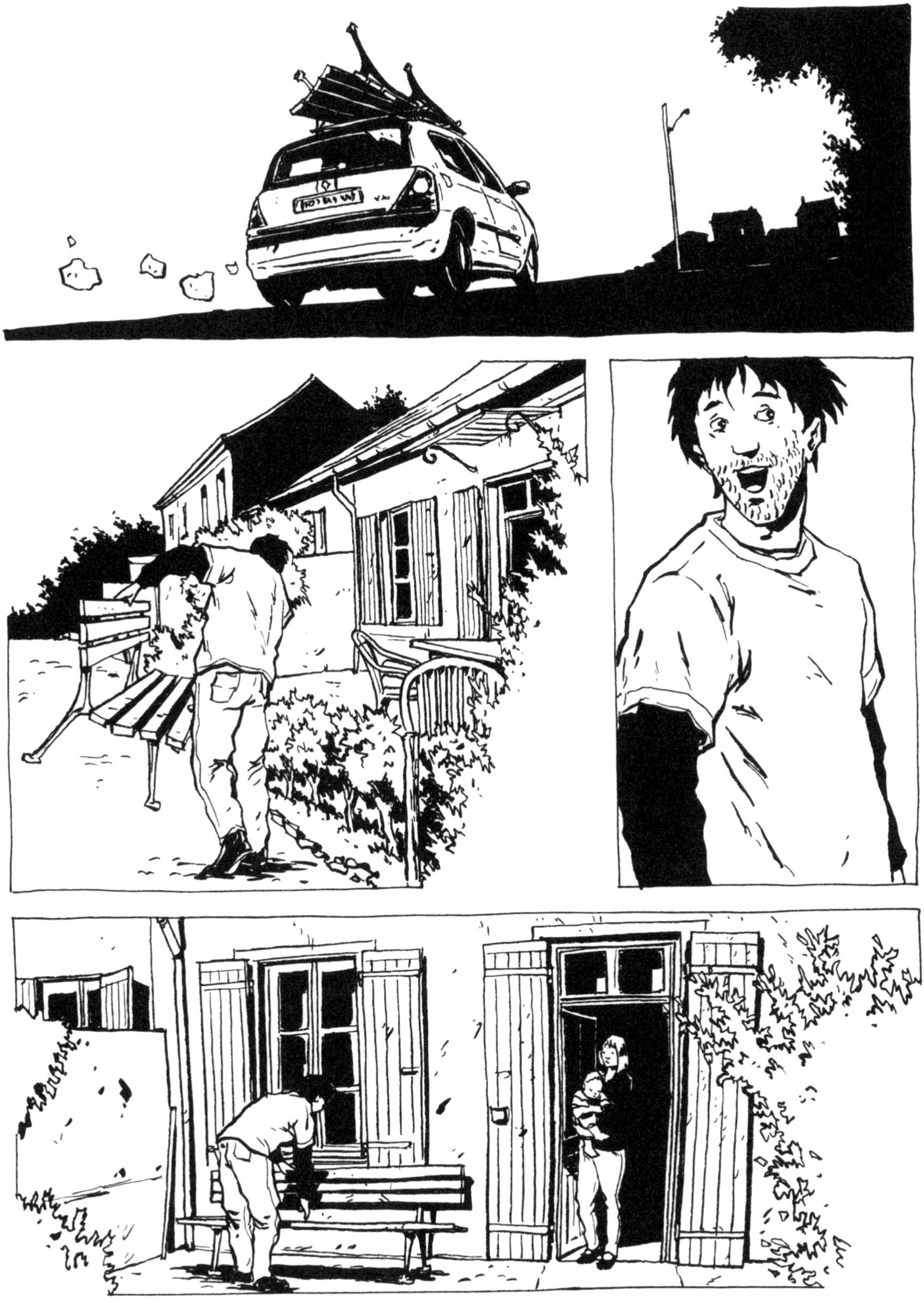

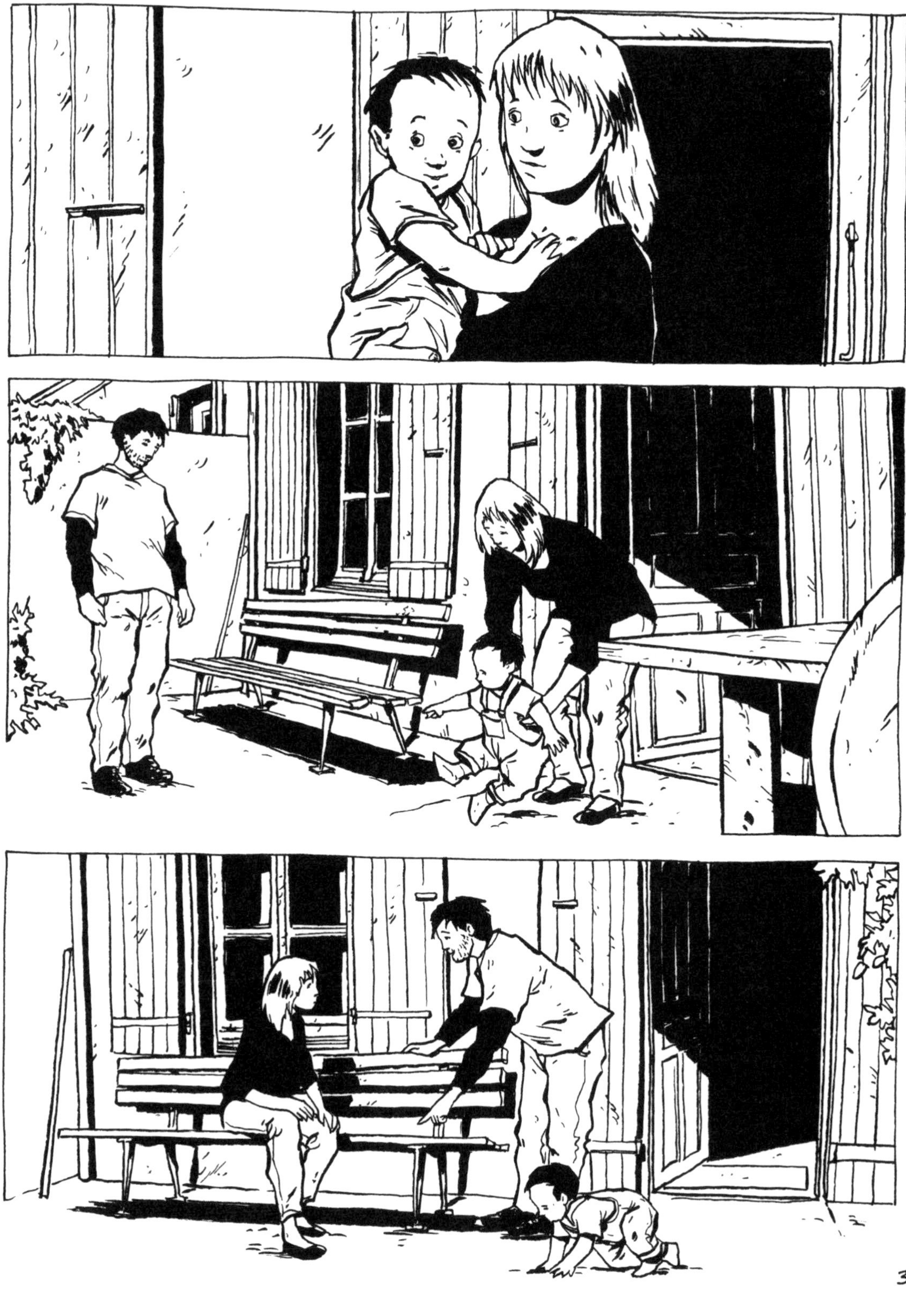

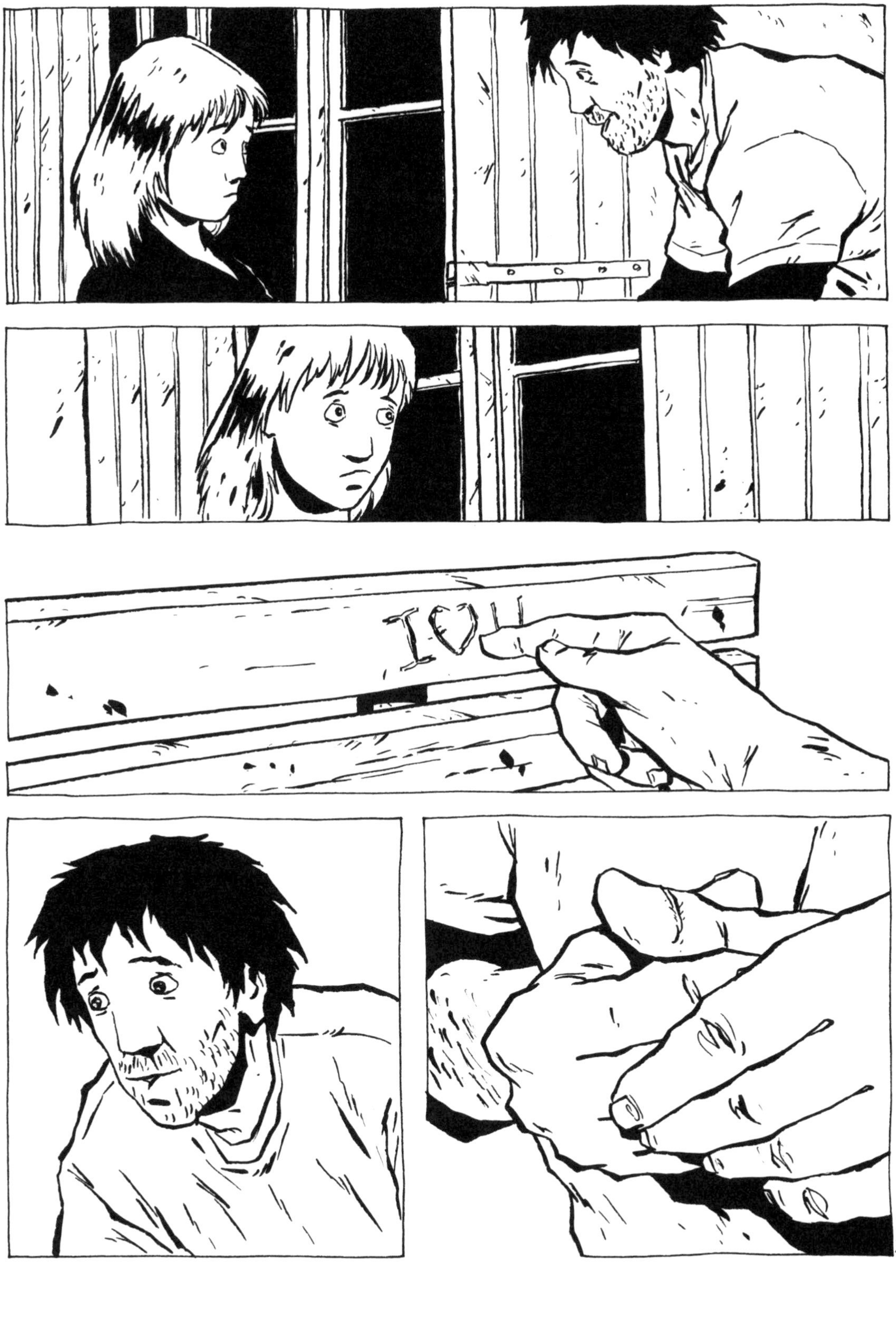
I ♡ U

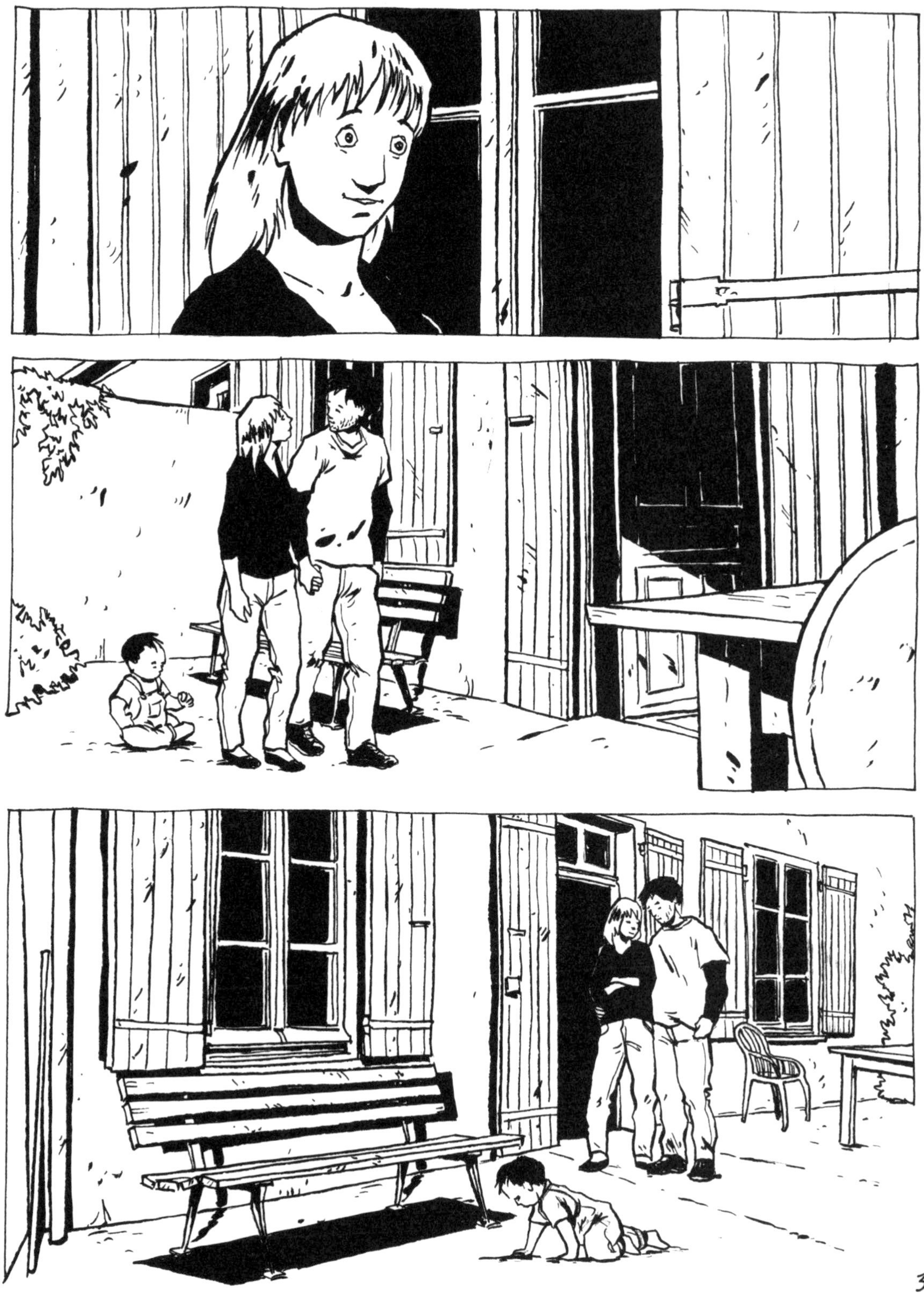

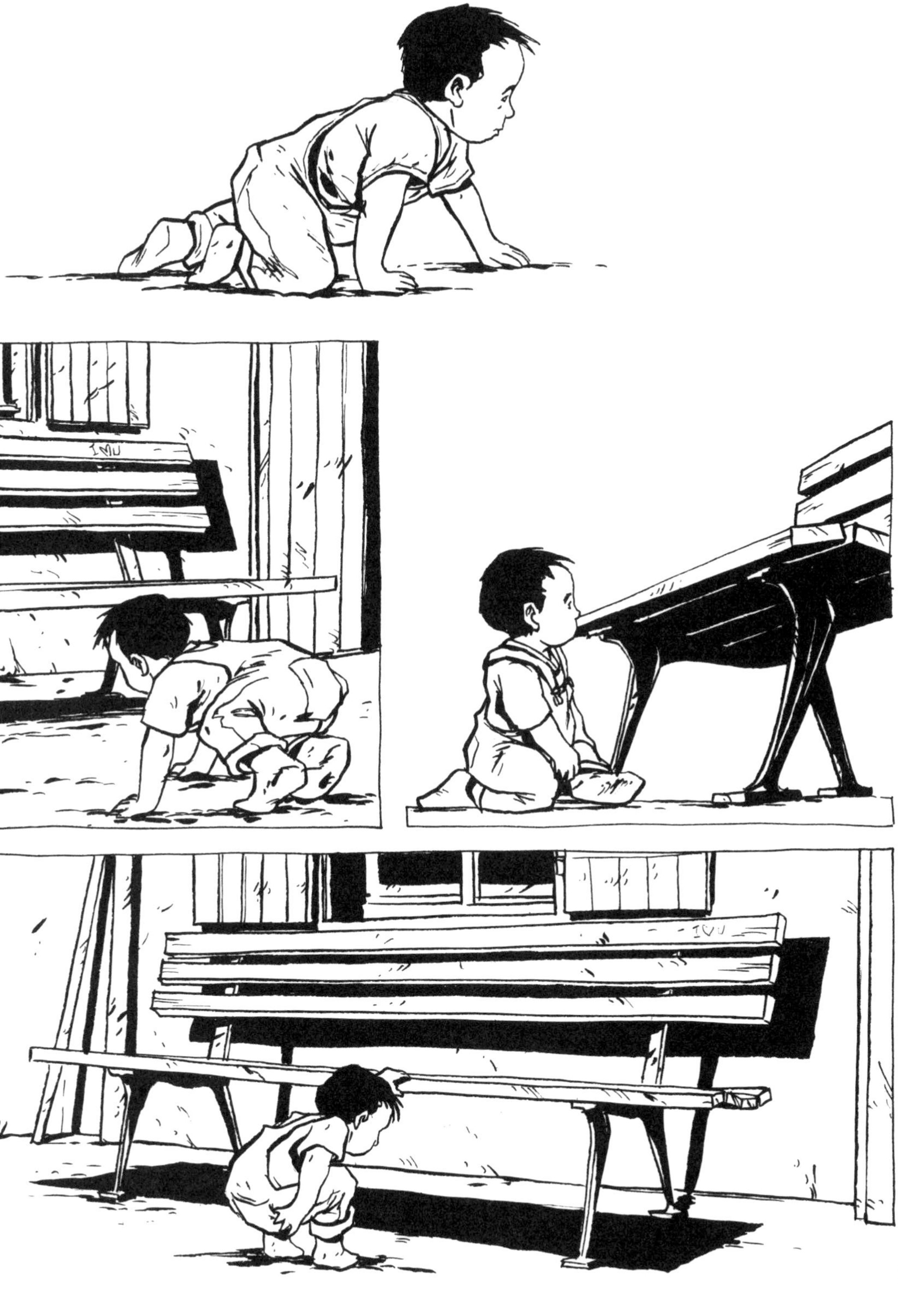

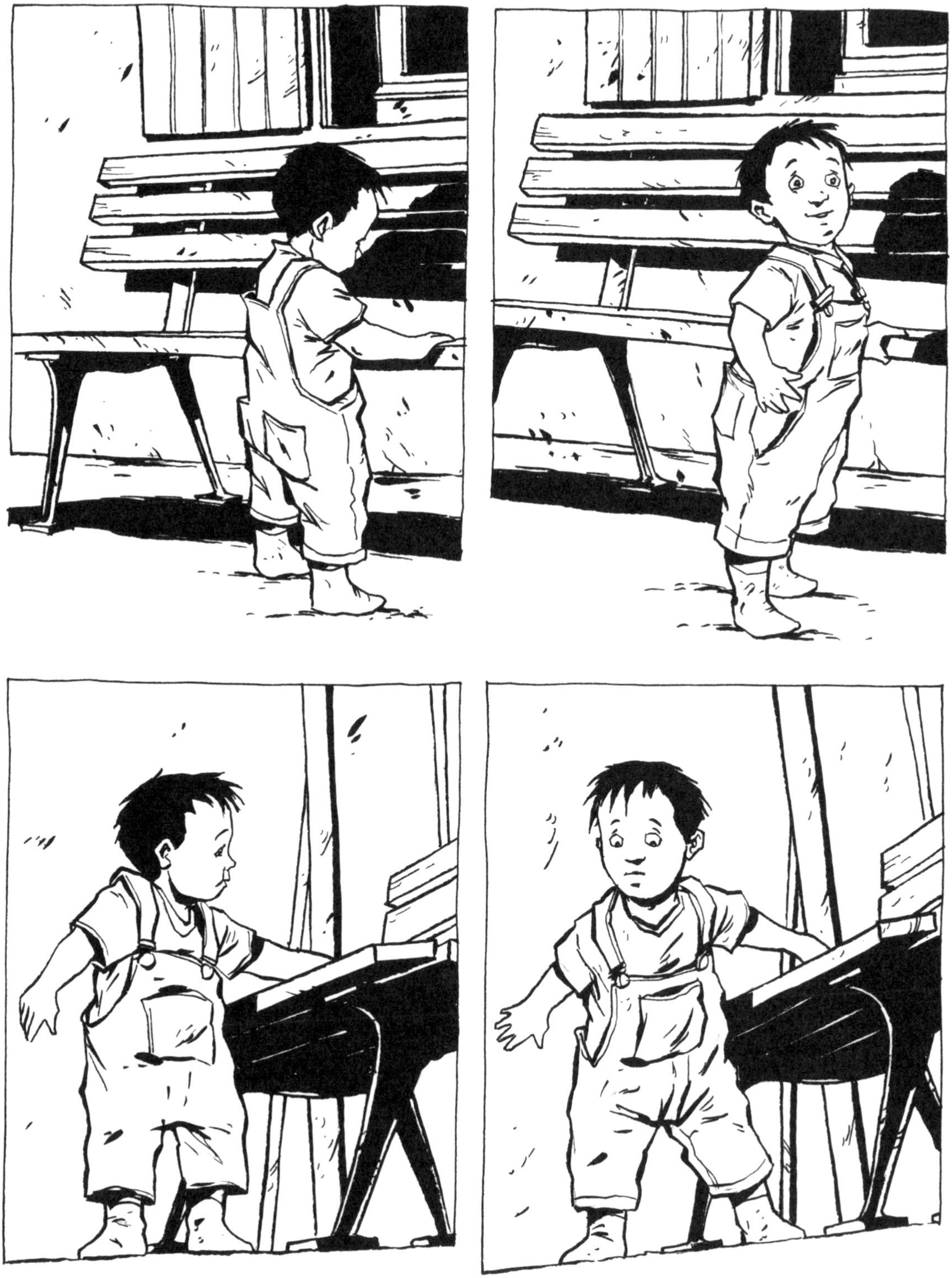

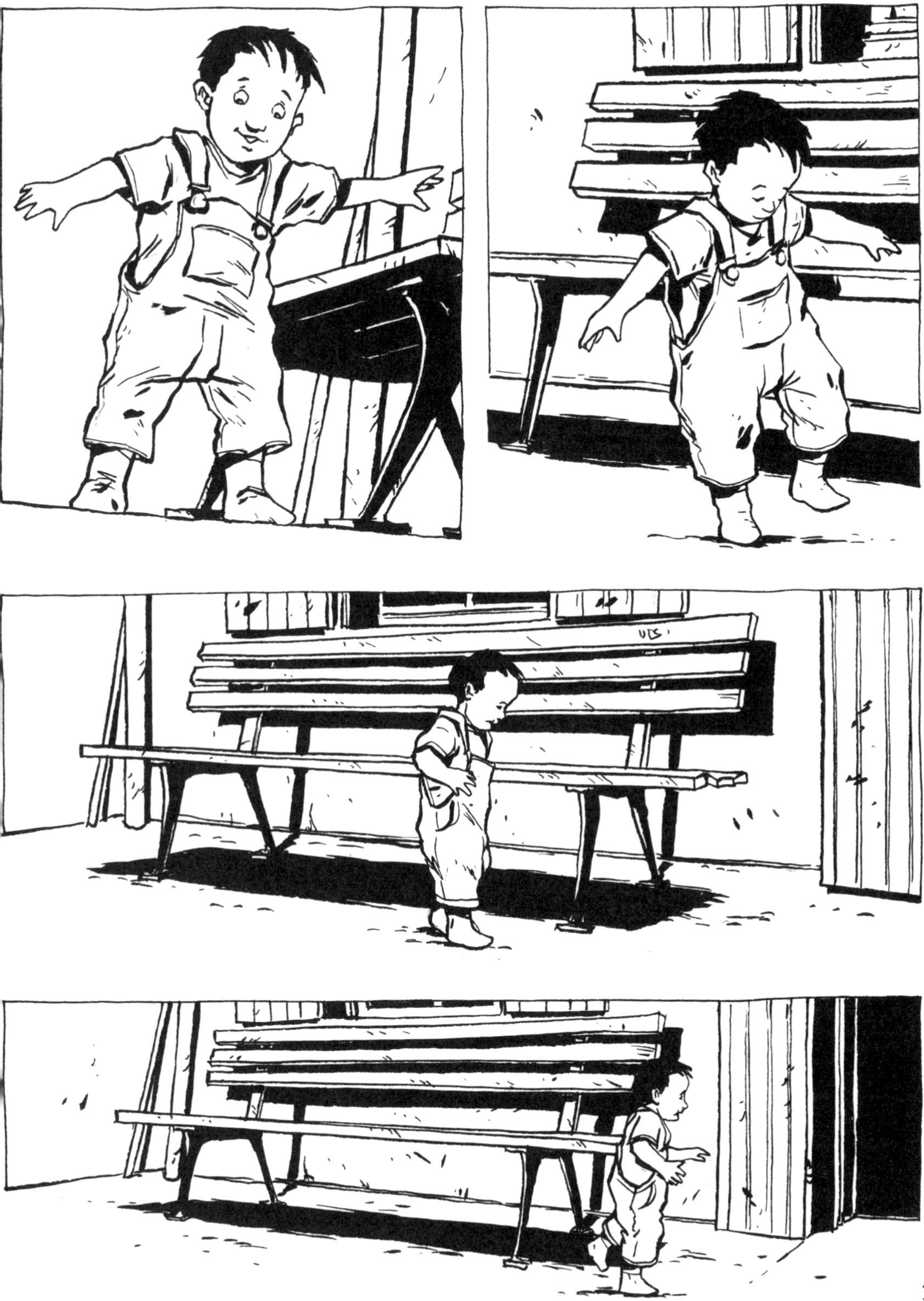

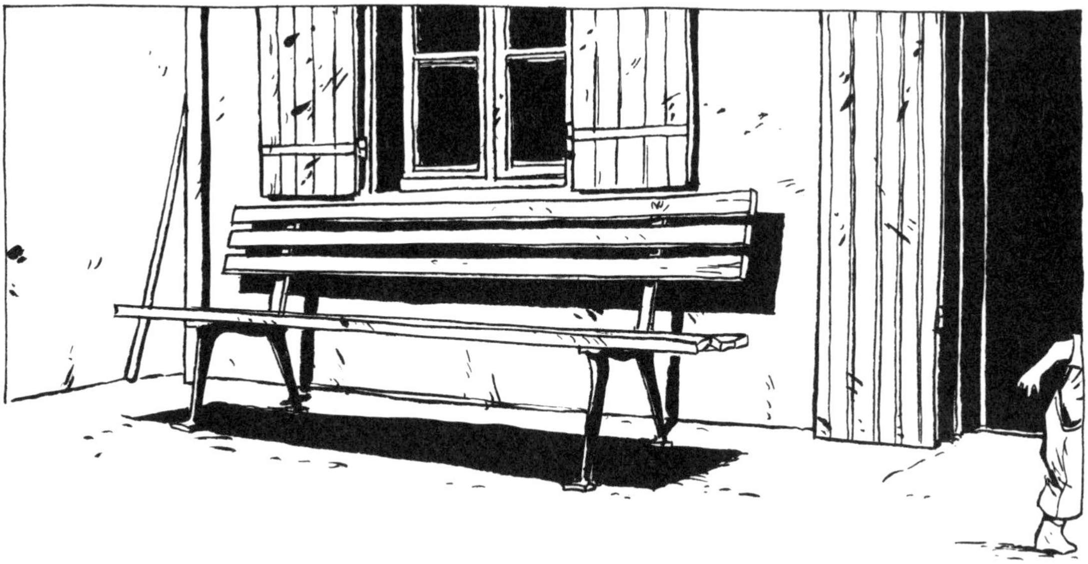

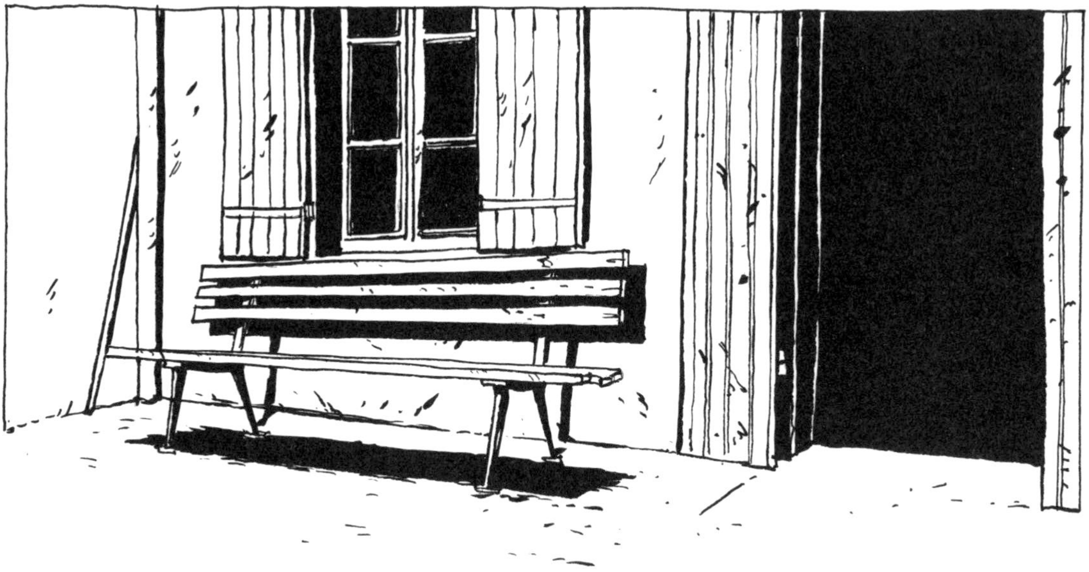

CHABOUTÉ_12

Gallery 13
An Imprint of Simon & Schuster, Inc.
1230 Avenue of the Americas
New York, NY 10020

First Gallery 13 trade paperback edition September 2017

GALLERY 13 and colophon are trademarks of Simon & Schuster, Inc.

For information about special discounts for bulk purchases, please contact Simon & Schuster Special Sales at 1-866-506-1949 or business@simonandschuster.com.

The Simon & Schuster Speakers Bureau can bring authors to your live event. For more information or to book an event contact the Simon & Schuster Speakers Bureau at 1-866-248-3049 or visit our website at www.simonspeakers.com.

Manufactured in the United States of America

10 9 8 7 6 5 4 3 2 1

Library of Congress Cataloging-in-Publication Data is available.

ISBN 978-1-5011-5402-7
ISBN 978-1-5011-5403-4 (ebook)